White Sun, Red Star

White Sun,

By the same author

Red Star

Robert Elegant

HAMISH HAMILTON: LONDON

First published in Great Britain 1986
by Hamish Hamilton Ltd
27 Wrights Lane London W8 5TZ

British Library Cataloguing in Publication Data

Elegant, Robert S.
  White sun, red star.
  I. Title
813´.54[F]   PS3555.L37

  ISBN 0–241–11956–1

Produced by Richard Clay (The Chaucer Press) Ltd,
Bungay, Suffolk

For Irene Booth
and also for
Eric Sampson and Cecil Coleman

Author's Note

A novel should cast light upon reality as well as telling an exciting tale. The author is therefore obliged to make his story very clear, particularly when the novel is set in a place unfamiliar to most readers and at some remove in time from them. But too much clarification can clutter the story of human beings amid dramatic and heroic events. Instead, here are brief explanations of the chief forces in the troubled life of China during the first half of the twentieth century:

Confucianism then dominated the behaviour and the thinking of almost all Chinese. That conservative political and moral code had been developed from the teachings of the Sage Confucius who lived in the sixth century B.C. It fostered authoritarian control within the home, as well as the nation, and it militated against change.

Warlords were ambitious generals who fought each other for power over China after the Nationalist Revolution of 1911 overthrew the Confucian Manchu Dynasty. Warlord rule was usually rapacious, inefficient, and cruel.

The National People's Party of Dr Sun Yat-sen struggled to sweep away the warlords and to create a unified, independent, and powerful Republic of China. Dr Sun's policies were initially inspired by his Christian faith and his belief in modified socialism, both acquired abroad.

Strong foreign influence throughout China was exerted from *treaty ports* like Shanghai, where the outsiders governed themselves under their own laws, having exacted the concession of such *extra-territorial rights* from the Chinese by force. The foreigners were chiefly interested in fat profits and the soft life – for themselves, not necessarily for the Chinese. Some idealists – and some missionaries – supported Dr Sun Yat-sen's Nationalists, but many foreigners wanted the lucrative disorder to continue.

Foreign ideas like democracy, science, feminism, individual liberty and universal equality, however, inspired the *students* at China's new universities and colleges. They exercised political influence wholly disproportionate to their numbers because of inherent Chinese reverence for learning, another legacy of Confucius (The common people treasured even scraps of paper bearing the intricate Chinese characters, called *ideograms* because each expresses one idea.) Therefore the natural leaders of the nation, the young intellectuals played the decisive role in its transformation.

* * *

Turmoil mounting upon occasion to anarchy wracked the world's most populous nation for decades. Even after the People's Republic of China was created in 1949, protracted periods of mass violence tormented the Chinese people.

The People's Republic has, however, during the past decade put aside both its fascination with ideology and its propensity towards turmoil to strive purposefully and intelligently for the well being of its people – and for a peaceful international order. That fundamental alteration is the most exciting – and most inspiring – political development of the latter part of the twentieth century. *White Sun, Red Star* is the story of the men, the women, and the extraordinary events that led to the development of today's China.

R. E.
Casalichiari
Torre Gentile di Todi
July 1, 1986

Prologue

The slender woman with the tawny hair twitched aside the curtain covering the limousine's window. She peered out, determined to impale on her memory the dark tenements and factories of Shanghai against the grey afternoon sky of May 2, 1952. Her face was pale, but her silk dress was of the same scarlet as the pennant that flapped above the chromium shark's grin of the limousine's radiator.

She did not turn when the man beside her said: 'I still don't see why you're determined to leave, Julia. Make sure you tell the world we didn't drive you back to America. Quite the contarary! I'm still wondering if I should let you go.'

The woman was still, evidently weighing his words. After half a minute, she turned, looked at the man in the elegant grey linen tunic, and said: 'Premier, I would stay if only I could. The best of my life has been here. But I cannot stay, Premier.'

'Why so formal, Julie?' asked the Chinese woman seated on the Premier's left. 'Among old friends formality is like a knife.'

'I'm not cutting myself off from you, Rosamonde,' the American woman replied. 'But it is portentous ... formal ... to me. The end of so much!'

'It's Tommy, isn't it?' the Premier probed. 'Always Tommy.'

'What do you think?' she answered.

'You can't forgive us, can you?' he persisted. 'Though no one knows for certain – not even I.'

'If I knew, perhaps I could forgive. But as it is ...'

*

1

Half a mile away, a pale man waited like an impatient lover at a rendez-vous. His narrow eyes remote behind rimless glasses, he hovered on the fringe of the workers overflowing the offices of the South Seas Spinning Corporation. Unlike the mill-hands he showed no interest in the inter-rogation booming from the loudspeakers on the lamp-posts. On that muggy late afternoon, the workers wore grimy singlets above baggy blue cotton trousers. The outsider nervously smoothed the lapel of his pin-striped suit and fingered the knot of his yellow foulard tie.

He turned to watch the deserted road and, head cocked, listened intently. The loudspeakers were relaying the voices of Communist cadres hectoring the owner of the South Seas Spinning Corporation. He waited for a sound other than the harsh accusations and the feeble replies.

After several minutes, the well-dressed man nodded and smiled thinly. Distant sirens heralded raucous motorcycles and the rumbling limousine. Surrounded by six outriders in the rumpled green of the Chinese People's Liberation Army, the black car turned the corner and bowled at sixty miles an hour towards the South Railway Station. The lean man noted wryly that the ponderous Soviet-made Zil was obviously copied from pre-war American Packards, like the touring car he had owned when a graduate student at Georgia Tech. He nodded with melancholy satis-faction when he saw the scarlet pennant above the radiator. That con-firmation was, however, hardly necessary, for private cars had virtually disappeared since 'liberation'. A limousine could only be carrying a senior official of the New China.

The white-capped policeman on the pedestal at the intersection snapped to attention, sounded his whistle, and windmilled his arms to halt the non-existent traffic. Officious People's Armed Policemen in khaki thrust back the crowd that spilled into the road.

The tall man slipped under the policemen's extended arms. His right hand was thrust deep into his side-pocket.

A policeman fumbled with the wooden holster of his Mauser pistol. The bodyguard in the front seat of the Zil snatched a Tokharin pistol from his belt.

They were already too late. Darting between the astonished outriders, the dapper man pulled a white envelope from his pocket − and hurled himself at the Zil's radiator. The impact flung him twenty feet. But a wheel crunched over his body before its screeching brakes stopped the heavy car.

The grizzled Premier instinctively grasped the arm-rest on the doors so that his extended arms shielded the women. When the limousine shuddered to a halt, he knocked on the glass partition of the front compartment.

'*Shen-mo shih, Li?*' he demanded. 'What is it, Li?'

'*Wo kan-yi-kan, Tsung-li. . . .*' Clutching the Tokharin, the bodyguard opened his door. 'I'll check, Premier. But it doesn't look dangerous. Only one man.'

'Another blasted suicide!' The Premier's voice was edged by exas-peration − and tinged with sorrow. 'We *must* crush the corrupt bour-geoisie, but . . .'

'Are you trying for a new record, old friend?' The woman on his right spoke Shanghainese with a slight American accent. 'Where is it all going to end?'

'What do you mean, Julia, a record?'

Imperious Premier Chou En-lai of the twenty-month-old People's Republic of China governed a greater number of human beings than any other statesman on earth. But he smiled at the jibe. The slender woman in the scarlet silk dress had been a friend and a political ally for many years. The Premier glanced affectionately at her cameo-like profile, but did not note, as had the Chinese woman, that the mahogany hue of her hair owed as much to art as to nature. Two years of 'proletarian dictatorship' had not quite driven every skilled hairdresser from the metropolis that was before liberation the most civilized – and most corrupt – city of Asia.

'What do you mean, a record?' he repeated equably when she did not reply.

'I was thinking of October 1929 in New York,' Julia responded. 'You couldn't walk down Wall Street for fear of falling financiers. You know we've already had many more suicides in Shanghai than after the crash in New York. And they haven't stopped yet!'

'We do not *enjoy* it, my dear Julia!' the older woman on the Premier's left said softly. 'I sometimes awake at night weeping. So *many* suicides, are they really necessary?'

'Not necessary, but unavoidable, Madame Sun . . . ah . . . Chingling.'

After three decades of friendship, the Premier sometimes still addressed the older woman by her title rather than her given name. Her heart-shaped face quite unlined, almost preternaturally youthful at sixty-four, she was a vice-chairman of the Chinese People's Political Consultative Council – and a living monument. The widow of Dr Sun Yat-sen, the great revolutionary who had been dead for twenty-six years, possessed unique prestige. Both the Communists and their perennial antagonists, the Nationalists, venerated Dr Sun as the father of the Chinese Republic.

'If it's unavoidable,' she temporized. 'Perhaps it *is* also necessary.'

'Do you believe that, Rosamonde, *really* believe it?' Julia indignantly used Madame Sun's foreign name. 'When you wake up weeping, do you really believe it's necessary? Driving hundreds of businessmen to suicide is unavoidable?'

The bodyguard slipped into his seat and nodded to the driver. As the limousine moved off, he reported to the Premier. 'The fellow was unarmed. Only this note. I found it near the body.'

'No name, but he addressed it to me – by implication, at least,' the Premier mused. 'I might as well read it, though no need to reply.'

That gallows humour revealed his ill-temper. He had not been unduly disturbed by reports of numerous suicides among the capitalists of Shanghai, which had previously been a capitalist's paradise. Today, for the first time, the campaign to stamp out 'the five evil practices of the bourgeoisie' had touched him directly. Suicide before an official's door or under his chariot's wheels had been the ultimate protest of Chinese

3

suffering injustice. The Premier was before all else Chinese – then an administrator and a Communist.

'Nothing new,' he remarked. 'Only the usual complaints. The wicked Communists promised to preserve Shanghai. They swore the New China would not destroy capitalist enterprise. They've gone back on their word.... What did the fools expect? The campaign to suppress the five evil practices, this Mr Liu Zoongvee says, has destroyed him – as it has destroyed free enterprise in China.'

Madame Sun looked pained, and her smooth porcelain forehead momentarily crinkled. Her plump, ringless hands stroked the blue silk of her modestly slit skirt. Although never formally a member of the Communist Party, she had concluded three decades earlier that the Communists offered the only hope for China's salvation. She was, however, upon occasion appalled by the ruthless régime she had helped bring to power. Seeing Julia's carmined lips part indignantly, she touched her friend's hand.

'It will be some time – perhaps a very long time – before we see you again.' She now spoke in English with the slurred accent of the American south. 'Please don't say anything you'll regret. Anyway, here's the station.'

The Premier and the ladies were greeted by uniformed railway officials drawn up before massed azaleas in great porcelain pots. The American woman took Madame Sun's hand and followed the station-master into an ornate waiting room banked with yellow and scarlet azaleas. When they were seated around a coffee table laden with bite-sized delicacies, the functionaries and the waiters withdrew in obedience to the premier's sweeping gesture.

'Of course the train's late again! Of course it's not ready for boarding.' His irony was strained. 'I must do something about the railways soon. Very soon. . . .'

'You can't solve all China's problems at once,' Madame Sun soothed him. 'But we must try. And some day . . .'

'Please don't wait for me,' Julia interrupted. 'I know how busy you both are. I can just about manage to get aboard alone.'

'A compartment is reserved for you,' the Premier said. 'But of course we'll wait.'

'I really would prefer second class . . . leaving Shanghai after so many years. Certainly not a compartment.'

'Think of the face Chingling and I would lose if you travelled second class,' the Premier joked. 'Besides, it's a long way to Hong Kong.'

'And much longer to America!' Madame Sun said. 'Julie, perhaps you'd better tell us what's in your heart. We shouldn't part on a false note.'

'*Wo lao peng-yu* . . .' Julia Pavernen said slowly. 'My old friends, my dear friends, I knew him, Liu Zoongvee who just killed himself. Not well, but I knew him. He was a lightweight, a social butterfly, the feckless son of a wealthy family. But he never did anyone any harm. And he was a first-class engineer. Have you so much talent to spare? How many more people can you afford to throw away?'

4

When neither answered, she added with apparent irrelevance: 'I still don't see why you wouldn't let me travel second class.'

'It's the least we can do for a *famous foreign friend of China*.' The Premier was savagely sarcastic, but he added gently: 'Please continue, Julie. I'm at your service.'

'You promised, my friend. You promised to preserve Shanghai. And now this!' The American woman's tone was bitter. 'Thousands dying. Everyday life totally disrupted. And you've gotten yourself into a stupid war against the Americans in Korea. Oh, I know they're dangerous. *Very* dangerous. MacArthur particularly. But war was *not* necessary. It helps only the Soviets. And you've purged your new officials only months after they took office. . . .'

'They purged themselves, Julie,' the Premier interjected. 'Purged themselves by intriguing, forming anti-Party factions. And by corruption, misusing their power.'

'Can't you see it?' the American woman pleaded. 'Can't you see it's unravelling before it's properly begun? That's why I'm leaving!'

'You *could* stay, Julie,' the Premier suggested. 'You're very welcome.'

'You know it wouldn't work,' she replied shortly. 'Not just Tommy ... It's over. The revolution is completed. And you, Rosamonde, will you stay?'

'I am Chinese,' Madame Sun responded. 'There is no choice.'

'It's really nowhere as bad as you think, Julie.' The Premier asserted. 'We can't be soft – no more than we could while we were making the revolution. You weren't soft then either. So much to be changed but the result will be wonderful. You'll see.'

'Of one thing, I'm certain,' Julia retorted. 'You'll never change Shanghai – not fundamentally. You'll never change the city's nature. It's too wild and wonderful, too evil and too delightful.'

'We hold Shanghai. And we will transform Shanghai.' The Premier was absolutely certain. 'It's a tough nut, but we'll crack it.'

'You may succeed – on the surface,' the American woman declared. 'But, in the end, Shanghai will defeat you!'

5

1

The moored warships of five nations were backlit by the setting sun against the skyline of the Bund. Turquoise butterflies and yellow crickets swarmed over the stark grey ships when the young woman in the blue-serge dress pirouetted across the cabin and stretched her diaphanous scarf over the round porthole. A welcoming present, the scarf was quintessentially Chinese, the embroidery so cunning that dew-drops glistened on its border of violets. The prospect seen through that transparent veil appeared hardly Chinese at all, except for the junks with mat-sails on the dark Hwangpoo River.

The young woman caught her breath when she saw the Stars and Stripes flying from both a buff-and-white gunboat and an iron-grey destroyer with four rakish funnels. The flag made her shiver with pride when she was for the first time so far away from the United States. Beyond that thrill, it was reassuring. She told herself again that Shanghai was not an unruly Chinese city, but an International Settlement under the orderly government of Americans and Europeans. Still Shanghai was undeniably in China – and thirteen thousand miles from Philadelphia.

Sheepish at feeling so much pleasure Julia Pavernen identified the white ensign with the Union Jack on blue-grey destroyers and a heavily-turreted cruiser of the Royal Navy. In the twilight's glimmer she made out the tricolour of France, the radiant sun of Japan, and the red, white and blue of the Netherlands.

No man of war, however, flew the flag of either of the two rival Republics of China. The capital in the north at Peking and the other in the south at Canton were the foremost contenders for power. But in late

7

June of 1921 several other well armed factions were also fighting for control of the world's most populous nation.

Julia reproached herself for her happiness at seeing the foreign flags. It was, of course, wrong for foreigners to impose themselves and their alien laws on the Chinese, even though the Chinese could offer no protection against the rapacious generals called warlords whose conflicts and looting imperilled everyone's life. The foreign warships patrolling the coasts and the rivers were a steel shield for Shanghai, which was the largest concentration of foreign individuals and foreign wealth in the Orient.

Behind Julia in the oak-panelled cabin, Emily Howe spoke vivaciously – and unintelligibly – in Shanghainese. Her buzzing z's and sibilant s's were echoed by her old nursemaid Ven Jyeh, who had come aboard the *Empress of Australia* from the pilot boat at the mouth of the Yangtze River. Listening to their conspiratorial laughter, Julia realized that the young woman who had been her closest friend for years lived another and totally alien life. Emily was Yuelin to the old nursemaid – and she was indisputably Chinese. She was not another American college girl with exotic features, but a daughter of the terrifying colossus of a country to which they had just come.

'Are you in a trance, Julie? One minute dancing around like crazy, the next frozen stiff. What's wrong?'

'Nothing, Emily. It's just that . . .'

'I was only teasing. I know exactly how you feel.' The Chinese girl smiled reassuringly. 'Just like I did when I first saw San Francisco, I was scared stiff.'

'But we're grown-ups now, past twenty. No reason to be afraid, especially not with you.'

'Shanghai's almost as strange to me, Julie. Ten years is a long time. I was only a child when I left and China was an Empire. I'm just as curious as you.'

'But you've hardly looked at the skyline.'

'Maybe I'm afraid, too. Anyway, we'll see it all later. Right now, I've got to pick the right dress for the party.'

'You'll never get packed in time,' Julia warned. 'Your things are strewn all over the cabin.'

'Nothing to worry about, Julie. Ven Jyeh'll take care of it. That's why she brought Ah Wong along to help.'

'Emmy, I don't understand it. Two maids to meet you . . . us. But nobody from your family. It isn't natural.'

'It's *not* natural, Julie. It's etiquette.'

Emily drifted towards Julia who stood at the porthole transfixed by the descent of evening upon China. The young Chinese woman glanced at the foreign men-of-war silhouetted against the Bund, but her casual gaze lingered on the British Consulate, the Maritime Customs House, and Jardine Mathesons. Those Western buildings were the façade of the foreign authority that ruled Shanghai's overwhelmingly Chinese population – making all those Chinese secure and some Chinese wealthy.

Was she, Emily Howe wondered, truly coming home? Or had America become her true home? After ten formative years abroad, she was profoundly, perhaps fundamentally altered. Was China still her home?

Perplexed by her own emotions, Emily nonetheless explained. 'Mom and Dad might have come to meet me, even though it would scandalize their elders. But they're giving that great big reception this evening. They're thirty years married. And they have to receive their guests.'

'I was afraid we wouldn't make it,' Julia said tartly. 'And what would they do if they couldn't show off their only girl child?'

'I thought I'd die with all those delays. So they couldn't meet us – and anyway they shouldn't. The older generation doesn't come out to receive the younger. None of my brothers could welcome an unmarried young woman like you. My two sisters-in-law I've never even seen. . . .'

'It sounds positively medieval,' Julia protested. 'I'm surprised you take it all so calmly, Emily Howe.'

'But Ven Jyeh came. She practically brought me up, and Ah Wong's always been her helper. They *are* members of the Howe family . . . will be till they die.'

'It must be nice to have such willing slaves,' Julia mused. 'Country parsonages in upper New York State barely run to a hired girl.'

'Your family's hardly poverty-stricken, dear,' Emily retorted. 'Even if they don't have hordes of amahs. I'll miss your folks.'

'They loved having you, Emmy. Even if they did get scared that my cousin Bobby and you. . . . Your folks would probably feel the same way. Emmy, you're a real mantrap. So dainty and demure the poor boys can't see the steel under the lace and perfume.'

'In Shanghai, they'll probably think I'm forward, not demure. Also too tall, gawky and overgrown. But this stupid race business. . . .'

'It's nonsense, of course. We're all God's children and . . .'

'Julie, honey, let's not have a deep philosophical discussion right now. Let's get ourselves dressed instead. The ship'll be mooring any minute now.'

Julia turned reluctantly from the spectacle framed by the porthole as the *Empress of Australia* groped towards her buoy. The pillared, domed, and pedimented buildings palisading the Bund reared against the violet twilight. None was more than seven storeys high, and their architecture ranged from the Romanesque through the Classical to the Byzantine. Not one was Chinese in inspiration.

Emily had once declared bitterly that the Bund was not only the gateway to China, but the symbol of China's subjugation. A Customs House with red-tiled roofs and upswept eaves had formerly stood among the aggressively alien buildings. But that single Chinese structure had been replaced by the present Customs House with its crenelated clock-tower like Taylor Hall at Bryn Mawr. The foreigners, Emily had said angrily, would not even leave the Chinese their own architecture.

You could never tell about Emily. Sometimes she was an ardent patriot who resented all foreign influence and swore to drive all foreigners out of China. Sometimes she sounded like a foreigner herself, remarking condescendingly that you couldn't expect Chinese to be honest

9

or clean or efficient. Taxed with her inconsistency, she would laughingly confess: 'I guess I've got a Treaty Port mentality. When the foreigners took over cities like Shanghai by forced treaties, they also took over our minds.'

As the breeze died over the *café au lait* river, the oblong sails of junks flapped. Grey smoke rose vertically from the braziers on the junks' sterns, while the musty fragrance of the city was seasoned by acrid coal fires and pungent garlic frying. A gong boomed, fire-crackers rattled, and a Chinese violin wailed. Treaty Port or not, Julia knew she had come to China.

'Stop mooning, Julie. We'll be getting off soon. And just look at you!'

Julia glanced down. Her lightweight blue-serge dress with its sailor collar and brass buttons followed the military mode inspired by the Great War. The travelling dress had flair. Though her father grumbled, her mother had ensured that her wardrobe, though meagre, would embarrass neither herself nor her hostess on the other side of the world.

'What's wrong with my dress?' she retorted. 'Why, you don't even have yours on yet.'

Although two inches taller than Julia's five foot three, Emily appeared fragile in the peach-coloured slip that hung just below her knees. Marvelling at that lace-trimmed wisp of a garment, the maidservant Ven Jyeh lifted the hem to cluck disapprovingly at the long suspenders that kept the gossamer silk stockings taut. Their delicacy pointed up by the slip's narrow straps, Emily's shoulders looked as if they would be bruised by a feather, much less an ardent hand. Her frailty was accentuated by her wide-set eyes and high cheekbones.

She had, however, been a robust forward on the Bryn Mawr hockey team. Emily was really as tough as old boots, Julia's mother had declared when exasperated by the imperious will beneath the appearance of docile, vulnerable femininity.

'I'm just deciding which dress to wear, Julie. What did you think was in the leather trunk Ven Jyeh brought?'

'Didn't notice. I was busy looking at the shoreline.'

'Well, have a look, dear!'

Noting peripherally that the spacious cabin was even more littered with clothing than before, Julia lifted the red-leather lid. She gasped at the rainbow froth that swelled from the trunk.

'There must be dozens!' she gasped.

'For both of us to choose from. Some for you and some for me. We'll have a wonderful time with them later. But, right now, we've got to decide what to wear tonight.'

'I've already decided,' Julia bridled. 'My sailor dress is fine. Anyway, I couldn't accept, and your mother couldn't know my size.'

'You can't wear that thing, dear. Now just let me see. . . .'

Emily rummaged in the trunk, but Julia objected: 'They couldn't possibly fit. Though that taffeta and lace *is* beautiful. A pity I couldn't squeeze into . . .'

'I told Mom roughly how big you are. Since she didn't know exactly about me either, she had the dressmaker run off four different sizes. But she's frugal. He left lots of material, so all can be altered.'

'Frugal? There must be thirty or forty dresses there. I can't possibly accept. . . .'

'You can't possibly offend my parents by refusing. Besides, I want you to look wonderful for the party. Now let me see. . . .'

Emily held up the taffeta and lace gown Julia had admired, but rejected it as too long. Ven Jyeh methodically folded the delicate fabrics, bringing order to the chaos her young mistress casually created. Just as deftly, she made minor alterations to the dresses they finally chose and, with Ah Wong's help, did their hair. When the junior officers of the *Empress of Australia* said farewell at the gangway to the tender, both young ladies were exquisitely groomed.

Tempted by the confections the dressmaker had whipped up from Parisian fashion plates, Emily had finally decided she must honour the occasion with a Chinese style. The sheen of the circlet of pearls that secured her chignon was reflected by the cream silk jacket with three-quarter sleeves. Adapted from the formal wear of the Manchu Dynasty, which had been overthrown a decade earlier, the collar did not confine her like a high Manchu stock, but rolled softly around her slender neck. A slim bell of tangerine silk, her skirt flaunted a wide band of antique embroidery above the hem.

After her initial resistance, Julia had also abandoned herself to the delight of dressing up. She floated down the gangway in a finely pleated cream-voile skirt with turquoise panels that matched its sash. Emily said she looked absolutely ethereal, despite her bold green eyes, with her translucent complexion and the mahogany hair that fell to her shoulders.

Lost in wonder at landing in China, Julia was barely aware of the deference that oiled their way or the bronze statue of Sir Robert Hart of the Chinese Maritime Customs Service that stood in the grassy triangle outside the Customs wharf. But no one could be unaware of the enormous motor-car glowing emerald green in the subdued light.

The Rolls-Royce Phaeton was bright with burnished brass, and its top was rich black canvas criss-crossed by leather straps. A chauffeur wearing a peaked cap, an emerald-green jacket, and breeches with leather gaiters bowed before headlights as big as silver salvers. A footman in the same uniform held the rear door open. Julia inhaled with delight the rich aroma of the split-leather upholstery, the sandalwood trim, and the white roses in the cut-crystal vases.

11

2

The footman seated beside the chauffeur was in constant motion, his head swivelling and bobbing as if he had St Vitus Dance. Although mystified, Julia did not like to question her friend, who was gazing raptly through the window. Her blasé air forgotten, Emily was obviously fascinated by the home she had not seen for a decade.

Nanking Road, Shanghai's chief thoroughfare, was a turmoil of glaring lights, ear-splitting noises, brilliant colours and pungent odours. Enormous advertising banners flapped above a multitude of shops, and streams of pedestrians in strange clothes flowed beneath neon signs.

The throngs parted reluctantly before the 'Hoo-oo! Hoo-oo!' of coolies trotting between the shafts of chrome-yellow rickshaws. Horse-traps commanded somewhat greater respect, and the people scattered for the tramcars' clanking bells. Around the majestic Rolls, Fords and Morrises darted at a foolhardy velocity of twenty-five miles an hour.

'Almost there now.' Emily remembered Chinese courtesy to a guest. 'The turn's a little way down Bubbling Well Road.'

She was breathing rapidly, and her ivory cheeks were flushed. After all was said, Shanghai *was* home. This was where she belonged. This was the focus of all her loyalty: China! *Not* America!

'Emmy, there are so many things I want to ask,' Julia ventured. 'But right now just tell me what's wrong with your footman. He keeps twitching like an epileptic.'

Emily Howe leaned back against the red-leather upholstery and chuckled: 'He's not really a footman at all. Only a bodyguard who . . .'

'A bodyguard?' Julia was fascinated – and a little frightened. 'What do we need a bodyguard for?'

'In times like these it's wise to take precautions against, for instance, kidnappers. Daddy's not exactly the poorest man in Shanghai.'

'For instance . . . kidnappers? And what else?'

'Well, things *are* unsettled. If your Uncle Jack hadn't sworn up and down it was safe, I bet your folks wouldn't have let you come.'

'If Uncle Jack hadn't paid the fare, I'd be back in Puxatawney right now. He swore there was no danger.'

'Not for you, perhaps. But for us.'

'Surely you're safe in Shanghai. In the Foreign Settlement.'

'Everybody knows Daddy contributes a lot of money to Dr Sun Yat-sen. And Dr Sun is fighting against the warlords and the reactionaries. He's fighting for a modern and united China.'

'Come off your soap-box, Emmy. So your father supports Dr Sun. So what?'

'So some people would like to shoot Daddy. So a bodyguard always sits next to the chauffeur. There are also guards around the house.'

Leaving Bubbling Well Road, the Rolls crossed Avenue Foch into Rue Pataro in the French Concession and turned into a lane shaded by plane trees. Gravel crunched before a red-brick gate-lodge beside a wrought-iron arch bearing the name Harmony Hall. The gilt spear-heads of the gates gleamed under enormous paper lanterns painted in scarlet with the intricate patterns of Chinese writing. Emily called those mysterious figures ideograms because each expressed a separate idea. Other lanterns lit the gravel driveway that wound among the fringed phoenix-tail bamboos and the towering rhododendrons with indigo-and-white flowers. Amid the dark-green foliage, Julia saw black figures, who she assumed were guards. The Rolls only drew up to the door after two full minutes. So brightly lit its outlines were indistinct, the house was clearly very big.

'Don't be surprised by the way my mother walks,' Emily warned. 'She only unbound her feet after I was born. She still hobbles a little, specially when she's tired.'

Eurydice and Donald Howe were receiving their guests in the circular panelled hall beneath stained-glass windows. The incandescent bulbs in the five-tiered crystal chandelier showered hard light, which was dazzling on the chequerboard floor of pink and grey marble. The electric fans hanging from the vaulted ceiling were lacquered emerald green.

His features bland and his black-rimmed spectacles gleaming, Donald Howe bowed slightly to his only daughter, whom he had last seen a decade earlier. He wore a well-cut Western tailcoat, but he was an old-fashioned Chinese father who did not display affection in public.

Eurydice Howe's mutilated feet were concealed by her floor-length skirt with gold-and-green stripes, and her plump chin rubbed against the high, stiff collar of her long Manchu-style jacket. She instinctively stepped forward to greet her daughter, but halted abruptly, her torso slightly inclined and her square face devoid of expression.

Chinese etiquette was far too rigid. Emily's mother was standing motionless when Emily had so long been so far away! Such restraint was almost inhuman.

Emily herself was quite motionless under the chandelier, her body bent in a profound bow. Her large eyes glistened, and her full mouth trembled.

'*Ching-ai di fu-mu* . . .' she quavered. 'Esteemed parents. . . .'

Donald Howe then moved almost as rapidly as did his wife on her crippled feet. Mother, father, and daughter embraced amid the rococo splendour of the hall, as demonstrative as a peasant family in a thatched hut.

'*Hsiu nue-nue*! *Waw nue-nue*!' Eurydice crooned. 'Baby! My baby!'

A half-minute later, the Howes stood once again apart. Their un-crumpled clothing hung perfectly; their hair was unruffled; and their expressions were mildly benign. Emily's features did not alter when she presented her guest to her parents.

'Delighted you could come.' Donald Howe's fluent English was distorted by a curious rhythmic intonation. 'Glad to have you.'

'You . . . are . . . very welcome.' Eurydice Howe always claimed she understood English, but did not care to speak it. 'I am . . . happy . . . you . . . come tonight.'

Julia realized that her hostess was repeating the formula with which she had greeted all the foreign guests at the thirtieth anniversary reception. The American visitor felt a surge of affection for the outwardly stolid couple who had dissolved into tumultuous emotion to welcome their daughter. 'I'm so happy to be here, Mr and Mrs Howe,' Julia said impulsively. 'So happy you let me come with Emmy. I'm just tickled pink.'

'Julie honey, I'm tickled pink at seeing you.' The male voice was American, and the spare man who had just entered was dapper in a white linen dinner jacket. 'You've turned into a mighty pretty girl, a fine little handful.'

Her oriental composure broken, Emily gaped like an American college girl. Julia, who was normally puppy-friendly, glanced at the newcomer frostily.

'But . . . you must be Uncle Jack.' She finally realized. 'You are John Pavernen, aren't you?'

The sleek black widow's peak, the long nose, and the cleft chin were totally unlike her father's features. That small-town parson was much bigger, and his remaining hair was still bright orange. But the newcomer's piercing green eyes were exactly the same as her father's – and, Julia saw, her own.

'None other, my dear.' He held out his arms. 'And how's my favourite niece?'

'Tickled pink to see you, too.' She laughed in his embrace. 'And very grateful for your invitation.'

'My pleasure, Julie. But let's leave the Howes in peace to welcome their last guests. We're a little late. . . . Where did that beautiful dress come from? I'd swear it was a Paris model.'

John Pavernen tucked Julia's arm under his own and, still chatting, led her down a long emerald-green corridor. The double doors at its end

14

opened into a circular room so large and so crowded she could hardly see the walls. Beneath a great glass-dome, she saw six many-tiered chandeliers around a massive central chandelier that cascaded light on the tightly packed guests.

'The ballroom,' her uncle stage-whispered. 'It'll just about hold the thousand-odd guests they're expecting. Of course, this is just the first act, mainly for *yang guei-tze*. . . .'

'*Yang guei-tze?*'

'Sorry. *Yang guei-tze* means barbarian devils. That's what they call us. The big burst next week's a gigantic banquet – mainly for Chinese.'

'Uncle Jack, what does Mr Howe do? Emmy said her father wasn't poor, but this . . .'

'Donald Howe's not the richest Chinese in the Settlement. As for foreigners, the Sassoons or the Haleevies could just about buy and sell him. But Donald's hardly poor, maybe the second or third richest Chinese. His father left him a string of native banks, silver shops as some people call them. He's also a big property owner, and he dabbles in textiles and matches. I'm trying to interest him in some projects, but he's darned conservative.'

'Conservative? But Emmy says he supports Dr Sun Yat-sen, the re-volutionary.'

'Conservative in business, Julie. Anyway, old Doc Sun's no big, bad Bolshevik. Maybe a touch pink, but no Bolshevik. He's even got a Christ-ian wife, one of old Charlie Soong's three beautiful daughters. And, I'll tell you, Charles Jones Soong was no Bolshevik, but a Methodist mil-lionaire, practically an American.'

'Then why does Dr Sun want a revolution?'

'Just to get decent government going in China, though I personally think . . . But hold on, baby. We're getting in too deep. Later we can relax and chew the rag, just you and me. I want to hear all about the family, but this is no place . . .'

'Whatever you say, Uncle Jack. We'll have lots of time to talk after I move in with you.'

'Well, not just now, I'm afraid. To tell the truth, my place isn't really up to snuff. And Eurydice Howe says it wouldn't be right for a young girl to move in with . . .'

'Her own uncle? Really, Uncle Jack, I didn't know Shanghai was so straitlaced.'

'Old Shanghai families like the Howes are very proper. So, you'll be staying with them for a while. And, Julie, Shanghai's *not* straitlaced – not at all. So you've got to be extra-careful.'

'I'll try hard,' Julia responded dutifully. 'Though I don't imagine Shanghai's any wickeder than Philadelphia.'

John Pavernen flushed, and his lips tightened. Giving up, he exploded in guffaws which went unnoticed in the noisy ballroom. He blotted his eyes with a linen handkerchief and said tremulously: 'You just cling to that idea, honey. Shanghai no wickeder than Philly! I've heard some good ones, but . . .'

15

Julia had not expected such spectacular success for her wide-eyed humour. She was, however, only half-jesting. The elite of wicked Shanghai looked sedate, self-important, and very respectable.

Manservants in ankle-length white robes were carrying silver trays through the chattering throng. Round tables around the walls were heavy with champagne, claret, whisky, brandy and port. The liquors stained the damask tablecloths when the harried waiters filled fresh glasses. Some tables were heaped with lobsters, oysters, crabs, and shrimps. On others carved-ice dragons with flashing electric-bulb eyes guarded mounds of shimmering caviar, smoked eel, and pickled salmon. Long buffets offered entire roast geese, ducks, pheasants, and sucking pigs.

'Not plopah Chinee fashion. Allee same *yang-guei* fashion makee walkee-walkee small chow,' John Pavernen remarked and then called out: 'Boy, two cup *shampiyen*.'

'Uncle Jack, what *did* you say? I hardly understood one word.'

'Male servants are called boy.' Jack Pavernen grinned. 'I simply asked for a couple of glasses of champagne. Don't you understand straight-forward pidgin?'

Julia remained prudently silent when he capped his revenge for her dead-pan humour by explaining ponderously: 'You'll learn pidgin soon enough. I said the Howes were deviating from Chinese custom and adopting foreign ways with the canapes – which are, logically enough, called small chow. Chinese always sit down to eat.'

'Very expressive . . . pidgin,' Julia agreed straight-faced. 'Concise, too. All that in so few words.'

'You'll do, Julie, you'll do.' John Pavernen raised his glass to her. 'Just remember Shanghai is a *very* wicked town.'

Although the louvres in the glass dome stood open and a score of ceiling-fans whirled, the ballroom was stifling. But additional guests crowded into the ballroom while the chatter – and the drinking – grew more hectic.

Several middle-aged Chinese men stopped to exchange greetings. Julia did not catch their names, but consoled herself that she would not have remembered them anyway. They addressed her with profound, almost fawning, courtesy. She might have been a visiting princess rather than an unremarkable young woman from a country parsonage. Traditional Chinese politeness, she concluded, was obviously heightened by general regard for John Pavernen. Her uncle must have carved himself a big niche in just three years in Shanghai.

When she congratulated him on his popularity, John Pavernen smiled non-committally. No reason to tell Julia that *she* was the object of respect and curiosity. Not because she was his niece, but because all Shanghai knew she was the intimate friend of Emily Howe and the guest of Donald Howe. Anyone that close to a throne, even a minor throne, commanded deference. Who knew when he might need a friend at court? Shanghai was no different from London, New York – or Puxatawney.

But Julia and John Pavernen were themselves courtiers when they joined the circle around a foreign couple. Although he was of middle height, the man's chest was massive under his formal tailcoat. Miniature medals shone on his lapel, and the blue-and-scarlet ribbon around his neck displayed the cross of a Knight Commander of the Order of St Michael and St George. His nose was assertively curved, and his blue eyes were commanding above his silver beard. The woman was voluptuous, and her blonde chignon was clasped with a circlet of amethysts and diamonds.

Julia estimated that she was an unlined fifty-five, five to ten years younger than the man. Her exuberant curves triumphed over the fashionable corsets meant to flatten bosoms and hips, and Julia remembered seeing her evening gown in the latest *Vogue* – a transparent chiffon overdress with beaded cuffs and hem. The sprays of flowers on the fragile fabric had obviously required hundreds of hours of painstaking needlework, and the petals of the tiny sunflowers on her black-satin pumps were apple-green jade with chip-diamond centres.

'May I present my niece Miss Julia Pavernen?' Her breezy Uncle Jack was unwontedly ceremonious. 'Sir Judah and Lady Haleevie, my dear.'

Julia instinctively bobbed a half-curtsey. Lady Haleevie reached out to clasp her hands, and Sir Judah patted her shoulder.

'We're delighted you've come, my dear.' Lady Haleevie's accent was very grand and imposing. 'Tell Emily to bring you to see us very soon.'

'That's very kind of you, Rachel,' John Pavernen was ingratiating. 'You mustn't let Julie become a nuisance to Judah and yourself.'

Delighted at calling the Haleevies by their first names unreprimanded, John Pavernen chatted animatedly with them. Julia accepted another goblet of champagne and a tidbit of crisp-skinned duck from an attentive waiter. A tiny linen napkin shielded the goblet, and the duck tasted of liquorice.

'The Haleevies are an old Jewish family from Baghdad,' Jack Pavernen whispered when they detached themselves. 'Been in Shanghai from the beginning. Old Judah's so rich he can hardly count all his shekels. They're very orthodox, but they don't act like Jews. Not just generous, but extravagant in their charities – specially for the Chinese. Old Judah's also very shrewd and very tough. *Never* get on the wrong side of the Haleevies.'

Many of the newcomers were young foreign men in dinner jackets. Naval officers, all foreign, were alike in blue and gold, but army and marine officers were gaudily diverse. Their scarlet, emerald and royal-blue tunics flaunted silver aiguillettes, fringed gold epaulettes, and rainbow medal ribbons.

Julia was very glad Eurydice Howe had sent such beautiful dresses to the ocean liner. Surrounded by young men irresistibly drawn by a new female, she would have felt a frump in her practical blueserge with the naïve sailor collar. Shanghai was obviously going to be great fun, despite the horror stories she had heard about foreign bachelors and their Chinese floozies. Confident that his niece would not be left alone, John Pavernen slipped away to pursue new contacts.

Repeatedly asked how long she was staying, Julia could only reply that she had no idea. She did not know whether she would want to stay more

17

than a few months – or whether she could. However, she would not think about it tonight. No more would she worry about her uncle, who was delighted to show her off, but reluctant to have her as his house-guest.

Tonight she would just enjoy herself. Frank male admiration was not new to her, but she had never attracted quite so many young men at once. She revelled in the opulence amid which the Howes lived, and she was impressed by their wealthy, powerful guests. The party was anything but stuffy, despite her first impression. Whatever it might lack, Shanghai had glamour.

'Miss Pavernen, are you reading me?' The fresh-faced American with the cornflower-blue eyes was apparently not annoyed but simply puzzled by her inattention to his tale of a flight from Nanking to Shanghai in a Jenny bi-plane. 'You look a thousand miles away.'

Julie recalled his rapid-fire self-introduction and the name on the visiting card he had pressed on her. Harrison Parker Smythe III ('Pronounced Smith,' he'd said) was a vice-consul of the United States of America. He had trained as an army aviator, but the Armistice had kept him from France. Flying was now a hobby, his escape from the bills of lading, the distressed seamen, and the visa applications that filled his working days.

'Of course I'm listening,' she protested. 'You were over Chinkiang, the wind was rising, and Nanking still more than a hundred miles away. . . .'

'Not as the crow flies. But I had to follow the railroad. My compass was out, dusk was falling . . .'

Finally caught up in Harry Smythe's adventures, Julia was disappointed when he broke off abruptly. She had never liked cliff-hangers. But the vice-consul was staring across the ball-room.

'Now that *is* interesting,' he mused. 'Very interesting indeed.'

'What's so fascinating, Mr Smythe?'

'You see the two Chinese men? Over there with the beautiful girl in the pale-blue *cheongsam*, the long dress with the slit skirt. The younger man, the one with the slicked-down hair and the round glasses. That's T.V. Soong. His father was Charlie Soong. Of course, you haven't heard. . . .'

'Charles Jones Soong?'

'You are a quick study, Miss Pavernen. Just arrived, but you know about Charlie Soong.'

'I only know his name. Also he was very rich and had beautiful daughters. Who's the other man? And the young lady.'

The lean man in the checked suit to whom T.V. Soong was speaking inclined his head attentively. His eyes were set square in his face, and they crackled with authority. The young woman in pale blue, who listened without speaking, was almost too perfect. Her features were symmetrical, and her complexion was flawless, while the slight fullness of her upper lip made her appear compassionate. Her chin was square, and it rose imperiously above her stiff collar, which was so high it brushed the black pearls in her earlobes.

'Very interesting!' Harry Smythe repeated. 'I thought the General was safely tucked away in the sticks.'

18

'I may be a quick study,' Julia objected. 'But I don't have the faintest idea what you're talking about. Who're the young lady and the other man?'

'She's Mayling Soong, T.V.'s youngest sister, a Wellesley grad. She's having her problems with those two chattering away so fast. Her Shanghainese isn't too good yet. The man's name is Chiang Kai-shek. No reason for you to have heard of him. He's just a hobby of mine.'

'How's that, Mr Smythe?'

'I just think he's worth watching. General Chiang's in his mid-thirties, and a trained army officer, one of the few. He serves Dr Sun Yat-sen in Canton way down south.'

'Why so surprised to see him here?'

'His mother died a few weeks ago. He should be home mourning like the filial son he is. This meeting could be damned important.'

'Why,' Julia persisted, 'so important?'

'Look, Miss Pavernen, Sun Yat-sen's the best hope of decent democratic government for China. He's also the best hope for the US. And he went to high school in Honolulu. T.V. Soong, his brother-in-law and financial supporter ... also pro-American, a Harvard man. If Sun Yat-sen can make himself president again, the US will be in clover – and General Chiang Kai-shek's bound to play a big role.' The vice-consul paused and innocently asked: 'Would you say the General's got his eye on Mayling? Miss Soong, that is.'

'Really, Mr Smythe, what do I know about such things in China? Off hand I'd say your General Chiang was so wrapped up in what T.V. Soong's saying he hardly knows she's there.'

'Well, you can't win 'em all. ... Miss Pavernen, my apologies for digressing. Can we have dinner this Saturday, then? I'll show you Shanghai by night.'

'I'd have to ask my hostess whether she has any plans, Mr Smythe.'

Shanghai ways, Julia reflected, were peculiar, if not necessarily wicked. Although she and Harry Smythe had not been formally introduced, they could in these free post-war days quite properly chat under the roof of a mutual friend. But it would be unthinkable for a young man she had just met in Philadelphia to suggest breezily that they dine *à deux*.

'Harry,' an English voice demanded, 'won't you present me to the lady?'

The American said with barely veiled antipathy: 'Richard Hollings, one of our local newshawks. 'Bye, Miss Pavernen. See you Saturday.'

'And will you?' Hollings asked.

'Will I what?' she responded absently.

'Will you see my friend Harry Smythe on Saturday?'

'I have no idea, Mr Hollings. It doesn't really concern you, does it?'

'Not yet. But it will, I promise you.'

'I haven't asked for any promises, Mr Hollings.'

'I am sorry. Sorry I've offended you and equally sorry I've confused you.' He laughed, and Julia felt a slight fraying of her first dislike. 'It's the language barrier. In England, promise in that context means simply to guarantee.'

'I don't see why my plans should concern you.' She flirted discreetly in spite of herself. 'Anyway, I don't want your guarantees.'

'I'm crushed, Miss Pavernen, utterly crushed!'

He smiled unrepentantly, and Julia felt her interest flare. The cocky Englishman looked more like a Frenchman. His hair and his eyes were dark brown, and his manner was intense. A hair's breadth under six feet, he appeared completely at home in his body, completely in control of himself. He was, she guessed, no more than twenty-three or twenty-four.

'You think I'm stuffy, don't you?' she capitulated abruptly. 'Tell me, Richard Hollings, why does Harry Smythe call you a newshawk?'

'An expressive Americanism, isn't it?' His dark eyes smiled. 'But you're not stuffy, and I'm not a full-fledged newshawk – only a little nestling. I do write occasionally from Shanghai for *The Times* because *the* China correspondent prefers to pontificate from Peking. But I earn my daily crust on the *North China Daily News*.'

'How interesting. I've never met a real live newspaperman before. You must . . .'

'. . . meet the most interesting people.' He completed the cliché. 'Everybody says so. But this time . . . you . . . it's true.'

3

The wiry man in the checked suit did not linger in the brightly lit doorway of Harmony Hall. General Chiang Kai-shek was annoyed at being bowed out by a houseboy because Donald and Eurydice Howe had abandoned the reception hall to join their own party. Stepping into a pocket of darkness among the rhododendrons, he reflected that one of the host's four sons might have bid a formal farewell to departing guests. The old courtesies were passing far too fast. Turning away, he did not see Thomas Tan-ssu Howe, the youngest son of the house, resume the post he had momentarily left to quell a squabble among the servants.

Despite his unattended departure, Chiang Kai-shek was well pleased with the evening. Political necessity had forced him to attend the Howes' anniversary reception when he should have been mourning at home a hundred miles away. He automatically used military terminology. Both the friendly and the hostile forces were in strategic flux, but he had just won a tactical victory.

The Provisional Government of the Republic of China, re-established at Canton only three months earlier, was in a precarious position, largely because President Sun Yat-sen was too trusting. Chiang Kai-shek had recently withdrawn to impress upon Dr Sun the the need to be resolute towards avowed enemies and cautious towards professed friends. Just after his return to Canton his mother's death had forced him to leave again. Dr Sun was now relapsing. He was temporizing with deceitful enemies and confiding in false friends.

Meeting in public with President Sun's brother-in-law T.V. Soong had reaffirmed General Chang Kai-shek's loyalty to the President and also reminded T.V. of his responsibilities to the cause. The millionaire, whose father had been Dr Sun's financial mainstay, now understood that he must urgently raise additional funds.

Alone and vulnerable in the secluded grounds, Chiang Kai-shek peered out cautiously from the cover of the ten-foot rhododendrons. When his eyes adjusted to the flickering light of the paper lanterns, he saw no danger. But a rustling in the dark shrubbery across the driveway drove him back into cover. Although he expected no enemy action tonight, his enemies were ruthless. He was, though, hoping to neutralize one enemy tonight – the big-bodied opportunist the foreigners called the Christian General because he baptized his troops with firehoses. Whatever else, the man was an original character among the warlords. This evening's meeting should produce a very useful alliance between the Christian General and the Canton government.

Chiang Kai-shek ran his sinewy hand through hair cropped short in the style of his officer-instructors at the Tokyo Military Academy. Aside from the Japanese, he disliked all foreigners – although the Americans were the brashest. T.V. Soong's sister Mayling had actually spent most of her life in America. She was a pleasant young woman, if a trifle flashy in her dress. In her demeanour she was, however, modest and unassertive, the chief virtues in a woman.

The General trotted towards the bend in the driveway where the small Hupmobile T.V. had loaned him waited just beyond the light of the paper lanterns. Although painstaking scrutiny had convinced him that no enemy lay in wait, he cautiously approached the boxy car from the rear. The chauffeur was asleep in the front seat, and his own peaked military cap was resting on the ledge beneath the rear window.

An arm clamped across his mouth, and many hands dragged him into the rhododendrons. His whipcord frame stiff, he threw himself forward to break away. When his surprised assailants loosened their grip, he groped in his jacket-pocket for the small Belgian pistol his blood-brother had given him earlier that day.

Before he could turn to face them, his invisible assailants tightened their grip. His hand was squeezed so hard the pistol cut into his palm, and a blindfold covered his eyes. But he could still kick out.

'Ta ma-di!' His shoe sank into softness, and he heard a harsh voice swear. 'Screw it!'

'I wear iron soles,' Chiang Kai-shek gasped. 'Are you blind?'

'I am not blind.' The precise answer was most welcome. 'My eyes are brighter than yours.'

The grasp relented. Unimpeded, the General removed his blindfold. He was ringed by four men wearing cotton long-gowns and wide-brimmed fedoras, the garb of Shanghai's toughs. The dappled moonlight seeping through the rhododendrons lit their stout leader. He was the Incense Master of the Mother Lodge, who was immediately subordinate to Chiang's blood-brother, the Supreme Lord of the Floodgate Fraternity.

'Excellency, you were too fast,' the Incense Master apologized. 'We had no chance to say the passwords. I deeply regret . . .'

'No harm done,' Chiang Kai-shek replied. 'But to wait till *I* spoke the

22

words was slovenly. And why assault me? Surely an exchange of re-cognition signs . . .'

'Excellency, the Supreme Lord instructed us not to approach you. We were to seize you so that any chance observer would not realize we were of one lodge.'

'There is, I assume, a purpose behind your eccentric performance?'

'Excellency, you must not keep your appointment with the so-called Christian General. And you must not ride in that car. Your life is at risk.'

Sometimes amused, Chiang Kai-shek was as often irritated by the conspiratorial mumbo-jumbo that attended all the doings of the Floodgate Fraternity, which foreigners called the Green Gang. Stringent precautions were, however, necessary. Always outside the law and usually opposed to the law, a secret society like the Green Gang had to ensure the loyal obedience of its members by threat of certain vengeance – supernatural as well as human. Otherwise, the secret societies would have perished, rather than enduring during the three centuries since they arose to fight the Manchu invaders and restore the Chinese Ming Dynasty.

The revolution of 1911 had toppled the Manchus, but no one dreamed of reviving the Ming. While a few diehards plotted to place a new dynasty on the Dragon Throne, true patriots now fought to unite China under a president. Badly maligned by ignorant foreigners, the secret societies had fought the Manchus effectively. They could now assist greatly in con-solidating the Republic. Their criminal activities Chiang Kai-shek was for the time being forced to ignore: prostitution, which he abhorred; extortion, which he despised; and narcotics, which he hated.

'Let's go, then,' he said. 'Doubtless my blood-brother will explain fully.'

'No need, Excellency,' the Incense Master replied nervously. 'An im-mediate meeting between yourself and the Supreme Lord would be peril-ous. I am authorized to explain. But, first, Excellency, send away the car.'

Chiang Kai-shek emerged alone from the darkness under the rhodo-dendrons so that any observer would believe he had gone into the shrubbery to relieve himself. He slid into the back of the Hupmobile and drew down the fringed shades. While the awakened chauffeur got out and cranked the engine, he slipped again into the darkness among the rhododendrons.

The stout Incense Master handed him a cotton long-gown and a battered fedora. Pulling the brim down to shadow his prominent cheekbones, the General became an anonymous strong-arm man. After three raucous failures, the Hupmobile's engine caught with a clatter.

'Excellency, the Supreme Lord has charged me to convey certain intelligence.' The Incense Master's diction was formal, though they were slinking through the shrubbery towards the gate-lodge. 'Quarrels among the warlord factions are, of course, unending. They are now clawing more viciously than ever at each other's throats for control of Peking, so they can claim the "legitimate presidency" in the eyes of the foreigners.'

23

'Peking is a symbol, not a capital,' Chiang declared sententiously. 'Never forget that the legitimate president of the Republic of China is Dr Sun Yat-sen, the *only* president elected by the National Assembly. Only usurpers proclaim themselves president in Peking.'

'I am grateful for your instruction, Excellency.' The Incense Master broke into Chiang Kai-shek's relentless didacticism. 'But time is short, and I am ordered to explain.'

'Proceed then!'

'I thank Your Excellency for his gracious permission.' The stout man retaliated by restating the obvious: 'The northern warlords are badly split among themselves. But they are united in hostility to the Canton government of Dr Sun Yat-sen.'

'Of course! How could it be otherwise?'

'The so-called Christian General claims to carry proposals from certain other warlords for an alliance with Dr Sun against the northern warlord clique. But he is not sincere. . . .'

'I do not expect sincerity,' Chiang snapped. 'Do you take me for a fool?'

'No, Excellency. However, we have learned that the Christian General is a stalking horse. Peking has sent assassins to Shanghai. You are their target – and he will lead them to you – knowingly or otherwise.'

'I'd better,' Chiang mused, 'confront him face to face!'

'Excellency, he is always ready to turn his coat. Why the comedy of fervent Christianity except to gain foreign support? The Supreme Lord bid me say: *Your life is too important to hazard in random reconnaissance.*'

'As always, my blood-brother is wise and prudent.'

Chiang Kai-shek fleetingly wondered whether the Supreme Lord was also in touch with the northern warlords and their assassins. But that suspicion was unworthy – worse, naïve. Of course his blood-brother was in touch with the warlords. Only a fool would fail to keep all his lines open. But the Supreme Lord would not assist the assassins. If the Supreme Lord's blood-brother were murdered in the Supreme Lord's stronghold, the French Concession at Shanghai, his own power would be badly shaken, and he would be reviled as a traitor. His blood-brother's self-interest, Chiang Kai-shek concluded comfortably, would ensure his blood-brother's loyalty.

The five men in long-gowns trotted through the rhododendrons to the gate-lodge. The Hupmobile rattled behind them, its feeble headlamps looming around the bend. As the Incense Master stepped boldly through the spear-tipped gates, he lifted his arms and joined his fingertips over his head. That gesture identified him to the guards, who were members of the Floodgate Fraternity. Chin down so that the brim of the fedora hid his features, Chiang Kai-shek followed. Behind the plane trees that fringed the narrow lane, they loped towards Rue Pataro.

When the boxy Hupmobile spurted through the open gates, its headlamps cast yellow beams and black shadows among the tree trunks. The five men in long-gowns were lit fleetingly as the automobile passed, the window blinds still drawn on the rear passenger seat. When the boxy

Hupmobile turned jauntily into Rue Pataro, the light of the street-lamps reached out to embrace it.

General Chiang Kai-shek had dismissed the vehicle from his mind, just as he would a regiment withdrawn from battle. He was intent upon reaching shelter, where he could analyze this latest thrust in the constant intrigue that was Chinese politics in mid-1921. A muffled backfire drew his attention back to the Hupmobile, and he stepped into the roadway to see better.

Two stocky men, anonymous in cotton long-gowns and felt fedoras, stood in front of the car. Elongated by bulky silencers, the Luger pistols in their hands spat at the windshield. They shifted their aim to the back-seat when the Hupmobile swerved, evidently out of control.

The peaked cap silhouetted against the rear-window shade tumbled to the floor, and the car hurtled towards the plane trees on the far side of the street. Headlights glowing, it piled headlong into a mossy trunk. When tongues of fire licked at the fuel tank, the assassins thrust their pistols under their long-gowns and trotted down Rue Pataro.

Careless of the rising flames, Chiang Kai-shek ran to the car and stubbornly tugged at the sprung handle of the chauffeur's door. He felt a hand heavy on his shoulder.

'Time to get out of here!' The Incense Master jerked his thumb at the chauffeur's slack form. 'You can't help him, Excellency. He's gone.'

Chiang Kai-shek's austere features softened for an instant while he mourned another life sacrificed to unite China. The next instant he resumed his habitual stern expression.

'I was planning to meet the Christian General in uniform,' he said inconsequentially. 'So I left my cap in the back.'

'They would have fired anyway. Pity about the driver.'

4

'Frenchtown they call it. The French Concession is a gilded playground for rich Chinese and foreigners. And hell for the poor.' Thomas Tan-ssu Howe was self-consciously eloquent. 'The misery of the common people is our first target.'

Feigning clinical detachment, Emily Howe's youngest brother peered at the lice crawling across the bony chest of the coolie who lay in a coma against the kerb on Avenue Joffre. They were like men from two different worlds. Tommy wore a starched cotton shirt and crisply pressed trousers, while the dying man was almost naked except for the tattered black trousers cut off above the knee. Though lean, Tommy was well nourished and well muscled. The coolie's ribs were sharp ridges beneath his greyish skin; his eyes were sunken; and his clawed hands twitched in feeble supplication.

'It's so bad here, it must be horrible in the countryside!' Emily exclaimed. 'I'm with you, Tommy. We've got to fight against human misery.'

Tommy's eyes snapped behind the black-rimmed spectacles of plain glass he wore to look older and scholarly. That effect was enhanced by his narrow skull, high forehead, and stubborn chin. It was, Julia decided, a strong face and a pleasant face, though not necessarily a biddable face. He was also heavily tanned, largely to demonstrate his solidarity with the common people who, unlike the well-to-do, could not shun the sun and wind.

'Lucky it's summer,' he said passionately. 'In winter, you wouldn't find just one dying man on Avenue Joffre. There'd be at least a dozen for the dustmen to pick up every morning.'

26

Tommy's accent sometimes made his low-pitched remarks hard for Julia to follow. Her friend's favourite brother, who was three years older, had acquired both his understated eloquence and his languid English drawl at Radley in Oxfordshire. Patriotic devotion, which his father called home-sickness, had, however, led him to return to China after that school for the privileged. He would forget not only his native land, he had argued, but his native language if he remained in England. Since Tommy would have become, at best, semi-literate in the complex Chinese ideograms, Donald Howe had permitted him to return. He did not want his son to become a deracinated Treaty Port Chinese, who spoke perfect English but was hardly acquainted with his own country's language and culture.

Now an advanced student at Peking Union Medical College, Tommy was home for the long summer vacation. Three days after his parent's anniversary reception, he was taking his sister and her American friend to a meeting of the National Federation of Students. Both were fascinated as they discovered Shanghai.

They were learning that not only business men but idealists flocked to the Treaty Port. The Students' Federation had its headquarters in the cosmopolitan city – like all progressive organizations. In the International Settlement and the French Concession they escaped the harsh censorship, the police brutality, and the instability that blighted political, intellectual and artistic life in China itself. The foreign-ruled enclave of eleven square miles was, therefore, a market place for new ideas as well as new merchandise from the outside world.

Despite his eagerness to get to the meeting at the Po Wen Girls' School, Tommy had paused on Avenue Joffre to point a moral for his sister and her American friend. Other pedestrians stepped over the emaciated figure that lay on its back with arms outflung, but the medical student stopped.

'The classic symptoms of malnutrition.' Tommy spoke like a professor lecturing a class. 'Dull eyes and swollen belly. Also, the raspberry rash of berri-berri around the lips. Tissue tone is lost. If you press his skin, the dent won't disappear for a long time.'

'Aren't you going to . . .?' Julia demanded.

'What?' Tommy asked. 'Going to do what?'

'To examine him, of course. You *sound* as if you could tell whether he'll live or die.'

Julia was almost as surprised by her outburst as Tommy was. She had never seen anything more horrible. The half-starved coolie lay unconscious among dog droppings, tea-leaves, and foul rags on a pavement so baked by the afternoon sun so that she felt the heat through her thin soles. Fighting her horror, she had instinctively spoken like her astringent Aunt Evadne, who was the scourge of negligent parents and cruel pet owners.

Tommy looked at her with new appraisal – and new respect. He nodded and dropped to one knee beside the wretched man. His movements were brisk and detached – in fact, professional, Julia felt. After laying his ear against the coolie's chest, he nodded again. The creature could be saved.

27

'What's the next step?' Julia asked.

'The next step?' he asked. 'What do you mean?'

'We are going to do something about the poor man, aren't we?'

'Julie's right!' Emily interjected. 'We can't just leave him.'

'Emily, do you know what you're asking?' Tommy directed at his sister the indignation he must spare their guest. 'If every one of the distressed, the starving and the injured on the streets of Shanghai. . . .'

'He's *not* everyone, Tommy.' Emily insisted. 'He's *this* one. And we can . . . we *must* . . . help him. If we don't, Julie'll think all Chinese are forever talking about saving the country and the common people, but doing nothing. And she'll be right!'

Thomas was shocked by the tirade. Since her return, Emily had appeared unassertive, almost docile, quite unlike the tempestuous ten-year-old he remembered. Yet she was now haranguing him like a fishwife – an *American* fishwife.

'Well, we could call the Red Swastika Society,' he conceded. 'If we can find a telephone.'

'You can, esteemed elder brother.' Emily was now ponderously respectful to her elder brother, as the Sage Confucius had enjoined. 'The tobacco shop over there must have a phone. You'd better call.'

'Why me?' He was still resisting the renewed feminine onslaught. 'Can't you manage a telephone call?'

'They won't pay much attention to a woman.'

'I suppose you're right.' He started for the tobacco shop, but turned to grin at them. 'You're a fine pair of harridans, you know. Is that what they taught you at Bryn Mawr – to bully your elders? But you're right. They're so many people, one forgets it's necessary to help individuals.'

'That *was* a handsome apology!' Julia exhaled. 'Emmy, I'm beginning to like your brother, even if he does think we're both shrews. By the way, who runs the Red Swastika Society?'

'The Buddhists, I think.'

'And people say the Chinese have no civic sense! If they can run a rescue service in a wild city like Shanghai!'

'Julie, the Buddhists *run* it!' Emily stepped into the torrent of her friend's indignation. 'But the funds, they come mostly from foreigners. You've got to realize . . .'

Her words were drowned by the hooting of an open truck crammed with slight Annamese soldiers displaying the anchor of the French Army of the Colonies on their basinlike sun-helmets. After it passed, they were uncharacteristically silent. Emily was embarrassed by her outburst, and Julia was abashed. She was still learning how many layers of misconception, misdirection, and misunderstanding concealed the truth in Shanghai.

After almost twenty minutes, Tommy finally returned. He was smiling, but his cheeks were flushed, apparently with anger.

'Took me almost ten minutes to get through – and ten more to talk them into sending an ambulance', he declared. 'I had to promise a donation on the spot. Now we'll be late for the meeting. That comes of meddling in other people's business.'

Julia did not point out that the ideals he professed made every one of his fellow four hundred million Chinese Tommy's business. He deserved praise, rather than more hectoring. Very few Chinese men – and not many foreign men – would have yielded so gracefully to the pleas of two young women. Beneath his jocular air, which was sometimes patronizing, Tommy was open-minded. Yet there was assuredly steel behind the velvet of his good manners.

'Now, Julia, tell me something,' he asked. 'Why've you come to China? Even Shanghai's no holiday resort, not to speak of the interior.'

Julia frowned and considered the question she had evaded even in her own thoughts before replying slowly: 'When Emily first brought it up, it sounded impossible. I only began to think seriously about coming when Uncle Jack offered to pay my fare. But why he . . .'

'He's becoming quite a friend of the family, isn't he?' Tommy's implication was unmistakable. 'All since it came up, your visit.'

'If you feel the Pavernens are crowding you out of Harmony Hall,' Julia flared, 'I'll leave tomorrow.'

'Hang on a second,' he protested. 'I never said that. If the others are even half as charming as you, I'd be delighted to have a dozen Pavernens. And you haven't answered my question.'

'I'm not awfully sure I can. I'm very fond of Emily, and I did want to be with her and meet her family. Your parents are delightful. . . .'

'But not her brother,' Tommy interjected wryly. 'He's a beast.'

'Not at all. Just stubborn and opinionated. Nothing that can't be cured.' Julia was astringently flirtatious. 'I also knew I'd never have another chance to see a foreign country from the inside. China is fascinating and . . .'

'You're stalling, Julie,' he persisted. 'Don't you know why you came?'

'Well, I majored in comparative civilizations. That's a fancy term for looking at different countries side by side. And what other civilization is more different from America? But the literature will be a problem. I could never learn to read Chinese, so Chinese writing will always be a closed book to me.'

'American civilization? What's that?' Tommy's mock hauteur dissolved into laughter when two indignant young women protested at once. 'I thought you'd bite at that. Julie, you'll learn the new Chinese literature through your pores if you stay long enough. Literature is very close to life itself: the struggle against foreign exploitation and the struggle to create a strong republic.'

Afraid of appearing to preach, Tommy broke off when the ambulance of the Red Swastika Society came into sight. It was only a sombre black cart pulled by two coolies. None the less, they skilfully transferred the patient to a stretcher after extracting two silver dollars from Tommy.

Julia gaped when the eccentric vehicle trundled again into the stream of carriages, rickshaws, and man-drawn carts with its brass bell clanging peremptorily. Tommy wondered if the patient would reach Shanghai General Hospital alive – and what care he would receive if he did. The friendless and penniless coolie, he concluded bleakly, was unlikely to see

29

tomorrow's dawn. He kept his own counsel while Julia and Emily praised him and congratulated each other for goading him to action. If his Americanized sister and her American friend wanted to play lady bountiful, he would not disillusion them.

Neither, however, would he deceive himself. If they had not insisted, he would have strolled away after using the dying coolie as the excuse for a political lecture. He was too like most Chinese intellectuals, Tommy reproached himself. He talked glibly – and abstractly – about the suffering masses and the coming revolution. When it came to helping a suffering individual, he hung back. But he was not too old to change!

Behind the undistinguished façade formed by two concrete arches, the Po Wen Girls' School on Rue Borgeat was pervaded by the musty smell of damp plaster. Not because it was new, but because plaster never quite dried in Shanghai's constant humidity. The classroom set aside for the Students' Federation faced a littered courtyard through narrow windows. Though thirty-odd students were seated on the narrow benches at 6:45, half an hour past the appointed time, none of the speakers had arrived.

The university students waited with irritable expectancy, their patience abraded by the clammy heat, which was not relieved by the slightest breeze. They all looked self-confident, and they all had soft hands. Obviously the privileged children of prosperous families, they were, Julia felt, a peculiar lot of radicals.

'Are they all students?' Emily whispered in English. 'The three girls, too?'

'Girls can now attend universities,' he replied. 'Quite a few.'

'But Emmy, you said you *had* to study in the States,' Julia interjected. 'You said no Chinese university would take a female student.'

'True then,' Tommy said. 'But Peking University finally admitted a couple of girls about a year and a half ago. Peking's our number one university, so others have followed. But Pater believes the best education is found abroad – aside from the snob value.'

'And Peking Union Medical College?' Julie asked. 'Why ever should you want to study there if it's inferior?'

'Everybody calls it PUMC. And it's different. It's really a foreign school in China. Almost all the professors are foreigners, mostly Americans.'

'Aren't you afraid of imperialist propaganda?' his sister teased. 'They're not corrupting your patriotism?'

'PUMC's nothing to do with politics, even if it is missionary-orientated. PUMC's interested only in medicine. Not like Peking University. It sometimes seems Peking is interested *only* in politics.'

'What's the joke about Peking U?' Emily asked rhetorically. 'Oh yes, it teaches reading, writing, and revolution.'

'Not completely off the mark,' her brother laughed. 'Though you just can't separate politics from education nowadays. Just as I remarked about literature a while . . .'

Tommy's attention was diverted by the voices raised in the corridor and the scuffing of cloth-soled shoes.

A young man entered the classroom, his mouth working and words pouring out. Somewhat above medium height, he was heavy-set and he swaggered. The collar of his homespun long-gown was undone to reveal the fleshy neck that supported his cannon-ball head. Parted in the centre, his thick hair was combed into black wings. His features were regular – and distinguished by a high forehead, heavy eyebrows, and a mole beneath the full lower lip. He strode towards the platform where five chairs stood behind a trestle-table and looked around as if expecting an ovation.

'Mao Tse-tung, a student leader from Peking,' Tommy whispered. 'Actually, he's a library assistant. This next chap's much more important.'

The second young man nodded to an acquaintance sitting under the windows. Though he walked like a peasant in a rice-paddy, his innate authority was as evident as Mao Tse-tung's assertiveness. Taller than his colleague, he was also better dressed. His dark-blue cotton tunic was lustrous, while starched white cloth showed beneath the cuffs and above the choker collar. His hair was close-cropped on his massive head, and his deep-set eyes were candid above his massive cheekbones.

'That's Chang Kuo-tao,' Tommy whispered. 'He was a real student. And he's been a leader of the progressive movement from the beginning. I'm really looking forward to hearing him speak. Do you know. . . .'

Leaning forward with her tawny hair falling over one eye, Julia listened intently. She was entering not merely a new country, but a new world. The electric atmosphere was thrilling. It was also frightening.

Women in China still fought for goals like attending university that had been attained long ago in the United States. Men, as well as women, were obviously inspired by fierce discontent with traditional restrictions upon personal freedom and by their country's near anarchy.

The gathering fell silent. Even wriggling and coughing halted, and Tommy's whisper was the only sound. Julia brushed her hair aside and saw that attention was focused upon themselves. Directed by the index-finger of Mao Tse-tung, every eye stared at her.

'Na ko nü-di . . .' he demanded shrilly in Mandarin, the language of Peking, and Tommy, unintimidated, murmured the English equivalent: 'Who is that female? Who has dared to bring a foreigner, a capitalist spy, to our meeting?'

Tommy replied in Mandarin, which the radicals were determined to make the common language of all China: 'I am Hsia Tan-ssu, a student at Peking Union Medical College. And this is my sister Yuelin. The foreigner is our American friend – our American sister. She's no spy. I vouch for her.'

'And who are you to . . .' Mao began hotly, but the other leader tugged at his jacket, and he finally conceded: 'Comrade Chang Kuo-tao tells me your guarantee is acceptable. Myself, I still wonder! The son and daughter of the biggest foreign-oriented capitalist . . . But Comrade Chang says it's all right.'

31

'A fine welcome!' Emily snapped. 'Just because Father's rich, are we not Chinese? Only ignorant servants think all foreigners are devils. This Mao Tse-tung also sounds convinced that all women are stupid! Why I could . . .'

'That's enough, Emmy!' Tommy was emphatic. 'You're holding up the meeting. Not many understand you, but they're all fascinated by a Chinese girl who spits out her anger in English.'

Decorum restored, the secretary of the Shanghai Branch of the National Students' Federation introduced the visitors from Peking. He began in Mandarin and was soon enmired in that alien language. He switched with relief to Shanghainese, when another student volunteered to interpret for the visitors from Peking.

'They're both in their mid-twenties, at most . . .' Emily whispered behind her brother's back. 'Mao, the sturdy-looking one with all the hair, could be a few years older, maybe just short of thirty.'

When the ceremonial preliminaries finally concluded, the assembly looked expectantly at Mao Tse-tung. He rose and began to declaim, his high-pitched voice soaring and plummeting in the manner of traditional Chinese oratory. Tommy interpreted the slurred Mandarin. Eliding and interjecting comments, he produced a telegraphic effect quite unlike the speaker's pompous sentences.

'I bring greetings to Shanghai from the Chinese people. (*Who does he think we are*? asked Tommy. *Abyssinians?*) Shanghai is a scandal, a reproach to the Chinese people. (*He's pretty scandalous himself*, said Tommy.)

'Shanghai is a reproach because its heart, where we now stand, is ruled by foreigners. How ironic that Chinese patriots need foreign protection to speak out for China's future. We can speak here much as we please – only because the foreigners live under foreign law, denying Chinese sovereignty over Chinese soil. (*The whole story*, Tommy whispered. *Might as well start in 600 BC when Shanghai was a fishing village on the coast instead of a great port on a river.*)

Emily spoke to her brother when Mao Tse-tung paused to sip tea from a covered porcelain mug. And Tommy promised to restrict his caustic comments.

'Shanghai's foreigners ruthlessly exploit the Chinese masses – helped by Chinese lackeys. (*Draw it mild, chum*! urged Tommy.) Industry prospers in Shanghai with sweated labour. Elsewhere, there are hardly any factories.

In less than a century, Shanghai has far outdistanced the rest of the Motherland. Yet an industrial and trading city has little connection with the real life of China, the peasants on the land. (*Does he want us all to go out*, whispered Tommy, *and wallow in pig-manure?*)

'Two years ago my colleague Mr Chang Kuo-tao helped lead the students of Peking University in a mass demonstration against the spineless acquiescense of the warlord government in Peking to the outrageous demands upon China made by the Japanese imperialists. That day, a new era opened, the era of the May Fourth Movement. Students learned

32

they could decisively affect political developments. Now we are becoming the masters of China. We . . .'

Tommy sat almost motionless, his acute boredom apparent only in his fingers restlessly tapping the bench. After almost two hours, he whispered: *'He's finally coming to the end, even he!'*

'Comrades, we must overthrow the warlords! We must drive out the foreign imperialists and punish their lackeys,' Mao Tse-tung exhorted. 'We must struggle particularly against Japanese imperialism. We must create a new China and a new Chinese people . . . unselfish, hardworking, dedicated, and clear-eyed! (*Well you get the flavour*, said Tommy. *I reckon he'll run dry in ten minutes or so. Thank God!*)'

He was wrong. It took twenty minutes for Mao Tse-tung to run dry.

Despite his harsh comments, Tommy Howe was eager to introduce Julia and Emily to the student leaders. Both smiled pleasantly, but neither acknowledged Emily's attempt to speak a few words of Mandarin. Yet neither displayed towards Julia the anti-foreign ferocity that had pervaded Mao's speech.

The long twilight was just giving way to darkness at ten in the evening. While they walked back to Harmony Hall, Tommy extolled the assembly he had derided while it was in progress. Though the National Federation of Students had no more than a hundred members throughout China, he declared, it was uniting all progressive elements. Both Chang Kuo-tao and Mao Tse-tung, he added casually, were avowed Socialists, probably Communists.

'Why didn't they say so?' Emily was indignant. 'It isn't fair. They didn't say a word about Socialism or Communism.'

'Well, they wouldn't, would they?' Tommy smiled. 'Not at this stage. Anyway, I suspect they've got hardly more idea than you and me what Socialism is – not to speak of Communism!'

5

June 30, 1921

The backbone of the International Settlement was Nanking Road, running from the Bund to the Race Course, which had once been the Settlement's western boundary. There, the avenue became Bubbling Well Road, called after the sacred spring that now marked the Settlement's boundary. Densely commercial, Nanking Road was lined by department stores, banks, and retail shops. Bubbling Well Road traversed more open and greener territory, though the tram tracks continued unbroken.

Sir Judah Haleevie's mansion, Jade House, stood in a park near the Western border with Chinese-administered Greater Shanghai. The nightclubs, dance-halls, and restaurants that catered to foreigners and to Westernized Chinese clustered at the eastern beginning of Bubbling Well Road. Among those haunts of pleasure, a blue neon sign on a clapboard bungalow recalled mortality: *Rafferty & Sons, Morticians and Undertakers.*

Just after ten on the last evening of June 1921, Emily Howe gazed through the moon-dappled night at the glow from Rafferty's display window. Illuminated by four arc lights and a rotating crimson spotlight, a coffin lined with white satin floated gently in the darkness. Emily shuddered and looked away. Her grandmother had kept her canoe-shaped coffin under her bed to ensure that she would embark upon her final journey in a fine vessel, but Emily was too Westernized. She found the spectacle macabre.

Her brother Tommy nudged her and pointed at the magenta-and-black motorcycle revving throatily beside their Rolls Royce. Despite the heat, the Chinese astride the saddle wore a serge tunic with a choker collar, serge knee-breeches, and leather puttees. The foreigner in the side-car

34

wore a white-shantung dinner jacket. His gold teeth glittered brighter than the burnished brass radiator of the Rolls, and his broad nose was twisted, apparently broken in the boxing ring. He raised a hand in benediction.

'Jeff himself!' Harrison Parker Smythe III, the American vice-consul, was perched on the jump seat. 'Jeff Jehosophat Geoffreys barrelling towards his new domain.'

Julia Pavernen looked towards Richard Hollings for enlightenment. But the Englishman was gawking through the other window at a US Marine in crisp khakis bestriding a second motorcycle. A slender young woman in a black-sequined evening dress was riding pillion, her long blonde hair streaming behind her. Julia was astonished when the blonde turned her head, for her features were wholly Oriental.

'Only in Shanghai a blonde Japanese.' Hollings chuckled. 'I'm told Suzuko's wig cost $200. But she's a very gifted tart. . . . I do beg your pardon, ladies.'

Neither Julia nor Emily had been offended, since neither knew what a tart was. Tommy Howe, who knew very well, grinned. He muttered in a mock-cockney accent: 'Watch it, mate!'

Hollings cheerfully answered in the same accent: 'Wash me mouf wiv soap.'

A Delage runabout that glowed the dark blue of a star-sapphire stood before the modishly striped awning on which hammered brass letters spelled out: St Andrew's Cafe. Tommy Howe's heart contracted in envy. His father insisted that a gentleman would no more perform the menial task of driving his own automobile than he would pull a rickshaw. Tommy stared covetously at the cherry-red leather upholstery, the hand-buffed brass headlamps, and the miniature body that flared to a point in back.

Joshua Haleevie stood beside the Delage, his light-blue eyes laughing. Before they left Jade House he had complained about the runabout's lack of doors, which made a footstool necessary as a mounting-block for any lady passenger. Since the minute Delage could not accommodate that furniture, the Haleevies' chauffeur followed Sir Judah's twenty-nine-year-old youngest son in a Marmon limousine.

Tall and dark-haired, Joshua was unaccompanied this evening – and Julia was not displeased. Her eye had been caught by the splendour of his tailcoat with two rows of miniature decorations won as a captain in the Royal Berkshire Fusiliers. His understated humour was also appealing. He gestured with ostentatious resignation at the vehicles that flanked – and dwarfed – the tiny Delage: Jeff Geoffreys's massive Daimler-Benz motorcycle combination and the mastodonic Harley–Davidson the US Marine rode. All the vehicles were brutal intruders in the balmy Shanghai night. The stench of motor-oil and rubber tyres was alien to the fragrance of incense, woodsmoke, and jasmine.

Tommy Howe was also different in the scented night. His black-rimmed spectacles discarded, the sleek man-about-town was a complete contrast to the ardent patriot of the Students' Federation. His shawl-

35

collared dinner jacket had been cut with passionate precision by Kilgour, French of Dover Street in London. Tommy disdained the evening clothes produced by Shanghai's tailors; he would never wear a white and double-breasted dinner jacket like Harry Smythe and Richard Hollings.

Emily had never before seen a night-club. Her mother would have been appalled at two young ladies, visiting St Andrew's Cafe, despite their four protective escorts. She wondered if they were not overdressed in the formal clothing they had worn for the reception at the Haleevies', elaborately attired for 'a night on the town', as Harry Smythe breezily called it.

Alighting from the Rolls on Joshua Haleevie's gallant hand, Emily was glad that she had discarded her yellow-straw cartwheel hat with the pink roses. Her many-layered voile dress and yellow-moiré sash were still too *ingénue*, as were the matching yellow shoes with cross-straps. Though the girlish look was the mode, Julia and she were quite young enough without affecting sweet-sixteenish costumes. Her friend was wearing a Lanvin model like the one she had chosen for her first night in Shanghai. The floor-length blue skirt exploded in a froth of ruffles from a tubular bodice with clusters of red roses. They looked, Emily saw with dismay, like bridesmaids rather than women of the world.

'You'll go upstairs, ladies and gentlemen?'

Jeff Geoffreys attempted a suave continental bow. The rough-edged former first sergeant of the US 15th Infantry Regiment had sunk the profits from his rough and ready American-style restaurant called Geoffrey's Kitchen into St Andrew's Café. Discreetly hidden by live plants and glass-bead screens, Jeff Geoffreys's favoured patrons could look down from the gilt-filigree balcony on the glass dance-floor. Through broad-leafed ferns, Emily finally glimpsed the glamour for which she yearned.

She could have been anywhere on earth. Only the waiter's sharp features and knowing glances were obviously Shanghai. When Tommy ordered, he spoke not Shanghainese but pidgin English, the common language of the treaty ports. The scene on the gleaming dance-floor was equally odd and equally cosmopolitan.

Nine young women wearing *décolleté* evening dresses in glaring electric colours were scattered like a splintered rainbow at four round tables beside the orange-and-yellow bandstand. Emily could not see their faces, but only the tops of their glossy black heads and their scarlet-tipped fingers twining around their wine-glasses. The musicians in the violet-and-gold uniforms of cavalrymen in an operetta were, however, clearly visible. Emily identified Filipino, Mediterranean and Scandinavian types, as well as Chinese. The band could have been pumping its slide-trombones, caressing its saxophones, and flaunting its clarinets anywhere in the civilized world.

Emily wondered with sudden revulsion why she had longed to return to Shanghai. The city was just a hodge-podge of peoples, customs, and languages drawn from a dozen nations. Shanghai was not China.

Yet the international community lived on Chinese energy and Chinese talent. The foreigners wrung her fellow Chinese dry and cast them aside

– like the dying coolie on Avenue Joffre. A few Chinese like her father could enrich themselves, but most were mercilessly exploited.

However, most Chinese in China were even poorer than those in Shanghai, for foreign rule provided employment, stability – and a degree of liberty. Even the revolutionary firebrand Mao Tse-tung acknowledged that. Until a Chinese government could guarantee liberty and security, Chinese would continue to flock to Shanghai.

Shanghai was also vilely corrupt, a paradise for unscrupulous adventurers. Every imaginable perversion was practised within its eleven square miles: from child prostitution, male and female, through exhibitions of torture and bestiality to the soul-destroying narcotics traffic. The human debris was finally shovelled into mass graves.

'. . . you care to?'

Emily smiled and looked up at Joshua Haleevie who was leaning towards her.

'I was wondering whether you'd care to dance, Emily.'

'I suppose we did come to dance,' she replied tentatively. 'But I wonder if I really should. . . .'

'Why ever not, Emmy?' Julia demanded. 'Why not if the boys want to dance?'

'The ladies on the dance-floor . . .' Emily began in confusion. 'The dancing . . . ah . . . partners, you know, they're . . .'

'They're not angels, Emmy, that's true.' Harry Smythe's innocent blue eyes apologized for his mildly risqué words. 'But each has her . . . ah . . . special friend, and they all behave . . . ah . . . decorously in public. Jeff Geoffreys wouldn't permit anything else.'

Men in dinner jackets from the candle-lit tables rimming the dance-floor rose and swarmed upon the hostesses. The band was playing a tune Emily half-recognized, but the melody eluded her. When the hostesses rose, she knew she could only be in Shanghai. The young women's faces, now revealed, were all Oriental. Most were Chinese, though she identified a Vietnamese, a Japanese, and a Korean as well.

The Filipino band-leader stroked the saxophone hanging around his neck and intoned: 'Please don't be offended if I preach to you a while. Tears are out of place in eyes that were meant to smile.'

Emily recognized the tune sung at every college dance that year: 'Look for the Silver Lining'. She laughed when Dick Hollings whispered behind his hand: 'And do forgive me for preaching to you.'

The band-leader threw back his sleek head and warbled: 'Look for the silver lining, whenever a cloud appears in the blue. Remember somewhere the sun is shining, and . . .'

Emily was half mesmerized. Indistinct forms whirled on the dance-floor amid smoke spirals, all dyed with rainbow light by the mirrored globe rotating above their heads.

An exceedingly tall Chinese in a black-silk long-gown stalked stiff legged towards the hostesses, his small head cocked awkwardly on his thin neck. A hostess in an ice-blue evening-dress with a plunging neckline raised her head and stared contemptuously when he spoke to her.

Emily blinked in surprise. Under the blue-black hair, which was drawn back in a chignon, the young woman's features were quite beautiful – and unmistakably European. Her enormous dark-blue eyes dominated a face that was a gentle triangle from marked cheekbones to a small, square chin. The skin of her broad, low forehead was so white it appeared to be tinged with blue.

The hostess rose, her contempt apparent in her rigid posture, and Emily saw that her dress was daring, but old fashioned. Her figure, too, was old-fashioned. A graceful abundance of hip and bosom was displayed by the V-necked bodice supported by silver straps. The bodice was fringed with tarnished silver tassles, as was the hobble skirt, which was slit in front to the knee to reveal nervous ankles in black silk stockings above scuffed silver pumps.

Although herself tall, the hostess barely came to the shoulder of the extraordinarily tall Chinese when they stepped onto the dance-floor. She took his hand mechanically and, unprotesting, permitted his arm to encircle her waist. Her own arm crept reluctantly around his shoulder. As they danced, she leaned backwards, straining away from his insistent embrace.

Emily watched in fascination from the balcony. She had never imagined that there were poor foreigners living in Shanghai, much less a European woman so impoverished she was forced to become a dance hostess.

When the band segued into a tango, the tall Chinese leaned down and spoke insistently. He pulled his reluctant partner closer, his big fingers splayed possessively on her naked back. She stiffened, snarled up at his angry eyes, and spat out a few words. Infuriated, the man shook her violently. Her head flew back like a rag doll's, and her tarnished silver pumps almost slipped from under her.

Bracing her clenched fists against his chest, she thrust him away. But she could not break his grip on her shoulders. In retaliation, he shook her even more violently while the other couples pranced around them unconcerned.

Her dark-blue eyes wide, the European hostess thrust her hand into her ice-blue bodice. Her scarlet-tipped fingers emerged clutching a pearl-handled pen-knife. She flipped the blade open and stabbed up at the eyes so close to her own.

The big man's bony hand closed over hers. His mouth slack with pleasure, he twisted the shining blade towards her face.

The silver point descended inexorably, weaving back and forth to show how he would carve a crescent on her vulnerable cheek. His yellow horse-teeth exposed in a malicious grin, the tall man deliberately prolonged her terror.

The woman's nails raked the back of the hand that still grasped her shoulder. Startled rather than hurt, the man loosened his grip – and she broke away. Turning to flee, she slipped on the slick dance-floor and fell to her knees.

The tall Chinese bent and grasped her shoulders again. Jeff Geoffreys moved between them, his shoulders and fists swaying and bobbing. A pair of stocky bouncers came to his aid and grabbed the arms of the big Chinese.

Joshua Haleevie, who had slipped down the staircase when the altercation began, swept up the young woman in his arms. With no apparent effort, he carried her up the gilded staircase to the balcony. He was setting her down in a chair at a vacant table when Emily intervened.

'Bring her here,' she directed. 'Who'd want to be on her own after that!'

The young woman smiled wanly. Her extraordinary dark-blue eyes flickered from Emily to the waiter, who was pouring a half-tumbler of vodka. Resting an elbow on the table, she tossed it down and smiled again. At close hand she was unquestionably beautiful: her hair fell in two crow's wings over her forehead; her skin was translucent; and her nose was arrogantly arched.

'It's very good of you.' The cultivated English accent surprised them all, and Richard Hollings's sensitive ear caught a hint of a burr. 'Truly, I wouldn't want to be alone.'

'Are you feeling better?' Emily strove to put their guest at ease, though her tea-party courtesies might ring hollow. 'More vodka, perhaps? I'm told it's a wonderful resorative.'

'Absolutely providential under the circs!' The young woman's smile was contentedly feline. 'Your good health! *Nasdroviya*!'

'You're Russian?' Tommy asked. '*Nasdroviya*'s the only Russian I know. My name's Howe, Thomas Howe. Tommy, actually.'

'Delighted, Mr Howe. I am Elizaveta Alexandrovna Yavalenka. My nanny called me Liz.'

'Your nanny?' Joshua Haleevie asked. 'And where was that, if I may ask?'

'Of course you may, my gallant rescuer.' Elizaveta Alexandrovna Yavalenka was candidly flirtatious. 'In St Petersburg in the old days. Her name was Annie, Annie MacCrossland. You've probably guessed she was Scots.'

'I had somehow suspected,' he grinned. 'By the way, I'm Joshua Haleevie. And I'm called Joshua, not Josh.'

'What else?' Elizaveta Yavalenka smiled. 'What else, indeed?'

'It must have been terrible for you,' Julia interjected impulsively. 'You were so brave.'

'Well, he wanted ... You all know what he wanted.' She sketched a gesture in the air. 'Frankly, I snapped back. I was a little impolite, you might say. But he *was* objectionable. Then I thought he'd shake my head right off my shoulders. At the least, break my neck.'

'How did you come all the way from St Petersburg?'

Frankly inquisitive, Richard Hollings noted with amusement that Vice-Consul Harrison Parker Smythe III was sitting primly erect in his cane-backed chair. The American's posture proclaimed his determination to remain aloof from this shady adventuress.

'Originally to Siberia with the Whites, the White Russian Army,' she replied. 'My brother Sasha was a major of Cossacks. Naturally, he was killed. He was his gallant father's son.'

She asked almost belligerently: 'Does not one of you know of Alexander Sergeiivich Yavalenko, the great Ukrainian millionaire and philanthropist? Have you not heard of his White Knights Sugar Company?'

Blank eyes and placating smiles confirmed their ignorance of her famous father. She, therefore, resumed with the rhetorical pauses and the dramatic gestures that demonstrated hers was a tale often told: 'I got to Siberia with a few poor jewels and a trunk of my mother's dresses. Paquin 1914, this little creation is. Finally I found myself alone in Vladivostok. The jewels were almost all gone. Otherwise, I had a handful of depreciated Imperial roubles and some evening gowns. The Whites were almost finished. No discipline and, even worse, no luck. So I bought a ticket to Shanghai.'

'What can you possibly do? What are your plans?' Emily's concern was as genuine as her tact was abysmal. 'There aren't many ways for a woman to make a living here.'

'Sometimes there's only *one* way.' Elizaveta ignored Emily's shocked expression. 'My plans? Quite simply, I plan to live. I plan to survive!'

6

July 9–12, 1921

The heat was brutal, and the political climate was stormy. A green-baize curtain was drawn for secrecy across the door to the minute courtyard, which was mottled with heat a little before seven in the evening. The front door was bolted, and the fourteen men choosing stools at the brown-shellacked table were already dripping with sweat. Intermittent thunderstorms made the atmosphere even denser, for steam rose from the baking pavements.

Strained goodwill was fast evaporating in the 90 degree heat and the 98 per cent humidity. Fear of discovery had impelled the delegates to transfer their conference down Rue Borgeat from the nearby Po Wen Girls School. Twelve of the fourteen men present resented this meeting in the spartan three-room, two-storey house behind the deceptively grand entrance capped by floral reliefs in sandstone. Those twelve were Chinese. All felt this session was not only superfluous, but hazardous.

The eldest among them only just thirty-four, the Chinese were markedly younger than their two self-invited guests. They felt they had been summoned like wayward schoolboys, and they were offended by the superior airs the Dutchman and the Russian gave themselves. Those foreigners were in turn angry at having been forced to plead for their belated invitation to the special session, convinced they should by right have participated from the first day of the conference. Their arrogance blinded them to the obvious. Today's session had only one purpose – to coddle their egos by allowing them to deliver speeches.

The older foreigner called himself Maring, a pseudonym deliberately nondescript. But his reluctant hosts knew he was actually a Dutchman with an awkward name.

41

I'd also call myself Maring or some such if I'd been born Hendricus Sneevliet, reflected the tall Chinese with the high forehead who stood at the head of the table. It did not occur to him that Maring might have found his own name ridiculous if he had known its meaning: Chang Kuo-tao, Mr Chang the Light of the Nation, indeed! Aside from his name, the Dutchman himself was peculiar. Heavy-set and powerful, Maring recalled a middle-aged Prussian general. His face was square and his hair short cropped. He wore a white suit and a high, stiff collar – as he had for many years in the heat of the Dutch East Indies.

An ardent Socialist, Maring felt great sympathy with the oppressed peoples of the Far East, who were exploited by both foreign imperialists and native ruling classes. None the less, his hectoring manner and his sneers at backward Asiatic races made his Chinese associates feel he had acquired a 'colonial mentality' in the East Indies.

In the shadow of Maring's formidable personality, the second foreigner, a Russian known as Nikolaevsky, was almost invisible. Small and dark, he rarely ventured an opinion.

None of his Chinese colleagues, Acting Chairman Chang Kuo-tao mused, was diffident. The most aggressive was Mao Tse-tung, the twenty-seven-year-old delegate from Hunan Province. Shortly after addressing the Students' Federation, Mao had contrived to send the senior delegate rushing back to Hunan by inventing urgent business at home. The dozen or so members in Hunan were therefore represented by the young man who held such a high opinion of himself. Looking again at Mao Tse-tung, who was already arguing with his neighbour, Chang Kuo-tao knew the Hunanese would prove troublesome. Pale and intense in his long-gown of coarse grey cotton, Mao looked like a fanatical Taoist monk. He knew little of either the world or the ideology, but carried himself with immense confidence. There was also something theatrical about his arrogant shrug and his contemptuous smile.

The delegates seated themselves slowly – as reluctant to open the meeting as they had been to attend. Only Maring was eager. He shuffled his notes and glanced imperatively at the interpreter who would render his English into Mandarin. The chief purpose of the special session in the Dutchman's eyes was clearly not the progress report he had demanded. It was his own speech. Although belatedly, he would tell the young delegates exactly how to conduct their affairs.

Acting Chairman Chang Kuo-tao glanced around again. Since everyone was finally seated on a low stool, he rapped the table to call the meeting to order. The sooner they began, the sooner they would be released from the sweat-box of this small room.

Before Chang Kuo-tao could speak, the green-baize curtain covering the rear door twitched, and a small man poked his head into the room. His features were obscured by the brim of his fedora, and his head swayed from side to side like a nervous cobra. He did not speak, but appeared to be memorizing every face.

'Oh, I'm sorry!' he finally apologized in Shanghainese. 'I must have come to the wrong house.'

42

The curtain closed when the stranger withdrew his hand. Sitting stock still, the fourteen delegates listened to the sighing of his felt soles across the tiny stone courtyard.

'Get your papers together!' Acting Chairman Chang Kuo-tao reacted first. 'He could be anyone. We've got to get out of here.'

After decades of conspiracy, Maring was also decisive. He rose, banged the table with his fist, and spoke rapidly: 'I propose that the meeting adjourn. Everyone must leave separately!'

No discussion was necessary. With the two foreigners in the van, the representatives scuttled out of the house through the courtyard and the back door into an alley. About three minutes later, Acting Chairman Chang Kuo-tao was the last to depart. Only two men remained: the occupant of the house and his close friend, who volunteered to stand by him.

Ten minutes later, they had barely set right the disorder left by their colleagues' hasty departure, the front door crashed open. The intruder had returned with a French inspector of police and five Chinese detectives in plain clothes. The spy was crestfallen at finding only two men where he had seen fourteen a quarter of an hour earlier. He insisted that he had witnessed a suspicious assembly.

'Why else were two foreigners present?' he demanded. 'Why, for that matter, did they disperse so fast?'

The inspector interrogated the remaining pair. He was insistent, but he was correct. His threats were implicit, and his manner was courteous. He was thorough, although he apparently did not quite believe the informer's allegations.

'What was the purpose of the meeting?' he asked. 'Who were the twelve men who left? Why did you break up so abruptly?'

'A cultural society,' the occupant of the house replied. 'We were discussing new trends in literature. The subject's a bit abstruse, perhaps, for a practical police officer, but it's of great interest to scholars and artists like my friends.'

'Why did they run away so fast?' a Chinese detective reiterated. 'What are they afraid of?'

'Their wives, I suppose.' The occupant smiled. 'Somebody said they'd catch hell if they weren't home on time. A new Shanghai opera's opening tonight at the theatre in the Great World. All the ladies are eager to see it.'

Although frightened by the detectives' persistence the delegate radiated serenity. He was, however, dismayed by his friend's behaviour. Instead of providing moral support, the man trembled with fear. His hangdog look and his chalk-white face virtually proclaimed his guilt. While the detectives ransacked the house his expression became ever more woebegone.

None the less, the inspector withdrew after his men had failed to find any incriminating evidence – or any indication of the purpose of the meeting. However, the French Concession police would obviously abandon neither their suspicions nor their surveillance.

*

It was truly an ill wind that blew no good! Acting Chairman Chang Kuo-tao congratulated himself as he skirted a handcart heaped with newspapers, satisfied that he had attracted no untoward attention. Having for once allowed enough time, he sauntered towards the waiting train. Puffs of steam from the black locomotive and the snorting of air-brakes recalled him to his first thought: *All was turning out very well indeed!*

The police intrusion upon the session three days earlier had proved beneficial. He did not believe in omens, for he felt that superstition was the curse of the Chinese people. But, if he did, he would have to admit the raid was an auspicious omen.

The overbearing Maring and his gray shadow Nikolaevsky had been virtually cancelled out. There was no need to invite them to the closing session, since they could not make the railway journey without making themselves conspicuous. The Dutchman's sole contribution to the conference was, therefore, destined to be the formal motion to adjourn the session that had not been formally opened.

Almost as gratifying was the defection of the fair weather friend who had volunteered to lend moral support to the tenant of the house on Rue Borgeat – and had almost given the show away. All the remaining eleven delegates felt the same way. That unaminity delighted Chang Kuo-tao, who had been repeatedly reprimanded by his father for holding excessively individual views about men and politics when he was barely twenty-four years old. He was not alone this time. All agreed that the defector was a dangerous weakling. No more than a wealthy playboy, he had insisted upon staying at an expensive and, therefore, conspicuous hotel. Fortunately he was now absenting himself from the final session because his wife was, he said, 'very nervous' after the police raid.

Chang Kuo-tao concluded as he climbed into the second-class carriage that differences of opinion were healthy – up to a point. At this stage the delegates could still disagree on strategy and even on doctrine. In the long run, of course, they would unquestioningly obey the majority's decision.

While waiting for the 7:02 express to depart, Chang Kuo-tao realized that the air was still fresh, not yet fouled by the stenches of high summer. Amid the throng bustling around the tea-vendors, the bun-salesmen, and the fruit-hawkers he had already seen six delegates board the train. Arriving one by one, they were all inconspicuously dressed – and all behaved discreetly. Even Mao Tse-tung this once refrained from strutting like a knight errant in a provincial opera. The Acting Chairman munched the fried bread-stick he had bought on the platform and sipped his green tea, which would be constantly replenished with hot water during the two hours it took the express to cover the sixty-odd miles to Kasing on the South Lake.

Although most of the work was completed, the journey would allow him to look over his papers undisturbed. He opened a file and began to read. But his chin sank slowly to his chest, and the pages remained unturned. He was astonished to find that he had slept when the conductor shook him awake at Kasing.

Chang Kuo-tao felt reasonably secure when he stepped off the train. The Chinese police of the lackadaisical resort town were most unlikely to be in touch with the police of the French Concession. Moreover, they would hardly act on some foreigner's vague suspicions – and they were probably incapable of effective action. Besides, it would be impossible for anyone to approach the houseboat unseen. Further, no delegate could leave before the session was over. Security was virtually perfect for the largely ceremonial closing of the conference.

It seemed just like a pleasure outing on the South Lake on that balmy mid-July day when the eleven young men embarked on the luxurious houseboat. Although he had been assured that the cook and the waiter were reliable, Chang Kuo-tao was pleased to find that they spoke their local dialect, but not the National Language, the Mandarin that was the common tongue of the delegates. Security was impeccable, and the essential work could begin.

The seductive beauty of the scene was, however, a distraction. Arched tile roofs peeped through the spruces on the hillocks, and the shore was obscured by bullrushes and pampas grass. The houseboat was itself a distraction. The carved rosewood panels and the gilded ceiling diverted the eye, and the padded couches and soft chairs diverted the will. For a time they drifted, enthralled by the charm of traditional China, which they all loved, though they hated its brutal exploitation of the masses.

Finally getting down to business, the delegates proceeded rapidly. They were assembled primarily to ratify decisions they had already discussed for almost two weeks. After they approved the Draft Constitution by a show of hands, only two matters remained: First, the labour movement must be the bedrock of their own power. They would not only strive to enroll working class members, but would organize their own powerful trade unions. Second, no reason to create a large Central Executive Committee for a movement that could, as yet, count no more than sixty or seventy hard-core adherents. Instead, a universally respected professor, who was unavoidably absent, was named Secretary-General; the oldest among those present was given responsibility for propaganda; and the energetic Chang Kuo-tao was made chief of the Organization Bureau.

As Acting Chairman of the First National Congress of the Communist Party of China, Chang Kuo-tao delivered the closing address. He announced that the fledgling Party would not affiliate formally with the Communist International in Moscow, the standing organization that in theory represented the joint will of the Communist Parties of all nations. He felt much personal satisfaction, for he detested the Dutchman called Maring who was the Commintern's chief representative in China. Nor would the Chinese Communist Party just yet inhibit its freedom of action by accepting the subsidy Moscow offered. After that agreeable business, Chang Kuo-tao formally closed the First Congress as the bright lights of the fishing boats began to flicker on the still waters of the South Lake.

The twenty-four-year-old lifted a cup of wine and quaffed it in triumph. He had just carried through the most taxing responsibility of his life with brilliant success. The warm spirits flowed down his throat, and joy tingled in his veins. Amid his exultation, he clearly foresaw the brilliant future.

45

The small group of congenial young men on the houseboat had just created a new organization. Though small and feeble, the Communist Party of China had emerged into a favourable environment. Widespread disorder was certain to nurture its rapid growth.

Chang Kuo-tao felt no doubts whatsoever. He knew beyond question that the Communist Party would win power over all China – and would then transform China. He also knew beyond question that the eleven men on the houseboat would all play major roles in the salvation of their country – himself, perhaps, above all.

7

August 28, 1921

Emily posed dramatically in the doorway leading from the small kitchen
into the shadowed loft. The severity of plywood partitions, Spartan
furniture, and sparse decorations was softened by the pot-plants, the
colourful silk cushions, and the Japanese prints with which Julia and
she had decorated Tommy's bachelor apartment on the sixth floor of
the tenement on Kiukiang Road. Emily steadied the blue-and-white
teapot on the slippery lacquer tray, unaware that the sun spilling through
the skylight backlit her brilliantly.

Julia stifled a gasp of surprise, then smiled resignedly. The sunlight
outlined her friend's body under her sheer voile dress with the slit skirt.
Noting Richard Hollings's gaze, Julia resolved to warn Emily that the
Englishman's interest was not confined to her intellect or her local knowledge.

Tommy, who was normally a stern guardian, ignored both his sister's
unintentional display and Richard Hollings's reaction. He had already
reproached Emily for the sheer fabric and the clinging cut of her new
dress, which she had believed would please him by its distinctively
Chinese style. Actually, Tommy had snapped, it was not Chinese at all,
but inspired by the slit riding-coats of the nomadic Manchus, who had
been the alien overlords of China until 1911. Worse, it had originally
been a masculine garment.

After that confrontation, brother and sister were curt with each other,
though they lavished charm on their guests. But Tommy grinned when
Emily stooped to place her tray on the coffee-table, which was a packing-
case covered with a lilac Indian shawl.

'One thing's unmistakable from your *cheongsam*,' he said in rapid

47

Shanghainese. 'You're unmistakably nubile, my dear sister!'

Thankful that the light concealed her blush, Emily replied in the same language: 'You were a dirty little boy. And now you're a dirty-minded big boy.'

'You've always been an exhibitionist,' he retorted. 'I remember at Grandma Li's house at the beach in Woosoong, you were always running around with no top and hardly any pants.'

'For God's sake, I was a tadpole, only nine,' she replied. 'You were naked as a jaybird that summer. Little boys can show their equipment, even flaunt it. Not little girls. *It* is dirty – and has to be covered.'

Richard Hollings leaned forward on the cushion-padded barrel that was his chair. His brown eyes crackling with amusement, he brushed a lock of brown hair off his forehead.

'They sound like fish-peddlers, don't they?' he observed. 'I'm truly sorry I listened to advice to study Mandarin instead of Shanghainese.'

'Last week,' Julia reminded him, 'you were bragging about all the Shanghai swear words you know.'

'Even so, I bet I don't know as many as your Russian friend Elizaveta.'

'*My* friend, Elizaveta! *My* friend as well as Julie's!' Emily interjected hotly. 'She's teaching me a lot about life – about men. I won't have Tommy and you casting aspersions on Liz. I'm fed up with your beastly male condescension and your sly male innuendoes. And they say women gossip!'

Amused, Julia reflected that three months in Shanghai had transformed Emily from a demure man-trap into a Chinese Emmeline Pankhurst, an ardent feminist. She nodded in forceful agreement, and Tommy glanced at her with his infuriating air of superiority. More prudent, Dick Hollings began an apology.

Her eyes bright with indignation, Emily over-rode him: 'Liz's friendship with Joshua is no different from our friendship, Dick. Just as fine as ours will be if you stop running down my friends.'

'Just as well,' Tommy interposed, 'since you two see so much of that Russian woman. How Joshua puts up with her moods, I don't ...'

'My dearly beloved elder brother couldn't put up with a living Kwan Yin.' Emily laughed, her good humor restored by his absurdity. 'Even the Goddess of Mercy would be too moody for you, you arrogant rooster.'

Julia was annoyed at Emily's denigrating Tommy – and, by implication, herself. Tommy and she were no longer casual friends, though she could not say more than that. The new tough Emily had implied that she was a doormat because she found Tommy attractive.

Of course she knew there could never be anything serious between them. Not primarily because they belonged to different races, but because of their utterly different backgrounds. Under the gloss of his British education, Thomas Tan-ssu Howe was Chinese to the marrow of his bones. He would never be happy outside China – and Julia could not imagine spending her life in exile from her own land.

Richard Hollings rose in the silence that followed Emily's outburst, and Julia again saw why her friend was attracted to the Englishman – though she took great pains to keep her parents from learning of that attraction. Dick was reasonably tall, and he was well set-up, as her mother would say, in the tan summer uniform of a lieutenant in the Shanghai Volunteer Force. A russet Sam Browne belt crossed his chest, and two small stars, which he called pips, shone on each shoulder-strap. He was an officer although he was a newspaperman, a 'pressman', as they were contemptuously called by the taipans, the senior business men who really ruled the Settlement and Frenchtown through the official consuls. But he was also a public school man and the special correspondent of *The Times*.

Despite her denunciation of male domination, Emily had not given up female wiles. She slipped her arm possessively through Dick's and drew him though the front door, murmuring to him: 'We mustn't be late for the reception, Lieutenant Hollings.'

'Emmy's so beautiful, so feminine, she'll always get her own way,' Julia reflected. 'No matter how she carries on about men dictating to her.'

'Don't take it so seriously, Julie.' Tommy spoke her thoughts aloud. 'Emmy and I've had spats since we were small. Sometimes even nastier than the parts you couldn't understand today.'

'Don't be too sure, Tommy. I'm working hard at my lessons. Before you know it, I'll understand every word you say in Shanghainese.'

'I sincerely hope not,' he laughed. 'Some of those words aren't fit for your ears – or Emmy's. She's not as emancipated as she thinks.'

'It's funny, Tommy. At Bryn Mawr we thought Emmy was a bit passive – almost subservient like a Victorian miss. But here . . .'

'Well, duckie, too ladylike for Bryn Mawr is practically wild for old-fashioned Chinese in Shanghai.'

'We're not really wild, Tommy. And we're very reserved about . . . ah . . . certain things. But educated American girls . . . young women . . . won't be treated as playthings or ninnies any more.'

'Emmy thinks I'm a radical, practically a Bolshevik,' he mused. 'That's nonsense. I'm still an old-style Chinese gentleman in some ways. So I'm rather conservative about young ladies and . . . certain things.'

Tommy's black-rimmed spectacles lay on the shawl-covered packing-case between the folding leather chairs in the style of the Ming Dynasty. He had found the chairs at a pawnbroker. Like his glasses, they were theatrical properites that enhanced his dignity, which was, however, laced by humour no more respectful of himself than others. Tommy emphasized the delicacy with which they were discussing the undiscussable by slipping his glasses on. His tanned face was intent when he cited traditional Chinese reverence for virginity. Though he looked a playboy ready for tennis in his linen trousers and short-sleeved shirt, he was truly an old-style Chinese gentleman.

Tommy had no more than touched Julia's arm occasionally. An American medical student to whom she had given the same mild encouragement would surely have tried to paw her. He would have stopped when rebuked, but he would certainly have tried. Tommy had not even tried. Perhaps because he was Chinese. Perhaps, Julia surmised with sudden dismay, because he did not find her attractive.

'You're in a brown study,' he remarked. 'Penny for your thoughts.'

'I was just thinking about . . . about what my father would call carnal knowledge,' she prevaricated gracefully. 'The rules aren't the same for a man as for a woman. Especially not in a backward country like China.'

She *was* attractive, and he *was* attracted. Julia had reached that gratifying conclusion after severe self-consideration. Although she had to protect her sensitive skin from the brutal Shanghai sun with broad-rimmed hats, her complexion had acquired a golden glow. Her shoulder-length hair, the colour of tawny port, was set off by her black-silk lounging pyjamas with the green beadwork. She had been afraid Tommy would think them too daring. But he had pronounced them 'Smashing!' – adding 'Snazzy!' to show off his growing mastery of American slang.

'China's already come a long way,' he bridled. 'You don't know how far.'

'In Shanghai – with the foreigners' pushing. But elsewhere, you must admit, China's terribly backward – and hardly moving forward at all.'

Tommy did not realize that Julia had intentionally turned the conversation, which was becoming too intimate. Unclear in her own mind how she felt about him, she was slightly apprehensive at their being alone in the loft apartment that was his hideaway from his parents. Yet it was with an involuntary twinge of regret that she saw he was suddenly diverted from himself. 'I'm going to tell you a story,' he said. 'I'll show you how fast we are progressing – and give you some idea of the obstacles we face. You remember that tall chap at the Students' Federation, Chang Kuo-tao? He told me this story. It's got funny bits and sad bits.

'Just across the Hwangpoo, just outside the Settlement is a district called Pootong.' He assumed a self-consciously narrative tone. 'The main factory of the British-American Tobacco Company is in Pootung: the biggest plant of the world's biggest tobacco company in the world's biggest cigarette market. As you've seen, Chinese are very heavy smokers. Naturally, BAT makes a fair penny. And BAT lavishly pays its directors, share-holders – and managers.

'But the directors don't want to spoil the workers, who put in twelve-to-fourteen-hour workdays. Besides, tens of thousands in the countryside are just panting to work in the big city – and be paid in cash, instead of rice and vegetables. So wages are abysmally low, and conditions are appalling.'

'You're leading up to the strike earlier this month,' Julia interjected. 'I thought the workers won.'

'Precisely, my girl,' Tommy replied. 'Their victory involved my friend Chang Kuo-tao and the secret society called the Floodgate Fraternity. Secret societies are . . .'

She nodded when he began describing those half-political and half-gangster brotherhoods. Sensing her impatience, Tommy returned to his superficially light-hearted account of events he took very seriously.

'Chang Kuo-tao is the boss of a brand new organization called the Labour Secretariat. The strike gave them a golden opportunity. Ten striker-leaders came to see my friend. They were grateful when he drew up a list of demands for them to present to the BAT management. They were fascinated when he told them how to organize a real union, which could unite all the workers behind those demands.

'Kuo-tao candidly acknowledged to the strike leaders that he was a Marxist. But they weren't troubled.

'"Every man," their spokesman declared, "is entitled to practise his own religion."

'They then got down to tactics. Their biggest problem was their senior foreman, who was a high up in the Floodgate secret society. He opposed the strike – and he was forcing the men to go back to work.

'The chief foreman and chief clerks of every major Shanghai firm are secret society elders. They're interested only in enriching themselves and in exploiting the workers on behalf of the management. Shanghai labour is totally controlled by gangsters.

'This particular foreman was extraordinarily powerful because he had for many years controlled all the hiring and firing. He hired secret society men, who naturally demonstrated their gratitude with regular gifts. But he constantly demanded bigger gifts, and he was always after their wives and sisters. Now he was determined to fire the striker-leaders who were conferring with Chang Kuo-tao.

'"You're already on strike," Kuo-tao told them "And the chief foreman's already made up his mind to get you. Since it can't be any worse, you might as well fight on. I'd go for a mass meeting. If you've got your mates' support, you can break the foreman's power. It's the only way!"

'The mass meeting held outside the BAT plant the next day wasn't a roaring success. Four hundred workers heard the strike formally proclaimed, listened in silence to its demands – and drifted away.

'Chang Kuo-tao was discouraged. But the strike-leaders were exuberant. Not *one* man had gone back to work, despite the foreman's pressure. Moreover, *all* key workers had attended the mass meeting, despite police threats.'

'What happened then?' Julia asked. 'Your strike's beginning to sound like a Chinese opera – no climax.'

'The climax came minutes later,' Tommy smiled complacently. 'The chief foreman was blustering, threatening vengeance on anyone who didn't go back to work immediately. A worker appeared carrying an enormous watermelon like a gift. He didn't say a word, but simply unpended the watermelon over the foreman's head. It was full of ripe, stinking night-soil. Drenched with human excrement, the great man was instantly transformed into a clown. He lost face – and all power over the workers, just as a Taoist idol loses its potency when thrown onto a dung heap.

'After that decisive farce, BAT couldn't cope with the union's aggressive tactics. Management shortly conceded all the workers' demands.'

'It's terribly interesting. But what's the moral?'

Tommy polished his glasses and observed: 'There is a moral. In Shanghai today modern capitalism and modern Marxism, medieval superstition and ancient notions of face – they're all muddled together. And China's even worse. But radical change is on the way. Even by strange means. Like a watermelon full of night soil. In time *everything* will change, I promise you.'

Although Tommy's enthusiasm was endearing, Julia was slightly disquieted. She loved the existing Shanghai so deeply that she did not want to see it change at all.

8

December 21, 1921

Shanghai, Julia had concluded, was unique. The metropolis on the Yangtze River, which drained the world's most populous river basin, was not yet eight decades old. Shanghai was a stripling among great cities – and as vain as a beautiful eighteen-year-old girl. Julia was happy to join the chorus of praise if that was a condition of living in the most exciting community on earth. Besides, in December of 1921 she truly believed Shanghai was as fascinating as its residents constantly proclaimed.

The International Settlement was, men said, a perfect example of many nations co-operating for the common welfare. Some 25,000 foreigners lived amid a total population of 800 thousand, which was expanding rapidly because the Settlement welcomed everyone – Chinese as well as a hundred other nationalities, races, and religions. Some extolled Shanghai's harmony, the lower orders labouring dutifully and the aristrocrats selflessly governing for the general welfare. Some boasted with perverse pride that Shanghai was the world capital of vice, all its vaunted glories based upon virtual slave labour. Yet even those detractors felt that the new League of Nations should model itself on the Settlement to assure worldwide co-operation, peace, and prosperity.

Sir Judah Haleevie's mansion, Jade House, was the epicentre of that truly international community. No Chinese epitomized Shanghai, because Chinese always belonged first to China. Few foreigners epitomized the city, because they owed their first allegiance to their own countries. The Haleevies were, however, archetypically Shanghai. They gave greater loyalty to no other place on earth, despite paying reverence to Jerusalem.

Since the doors of Jade House were open to all, Joshua had casually

53

asked his own friends to his mother's At Home four days before Christmas of 1921. He was, however, dismayed when Emily Howe and Julia Pavernen brought Elizaveta Alexandrovna Yavalenka unannounced to enjoy the Haleevies' hospitality.

That astute young lady, who was precisely the same age as the twentieth century, had weighed her friends' impulsive invitation against Joshua's failure to ask her. Moved as much by curiosity as by calculation, she had finally decided to go. Her self-assurance did not, however, totally conceal her trepidation.

Elizaveta's prejudices were complex, but flexible. She hated the Bolsheviks and the disproportionate number of Jews among the Bolsheviks for their violent disruption of her life – and the cruel deaths they had inflicted upon her friends and relations. She did not, however, despise *all* Jews.

Her restraint derived from her father, the Ukrainian count and multimillionaire who had taken far more seriously than his presumed profession of soldiering his hobbies of painting and chamber music, as well as his avocations of finance and manufacturing. It was not only stupid, he had taught her, but self-destructive to scorn an entire group. He had advised Elizaveta to save her scorn for the contemptible and to give her esteem to the admirable – regardless of their origins.

Elizaveta had, however, learned that Shanghai Jews hated Russians, particularly the Russian aristocracy. She was glad she did not call herself Countess, not only because the title would be ridiculous in her circumstances, but because it would further inflame the Haleevies' prejudices.

Even if they did not object to a White Russian aristocrat, Joshua's family was unlikely to welcome a young woman of her own curious profession. She decided none the less to attend Lady Haleevie's At Home, after warning Julia and Emily that her presence might be embarrassing. Their naïveté dismissed her fears, and she decided that the worst that could happen was that she would be snubbed. At best, she would meet men who would further her purposes. She was determined not merely to survive, but to survive comfortably.

Accordingly she chose from her mother's wardrobe a dress of crimson satin, demurely cut. The Callot Soeurs model accentuated her voluptuous figure and set off both her porcelain-white skin and her crow-black hair.

Azaleas in porcelain jardinières made the long corridors of Jade House glorious with their bronze, gold, and vermilion flowers. Scarlet poinsettias and winter-flowering cacti fringed with mauve flowerets adorned the dove-grey drawing room where Rachel Haleevie was receiving her guests.

Elizaveta Alexandrovna Yavalenka was shocked by her own response to the mansion. She resented the multiplicity of rooms, and the lavish furnishings struck her as vulgar. A moment later she realized that she was envious – and intimidated.

Envy she might reasonably feel because of the tawdry surroundings in which she now lived. But why, Elizaveta wondered, should she be intimidated by a bourgeois mansion? She who had danced in the Winter Palace in St Petersburg, she who had ridden for three days in a straight line without reaching the boundary of her father's estate.

Sorrow washed over her. She would never again know the splendour that was her birthright. She would never enjoy even the bourgeois opulence of something like Jade House. She realized with anguish how far she had fallen.

Lady Haleevie received Elizaveta warmly. She was fond of both Emily and Julia, who had presented their good friend. Rachel's blonde head inclined towards Elizaveta's blue-black head. They sat side-by-side on the gold-brocade sofa talking of the splendour of St Petersburg, which the older woman had seen with her banker father decades earlier.

A mist of tears made Elizaveta's eyes glow like sapphires. She mourned the days now forever lost, and Rachel Haleevie patted her hand consolingly.

Five years earlier the adolescent Elizaveta would have resented that patronizing gesture from a bourgeoise Jewess. In her troubled twenty-second year, Elizaveta clung for an instant to Rachel's soft white hand.

Finally rising to leave the place beside the hostess free for another guest, she marvelled at the misgivings that had almost kept her from coming – and she responded eagerly to Lady Haleevie's warm invitation: 'Do come again. Any time, not only Thursdays.'

'You were right, and I was wrong,' Elizaveta confided happily to Emily and Julia. 'She's lovely, and she asked me to come again soon. Sometimes it's folly to be too wise.'

'I still don't see why you were so worried,' Julia observed. 'You're perfectly presentable. Not just presentable, but beautiful. No wonder Lady Haleevie wants you to come again. You'll brighten up her soirées.'

'You're both far too generous.' Elizaveta bestowed a delighted smile upon the entire crowded room. 'But I wonder . . .'

'Wonder what, Liz?' Emily was impatient with Elizaveta's pensive pauses.

'She doesn't know who . . . what . . . I am,' Elizaveta declared lugubriously. 'If she finds out . . .'

'The Café, you mean? St Andrew's Café and dancing with . . . with all kinds of men?' Julia dismissed her fears. 'Lady Haleevie will understand.'

Irritated by Julia's ignorant optimism, Elizaveta said sharply, 'Surely, my dear, you're not that naïve! Or are you?'

Julia was wounded. She had surmised that Elizaveta might not only dance with strangers, but dine with men who were unpleasant and, perhaps, accompany them to theatres or casinos. Her sheltered American imagination was incapable of casting Elizaveta in any other role. Other things happened in novels to bedizened harridans; they did not happen to a well-spoken, old-world aristocrat she was proud to call her friend.

Subsiding into hurt silence, Julia was pleased to see her uncle across

55

the Victorian drawing room. Sleek and charming, that quintessentially twentieth-century man, John Pavernen, wound among the ponderous tables and overstuffed brocade sofas of the Victorian era.

'Why, Julia, honey,' John Pavernen said. 'I didn't realize you knew . . .'

Over his left shoulder, Elizaveta scornfully contemplated a plump Italian matron, whose beaded dress was the same scarlet as her own. Emily caught the fleeting recognition that crossed John Pavernen's features. But Julia was caught up in her delight at seeing her uncle, whom she idolized as the archetype of the Shanghai go-getter, the man of the future.

'. . . knew the Haleevies so well,' John Pavernen improvised smoothly. 'Emily, you're as lovely as ever. Won't you introduce me to your gorgeous friend?'

Elizaveta smiled coolly and extended a hand tipped with crimson nails.

'Elizaveta? Do they call you Liz?' Jack Pavernen twinkled. 'But Elizaveta Alex . . . an . . . an . . . Hell! I can't get it.'

Elizaveta repeated her full name, rolling her r's like a tragédienne of the Moscow Arts Theatre. Julia giggled at her uncle's drollery. Emily marvelled that John Pavernen's over-acting did not reveal to his niece that the Russian and he had already met. Perhaps, Emily speculated naïvely, John Pavernen wanted to conceal that acquaintance because Elizaveta and he were mixed up in some confidential business dealings.

'Uncle Jack! Just the man I wanted to see!' Julia burbled. 'Liz needs . . . would like to find work. I thought with the new project you might . . .'

'I'll see what I can do,' he smiled. 'Though Miss . . . Miss Yar . . . vava . . . oh, Hell! Liz herself is mighty quiet. Is she really interested in a dull nine-to-five job?'

'I am interested in work, Mr Pavernen.' Elizaveta did not smile. 'I'm sorry I'm not on the phone. May I ring you?'

'Sure. Julie knows my number. She's really got my number. Makes me jump through hoops. Now, if you'll excuse me, I've got to see a man about a dog.'

'A man about a dog?' Elizaveta asked.

'Some business he doesn't want to mention,' Julia explained. 'Isn't he a scream?'

'A *bolshoi* scream,' Elizaveta agreed gravely. 'What's that word you taught me? Ah, yes, humdinger. Your uncle is really a humdinger.'

'You must be talking American.' Joshua Haleevie presented a salver laden with silver goblets. 'Now I'm *not* offering you ladies eggnog. *Never* serve *Christmas* eggnog in this house. But the milk punch bears a certain resemblance.'

'How lovely, eggnog . . .' Julia began, but yielded to Elizaveta, whose eyes were shining with nostalgia.

'Nanny always gave us eggnog for Christmas. With a nip of rum and a spoonful of brandy. It's five years since I tasted eggnog.'

56

'Eggnog with rum and brandy?' Julia sipped inquisitively. 'We never had liquor in our eggnog. It does taste . . .'

Julia's delighted discovery went unremarked, for Emily was staring speculatively at a newcomer. Jade House was an odd setting for the favourite general of President Sun Yat-sen of the Canton Republic of China. But the red-haired American Vice-Consul Harrison Parker Smythe III was unquestionly conversing with Chiang Kai-shek. The General spoke no English, and his Mandarin was virtually unintelligible. Emily revised her assessment of Harry Smythe's brash ignorance and drifted towards the pair. Joshua linked his arm through Elizaveta's and led her away.

'I want you to meet some interesting people,' he told her expansively. 'You've been hiding your light too long.'

Elizaveta wondered at his altered attitude. Patently uneasy when he greeted her, he had disappeared for three-quarters of an hour – to re-appear abruptly with the eggnog. What, precisely, had he feared?

Dreading Elizaveta's inevitable humiliation, at the hands of his beloved – though shockingly conventional – mother, Joshua had retreated to the conservatories. Impelled by his concern for Elizaveta, he had returned to find them taking obvious pleasure in each other's company. He concluded that he had once again underrated his mother. Repentant and exuberant, he had then chosen to display Elizaveta to the company.

'Herr Graf von Schweinitz and Madame Lollard, Mr Chow the match-king, and General Li. . . .'

Elizaveta automatically filed every name in her memory. Any one might in the future prove vital to her survival. She disliked weighing the potential usefulness of everyone she met, particularly every male. But that calculation was necessary.

For the first time since fleeing Vladivostock fourteen months earlier, Countess Elizaveta Alexandrovna Yavalenka considered the possibility that she might be able to lead a normal life. Not the splendid existence of the Russian aristocracy, which had been eclipsed forever by the Bolsheviks. Perhaps, however, a normal bourgeois life, at least, a comfortable and decent life.

The Christmas spirit, though formally ignored by the Haleevies, was palpable in the overheated room where a string quartet alternately played Bach cantatas and popular tunes like 'Dardanella'. The glow of candles and the fragrance of flowers contrasted poignantly with the glare of the neon and the reek of the cheap perfumes among which she worked at night. Caught up by the atmosphere, Elizaveta loosened the reserves that normally constrained her emotions.

She had been given a warm welcome at Jade House. Lady Haleevie had offered feminine solidarity rather than the humiliation she had feared. Perhaps, Elizaveta mused, Shanghai was not entirely a heartless wasteland.

John Pavernen she had snubbed automatically, though she had initially recalled only his face. She now remembered meeting him in a sumptuous apartment on Szechwan Road at a cocaine-and-roulette party attended by eminently respectable men – and not a single respectable woman. Although he had obviously recognized her, Julia would plead her case. Why should she not take a respectable job from John Pavernen – and gain time to contemplate her future?

As she frankly declared, Elizaveta was above all determined to survive. The wealth and power she would certainly acquire in her present calling would eventually make her invulnerable. The obvious alternative was abhorrent – and probably unattainable. Marrying to survive was voluntary slavery. Besides, what man she could stomach would offer *her* marriage?

Yet Rachel Haleevie's unaffected welcome had made Elizaveta feel she was not irretrievably lost. John Pavernen's promise to do what he could for her encouraged her to envisage a new life. When she left with Emily and Julia, half an hour later, she was bubbling with gaiety.

Her friends were going to a pre-Christmas dinner with those devout Methodists, the Soongs. Elizaveta decided to ride with them in the emerald-green Rolls. She chatted brightly, repeatedly reminding Julia to remind John Pavernen of what he had said. Elizaveta's volatile Russian spirit soared. The job was already a reality in her imagination. Her exhilaration was not diminished by the cold ride in a rickshaw to her dingy bed-sitter at the wrong end of Kiangse Road.

After climbing five flights of stairs, Elizaveta found the creaky wooden door half-open on the small room that the landlord, with heavy commercial enthusiasm, called a studio apartment. His navy-blue cashmere overcoat still buttoned, Joshua Haleevie sat in her dilapidated wing-chair beside the convertible studio-couch under the high window. He had lit the gas-fire, which was fed by a coin-operated meter, and the dank chill was just yielding to the jagged blue flames.

His light-blue eyes gazed an instant longer into those flames, reflecting their sombre shadows when he looked up. Elizaveta saw that his lips were compressed as if guarding a secret, and a minute frown creased the skin between his dark eyebrows, he stared at her, and smiled without joy.

'What a delightful surprise!' Elizaveta was still gripped by exuberance. 'I've got a bottle of vodka somewhere . . . and a smidgin of caviar. Do take off your coat, my brave captain.'

'It's not really a social visit, Elizaveta.' He dutifully hung his coat in the minuscule foyer. 'It's more of an anti-social visit.'

'And what does that mean, my captain?' She remained kittenish. 'This uneducated Ukrainian peasant girl does not know such an English word.'

'Harry Smythe let it slip. Unintentionally, I think. He told my mother where we'd met you. And she . . .'

'And she?' Elizaveta stood stockstill amid her shattered illusions. 'What has she said?'

'She said . . . she said she was very sorry, distressed, but she had no choice. She wanted to write you a note. But I said I'd come myself. Well, you can guess . . .'

'I can – assuredly. However, since you've come all this way you might as well tell me. What is the message?'

'Mother wants you to know she liked you enormously . . . and she was looking forward to seeing you again. She had thought of helping you find some congenial position. But . . .'

'But, Joshua?'

'It is nothing personal, she stresses. Under other circumstances, she would like nothing better than to have you as a friend. She may still be able to help you find a position. So could I, for that matter. But . . .'

'But, Joshua?' she probed. 'Be done with your buts!'

'But there can, of course, be no question of your ever coming to Jade House again. She regrets it, but she must make that clear.'

'Why this great hurry to tell me, Joshua?' she flared. 'Apparently you couldn't wait to rush over here to give me the glad tidings!'

'I didn't want you embarrassed further,' he declared. 'I didn't want you to make plans . . . to talk about seeing us. I didn't want you to be shown up for bragging and fantasies like the other . . . the other . . .'

'The other whores, you mean. Why don't you say it?' Her emotions swung wildly. 'You do have a good heart, my dashing captain, don't you? I'm grateful.'

He stared at the threadbare carpet and stammered: 'Of course I'll do everything I can to help you. My God, I had no idea you lived so . . . meanly. I'll push Pavernen about a job for you. Or find you something myself, I promise. Whatever I can do . . .'

'I really don't think there's any need.' Elizaveta coldly swept up the rubble of her illusions. 'I'll make my own way, thank you. Be assured that I can.'

Joshua stood mute when she locked the door of the studio apartment. Reaching behind her, she undid the topmost of the row of hooks that fastened her crimson dress. She then turned her back to him.

'Well then, back to work,' she said gaily. 'Do be a dear and undo me.'

'For God's sake, Elizaveta!' he protested. 'Don't be mad. For my sake! I promise you I'll find something. . . . In time maybe even . . .'

'Maybe nothing, my dear.' She laughed. 'Just undo me, please. It's what I want, I assure you.'

9

The distant hammering invaded Julia's sleep, not quite awakening her. She pulled the pillow over her head, but could not shut out the knocking on the door. Resignedly, she stretched out her hand to grope for her cotton dressing gown. Reluctantly, her eyelids parted on the opalescent morning.

An instant later her green eyes opened wide, and she slipped the dressing gown over her lace nightdress. She was not in the airy bedroom in Donald and Eurydice Howe's Harmony Hall, which she had occupied during the nine months since her arrival in Shanghai. Taking in the sparse furnishings and the high, sloping ceiling, she remembered. For the first time, she possessed an apartment all her own. That independence, too, she owed to her friendship with Emily.

Tommy had offered her the apartment when he saw that she felt she could no longer impose on his parents' hospitality. His mother had urged Julia to stay indefinitely, delighted at having not one but two daughters in the house. Despite her affection for Eurydice, Julia pointed out that she was no longer a lady of leisure. She could not reside so far from her employment in John Pavernen's office in unfashionable Hongkew.

After his mother left the room, shaking her head sadly, Tommy had suggested: 'Julie, why don't you take on my attic? I'll be in Peking for another year – and then interning at Shanghai General. The rent's very low because it belongs to Pater. Fortunately, he can hardly remember every property he owns. I fixed it with old Lau, his office manager. Do take it, Julie. I'd hate to see the old flat go to waste.'

Although the alarm clock on her bedside table read 6:45, the hammering still resounded through the loft. Julia's slippers glided across the

60

polished floorboards of the cavernous sitting room. She pushed the folding steel grate and mechanically opened the five bolts, deadlocks, and chains that secured the front door.

These ample safeguards were not really necessary, for foreigners were virtually sacrosanct in the Settlement – unless they sought out trouble. The ordinances of the Shanghai Municipal Council, enforced by the foreign-officered police, ensured her security. She felt no apprehension of her dawn visitors, although the building was far downtown at the junction of Kiukiang and Honan Roads around the corner from commercial Nanking Road.

'*Dieh-wuh gun-ssi* . . .' a male voice called. 'Telephone company for installation.'

After tightening her sash, Julia swung the door open. The three smiling men in the grey uniform of the Shanghai Telephone Company proffered identification cards bearing their pictures and their descriptions in Chinese and English.

The United States was efficient, Julia felt, but Americans did not run to such cheerful service so early on a Sunday. Their detractors said the Chinese could never master modern inventions, but would always require supervision by mechanically minded foreigners. Their grudging champions replied that the Chinese were clever as monkeys; show them how, and they'd do the job perfectly ever after – as long as there was no need to make changes. Julia herself found the Chinese remarkably ingenious and adaptable, extremely willing and hard-working. The old China hands said she was blinded by her newcomer's enthusiasm and would learn better. It was only monkey-cleverness.

'Not monkeys, but donkeys,' Tommy had commented meditatively. 'Awkward, intelligent donkeys . . . not graceful, stupid horses. Like donkeys, we Chinese won't work unless we know why – and we're decently rewarded. Like donkeys, we're hellishly independent. That's why it's so hard to govern the Chinese.'

Smiling reminiscently, Julia showed the workmen the corner where she wanted the telephone and returned to her tiny bedroom to dress. They were soon pounding again, although she had assumed that laying telephone wires was a relatively silent task. The din sounded as if they were tearing down the walls.

She emerged into clouds of plaster-dust, through which wafted the beguiling smells of bacon and coffee. Her amah had obviously arrived on the heels of the workmen. Lao Zee, introduced by Emily's old nursemaid Ven Jyieh, was preparing fruit, toast, and scrambled eggs with bacon. A straw suitcase and a cloth-wrapped parcel lay at her feet in the small kitchen, but she was already wearing the amah's uniform of white tunic and black trousers.

'No pay Missy porridge and kippahs. More bettah, Missy not eat too muchee,' Lao Zee declared. 'Fat Missys nevah catch man. Europ'en mastah very funny. Chinese man very much like fat lady.'

The amah had taken command. Julia contentedly watched her bully the telephone men and tell the delivery coolies where to place the furniture. The Shanghai Secondhand Store paid no heed to Sunday and boasted in advertisements that it 'commanded the resources of over one hundred of the leading pawnshops, thus guaranteeing low prices and high quality'.

Emily had, however, declared that the prices were outrageous, only for credulous foreigners. Emily loved protracted shopping expeditions, although Julia hated the interminable bargaining. Emily was alternately so Chinese or so emancipated it was hard to pin her down. Predicting her reactions was like picking up the quicksilver from a broken thermometer.

Lao Zee eagerly trotted to answer the ringing telephone, but returned chopfallen to announce: 'Only silly test'. For half an hour, the instrument pealed at intervals, and Julia was unprepared when the grey-haired foreman with silver-rimmed glasses suddenly informed her in English: 'Mr John Pavernen has rung through. He would be glad to talk with Miss Julia Pavernen.'

Marvelling at that formal summons, Julia saw with surprise that the sitting-room wall was again intact, the telephone wires completely hidden. The foreman waved her to the extension in the bedroom.

She dubiously lifted the candlestick base with the conical mouthpiece. Although invented forty-five years earlier and rapidly developed in the Great War, Alexander Graham Bell's telephone was still largely confined to offices. It was rarely seen in homes. Ladies and gentlemen would never prefer it to handwritten notes for social communication.

'Julie, is that you?' John Pavernen's baritone crackled metallically. 'How are you, honey? Snug in your new little nest?'

'Hello, Uncle Jack. It's lovely. They just put the telephone in. You're the very first caller.'

'I just thought I'd give you a tinkle. Now you're working for me, you've got to have a phone. See how convenient it is?'

'Convenient? A little early to tell, I'd say.'

'You bet your life it's not too early to tell. Julie honey, a message just came to my cable address. *Happy Easter darling stop when planning come home questionmark all our love mother and dad.* You want to answer? The messenger's waiting.'

'Not now, Uncle Jack,' she replied after a pause. 'I'll send an answer later, when I've had time to think. I don't want to go home – not for a while, anyway. But I'm not sure how to tell them.'

'Okay, honey. Whatever you want. Just as long as you don't leave me in the lurch. I'll try to get to your house-warming party. But I've got a big deal cooking.'

'On Easter Sunday? Well, I guess that's what it takes. Oh, Uncle Jack, what about Elizaveta? It's been a long time since . . .'

'I haven't forgotten. I can find something for her in real estate. A lot more Russians will be coming soon – and they can't *all* be broke.'

'Thanks a million, Uncle Jack. You're wonderful.'

Replacing the earpiece on its wishbone rest, Julia glanced at the clutter of valises and trunks in the bedroom. Lao Zee would make short work of reducing that chaos to perfect order. Julia grinned in self-mockery. A year earlier, she would without thinking have cleared up herself. She could almost hear her mother's voice: 'Darling, you can't leave your room like this. Ladies just don't.'

Julia dropped to her knees before the big steamer-trunk. Her mother would hardly have approved of her blowing her last penny on new clothes to celebrate her job with Uncle Jack's new company: JPEnterprises. After heedlessly tumbling garments out of drawers, she rose clasping a froth of lime-green satin.

The new lounging pyjamas, which she had designed herself, were more sophisticated than the green-sequinned, black-silk pyjamas she had worn to death last summer. The narrow trousers flared at the ankles, while both the cuffs and the stand-up collar of the slim tunic were edged with bands of embroidered asters and butterflies.

The pale green silk contrasted provocatively with her tawny hair, and she no longer felt guilty at applying a film of face-powder and a touch of lip-rouge. Further self-adornment would, at twenty-one, be excessive. Her forte was simplicity. She slipped on a chunky bracelet of old ivory with a silver clasp. After inserting a Chesterfield into a six-inch ivory holder carved with dragons, Julia was ready for the day.

In dismay she dropped the holder, clapped her hand to her mouth, and looked fearfully at her bedside clock. In great haste she pulled a linen duster over her lounging pyjamas, jammed a felt cloche on her head, and raced down the creaking stairs.

Fortunately, a yellow public rickshaw was passing outside. She promised the coolie an additional fifty cents to hurry and sat back, hoping she would not be too late for the Easter Service.

Joshua Haleevie's Delage runabout gleamed sapphire before the door when Julia returned shortly after noon. Behind it, the Haleevies' pearl-grey seven-passenger Marmon stood at the kerb like a berthed ocean liner. Perhaps Joshua was enacting his fantasy; perhaps the limousine actually did carry a footstool for his female passengers to alight on. The enormous motor-car certainly carried his house-warming presents.

Smiling in anticipation, Julia climbed the splintered staircase. She was tired after failing to find a rickshaw to carry her back from church. Her feet hurt because she had not changed her spike-heeled mules, and she was perspiring because she could not take off the linen duster that concealed her frivolous pyjamas. That garment would have affronted the pious and fashionable ladies in their Easter bonnets and new dresses. Besides, she might have been mistaken on the street for a 'dance-hall hostess' returning from a night of work or hurrying to an early assignation.

Julia had learned much during the nine months since her arrival – not all of it pleasant. She felt as far removed from the naïve girl who had disembarked from the *Empress of Australia* as her present exquisite costume was from the gauche black-silk pyjamas she had earlier prized.

Above all, she had learned exactly why Shanghai was called the wickedest city in Asia, where even foreign women sold themselves as harlots. Still, she could not believe that Elizaveta did that sort of thing, regardless of her Russian friend's bravado.

A catchy melody was tinkling through the loft. Joshua was cranking a Victrola, and a black-bakelite disc was pouring the brassy strains of Cole Porter's 'China Doll' through its curved horn. Elegant in a blue-linen Norfolk jacket and wide-legged trousers, he kissed both her cheeks. She would have been shocked by that effusive greeting nine months earlier. Now she laughed in delight.

Her small head balanced on her swan's neck, Elizaveta threw her arms around both her lover and her friend. Before she was enveloped, Julia took in the long white kaftan crossed by bandoliers and cut close to Elizaveta's voluptuous figure. Red half-boots and the karakul hat cocked on her black hair completed the image of a daredevil Cossack.

'I weep that it's not Russian Easter!' Elizaveta parodied the Slavic melancholy that sometimes overwhelmed her. 'But I'll try to be jolly. I know you'll be very happy in your new flat, Julie.'

'Tho' I says it as shouldn't, we're gonna make you happy, luv.' Joshua was an unconvincing Cockney. 'Lookee there!'

Beneath the long north window, ten cases of Pommery champagne were stacked. The long table bore a big silver tray laden with smoked salmon and smoked sturgeon. Through the loft drifted the smells of the two delicacies Julia liked best. The rich scent of braised meat came from Russian *zakuski*, as she had learned to call the small horns of pastry. The scent of sweet vinegar and ginger heralded the miniature purses of translucent dough the Shanghainese called 'little steamer dumplings'. The Haleevies' chauffeur emerged from the minuscule kitchen bearing a salver of fresh caviar and buckwheat blinis. Another manservant carried a block of ice that encased a bottle of vodka.

'I didn't expect *this* when you said to leave the arrangements to you,' Julia protested. 'It's just too much. . . .'

'Never too much! Never!' Elizaveta's normally crisp English was today furry with Slavic consonants. 'It is men's duty to give – lavishly! It is women's duty to enjoy – delightfully! Never say *too* much. Only drink and eat, laugh and sing – and *drink*!'

Since both her friends had obviously acted on that advice, Julia lifted a thimble-glass of vodka.

'And also eat!' Elizaveta admonished. 'If you take a little bite with every sip, the vodka will make you merry. If you don't, you'll become depressed and weepy and . . .'

'. . . Russian!' Joshua interjected. 'Mad Russian!'

The footsteps that clattered on the stairs were muffled by Fyodor Chaliapin singing the clock aria from *Boris Godonov* through the Victrola's scalloped horn. Hearing Harry Smythe shouting his greetings from the corridor, Julia took Elizaveta's arm.

'Come see my new dress,' she invited. 'Before too many arrive.'

'But while she can still see,' Joshua grinned. 'I'll hold the fort while you two exchange the secrets of the boudoir.'

'We had a couple of bottles of bubbly before we came,' Elizaveta confessed as the bedroom door closed. 'Now where's that new dress? Your taste is really improving, pet. Those pyjamas are fabulous.'

'It's not about dresses,' Julia answered. 'Liz, Uncle Jack says he can find a job for you. Also, maybe you'd like to move into my spare bedroom. As a favour. I could use a little help with expenses.'

'A job? What job?'

'Something to do with real estate, selling or renting houses and apartments, mainly to Russians.'

'I shall talk with him,' Elizaveta decided judiciously. 'But I think not. I do not know that I shall have time.'

'Time? Are you that busy? With what?'

'Many things, pet, many things. Life is real and earnest. Not all champagne and caviar by any means.'

'If you really don't need the job any more, I'm happy for you. But do think about it. And what about moving in? It would be fun, wouldn't it?'

Elizaveta Alexandrovna Yavalenka stared at Julia Pavernen. Her full lower lip trembled with suppressed laughter.

'I'm touched by your offer,' she finally said. 'It could be great fun. But I'm afraid you'd cramp my style.'

Believing that reluctance to be mere politeness, Julia persisted. Elizaveta rejected all entreaties, though she refused to explain how her style would be cramped.

'Look, Julie, there's no point in going over it again. And I want a drink. Anyway, I love my present way of life. Wouldn't change it for the world.'

Hurt by Elizaveta's rejection, Julia bit back the obvious retort. The wild Russian would have to change her way of life when Joshua proposed and they were married.

The big loft was filling up with guests. Julia shook hands with Harry Smythe, who introduced a fluffy Belgian blonde. She offered her cheek to Richard Hollings. The Englishman's dark eyes searched the room and, for an instant, his straight-planed face was desolate.

Hollings's occasional melancholy, Julia firmly believed, was due to the horrors he had seen as a lieutenant on the Italian front. But he said he'd had a 'cushy job in intelligence'. Finding that Emily was not among the throng, he pushed a lock from his forehead and asked.

'Who is that big Chinese chap?'

Following Richard's gaze, Julia saw a striking figure placidly sipping champagne under the north window. The big oval head with the shrewd eyes above the massive cheekbones was tantalizingly familiar, and authority clothed him almost as palpably as his lustrous light-blue cotton tunic. Still striving to remember him, she saw that he was cradling a black-and-white puppy in his left arm.

When he bowed in greeting, Julia remembered him: Chang Kuo-tao, Tommy Howe's mysterious radical friend. She had met him at the students' meeting that was interminably addressed by the zealot in homespun whose name she could not remember.

'Hsia Tan-ssu Hsien-sheng chiao wo lai kao-su. . . .'

He was obviously perplexed by her obvious incomprehension of the tide of Mandarin. But Julia, who recognized Tommy's name, Hsia Tan-ssu, begged him in her hesitant Shanghainese to continue. He replied in slightly more fluent Shanghainese, and, somehow, they understood each other.

He had, he said, seen Tommy in Peking on his way back from Moscow. Moscow? Julia wondered what on earth a young Chinese labour leader was doing in the Bolshevik capital.

The puppy was Tommy's house-warming present. Although a nuisance on the train, it was really a good little chap. The lion dog was prized as a temple guardian in its native Tibet, he said, though it did not grow very big. The puppy's name was Tang Jo-wang. When she took it in her arms, a pink tongue kissed her fingers.

'Take care,' Chang Kuo-tao warned. 'And before I forget, I've also got a letter for you.' She put the puppy down just in time, and a small puddle appeared on the floorboards. After asking Lao Zee to put both puppy and letter in the bedroom, Julia turned back to the mysterious Mr Chang.

He had, it emerged, been to Moscow to attend the First Congress of the Toilers of the East. He replied without hesitation to her direct questions and pronounced that pretentious name in clumsy English. He added that he was the delegate of the All-China Secretariat of Labour, though himself no *toiler* (again an English word), but only a *clerk* (once again English). Neither secret nor specifically Bolshevik, since Dr Sun Yat-sen's National People's Party had also attended, the conference had launched a 'campaign to unite the exploited masses of Asia.'

They parted with mutual congratulations on having communicated so clearly. He hoped to see her again, Chang Kuo-tao said. Perhaps she would have time to teach a few classes at the Foreign Languages School his group was organizing.

'And what group is that?' she asked.

'Just the Secretariat,' he replied promptly, 'the Secretariat of Labour. I'm the director.'

'Oh,' Julia persisted, 'I'd heard of another organization as well? A political party?'

'*Ah-la fu hsiu-deh!*' he replied in emphatic Shanghainese. 'I don't know anything about that!'

A sense of housewifely duty drove Julia into the kitchen, but Lao Zee expelled her: 'More bettah Missy go talkee guests. Catchee small piece drink and makee merry. But no watchee drink too much!'

The loft no longer appeared cavernous when filled with chattering guests. After patting her hair into place, Julia lit the Chesterfield in her ivory holder and made her entrance.

Richard Hollings smiled at her fleetingly. His gaze returned to the front-door, through which Emily Howe was just entering. She revealed a

66

striking blue-crêpe *cheongsam* when she removed her black-velvet coat, and Richard's eyes glowed.

Julia recognized the Chinese brother and sister behind Emily. T.V. Soong wore a double-breasted blue suit with businesslike tortoise-shell glasses balanced on the bridge of his broad nose. Mayling Soong was even more striking than Emily, though somewhat shorter. Beneath jet bangs her face was heart-shaped, and her complexion justified the cliché 'skin like a camellia petal'. A red-felt pill-box perched saucily on her glossy hair, she was the first Chinese woman Julia had seen wear a hat. Her green-silk *cheongsam*, barely nipped at the waist, did not really display her figure.

'Julie, here's Mayling Soong.' Emily asked. 'You do remember her big brother Tze-ven? Everybody calls him T.V.'

Richard Hollings came up and whispered urgently in Emily's ear. She allowed him to lead her away.

'And how are you enjoying Shanghai, Miss Pavernen?' Mayling Soong asked. 'It's been some months since you came to dinner with us.'

'I adore it. I think Shanghai's wonderful. I wish my Shanghainese was better. I'm studying hard, but . . .'

'We prefer to speak English.' T.V. Soong's prized American accent was minutely marred by slurred consonants. 'My sisters and I always speak English to each other. You know I was at Harvard when May was at Wellesley.'

Mayling added: 'It's just natural to speak English. We're all American-educated. Ailing, my oldest sister, we usually call Nanny. And Chingling . . . Mme Sun Yat-sen, you know . . . is Rosamonde. I'm only May, little May, the youngest. And T.V. is . . . T.V.'

'A friend's just sent me a puppy . . .' Julia began.

'Hiya, T.V. How you doing?' Vice-Consul Harry Smythe offered a tray of glasses. 'Miss Soong . . . Mayling . . . how're you?'

'Yes, Miss Pavernen?' Mayling ignored him. 'You were saying?'

'The puppy, he's adorable. From Tibet, I'm told. He's called Tang Jo-wang.'

'What a funny name for a dog unless . . .' Mayling almost giggled.

'. . . unless he's a religious dog,' T.V. completed her thought.

'A religious dog?' Julia repeated blankly. 'Well, they do say lion-dogs guard the temples in Tibet.'

'Lamaseries,' Harry Smythe corrected automatically. 'They have lamaseries in Tibet, not temples.'

'Tang Jo-wang is the Chinese name of a German Jesuit who came in the seventeenth century,' T.V. recalled. 'He was a great teacher of science, theology – and gunnery. His original name was very long: Johann Adam Schall von Bell.'

'I'll call the puppy Adam,' Julia decided. 'I could hardly call him Father Schall.'

'How come you're up on this Father Schall, T.V.?' Harry Smythe's carrot hair gleamed in the afternoon sun streaming through the skylight. 'Never heard of him myself.'

67

'Then he couldn't be important, Mr Smythe!' T.V. Soong pointedly turned to address Julia. 'An ancestor on our mother's side was Schall's greatest disciple. He became Grand Chancellor of the Ming Dynasty. Prime Minister, we'd say today.'

'But you're not Catholics, are you?' Harry Smythe could not recognize a snub, a failing that was a great advantage for a diplomat. 'I know your family's not.'

'You *are* well informed, Mr Smythe.' T.V.'s distaste was tempered by his respect for the brash American's official position. 'We Soongs are all Protestants. So are my brothers-in-law. Rosamonde's husband, Dr Sun Yat-sen, was converted in Hawaii. Eileen's husband, H.H. Kung, is the seventy-fifth lineal descendant of Confucius. But he doesn't call himself Duke, which is the Kungs' hereditary title. He's prouder of being a Yale Ph.D.'

Some Chinese really did worship their ancestors, Julia decided. T.V. Soong obviously worshipped not only his own, but the ancestors of his brothers-in-law. A pity the redoubtable Dr Sun Yat-sen was known to be descended from Cantonese peasants. However, if he tried, T.V. could probably dredge up a minister and a general or two among the President's ancestors.

'Not very Christian, though, cosying up the Bolsheviks, is it, T.V.?' Harry Smythe was unimpressed. 'If Sun Yat-sen's such a good Christian, how come he's hobnobbing with the Comintern agents?'

'You know, Harry,' T.V. replied candidly. 'Socialism may be necessary for China.'

'What do you expect?' Mayling added. 'England and France aren't interested in helping the President. Even America won't. Dr Sun Yat-sen stands for progress, but only the Bolsheviks want to help him.'

'Don't give up hope,' Harry Smythe advised. 'Some Americans are trying to help Dr Sun. Some have also got a lot of faith in General Chiang Kai-shek.'

'He *is* a remarkable man,' Mayling said softly. 'I, too, have much faith in General Chiang.'

The party was thinning out, and Julia went into her bedroom to repair her make up. She recalled Emily's tart observation: 'The worst thing about being the hostess is having to wait for the last guest to leave before you can take your shoes off.'

But she was still enjoying her own party. She felt delightfully un-inhibited and exhilarated. But she was not drunk, not even slightly tiddly. And she could prove it: out of all the bantering conversations, the laughter, and the jokes, she remembered best her serious discussions with Chang Kuo-tao and T.V. Soong.

Before rejoining her guests, she re-read the note that had accompanied the puppy Adam. Tommy wrote that he was working hard. He could evidently not quite breach his reserve enough to tell her outright that he missed her, but he did say he was greatly looking forward to seeing her.

From the reticent Tommy that was virtually a declaration. Tucking Adam under her arm, Julia returned to the loft.

'Where's Liz?' she asked Emily. 'I want to drink a toast – to the three of us.'

'She's just left, Julie. Richard and I are also going to run along.'

Julia heard an unidentifiable male voice murmur: 'Elizaveta Alexandrovna Yavalenka, the tart with the heart *for* gold.'

She was, however, too tired and too happy to take the remark as anything but a joke in poor taste.

10

May 16, 1922

The approach to Harmony Hall always cast a faint shadow over Emily's normally blithe temperament. The process of unlocking the ponderous iron gates was positively medieval, as was the ritual search of the emerald-green Rolls-Royce, in which a bodyguard always rode beside the chauffeur. The dark figures visible among the bright rhododendrons of mid-May were like the henchmen guarding the castle of an evil prince. Accustomed to the casual freedom of America, Emily felt stifled by her own home.

Emily fiercely resented men's oppression of women, but her nature was optimistic. After her momentary depression, she was again cheerful when she alighted from the Rolls with an armful of text-books. Visiting Julia in the loft on Kiukiang Road always left her in good spirits. The black-and-white puppy was very funny, and his mistress was perturbed because he was at three months as big as a full-grown spaniel. Adam somehow seemed to possess the same naïve and good-hearted enthusiasm that made Julia herself such a delight.

Julia was dedicated to her new job – and comically secretive about her uncle's business. John Pavernen had decreed that she must continue her study of Shanghainese for the sake of JPEnterprises. Eager to regain command of her neglected native tongue, Emily was happy to join those private lessons – and to escape the confinement of Harmony Hall.

The tutor's rudimentary English made her assistance essential, and her advanced lessons did not interfere with her friend's elementary lessons. Moreover, Venerable Master, as they addressed the forty-two-year-old scholar, had opened a door to an exciting prospect. He wrote popular articles on classical themes for a number of the hundred and forty-four newspapers and magazines that Greater Shanghai's two and a half

70

million Chinese insatiably consumed. At his suggestion, Emily had written about her experiences in America for the *Women's Weekly*. Venerable Master's enthusiasm was only in part inspired by his fees for placing her articles and polishing her writing, for he had great faith in her ability. With his encouragement, Emily also rediscovered her joy in telling stories.

After starting with fairy tales for children, she was now writing light romances to enliven the dreary toil of shop girls and factory girls. Not daring to write under her own name, she was gratified by the growing popularity of her pen-name: *Je Hsin*, which meant Enthusiastic (literally 'Hot-Hearted').

Venerable Master's enthusiasm diminished slightly when the bi-monthly *China Today* asked his protégée to write regularly on the plight of women. Her increasingly strident tone was distressing to a gentleman-scholar of the old school.

She herself was not a gentleman, Emily replied reasonably, and she was not much of a scholar either. He should, therefore, not reproach her for lacking the literary polish or the judicious restraint expected of a gentleman-scholar. Besides, she countered, Chinese of the old school required of their women, above all, fecundity; secondly, subservience; thirdly, chastity – and no more. Having developed that theme in her latest article for *China Today*, she had earlier that afternoon taken mildly malicious pleasure in watching Venerable Master cluck with indignation while he dutifully – and scrupulously – corrected her prose.

Stepping out of the Rolls into the late afternoon sunshine, Emily was a little ashamed of her enjoyment of Venerable Master's distress. None the less, she reminded herself, men like him – well-meaning, decent men – must be forced to change their attitudes radically before China's downtrodden women could be free. Actually, his anger was encouraging, for it proved her arguments were hitting home. She was already fighting the opening battles of the arduous campaign for feminine emancipation.

In her preoccupation, Emily hardly realized that the door of the circular reception-hall was, quite extraordinarily, being opened by Old Woo himself. The six-foot-two major-domo was imposing with the green-and-gold seal of the Howe family glowing on the breast of his white long-gown, which was lighter by only a shade than his silver mane. Born into the service of the Howes, Old Woo would condescend to welcome an ambassador or a governor – if he approved of them. Even the master of Harmony Hall did not expect that his major-domo would always greet him in the hall.

'*Yuelin, Yuelin Siu-jyeh* ...' Old Woo's tone was portentous. 'Emily, Miss Emily, your parents are waiting in the study. The Master wishes you to come immediately.'

Emily's heart skipped a beat. Something terrible must have happened in the few hours she had been away. Perhaps Tommy was injured – or worse. Perhaps her mother or her father had been found to be afflicted with a critical illness. Perhaps the Howe enterprises had encountered a great setback.

Emily's hurried heels clicked on the marble floor of the hall, drummed softly in the hardwood corridor – and were muffled by the blue-and-white Tientsin carpet in the study. Donald and Eurydice Howe sat side by side on the purple-flowered cretonne sofa. They were modern parents, but today they looked terribly old-fashioned. Despite his black-rimmed spectacles and the lavalière watch pinned to her imposing bosom, their severe expressions made them look like a Manchu Dynasty ancestral portrait.

'*Ah-ba! Mng-ma! ...*' Emily spontaneously spoke in the slurred Shanghainese of her childhood. 'Daddy! Mamma! What's wrong? Why are you looking so sad? Is it something awful?'

Her mother's stern mien did not alter, but her father's eyes blinked behind his thick lenses.

'Nothing is wrong, Yuelin.' Her mother's lugubrious tone belied that reassurance.

'Nothing at all's wrong, Yuelin.' Her father's smile was strained. 'It's just that . . .'

'Actually, daughter, this is an occasion for joy.' Eurydice casually interrupted her husband, as she would never in public. 'We're all very happy. It's an occasion for rejoicing!'

'Well, you don't look it.' Emily was blunt in her relief – and her suspicion. 'You've frightened me half to death. What's it all about, Daddy?'

'We wanted you to know immediately,' he replied. 'So I told Old Woo to send you in the instant you got back.'

'Something to do with me, is it?'

'Something wonderful for you,' her mother replied. 'We are delighted to tell you that you will be married in October just after the Mid-Autumn Festival. Oh Yuelin, we're so happy for you.'

Emily stood rooted to the blue-and-white carpet, her lips parted in astonishment. Through the blood pounding in her ears she half-heard her father add: 'It's a wonderful match, Yuelin. Nien-lao's a fine young man. And the Lis are a deeply respected family – old scholarship and old money, too. It's a magnificent alliance for both families!'

'Isn't this . . . Don't you think . . . I can't see . . .' Emily stammered in shock. 'Isn't it all . . . so abrupt? I can hardly think. . . . It's so sudden.'

'You've known him all your life, my dear,' Eurydice placidly pointed out. 'You were betrothed to Nien-lao when you were four. You've always known that you two would marry. Seventeen years ago is hardly abrupt, is it, my dear?'

'Mother, that . . . that was . . . only a formality. Daddy told me so over and over again. When I was old enough, he used to say, *perhaps* I'd marry Nien-lao – only if I wanted to. Daddy always promised. And now this . . . this avalanche! I can't believe it! I just can't!'

'Your father has always been far too indulgent.' Eurydice's lips hardly moved. 'He's always allowed you too much rein. But what could you expect? His only daughter! His thousand taels of gold!'

'Formality or not, Yuelin, the engagement stands.' Donald Howe ignored his wife's sour outburst. 'It was never amended – and certainly not cancelled. The Lis and the Howes have now decided that the marriage will take place in October. It is only May now, so it's hardly abrupt. Yuelin, marriages have always been arranged by parents who seek the best for their daughters.'

'The best for their daughters?' Enraged by his unblinking assumption that she would do exactly as he directed, Emily was appalled by the sudden realization that she probably would. 'Why don't you say the best for themselves and their families? Or what *they* think is the best. Daughters don't matter at all! This daughter matters least of all!'

Eurydice Howe's lips clamped shut. Parental authority had declared its will, and there was no more to be said. The marriage would take place as arranged. Further discussion was not merely unnecessary, but could lead to acrimony – perhaps to unfilial protests and unladylike tantrums Emily would later regret. Children had to be told what to do – particularly female children.

'Now, dear, you know very well we're only thinking of what's best for you.' Her father still tried to placate her. 'And we gave it a lot of thought.'

'But *you* decided, Daddy. You didn't even talk to me. You simply decided what was to become of my life. You *disposed* of me.'

Father and daughter stared at each other apprehensively. Both feared a head-on confrontation, and both strove to quell their anger. Donald Howe studied the plump, powerful hands crossed on the paunch that distended his grey-silk long-gown. Still standing stock still on the blue-and-white carpet, her text-books clutched to her bosom, Emily felt her knees tremble.

'Father and Mother, Esteemed Parents, won't you open your hearts?' she pleaded. 'Only listen to me for a few moments? Could you not reconsider? Why, I can't even remember what Nien-lao looks like. It's *so* desperately important to me. Can't you just . . .'

Her father and mother faced her like implacable Buddhas, stone-faced, immobile, and unreachable. Their ears were deaf to prayers, and their hearts were closed to mercy.

She had no choice, Emily realized in despair, not in their world. Since she *must* submit, she should submit with good grace. Bowing to the two remote figures, she began to compose in her mind a litany of self-abnegation. The years fell away, and the centuries unwound. She prepared to submit to the fate she hated just as a weeping princess of the Han Dynasty had two millennia earlier submitted to the Emperor's command that she marry a chieftain of the Hunnish barbarians.

No, not like that princess at all. Like a peasant girl called from feeding the chickens to be informed that she was to be sold to a lecherous old landlord. The Emperor had explained to the protesting princess the reasons of state that made her distasteful marriage necessary – because that explanation would induce her to serve the Dynasty's purpose more effectively. The grasping peasant father would curtly pronounce the life sentence – as had her own urbane banker father.

She was, Emily realized with horror, on the verge of bending openly to her father's will – as she had already bent in her thoughts. Then rage flamed in her heart. She raged at her own slave-mentality, the age-old docility of the Chinese woman who would accept humiliation, privation – even death – rather than raise her voice in defiance.

She had almost betrayed everything she believed. After raising the banner of women's rights, she had almost given way meekly at the first assault. Stronger than her righteous anger at her parents, Emily felt white-hot contempt for herself.

Her books dropped from her arms, and her hands rose as if in imprecation. Eurydice Howe stared impassively, but Donald Howe dropped his eyes before his daughter's fierce gaze.

'Why? . . . Why?' Emily demanded. 'Why are you doing this to me? Have I hurt you so that you wish to punish me? What have I done to deserve such treatment?'

Donald Howe did not reply, but sat still as a carved image of the God of Wrath. He flushed scarlet, and an instant later turned so pale that his grey eyebrows stood out dark. His hands clutched his chest, and his face turned putty-grey – lustreless and flaccid.

'You . . . must . . . be . . . married!' He wheezed as he pushed each word off his tongue. 'And *very* soon!'

'Your poor father!' Eurydice interjected sternly. 'What you're doing to him! He'll have a heart attack if you're not careful. And all because he loves you and wants the best for you, you foolish girl.'

The chief antagonists ignored her interruption like two gladiators who cannot allow themselves to be distracted for an instant from the mortal threat of the other. His leaden colour hardly altered, Donald strove to speak calmly. But his tenor voice rose in fury.

'You force me to tell you the reasons, ungrateful child. Of course the engagement was a formality, a convention, no more, as I used to tell you. However, I have now made it binding and irrevocable. You cannot . . . absolutely cannot . . . cast it off.'

Emily had never before seen the implacable face behind which her father now continued his reprimand: 'Why have I done so? Because this is your last chance. No other gentleman of good family would marry you after the revelations I am in honour bound to make. But the Lis – in their great magnaminity – are prepared to overlook your notorious behaviour. They will honour the contract of betrothal despite your . . . your ill fame. You should get down on your knees and thank Heaven for the Lis' tolerance.'

Stunned by his tirade, by her father's incomprehensible accusations, Emily at length replied: 'Father, I don't know what in Heaven's name you mean. My notorious behaviour? My ill fame? What on earth *are* you talking about? Tell me! Please tell me! I'm afraid you've both gone mad.'

'He's talking about your disgusting behaviour,' Eurydice Howe declared. 'Your secret trysts, your assignations with that long-nosed Englishman. He's also talking about . . .'

'. . . your shameless articles for the filthy mosquito papers,' Donald roared, his colour again high. 'A daughter of mine writing pornography!

74

I can hardly believe it even now. And you dare . . . you dare say we are mad!'

'I am deeply sorry, Father. Saying that was unforgivable.' First contrite and low, Emily's own tone rose with her temper. 'I swear to you I've done nothing to be ashamed of. Nothing! I made no secret of seeing Dick. Why should I? We've done nothing. *Nothing*, I tell you, in any way shameful. And – pornography? Pornography you say! My God, how could a virgin write pornography? They're only little tales of girls and young women – only to amuse them. Have you read them, even one?'

'We would not allow them into the house, much less sully our eyes,' Eurydice replied flatly. 'Your father *has* read your political articles. Red Bolshevik propaganda! Nothing less!'

'Bolshevik propaganda, Mother? Why, they're only to tell women about their rights.'

'Next,' Eurydice continued, 'you'll be advocating naked parades to show that women are equal and unashamed. Probably marching naked yourself. Just like the Bolsheviks. I always told you, husband. This comes of giving girls education. Letting her go abroad, that was madness. Perhaps *your* daughter is right. Perhaps we are mad to try to do the proper thing for her.'

'Is it proper to force a young woman into an arranged marriage she detests?' Emily retorted. 'Proper to berate her like a clumsy scullery-maid for writing a few little tales? My God, I thought you'd be proud of me.'

'Well, you didn't rush to show them to us, did you, dear?' Eurydice continued complacently. 'But all that's past now. You'll forget about your scribblings after you marry Nien-lao. Think of the lovely ceremony. You'll see how happy you are.'

'Mother, I'm not an infant or a fool,' Emily retorted. 'Please don't talk to me like that.'

'How else should your mother talk to you when you act like a fool?' Donald demanded. 'She's right. Six months after your wedding all this nonsense will be totally forgotten.'

'You're assuming, Father, that there'll be a wedding. I'm not so sure.'

'Don't be completely foolish, my daughter,' he counselled. 'What else can you do, even if you dare disobey me? What else can you possibly do?'

'I can *not* marry Nien-lao, I tell you!' she cried. 'I just can *not*!'

Emily dashed out of the study. Her initial reaction was much as her parents had expected, although her outburst surprised them slightly because it was so virulent and so vulgar. The American influence, naturally. None the less, she would in time obey them.

Stumbling up the stairs to the sanctuary of her bedroom, Emily paused stricken on the landing. She demanded aloud of herself: 'Good God, what shall I do? What could I *possibly* do?'

75

11

The black pencils bristled stiletto-sharp in the jar of the same pink marble as the half-moon blotting-paper holder and the inkwell with its black and red pools. The new telephone, which ingeniously combined mouthpiece and earphone in one handset, stood on the mahogany desk beside the brass sign reading: MISS J. PAVERNEN. The Underwood typewriter stood against the wall on its wheeled stand, concealed under its black rubberoid cover.

John Pavernen wished the typewriter to be inconspicuous. Julia was his office manager, far above a mere typewriter clerk. She was also first vice-president and a director of JPEnterprises, Inc. Since she was emphatically not a secretary, she was not to display the typewriter. It was, he said, the symbol of the 'emancipated' women who declared: 'We will not be dictated to by men' – and promptly got themselves jobs taking shorthand dictation.

In late May of 1922, Julia was delighted by her new position and exhilarated by the excitement of her Uncle Jack's business. She had heard him called 'Quick Jack', and she resented that nickname. But it was also a tribute to his live-wire ways.

Nor was she disconcerted because the office was situated in a somewhat rundown tenement in Hongkew. Although that name rather romantically meant the Beginning of the Rainbow, the district north-east of the juncture of the Hwangpoo River and Soochow Creek, which had once been the American Settlement, was now largely Japanese and thoroughly unfashionable. John Pavernen maintained he had 'gotten in on the ground floor' of an area that would soon prosper again. Julia sometimes wished the office was on the ground floor, not up four flights of rickety stairs.

She was, however, not disturbed at being not just the first vice-president, but the only visible director aside from President John Pavernen. A Mr Chow Kasing was second vice-president and secretary-treasurer, but ceaseless illnesses kept him from the office – and the single board meeting she had attended. Julia was, in fact, not only office manager, but filing clerk, typist, and telephonist – the only employee of JPEnterprises aside from Little Pow, who was just ten years old. That wide-eyed waif ran errands and energetically swept out the office, all the while chattering rapidly in Shanghainese so slangy she had originally understood no more than one word in five.

Julia's grasp of the language had advanced in the last four months. She had not, however, learned to pretend not to understand hard luck stories like the one that preceded Little Pow's plea for a rise of a dollar a month. Instead, she responded with a colloquial rebuff that might have raised eyebrows in some Shanghai dives.

The waif grinned good-naturedly, shrugging his frail shoulders within the cut-down long-gown that enveloped him. It was a hand-me-down that had faded to a pale cerulean blue after laundering that, though infrequent, had extended over two decades. Winter and summer, Little Pow wore the tattered cotton garment to show that he was one of the elite employed in offices – rather than in manual labour.

Julia fished in her purse and handed him a shiny silver dollar bearing the eagle-and-snake emblem of Mexico. Among the coins of many nations circulating in the International Settlement, the Chinese favoured the 'dollar Mex' because of its high silver content.

'A present from me,' she told him. 'Not from the company.'

She knew he would hardly believe that any sane person would freely give that immense sum, equivalent to fifty cents American, out of her own purse when she could charge it to the company.

Actually, one dollar Mex was no small sum to Julia either. She realized that it was conscience money. Shanghai was not only champagne, caviar, and dancing, but cholera, starvation, and sixteen-hour workdays in squalid factories. The silver coin was her sincere offering to the jealous gods of fortune. Although she revelled in her work, Julia, no more than Little Pow, could not expect a rise for some time.

Behind the smoked-glass panel in the yellow-shellacked partition wall, the president's office was hardly larger than her cramped anteroom. The fragrance of Havana cigars and Scotch whisky was gradually overcoming the reek of new paint and the ripe cabbage smell of the cheap sisal floor-matting.

John Pavernen repeatedly impressed upon Julia and upon those suppliers or customers who climbed to his eyrie that JPEnterprises was not concerned with display, but with quality. That meant the finest materials, the best craftsmanship, and absolute integrity in endeavours ranging from real estate through rattan furniture to insurance.

The most exciting venture was the most recent. Riverview Manor was the biggest prize that had come John Pavernen's way in years. An absentee German owner had commissioned JPEnterprises to renovate and then sell sixty-five Chinese-type houses on the outskirts of Hongkew. The potential profit was great, and the business reputation to be gained by Jack Pavernen was even more valuable.

Julia frowned, and her tawny eyebrows drew together – for she would not pluck them into the half-circles of astonishment that were fashionable. Before leaving for Canton to sell second-hand machine-guns to Dr Sun Yat-sen's Nationalist Army, her uncle had given her a lecture on Shanghai's ways.

'Everybody in this town is a crook, remember that,' he had told her. 'Everybody from the chairman of the Municipal Council and the British Consul right down the line. Even the judges of the American Court and the Mixed Court. Not criminals, maybe, but definitely crooks. There's only one exception. The US Consuls aren't crooks. But they've never been very bright.'

She smiled wryly, though he had been deadly serious. The door-bell pealed and diverted her thoughts, but no shadow obscured the gold-leaf lettering on the glass-panelled door. When the bell pealed again, she realized that it was the unfamiliar ring of the new telephone. She gingerly lifted the handset.

'Halloo! Halloo!' A guttural voice bellowed. 'Iss dot Pavernen's ... Yut Pay Enterprises? I had better like speak Herr ... Mr Pavernen ... *sofort* right now.'

'Yes, Mr Vass, this is JPEnterprises,' Julie answered the mercurial German building contractor. 'But Mr Pavernen isn't in.'

'Pavernen! Pavernen!' Vass shouted. 'I must speak Pavernen right now. *Sofort!* No time to waste.'

'I'm very sorry, Mr Vass. Mr Pavernen is in Canton and won't be back for at least a week. Can I help you?'

'Help? Are you architect? Are you sanitary inspector? Are you plumber? How can you help?'

'If you'll tell me what's wrong, Mr Vass, I could at least try. Perhaps I could get in touch with Mr. Pavernen if it's absolutely essential.'

'Who's there?' he demanded. 'Is that 9147? Whom do I speak?'

'This is Julia Pavernen, Mr Vass.'

'Ach, the little niece. So, is your problem too. It gives no baths. I could not get bath anywhere in Shanghai.'

'Are you sure?' She stalled, uncomprehending. 'Quite sure?'

'Am I quite sure? Of course. I need bath very bad. But I cannot get bath anywhere. And I need sixty-five.'

'Sixty-five? Sixty-five baths?'

Before grasping his meaning, Julia was struck by her mental image of the porcine Vass attempting to wash away the cumulative guilt of his many years of chicanery by sixty-five successive immersions.

'So, you see, young lady? Where can I take sixty-five baths when there is not one in Shanghai? I even tried Hankow and Ningpo. But nothing! All gone and no imports since three months.'

'And there's nothing else you can use?' Julia asked. 'Of course not. A bathtub's a bathtub and nothing else'll do. Doesn't anyone *make* bathtubs?'

'*Make* baths? I think not . . .' Vass paused portentously. 'But maybe can do. I have idea. Is all right if a little heavy, no?'

'Why not, Mr Vass? Bathtubs are supposed to hold water. It doesn't matter if they're a little heavy?'

'Have idea of genius, I believe. I call and report myself later. Goodbye.'

Immediately after Julia returned the handset to its cradle, the bell rang again. Removing her right earring for comfort, she lifted the handset again.

'Julie? Julie darling? I'm so glad I found you.' The cool Emily sounded distraught. 'I must see you! I must talk with you!'

'Of course, honey. I can't get away from the office till six. But any time after . . .'

'Thanks, Julie. I don't know what I'd do without . . .'

'You're not . . . not in trouble, Emmy?'

'Of course not. Not *that* way. I'm . . .'

'Sorry for asking, but you sound desperate.'

'Desperate?' Emily replied. 'I may very well be desperate. But I'm still a pure and virtuous maiden – worse luck.'

'What *is* bothering you? Still the deadlock with your folks?'

'Julie, it's not a deadlock any more. When they sprang this crazy marriage on me a couple of weeks ago, you remember, I told them I just wouldn't. And they haven't said a word about it since.'

'Then, you've won, Emmy. Why so blue?'

'It's not that simple,' Emily sighed. 'They're making preparations just as if I'd agreed. They're going to steamroller me – no matter what I say.'

'Now be sensible, Emmy. How can they? Just make it absolutely clear you *won't* go through with it. They can't risk the loss of face . . . the scandal . . . of your refusing at the last minute.'

'You don't understand at all,' Emily exploded. 'If I make a scandal, I'll be branded a scarlet woman. People'll say I'm *afraid* to marry because I'm shop-soiled. Sure my parents will suffer, but it'll be ten times worse for me. They're counting on that. Besides, they know I cannot, just cannot, make the family lose face.'

'So there's nothing you can do? Absolutely nothing?'

'I can hardly run an ad saying: *The marriage arranged between Miss Emily Yuelin Howe and Mr Li Nien-lao seventeen years ago will not take place.*'

'Emmy, suppose . . . just suppose you disappeared. One fine morning you're not there. Then what?'

'They'd have to call it off,' Emily answered immediately. 'Invent a plausible excuse and call it off. Or risk looking like perfect fools.'

'Well, why don't you?'

'Why don't I what? I don't get you.'

'Why don't you disappear?'

'How can I?' Emily was irritated. 'Julia, you're obviously not taking this seriously. Please don't play games with me.'

'I am serious. Not disappear so no one knows where you are. Disappear so everyone knows where you are, but . . .'

'Julie,' her friend interrupted, 'please get to the point!'

'Why not move into the loft with me? Your folks'll have to pretend they agreed – or lose more face. But they can't steamroller you if you're not under their roof.'

'They'd just go right ahead!' Emily replied after a moment. 'They're blind stubborn – about as flexible as dry old bones.'

'I'm sorry.' Julia was crestfallen. 'I really thought for a moment it would work.'

'Just a minute, Julie. You know, it just might. If I'm not under my parents' roof, the Lis are sure to ask questions. And Daddy wouldn't lie outright. Not about something so important.'

Julia prompted. 'What could happen then?'

'I'm not sure, but it *could* go this way: Daddy decides to get out from under when he sees he can't win. So he regretfully breaks off the engagement. He tells a plausible story. No one believes it, but it saves everyone's face.'

'So it could get you off the hook?'

'Could be. I'll try to come around about seven. But I can't promise. Not the way things are.'

'Oh, Emmy, how's Richard? Do you think . . .'

'Stop it.' Emily managed a laugh. 'I'm trying to wriggle out of one match, and you're plotting another – with even more problems.'

Laughing, Julia replaced the handset. Abstractedly pushing her hair into place, she felt her earlobes bare and began scrabbling on the desk in search of her earrings. Smiling triumphantly, Little Pow produced them from his sleeve. The brass hemispheres were bright after his assiduous polishing. She did not have the heart to tell him that she much preferred the patina of apparent antiquity.

Julia pulled out the typewriter and briskly whipped off the rubberoid cover. A pile of unanswered letters lay on her desk. Although the most ambitious, Riverview Manor was by no means JPEnterprises' only iron in the fire. Aligning a sheet of paper, she rolled it into the black-and-chrome machine.

Dear Mr Sylvester, she began a letter to the export manager of United Metal Fasteners, Inc. of St Louis. *I was happy to have your letter of the 16th of* . . .

The telephone pealed. Grimacing at Little Pow, who was sweeping imaginary cobwebs off the wall, Julia resignedly lifted the handset again. No wonder some firms still refused to install telephones. The calls did intrude without warning upon regular work.

'Here is Smidgelou . . . Smidgelou Tomas,' a ripely accented Middle European voice announced. 'My wife is very angry. She says she will kill me.'

'I'm so sorry to hear of your problem, Mr Smidley.' Julia was pert, never having heard the name before that instant. 'I wonder how I can help you.'

'Smidgelou . . . Smidgelou Tomas,' the voice reiterated, as if that name must command immediate respect. 'What are you going to do? Manya cannot be unhappy. She will come out in bumps – and my life is a misery.'

'I'm so sorry, truly I am.' On the verge of giggles at the absurd conversation, Julia none the less asked as solicitously as she could: 'What can I do to help?'

'You are Jay Pay Ay Ink, are you not that?'

After pondering for an instant, Julia acknowledged that she was JPE Inc., and the voice resumed: 'It is about my house in this Riversdells . . .'

'Riverview,' she corrected automatically.

'Riverview or Mountainside is no difference. Might as well be Riverbottom all the good it does me. When do I get my house, young lady? I have paid all instalments to datum, excepting ten percent disconto. Two months ago I was promised, but still no house. Manya says we'll soon be sleeping in streets. She comes out in red bumps – and my life is a weariness.'

Cradling the handset in the hollow of her shoulder, Julia leafed through the Riverview Manor receipt file. She found *Smidgelou T.* and a record of payments.

'I have it now, sir. Yes, all appears to be in order. Your house has been allotted. . . .'

'When can we move. Two days? Three days? A week?'

'I regret, Mr Smidgelou, that we are experiencing minor problems with plumbing. Our suppliers have let us down.' She could not tell him they had *no* suppliers of bathtubs. 'However, I have just talked to our chief architect, our superintendent of construction, and our technical manager. They hope that in two weeks . . .'

'In two weeks we can move? We shall have our little house?'

'Most likely, sir.'

No reason to tell him she had that instant fished that date from the well of her optimism. No more reason to inform him that architect, superintendent, and manager were all one: the choleric Gustav Vass, who was also senior hydraulic engineer, supervising decorator, and master electrician. Such relevations would not help Manya's bumps.

'Let me check your address. . . . Yes, we have it right. You'll be hearing from us very soon, sir. . . . Oh, there's nothing to thank me for. I'm glad to be of service. . . . Goodbye, sir. By the way, my mother always applied apple vinegar to hives, but I imagine Shanghai vinegar will do. . . . A pleasure, sir.'

She was getting to be as plausible as her Uncle Jack. Not a liar, of course, but a comforter of those suffering from long deferred expectations. It would neither have soothed Manya Smidgelou's rash nor relieved Tomas's weariness to learn that she had no idea when the house in Riverview Manor would be ready for occupancy. Two weeks perhaps – if the terrible Gustav Vass solved the bathtub problem. Tomorrow she would go to see the slippery Herr Vass about the missing bathtubs.

Dear Mr Sylvester, she resumed the letter to United Metal Fasteners. *I was happy to have your letter of the 16th. I can assure you that we could sell many times the present volume of thumb-tacks if they were gold-coloured. The Chinese, who are obsessed with that metal, will undoubtedly purchase many thousand gross to imbue their household shrines and their conveyances with the aureate hue of prosperity.* (She had been unable to talk Uncle Jack into striking out that last pompous phrase.) *Your brass screws, for example, are already selling briskly because . . .*

'Good afternoon, JPEnterprises. . . .' Julia automatically responded to the telephone and automatically removed her left earring. 'Oh, hello Liz. How are you?'

'I'm in trouble, big trouble!' The Russian woman's voice was incongruously blithe. 'I must talk with you.'

'Twins is it, dearie?' Exasperated at this latest interruption, Julia was tart. 'But why come to me, innocent little me? You of all people should know *that* kind of doctor.'

'Not *that* kind of trouble, silly,' Elizabeth laughed. '*Real* trouble. Joshua wants to reform me. He wants me to give up my present way of life and marry him.'

'Oh Liz, how wonderful! I'm so happy for you. When's the wedding?'

'Hold on, Julia. We haven't talked about a date yet.'

'Grab him!' Julia advised. 'Set the date right now. Don't let him get away.'

'I'm not sure I've got him. Rachel Haleevie's not likely to let her precious son marry a . . . a woman like me. She won't have me in the house, you know. Besides, I'm not Jewish.'

Julia marvelled at her sudden elevation to the wise woman of Hongkew, but counselled: 'Let's take it step by step. First, you're not absolutely sure Lady Haleevie will say *No*. Joshua's only one of seven sons, so perhaps she can spare one to a Gentile. Last – and most important – Joshua loves you very much. Let him decide. It's *his* family and *his* problem.'

'I'm not sure Joshua could stand up to his mother, Julie. Suppose he swore he was going to marry me and she then forced him to back down. It would be worse than humiliation for him, more like castration.'

'You're absolutely wrong, Liz. Joshua will stand up to his mother. And Sir Judah's a great romantic. He'll be on your side when it comes to the crunch. Grab Joshua, Liz. Not to speak of the money.'

'Also, there could be no money,' Elizaveta mused. 'If Rachel works hard on Sir Judah, he could cut Joshua off. And money is important, Julie.'

'Oh, money! No Haleevie will ever starve in Shanghai.'

'I'm serious, Julie. I'm not interested in love in a hovel. And Joshua's incapable of making a living on his own. I may be mercenary, but nothing kills love quicker than poverty.'

'If you truly loved him . . .'

A sigh of exasperation floated out of the handpiece to preface Elizaveta's reply: 'Love is love – and life is life. There are many different kinds of love, my wise little kitten, as you will learn. I won't risk ruining Joshua's life, not to speak of my own. Anyway, I'm not absolutely sure I *want* to marry him. Why should I change my present way of life? I rather enjoy it.'

'Oh, Liz, what a foolish thing to say when . . .' Julia stopped in mid-sentence when she realized her Russian friend was not necessarily indulging in bravado. 'Then what *do* you want?'

'I'll tell you. I've been approached by a group of White Russians. They want to start a small hotel and night club called Ikra.'

'What does that mean?'

'Ikra is caviar. A good name, isn't it? But their funds aren't quite enough. I'll need to put up a hundred thousand Mex myself. I thought JPEnterprises might be looking for a good investment. My Russians will guarantee occupancy of forty per cent of the rooms. They travel and have travelling friends. So I thought, perhaps, your uncle, after the bits of business we've done in real estate . . .'

'Darling, you might just as well go to Manchuria for coconuts as to us for something like fifty thousand US dollars. Between us, JPEnterprises is something like overextended. Every penny we've got is invested. We're borrowing, not lending. I know Uncle Jack would like to, but there's no hope here.'

'Oh, dear, and I thought . . . Perhaps Emily could help. Her father might . . .'

'Maybe I shouldn't tell you, but you'll know soon enough. Emily might be trying to touch you for a loan soon. She's thinking of moving out of Harmony Hall. The parents are pressing her to marry someone she despises.'

'That is bad news – for both of us. You'll soon be the only one with a regular income. How ironic!'

'Liz, why don't you come around for a drink about seven? Emmy'll probably be there, and we can really talk, the three of us.'

'I do have a tentative appointment.'

'Tell him you can't make it. If it's Joshua, he'll understand. If it's not Joshua, it's not important.'

Julia hung up decisively. Without being asked, Little Pow placed her earrings on her desk. He had polished them so diligently that they sparkled gold – or, as Quick Jack Pavernen would say, with the aureate hue of prosperity.

12

John Pavernen was very tired. His eyes were dull, and the aura of his charm flickered feebly. Worse, he displayed none of his normally insatiable appetite for the minute details of his varied ventures – and his niece's personal affairs.

He had come directly to the office after disembarking on the Bund from the coastal steamer. Julia already knew that his effort to sell arms in Canton had failed, despite a fulsome letter of introduction to Sun Yat-sen from the President's brother-in-law, T.V. Soong. Even allowing for that disappointment, her uncle still seemed extraordinarily depressed. Having returned in haste, he was apparently unconcerned about events since his departure.

Julia eased her shoes off and curled up in the cracked red-leather chair in the inner office. She casually lit a Chesterfield, shook out the wooden match, and blew a cloud of smoke. Her uncle only raised his eyebrows, and continued the ritual selection of an Upmann panatella from the crystal humidor on his desk. Finally satisfied, he pierced the tip and lit the cigar with a lighter set in a gold-plated fifty-calibre cartridge. His hand trembled wearily.

This was obviously not the time, Julia decided, to trouble him with her friends' problems. She had heard nothing from Emily since the frantic telephone call several weeks earlier. Moreover, Elizaveta was getting into dubious company in her search for capital for her private hotel, the Ikra. When John Pavernen looked distastefully at his cigar and laid it aside in the cloisonné ashtray, she was reluctant to intrude even business matters upon his preoccupation. But one pressing matter she could not put off – not if the plaintive Smidgelou Tomas was ever to occupy his house in

84

Riverview Manor.

'Uncle Jack, I hate to bother you,' she said hesitantly. 'But Vass the builder's been after me. And I can't make the decision myself.'

'What's up?' he asked brusquely.

'Bathtubs, Uncle Jack. Vass can't find a single bathtub anywhere on the China Coast.'

'Not another red cent for that old horse thief!'

'He has come up with a solution,' she replied. 'Says it'll be cheaper than regular tubs and he'll use the money left over to install light-sockets in the kitchens. You forgot to specify, he says, so he didn't include them in his original estimate.'

'Up to his old tricks, I see. How could I forget to specify lights in the kitchens?'

'Uncle Jack, I looked through all the correspondence as well as the specifications. And there's no mention of lights in kitchens.'

'Oh well, we all make mistakes. But what's all this about bathtubs?'

'Mr Vass wants to make them out of concrete. He says . . .'

'Concrete! Absurd! Riverview's not the Ritz, for sure. But concrete bathtubs'll look like hell.'

'He's thought of that. He plans to mix in marble dust for a smooth finish. Like a Roman bath, so beautiful it shall be, he says.'

John Pavernen grinned at his niece's mimicry of Gustav Vass. Though the shadows lingered in his green eyes, he relit his Havana cigar.

'Marble bathtubs in Riverview Manor in Hongkew!' he exclaimed. 'That'll knock some people's eyes out. Why did you hold off?'

'It's never been done. I just didn't . . .'

'Tell him to get started right away. I don't need angry subscribers knocking down our doors, maybe defaulting on their payments.'

'I've had a few angry subscribers. Otherwise, there are just one or two little things. Everything else can wait.'

John Pavernen dealt competently, but abstractedly, with the other problems Julia presented.

He then inquired querulously about the oscillating electric fan they had received as a sample from Cleveland, Ohio. Since her thin shantung dress was clinging damply to her shoulders, Julia happily fetched the fan from the cupboard where Little Pow stowed it each evening. The waif was absent, having pleaded illness. He was generally ill on race-days.

When she returned, her uncle had taken off his butternut-yellow nankeen jacket, although his striped tie was still tightly knotted. A tumbler of Scotch and water was clasped in his right hand.

'Are you wondering why I'm a little shook up?' he began almost shyly. 'Wondering what's happened to old Uncle Jack?'

'You don't seem your usual self.'

'You can say that again, honey. You know they ran President Sun Yat-sen out of Canton?'

'I saw a report in the *North China Daily News*, but it was vague. Dr Sun seems to pop in and out of power just like the warlords.'

'I never paid much heed to warlords. A few dollars here, a few dollars there – and they let you get on with business. As long as the Volunteer Corps kept them from bothering the Settlement, I figured they could fight each other all they want. Good for the gun business. But one of these days some bozo's going to take over China. And with one fellow running the whole shebang, it could be a different story for you and me, Julia.'

'Uncle Jack, why don't you tell me what happened in Canton?' she suggested. 'And what happened to you.'

'Well, after they let me out of jail . . .' He raised his voice over the buzzing of the fan. 'That, mind you, was *after* they put me up against the wall in front of a firing-squad. Maybe I better begin at the very beginning. . . .'

Proud of his new knowledge, John Pavernen described to Julia the rival factions of warlords fighting each other for mastery. Dr Sun Yat-sen, with his National People's Party, who loosely held Kwangtung Province in the south, was strictly speaking not a warlord. He was, however, allied with the dominant warlord of that province, and he was seeking other allies against the grand coalition of northern warlords.

It was confusing, Pavernen acknowledged. Besides, the present warlord alliances would soon shift – as they had been continually shifting since 1915. There were rich pickings in the provinces, but the great prize was Peking. Whoever controlled the old Imperial capital appointed the nominal president – and enjoyed the benefits of foreign recognition. One benefit of that status was the substantial income from the Chinese Maritime and Inland Customs, which was administered by foreigners 'on behalf of the government of China'.

'Anyway,' John Pavernen said, 'Dr Sun Yat-sen's been cosying up to the warlord of Manchuria way up north, the one they call the Old Marshal. The Doctor wants them to join up and squeeze out the others, especially that pious fraud they called the Christian General. You know, old Sun's not all that different from the warlords.'

'Uncle Jack, that's just not true! The Nationalists *are* different!' Julia's indoctrination at the hands of Emily Howe and Mayling Soong revealed itself. 'Sun Yat-sen was actually *elected* president by the National Assembly, even if it was ten years ago. The Nationalists are fighting for an ideal. And they'll win in the end.'

'Nice little speech, Julie. But what the good Doctor needs right now isn't ideals. It's more troops, more guns, and a secure base. He's not looking too chipper. I'll tell you what happened in Canton. It started off fine. . . .'

The Victoria Hotel in the minute British Concession on Shameen Island a few yards from the city of Canton had welcomed John Pavernen warmly. The rattan furniture company he served as export agent had left gifts of tropical fruit and bourbon. He slept well in the high-ceiling bedroom beneath the big ceiling fan and the ghostly cloud of the mosquito-net. He was awakened by an invitation from the Office of the President

86

of the Republic of China. Quite remarkably, the letter was written in idiomatic English with American spelling. Madam Sun Yat-sen, the former Rosamonde Soong, was obviously still acting as her husband's English secretary.

John Pavernen was, however, received by neither the President nor the First Lady in the Presidency atop Kwangyinan Hill. Instead, he waited seven hours before he was shown into a small office crammed with files, field telephones, maps, and a squat hardened-steel safe. It almost overflowed with the ruddy corpulence of a middle-aged foreigner in a Nationalist uniform, who introduced himself in fluent, though heavily accented English as Colonel Bowe, the President's military secretary.

John Pavernen never learned whether Bowe was the Colonel's original name or a pseudonym – and did not much care. Although both foreigners had lived too long in China to commit themselves in an initial discussion, Pavernen soon sensed that Colonel Bowe was eager to purchase at least four hundred Vickers machine-guns with spare parts and 100,000 rounds of ammunition for each – as well as large quantities of grenades, rifles, and pistols.

He had feared that payment would pose problems. But the magic name Soong was invoked. T.V. Soong, who was financial advisor to his brother-in-law, the President, was collecting substantial funds from forward-looking capitalists – foreign as well as Chinese. Besides, both Colt and Vickers were anxious to get a foot in the door of the leader they vaguely understood was 'the legitimate President of China. Their profits could be immense if the Nationalists actually mounted a further Northern Expedition to crush the warlords. The gun-makers were, therefore, offering exceedingly generous terms – as well as lavish 'finder's fees' under the table to the buyer's agent.

At that stage, John Pavernen knew no more of the warring factions than their need for arms. He, therefore, accepted without a thought Colonel Bowe's unsolicited assurances that the indiscipline among the garrison of the city of Canton was not serious. Nor did he ask why President Sun had just felt it necessary to leave the fighting front and hasten back to restive Canton to restore order.

Yes, Colonel Bowe volunteered, some twenty-five thousand unruly soldiers in Canton could be a problem, for they obeyed the local warlord. But that warlord was a devoted member of the National People's Party and an unswerving supporter of the President. Only a week earlier, he had called formally upon Dr Sun to congratulate him on the Northern Expedition's victories. And only yesterday he had telegraphed from his field headquarters to reaffirm his loyalty.

'Ugly rumours, no more than ugly rumours!' Colonel Bowe exploded. 'Nonsensical rumours that our Cantonese warlord is encouraging his troops to loot and riot in the city in order to undermine Dr Sun's authority. The same liars even say that he is plotting with the President's enemies. Tommyrot!'

'Why are you telling me all this?' John Pavernen asked. 'Aren't you worried about scaring me off?'

'Better you should hear the truth from me than falsehoods from others. And we shall prevail.'

Gladly accepting an invitation to dine with Colonel Bowe the following night, John Pavernen seated himself in a sedan-chair to return to the Victoria Hotel. Soldiers in mustard-yellow uniforms were swaggering through the crowded streets. They pushed aside civilians with their rifles, and they lifted goods from those shops whose proprietors had failed to put up padlocked wooden shutters. The chair-coolies twice darted into narrow alleys to avoid squads that were searching passers-by for valuables.

At seven most evenings, the streets of downtown Canton would have been tumultuous with colour, light, and noise. Tonight those streets were emptying rapidly. The stream of pedestrians dwindled as the last furtive walkers hurried home to escape the rampaging troops. Light streamed only from those restaurants and tea-houses that had been forced to remain open. Even the painted sing-song girls and the swaggering pimps forsook the soldiers who were their natural prey to retreat behind barred doors. At major intersections the miniature iron-pagodas of the traffic police were deserted, as were the theatres, taverns, and cafés on the four corners of the intersections. The funereal stillness was occasionally enlivened by shots, by the laughter of drunken privates, and by the screams of terrified women.

After he showed them ten silver dollars, John Pavernen's chair-coolies loyally bore him towards Shameen Island through the sodden heat that blanketed the city. For the first time since he came to China, he was fearful for his own safety. Why had Colonel Bowe allowed him to brush aside the offer of a military guard as if it were an empty courtesy? Or did the Colonel feel that any Nationalist escort would be more provocative than protective?

The sedan-chair finally crossed the hump-back bridge to Shameen Island. Though it could not offer the security of the International Settlement, the British Concession on the man-made sandpits in the Pearl River was a refuge. Among the Victorian bungalows with their tennis courts and English gardens the toytown streets, the frenzy of the native city was no longer frightening. When the coolies trotted past Grimaldi's Café to leave him at the pillared entrance of the Victoria Hotel, John Pavernen had convinced himself that his fears were groundless.

He dined well on *canard à l'orange* and drank a reasonable claret in the velvet-curtained dining room. Well fed, he was ashamed of his near-panic. He had, after all, advised so many newcomers not to be alarmed by the ferocity of warlord troops. The officers, he had always said, knew that foreign soldiers and foreign gunboats were never more than a day or two away – and would wreak terrible vengeance if foreigners were molested. Even today the brutish soldiers of the local warlord had not dared to stop him.

He carried a brandy-snifter to his room and sat contentedly pulling on an Upmann panatella and calculating again the likely profits of the arms deal. But it had been a long and wearing day. Just after ten he climbed into the high brass-bedstead and drew the mosquito-net.

John Pavernen was only mildly alarmed when he was shaken awake at half past eleven. He recognized the tan Nationalist uniform, and he listened patiently to the lieutenant's halting English: Colonel Bowe apologized for the intrusion, but wished to see the gentleman immediately. Since he could imagine no other reason for the summons than quick agreement on the deal, Pavernen hurriedly dressed. It was an odd hour, but politicians were odd people. Besides, many Chinese liked to do business in the middle of the night.

Humming with anticipation, John Pavernen smoothed his hair with his brushes to its normal patent-leather sheen. He reknotted his blue-foulard tie and shook the creases from his seersucker jacket while following the officer through the moonlit tranquillity of Shameen. After nodding amiably to the startled British sentries at the hump-back bridge, he crossed into Chinese territory.

Six soldiers trotted alongside the sedan-chairs carrying the lieutenant and himself. The chairs' swaying was hypnotic. His eyes closed, and he dozed as he was borne through the dark, deserted streets.

When the coolies halted abruptly, he awoke with a jerk. The wicker and bamboo sedan-chair dropped to the cobblestones. He heard a shot, then two more. He could see little, for he was virtually seated on the ground. But the Nationalist lieutenant floundered out of his sedan chair, snatching at his holstered pistol. A rifle fired ten feet away. Incredulity painted on his broad face, the lieutenant was flung backwards.

A captain in the mustard-yellow of the warlord army stepped out of the shadows. His revolver was drawn, and he was followed by a sergeant with a bayonet fixed to his rifle. The blade plunged into the lieutenant's throat just above the collar bearing the gold bars of his rank. The dying man's hands clutched the bayonet, but fell away with lacerated palms. He squeaked once and fell forward, bending from the waist in the attitude of prayer.

Pavernen saw that two Nationalist privates lay unmoving on the cobblestones. The remaining four had vanished into the night with the chair-coolies. The warlord captain looked down at him, and he felt his stomach turn over.

'I've never been so scared in my life,' he recalled in the shelter of his office in Shanghai. 'I didn't find out for days, but I was really pretty safe. Colonel Bowe wanted to get hold of me for exactly the same reason the warlord captain grabbed me. Both thought they could use me – as an American. Colonel Bowe had the notion that I could protect Dr Sun and Madame Sun by my presence. The warlord outfit was afraid I could get the US Marines to avenge myself and the Suns. So they locked me up. But I'm getting ahead of my story. While I was cooling my heels in a cell that night, the Cantonese warlord made his move against the President. Madame Sun Yat-sen told me about it later in Hong Kong. It was the early morning of June 16th. . . .'

Rosamonde Sun knew she was dreaming. She therefore dismissed the distinct shrilling of a telephone as an embellishment of her own imagination. She was walking on the campus of Vanderbilt University under autumnal foliage when her husband's hand on her shoulder awakened her.

'They're coming!' he said tersely in English, the language of their intimacy. 'I've just had a telephone call. We've got to get out of here right now.'

Her voice still muzzy with sleep, she replied: 'Darling, *you* must go. I'd only be a hindrance, slow you down. I'll stay here. No one will hurt a woman.'

The President finally agreed. If he were killed, all the hopes of China would die with him. Sun Yat-sen slipped through the gates accompanied by just ten soldiers. Fifty men of his bodyguard remained under Colonel Bowe's command to protect his wife. Fortunately, their mansion was several hundred yards from the imposing Presidency, which was certain to be the mutineers' chief objective. With luck, the rabble would overlook the mansion and the long bridge that connected it to the Presidency.

But the first volleys raked the mansion half an hour later. The assailants were firing from the slopes above and below. Through the shuttered windows, Rosamonde Sun and Colonel Bowe heard high-pitched shouts: '*Saat! Saat! Saat Sun Yat-sen!* . . . Kill! Kill! Kill Sun Yat-sen!'

The supposedly devoted warlord of Canton had not only ordered the assault, but had told his troops they could loot the city for three days if the coup succeeded. He had also promised $200,000 Mex to the soldier who could prove he had killed the President.

Colonel Bowe ordered his men not to reveal their positions and exhaust their ammunition by returning fire in the darkness. But dawn came at 5:46, and a storm of metal swept the mansion. Surprisingly, the rifles and machine-guns of the defending troops briefly squelched the assailants' volleys.

Field-guns then began to pound the vulnerable target. Most of their shells fell wide, though a few exploded in the upper stories of the mansion. By eight in the morning, the sun lit the breaches in the walls. The defenders' ammunition was almost exhausted. Twenty had been killed and almost all the rest were wounded.

The only possible escape was by the bridge to the Presidency. Colonel Bowe warned they might be 'leaping from the frying pan into the fire'. But there was no alternative.

Accompanied by two volunteers from the bodyguard, Rosamonde Sun and Bowe crept along the bridge. They were shielded by the four-foot-high railing, but the assailants glimpsed a raised head and redirected their fire. Although most bullets flew wide, a lucky shot smashed the railing and wounded Colonel Bowe in the thigh.

The two soldiers dragged him into the Presidency and were welcomed by its relatively unscathed defenders. They carried Colonel Bowe to a bedroom and staunched the bleeding. If they fled the Presidency, they would have to leave him behind. The warlord troops were virtual savages – and poor marksmen. They had inflicted no major damage on the Presidency after seven hours, but the commander of the guard chose to

90

throw in with them rather than fight on. To sweeten that appalling news, he offered to speak up for Madame Sun. But he could not guarantee her security. The two privates of the President's bodyguard chose to remain with her.

By four that afternoon, Rosamonde was close to despair. Bleary with exhaustion, she was seeing the reality of violence for the first time in her sheltered life. She almost broke down when the drawing-room ceiling collapsed under the shell fire thirty seconds after she had scurried out. She stumbled into the courtyard between her two bodyguards when it became obvious that the Presidency could hold out no longer.

A stream of soldiers in mustard-yellow was pouring through the battered iron gates. Their bayonets were dark with blood, and their faces were black with gunpowder burns. Defying their officers' feeble discipline, they swarmed to loot the riches of the Treasury and the Customs Office. Amid the turncoats in tan Nationalist uniforms, the victors overlooked the woman who staggered towards the street between two Nationalist privates.

Rosamonde Sun and her bodyguards limped into a narrow lane. They saw mass slaughter in the streets. Bayonets, small-arms, and random artillery shells had made a bloody shambles of the district surrounding the Presidency. Limbless torsoes lay on the cobblestones, and a severed head grinned toothily atop a broken gate. Soldiers and civilians lay together in death, their blood intermingled in the pink dust of shattered brick walls. Two men squatted in the ruins of a shelled hut and gazed into each other's eyes like children staring each other down. Both were unmarked, and both were dead – killed by the shock-wave.

'Shoot me! Shoot me now!' Rosamonde pleaded through cracked lips. 'I can't possibly escape. Shoot me now! Don't let those savages get me!'

'Now, Madame!' The senior guard's plump features twisted in concern. 'Now, Madame, it will be all right. You'll see. Just come along now.'

They supported her between them, the plump guard and the youthful guard. They lifted her over the rubble and swung her across shell-craters. When they heard a column tramping towards them, they hid her with their bodies.

'Play dead!' the plump guard commanded. 'It's our only chance!'

The three fugitives lay still amid the corpses till the column had passed. Although Rosamonde stumbled and retched, they finally carried her into an isolated farmhouse on the edge of the city. The middle-aged farmer recognized her and demanded that they leave. She did not see her guards threaten him with their bayonets because she had collapsed. When she awoke, the younger guard was sponging her face. The elder was holding the door open and peering out. A shot sounded, and he crumpled to the packed earth floor.

'Don't look Madame!' counselled the stripling. 'Don't look. He's finished.'

At her lowest moment, Rosamonde Sun heard above the irritable clamour of field-pieces the unmistakable roar of naval guns. She knew the warlords had no warships. She smiled for the first time in twenty-four hours. Loyal gunboats were bombarding the traitor forces. Lulled by the guns, she finally slept.

Their unwilling host was so delighted to see them go early the next morning that he offered patched trousers and a torn shirt to the guard. He also gave Rosamonde Sun his wife's cast-off black pyjamas and old conical straw-hat. Clutching a basket with a few vegetables and eggs, she looked like a farm woman earning a few extra coppers.

'And that was about it,' John Pavernen said. 'She got a sampan to take her downriver, where the President had found refuge on a Nationalist gunboat. Old Dr Sun had gotten away without a scratch. If she'd gone with him, Rosamonde would have had a smooth passage. He's still on that gunboat – hoping to rally his forces and retake Canton. She later left for Hong Kong in her old lady's disguise to look for outside help.'

'Only one thing you left out, Uncle Jack,' Julia observed. 'What the rebels did to you.'

John Pavernen looked at his niece abstractedly for a moment before replying: 'What they did to me? Oh, yes. They put me up against a wall in front of a firing-squad. I think they were just trying to scare me. They sure succeeded. Then the Cantonese warlord decided to let me go. He apologized personally for his officer's mistake. Wanted no trouble with the Americans, he told me. God bless the Stars and Stripes!'

13

Julia squirmed on the raw-silk cushions of the roomy rosewood chair that was her latest acquisition from the Shanghai Secondhand Shop – and decided her skin was not quite a perfect fit. In places it felt as loose as an elephant's hide; elsewhere it was painfully taut over her bones.

Naturally, she told herself with limp sarcasm, the early August climate of Shanghai had nothing to do with her alternating irritability and lethargy. The temperature was only 84 degrees at nine in the evening, and the humidity was actually below 80 per cent for the first time in weeks.

So Richard Hollings had told her when she impulsively telephoned him at the *North China Daily News*. He had been glad to relieve the boredom of the late shift by chatting. He had, of course, repeated the question about Emily's whereabouts he had been asking for the past two months. Once again, she had been forced to confess her total ignorance.

'Damn it, Julie, I miss her – badly,' he had confided and hung up.

If only Tommy would return from Peking. Though he was to begin his internship at Shanghai General Hospital in mid-September, mysterious concerns still kept him in North China long after receiving his MD in June. Although Julia had avoided prying in her semi-weekly letters, she had of course told him repeatedly of her anxiety over Emily's disappearance. His replies were reassuring – and vague. Emily would be all right, and he would come to Shanghai just as soon as he could.

Damn it, she wryly imitated Dick Hollings's tone, she did miss Tommy badly – and not just because of her concern for Emily. She missed the laughing eyes behind the black-rimmed spectacles he wore to look older; she missed his stubborn chin with the minute cleft; and she missed his slow smile. She missed Tommy Howe more than she had thought it

93

possible to miss any man. Yet they had no more than kissed chastely once or twice.

Then there was Emily, unheard of since her frantic telephone call in late May. Donald Howe had refused to discuss his daughter when Julia ran into him at the Columbia Country Club. Family matters, he had said frostily, were not meant for gossip at a charity ball. She had even bearded the major-domo at Harmony Hall. Old Woo had shaken his head and replied: 'Miss Emily is not available!' She had only one clue: Eurydice Howe was spending much time away from Shanghai, but where – or why – Julia could not find out. She could, therefore, only wait and hope, marginally reassured by Tommy's confidence.

Julia was also concerned about Smidgelou Tomas. Now a familiar voice on the telephone, he was still homeless because Riverview Manor was still not ready for occupancy. Gustav Vass had quickly manufactured the sixty-five concrete bathtubs. Electrical wiring and water-pipes were now the problem.

If John Pavernen and Gustav Vass did not solve *all* those problems very soon, JPEnterprises could collapse. After Little Pow, she would be the next casualty. After arriving a year earlier for a brief visit, she now felt herself part of Shanghai. Somehow, she would earn a living so that she could remain.

What would Uncle Jack do? He had other irons in the fire, but the fire was dying. No longer fooling herself, she recognized that he was essentially 'a small piece taipan'. Although the several civil wars always raging in China created a lively market, even his arms deals were in the doldrums. He had smiled unhappily and explained: 'I could sell ten million dollars worth of guns tomorrow. It's easy to find buyers. But it's damned hard to find payers!'

Although John Pavernen had promised to think about Elizaveta Alexandrovna Yavalenka's need to match the capital promised by the Russian syndicate for the private hotel Ikra, Julia could not press him now. Elizaveta was obsessed with the Ikra, which Julia – who was learning fast – suspected was also to be a *maison de rendezvous*, a house for assignations. Having survived handsomely, the Russian now wanted the wealth and power that would give her total independence. She had confided with breathtaking candour that she was trolling for cash among the secret societies, even hoping to convince the Supreme Lord himself.

Elizaveta laughed when Julia urged her to marry Joshua and give up her dangerous association with murderers, drug peddlers, and extortionists. She loved her work, she said, though she also loved her man. How long Julia wondered would even Joshua put up with his mistress's capricious behaviour?

She sipped green tea and wriggled into a more comfortable position, quite happy to be alone. Unless it was Tommy, she would rather be alone. That unbidden thought was disturbing. What did she actually expect of Tommy? Where were they headed, *if* they were headed anywhere together?

The front-door bell shrilled imperiously through the loft. And where was Lao Zee? The amah should already have come back from the meeting of her Buddhist Sisterhood. Julia laughed aloud at herself. How quickly one became accustomed to being waited upon.

'I'm coming!' she called out. 'Just keep your shirt on.'

She swung the heavy door open and stared in amazement at the slender figure standing in the gloom of the hall.

'Well, aren't you going to say hello?' Emily Howe smiled. 'May I come in?'

'Emmy! Emmy darling!' Julia hurled herself at her friend. 'Oh, Emmy, I was afraid something terrible had happened to you.'

'In a way, it has. But let me sit down and have a drink first. Talk later. Catastrophes seem to make me very tired.'

Julia busied her hands preparing the gin and tonics they had learned to drink after leaving the United States. Though the quinine in the Indian tonic water was bitter, it was refreshing on a sweltering night. Mechanically chipping ice from the block delivered daily and squeezing the lemon, Julia studied her old room-mate. Her expression dejected, Emily was staring at the squares of light from the high north window.

'Well, here you are.' Julia's exuberance was forced. 'And here's your drink. Now, then, where have you been?'

'I tried, Julie! I really tried, believe me!' Emily blurted. 'I tried hard to make myself do what they wanted. I knew I shouldn't, but I made every effort. And all I did was postpone the catastrophe.'

'You're not ill, are you?' Julia was determinedly hearty. 'No, just tired, I see. We'll soon take care of that. What's this catastrophe?'

'I'm fine . . . just fine physically. You know I always look as if a breeze could carry me away. I'm just a little thinner, but *maskee*.'

Julia grinned. The Shanghai expression *maskee* could convey a realistic 'Nothing can be done!', a consoling 'Don't worry!', or a defiant 'What the hell!'. Emily was, however, not just a little thinner. She was haggard – and her hands were almost transparent.

'The catastrophe is breaking with my parents. A blazing row before they threw me out of the house! For me . . . for any Chinese . . . a break with the family is like being half-dead. I'm not certain I really exist any more. My fine Western notions don't count for much – all that talk about individualism. I feel like dirty jetsam cast up on a rocky shore.'

'You're eloquent tonight, Em. You so rarely talk the way you write. But tell me more. Why did you disappear? What's been going on?'

'There's not much to tell. I promised my parents I'd think very seriously about marrying Nien-lao. First, though, I had to get to know him. It was medieval, but my father found a way that would avoid scandal.'

Emily and Nien-Lao had stayed with their respective cousins in Hong Kong. Eurydice chaperoned her daughter, who had a year earlier crossed the Pacific Ocean unchaperoned – and unscathed. The British Crown Colony was even more old-fashioned than Shanghai.

'I couldn't stand him, Julie!' Emily erupted. 'He's ghastly, far worse than I thought. A brainless playboy. But what could I do? Then Mayling

95

Soong turned up – and advised me to say *No*. To have nothing more to do with Mister Li Nien-lao.'

Emily gulped her drink. 'It's funny about May. Under that demure exterior, she's very tough. And she believes strongly in women's rights. No arranged marriage for her, no sirree! But she's sweet on General Chiang Kai-shek. She's worried because he's living with Sun Yat-sen on that gunboat near Canton.'

Emily talked compulsively, as if their reunion were a casual social occasion that would be marred by awkward silences. Her appearance belied her breezy manner. Her normal slenderness was now almost emaciation, and her frailness was swallowed by the big rosewood chair. She had curled herself into a boneless posture as graceful as an Utamaru print of a serene geisha, but she babbled like a nervous hostess.

'What's so funny about May?' Julia demanded. 'You're mystifying me.'

'Oh, yes. May swears she'll never marry by arrangement. She's half in love with Chiang Kai-shek, but he's already got a wife. So there isn't much hope for a good Methodist like May. Women are funny, aren't we?'

'I guess so, Emmy. What happened to you then?'

'Father joined us when I said flatly there was nothing doing. He was even angrier. I thought he was going to beat me.'

Donald Howe had raged and stormed. He had called upon the Heavens to redeem his unfilial daughter. He had raised his right hand to chastize her misbehaviour, but his arm had fallen back to his side. He was remiss in his duty, but he loved his disobedient daughter too much to strike her.

She was disobedient, but not defiant. Aside from her refusal to marry the man her parents had chosen, Emily was perfectly responsive to their wishes. Her father accordingly directed her to spend the summer away from Shanghai in North China. She was to think about the consequences of her behaviour – and to consider her decision once again.

She had replied in anguish: 'Can't you see it? Can't you see you want to inflict a life sentence on me? Oh, Daddy, *why* can't you see?'

Emily languished in the unfamiliar north for two months. At least Tommy had remained to be with her. And he wholeheartedly urged her to reject the arranged marriage.

Upon returning to Shanghai only a few days earlier, Emily had side-stepped a confrontation by telling her father she was still thinking. She was thinking – above all thinking how much she loathed Li Nien-lao. But her father could no more reconsider his decision than he could leap over the Great Wall of China.

The crisis had broken just after supper that same evening. It was almost an anti-climax. Passion was already spent on both sides, leaving only the bare bones of obstinate resolution. Eurydice wept quietly, her well of tears almost exhausted. Donald declared hoarsely that he would disown Emily if she did not comply. But she could no more surrender than he could relent. Without rancour, he had finally told her to leave Harmony Hall.

'Well, what now?' Julia was briskly practical. 'Where do you go from here?'

'I was hoping you'd ask me to stay a while.'

'Don't be silly, Emmy. It's practically your apartment. It's certainly Tommy's. I was getting a little lonely. I'd love to have an apartment-mate, specially you.'

'Thanks, Julie.' Emily smiled pallidly. 'They're sending my clothes over in the morning. All due courtesies, you see. It's just that I am no longer their daughter.'

'What'll you do, Emmy?'

'Oh, that's taken care of. You won't have to support me.'

'Taken care of? You're a fast worker.'

'You remember the Women's Commercial and Saving Bank on Nanking Road, don't you? The first bank in the world run entirely by females. Well, I've bought myself a junior partnership. Grandpa Howe left a little money just for me. He was unusual. He felt a girl needed a nest-egg of her own. So now I'm a banker.'

'Well, that's not so bad, is it? Except, of course . . .'

'You remember, Julie, how we used to talk of being pushed around by our parents? How we swore we'd stand up to them? Well, I've stood up to my parents. And I'm devastated! Heartbroken!'

'It'll be all right, Emmy. They'll come round. You'll see.'

'Stop making soothing cow noises, Julie!' Emily flared. 'They *won't* come round. You don't know Chinese pigheadedness.'

'Hold it, Emmy! I was just trying to be friendly after being worried sick about you. So get off your high horse.'

'Sorry, Julie!' Emily was contrite. 'I guess I'm overwrought.'

'I know, I can see that. But do you know who else has been worried sick? Dick Hollings is always asking if I've heard from you. Why don't you give him a ring? He's usually at the office till midnight.'

'I couldn't, Julie. I'm too drained. Why don't you? Just tell him I've turned up none the worse for wear and popped off to sleep. I'll definitely ring him tomorrow.'

14

October 25, 1922

'Keep it light, my girl!' Julia had cryptically advised as she discreetly left the loft-apartment a half-hour before Richard was expected. 'Don't get too intense!'

That well-meant advice was at least a month too late at the end of October 1922. Besides, Julia was herself intensely involved with Tommy Howe – when he managed to escape from the Shanghai General Hospital, where a junior intern was expected to work a hundred hours a week. But Emily and Richard were oblivious to other human beings.

'If we'd kept it light,' Emily sighed after Julia had gone. 'I'd have missed this . . . this pure pleasure.'

'Don't say pleasure, Em, though it is pure – much too pure,' Richard grinned. 'But pleasure has a specific meaning in this context. I imagine your American education didn't run to such fine distinctions.'

'Imagine what you please, Richard. Just don't be so stuffy and patronizing. You sound like a sixty-year-old grammarian with the gout.'

She plucked a small orange cushion from the rosewood chair and flung it at his head. It sailed over the rattan sofa and grazed the standing lamp which had been made from a five-foot-long Tibetan brass horn. He rose from the sofa and scooped her out of the chair. Her head cradled in the curve of his neck, he buried his face in her musky hair.

'Just don't tease me with talk of *pleasure*,' he complained lightly.

Emily chose to ignore the double-entendre. Neither stupid nor ignorant, she did not lack the courage of her emotions. She was, she concluded in exasperation, just inhibited – badly inhibited.

It was 1922, not 1822: not only manners, but morals had altered radically. Intelligent young women now sealed with their bodies the pledges made by their hearts.

Yet she hung back. Although Dick was not insistent, she felt guilty at thwarting his natural desires – and her own. But the inhibitions passed on by a hundred generations of Chinese ladies were too strong.

She gave herself to his caresses – and tingled with pleasure. She loved his hard kisses, and her tongue darted in return. The rough touch of his hands against her skin and the prickle of the stubble on his jaw made her feel small, fragile, and protected.

None the less, she froze when his hand moved towards the delta between her thighs. In spite of herself, she stiffened – and he felt her involuntary revulsion. She could neither feign receptivity nor give herself wholly.

Richard never blamed her, and his good humour naturally made her feel even more guilty, rather like a miser of emotions. Though he seemed resigned (if not content) to wait, she feared that indefinitely postponing physical consummation could destroy their love.

None the less, the excitement that flared in her whenever they met – even if they had been apart only an hour or two – made the sky itself bright. His cynicism and reserve dissolved, Richard had told her he felt his heart leap against his ribs whenever he saw her again.

He was telling the literal truth. They were already bound together, despite their differences. He was an Englishman who had come five years earlier to the alien culture of China, while she was a Treaty Port Chinese who had spent most of her aware life in the United States. Yet they had discovered large areas of knowledge and attitudes held in common. For the first time in his extensive – though hardly profound – experience of women, Richard Hollings loved a woman with his mind as well as his body. The interplay of their minds offered delights almost as exquisite as the interplay of their emotions. The complete physical intimacy they both desired, he concluded, he must attain through her mind. Not to seduce her intellect, but to seduce her body *through* her intellect – and thus overwhelm her inhibitions.

He set Emily down in the rosewood chair. Though she felt regret, she was inured to his breaking off their embraces when, as he had explained with slight embarrassment, he could no longer bear the physical tension they aroused. She smiled, penitent and silent.

'You'll never succeed.' He abruptly – and calculatingly – initiated an abstract discussion. 'It's against nature. Men want baubles as much as women do, maybe more.'

'What *are* you talking about, Richard? I don't want baubles. I only want you.'

'Would to God that was completely true, darling. But I was thinking again China would never succeed as a republic. Men – and their wives – want gewgaws. The old Confucian dynasties cleverly handed out the bribes we English quaintly call honours: medals, peacock feathers, titles of nobility, and cloaks of honour. Britain does the same today. It's the cheapest – and not the worst – way to run an empire.'

'That nonsense has nothing to do with running the country.'

'If a man hopes to become Sir Alfred Smith or Lord Puddleby, he'll work hard. He might even stay reasonably honest. It's economical, too. A few quid for decorations and sashes – made up many times over in taxes when the chump buys his robes, his calling cards and his champagne.'

'I just don't believe titles make so much difference,' she retorted. 'Shanghai is far more enterprising than Hong Kong, though my father can't hope for a knighthood – as he could in Hong Kong.'

'But the Sassoons and the Haleevies both have baronetcies, hereditary knighthoods.'

'Dick, that's not why Shanghai makes Hong Kong look like a sleepy backwater.' Emily stalked back and forth as she spoke. 'I'll tell you why. Many nationalities, not just stodgy British and cheeky Cantonese. And they all compete. They rub against each other, and the friction makes the atmosphere electric. That electricity galvanizes the Chinese of Shanghai – whether coolies or capitalists. They're all here because the Settlement offers freedom for enterprise, not just security. Not titles, just good profits and wages.'

'Riding your hobbyhorse again? Adam Smith, invisible hand, and all that.' Richard mocked gravely. 'And how are things at the ladies' bank?'

Emily detested the smugness in his voice when he spoke of the Women's Bank. A self-declared Bohemian, Richard despised all commerce – and savagely condemned the misdeeds of taipans and consuls. He agreed with Jack Pavernen that all were crooks. Particular condescension coloured his tone when he discussed the modest premises at 219 Nanking Road where Emily spent her working days. His dark eyes sparkled maliciously; his mobile lips curled scornfully; and his lean body slouched even lower on its spine to signal his contempt. Only a foolish woman, he had once said unguardedly, would surrender her birthright of femininity to compete in the grubby realm of commerce.

Emily looked at him wide-eyed, still puzzled by his attitude. How could he allow himself to show such contempt for her work when he was insistently wooing her? He could not be jealous of her titles: assistant cashier and chief loan officer. After all, he knew how small the staff was. Perhaps he begrudged the time she spent behind the fumed-oak counter. Perhaps it was something fundamental. Although his avowed Bohemianism compelled him to endorse her public advocacy of women's rights, she sensed that her feminism irritated him.

Emily shivered. The damp October chill was creeping into the loft despite the pot-bellied stoves glowing at either end of the cavernous living-room. She shivered despite the grey flannel suit with the full skirt she had worn to the office and the quick supper at Jeffrey's Kitchen. Her eyes unfocussed, she stared pensively into the distance.

'I didn't mean to annoy you.' Dick was always sensitive to her mood. 'I'm sorry, but I am honestly concerned. You say you like the work. But do you truly?'

'Of course I do, you ninny!' The weight of her resentment lifted and she laughed. 'I'm also earning a few dollars to keep body and soul together.'

'You must enjoy it thoroughly. How many times have I offered to help? And there is your writing.'

'My writing couldn't keep that great oaf of a puppy Adam in bones. Anyway, you're not much better off than I am. How could I accept your help? I don't even know what you mean by help.'

'I mean we could marry.' He was aggrieved. 'Not tomorrow, but some day very soon. As soon as I get the deputy editorship and the rise that goes with it.'

'If we wait for old Putnam Weale to give you that raise, we'll wait forever. Anyway, I've told you over and over I don't even want to think about marrying now. There are too many things I want to do. Meanwhile, I do thoroughly enjoy the Bank. It's a new world, as exciting as Tibet or Timbuctoo.'

'Only chap I met who'd been to Timbuctoo said it was duller than Swansea on a wet Sunday after chapel.' He bantered guiltily, relieved despite himself by her refusal to discuss marriage. 'Why is the Bank so fascinating? Tell me, for example, what you did today?'

'It may surprise you. I talked the Loan Committee into putting up a hundred thousand for a new hotel on Kiangse Road.'

'A hundred thousand's not small change. But why so cock-a-hoop? If your feminism will allow me that expression.'

'Can we declare a truce in the war of the sexes?'

'None of my doing,' he replied. 'I'm not a masculinist – or a phallocrat. But you are a feminist.'

'Peace, Dick! The hotel's to open next month. It's to be called the Ikra. That means caviar in Russian. The proprietress is Elizaveta Alexandrovna Yavalenka. Now what do you . . .'

'You've torn it now. You've really torn it. Indignant husbands and fathers will swoop down in moral outrage and carry all you innocent ladies of the bank back to your homes. Don't you know . . .'

'We're not *that* innocent!' she flared. 'We're all quite aware of Liz's profession. Even old Mrs Wang the manager knows. So don't . . .'

'Hold, enough!' He raised his palm defensively. 'You know I was joking. How in the name of God did you get respectable ladies to put up money for . . . ah . . . a *maison de rendezvous*?'

'A cathouse, they say in South Philadelphia.' Her eyes flashed, and her gestures were dramatic. 'It was easy. I argued that our business was doing business. Profits for the Women's Bank first, promoting female business interests second. No reason to base loan policy on personal morals – unless the applicant's morals affected her credit-worthiness. I said we'd received a businesslike application from a businesswoman in need of additional capital – and we should consider it on its merits. If the figures checked out, how could we refuse the loan? Turning Miss Yavalenka down would prove what the men said: women in business were ruled by their emotions, rather than hard-headed commercial considerations.'

'*Brava!*' He applauded lightly. 'What a magnificent performance. I take it they granted the loan.'

'Of course. What else could they do?'

Richard partially shared her exhilaration. Although he regarded the Women's Bank as comical, he was delighted by the growing self-confidence that sprang from Emily's business success. Whatever love might be, he knew he loved the deceptively frail-looking Chinese girl. How, otherwise, could he tolerate his peculiar position? He was her lover, but not wholly, because the emancipated young woman was not wholly emancipated. She was inhibited by traditional restraints, just as her fervent feminism and her burgeoning self-assurance were clouded by her femininity and her diffidence.

'So what's next?' he asked gravely.

'As a matter of fact . . .'

Emily darted into the kitchen. She returned with two champagne flutes and two frosted bottles of Krug 1912, the last of Joshua Haleevie's housewarming present.

'I'll do that,' he offered. 'Opening champagne is a man's job.'

'Not tonight, darling. To Elizaveta and the Ikra! To success! To the Women's Bank!'

The wine frothed in the crystal flutes, paler than moonlight. Bubbles beaded the sides, constantly forming and dissolving, always rising towards the rim.

Through the crystal Richard surveyed Emily's features, as pale and patrician as the champagne. It was ironic that he should give her his affection unreservedly after years devoted to ladies who were far more adventurous sexually. Odd, too, that the lady to whom he wished to dedicate his life was Chinese.

Suppose he brought Emily home? His bigoted father would scorn her as 'a yellow bint'. His genteel mother would sniff bronchially and flutter in fear of the neighbours' disapproval. No, they wouldn't have the chance to humiliate his wife. He would never bring Emily home to them. Assuming that she finally consented to marry him – as he passionately wished.

Besides, she could well look down on their meagre manner of life compared to her parents' gilded luxury. Now chief clerk to the leading solicitors in Leeds, his father had moved a world away from his grandfather, a shepherd who owned only his crook and his dog. His own ascension, first, to public school on a scholarship and subsequently to the University of Cambridge after attaining a lieutenantcy in the Intelligence Corps, created an even greater distance between his parents and himself.

They now felt he had thrown nearly all his advantages away. After working briefly as a junior reporter on the *Yorkshire Post*, he had accepted an offer from the *North China Daily News*. It was only his connection with *The Times* that saved him from his parents' total condemnation. To them *The Times* was not a newspaper, but an institution, less than the Crown, but almost as imposing. He was otherwise twice damned: first, a despised pressman, and second, a resident of that abyss of evil called Shanghai.

In truth, he had come to Shanghai as much to escape their withering respectability as to find a new world to conquer. He knew that he would conquer. He would throw their condemnation back in their teeth by excelling publicly. For his own sake, too, he would fight to become one of the best known newspapermen in the world. Would marrying Emily help or hinder him? He did not really know and, at that moment, he did not really care.

'You're far too pensive.' She broached the second bottle. 'No thinking allowed tonight. I'll fix you.'

She sprang exuberantly to her feet and circled the loft, her arms extended like wings. 'We're celebrating, my boy!' she burbled. 'Celebrating my victory. I strafed them. And now I'll strafe you.'

Rasping staccato in the back of her throat, she imitated either the roar of the airplane's engine or the rattle of its machine-guns. She shouted exuberantly and hurled herself head first onto his lap. Her skirt rucked up around her thighs when she turned over and twined her arms around his neck. He recalled that she had been reading a biography of Catherine the Great when she demanded huskily: 'Kiss me, my fool!'

He touched his lips to hers, tentatively at first, and he marvelled at her madcap exuberance. The heady taste of champagne in her mouth was the answer. A few glasses of bubbly, which would only steady his head, could exhilarate a slender girl who was, despite her bravado, unaccustomed to its insidious sparkle. He regretfully drew back his head and reluctantly loosened his embrace.

'What's the matter?' she demanded. 'Don't stop now. If we're ever to . . .'

He still hesitated, and she declared hotly: 'Don't be so damned gentlemanly. A little Dutch courage doesn't mean I'm drunk.'

She pulled her skirt up around her hips and took his hand in both of hers. After gravely kissing his palm, she placed it on the long forbidden, silk-covered delta.

'Now show me!' Her breath tingled in his ear. 'Show me everything!'

He slipped his arms under her and rose from the sofa, gasping involuntarily as he took the weight of the body that appeared so frail. Liquid in their minutely oblique setting, her eyes gravely studied his face. Silent for fear of breaking the mood, he placed her on her bed and pulled the quilted coverlet over her. She seized his hands and drew him down to her.

'I'm not drunk, you know, not even tiddly.' She kissed his ear and whispered. 'I'm just pretending a little.'

He had seen her take more wine with less effect. But it was too late for scruples. One way or the other, she might never forgive him. He began undoing her grey flannel jacket, kissing her lips after each button.

'It's just like peeling an orange.' She chuckled in her throat as he drew off her skirt. 'I'm Nell Gwyn, the orange girl.'

He gasped in delight when she was naked on the aquamarine coverlet. Her mouth was faded carmine with the lipstick almost kissed off; her skin was pale ivory; and her nipples were light pink. He laid his head on

103

her breast, and she clutched him to her. An instant later, she stiffened and drew away.

Too late, Richard decided, believing himself cool in judgment despite the blood pounding in his ears. If he drew back now, they would never come together again. Whatever she thought she felt, he would not falter unless she resisted with all her strength.

He might be utterly wrong. She might afterwards be infuriated and disgusted. But he must risk that – or they would never again be so close, physically or emotionally.

Emily was acutely aware of his every movement, although her eyes were closed. She felt him heavy upon her. Beyond conscious control, her hips moved tentatively, and her thighs parted hungrily.

A high-pitched trilling welled from her throat. She screamed in fleeting pain an instant later.

Richard kissed her breasts and drew the coverlet up. Her lips in the hollow of his throat, his cheek against her temple, they lay quietly for a time. The tears seeping from her eyes were damp on his shoulder.

'That was nice, very nice!' she finally whispered, kissing his shoulder. 'I'm not disappointed at all. But why do people make such a fuss? Is that all there is to it?'

He smoothed the damp tendrils of black hair off her forehead and kissed her eyelids before replying: 'No, that's not all. Not by a long shot. Especially for a woman. Women can feel so intensely. . . .'

'Who told you?' she interrupted. 'No, don't say. I don't want to know. You're sure?'

'Quite sure. Feelings . . . sensations so intense they almost consume. . . .'

'Well, that won't be necessary!' she declared judiciously. 'Though it could. . .'

He leaned over to kiss her, but she pushed him away and finished with a gamine grin: 'I was saying it could be true. We must try again very soon. I suspect I could get to like it!'

15

December 22, 1922

The house was unpretentious, almost shabby: just another six-storey tenement on Kiangse Road. That plain red-brick façade belied the Edwardian opulence within. The old-fashioned brass bell-pull had been burnished by many palms over the years. Beneath it, IKRA was engraved on a brass plaque which, after four weeks, was already worn by assiduous polishing. Discreetly lowered blinds confirmed the house's respectability. To its habitués the appearance of solid bourgeois virtue guaranteed discretion.

The raffish coupé standing at the kerb marred the impression of stolid bourgeois virtue. The jaunty Delage gleamed sapphire as the street-lamps came on at five in the afternoon. The Marmon limousine behind it was discharging a cargo of champagne, brandy and claret. The chauffeur chivvied the liveried porters who were carrying the cases into the bijou elevator with the heliotrope-velvet curtains. The man who drove the Delage was fretting in the red-plush parlour.

Joshua Haleevie concluded wryly that his Christmas presents were more welcome than himself. The wine bottles were going directly to the private apartments on the top floor, but he awaited a summons. The concierge had passed on Elizaveta's regret that she could not at that moment even say a word on the internal telephone system, whose installation he had supervised. Smiling in strained resignation, Joshua flung himself down on the cream-and-red striped sofa to sip a brandy and soda.

All intrusive males were excluded from the private sitting-room where Elizaveta Alexandrovna Yavalenka was entertaining Julia Pavernen and Emily Howe. After the Edwardian pomposities of the public rooms, the simplicity of the white rattan furniture with the mint-green cushions was refreshing. With her closest friends, her only true female friends, Elizaveta could relax – she could even show her true face beneath the professional hauteur modelled on her god-mother, the Grand Duchess Olga, who had been murdered by the Bolsheviks with her parents the Czar and Czarina in 1918.

None the less, Elizaveta dramatically drew deep on her aromatic Egyptian cigarette through a lapis lazuli holder. Gliding towards the window, the sable-trimmed train of her evening-gown swirled. Her guests' afternoon dresses seemed drab, and their subdued make-up pallid.

'It's all theatre, of course.' Even in her professional regalia, Elizaveta was not above self-satire. 'I'm selling illusion, you know. Fortunately, I've got all my mother's pre-war dresses. How do you like this little number?'

The chartreuse tunic with the hexagonal diamanté pattern was displayed dramatically by the old-rose mantle with the sable border. Gold-mounted osprey feathers soared from the diamanté chaplet around her forehead.

'Mummy's favourite court dress. Properly worn with a tiara. But I thought that would be going too far.'

Elizaveta poured Lapsang Souchang from the silver teapot into bone-china cups and served lemon slices with silver tongs heavy with silver grapes. No prop had been omitted that would complete the illusion of an opulent mansion during the reign of naughty King Edward VII.

'Smashing, isn't it?' Elizaveta almost dissolved into giggles. 'My dears, it's great fun. Such a lark!'

Emily's Confucian puritanism kept her from speaking, and newly acquired tact sugared Julia's comment: 'It's brilliant, Liz. The Ikra even smells just right. Those musky perfumes . . .'

'. . . just like rutting deer . . .' Elizaveta interjected.

'. . . and the aroma of cigars and cognac.'

'I've built a playground for our lords and masters. It's going to be a very jolly Christmas.'

Julia assured herself she was not shocked by the Ikra's purpose. Even Emily had primly noted in her office diary that she was 'inspecting premises on Kiangse Road on which a mortgage is held'. Elizaveta had already led them on the tour of inspection.

The suites on the fourth floor, sealed by formidable padlocks, were reserved for permanent guests. The salons and dining rooms on the ground and first floors were public, as were the casino and the ballroom in the big circular extension in the rear. The bizarre splendours of the suites on the second and third floors were designed for the most private of activities.

The Caligula suite was built around a nine-foot-square sunken marble bath which was flanked by a marble slab for massage and a marble dais with a marble bench 'for a lute player'. The bath-chamber was panelled with creamy Travertine marble and heated by gilded radiators to 78 degrees.

Behind other doors lay a Japanese pavilion and apartments in the styles of the Egypt of Amenhotep and the France of Louis XV. Elizaveta did not comment on their furnishings. A cubicle chamber, half-lit by red strip-lighting, featured a nine-foot wooden cross, a gridiron above a brazier, and a chain-festooned post hung with knouts, quirts, and whips. Julia had not dared asked about the enigmatic black-and-silver machines in the bathroom, and Emily had turned her eyes away.

'It's nearly six.' Elizaveta announced when they left those dark, male-orientated fantasies for the immaculate femininity of her sitting-room. 'Sun's over the yard-arm. I've just time for a drink and a gossip.'

'Only one ship in the Hwangpoo today with a yard-arm. An old four-masted grain-carrier from Southampton.' Emily was tart. 'And the sun's been over that yard-arm for an hour. It's already dark outside.'

'Yard-arm or hard-arm,' Elizaveta snapped, 'I want a glass of Joshua's champagne. Fit for a boardroom, he says, or a bawd's room.'

Emily smiled thinly at the defensive joke, and Elizaveta looked at her speculatively. Emily was markedly more attractive, her bosom fuller and her skin glowing. There was an obvious explanation for that radiance – and for Emily's casual understanding of the double-entendres. The Englishman who looked like a Frenchman must have finally succeeded in getting her into bed. Why did the Chinese make such a fuss about sex?

Julia was blushing, and Elizaveta asked slyly: 'Still a virgin, Julie? What's the matter with Tommy? Does he need guidance from his sister?'

Having reduced both her guests to appalled silence, Elizaveta demurely sipped her champagne. Her friends expected her to be outrageous.

'Liz, time will cure most things, including my virginity.' Julia recovered resiliently. 'I won't tell you how to run your business if you don't tell me how to run my life.'

'I'd welcome suggestions, my dear. Though I've had a lot more experience of both.'

'Then tell me something, comrade.' Julia knew the Bolshevik salutation would annoy Elizaveta. 'Those padlocked rooms on the fourth floor. Who uses them? And what do they do there?'

'Not what you think, my snappy virgin. They're very respectable Russian gentlemen, who, Emily knows, put up half the capital for the Ikra. Though the Whites have been forced out of Siberia, they still hope – and plot. Certainly they buy arms. Your Uncle Jack's often here to see them.'

'Aren't you giving away secrets, Liz dear?' Emily's tone was barbed. 'I thought ladies like . . . like you . . . never told who their . . . ah . . . clients were.'

'I didn't say he was a client, Ice Princess. Only that he visited my fourth-floor lodgers. And I do not require instruction from . . .'

'Poor old Uncle Jack could use some new business.' Julia headed off an open quarrel. 'He's still got his Korean girl friend, and she's expensive. Anyway, the armament business is so slow, he probably couldn't afford your . . .'

'What about Riverview Manor? Solved your problems there?'

Elizaveta's insatiable appetite for gossip was a professional asset. 'I warned you that builder fellow Vass was a rascal.'

'My dear girl, Vass finished everything two months ago, even those scrumptious concrete bathtubs. Marbleized he calls them. Everyone's all moved in. But the banks've taken all the money.'

The telephone tinkled remotely, and Elizaveta lifted a brass-and-malachite instrument from behind a cushion.

'Yes, my love, do come up now,' she said throatily. 'I'm afraid I forgot about you. We were having such a good time. . . . No, I won't. Never again, I promise. . . . He is? When? Just now? That *is* interesting. . . . Goodbye, darling. Hurry!'

Julia was again disturbed by Elizaveta's casual treatment of her faithful cavalier. Elizaveta was amused by Julia's distaste for the business of the Ikra, in contrast to her forthright acceptance of the business in guns. Yet the commerce in flesh was, at worst, a simulacrum of love, while the commerce in armaments was, ultimately, death.

Elizaveta considered her trade moral, indeed benevolent, compared with John Pavernen's traffic in guns. A good house gave much pleasure and no pain to either patrons or practitioners, unless they wanted pain. A good war was impossible, for all war inflicted pain and death – even the mock wars of the warlords.

The Countess who rarely used her title felt aristocratic disdain for bourgeois sexual morality. She did not, however, believe in the 'free love' that was as bad for the heart as it was for her business. She did believe in love, and she was amused by the middle-class inhibitions that disturbed her friends. But she did not speak of her reflections on love and war. Her lover was on the point of arriving, and it was her inflexible rule not to discuss serious matters with men.

'Joshua's on his way up,' she instead remarked. 'He says General Chiang Kai-shek is also honouring my humble establishment. Natty as an organ-grinder in a velvet-collared chesterfield and a checked suit.'

'Poor May Soong, she must not ever know he comes here,' Emily decreed. 'How she can moon after a man who has a wife and a couple of half-grown sons? It's beyond me.'

'You've done it now Liz,' Julia taunted. 'You've told us the name of a client.'

'Hardly, my dear. General Chiang Kai-shek visits a gentleman on the fourth floor. Though he does patronize other houses, I hear. When he comes to the Ikra on *my* business, my lips will be sealed. But in Shanghai, *everyone* talks about business and politics.'

'. . . and love!' Emily retorted, while Julia insisted: '. . . and sex!'

'If I'm not mistaken,' Joshua Haleevie interjected, stepping out of the elevator, 'you're talking about my favourite subject.'

'What's that, my darling?' Elizabeta lifted her face for his kiss. 'Business or politics?'

'Neither,' he replied. 'Only love.'

'And sex?' she teased. 'They don't always go together.'

'With me, they always do,' Joshua declared. 'But we're embarrassing your guests. Good evening, ladies.'

The accent Joshua had acquired at Harrow and Cambridge was, Emily decided, even more posh then Tommy's. To American eyes, Joshua's manner was typically English – restrained, almost inhibited. He never wore his Distinguished Service Cross, not even when in the uniform of a major of the Shanghai Volunteer Corps. Yet his bow was continental, almost Levantine. He was by just a hair's breadth too sleek to be perfectly English. He was devoted to the Russian mistress who treated him so casually. Although his words were light and sometimes cynical, he was always kind and, Emily sensed, vulnerable.

General Chiang Kai-shek would have been appalled to learn that Joshua Haleevie had recognised him. His fedora was pulled down, and his collar was raised to conceal his features. Later all would come out, but not yet.

There was little danger of premature disclosure. The White Russian madam, who was young and naïve, believed her sponsors were White Russian loyalists drawing on the gold hoard of the Czars. Should she learn of his presence, she would assume that he was involved in those childish schemes.

Chiang Kai-shek was repelled by the Ikra's overwhelmingly foreign character, exemplified by the wreaths, the mistletoe, and the red-and-green ribbons celebrating the Christmas season. But his mood was still buoyant. President Sun Yat-sen had entrusted the life-or-death negotiations to him. They had learned to depend on each other during fifty-three days on the gunboat off Canton – before the Old Man finally agreed to retreat to Shanghai. The house at 29 Rue Molière was not only more comfortable but a better base than the gunboat. Dr Sun was in touch with both the Christian General and the Old Marshal of Manchuria. But he was fed up with warlords. He had virtually concluded that all warlords must be crushed before China could attain his three goals: nationalism, prosperity, and democracy.

Undeterred by past failure or the gory Canton Mutiny, the President was now seeking allies abroad for a new Northern Expedition. Sun Yat-sen was a Christian, but the Christian powers would not help him. Present disorder was too much to their liking. He now believed his best hope was an alliance with the Communist International in Moscow and its protegé, the Chinese Communist Party.

The Comintern offered not only gold and guns, but agitators, and generals. The Communist Party of China was, moreover, growing powerful. Controlling the expanding labour movement, the Communists instigated strikes by miners, railway workers, and seamen. Since working with the Communists would strengthen the National People's Party, Chiang Kai-shek had been entrusted with securing the best possible terms.

When he ascended to the fifth floor of the Ikra amid the irritating Christmas decorations, most members of the Communist Party had already become members of the National People's Party – *after* the Comintern had commanded them to join.

If Nationalists and Communists today agreed on several outstanding issues, the two parties would announce their new alliance – and would soon rule China together.

'Come in, General.' A small, bearded European responded to Chiang-Kai-shek's peremptory knock. 'I believe you know Mr Chang Kuo-tao, the labour organizer.'

The heavily padded door ensured against eavesdropping. When it closed, hidden microphones relayed the conversation in the room to the two plain clothes men concealed in the basement who listened through bulky earphones and frantically jotted notes in Chinese shorthand. Joshua Haleevie had implanted those microphones when he installed the internal telephone system.

Joshua was to report to London that the Nationalists and the Communists had finally agreed. All members of the Communist Party were also to become members of the National People's Party – as individuals. Whatever that formula meant, the Communist leaders were to hold high rank in the Nationalist hierarchy.

Joshua was to point out: First, the Soviet Union, working through the Communist International, had won a decisive victory by joining with Dr Sun Yat-sen, who possessed both great personal prestige and a standing army. Second, a new phase had begun in the struggle for China.

A sealed envelope passed from the Comintern agent to General Chiang Kai-shek to seal the pact. Joshua could not, therefore, tell his friends the amount of the first instalment of the subsidy Moscow was to pay the Nationalists. He could, however, report that it was 'very substantial – a heavy weight to tip the balance of power.'

16

January 27–February 7, 1923

The errant thought insinuated itself into Emily's mind while the rickshaw jolted across the cobblestones. Her brother Tommy was actually three persons: the playboy, the scientist, and the patriot. Since she could not tell which of them would be dominant at any particular moment, it was sometimes like dealing with three different men.

Emily was flung against Julia on the rickshaw's hard seat behind the canvas screen that protected them from the chill drizzle of late January. The rickshaw-puller was feeling his way through the dusk from the South Station, where they had seen Tommy off to Hankow. That city was 450 miles south-east of Shanghai in a direct line. He would, however, travel some 250 miles north-east to Nanking, cross the Yangtze River by boat, and board a new train that would carry him a circuitous 500 miles to Chengchow. From Chengchow, China's only major railway junction, Hankow was somewhat less than 400 miles due south.

The alternative to that roundabout journey of more than a thousand miles was a long voyage aboard a Yangtze River steamer from Shanghsi to Hankow. Neither public buses nor private cars could attempt the journey on the dirt-track roads, for medieval China began just outside modern Shanghai.

As Tommy began his long journey, Emily reflected on the complex brother she had rediscovered only two years ago after a decade-long separation. Most people saw the playboy Tommy who joked in Shanghainese or drawled sarcastically in English, hiding both his intellect and his convictions beneath a cloak of banter. That public Tommy was endearing – and always amusing. The other two Tommies were more interesting.

111

His natural habitat the linoleum corridors and draughty wards of Shanghai General Hospital, the crisp scientist believed himself detached from both compassion and anger. Emotion would only interfere with his mission, which was to heal patients. None the less, the concern he actually felt for his patients drained him more than did the physical demands of his work, sometimes leaving him virtually unable to speak.

Tommy the patriot was a strange blend of fiery passion and ice-cold dedication. He put China above all else, but he could not say exactly what was best for China. Which was most important, national dignity or the well being of the people? Which should come first, popular government or industrial development, military power or social justice? Tommy knew that China could not attain all those goals at once, though Sun Yat-sen had implied that she could in his book *Three People's Principles*. Family solidarity, moreover, inclined Tommy towards Dr Sun's National People's Party, to which his father contributed lavishly. But he was also deeply impressed by the extraordinary vitality of the young men who called themselves Communists.

Staring through the grimy window as the train clattered towards Soochow, Tommy wondered if he was wise in accepting the invitation of Chang Kuo-tao, the Communist leader Julia always remembered fondly as 'the big man who brought me Adam'. The lure was, however, irresistible.

His friend was to preside over the Inaugural Congress of China's first major labour union. With the blessing of the warlord who currently controlled the Northern Capital, Peking, the Peking-Hankow Railway Worker's General Union was already sprouting regional Workers' Councils. It was the core of the rapidly expanding labour movement, which was dominated by the fledgling Communist Party of China.

And Chang Kuo-tao was the kingpin. No patriot could reject his invitation, Dr Thomas Tan-ssu Howe concluded as the train rumbled north at twenty-six miles an hour.

When he finally reached Hankow astride the Yangtze River four days later, Tommy knew he should have come by steamer. He had in those four days seen so much poverty, squalor, and suffering that he was almost numb with despair. The wretched peasants doggedly ploughed the meagre soil – to keep death at bay for another year or two. Their lives were not even medieval, but simply primitive.

Hankow was far more advanced. Its people lived in relative comfort – in good part, Tommy acknowledged, because it was a treaty port, which like Shanghai had been developed by foreigners. His view of foreign imperialism was for the moment somewhat less scathing, and he was delighted to alight at Hankow from the bone-shaking railway carriage.

The station-master, self-important in a red peaked cap, strode across the wind-swept platform. Swivelling beneath the patent-leather visor, his eyes came to rest on the young doctor who was stepping down to the platform. The station-master produced a small envelope and waited while Tommy read the curt note: *In haste: Plans changed. Return immediately Chengchow. Kuo-tao.*

'Same compartment, Doctor,' the station-master said. 'The train turns around here. Only twelve to fifteen hours back to Chengchow. Not even 400 miles. You'll get there in plenty of time for the Congress.'

During the long journey to Hankow, Tommy's mind had been crowded with new insights into his native land. During the monotonous return to Chengchow, his thoughts focused on Julia and their last evening together in the loft-apartment. She had for the occasion ejected not only his sister Emily, but the amah Lao Zee.

It had, he realized, been a close call, a damned close call. He had almost asked her to marry him.

Not that he wasn't fond of Julia – very fond of her. Actually, he thought he loved her. He knew he was never completely happy except when they were together.

But marriage was another thing. Would be even if his parents weren't poised to come down on him like ten tons of bricks if he ever breathed any notion of marrying as he pleased – and, infinitely worse, a foreigner.

Besides, he wasn't ready for marriage yet, not even ready to think about marrying. He had too much before him – too many challenges in his profession and too many tasks for his country.

If he could only take it as lightly as most fellows did, he would probably be better off. But he couldn't treat Julia as if she were a superior sing-song girl. He couldn't just use her when he could not possibly marry her.

He would have to give her up. Yet the mere thought of never seeing her again made him feel hollow and frightened. Heaven knew what would become of them!

Five hundred miles away, Julia was remembering the same evening. She spent a lot of her time thinking about Tommy.

She had no idea what future, if any, lay before them. But no woman of twenty-two could avoid speculating on marriage. However, she knew her own mind. She might perhaps, some day wish to marry Tommy. But not today, not tomorrow – not even a year hence, which was as far as she could project her thoughts into the future.

Besides, Tommy had never expressed any hope of their being together even in a year's time. Marriage evidently never entered his mind. Perhaps she was only a passing entertainment, more diverting because she was a foreigner. In that case, why in God's name didn't he at least *attempt* to seduce her?

He had that evening complained rather proprietorially of her closeness to Elizaveta. When she reminded him of their meeting at the St Andrew's Café he had growled: 'How was I to know you would become such friends? Or that Liz would become ... ah ... what she's become? Everything was different then.'

113

'What do you mean, everything?' she asked. 'What else has changed?'

'Blast it, you know what I mean. I didn't then feel about you – not the way I feel now.'

'Tommy, you almost make me *want* to obey you,' she said. 'You're so nice when you come down off your high horse.'

The telephone shrilled, destroying her hope of inducing him to expand the strongest declaration of affection he had ever made. The mood shattered, she sighed and lifted the earpiece.

She was rewarded by crackling and Central's cheery greeting: 'Is that 90654? Just a moment. I'll connect you.' Then Central reported: '90654? I'm sorry. Interference on the line. Your caller has been disconnected.'

Although the interference had also broken the emotional connection, she seated herself again on the sofa. Tommy took her hand, and it seemed he would continue his declaration. His gesture was, however, meant to soften his next words.

'Actually, I'm not so worried about your being corrupted. Not . . . ah . . . physically. But the false values of a place like the Ikra are very dangerous. So . . .'

'Tommy, Shanghai *is* false values,' she interrupted. 'The champagne and the bright lights and the caviar. I love it, but I don't kid myself it's real. . . . I'm so glad you're jealous.'

Julia exuberantly hugged Tommy's arm. She was intensely aware of his shoulder pressing against her breasts. How did it feel to him, she wondered, raising her face. His lips were taut against hers, and, for the first time, his tongue probed her mouth. Her entire body floated on the ripples that swelled outwards from its centre. She waited expectantly. He would certainly repeat his declaration. She was wondering how she would reply when the telephone shrilled again.

'Drat it!' Julia exploded. 'Damn it to hell!'

None the less, she obediently rose and answered: 'Yes. Yes I'll wait. But do connect them as soon as possible. . . . Yes, who's calling?'

'Smidgelou Tomas here!' In spite of herself, Julia smiled at that heavy Czech voice. 'I am warning you. It is too bad. I warn you.'

Inured to his bizarre English, she responded lightly to the apparent threat: 'Hello, Mr Smidgelou. What seems to be the trouble?'

'We are having fires, two fires in one night. So, I am calling you at your house so I can tell you. Two fires in one night!'

'You mean the stove draws well? And the house is warm? I'm so glad, Mr Smidgelou.'

'Is not fire in stove, Missy. Is fire in walls. Two times. I am warning you because you are always so kindly.'

'In the wall, Mr Smidgelou? Fires in the wall? How can that be?'

'I do not know, Missy Pavernena. Manya and me are sitting peacefully, so happy to be in new home. And then, boom, fire is coming out of wall.'

'Was anyone hurt? Is it all right now? Is there much damage? I'm so sorry, Mr Smidgelou.'

Resting his chin on his crossed arms, Tommy leered over the back of the rattan sofa and intoned sepulchrally: 'Never admit liability! Never acknowledge fault! Never accept responsibility! Golden rules for young doctors also apply to embryo real estate taipans.'

She waved him to silence and, ignoring his admonition, continued: 'Naturally we'll take care of it. Probably a minor fault. I'll call Mr Vass first thing in the morning. You're sure everything's all right now?'

'I have thrown water at fires, and all is right. Only underneath where paint is washed off, wall is a little green. But not important. Thank you, Missy. Manya will sleep more happier this night.'

Since there had been no injury and no significant damage, Julia dismissed the incident as a laughable freak. To her surprise, Tommy frowned and hummed under his breath. But men loved to make a fuss about anything mechanical. Automobiles, plumbing, and electricity were the sacred mysteries they cherished as women cherished the mystical travail of childbirth.

'Spontaneous combustion?' he muttered. 'Don't see how, unless there's sulphur in the plaster. But that's ridiculous.'

Julia listened in fond amusement while he mused aloud: 'Jack Pavernen's very proud he put in electricity – points and sockets throughout. It's not my line of country, Julie, but your man Vass better take a good look at the wiring. I'll be blowed if I know exactly how a fire could start after several months. The insulation perhaps.'

'And the green on the walls, Tommy?' She was marginally alarmed. 'What could that be?'

'Green walls? I'll be bug . . . I really couldn't say. Mould perhaps. But *under* the paint, which doesn't sound terribly durable if water washes it off? Sorry old girl, I really couldn't say.'

Tommy laughed at that recollection, still puzzled by the inexplicable phenomena. At least his recollections provided a diversion on the apparently interminable journey that finally ended at six p.m. on January 31st. Chengchow, once an ugly market town, had swollen into a hideous semi-industrial city because it was the single place in China where north-south and east-west railway tracks crossed.

Coughing in the soot-laden dampness, Tommy was led along a snow-banked platform to the station-master's office. He found Chang Kuo-tao ensconced like a feudal potentate among enormous white canvas sacks crammed with propaganda pamphlets. The labour leader offered brisk greetings and flicked coal dust off the wooden bench with a grimy handkerchief. Without further preamble, he asked: 'Do you remember Mao Tse-tung? The thin fellow with the mole on his chin. Always wears an old-fashioned long-gown of homespun cloth. Always was a country bumpkin, a real yokel!'

'Why are you so hot under the collar about old Mao?'

'Damned fool thinks he can make a revolution and seize power by organizing the peasants. The peasants have got no more coherence than a sheet of sand, as Sun Yat-sen would say. Helluva foundation for a

115

revolution. Well, let Mao pick hayseed out of his hair. We're on the right track to power here, the railway track. I'm organising the industrial workers, transport and mining workers, the proletariat. Immense power nicely concentrated. I've got the revolution in my palm.'

Chang Kuo-tao cupped his hands, and Tommy noticed that they were not calloused like a worker's, but soft like a scholar's. The big man was, however, wearing the quilted cotton jacket of a manual labourer. His broad face was grimy, and a light stubble sprouted beneath his heavy cheekbones.

'Protective colouration.' He grinned at Tommy's frank scrutiny. 'The big warlord in Peking is friendly, the one they call the Scholar General. But some of his cops aren't so friendly.'

Tommy had himself worn old Chinese-style clothing to make himself inconspicuous on his long journey. He chuckled, remembering the stringy American missionary with a baggy skirt down to her ankles who had demanded that he fetch tea *chop-chop* – and blushed when he answered in an upper-class English drawl. Noting Chang Kuo-tao's flushed cheeks, Tommy knew his friend had fortified himself against the damp cold with *baigarh*, the foul smelling Chinese vodka.

Normally expansive and talkative like most politicians, Chang Kuo-tao was now ebullient – with *baigarh* and with optimism. Walking to the Wuchou Hotel in the centre of Chengchow, the bourgeois doctor listened attentively to the revolutionary, who was the son of a rich country landlord. The radical had directed the station-master to send coolies to the hotel with their luggage. He took for granted the services of the proletariat he had sworn to free from its chains.

Chang Kuo-tao asked after Tang Jo-wang, the Tibetan dog, and after Joo-li, the foreign woman. He grinned at Tommy's account of Julia's dismay over Adam's bounding growth. He laughed when Tommy reported the amah Lao Zee's dire prediction that the dog would be bigger than a water-buffalo when full grown. The acting secretary-general of the Communist Party of China was in roaring good humour, exuberant as a schoolboy on the first day of the long summer vaction.

Though the moonlight could not penetrate the cramped alleys, an occasional paraffin lamp glimmering through an oiled-paper window lit the slimy cobblestones. Their cloth shoes could not always avoid the sewage from the ditch that ran in the middle of the alley. The shuttered houses, which were the repellent black of decaying sponges, reeked of rotting excrement, putrifying vegetables, and rancid peanut oil.

The Communist ignored the squalor from which the Shanghailander involuntarily shrank. He only halted his spirited analysis of Chinese society when a mangy dog darted across the alley in pursuit of a sleek rat with a whip-like tail. When the rat took refuge in a wicker basket, a lid dropped automatically. A lean arm reached out of a window and took in the trap.

'For his pet snake!' Chang Kuo-tao smiled. 'When it gets fat enough, he'll eat the snake.'

Except for that aside, the revolutionary talked solely and compulsively of politics. He spoke of the forthcoming Railways Workers' Congress like a proud father. He treated Tommy like a good luck mascot and addressed him as 'My boy!', though Tommy was the elder by almost a year.

In deadly earnest he recalled the critical events of the past month in which he had participated. Fascinated, Tommy filled his meerschaum pipe from his oilskin pouch. He was puffing meditatively as they emerged into the square on which the Wuchou Hotel stood.

'Of course, you know the declaration of January 1st on the Communist-Nationalist alliance. But do you know agreement was reached in the Ikra Hotel?' Chang Kuo-tao revelled in his disclosures. 'We also agreed to reorganize the Nationalist Party, make it disciplined like a Communist Party. The chairman of the reorganizing committee is the Secretary-General of the Communist Party.'

Tommy bit hard on his pipe when he learned of the Ikra's role. His friend continued compulsively: 'I hate taking orders from foreigners. But Moscow really tightened the screws, insisted we join the Nationalist Party. I don't trust this new alliance. But the Comintern's paying the cook, so it can choose the menu – for the time being.'

'Hard cheese for your lot, isn't it?' Tommy probed. 'The Comintern joining Dr Sun Yat-sen in a declaration that China isn't ready for Communism.'

'The Comintern has practically switched its support to Sun Yat-sen,' Chang Kuo-tao conceded. 'But not for long. Tomorrow we Communists will show those idiots in Moscow where the power in China really lies.'

'With, say, four hundred Party members?' Tommy asked quietly. 'Among four hundred million people that's not much power.'

'A single spark starts a forest fire!' The Communist quoted the traditional saying with gusto. 'Just watch the sparks fly tomorrow.'

The delegates to the Inaugural Congress of the General Union of the Peking-Hankow Railway Workers began entering the Pulo Theatre near the Wuchou Hotel early on February 1st. They were confident because they were supported by the warlord who controlled North China and Peking, the traditional capital. Noted for his reverence for the teachings of Confucius, he was called the Scholar General – admiringly by his friends and derisively by his enemies. Inspired by the Sage's concern for the common people, he wished to encourage the labour movement.

The Scholar General had already appointed six Communist railway-inspectors to investigate corruption and inefficiency. He planned to use those cat's paws to get rid of his enemies on the railway, so that he could impose his own absolute control. In return for that service, the Communists were permitted to organize unions – and the Railway Workers' was already the biggest, the best organised, and the most powerful trade union in Chinese history.

Preparations for the Inaugural Congress were meticulous. The organizers had even inserted announcements in the newspapers of Peking,

117

Tientsin, Shanghai, and Hankow. Their candour informed not only the workers, but the railway management, the local garrison, and the police.

Under pressure from those conservatives, the Scholar General had ordered the Congress banned. But he had only yesterday explained to a special union delegation that his reluctant decision was conditional. No *formal* Congress was possible because Chengchow lay in a military zone, but he would not object to a simple inaugural ceremony.

Tommy Howe was puzzled by the fine distinction between 'a formal meeting' and 'a simple ceremony'. He was also puzzled by the assurance with which the Communists were preparing to convene the full Inaugural Congress. He was not convinced, as they were, that the Scholar General had prohibited the formal Congress only as a gesture to placate his conservative allies. However, Tommy concluded with some complacence that Chang Kuo-tao knew the situation far better than he did.

Dressed like his friend in a blue worsted jacket with a choker collar, Tommy was borne into the Pulo Theatre on a wave of hope, but he naturally clutched his leather Gladstone bag with the essential drugs and instruments he always carried. He was immediately enveloped by the nostalgic smell of the theatre. The rank odour of performing bears mingled with the chalk dust from acrobats' shoes and the harsh perfume of the hot hand-towels vendors flung to the audience.

At nine in the morning, the first tiers of benches were already filled with delegates in their shiny best clothing. Their faces were scrubbed, but their calloused hands were grease-stained, for they were true working-men. On the stage, a long trestle table stood before the row of folding wooden chairs that awaited the leaders. Men in the dark-blue uniforms of the theatre staff were putting the last touches to the preparations.

Chang Kuo-tao strode stiff-legged towards the stage, where a half-dozen labour leaders were speaking spiritedly to the blue-uniformed attendants. At their centre was a small man with a hooked nose, a villainous moustache, and a sickly complexion. His uniform glittered with brass insignia. He wore a holstered revolver on his hip, as did all the other men in blue uniforms.

They were not attendants, Tommy saw, but policemen, and a file of police reinforcements was streaming down the aisle. Through the open doors, he heard marching feet and a blaring bugle.

'What's all this?' Chang Kuo-tao scrambled onto the stage. 'What the devil's going on?'

'. . . it's very simple,' the police chief was repeating. 'You can all get the hell out of here. Get out and disband. There will be *no* meeting and *no* inaugural ceremony.'

'The General himself assured us we could hold a simple ceremony,' the union's heavy-bodied first secretary persisted. 'No Congress, but a plain ceremony was okay.'

'What's the difference?' the police chief demanded. 'I'll give you five minutes to disband. Any longer and someone's going to get hurt!'

Chang Kuo-tao stepped between the first secretary and the police chief. He peremptorily directed his colleagues not to argue, not with the police inside and the soldiers outside. The Inaugural Congress would, he added, assuredly meet elsewhere under more favourable conditions. The organizers obediently shouted out to the audience that the meeting was postponed and advised them all to leave peacefully.

A few men rose, but most stubbornly remained seated. The diehards stamped their feet, shouted, and hissed. Emboldened by that outcry, the first secretary made a megaphone of his hands and screamed: '*Kung-hui wan sui!* . . . Long live the Union!'

'Long live the Peking-Hankow Railway Union!' The crowd responded. 'All hail the First Congress!'

His face pale with rage, the police chief clapped his hand over the secretary's mouth. He declared furiously that the outcry had violated the ban on a meeting, and he clung to the stout secretary like a terrier attacking a bear. Still shouting slogans, the delegates trickled out of the Pulo Theatre into the rainy morning.

The police chief's anger remained high because he feared severe punishment for permitting the exchange of slogans. Raging, he ordered the police and the troops to seize the banners and placards the workers had made for the joyful inaugural parade.

Neither policemen nor soldiers were gentle. They tore apart the big floral tributes and ripped up the well wishers' good luck banners. As a final gesture, they occupied the Union's headquarters and manhandled the staff.

The magical smell of the theatre was washed from Tommy's nostrils by the sour drizzle outside. He had come a thousand dreary miles from Shanghai, and he had wasted his time and his energy on a fiasco. The first test of the Communists' trade union movement had just ended in humiliating defeat. Although he agreed with his friend Chang Kuo-tao that they had to withdraw before greatly superior power, Tommy was bitterly depressed. The Communist leaders, especially his supremely self-assured friend, were criminally naïve. How could they have believed that a reactionary Confucian warlord would even tolerate – much less encourage – a radical labour movement?

Swinging his Gladstone bag in dejection, Tommy slowly walked back to the hotel to pack his belongings. He found all the leaders of the trade union movement, both young Communists and older workers, crammed into the big room on the second floor he shared with Kuo-tao. They were talking of retaliation, rather than retreat. Restored to his normal ebullience, Chang Kuo-tao was not restraining the hot-heads, but backing their demands for a total strike.

The workers' requests had been moderate: the police chief and senior railway officials to be formally reprimanded; the police to withdraw from the Union's offices; finally, a full day off with pay once a week and a week's paid vacation once a year. When the Scholar General flatly refused to consider these requests, the strike became inevitable. Even tactically cautious Chang Kuo-tao was convinced that a forceful demonstration of the workers' power would bring the Scholar General to his senses. Tommy felt it might actually succeed when he heard that the Chengchow Railway District had provided two special cars to carry the union leaders south to Hankow, which was the storm-centre.

Demonstrating remarkable solidarity all the workers walked out and closed down the Peking-Hankow Railway. By the evening of February 6th, the optimists who foresaw a quick victory were cock-a-hoop. Facing the might of organized labour for the first time, the demoralized authorities were coming around.

The army had signally failed to get the trains rolling. Many engineers were arrested and threatened and beaten. But they had still refused to man locomotives, and the Provincial Garrison Commander had finally backed down. On the morning of February 6th, the Provincial Council of Trade Unions held a mass demonstration in Hankow to demonstrate its total support for the Railway Workers. Some 10,000 militants marched to the industrial suburb of Kiangan,where the railway workers lived near the carriage and locomotive repair shops. Speaking in front of Kiangan Station, the Trade Union Council's leaders pledged a walkout by every worker in Wuhan. Hankow and its two sister towns, collectively called Wuhan, were second in industry only to Shanghai itself. Wuhan would be paralyzed if the strikers' demands were not promptly granted. That evening, the Provincial Governor proposed that serious negotiations begin the next day. The authorities, who had initially refused to talk at all, were begging for talks.

Tommy Howe watched the Railway Union's resurgence with wonder. From the window of his improvised clinic for workers' families in the schoolhouse that was the strike's headquarters, Tommy contemplated the gaudily decorated town-square – and his heart lifted.

As the dusk of February 7th descended, a festive spirit swept the square. Children swarmed around hawkers of chestnuts, toys, and candy-apples. The shadows of leather puppets projected on a screen enthralled an audience with the adventures of the grand-master of deception, General Tsao Tsao. Two dumpling vendors, unable to meet the demand, retired with their stocks exhausted and their cooking-fires banked.

Four scrawny dogs chased a phantom cat through the half-light, and a two-stringed violin shrilled joyously from the crowded teahouse. Workers in their best clothes squatted to watch single-stick fencing. Their wives gossiped as they strolled around the bamboo stage in the centre of the square. Bystanders discussed every move in a game of Chinese chess, but the players were unperturbed. The news blew like a breeze across the square: 'They're coming. . . . They're coming to talk. It's all over bar the talking! Time for a victory party.'

Tommy's friend Chang Kuo-tao was once again cautious. He instructed the representatives the Union had chosen to talk with the Provincial Governor's delegation not to reveal their identity until the official delegation actually arrived. But that was just prudent tactics.

Thunder rumbled in the north, and Tommy instinctively glanced at the sky. The pallid sun was setting at five o'clock, and there were no dark thunderheads among the white cloud tufting the sky. Thunder rumbled again. A prolonged peal closed with staccato cracks.

As if summoned by the thunder, two youths wearing red armbands loped across the crowded square to the strike headquarters. Though flushed and panting, they displayed the self-importance of men bearing portentous news. One dashed into the office, but the second addressed Tommy.

'*Daifoo, ta-men....*' He used the respectful old word for a doctor. 'Master Physician, they're attacking the union offices at the station. Police and troops with big guns. It's all over. You must get away.'

The strike leaders pelted out of their headquarters into the alleys. The news raced through the square, and the revellers dispersed. No more than fifteen minutes after the messengers' arrival, Chang Kuo-tao and the first secretary of the Railway Union left the empty schoolhouse. In the square, the puppet-master and his apprentice were still packing up their little leather actors.

'Come on, Tommy!' Chang Kuo-tao urged. 'The troops'll make a house-to-house search. We're all getting out. Our rendezvous is the Blue Phoenix Teahouse in the French Concession. But you'd better come with me.'

'I'm not coming.' Tommy made his decision as he spoke. 'I've been deadweight for a week, a passenger on the railway strike. If there's going to be shooting, I can be useful. My business is looking after the sick and injured.'

'If that's what you want.' Chang Kuo-tao shrugged. 'Just don't kid yourself your profession'll protect you. *My* business is to survive.'

'*I-lu ping-an!*' Tommy replied. 'A peaceful journey then!'

Assisted by women whose children he had treated, Tommy laid out bandages and the few drugs remaining in his Gladstone bag, along with some bottles of *baigarh*, which would serve as anaesthetic as well as antiseptic.

A ruffle of rifle fire heralded the arrival of the Scholar General's troops. Tommy dropped to his knees behind the schoolhouse's stone wall but peeped over the window-sill when hobnailed boots crashed in the square. Smart in dark-green woollen blouses, their matching breeches tucked into rolled puttees, the garrison troops halted with the finicky precision of carriage-horses. Under their sergeants' command, they split into small units to search the lanes and houses.

Tommy rose and clasped his grimy hands together. The gut-griping fear was seeping away. His crude array of medicines and instruments would, after all, not be needed. The door crashed open behind him, and he heard the clatter of rifle-bolts.

He turned to see a weedy young officer pointing an enormous pistol at him. The muzzle's erratic wavering terrified him once more. The officer, who was evidently just as frightened as himself, might well shoot him accidentally.

'I'm a doctor.' His voice did not quaver. 'A doctor visiting from Shanghai. Nothing to do with this ... this strike.'

'A doctor?' the officer retorted. 'Also a Communist, no doubt. All you Shanghai scum are Communists.'

'A Communist? Never! Just a doctor visiting friends in Hankow. The Reds seized me and forced me to treat their people.'

'Come along!' the weedy officer snapped. 'I've got my orders. Round up all suspicious types.'

As he turned towards the door, Tommy heard glass breaking. He glanced back to see soldiers snatching up the *baigarh* bottles. The darkness outside was lit by the flare of bonfires and by occasional muzzle-flashes. Hands tied behind his back, he was turned over to a stout sergeant who wore a smile of great benevolence. Tommy squatted on the rock-hard ground and realized he was not to be shot immediately. He clamped his hands between his thighs to still their trembling.

In the light of wind-blown torches, he witnessed a cruel medieval spectacle. The dark mouths of alleys spewed out search parties of soldiers dragging back the strikers who had been found in hiding. The shiny black patches on the workers' holiday clothes were blood.

He rose and asked the benevolent sergeant to allow him to treat the wounded. The sergeant's hand slammed him hard across the face. Toppled by shock as much as the blow, Tommy sprawled on the ice-frosted ground. For the first time in his life an inferior had struck him.

He squatted again, waiting for an officer to approach, and watched the search parties returning with their prey. Not all, he consoled himself, were wounded, not even most. Smiling wryly at his altered perspective, he reminded himself that even one injured man denied treatment was a tragedy.

'They killed Lee and Wang, chopped off their hands.' The prisoners' voices murmured behind him. 'Got old Liu, too. There was one union leader who didn't run away.'

Eighty-odd prisoners were finally assembled in the wavering glare of the torches. The thin colonel shivered in his fur-lined trenchcoat and instructed the guards: 'Bring them inside in batches of five.'

Shouldering his way into the first group, Tommy was surprised by his own temerity. He was determined to plead that he be permitted to treat the wounded. To his surprise, the colonel agreed immediately.

Working with his few instruments and using *baigarh* as an antiseptic, Tommy cut and stitched mechanically. In his professional role he felt himself, again secure. His eyes were on his work, but his ears were cocked to the sharp questions and the stumbling replies of the workers' interrogation. He glanced up to see officers examining the men's hands under an oil-lamp. Soft palms would reveal the professional agitators who pretended to be working men.

Prodded by rifle butts and bayonets, most of the captives were turned out of the schoolhouse almost as rapidly as they were led in. After two hours, only four remained. Tommy recognized three as union leaders. A man called Lin was chairman of the Kiangan branch of the Railway Union. Concentrating on a suture, Tommy missed the next round of

122

questions and answers. When he looked up again, the thin colonel was motioning the four towards the door.

'After you, gentlemen!' He was elaborately ironic. 'We'll soon see if you don't change your minds. You will damned well tell the men to go back to work. And they'll obey you. After all, you are their union leaders. A few words or your lives, gentlemen?'

Tommy peered through the window as the union leaders in their holiday best walked between lines of glittering bayonets. Now lit by the serene moon as well as the torches, the drama he saw was mute. Those words not swallowed by the distance were cut off by the murky glass of the window.

The colonel spoke at length to Union Chairman Lin, obviously pressing him to use his authority to end the strike. A word from their leader would presumably send the workers back to their trains and their workshops. When the colonel paused, Lin shook his head stubbornly.

The sinister drama played itself out in silence. The colonel made a final appeal, and for the tenth time the union leader shook his head.

The colonel nodded sadly and beckoned. A squat sergeant trotted into the circle of torchlight. With one flowing motion he reached over his shoulder to extract a two foot-long half-moon blade from its sling on his back. He twirled the enormous knife, and it caught the moonlight. Graceful as a ballet dancer, he lifted the half-moon blade high with both hands.

Chairman Lin's eyes followed that movement, blinking rapidly. The sergeant swept the knife down. An arc of fire in the torchlight, the blade chipped the half-frozen ground three inches from the union leader's toes.

The colonel repeated his demand once again. He received the same reply – an obdurate shake of the head.

Resignedly, he turned away. While Chairman Lin's eyes still watched the colonel, the half-moon blade descended. His head tumbled to the ground, and blood spurted until his heart stopped beating.

The remaining union leaders were not accorded the same kindness. The sergeant did not kill them unawares. Another half-hour passed while threats and demands evoked the same blank refusal before the last leader was beheaded.

Turning in disgust, the colonel returned to the schoolhouse. Despite his fur-lined coat, he was suffering from the intense cold. He flailed his chest with his palms, nodded to Tommy, and demanded *baigarh*.

'Cretins! Idiots! What makes them do it?' he demanded. 'All that rabble'll be back at work in a day or two, anyway. Why didn't they buy their lives? Only a word! I can't understand it.'

A deferential junior officer spoke in a low murmur.

'The heads?' The colonel negligently pronounced an epitaph. 'Why, the dogs will be glad. . . . No! Hang their heads on the telegraph poles in front of the station. A salutary lesson for all concerned!'

17

'By Shanghai standards she's just a good plain cook.' Tommy veiled his appreciative belch with his napkin. 'But by English standards she's a genius, your Lao Zee.'

The prodigal was visiting the loft-apartment for the first time since his return from his adventures a week earlier. He had only in the last week of February been released by the colonel who was convinced all Shanghailanders were Communists, particularly intellectuals like lawyers, teachers, and doctors. The colonel had not been blind to the benefits of holding a competent physician captive. Tommy had treated complaints ranging from syphilis through tuberculosis to shrapnel wounds – to his professional benefit. He was almost sorry to board the Yangtze River steamer for Shanghai when the colonel was forced to release him by the peremptory telegram from the Scholar General.

That warlord had come under pressure from the Supreme Lord of the Floodgate Fraternity, acting at the behest of the gangster's blood-brother, General Chiang Kai-shek. That military politician was responding to the pleas of Mayling Soong, who had been swayed by Emily Howe and Julia Pavernen. General Chiang Kai-shek anticipated a further large contribution from Donald Howe to the war-chest of the Nationalists, who were campaigning to destroy all warlords in alliance with the Communists, whose strike the Scholar General had ferociously crushed.

Relaxed after the river voyage, Tommy had defied his mother's command to rest before returning to Shanghai General Hospital. He was so appalled by the effect of his absence that he spent the next five days – and most of the nights – in the wards and the laboratories. He had finally found time to dine in the loft-apartment on a damp evening in early March.

124

Richard Hollings was less solicitous than Emily and Julia. He was, however, eager for a first-hand account of the strike, which had been obscured by rumour, censorship, and bad communications. Although a flood on the Yellow River that killed tens of thousands was hardly worth a paragraph in *The Times*, much interest had been aroused by the 'firm suppression of the anarchist-communist plot to paralyse China's railways'. London was now sensitive to the Red menace.

Yet no other reporter had the details. Richard smugly stroked Adam, the black-and-white Tibetan dog Tommy had given Julia. Almost eighteen months old, Adam was as big as a calf. Though his bushy black tail knocked ashtrays off the coffee table, his great brown eyes looked at the world with melting tenderness. Julia had forgiven Tommy for mistaking an enormous mastiff for a small lion-dog.

'Plain cooking or not,' Julia answered Tommy's left-handed compliment, 'everything's *so* good.'

'I do like a hostess who isn't afraid to blow her own horn,' Richard Hollings remarked drily. 'This is delicious. What is it, Julie?'

Julia blushed. She had no idea of the name of the dish in the earthenware casserole. She only knew the big meat balls were enticing in their nest of braised Chinese cabbage.

'Do stop teasing, Dick,' Emily directed. 'You should know it's *shiz-tzu tou*, lions' heads.'

Though the lions' heads were really too hearty, Emily would have served ten more courses if they made Tommy happy. They were followed by another equally hearty dish: 'upside down meat', anise-steamed fat pork over mustard greens. Then 'quail eggs in tiger's skin'. The tiger's skin, deep fried until crunchy, was thin-rolled bean curd. Men, like children, loved chewy things with plain flavours.

Julia was also indulging her own cruder tastes although Tommy, too, loved sautéed eel topped with bubbling oil and garnished with coriander. Since the eel was on the heavy side, the next-to-last dish was light: tiny shrimp with *mao tou*, miniature lima beans with a distinctive nutty flavour.

Emily had really planned the meal. Having been indoctrinated in the rituals of the table by her old-fashioned mother, that emancipated young woman firmly believed that a whole fish must precede the soup that ended a meal. But Lao Zee had been unable to find a suitable fish in the market on a stormy day. Fretting because the welcome dinner for her brother was ending with shrimps, Emily was irritated by Julia's intemperate chuckle when the amah ceremoniously presented the eight-treasures soup.

'The beans reminded me,' Julia said contritely. 'I can't help laughing every time I think of Gustav Vass and the hanging gardens.'

The men looked up enquiringly. But Emily cut off their questions with a wave of her hand while Lao Zee ladled the broth out of the big green squash called winter melon. The eight treasures were dried scallops, black mushrooms, smoked ham, duck breasts, straw mushrooms, deer tendons, duck gizzards, and lotus seeds. Although Cantonese in origin, the soup was a favourite of Tommy's.

'That's Chinese genius.' He repeated the same words every time winter-melon soup appeared. 'You eat the tureen, too. Nothing wasted and no washing up.'

After they had raised their cups of yellow rice-wine to salute the soup, Emily's smile gave Richard permission to ask: 'What's all this about Gustav Vass and hanging gardens?'

'Dick, you mustn't write about it,' Julia cautioned. 'Tommy, do you remember when my telephone pal Smidgelou Tomas complained of fires in Riverview Manor and the walls turning green?'

'Yes, and what,' he asked, 'did it turn out to be?'

'Well, the fires were serious – or could have been.' Julia no longer smiled. 'Vass had used old wiring to save money. His workmen simply twisted the bits of wire together to join them. No insulation at all. Those joints flexed and rubbed as the new walls settled – so sparks flew. Presto, mysterious wall fires. Fortunately, most of the wiring's external so it was easy to check. Vass swears it won't happen again. He also avoided water dues by tapping into the neighbours' main – till they found out.'

'The hanging gardens, Julie?' Richard reminded her.

'That is strange. Grass and wild flowers growing out of walls.' She laughed again. 'Gustav Vass said dead-pan: "Miss Julie, I congratulate you! Such beautiful gardens – and indoors in winter! Like the wonderful hanging gardens of Babylon."'

'How did the plants get there?' Richard persisted.

'Mr Vass didn't waste money on plaster. Instead, he scooped up mud from Soochow Creek. "Very clean mud," he claims. No wonder the walls are sprouting plants.'

'It's very funny,' Tommy said. 'But it could be damned serious for Jack Pavernen.'

'Maybe, Tommy. We only learned today. Uncle Jack's still joking about advertising an indoor garden with every house.'

'I'm glad you're relaxed about it.' Tommy shook his head. 'Quick Jack Pavernen could be in more trouble than he knows.'

'Uncle Jack'll find a way out,' Julia replied. 'He always does. Maybe spray the walls with weed killer.'

'Let's move and let Lao Zee clear up,' Emily interjected. 'Then, brother dear, you can tell us about your adventures. Or are you tired of talking about it?'

'Hardly. Nobody wants to hear my boring story.'

'Let us judge that, old boy,' Richard Hollings urged.

'If you insist. It all began, you know, when Julie and Em dropped me off at the North Station . . .'

Adam thumped his plumed tail on the floor. The light was subdued, and they were seated around the glowing pot-bellied stove. Intently watching Tommy's shadowed face, Julia was reminded of enchanted winter evenings when she and her cousins would demand: 'Tell us a story!' The atmosphere was electric with anticipation. Julia realized that she was already half in love as Tommy began the tale of his adventures in the interior.

*

126

Tommy described the forcible end of the Inaugural Congress and the decision to call a total strike. He told of the high hopes that ended with the slaughter of the strike leaders – and how he himself was spared by the warlord colonel. He was talking of his friend Chang Kuo-tao's escape to Hankow disguised as an illiterate peanut vendor when the telephone shrilled. Rising to answer the summons, Julia realized that Richard was pumping Tommy. She would have to warn him, she decided, lifting the earpiece.

'Hello. Is Smidgelou here. Smidgelou Tomas speaking.'

Julia smiled at the absurd accent, although she was slightly apprehensive. Smidgelou Tomas loved the telephone, but he would call her at home only in an emergency.

'Hello, Mr Smidgelou. Is everything all right?'

'Oh, is fine. Everything all very fine. Donkey dorey, since no one is killed.'

'Killed, Mr Smidgelou?' Julia sometimes suspected that Tomas Smidgelou played up his mangled syntax.

'Is the bathtub, Missy Pavernen. So beautiful the bathtub, all marble like baths of Caracalla. Bathtub is still beautiful and shining.'

'I'm delighted, Mr Smidgelou. I did wonder about mixing marble with cement.'

'No questions whatsoever. Is very strong and very beautiful bathtub. Is making wonderful centrepiece, but is not good for eating off.'

'Eating off, Mr Smidgelou? Why in the world would anyone want to eat off the bathtub?'

'Because it gives no more a table in dining room. Is, thus, necessary to eat off bathtub.'

'I'm sorry about your dining-room table.' Julia knew he would shortly get to the point. 'Can't you find another? I know a very reasonable furniture shop.'

'Must be very special table to fit over bathtub. Not finding such all so easy.'

'Why must it fit over the bathtub? Do, please, tell me.'

'Is simple, Missy Pavernena. Bathtub is now where table once was. Hole in ceiling is making house airy, though not so very nice in cold March weather. Lucky no one is hurt when bathtub falls down.'

'Oh, my God! The bathtub fell through the ceiling into the dining room?'

'Just so, Missy. Because very heavy. Marble is heavy, and cement is heavy. Together twice as heavy. Also, Mr Kratcher next door has not telephone, but asks me tell you no one is hurt by him either.'

'You mean you're not the only one? Those blasted bathtubs. We'll certainly set that right just as soon as. . . .'

'I am sure, Missy Pavernena. Especially when no one is paying any more money in Riverview. No instalments till all bathtubs is fixed – and no more is falling. Sorry, Missy Pavernena, but all tenants ask me to tell you: *No more money!*'

18

June 23–August 15, 1923

'If only you could write,' Emily explained, 'you could join my one-woman syndicate.'

'Well, I can't,' Julia replied. 'So I've got to find some other way to make enough money to keep going. Or else, I guess, go home.'

Emily sighed in exasperation. She could once have taken the sums her friend needed from her allowance – and hardly felt the pinch. Nowadays, she was hard pressed to pay her own share of the housekeeping.

Otherwise, she was gloriously alive – emotionally, intellectually and politically. She had never been happier, and she had never faced so many practical problems. Alienation from her parents – and their support – was the price she paid for refusing to marry the bridegroom they had chosen.

Since Julia and she were often taken out to dinner, they could just meet the cost of necessities like food, the amah, and electricity. Although their friends rarely appeared without gifts, the essential luxuries were almost beyond reach: the telephone, clothing, hairdressing, and books. If Tommy had not secretly paid the small rent from his allowance, they might have had to move out. As it was, her articles for Chinese-language periodicals almost covered the necessities, while luxuries came from occasional pieces for the *Philadelphia Public Ledger*, a connection Harry Smythe had arranged.

Although those pieces had evoked inquiries from *Liberty* and the *Ladies' Home Journal*, she was afraid to take time from writing for the Shanghai publications. Since those Chinese articles provided their daily rice, she would not gamble on the American magazines, which paid immeasurably better but would not promise acceptance unseen.

Tommy was astonished that she was not drawing a comfortable salary from the Women's Bank, particularly since she had sunk her legacy from their grandfather into that idealistic venture. Herself somewhat dismayed, Emily championed the board's decision to operate as a co-operative. Since all could obviously afford the deprivation, shareholder-employees would receive a token $5 Mex a week until the Bank began making a profit.

Most frustrating was Julia's inability to solve the financial problem Julia had largely created. J. B. Powell of *Millard's Weekly Review* was looking for another American reporter. But Julia swore her mind became a vacuum the instant she tried to compose anything more ambitious than a short letter.

Of course it was Julia's uncle, not Julia herself, who was at fault. John Pavernen had fought to stem the tide of disasters raised by Gustav Vass's carefree ingenuity. Quick Jack could talk his way out of spontaneous fires and 'hanging gardens'. But even Vass's invention could not rise to the challenge of ceilings collapsing beneath ponderous concrete-and-marble bathtubs.

Smidgelou Tomas's threat was no less lethal for being comical. All instalment payments ceased – and an impromptu residents' association sued JPEnterprises for fraud.

John Pavernen promptly dissolved the company. Since a non-existent company could not employ an office manager, Julia was out of work. A severance payment from JPEnterprises's sparse remaining funds would have been considered stealing from the company's creditors – and John Pavernen had no personal funds. Retiring to his flat and his Korean mistress to recoup, he fortunately remembered that the solid Underwood typewriter did not belong to JPEnterprises, but was a loan from a long absent friend.

Not Julia, but Emily fell on the typewriter with delight. Within a week, she had taught herself to type. Emily was less enthusiastic about another remnant of JPEnterprises. Little Pow, the office devil, had followed Julia home like a lost dog after she locked the office door for the last time. He was sleeping beneath the kitchen table and trying with inexhaustible energy and good humour to make himself agreeable – and indispensable.

'Little Pow makes five, you know,' Emily observed pointedly. 'The two of us, the amah, and him. Five mouths to feed on a guaranteed $5 Mex a week. Including Adam, who eats twice as much as anyone else.'

'At least Adam earns his keep,' Julia laughed. 'We'll never have burglars with dog-same-size-pony on guard.'

'Julie, why can't you be serious? It's no laughing matter.'

'Em, why not let Lao Zee go? I'd hate to see her leave, but . . .'

'Are you mad?' Emily demanded. 'You know it's impossible to keep house in Shanghai without an amah.'

'Lots of poor folk manage, dearie. Anybody'd think you'd never left Shanghai – much less spent years in the good old US of A learning the pleasure of doing for yourself.'

'Some pleasure!' Emily snorted. 'I haven't noticed you doing much for yourself.'

They were chatting in Emily's minute bedroom while she dressed to attend the Shanghai Amateur Theatrical Society's presentation of *HMS Pinafore* at the Grand Theatre. (*The Mikado* had been ruled out as possibly offensive to the Japanese.) Julia picked up a cut-glass bottle and waved the stopper in the air as she sniffed the perfume. Emily twisted her head to glare at the crooked seams of her smoky-grey silk stockings in the mirror on the back of the door.

'Put that down, you slut,' she commanded. 'Richard swore I'd never get another present if I let you anywhere near the Shalimar. Anyway, we can't both use the same perfume.'

'We won't, dearie.' Julia grinned. 'Different skins give different scents to the same perfume. You were saying?'

'Oh, yes! We can't possibly let Lao Zee go. She eats very little – and her wages are laughable. Besides, what would become of her?'

'*Noblesse oblige*, eh? Anyway, Lady Emily could never get her own breakfast.' Despite that bravado, Julia suddenly appealed: 'Oh, Em, what *are* we going to do? And it's all my fault!'

'Don't be foolish, Julie. Anyway, I'm trying to find something for your uncle. Without Dad's help, it's hard, but . . .'

'If you could put us in the way of selling a few guns, things would be better. Uncle Jack could open a new office, and I . . .'

'Don't count your chickens. I'm afraid I'm not getting far. T.V. Soong promised to speak to Dr Sun Yat-sen, and Mayling will talk to Chiang Kai-shek. But the Nationalists are a faint hope. Russian money means they buy what the Russians say. And with Comintern advisers pouring in. . .'

'If you could only get me in to see Dr Sun, I'm not a bad sales-man. . . .'

'You're not serious, are you? It's hardly worth the gamble, even if we could raise the fare to Canton.'

'I forgot he'd gone back there. Of course! That's why Tommy's Communist friend Chang Kuo-tao was on his way to Canton. Do you remember Chang Kuo-tao, Emily? He's offered me some work.'

'Unlike you, I don't forget Chinese names, Joo-li.' Emily laughed. 'What kind of work?'

Even the thought of Chang Kuo-tao was incongruous in the bower of carefree femininity Emily had created. Never happy tidying up after herself in America, she had happily reverted as soon as she returned to Shanghai. Her negligence about her room contrasted with her orderly mind and the primness that sometimes frosted her demeanour. Face-powder swirled around the half-used lipsticks and the cut-glass vials on her tiny dressing-table. Three odd stockings were flung across a gilt chair. A crêpe de chine slip lay in a foam of lace on the pink coverlet, and two dresses of emerald green and old rose cascaded out of her wardrobe.

None the less, Julia recalled Chang Kuo-tao – and his offer. He was very earnest, though he was only twenty-six. That was a ridiculous age for a major political figure in a society that still believed men reached the years of discretion only at sixty. But the big man's colleagues were hardly older. Only the Secretary-General of the Communist Party was over forty. Young men were striving towards a new world in mid-June of 1923.

Chang Kuo-tao had come by to take tea, pat the enormous Adam, and recall his earlier suggestion that Julia might like to teach at the Communist Party's Foreign Language School. He could now invite her to teach English at Shanghai Labour University. That new institution boasted a veteran Nationalist author as president. A brilliant young Communist journalist was dean of studies. The University would not, Chang Kuo-tao promised, make excessive demands on her precious time. It would, however, pay her travelling expenses and provide evening meals with other faculty members on the days she taught.

Julia was attracted by the cause – and by the certainty of meeting fascinating people. She did not tell him that she suffered from lack of money, not lack of time. Although his own father was well-to-do, Chang Kuo-tao's puritanical eye had obviously judged her, like all foreigners, to be so wealthy that offering her a wage would be insulting. She could not disillusion him without appearing grasping.

'Well, if I do teach at the Labour University, Harry Smythe'll be happy,' Julia mused aloud. 'He's always probing me about the Kuomintang. He thinks you know *all* about the Nationalists. And he's always urging me to get closer to the Communists.'

'So you're going to spy on the Communists, are you?' Emily laughed. 'Just look what happened to Mata Hari!'

'Anyone less like a spy than me I can't imagine. And nothing's going to happen to little Julia.'

Tommy Howe watched the waiter descend the spindly iron stairs of St Andrew's Café carrying meticulous directions to the bartender for the Brandy Alexander that was Julia's new passion. He was humming 'Poor Little Buttercup' from *HMS Pinafore*, but broke off abruptly to declare: 'Julie, you know that's not the reason.'

'What's not the reason for what?' she demanded. 'Did I miss something you said?'

'No, I missed saying something,' he confessed. 'It's not easy though.'

'Just tell me like a brave little lad.' She laughed. 'You'll feel much better when it's out.'

'Damn it, woman!' Tommy exploded. 'Don't mock me!'

Julia recoiled from his vehemence. She was never quite sure where the histrionics began when he played the choleric Edwardian gentleman. He had, after all, begun school in England when the old King was at the mid-point of his reign.

'I was attempting to say,' he resumed, 'that Richard wasn't the *prime* reason the parents cast Emily out.'

'I don't understand, Tommy.'

'Not because Richard wasn't Chinese, but because she wouldn't marry Li Nien-lao. So, you see, not because of Richard. But because she humiliated them by refusing to marry the man they chose.'

'And if Richard weren't European? If he was Chinese?'

'It would've been the same. They wanted her to marry Li Nien-lao, not *anyone* else.'

'Suppose she hadn't been seeing so much of Richard?'

'Yes, they might not've insisted on her marrying *immediately*. But that's not the point. What I'm endeavouring to convey is that I want you to understand it wasn't because Richard was European that they disowned her.'

'What's all this got to do with the price of beans in Boston, Tommy?'

'Now, Julie, don't get skittish. Since it wasn't because Richard was European, it wouldn't affect you and me. You do see, don't you?'

'Through a glass darkly.'

For the twenty-fifth time that hot, damp evening, the wizened waiter in the outsized white coat trotted up the wrought-iron staircase. But he did not spill a drop of the creamy Brandy Alexander.

'I'm not doing brilliantly, am I?' Tommy took a long pull on his tankard of vodka-and-lime juice. 'Please bear with me. The break between Em and the parents was not primarily because Richard was European. I've proved that, haven't I?'

Julia was delighted – and uneasy. He was evidently leading up to a proposal of marriage. Although his rationalization regarding his parents' presumed attitude was hardly convincing, it really didn't matter. His excessive concern with their reaction in itself put her off. Regardless of affection, she could never marry a man who was more concerned about his parents' feelings than her own.

'And the parents haven't objected to you,' he added. 'Not at all!'

'I'm so glad, Tommy.' Her smile was forced, and she asked disingenuously: 'Did you ever think my parents might object?'

'How could they?' He was genuinely puzzled. 'We haven't done anything anyone could object to. Worse luck!'

Pleased by his gallantry, Julia was appalled by his blindness. Although educated abroad, Tommy could not see that Caucasian American parents might object to their daughter's marrying a Chinese. He was blinded by the millennia-old Chinese conviction of absolute Chinese superiority.

'So, mine wouldn't object,' he resumed doggedly in the face of her silence. 'If we married . . . I mean, you can see.' He paused, then blurted: 'Could you ever, Julie? Will you, Julie darling?'

Like most young women, Julie had envisaged this magical moment. In those fantasies she had sometimes sacrificed Tommy's love because it was unfair to bring Eurasian children into a world bristling with racial prejudice. Sometimes she had accepted blissfully, disregarding all practical considerations including her own parents' shock. But she had never known precisely what she would say, for she had never really believed the moment would come.

'I'd love to, Tommy, if I could.' Her own words astonished Julia. 'But I don't . . . that is, I wonder . . . just who is asking me – you or your parents? Who am I supposed to marry, you or them?'

'Julie, I'm so sorry.' Tommy was, as ever, quick – and again sensitive

132

to her feelings. 'I never thought. Only that you were troubled by the way they treated Emmy. Me, of course, Julie. Only me! Julie, I do love you so.'

Not merely mollified, she melted under his first avowal of love. She knew that her reply had been churlish. Tears of joy made her green eyes brilliant.

'Tommy darling, you're magnificent,' she said softly. 'And I love you, too. Truly I do.'

'That's wonderful! Then everything's all right. I'm so happy! Delirious!'

'I'm very happy, too, darling. I'm so delighted I'm floating on air.' She leaned across the table and kissed him and after a long silence, added slowly: 'But I can't marry you now. Perhaps some day, but not now.'

'Why ever not?' Tommy was astonished. 'You say you love me. And you know I'd be a good husband. Tell me why not now, Julie!'

'Because it's the wrong time.' Her thoughts became clear as she put them into words: 'You're on a rescue mission. You're a knight errant saving a maiden in distress. Just because I'm down on my luck doesn't mean I need to be rescued. So . . .'

'What possible difference does that make? You know I desperately want to marry you. No matter what your luck, I'd want to.'

'If I said *Yes* now, I'd always wonder was it love or misplaced chivalry. I'd never be sure. And, perhaps, *you'd* never be sure.'

'Then when, Julie?' he demanded. 'When will you get over the vapours?'

'I don't know, Tommy. And I certainly can't promise to tell you. I could hardly say: *Now it's all right to propose!* I'm honoured and touched, Tommy, more than I can say. But let's just go along as we've been. And I . . . I do love you very much.'

Indigo in the east and violet in the west, dusk fell like a benediction on the city. The street-lanterns were a string of luminescent pearls along the Bund, and even the seagulls soaring over the Hwangpoo were momentarily silent. Tommy sauntered slowly through the mid-August heat to clear the ether fumes and the antiseptic stenches of the hospital from his head. His imagination caught by the fairyland atmosphere, his memory roved over the magical season just closing.

All summer the familiar streets had glowed with other-worldly radiance, and enchantment had touched the commonplace housefronts. Poets, it seemed, knew better than neurologists. Love could actually alter one's perceptions.

Despite Julia's gentle rebuff a month earlier, he was profoundly content. For her part, Julia was blithe and vivacious, even though her finances remained precarious. They knew they might not now – if ever – marry, but they also knew that they loved each other.

On the practical level, he thoroughly approved of her teaching at the

Foreign Languages Department of Shanghai Labour University. She was not only helping China, but was expanding her political consciousness through her contacts with faculty and students. He was amused because her truly gainful employment, which had been arranged by Joshua Haleevie, was diametrically opposite in political character. Julia earned fifty Mex a month by teaching occasional classes at the Maritime Customs College, where Chinese youths were trained to serve as pillars of the *status quo*. The foreign-officered Customs Service was a handmaiden of imperialism – and the warlord government in Peking. But she would not accept financial help from himself.

Such practical matters were, however, peripheral to their common joy. Their intense happiness refuted the theories of Dr Sigmund Freud of Vienna and prurient 'sexologists' like Krafft-Ebing and Havelock Ellis. Although they had not slept together, Julie and he were rapturously happy with each other.

Moved by Emily's example, which a presumably ignorant brother deplored but could not affect, Julia had shyly offered herself. Although severely tempted, he had forced himself to draw back at the brink. His restraint sprang naturally from the love he bore her. Yet he knew in his heart that marriage was out of the question – however he might deceive himself with hope.

Still, Tommy mused as he side-stepped a rickshaw, Emily and Richard seemed as happy as Julia and himself. Perhaps they were not as fine-grained. Whatever the reason, his sister was evidently not troubled by her behaviour, which was still unconventional in the 1920s, having earlier been unquestionably immoral. Perhaps it was because she and Richard could eventually marry. Emily had told him she would, in principle at least, not hesitate to marry a foreigner. Of course her children would *not* be Howes.

Tommy nodded tolerantly. Let them do as they thought best, though Julia and he thought otherwise. The enchanted summer of 1923, he realized suddenly, was coming to an end far too soon. Despite his contempt for folk superstition, he feared that retribution must follow such great joy. Who, he wondered, would pay the inevitable reckoning?

Transition
1924–1925

Julia's memory for dates, telephone numbers, and addresses was so precise that her Chinese friends, whose own memories had been trained by learning thousands of ideograms, called her a living encyclopedia. Yet she could never recall whether she had first met Madame Sun Yat-sen in late 1923 or early 1924. But she perfectly remembered both Rosamonde Sun's dress and the place, since both were so incongruous. While Sun Yat-sen's wife danced at the Americans' Columbia Country Club, Sun Yat-sen was repudiating the free enterprise system which had given him an education, a profession, and a career. He was also denouncing the capitalist nations – and lauding the sympathetic Soviet Union.

The Country Club was, however, the natural locale for a banquet given by the American Chamber of Commerce. Although her husband was in Canton conferring with his Bolshevik advisers, Rosamonde appeared on the arm of her brother T.V. Soong in a *cheongsam* adorned with diamanté lotus flowers. She was not only soigneé, but spontaneously gay.

The banquet had reached the stage where hearty Americans and jovial Chinese were vying to prove their amiability by the volume of their conversation. Rosamonde's high-pitched voice pierced that din when Julia was introduced by her sister Mayling. A smile lit her face, but, almost miraculously, not a single line appeared. She still looked like a painted porcelain doll, though she spoke like a philosopher. Rosamonde introduced Julia to the real China, which lay beyond Shanghai – and beneath Shanghai's surface glitter. Without Rosamonde's encouragement, Julia might not have brought herself to teach at Shanghai Labour University. If she had never known the University's hectic political and social life, she would have missed a profound experience which was to shape her own life. She had first to overcome her ingrained fear of those bogeymen of the bourgeois American imagination, the bomb-throwing Wobblies and Bolsheviks. The Labour University was quite openly run by the Communists with their new allies, the Nationalists.

Both Chinese parties were now very close to the Russian Bolsheviks. Mayling Soong's suitor, General Chiang Kai-shek, who was inherently conservative, had just spent three months as an honoured guest in the Soviet Union. He had studied the organization of the Red Army and the Communist Party, which Sun Yat-sen was imitating. Perceptive despite her naïveté, Julia knew that Rosamonde Sun had to champion her husband's inclination towards Moscow. However, Rosamonde spoke candidly of her initial misgivings regarding the Nationalists' leftward drift.

'God knows, it wasn't for want of trying the others,' she confided. 'My husband pleaded with America and Britain to support the Nationalist Revolution. America was the land of his youth, and England saved him from execution by the Manchus. A little while ago, he made a last desperate effort. He suggested to the American Minister that Washington join with London and Paris to mount a military occupation of all China's major cities. And also send technical, judicial, educational, and military experts to help administer the country. After five years the foreign powers would withdraw, leaving behind a united, prosperous and democratic Republic of China.'

'Was he serious?' Julia asked.

'He was deadly serious!' the First Lady replied. 'But the American Minister thought he was joking – or mad. And that was that.'

The Nationalists had no alternative to the alliance with the Communist International, Rosamonde insisted, not if they were to free China from imperialism and warlordism. The National People's Party had to become a centralized, disciplined party like the Communist Party of the Soviet Union. But it would never become the party of atheism. Her husband, like herself, was a devout Christian.

'You know Chiang Kai-shek doesn't stand a chance with Mayling!' Rosamonde appended inconsequentially. 'Not as long as he's a pagan. My mother, Mammie, would *never* stand for it!'

Although curious about the General's stealthy courtship of Mayling Soong, Julia could not pursue that opening. As if regretting her indiscretion Rosamonde turned the conversation sharply.

'You, too, can serve the future, Julia,' she said. 'You can help China by teaching at the Labour University. Not to help the Communists or even the Nationalists. Just to serve China – and the future.'

Julia felt it would be churlish to rebuff this frank appeal from a woman whom she admired extravagantly. She yielded completely when Rosamonde Sun spoke of the vital role China's women were playing in the Nationalist revolution.

'Chinese women have always been exploited – even if some exercised great influence through husbands and sons,' Rosamonde declared. 'But that's all changing now. Whether men like it or not, Chinese women are

136

striking off their shackles. I'm forming women's unions and starting a school for women propagandists. After fighting alongside men, women will be entitled to *demand* their full rights when the revolution triumphs.'

Rosamonde insisted that Julia must join that heroic movement. Many women were enrolled in the Labour University. By teaching them English, Julia would promote not only China's welfare, but the worldwide crusade for female emancipation.

Rosamonde Sun dominated Julia's thinking for a considerable time. Her example and her inspiration were paramount. The American recruit to the Chinese revolution was only a little dismayed when she learned that her heroine could also be ruthless, almost brutal.

Women's unions were springing up under the Nationalists' aegis. The hundreds of maltreated slave-girls who fled to the protection of those unions were immediately given new names to mark their liberation – and to conceal their identity from their owners. But Rosamonde ordered that no publicity be given to the homes of refuge. 'Otherwise,' she warned, 'a multitude of runaways could overwhelm the homes – not only girls sold into bondage by their desperate parents, but pitiful child labourers.'

Thousands of young Chinese flung themselves into the women's movement. The militants dramatically cut off their long tresses – and inflicted the same sacrifice on their unwilling elder sisters. They were called 'the bobbed-hair girls', and they suffered for their beliefs. Ridiculed in the cities for mutilating their femininity, they were stoned by shocked peasants in the countryside.

None the less, cracks were appearing in the citadel of masculine supremacy. Whether grizzled farmers, sleek grey financiers, or ardent young patriots, few responsible men could now ignore the plight of their women. Moreover, Communist political training schools like Shanghai Labour University trained female agitators and propagandists to rally popular support for the Nationalist-Communist armies that would soon march north to sweep away the warlords.

Although the Labour University operated in the open, most Communist activities in Shanghai were still secret. But in Canton, the metropolis of the south, the Communists openly ruled alongside the Nationalists. Julia travelled to that provisional capital of the resurgent Republic of China in the early autumn of 1924 – sent by her Uncle Jack.

Resilient, courageous, and never prudent, John Pavernen was back in business. Although her uncle was perhaps 'a flea in the seams of the golden shirt of capitalism', as Tommy said, she still loved him. She was therefore happy to accept his challenge to sell armaments to the joint Communist-Nationalist armies. Her Uncle Jack believed that Julia's intimacy with Madame Sun, and her friendship with a number of Communist leaders would serve her well.

Julia was intrigued by Canton. The sub-tropical city hardly appeared Chinese at all after the more temperate Yangtze Delta. The colonnades that sheltered the sidewalks from rain and sun seemed as alien as the banana plants, the hibiscus bushes, and the palm trees. Smaller, darker, and even more frenetic than Shanghailanders, the Cantonese seemed more like South-east Asians than Chinese.

Canton was dominated by the heavily moustachioed Dr Sun Yat-sen and his cherished advisor, the even more heavily moustachioed emissary of the Communist International who was called Michael Borodin. Borodin happily confessed to Julia that he had been deported from Chicago. 'But that was under another name,' he added. 'So it doesn't count.'

Canton took the young American woman to its heart. Rosamonde Sun warmly welcomed Julia into the company of the young idealists who clustered around her. But Julia was invited to tea by Chiang Kai-shek as a friend of Mayling Soong, rather than a protégée of Madame Sun Yat-sen. General Chiang initially appeared reserved, almost cold. But he warmed when she addressed him as 'Commandant'.

The Chief of Staff of the National Revolutionary Armies was delighted, he said, to find that one who was both foreign and female understood the importance of his recent appointment as Commandant of the newly established Whampoa Military Academy. It was a great honour to train the officers who would shape the future of China. In that responsibility, he added with forced joviality, he was happy to have the assistance of the director of the Academy's Political Training Department, Comrade Chou En-lai. After Chiang Kai-shek spat out that name like a bad oyster, Chou En-lai came into the office – and Julia was smitten. She knew his reputation as a brilliant Communist leader still in his mid-twenties who had recently returned from France. She had not expected such compelling, mobile features or such dark, expressive eyes. When he spoke in slurred Shanghainese, she gave part of her heart forever to Chou En-lai.

'I've heard about you, Miss Pavernen,' he smiled. 'Your work is greatly appreciated. It's much like my own.'

'But you're directing political training, aren't you?' she asked.

'It's still like your own teaching. We're not only raising the cadets' political consciousness, but training agitators to undermine enemy morale. Also actors and poets, newspapermen and musicians, bill-posters and orators. . .'

'What a strange collection!'

'All have the same purpose: to mobilize the spontaneous support of the common people. Why, one troupe of actors is worth two infantry companies, and a good poster campaign . . .'

'Some people can't talk about anything but politics,' General Chiang Kai-shek interrupted. 'I hear you're peddling guns. Funny job for a lady, but what have you got?'

'The rifles are 1903 Lee-Enfields, Commandant, with plentiful ammunition.' Julia was momentarily taken aback by his abruptness. 'Also assorted Vickers and Maxim machine-guns . . .'

'I'll take two hundred Maxims.' The Commandant had obviously made up his mind beforehand. 'If the price is right – and you can deliver promptly. Delivery's always a problem.'

Julia was calculating the earliest delivery she could promise when Chou En-lai interjected: 'Commandant, I believe that all arms purchases must be approved by . . .'

'Now, Comrade, we mustn't trouble our visitor with our administrative arrangements.' Chiang Kai-shek's reprimand was silky. 'I'll take ten thousand Lee-Enfields, always assuming prompt delivery.'

'Prices naturally depend on quantity and delivery dates,' she ventured. 'Also how much ammunition and . . .'

'I never haggle! I'm not a merchant.' Chiang Kai-shek was haughty for one who had failed as both merchant and stockbroker. 'Just give my chief clerk the details. More tea?'

Julia was distressed by the cruel loss of face inflicted on Chou En-lai. When Chiang Kai-shek again offered tea, she hurriedly rose. In his mouth the reiterated invitation seemed more like a dismissal. When she left, her admiration for the General was tinctured with exasperation. He was a maddening mixture of incompatible elements: courtesy and insensitivity, deftness and maladroitness, generosity and callousness, patriotism and egotism.

Only Tommy Howe did not join the chorus of congratulations when Julia returned to Shanghai brandishing a contract ratified by eight square vermilion seals. Everyone else was virtually ecstatic – each for his own reason.

Pleased that the Nationalists' arsenal was to be augmented, Emily Howe and Mayling Soong were both delighted that those guns were to come from capitalists, rather than Bolsheviks. Besides, Emily pointed out practically, Julia's share of the commission would keep her for a year. Richard Hollings had decided coolly that the Nationalists were the best of a bad lot, 'the least worst faction in China', as he put it. Elizaveta Yavalenka and Joshua Haleevie's congratulations were only slightly soured by Elizaveta's dire warnings that the arms sale would make the Bolshevik threat worse.

Even Tommy's Communist friend Chang Kuo-tao confided his satisfaction. The arms were *not* coming from Moscow and thus *not* making the Republic of China and the Chinese Communist Party even more dependent upon the Soviet overlords he despised and feared.

Only Tommy growled his felicitations in a tone that left little doubt regarding his true feelings. When Julia demanded to know what was bothering him, he asked what she could possibly mean. When she pointed out that his tone of voice belied his words, he mocked: 'Me only poor mis'able Chinee boy. No talkee English so good like Missy. Me no savvee what thing b'long tone o' voice.'

Though exasperated, Julia laughed. None the less she sensed that he was put out by her emergence as an independent woman who had brought off a remarkable stroke of business. She never carried on about women's rights as Emily did, but she resented his assumption that she was a charming incompetent. Tommy was showing a side of himself that was very Chinese – old-fashioned Chinese.

'Tommy darling,' she finally said. 'I know something's bothering you. Why can't you tell me?'

139

'Julie, I'm really very happy,' he replied. 'And delighted by your triumph.'

'Yes, but what *is* bothering you?'

'Since you must know, I'm not madly happy about your peddling guns.'

'But these guns will fight for a better future – for a unified China. You can't make an omelette without breaking eggs!'

'My Lord, Julie, spare me the clichés. You've never seen those broken eggs.'

'What *are* you talking about?'

'I suppose broken heads, not eggs. I saw too many heads broken and too many lives snuffed out during the railway strike. I can't parrot slogans anymore.'

'You can't be a pacifist, Tommy,' she protested. 'If we . . . intelligent, right-thinking people, I mean . . . if we give up violence, the warlords and imperialists will run roughshod over China.'

'You mean *left*-thinking people, don't you? The Communists have got all the answers for China – for the whole world. But they can't run their own party. As for Communist-led strikes, they're disasters.'

'The Communists are still the best hope for China.'

'Perhaps the best *available* hope, Julie.'

'You've changed, Tommy.' She was disturbed. 'You've really changed.'

'Perhaps I have. I'm appalled by some of the deeds that are done in the name of China. But I'll soldier on somehow. And you? Haven't you changed too?'

'A little, maybe,' she conceded. 'I've learned a lot, especially from you.'

'I won't take a bow, I never meant to lead you so far left. You've gone way beyond me.'

She pondered her reply to that gentle admonishment. But there was no suitable reply. She could not refute Tommy, who knew more about China and the world than she did. Neither could she humbly promise to cut her ties with the Communists. She had invested too much of herself in the progressive movement. She would feel a traitress if she deserted now.

She also resented his patronizing her. He had introduced her to the Communists' world, and he was now talking as if she were incapable of reaching any important decision unaided. Her inherent good sense and her good nature, above all her deep affection for Tommy, kept her from exploding. But they did not discuss politics again for some time.

Political concern – if not necessarily political commitment – was the background to the life of every intelligent young man and woman in China in an era of violent change. Politics did not, however, preoccupy Tommy and Julia in the middle of the hectic 1920s when he was twenty-six and she was twenty-three. They were endowed with too much vitality and a saving measure of frivolity. Their emotions were also tossed by violent emotional storms. The great affection that bound them was shot

140

through with almost equally great tension. The physical act of love, they both believed, was no more than the natural extension of the great affection between them. In theory they already knew everything about it except its realization. In practice they knew nothing. Only natural it might be, but her puritan restraint and his Confucian prudery were towering obstacles.

When they finally slept together after a blessed excess of champagne, it seemed no more than inevitable. Julia initially felt the act was pleasant. Later she learned that it was delightful. And the earth occasionally shifted beneath them. Above all, they saw each other in a wholly new light: the familiar companion was virtually transfigured into a new being. After their unity was thus sealed, their indecision regarding the formal commitment of marriage was curiously protracted. They felt as if they were already married – only without the compulsory lifelong responsibility that stifled spontaneity.

Afterwards, Julia realized that Tommy's short temper and her own irritability had arisen largely from the physical frustration of two adults who were deeply in love. Professionally, Tommy derided those modern theorists who ascribed almost all ailments to sexual origins. But, afterwards, he too conceded that their unnatural restraint had contributed to his deep annoyance with Julia when she returned from Canton flourishing her contracts for guns. Their relationship might have appeared calm to their friends, but it was hardly unruffled. The stream of their joined lives flowed strongly, raising waves and sometimes whirlpools.

Their union was, however, placid beside the turbulent relationship of Emily and Richard. Those two never bickered before others, but their tumultuous private quarrels were always revealed in public by her excessive sweetness and his savagely cutting humour. Their intense relationship, as Julia gathered from Emily's infrequent hints, sometimes soared to heights Tommy and she never experienced – and as often plumbed depths unknown to Tommy and herself.

Twice Emily confided from the depths of her despair in the aftermath of a quarrel that Richard was wildly jealous of her professional life. He constantly made sour jibes at the Women's Bank, viciously deriding not only the earnest lady manager, but Emily's own accomplishments.

He asserted quite accurately that Emily had set Elizaveta up in a gilded brothel with the Bank's funds, and then asked: 'What's actually the oldest profession for women – whoring or banking?' When his inhibitions were short-circuited by whisky, he denigrated Emily's writing, indiscriminately belittling both her journalism and her fiction. Julia could see him bristle whenever conversation turned to Emily's work, although his saturnine charm dazzled others.

'Emmy, why do you put up with it?' she asked one dreary afternoon in the autumn of 1924. 'No one's worth so much grief!'

'Don't say that, Julia Pavernen! Don't *ever* say that! Richard is well worth it – and I give as good as I get,' Emily retorted with a complacent smile. 'He was furious when I scooped him.'

'Scooped him?'

'The *Philadelphia Public Ledger* had the story before *The Times* of London when T.V. Soong became Finance Minister in the Canton Government. Hardly an earth-shaking development, but it was a small step away from Moscow.'

'Just the sort of thing that fascinated poor Harry Smythe,' Julia remarked. 'Until they sent him to Rome.'

'Rome? Harry's Mandarin will be a great help there!' Emily observed and returned to her personal concerns. 'That argument's finally blown over. But Dick still can't understand why I didn't realize I had an obligation to tell him *before* I filed my story. Lately, though, we've been clashing about something else – marriage.'

'You mean he won't marry you?'

'Well, not quite. That was true a couple of months ago. But, for the past few weeks he's been after me. He's badgering me to "agree in principle" to marry him – even if I won't set a date.'

'There's nothing wrong with that.'

'Yes, there is, Julie. I'm hardly ready to marry Dick or anyone else just now. And he is a foreigner, you know.'

'It hadn't quite escaped my notice. You mean that still bothers you? I thought . . .'

'I guess I'm more old-fashioned than I thought. It's funny. I'm happy . . . delighted to . . . ah . . . you know . . . go to bed with him. But the thought of marrying . . . having children with blue eyes. Ugh!'

'That's impossible, Emmy. Genetically, you know. Don't you remember old Brother Mendel and his sweet peas? You both have brown eyes, and brown dominates. So you can't have blue-eyed children. Not unless some ancestor left you a blue-eyed gene. Someone who did *not* mind foreigners.'

'Now don't you be huffy. You know exactly what I mean. Even if *you* don't feel the same way with Tommy or . . .'

'. . . I'm not so sure I . . .'

'Anyway, Dick and I are even.' Emily over-rode her. 'Sometimes he doesn't want marriage. Sometimes I don't.'

'That's a fine basis for a continuing relationship!' Julia laughed despite her irritation at Emily's racism. 'You can go on forever that way – if you don't kill each other first. It's a little too rich for my blood.'

'Anyway he's going north next week to cover the new war between the Old Marshal of Manchuria and the Scholar General. Oh, Julie, I'm so worried about him – and so miserable.'

It wasn't much of a war. Still, they called it the Northern Warlord War of Autumn 1924. So many such warlord wars were being fought in China they were handily classified by location and date.

Richard had been drawn to the battlefield because Dr Sun Yat-sen was marginally involved as a nominal ally of the Old Marshal of Manchuria against the Scholar General at Peking. He was, moreover, delighted to be employed by *The Times* of London because the permanent correspondent from Peking was on home-leave.

It should have been a spirited war, for it involved the largest armies ever assembled in modern China. The Scholar General mustered more than 170 thousand soldiers and a powerful naval squadron. In addition to his ground forces, the Old Marshal possessed an air force of canvas-and-wood warplanes flown by foreign pilots under the nominal command of his son, inevitably known as the Young Marshal. Further, the Japanese lavishly provided the Old Marshal with funds, as well as many batteries of artillery and virtually unlimited ammunition.

Yet all that brave display ended without a single battle – primarily because the Christian General, who was officially on the side of the Scholar General, turned his coat. Encouraged by the Japanese, that seasonal opportunist quietly seized Peking, China's nominal capital behind everyone else's back.

In Peking Richard Hollings saw the unkempt troops of the Christian General singing 'Onward Christian Soldiers' in Chinese and warily eyeing the populace. Shopkeepers barricaded their premises, and householders withdrew into their walled compounds. Another moustachioed military politician was installed as President of the Republic of China – and the foreign legations duly recognized his government, which did not even rule Peking effectively, much less all China.

The Christian General, however, thereupon invited the Old Marshal of Manchuria and President Sun Yat-sen of Canton to confer in Peking. That tripartite summit was encouraged by the Japanese, who had armed the Old Marshal, instigated the Christian General's *coup d'état* – and also encouraged Sun Yat-sen. All Tokyo wanted in return was a pre-eminent position in China.

Sun Yat-sen confided a different vision to his wife Rosamonde. He foresaw a reconciliation of all the warring factions under his own leadership, a reconciliation that would make unnecessary the anti-warlord campaign for which the National Revolutionary Army was training in Canton. He would again be president of a united China, as he had been briefly after the Revolution of 1911.

The presidential party arrived in Tientsin on December 12, 1924, and Dr Sun conferred with his ally, the Old Marshal of Manchuria. After the toasts he retired to his bed, for he knew he was suffering from a liver complaint. He nevertheless went by train to Peking on the last day of 1924. But he conducted no political negotiations. Instead, doctors flowed into his suite at the Hotel de Pekin –and dire rumours flowed out.

On January 26, 1925, Dr Sun underwent surgery at the Peking Union Medical College Hospital, Tommy Howe's alma mater. Having a few weeks earlier in Shanghai denounced all missionaries as 'agents of imperialism', the patient entrusted his life to an American missionary surgeon. The surgeon's skill was not really tested. Because cancer had already invaded the liver, he simply closed the incision.

Dr Sun Yat-sen was a long time dying. He lingered through February in a private house in the quarter called the Tartar City, and the vultures gathered. Michael Borodin, his Comintern adviser, hurried to Peking. Among the Nationalist leaders only Chief of Staff Chiang Kai-shek

143

remained in Canton to press the campaign against the local warlords and to run the Whampoa Military Academy. Richard Hollings was fascinated by the ritual dance of heirs – presumptive, aggressive, and importunate – around the dying President's bed.

The President died on March 12, 1925. His magnetism and his warmth perished, but not his capacity to inspire upheaval. The day before his death he signed a political testament drafted by his heir-presumptive Wang Ching-Wei, whom Richard Hollings always compared to the Athenian Alcibiades because of his great beauty, his great talents, his corruptness, and his ultimate ineffectiveness. The sentence '*Ko-ming shang wei cheng-kung!* ... The revolution is not yet completed!' was a time-bomb. It was to give sanction to the discontented to undermine all authority for the next two and a half decades.

The open letter to the Soviet leadership Michael Borodin wheedled out of the dying man expressed profound gratitude for Moscow's staunch support against imperialism. That document, the second Dr Sun did not write but did sign, was another time-bomb. It foresaw the day 'when the USSR will welcome a friend and ally in a powerful and independent China – and the two allies will advance hand-in-hand to victory in the great struggle for the liberation of all the oppressed peoples of the world.'

Donald Howe was alarmed by the continuing leftward drift of the Nationalist revolution, as was his wife Eurydice's close friend, Mammie Soong. Having lost her powerful son-in-law, the matriarch was not particularly cheered by General Chiang Kai-shek's strengthening his grip on the levers of power. Mammie Soong was not interested in General Chiang Kai-shek. Her daughter Mayling could never wed that ardent suitor. He was not merely a pagan, but was firmly tied to his second wife.

The bizarre symbolism of President Sun Yat-sen's protracted obsequies moved Richard Hollings to flights of descriptive reporting. That sometimes negligent Christian was given a pious Christian burial on his devoutly Christian wife's insistence. But the religious rites were preceded by a Bolshevik rite. Like the Soviet leader Lenin, Sun Yat-sen was embalmed by a process designed to preserve his body indefinitely for public veneration. Despite missionary misgivings, that macabre service was rendered by the Peking Union Medical College, which also offered its chapel for the funeral service. Nationalist zealots, who equated Christianity with foreign imperialism thereupon threatened to blow up the chapel, and prudent Chinese absented themselves. Thus foreigners were the majority among the mourners for the anti-foreign firebrand who had been educated by Americans and Britons.

Afterwards, Dr Sun Yat-sen finally conquered Peking. He lay in state in the Imperial City, and tens of thousands shuffled past the bier to gaze at the sallow face with the iron-grey moustache. The white-sunburst flag of the Nationalists draped the coffin and flew for the first time in Peking. Shepherded by university students, thousands of school-children gazed in awe at their lost leader and heard phonograph recordings of his speeches hiss from loudspeakers hanging in the trees.

After three weeks of adulation, the body was transferred to the Buddhist Temple of Azure Clouds in the Fragrant Hills north-west of Peking, where the maple leaves were tender green. Nationalists and Communists, students and intellectuals, artisans and labourers marched in thousands behind the catafalque, muffled against the chill April wind. The cortège moved slowly, and the white mourning bands pinned to men's jackets were bright in the afternoon sun. Above their heads banners flaunted anti-imperialist and anti-warlord slogans – while the warlord's police stood by impotent.

If popular sentiment had been decisive, the National Revolution would have triumphed that cold April afternoon – and Dr Sun's dream of uniting China without bloodshed would have been realized. But the warlords still dominated the country. They soon put down the demonstrations, and China apparently reverted to its uneasy *status quo*.

Richard Hollings reported these extraordinary events brilliantly, and he was justly rewarded. But not as he had hoped by the deputy editorship of the *North China Daily News*. Choleric with fury at the anti-foreign demonstrations that rocked Shanghai after Sun Yat-sen's death, the editor singled out his best reporter for retribution. His reasoning was simple: Richard Hollings had written sympathetically about the last days of the Nationalist President, who was sworn to drive the foreigners out of China. Richard Hollings was, moreover, involved in a scandalous liaison with a Chinese woman whose father was a major contributor to the Nationalists. Richard Hollings had obviously been seduced into championing the anti-imperialist and anti-capitalist movement. He was, therefore, no longer fit to report for the newspaper that was a bulwark of the *status quo*. Accordingly, Richard Hollings was dismissed from the *North China Daily News* as a traitor to his countrymen, his class, and his race.

For several months he lived on his meagre savings and the meagre cheques for his occasional contributions to *The Times*. Introduced by T.V. Soong, that perennial Harvard man, he was also invited to write a series for the *Boston Globe*. Except for simple, dramatic events, the complex turmoil in China was hard for outsiders to follow. But the *Globe* was a serious newspaper. It believed in educating its readers as well as entertaining them.

Late one April evening, Richard appeared at the loft-apartment waving a small white envelope scrolled in blue: *Mackay Radio and Telegraph Company*. He gestured expansively and demanded: 'Listen to this cable from the *Globe*: HOLLINGS: INTERESTED STAFF JOB COVERING CHINA AND FAR EAST? SALARY THREE THOUSAND FIVE HUNDRED DOLLARS YEARLY PLUS REASONABLE EXPENSES, ADJUSTABLE UPWARD DEPENDING SUCCESS OF NANA SYNDICATION OF YOUR STUFF. SMITHERS.'

'What's NANA?' Julia asked while Emily was momentarily speechless in delight.

145

'The North American Newspaper Alliance – and it services hundreds of papers.' Emily replied from the summit of superior knowledge. 'Oh, Dick, it's wonderful!'

Hollings exuberantly threw his arms around both of them. Disentangling himself, he waved the telegram again and asked: 'Do you know what this means?'

'You're a success, Dick, a great success!' Emily totally regained her power of speech. 'You're on your way up, I knew your pieces for the *Globe* were brilliant. I'm so happy for you.'

'For us, Em, for *us*! With $3,500 from the *Globe* and £200 to £400, say $1,000 to $2,000, from *The Times*, I'm really independent. *We're* independent! We can go anywhere we want in Asia.'

'China and Far East, they do say. But I can't just be away from the Bank any time I please. Does this mean you'll be away a lot?'

'Of course not,' he reassured her. 'It only means I have *carte blanche* to travel when I want to. It's wonderful.'

Smiling at the exhilaration displayed by the cool Englishman, Julia slipped into the kitchen. She wanted to leave the lovers alone, and she wanted to get out the champagne kept in the ice-box for 'emergencies'. She waited ten minutes before returning to hear the tail-end of Emily's incongruously glum remark: '. . . that case, we'd better leave it for a while.'

Richard nodded in equally glum agreement. None the less, both he and Emily joyfully lifted their glasses to Julia's toast: 'To the great foreign correspondent! The new William Henry Russell.' Emily later refused to tell her inquisitive friend precisely what she and her lover had discussed during those crowded ten minutes. She would only say that they had prudently decided against immediate marriage.

Tommy did not share Julia's exhilaration when scarlet flags with white stars were hoisted over Chinese-ruled Chapei to taunt the foreigners. The Settlement's Municipal Council, of course, had no power over the industrial quarter that lay immediately to its north. Yet, rather than rejoice, Tommy recalled the Communists' tendency to bring down gory retribution upon their own heads by their recklessness.

While he reserved judgment, Julia was drawn into the twilight realm of espionage and subversion where the Communist revolutionaries secretly manipulated the labour movement. Controlled by secret societies, unions were largely syndicates to extort money from both workers and employers. Controlled by the Communists, they were a political weapon – and playing with guns was dangerous.

'You know, this isn't a frolic for Girl Guides,' Tommy warned Julia possessively. 'The Municipal Council isn't shooting Red agitators – not yet. But that time will come. The other lot have never hung back from murder. Not the warlords, the Japs, and the Floodgate Society. Only they call it assassination.'

'My dear idiot, I'm only running a few errands,' she replied with feminine practicality. 'No one knows about it. I live exactly as I always have. Anyway, I'm much too small a fish for anyone to bother with.'

'Julie, *you're* the idiot!' His tone was no longer jocular. 'An idiot to get so mixed up in things you don't understand. They're playing for high stakes – power and death. You're only a pawn – an impulsive pawn. And you could suffer horribly. Sometimes, I wonder why I put up with you.'

Momentarily abashed by that lecture, Julia still happily served as a courier and an informer for the Communists, who were inciting strikes in Japanese-owned factories. She often carried messages, sometimes melodramatically tucked into a stocking-top, from the 'leading cell' of Shanghai Labour University to the Ikra. She would slip these missives into the doorman's hand. He, in turn, tucked notes into the parcels she left in his keeping when she took the elevator to the private apartment on the fifth floor to see Elizabeta. Her chief value to the conspirators was, however, not carrying messages, but her access to foreign circles they could not penetrate. Jade House was particularly useful. Rachel Haleevie's At Homes were, as ever, well attended, and influential men talked freely to the impressionable young American woman.

As the last muggy week of May drifted by, the new wave of strikes against Japanese-owned factories mobilized all militant workers and intellectuals. Glad that they were not the target, other foreigners tolerantly watched strikers and students parade their anti-Japanese message through the Settlement and Frenchtown to the rhythms of hired funeral bands. Chinese policemen happily waved the processions on. They, too, hated the arrogant Japanese.

The police stood by when locked-out workmen smashed the gates of the Nagai Cotton Mill, which had closed down because of lack of the raw materials produced by the striking factories. Raging against the machinery that had broken their rice bowls by lying idle, the workmen smashed spindles and looms with crowbars and hammers. Japanese foremen ordered them to leave – and pulled out revolvers. Terrified when the workmen attacked with their iron weapons, the foremen fired. Seven workers were hit, and a Chinese fitter who was wounded four times died amid the smashed looms.

In Canton, Tommy's friend Chang Kuo-tao received an urgent message from the Central Committee of the Communist Party in Shanghai: RETURN IMMEDIATELY TO TAKE CHARGE OF THE NEW WAVE OF AGITATION. WE HAVE A MARTYR TO EXPLOIT. On May 27th, even before he arrived, the students of Shanghai Labour University staged a mass rally against the Japanese murderers – and formally resolved to expel all foreigners from Shanghai by force.

No longer complacent, the Settlement authorities arrested a number of student leaders and called up the Volunteers – to the disgust of Richard Hollings. He could not report the greatest crisis the city had known for decades because he had neglected to resign his commission. He was, moreover, thoroughly bored, for the Volunteers were ordered to remain inconspicuous in their barracks until they were needed.

On Saturday, May 30, 1925, a day of alternating sunshine and showers,

147

neither side was prepared for a confrontation. Senior police officers were either shooting small birds or watching a football game that afternoon. The designated commander of the radicals, Tommy's friend Chang Kuo-tao, was on a coaster just entering the mouth of the Yangtze. Lesser individuals were at their own tasks. Tommy Howe was on duty at Shanghai General Hospital, and Joshua Haleevie was meeting one of his informers behind the Race Course.

Julia Pavernen was waiting on Nanking Avenue with Emily Howe for the procession demanding the release of the arrested student leaders. The two women were uncomfortably conspicuous among the male throng near the mouth of Kweichow Road, which was the way to the Laoza Police Station.

A mushroom field of oiled-paper umbrellas sprouted in the rain. Other spectators crowded under the balcony of Yung Chang Hsiang, Haberdashers and Outfitters, on the corner. Only the corrugated-iron roof of the tram shelter in the middle of Nanking Road was visible, an island in a sea of demonstrators. The shelter gleamed slick green when the sun emerged for a few minutes.

The policemen guarding narrow Kweichow Road, which led to the Laoza Police Station, were rigid in apprehension. Yet the militants' mood was jovial, almost holiday-like. Despite the anti-foreign slogans they chanted, several waved gaily when they recognized Julia. The Propaganda Section of the Protest Committee had, however, provided fierce banners: TOPPLE IMPERIALISM! DRIVE OUT THE FOREIGNERS! ABROGATE ALL UNEQUAL TREATIES!

Inspector John Everson, the duty officer at the Laoza Station, was not concerned with political issues. He was remembering the dismissal of the officer who had failed to prevent the same police station's being burnt by a Chinese mob twenty years earlier. He was worrying about his career – and the welfare of his plump Chinese wife and their six-year-old son.

The tide of demonstrators lapped at the thin khaki line spanning the mouth of Kweichow Road. Julia recalled meeting John Everson at a drinks party. She had found him dull – and very nervous about the Communist threat. His broad head and blunt features had seemed sheeplike, particularly since his centre-parted hair curled into two stubby horns.

Standing straddle-legged in the side-road, his solar topee pulled low over his forehead, John Everson roared commands through a mega-phone. After repeatedly – and vainly – warning the mob to disperse, he ordered his constables to arrest the ringleaders. Snatched at random from the front row, three students were frogmarched down the road and into the Laoza Police Station. The tide of demonstrators flowed behind them through the gates and the courtyard into the charge room.

Through the open windows of the black-banded redbrick station, John Everson could hear agitators denouncing foreign arrogance. In his own charge room, other agitators were stridently demanding the release of his prisoners. He ordered his constables to drive the intruders from the station. After several minutes of scuffling, the charge room was cleared – and Everson realized that his prisoners had also vanished.

Jubilant at outwitting the foreigners, the good-natured crowd flowed back into Nanking Road. Two youths paused to chat with Julia and Emily. They laughed as they described the mêlée inside the Laoza Station. Smiling broadly, they rejoined the crowd, which was chanting: 'Drive out all foreigners!'

All in all, Julia felt it was more like a high-spirited football rally than a political demonstration. But Emily apprehensively pointed out: 'They're much too pleased with themselves. Drunk with their petty triumph. Anything could happen!'

A formation of thirty or so foreign policemen appeared on Nanking Road and pushed through the crowd to reinforce the Laoza Station. Shouting in glee, the demonstrators surrounded the marching constables and playfully taunted them. As if in fun, students elbowed them and snatched at their holstered revolvers. Drawing their ebony truncheons, the disciplined police beat back their blithe assailants with grim pleasure. The mood of the crowd altered violently in that instant. Seconds later, the demonstrators surged again towards the Laoza Station, screaming: '*Sah yang-guei! Sah!* Kill the foreign devils. Kill!'

The line of constables strung across the mouth of the side-road buckled under that renewed pressure. When the khaki figures were swept back by the throng, John Everson ordered police carbines cocked. He then shouted a final warning, which was drowned by the screaming mob. Released by fear, the adrenalin in his veins throbbed a command: *The Laoza Police Station must not be sacked again – not with Everson in command.*

'Ready!' he cried. 'Aim!'

The curt orders were inaudible to the mob.

'Fire!' he screamed. 'Fire!'

Twenty-two carbines crashed. A second volley ripped into the throng before John Everson could halt the firing.

For an instant, all was still. In the next, the silence was trampled underfoot. Sandals scuffed, wooden soles clacked, and leather shoes slapped as the demonstrators fled.

Twelve did not flee. They lay still on the damp black tarmac. Blood seeping into puddles of rainwater swirled iridescent in the sunlight. Other wounded were dragged or carried away.

Within two minutes, Nanking Road was deserted. The half-dazed John Everson stared uncomprehendingly at the corpses. Minutes later, a detachment of the Volunteers arrived on the double. Their Sam Browne belts gleamed; their voluminous khaki shorts flapped; and their bayonets glittered balefully. They set up their Bren machine-guns amid the unearthly peace. Nanking Road had never been so still.

The city's foreign overlords had been spared the embarrassment of the Laoza Police Station's being put to the torch a second time. Nine dead and sixteen wounded were a small price to pay for maintaining foreign prestige. The date of the massacre was, however, to become a rallying

149

cry of the Chinese revolution as the Five Thirtieth Incident. May was the fifth month, and the atrocity occurred on the thirtieth day of May. In English, the fateful event was to be simply called the May 30th Incident.

Since students in China evoked the same awe and reverence that elsewhere attended royalty, boxing champions, and successful confidence men, the May 30th Incident was not merely an atrocity, but a desecration. The British were the butt of universal anger. A seamen's strike in Canton cut off British imports, and a general strike paralyzed the British Crown Colony of Hong Kong. Recruits swelled the Chinese Communist Party and the National People's Party as liberals abroad began to talk of pulling out of Shanghai. The campaign to exploit the new martyrs, orchestrated by Tommy's friend Chang Kuo-tao, was thus brilliantly successful – as was initially the general strike in Shanghai.

Tommy expressed scepticism. His blood was up, but he was still not convinced that either the Communists or the Nationalists offered solutions to China's profound problems. When Julia charged him with reverting to the values of his conservative multi-millionaire father, he replied: 'Whatever made you think I had abandoned *all* his values?'

Tommy none the less volunteered to serve as a medical officer when the Nationalist Army embarked on its Northern Expedition. He further heartily welcomed his Communist friend Chang Kuo-tao back to Shanghai, for friendship transcended politics in his eyes. He, but not the Communist sympathizer Julia, was invited to the tenement in Chapei where Chang Kuo-tao and his bride lived. Julia was still an outsider.

She felt a profound loss when the Municipal Council closed down Shanghai Labour University. Foreign-owned mills and factories were, however, forced to suspend operations – as were even foreign-language newspapers – by popular support for the general strike. Wheelbarrow, mancart, rickshaw, and wharf coolies stopped work and halted all trade.

Though Chinese-owned, the Women's Bank was badly damaged by the slowdown. Emily had plenty of time to write for Chinese-language periodicals – and plenty to write about for the *Philadelphia Public Ledger*. Julia was again unemployed after the Labour University's suppression, for the Customs College suspended classes.

The times were, however, glorious and exciting, for street demonstrations never ceased. Moreover, plays, skits, and cabarets bitingly attacked the foreign imperialists. The patriotic actors were, like the patriotic press, supported by patriotic capitalists like Donald Howe.

Britain had, however, not maintained her pre-eminence in Shanghai for almost a century by faint-heartedness. At the beginning of September, the Power Company cut off electricity to the patriotic capitalists. By the end of September, the general strike was over. Stubbornness and ingenuity had again won the day for the foreigners.

A week later, Shanghai was again booming. Millionaires became even wealthier – and more arrogant. The poor toiled even harder for their pittance. Abandoning his detachment, Tommy was in a state of barely controlled fury. Julia swore she would not be a sunshine soldier deserting at the first setback. Victory was certain, though it might be slow.

Emily candidly confessed that she was confused. Although strongly anti-imperialist, she had been sickened by the massacre the Communists provoked to create political martyrs. The May 30th Incident had also affected her personally. Richard, she confided to Julia, had never behaved more abominably. He could not forgive her for having witnessed the massacre while he was confined to barracks with the Volunteers. Nor could he forgive her for filing her eye-witness story to the *Philadephia Public Ledger* before cabling third-person reports in his name to the *Boston Globe* and *The Times*.

'He's wild. Somehow he blames me for his not being on the scene,' Emily told Julia. 'He's so ambitious, so tied up with his new job, nothing else exists for him. You'd think the whole sad business was staged just for his benefit. But he wasn't there. How could I possibly write an eye-witness story for him?'

'Perhaps you should have, Em,' Julia replied. 'If you really want him, don't stand in his light again.'

'Stand in his light? Oh, I see.'

Emily took that advice to heart – and adroitly acted upon it. Feigning feminine helplessness, she quickly recaptured his affection.

19

January 1–March 3, 1926

General Chiang Kai-shek knew that destiny had spared him from the assassins' bullets five years earlier. On January 1, 1926, when the Second National Congress of the National People's Congress convened in Canton, he stepped into the limelight he was rarely thereafter to escape. His big teeth shone in his bony face, and his long cavalry cloak swirled dramatically when he raised his arms to acknowledge the cheers of the crowd. He did not, however, yet wear the cloak of the undisputed successor to Dr Sun Yat-sen. His military victories had already won him greater prestige than any other Nationalist leader, but he was still pursuing the personal political supremacy he believed essential to the triumph of the National Revolution.

Public acclaim was echoed in the private sessions of the Party Congress. Chiang Kai-shek reported the graduation of the second class of the Whampoa Military Academy and the expansion of the National Revolutionary Army to 100,000 men under his command. He was cheered when he declared himself now ready to launch the Expeditionary Army northward, from the firm revolutionary base in the south. He was, further, raised by acclamation to first place in the Standing Committee of the National People's Party and appointed chairman of its Military Council.

On January 3, 1926 in Shanghai Mayling Soong heard with muted joy that Chiang Kai-shek had been formally designated the supreme military leader. Since he was already married, her mother, whom they all called Mammie, had recently rejected the General's formal plea for May's hand. May had not demurred. She was a good Methodist, and Chinese Christians, unlike traditional Chinese, were, of course, monogamous. No one had spoken of divorce.

152

None the less, May was warmed by Chiang Kai-shek's frequent letters, to which she returned long, thoughtful replies. Bored by the aimless life of a socialite, she was herself attracted to politics. Her head confirmed her heart's judgment: the thirty-eight-year-old professional soldier was the best hope for the nation – and for herself.

'The country doesn't need just a leader, but a saviour,' she earnestly told Emily Howe. 'I'm convinced Chiang Kai-shek is that man.'

'Don't go overboard, May!' her friend replied. 'He's only a man, not a demi-god.'

Enjoying a stretch of relative calm with Richard Hollings, Emily was pleased because the New Year's audit had shown the Women's Bank moving steadily into profit despite the strikes following the May 30th Incident. Aside from nagging concern for Julia and Tommy, who seemed to have no concept of the future, her mind was at ease.

But on January 8, 1926, a frosty sunlit Friday, Elizaveta Alexandrovna Yavalenka was close to despair. She knew she was the victim of a conspiracy – and the Ikra was threatened.

Sometimes she felt far older than twenty-six, for she had endured too many hardships too young. The private hotel was her pride – and her consolation. The Ikra was also her family, for she employed her fellow Russian refugees as cooks, guards, doormen, and, inevitably, courtesans. Although she loved Joshua Haleevie, she would not perish without him. Without the Ikra, she would be inconsolable. And the Ikra was threatened.

The opulent hotel was hellishly expensive to run, and receipts were dwindling. Despite the building boom, her clientèle was falling off. Worse, her Russian sponsors had abruptly cut off their subsidy.

Discreet access to the Ikra's private rooms was no longer necessary for them. The Russian Consulate in Hongkew had become an extraterritorial sanctuary after the Peking government's recognition of the Soviet Union. Instead of the Ikra, the Chinese Communists and the Comintern's agents now met at the Consulate in secret – and in safety. Yet they still instinctively preferred to enter through the side-doors at night.

Elizaveta acknowledged ruefully that she had for years deceived herself. The Ikra had been subsidized not by the White Russians, but by the Reds, who were now demanding immediate repayment. The sum was immense: $100,000 Mex, about £10,000. On Joshua's advice, she had told the Bolshevik lackey who passed as a diamond merchant that she would not give him a single copper cash. He threatened violence while his perpetual smile still curled his lips.

The $75,000 Mex she owed the Women's Bank must, however, be repaid on schedule. An aristocrat turned hotel keeper could not indulge herself with aristocratic disdain for her debts. Joshua remained her prop. He would do anything for her and the Ikra except pay its debts. When her name was clouded by whispers alleging virtually impossible vices, he remained staunch. Through his own particular channels he traced the slanders to the jolly diamond merchant. Mobilizing the same mysterious resources, he damned the malicious gossip.

Just when Elizaveta's volatile Slav spirit was rising she suffered a new blow. Joshua thoughtlessly repeated information acquired during a lunch with Sterling Fessenden, the powerful American Secretary-General of the Municipal Council. The International Settlement was under pressure from both England and the United States to ban prostitution. Church groups in those puritanical Anglo-Saxon countries were horrified by their missionaries' reports of debauchery and vice.

'As soon ban chopsticks!' Elizaveta snorted. 'Either way Shanghai would collapse.'

'Sterling says he's got to put up a good show,' Joshua now told her. 'The pressure's coming from the White House and Number Ten Downing Street.'

'What can they do, my darling? Pass an ordinance against sin? Issue a decree making virtue obligatory?'

'Actually, Sterling's hit on a rather novel scheme. It'll shut up the toffee-noses – and do the least possible harm.'

'And this miraculous scheme is?'

'A lottery to decide which houses are to close. The missionaries claim there are more than six hundred in the Settlement.'

'A little low, that figure.'

'You needn't worry,' he assured her. 'Nothing to do with you, of course.'

'Nothing, of course.' Elizaveta echoed Joshua's uncharacteristically hearty reassurance – and shivered with fear. She had made some good friends – and some bad enemies.

She drew what confidence she could from the Ikra itself. She found sanctuary in her sitting-room, which was cool in summer and bright during the dreary winter, when rain and fog were broken only by snow flurries. Despite the concealed radiators, coal was burning in the white marble fireplace in mid-January to provide warmth for both the eye and the spirit. None the less, she nervously pleated her quilted orange skirt between her thumb and forefinger.

'There's no need to be afraid, Bess,' Joshua, who hated hearing her called Liz, used his own fond nickname only in private.

'But I am afraid,' she confessed. 'Can you find out exactly how Sterling Fessenden plans to run his raffle? I must make the Ikra absolutely secure.'

'The Council's leaving the mechanics to the Revenue Department. Old Sampson has run dozens of lotteries.'

Although Elizaveta liked the brisk Englishman who was, she felt, wasting his talents in the municipal service, she asked suspiciously: 'But will he fix it for me?'

'Probably not, but there's no need. There'll be five drawings spread over as many years as possible. So, no more than twenty percent of the ... ah ... houses will go to the wall each time.'

Joshua saw that the Ikra was indeed in danger. A foreign-owned bordello would be a sacrifice particularly pleasing to the missionaries. He did not himself wish to preserve the Ikra, which was his only rival.

If the hotel were closed, Elizaveta might finally accept his proposal. Yet he feared she would not even then marry him. Regardless, he could not inflict on her the monstrous unhappiness she would suffer if the Ikra went under.

In any event, he first had to break down his parents' opposition to such a patently unsuitable marriage. Elizaveta would not defy them; she said candidly that she had no desire to have a pauper for a husband. Joshua desperately feared losing her. He would, therefore, take her on any terms – as he did now. How would she react to the eminently suitable marriage which his mother was pressing upon him? Would it destroy their relationship? At thirty-two it was past time he was married. But he would never give up the mercurial Elizaveta, who alone could dispel the occasional melancholia that still oppressed him eight years after the Great War.

On March 5, 1926, General Chiang Kai-shek knew he was in grave danger. Not only his power was threatened, but his life. The Communists were brazen. A week earlier, assassins had tried to shoot him inside the walls of the Whampoa Academy itself. He had lived with the threat since the so-called Christian General sent assassins to Shanghai in 1921.

Chiang Kai-shek's wide mouth twisted in distaste. The Christian General was just as constant in his religion as he was in his alliances – that is, not at all. On the defensive against the warlord allies he had betrayed, the opportunist had deserted his beleaguered army and slipped away to Moscow to plead for help. As usual, the Russians were playing all sides against the middle.

The treacherous Christian General was, fortunately, no immediate threat. More worrying, Michael Borodin, the Comintern's senior agent, had also slipped away, probably to hatch new plots, Chiang Kai-shek felt.

Borodin had certainly approved the attempts on the life of the only man who could save China from Communism. The Comintern's agent would also return very soon, for he directed all Communist activities in China. He was a member of neither the National People's Party nor the Chinese Communist Party. He was not even Chinese. Yet the adventurer had exercised greater power over the National Revolution than any other man since the death of Dr Sun Yat-sen.

Foreign influence was too great in the revolution. The mongrel city of Canton, which looked abroad, had intermittently been the capital of the Provisional Republic of China since 1915. Then there was Hong Kong, only ninety miles away. The British occupation must be smartly dealt with after the final victory – as must Shanghai. Only by reclaiming those foreign-occupied territories could the Motherland redress past humiliation and curtail Western influence.

General Chiang shook his head in self-reproach for permitting his mind to wander. He selected a bamboo writing-brush from the five bristling like rockets in the burnished brass tubes of his penholder. After swirling the bristles in a pool of black ink, he jotted notes on the intelligence summary before him.

155

Canton was his immediate concern. Canton was intractable, as stubborn as the ram that was its symbol. What was that word he had first heard in his cadet days in Tokyo? Yes, Canton was schizophrenic. The city had a split personality and was always showing a different face.

On the waterfront, Western structures like the colonnaded Post Office looked over both the modern white steam-ferries to Hong Kong and the thousands of sampans where families lived exactly as their ancestors had for millennia. The metropolis reeked sweetly of decaying vegetation, yet its cuisine was emulated throughout the world. Both innovative and conservative, the Cantonese were also energetic and outward looking. Yet, behind modern department stores like the many-cupolaed Sun Company Building there flourished opium dens run by secret societies and by local warlords – both sometimes allies of the Nationalists and sometimes their foes.

Over that schizophrenic metropolis the revolution had daubed a red hue. Crimson propaganda banners spanned medieval lanes, and scarlet pennants with fiery slogans hung from ancient temples. Two groups monopolized the few automobiles: revolutionary personages wearing red neckties around choker-collars; and warlord generals with bristlingly armed bodyguards standing on running-boards and sprawling on mudguards.

The Kwangtung Province Committee of the Chinese Communist Party had its headquarters on Wen Teh Road, which ironically meant Civic Virtue. The only overtly Communist offices in China were hung with red bunting, as were their satellites, the numerous trade unions and mass organizations. At the bright crimson doors, young women with bobbed hair and fanatical eyes were jostled by officers with gleaming Sam Browne belts, by grimy workers, and by barefoot peasants.

Elated by the strikes that had been shaking China since the May 30th Massacre of the anti-Japanese demonstrators in Shanghai, the Communist Party believed the labour movement would carry it to power. The Communists also boasted of the economic noose drawn around Hong Kong by the seamen's walkout and the boycott of British trade. Professional officers laughed at the thought of workers standing up to the regular troops' bayonets, not to speak of rifles. How could they take the Communists seriously as soldiers when the inexperienced twenty-eight-year-old called Chou En-lai was Chairman of the Military Committee of the Communist Party?

The peasants saw an awkward fellow from Hunan Province called Mao Tse-tung, who was director of the National Peasants' Institute. That thirty-two-year-old bumpkin actually believed the peasantry would carry the Communists to power. Chiang Kai-shek found the Hunanese extremely irritating. Something about Mao Tse-tung made his flesh creep.

Like Napoleon, whose campaigns he had studied at the Tokyo Military Academy, Chiang Kai-shek could do several things at once. He looked down to find that his mind had been operating on three separate levels simultaneously. While reading the intelligence summary and considering the problem of Canton, he had defined the strategy to solve that problem.

The Russians are essential [He read his succinct summation with pleasure]. *They provide arms, gold, and advice. Only the last can we dispense with.*

Borodin I must, therefore, tolerate; the Chinese Communist Party I can very happily do without.

The weasels of that Party are trying to split us Nationalists by dividing myself, the military arm, from the political arm. They even wanted me to lead a force north to intervene in the latest warlord squabble on the side of the Christian General. I was supposed to subordinate myself to that buffoon, the Christian General! The Red weasels are smearing my name and wooing the civilian authorities of the National Government.

Ultimately, I must assume civil power, as well as military power. Immediately, I must crush the Communist menace. I cannot drive the Communists out of the National People's Party right now. That would alienate Moscow, our supply sergeant. But, I must strike at those Red conspirators just as soon as I can find – or create – a plausible pretext.

Chiang Kai-shek knew from agents' reports, from the letters of Mayling Soong, and from his blood-brother, the Supreme Lord of the Floodgate Fraternity, that Dr Thomas Tan-ssu Howe was a close friend of the Communist Labour leader Chang Kuo-tao. But the young doctor's father was a great patriot – a major financial supporter of the Nationalists. Moreover, his three older sons had performed valuable services, and even his daughter Emily served the cause by her writing. Dr Howe was therefore to be spared. Had he not been his father's son, he would already have been classified as a suspect – and quietly 'cleared away'.

After volunteering to serve as a medical officer with the Northern Expedition, Tommy reported to Canton early in March 1926. He was astonished at being appointed a deputy surgeon-general with the rank of colonel. When he delivered a letter from his father, Commanding General Chiang Kai-shek dismissed his misgivings, but offered: 'If you insist, I can demote you to divisional surgeon with the rank of lieutenant-colonel. But no lower.'

Amused when Tommy did insist, General Chiang jotted a note for his chief of personnel. He also made a mental note: *Whatever his political errors, young Howe is a man of personal honour. By rejecting higher rank for a more dangerous post, he has displayed true Confucian virtue.*

After refilling Tommy's teacup the General opened the large envelope bearing Donald Howe's vermilion seal. He smiled fleetingly in pleasure when a smaller envelope scented with jasmine fluttered out. But, duty demanded, he put aside Mayling Soong's letter in order to read Donald Howe's.

Tommy Howe found Chiang Kai-shek a vital and surprisingly genial presence. Hair cropped in the Japanese fashion proclaimed him a professional officer, and his uniform was plain. The deep-set eyes above his flat cheekbones were bright with intelligence, and his new moustache did not conceal his sensitive lower lip.

157

To Chiang Kai-shek young Howe seemed the prototypical Chinese intellectual: intelligent, passionate, and naïve. The narrow eyes in his long face were vulnerable, and he was pallid after two years in the wards of Shanghai General Hospital. The General noted with approval his visitor's pains to make himself look older and more responsible: the curved meerschaum pipe, the spectacles with black frames, and the worn brown-leather Gladstone bag.

'Your esteemed father commends you to my care,' Chiang Kai-shek said drily. 'He expects your return unscathed as soon as the Northern Expedition ends. He'll be pleased if I can dispense with your services earlier.'

'A parent's natural concern, sir.' Tommy responded to the oblique censure. 'But I'm a grown man. I know a soldier serves where assigned – until relieved.'

'I'm assigning you as a divisional surgeon. Even division headquarters can be shelled or overrun.'

'Yes, sir.' Tommy understood the tacit message: the General would not offend an influential backer, but would not be dictated to. 'Though I'd prefer regiment or battalion.'

'I don't have so many doctors I can assign them to battalions. Now tell me, Doctor Howe, what's the situation in Shanghai? I want your own impressions.'

Tommy hesitated, fearful of antagonizing his commanding general by excessive candour. Yet their goals were the same. He could, therefore, speak frankly.

'Everything's going well. Smooth co-operation between the Nationalists and the Communists. The leaders meet regularly in the Soviet Consulate, so there's little danger of misunderstandings.'

Chiang Kai-shek commanded: 'Tell me more about those meetings.'

'Not much to tell, sir,' Tommy responded. 'At first the Nationalist moderates were suspicious of the Communists. But through those meetings, they are becoming a united force.'

Chiang Kai-shek was himself wooing the key moderate faction within his National People's Party. Preoccupied with Canton, he had overlooked the moderates' meetings with the Communists in the Russian Consulate in Shanghai. The tendons of his neck stood out, but his benevolent smile remained unaltered.

As the door closed behind Tommy, the general re-read the key passages of Donald Howe's letter. *We look to you alone. The civilians in the Nationalist Movement, are weak and wavering. Matters are not good here. The strike and the boycott last year showed how powerful the workers and the intellectuals could be when united. We businessmen fear that that new force will attack us. We depend upon you to ensure that it does not. Additional funds are, of course, available.*

Chiang Kai-shek grimaced and rubbed the back of his neck. He was emotionally depleted and physically worn by his constant struggle to throw back the Communists' ceaseless attacks. It was time for the counter-attack. But first the disciplined soldier allowed himself a diversion. Slitting the unopened envelope with an impatient thumbnail, he leaned back to read Mayling Soong's somewhat childish ideograms.

Esteemed General, You must strike very soon. [She had written.] *We cannot permit events to pass us by. Your destiny is at stake. Our future is also at stake, for my mother will never permit me to marry a nonentity. We must be worthy of each other!*

Mayling Soong's letter galvanized the General. All the information he had received pointed to the same conclusion. He must move immediately. The problem was no longer strategic, but tactical: Precisely what pretext to employ? Precisely when and where to strike?

20

The Ides of March were kind to Elizaveta. The Ikra was taking in more than enough to cover its substantial outgoings as well as her unchecked personal expenditures. The day the first tour group checked in, she resumed her practice of giving a tenth of her income to the Orthodox Church, which served the White Russian community's material needs as well as its spiritual needs.

Elizaveta owed her relative peace of mind to John Pavernen, who, even his nice Julia acknowledged ruefully, was 'more likely to bring tears than sunshine into other people's lives'. Naturally, he collected a commission each time a string of Bentleys, Hispano-Suizas, and Cadillacs deposited a party of wealthy round-the-world trippers at the Ikra. When Quick Jack first proposed that he arrange for passengers off cruiseliners to stay at the Ikra, he had also advised Elizaveta to give the place more flavour. The private hotel, he had explained, was too strait-laced – too tame for sensation-hungry plutocrats who hoped to dispel their boredom by taking an exotic cruise.

Since he demanded much less stuffy respectability, Elizaveta had for the first time admitted her professional ladies to the casino and the public parlours. But she gave them much leeway. She did not insist when two of her ladies, a Javanese and a Greek, declared they wanted no part of the raddled French *comtesse* with the purple hair who proposed they make a foursome in the Caligula Suite with her lightly moustachioed travelling companion, who claimed to be a Rumanian baroness.

Although she regretted the respectability she had enforced when the Ikra was a discreet brothel, Elizaveta was happy again for a time. But her volatile Slavic temperament lit upon other worries: the absence of

160

any further news – or even gossip – about the lottery to close the brothels; and Joshua's excessively good humour, unmarred by either depression or anger for several months.

Fearing unpleasant surprises on both fronts, she was not surprised when the first unpleasantness occurred. She was, however, surprised at learning about it not from gossip, but from the press. The *North China Daily News* report under the cryptic headline RAFFLE SCHEME ENSURES EQUITY read:

The Municipal Council has arrived at a method to ensure perfect justice in the lottery to determine which houses of pleasure are to close to elevate the Settlement's moral tone.

Establishments in the French Concession will not be affected. The French Consul observed: 'To be French is moral tone enough.'

During the next ten years, all brothels in the Settlement will be shut – at the rate of twenty per cent every two years. Twenty-five per cent of those closed in the first drawing will be foreign-owned.

'The Settlement has a responsibility to entrepreneurs,' a spokesman of the Municipal Council declared. 'We cannot wantonly close brothels any more than we can arbitrarily close other businesses. Shanghai lives by trade.'

Elizaveta threw down the newspaper and lifted the telephone. Her fingers trembling, she thrust a Murad into her lapis lazuli holder. That indulgence she normally reserved until after six o'clock.

'Yes, I've seen it. I was on the point of ringing you.' Joshua could visualize the angry flush mantling her cheekbones. 'Don't get excited, Bess. It's still a long way off. Somehow, we'll . . .'

'I'm not excited. Not really.' She stubbed out the Murad. 'Just curious actually. What more have you heard?'

'Nothing. But I'll make it my business. Don't fret about that twenty-five per cent foreign business. There's always a way.'

'Why in the name of God throw that in? Your Anglo-Saxon morality is still a mystery to me!'

'I'm not an Anglo-Saxon, Bess. But closing down only Chinese houses would hardly placate London or Washington. The killjoys want to make Shanghai foreigners paragons of morality.'

'Don't you worry about the others,' she directed. 'Just put your big brain to working out what I can do.'

'All right, darling. But it'll have to be tomorrow. I've got a Volunteers' dinner tonight. Perhaps I'll hear something there.'

Elizaveta was somewhat happier when she replaced the malachite-and-brass handset. Was the Ikra, she wondered, really worth all the anguish? Perhaps she should simply get rid of her professional ladies. But could the Ikra support itself if it were only a hotel? But besides, life could be intolerably dull if she embraced such respectability.

What would life be like as Joshua's wife? Fat chance, though, that his mother would ever approve his marrying a gentile procuress who had been a harlot. Other Russians had left the profession to become virtuous wives and beloved mothers. But none of the families that accepted them

161

was even remotely as powerful – or as pious – as the Haleevies. Nor had any of those women made themselves quite as conspicuous as she had.

Elizaveta smiled ruefully and lit another Murad. So much for achieving spectacular success in one's chosen profession! She chuckled, and mischief lit the classic features that appeared designed only for noble emotions. Perhaps the Haleevies would give Joshua a handsome allowance to leave Shanghai. There were worse things than living comfortably in London, Paris or Rome. Even New York at a pinch. But how could any nation voluntarily prohibit wine and spirits?

Marriage might not be such a bad idea. It was, in fact, rather tempting. How nice to be cosseted, instead of contending with paranoid bartenders, temperamental cooks, and mercurial ladies of pleasure – not to speak of mothering the entire White Russian community.

She did love Joshua – insofar as she was capable of unselfish emotion. He said she was denigrating herself when she talked that way. And he undoubtedly loved her, yet it has been several weeks since he last pressed her to marry him. Although he said his proposal always remained open, he must be induced to press her again of his own volition, of course. Perhaps he felt discouraged. She could soon fix that. *If* she really wanted him – or any one man – for life.

Shortly after Tommy Howe's visit, Chiang Kai-shek deployed his forces to counter-attack the Communists. He would manufacture a pretext if necessary, but his enemies would probably provide one. They were growing more insolent every day. Furthermore, it was imperative that China have a strong leader to deal with the Japanese, who were growing more aggressive every day. The warlord government in Peking was actually shooting down students who rioted to protest Japanese incursions.

On the same fateful March 18th, General Chiang Kai-shek received a puzzling telephone call from a junior officer. The *Chung Shan* had just arrived at the Whampoa Military Academy, which lay south of Canton. What were the Commander-in-Chief's orders?

'On whose instructions did the gunboat *Chung Shan* leave Canton?' Chiang Kai-shek demanded.

'The Commandant's,' the officer replied. 'The Commandant of the Whampoa Academy.'

Chiang Kai-shek replaced the telephone and stared in speculation at the wall-map. He was himself Commandant of the Academy, and he had given no orders to move the gunboat. His instinct, which never erred, told him the unauthorized voyage was connected with the threats against his life. How better kidnap – or kill – him than by luring him aboard the *Chung Shan*?

On the morning of March 20, 1926, Chiang Kai-shek proclaimed martial law. More than twenty Communist leaders were summarily detained, Chou En-lai among them. Soldiers boarded the *Chung Shan*, which had dutifully returned to Canton. An infantry regiment officered largely by Communists was disarmed, and the rifle-carrying militia of the Communists' Hong Kong Strike Committee was ordered disbanded.

Canton, the provisional capital of China, lay in Chiang Kai-shek's palm. Although he was by far the most powerful figure among the Nationalists, he did not immediately assume the rank of Generalissimo. But the labour leader Chang Kuo-tao explained the new political reality to Tommy: 'Chiang Kai-shek is supreme – for the moment. We Communists will go on talking with him for the time being. But we'll soon be fighting him.'

'It's a matter of principle, you see!'

Joshua Haleevie threw out that cryptic remark as the brilliant-blue Delage bowled south along Honan Road towards Avenue Edward VII, where the French Concession began. Beside him in the open cockpit, Elizaveta Alexandrovna Yavalenka clutched at her wind-whipped head-scarf. Still chuckling at the unique sandwich-man they had just passed, she only half-heard Joshua's casual remark.

For a decade the coolie wearing a long-gown had tolled his town crier's handbell through the streets. He sported a large tricorn hat crowned with white ruffles, which an eccentric Edwardian lady might have worn. Two glass showcases slung on his carrying pole displayed the fine needlecraft of blouses, tea towels, and kimonos. From time to time, he cried out: 'See the skills demonstrated at the Singer Sewing Machine Centre!'

'I said it was a matter of principle.' Joshua raised his voice over the rush of the slipstream. 'Whether you're for it or against it.'

'For or against what?'

She noticed inconsequentially that his clear eyes were the same light blue as the linen blazer she had finally persuaded him to wear, when he smiled and explained: 'On this day, April 14, 1926, the Shanghai Municipal Council for the first time seated three Chinese members.'

'It *is* a Chinese city.'

'Is it *really* a Chinese city, my love? Europeans built most of it. Remember the Council's Chinese Advisory Committee resigned *en bloc* a year ago to protest the May 30th Massacre. Some people argue that no Chinese – not even rich, tame Chinese – should now be allowed on the Council.'

'And what do you say?'

'I say all Shanghai must ultimately belong to the Chinese – and it will. But not just yet, may it please the Lord. I'd favour a few trivial gestures towards Chinese self-esteem. And meanwhile, I'd get away with everything I could – just as long as I could.'

While the Delage rolled along Avenue Edward VII Elizaveta marvelled at Joshua's characteristically British reconciliation of lofty principle with unabashed practicality. She also wondered again why Joshua was silent about the sex lottery, as the Chinese called it, that would decide the fate of the Ikra. A month had passed since the article in the *North China Daily News*, but Joshua still said that he knew nothing more. When she pressed him earlier that afternoon, he had patted her shoulder reassur-

163

ingly and infuriatingly advised: 'Not to worry, old girl. It'll all come right. I'll explain later.'

The open runabout, so grand when new five years earlier, was now rather quaint. None the less, pedestrians stared at the Delage, for the smoothly curved body was still extremely elegant and striking.

The streets of Frenchtown exuded the same faded Gallic elegance as the runabout. As in France, kerbside pillars displayed advertisements, and Chinese, as well as foreigners, were strolling homeward with long loaves of bread tucked under their arms. Even the smells were subtly different in Frenchtown. Beneath the universal vinegar, incense, and mildew of Shanghai floated heavy floral scents and the acrid smoke of dark Gauloise cigarettes. Paris on the Hwangpoo!

The sapphire runabout entered the drive of the Cercle Sportif Français, which everyone, including the French, called the French Club. In the circular white building, which was monumental and crowned with a roof garden, fashionable Shanghai relaxed and played under the jaunty *tricoleur*.

Shanghai was a city of clubs, but the Cercle Sportif was the only one to which Joshua could take Elizaveta without fear of rebuff or insult. Like the Americans' self-consciously virtuous Columbia Country Club, the self-consciously tolerant Cercle Sportif imposed no racial restrictions. Moreover, the flexible French did not inquire into a woman's professional or marital status. Elizaveta had declared that she no more regretted the other stuffy clubs than she did her exclusion from Jade House. But Joshua knew she bitterly regretted Jade House.

Bright summer dresses and white-linen jackets flowered around the round metal tables behind the bamboo sun-screens shading the verandah. A pair of vivacious Frenchwomen chattered in tennis dresses that barely came to their knees. Elizaveta momentarily felt out of place in a beige-lace cocktail dress with a circular neckline that demurely framed a single strand of pearls. Then she spied the wife of the managing director of the Banque de l'Indochine, who wore an evening gown with a plunging V-neckline and a scalloped hem outlined by gold sequins. That splendour at half past six in the afternoon was justified by an early dinner-party before a charity dance.

Elizaveta was beset by the regrets she normally held at bay. How lovely to attend a grand ball again! Once again to be a welcome guest who stirred the other ladies to envy, rather than a professional hostess to men escaping from their own women. For an instant, she despised the Ikra.

The typical Shanghai waiter wore the invariable black trousers and white tunic. Joshua normally ordered in French to avoid both condescending pidgin and the comments provoked by the colloquial Shanghainese of his boyhood. But he hailed the waiter as '*Woo Doo-kuh-tow!* . . . Fatty Woo!'

After the two had chatted like the old friends they obviously were Joshua remarked: 'Good chap, old Fatty! His father worked for us for donkey's years. But he wanted to better himself. He's a captain here, which isn't bad.'

'Joshua, isn't it time to tell me?' She sipped her *citron pressé*, a pretentious name for fresh lemon juice and Vichy water. 'You said you'd heard something new about the sex lottery.'

'Sorry it took so long, Bess. My blasted mother shut up the chaps who usually drop a word to me. How? Same way I get them to talk – with silver. The Council doesn't pay princely wages.'

'My Lord, why did *she* interfere? What's it to do with her?'

'Nothing? But she thought it did. . . .' He added irrelevantly: 'Actually, you know, she's quite fond of you, sorry she can't have you to the house. She thinks highly of you. But *not* for her precious son.'

'That's rather obvious,' Elizaveta replied icily. 'Though not her fondness. But what's she to do with the lottery?'

'You won't like this!' Joshua's cloak of insouciance slipped. 'She wanted the Ikra to close, so you'd cease to be a threat. So you'd quietly vanish into . . .'

'Find my own level, you mean?'

'Perhaps that's what she meant. But she never used those words, not at all. I got the impression she hoped you'd marry.'

Joshua believed he had drawn Elizaveta off the scent. Since he still hoped she would some day marry him, he could not acknowledge that her intuitive guess was correct. Her prospective mother-in-law had declared that Elizaveta's place was in the gutter.

'Marry anybody but you! Is she still pressing you to marry a good Jewish virgin?'

'She's got three or four candidates, all nubile Jewish maidens with wealthy fathers. But there's safety in numbers. Time to worry when she narrows it down to one.'

'And your father? How does he feel?'

'Marrying is women's business, he says, though he doesn't believe it. But he's bloody annoyed at her plots and machinations.'

'Plots and machinations! How fascinating! Tell me more.'

'I suppose I must. She tried to rig the lottery – make sure the Ikra would be padlocked.'

'That wasn't too clever. From her point of view, I mean.'

'So my father said!' Joshua chuckled. 'Believe me, I had no idea all this was going on. . . . Look here, Bess, let's get married tomorrow. You know old Captain Hyde, my step-grandfather, left me a fairish sum in my own name. It's no fortune, but . . .'

Though her heart was melting, she steeled herself to answer: 'Later, darling, please. I'd love to talk about it – later. Right now, I want to hear about these plots. They're a real threat. They could alter my life.'

Joshua's heart sank, but he bit back the obvious retort: *So could marriage alter your life!* Instead, he replied in a light tone: 'Father pointed out to her that closing the Ikra could well drive you into my arms. When I told him I'd asked you to marry me, he only smiled and said: "Every man goes to the Devil in his own way – or to Heaven."'

'Charming, I'm sure! At least he didn't condemn me outright.'

'The opposite, perhaps. Any rate, he's now vetoed all plots. There'll be no pressure to close the Ikra – and no pressure to keep it open either.'

'How nice! And when do I learn my fate.'

'I'm available any time, but you'd be well advised to move fast!' His laugh held little mirth. 'But I gather it's the lottery that interests you – not me. It'll be some months before the drawing. Of course, everyone's hoping it'll be forgotten.'

'That's a great relief, darling. I'm so relieved! So happy!'

'Then let's have a word about you and me, shall we? I do so . . .'

'A moment, darling, just a moment or two.' She smiled winningly. 'First, I'd like a very cold bottle of Krug 1912. To celebrate.'

After dutifully ordering the champagne from his friend Fatty Woo, Joshua said: 'Of course, Elizaveta, to celebrate!'

21

July 9, 1926

Although fully occupied by his duties as acting deputy surgeon-general of the National Revolutionary Army, Tommy Howe still watched with fascination the sky-rocket rise of Mayling Soong's admirer. By July 1926, Chiang Kai-shek had been confirmed as Commander-in-Chief with the rank of Generalissimo and garlanded with other dignities. He was chairman of both the Executive Council and the Military Committee of the National Government, as well as director of the Organization Bureau and the Military Bureau of the National People's Party. His personal authority was supreme, primarily because of his decisive action against the Communists. They, none the less, remained partners in the revolutionary alliance.

Tommy was himself building a medical service for the Northern Expeditionary Force of some 100,000 men, which was to challenge warlord armies a million strong. Concerned with politics rather than medicine, the surgeon-general had given to his enthusiastic subordinate all responsibility for 'organizational matters'. Still struggling with shortages of medicines and instruments, Tommy was alleviating the dearth of doctors by appealing to his classmates at the Peking Union Medical College.

He was exhausted at the end of the long days spent contending against an implacable opponent: the obstructive bureaucracy of the fledgling Nationalist movement. He longed for the loft-flat in Shanghai and for Julia. Being compulsively virtuous, he found his diversion in Canton's improvised motion picture theatres. Though he often fell asleep, he also picked up the jargon. In Chinese leading players like Charlie Chaplin were called *ming-hsing*, bright stars.

Most of the bright stars of the National Revolution had already been eclipsed by the brightest star, Generalissimo Chiang Kai-shek. His chief rival, the head of the civilian government, had gone to France to be treated for chronic diabetes. After brief detention, reinstated as Deputy Chief Political Commissar of the Expeditionary Force, Chou En-lai had gone north with the first regiments. Deprived of his position in the hierarchy of the National People's Party, Mao Tse-tung had gone to Shanghai as director of the Peasant Section of the national headquarters of the Communist Party.

One star had, however, reappeared. Michael Borodin, the Comintern agent, had returned in haste to Canton to play a supporting role where he had been the star-maker. His orders were to patch up a compromise peace with the Nationalists. The Communist International was anxious to retain all possible influence, even if that meant sacrificing the Chinese Communists. Since the anti-Communist Generalissimo still wanted Moscow's gold and guns, the Kremlin still held a strong hand. The Comintern, therefore, forbade the Chinese Communists to leave the National People's Party – and the Communists reluctantly obeyed.

Tommy's friend, Chang Kuo-tao had roundly denounced Moscow's obduracy. Although the second man in the Communist Party, he was powerless to fight that decision. Accordingly he was leaving for Shanghai the next morning.

Canton was being deserted but the acting deputy surgeon-general awaited the pleasure of his Commander-in-Chief. The Generalissimo would not take to the field until he had extracted the $500,000 pledged by the Chamber of Commerce and the 4,000 coolies promised by the unions. Nor could Michael Borodin leave Canton until the Generalissimo did.

On the evening of July 9th, Tommy was watching a moving scene beside Chang Kuo-tao and Michael Borodin. The last graduating class of the Whampoa Academy was taking the oath of loyalty and receiving their commissions.

The tousled palm trees were black against the violet twilight. As the dusk deepened, the candles on the altar cast an otherworldly glow over the khaki ranks drawn up before the shrine at the front of the square.

'Like young crusaders,' Borodin commented. 'Medieval squires on the eve of being knighted.'

Tommy duly translated for Chang Kuo-tao, who was uneasy with the Comintern agent's romantic streak. The labour leader knew as much about medieval European history as he did about the reproductive cycle of the trout. 'Let's hope they have the same success,' he replied.

Their smooth faces taut with emotion, the new lieutenants bowed to the portrait of Dr Sun Yat-sen enshrined on the altar between crossed Nationalist flags bearing the jagged white sun. The pale smoke of incense sticks drifted over the stubbled heads they revealed when they reverently doffed their caps. They bowed in unison, and their stiff new Sam Browne belts creaked.

Hobnails scraped the pavement when they marched off. The National Revolutionary Army boasted that even privates now wore leather campaign boots. It was the first Chinese army ever to make that modest claim. Their allies, the warlords' soldiers, still campaigned in cloth shoes or home-made straw sandals.

The ghostly files vanished into the dusk. Tommy and his companions turned towards an alley half-lit by the tentative moonlight that spilled over the scalloped grey-tile roofs on either side.

Between Michael Borodin and Chang Kuo-tao, Tommy felt like the middle of three steps. He was taller than the foreigner, but the Chinese overtopped him by almost two inches.

'Well, Comrades, we'll all be moving north tomorrow.' A nasal American tone overlaid Borodin's Middle European vowels. 'A pity you're going to Shanghai, Kuo-tao. Dr Thomas and I will miss your . . .'

A rifle shot nearby interrupted him. An instant later, two more reverberated in the distance. After waiting for a time, Borodin shrugged and picked up his remark: 'We'll miss your company and your counsel.'

Tommy was not so casual. He had not learned to ignore the exchanges of fire between the police and the Communists' armed militia that so frequently disturbed Canton. Hearing no further shots, he began to interpret Chang Kuo-tao's reply: '*Tung-chih, ming-tien wo-men tou* . . . Comrade, tomorrow we'll all . . .'

The rattle of a sub-machine gun emphatically halted him. A heavy machine-gun began firing bursts, and red tracer bullets sprayed across the moonlit sky. Men shouted hoarsely in the distance, and a woman screamed in terror.

'*Bo-lo-ting, che chiu shih* . . .' Chang Kuo-tao shook his clenched fists at the sky. 'Borodin, is *this* what you want? Police crushing the workers in the name of the National Government – the government the Comintern demands we support! By Heaven, it's past time for us to break with the murdering Nationalists!'

'My friend, you're too impatient,' Borodin replied equably. 'Communists can only work with the tools to hand. The revolution hasn't yet reached the stage where a break is . . .'

'No matter what stage, there's no excuse for this!' Chang Kuo-tao was impassioned. 'How can you justify supporting the man who is crushing the workers? That's madness – strategy run wild.'

'My friend, I share your indignation. But we must ensure a firm rear base for the Northern Expedition.'

'Is that all important, Borodin? How can the Comintern still urge the Chinese Communist Party to become part of the National Party? Are they *all* mad in Moscow?'

Neither man looked up at the red glare of flames on the tiled roofs a few streets away. Though himself distracted, Tommy drily translated the Comintern agent's reply: 'Moscow's not mad, just obsessed with its own problems. But what would *you* do, my friend?'

'It's too late!' Chang Kuo-tao exploded. 'Far too late. I would have moved earlier. I would have seized Canton. I urged it. We were certainly strong enough.'

'Many believed so. Perhaps we actually were strong enough. Yes, I suppose we were.'

The Comintern agent fell into meditative silence. Chang Kuo-tao's big face was pallid in the moonlight as he stared at Borodin, astonished by that admission. The flames balefully reflected by the low-lying clouds painted both men's faces red. They confronted each other like Titans beneath an erupting volcano.

'Then why didn't we act?' Chang Kuo-tao demanded. 'Why did you forbid us to seize Canton?'

'Because, my dear comrade-in-arms,' Borodin spoke very slowly, 'Because we could not have held it. If there had been one chance in four that we could maintain control of Canton for even a year I would have been the first to attack the Nationalists. I would have ignored the Comintern's instructions and led the assault myself.'

After pausing to let Tommy finish translating, Borodin declared passionately: 'Since there was *no* chance whatsoever I blocked any foolhardy action. Yes, I went along with Chiang Kai-shek. And I would do it again. We can always break with the Nationalists. We can always attack Chiang Kai-shek. If we do so prematurely, if we do not possess a secure power-base, far greater disasters will follow. We would face a catastrophe!'

22

January 27–February 28, 1927

The grubby index-finger with the ragged cuticle nudged aside Julia's crimson-varnished nail and stabbed decisively at the three cities huddled in the bend of the Yangtze River several hundred miles west of Shanghai on the big wall-map. Little Pow, the boy of all work who had attached himself to Julia after JPEnterprises' failure, beamed in triumph. The triplets Wuchang, Hankow, and Hanyang were collectively called Wuhan, and they were the provisional capital of the Nationalists' Republic of China.

'All b'long Chinese now. Never b'long British again!' He abandoned his rough English for Shanghainese. 'Never again a British Concession in the Wuhan cities. The National Revolution has seized back our territory. We will never surrender Wuhan. We will die, but not surrender!'

'Shall we get back to the lesson, Little Pow?' Julia, who shared his sentiments, was amused by his oratorical flourishes. 'You won't agree with the editorial, but you must understand it.'

Little Pow resumed his chair at the rosewood desk under the high north window of the loft-apartment. Despite the smoky paraffin heaters that supplemented the pot-bellied stoves, the cavernous living room was chilly that late January evening. Julia was, however, reasonably warm in a blue silk *cheongsam* padded with raw silk. Little Pow's quilted long-gown had been cut down after being cast off by Tommy Howe, who was almost a foot taller.

'By all means, venerable teacher.' The waif grinned and switched back to English. 'Almost half my country, already Generalissimo Chiang Kai-shek freed from warlords. Pretty soon Generalissimo also take back Settlement and Frenchytown.'

'We must get back to the lesson.' Julia knew it was useless to correct

171

his mangled syntax when he was so exuberant. 'You remember the editorial said Generalissimo Chiang was wrong to occupy the British Concession at Hankow.'

Little Pow picked his way though the *North China Daily News*, finally exclaiming: 'Ai-yah, here it is! I speak first like always?'

Julie nodded, and he cleared his throat importantly before reading aloud: 'When groups of Chinese like those whose adherence Comrade Borodin has bought declare war on us, we should have the courage to admit to ourselves and to one another that we are facing war.'

Enthusiasm glowed on Little Pow's bony face, and his scarred little hands clutched the newspaper hard. The hysterical text from the newspaper Richard Hollings called 'the mouthpiece of the plutocracy' was not a happy choice for their semi-weekly lesson. Still, it was too late to correct that mistake. Julia made a mental note to ask him the meaning of adherence and nodded to him to continue.

'It's already war,' Little Pow instead declared. 'We don't have much time, the teachers at the Workers' Night School say. The Settlement Police could close us down any minute. But we are vigilant, and we are well organized now.'

While Julie protested feebly that they must get back to the lesson, Little Pow reached inside his enveloping long-gown to produce a white arm-band bearing two red ideograms: *Min Ping* – People's Militia. He confided: 'I carry messages for the leaders.'

She was thrilled. Generalissimo Chiang Kai-shek's army of Nationalist and Communist troops fighting as one was moving eastward from Wuhan towards Shanghai. Even before the National Revolutionary Army arrived, however, the aroused masses led by the Communists would already have taken much of the city. The Dean of Shanghai Labour University had drawn up a brilliant 'Plan for the Shanghai Uprising'. Little Pow and his fellows were the couriers for the underground army that would seize Chinese-ruled Greater Shanghai, the populous districts surrounding the foreign concessions.

Julia knew of no plan to seize the foreign concessions. She did not know everything, but the Municipal Council knew rather less than she did. As the National Revolutionary Army rolled from south to central China, the foreigners had swung from disdain to near panic. As a quarter of a million fearful Chinese crammed into the concessions, the foreigners swore to defend their property to the death. Some discovered urgent business elsewhere, and the taipans sent frantic cablegrams pleading for reinforcements against the Red hordes. Neither the Volunteers nor the Yangtze gunboats could defend the enclaves from mass attacks. The foreign powers were sending regular ground forces and naval flotillas. But the build-up could take months, and the National Revolutionary Army was already marching on the old capital of Nanking, two hundred and fifty miles upriver.

And what was she, Julia Pavernen, spinster of twenty-six summers, doing while, as the Chinese said, 'the earth reeled and heaven shook'? While a new era was emerging from the womb of history, she was earning a bare living by teaching the future servants of imperialism in the Maritime Customs College. Though the pay was a joke, she was also reading news bulletins and interviewing prominent visitors for XMHA, the lustiest of the new wireless stations competing for advertising. In addition, she was hoping for commissions on future arms sales to the Generalissimo, although John Pavernen was presently honouring the foreign powers' embargo against the Nationalists.

She was, however, also teaching at the Shanghai Labour University. Finally she was tutoring Little Pow in the unwelcome leisure time left by Tommy's protracted absence. Tutoring a fifteen-year-old when China was in flames! While not as callous, it seemed almost as futile as Nero's fiddling while Rome burned.

But not quite. Little Pow's talents were well worth developing. He was dedicated to the Communist Revolution. He was also a flesh-and-blood symbol of that revolution, a son of the masses who were rising in wrath after centuries of oppression.

Little Pow, who had never really known his parents, cherished dreamlike memories of a thatched hut beside a pig-pen among silver paddy fields. He recalled a father with strong hands helping a sweet-faced mother feed her chickens. Julia discounted that idealized vision as the fond fabrication of his Auntie Vee, who had taken refuge with Pow in the industrial slum called Pootung when he was no more than two years old.

'The revolution against the Manchus uprooted me,' he had learned to declaim at the Workers' School. 'But the National Revolution will restore my ancestral acres.'

Actually, Little Pow had no desire to return to the countryside. He did not even know where his ancestral acres lay, since Auntie Vee had died when he was just five. It sounded very much like cholera, Tommy had concluded from the waif's graphic description. Bereft of family in a family-centred society, Pow became a creature of Shanghai's alleys.

For the next five or six years, he had somehow survived while drifting friendless through the city. Although he was reticent about that period, certain allusions led Tommy to suspect that he had spent several years in a 'small-boy house', a homosexual brothel in Frenchtown. Only because the Workers' Night School encouraged its students to 'cry out the bitterness of oppression' had Pow recently talked more freely about his life before John Pavernen found him begging on a corner.

The bright, undefeated eyes in the haggard child's face had attracted the attention of the man Little Pow reverently called 'Mastah Jon'. Pow's hands had quickened John Pavernen's interest. Scalded scabrous pink, they were so raw he could hardly pick up the occasional coin or perforated copper cash that passers-by flung him.

The waif had later grown sturdy on the casual bounty of the Pavernens, a diet far richer than half China's four hundred millions ate. But Pow had been stunted by his early deprivation. Perhaps five foot six in high heels, Julia looked down on his five foot one in cloth soles. If he lived to be ninety, he would always be called Little Pow.

The waif's reserved dignity was formidable, though he would now talk about the misery of his early childhood. Drawn out by Tommy, he had almost a year earlier revealed why his hands, now seamed with scars, had been so hideously scalded when John Pavernen found him. Pow instinctively reverted to Shanghai colloquial so thick that Tommy had to explain many expressions to Julia – and had to suppress some searing obscenities.

'For maybe two years or so after Auntie Vee passed from the world, I do not remember anything at all.' Tommy believed Pow had erased from his memory his time spent in the small-boy brothel. 'After . . . after I ran away . . . I knew I would die. I did not die because the foreigners' cigarette factory gave me work. Then I almost died *because* of the factory. The work so hard and so dangerous. Sometimes only fourteen hours a day, but mostly sixteen. And so little food, scraps not good for pigs – rotten cabbage with maggots crawling. Sleeping on cold, wet stones.'

'Your hands?' Tommy had probed gently. 'Did they get burnt and broken in the cigarette factory?'

'No, Doctor Tom, not in the cigarette factory. In the silk mill after I became foreman.'

'Foreman?' Julia had exclaimed. 'How could you be a foreman when you weren't even ten?'

'Most workers are much younger, Missy Joo-li. Small girls of six or seven. Maybe eight, but no more. Little fingers can better unreel threads from silk cocoons. And girls get no pay, because they must work off the buying-in price the bosses pay their fathers. It can take four, maybe five years. All the time they are fined if the work isn't perfect. But the bosses usually let the girls go after four years. Their fingers get too big and clumsy. Their eyes are spoiled by always looking for tiny threads in dark rooms.'

'It must have been horrible, Little Pow!'

'Like pictures of Buddhist hell, Missy Joo-li. Only one tiny window high up, so no air at all. No breeze, because even the tiniest breeze can snap the very thin threads. Small girls stand all day and long into night at child-size machines unreeling threads over basins of boiling water that make cocoons soft. They must all the time dip hands into water. So all are scalded, all red and bleeding and puffy with boils full of pus.'

'And *your* hands, Pow?' Tommy asked. 'Did you have to unreel cocoons in boiling water, too?'

'How could I, Doctor Tom? My fingers were already too big, too clumsy. No, my hands were my own fault. I did not so quickly learn I must look out for myself – only myself always. You see, bosses always beat small girls who work too slowly. One day a man and a woman came into our room very angry. All are useless little mouths, the woman says. Their mouths are always eating – but their hands are not working. Small girls, she says, are only fit to be whores.'

Julia took Little Pow's scarred hand when he closed his eyes as if to shut out the memory. 'The woman is worse than the man.' He resumed without prompting. 'She says they will make example of smallest girl. So they tear off her little trousers and the man beats her with bamboo cane till blood runs. To show everyone the punishment for laziness. The woman is crazy mad. She holds the smallest girl over the boiling water and starts to throw her in.

'I do not think, but jump at the woman – and the smallest girl runs away. The man swears he will make an example of me. But I wriggle too much for them to lift. So they grab my hands and hold in boiling water. Then the woman beats my hands with the bamboo cane till blood runs and bones crack. Afterwards I run away – and Mastah Jon finds me. Otherwise, I will surely die.'

Recalling the terrifying account, Julia studied Little Pow, who was still frowning at the newspaper. He was now self-reliant, though he still slept under the kitchen table companionably nestled against the Tibetan mastiff called Johann Adam Schall von Bell. He more than repaid the small expenditure for his keep by running errands, helping the amahs with heavy work, and gathering information for Emily Howe's articles. Julia was confident that he would in the future render great service to the Chinese people. He already served as a courier for the People's Militia because the myriad street children of Shanghai could go anywhere almost unnoticed. Besides, little of importance escaped the big black eyes prominent in his triangular face.

The telephone bell intruded into Julia's thoughts, and she reluctantly rose. Fear for Tommy, who was campaigning somewhere, tightened her throat every time the telephone rang. Before she could lift the earpiece, the ringing stopped. The enlarged and improved exchange was still temperamental.

The kitchen door crashed open. Responding to the telephone's summons, Adam bounded into the living room. He was three feet high, and his plumed tail wagged violently. Fortunately, the ashtrays and ornaments on the cofee-table were now beneath its arc, but Julia trembled for the lamps.

Disappointed because the telephone was silent, Adam opened his great jaws and clamped them shut on Little Pow's arm. The laughing youth could not resist the mastiff's strength, and they sprawled together on the hardwood floor. Adam's playful bellowing almost drowned out the telephone's renewed ringing.

Julia snatched up the instrument and shouted into the mouthpiece, 'Just a minute!' She rolled up a newspaper and attacked the mastiff. With Little Pow, who was still laughing, pulling at his iron-spiked collar, Adam finally stopped barking and allowed himself to be dragged into the kitchen.

'I'm very sorry,' Julia told the instrument. 'A slight disturbance here.'

'That cussed dog again?' John Pavernen asked. 'Why don't you get rid of him? He's nothing but a confounded nuisance.'

'Hello, Uncle Jack, how are you? ... No, I certainly won't. Adam is the world's best burglar insurance. Anyway, I'm very fond of him – and Tommy gave him to me.'

'You *are* edgy today. What's up?'

'Sorry again, Uncle Jack. Every time the phone rings I just *know* something terrible's happened to Tommy. How are you, really?'

'Fine, just fine!' His tone was elaborately casual. 'As a matter of fact, tickled pink. You see, they've made me an ambassador!'

'That's just wonder . . .' She broke off in mid-word. 'You're teasing. Who's made you an ambassador?'

'Why, the Municipal Council. An ambassador for the Settlement.'

'Now I know you're teasing. How can the Settlement appoint an ambassador? It's not a country, you know.'

'For present purposes it is. A semi-autonomous entity which stands in peril. So the Council needs an ambassador.'

'Ambassador to whom? To where? Are you going to Peking to the old régime? Or to Wuhan to the new régime? This is a silly conversation!'

'It's all true, Julie, believe me.' His self-esteem was wounded by her persistent disbelief. 'I may need your help. Naturally, I can't say any more on the phone.'

'Not even a hint?'

'Well, let's just say I'm the ambassador to a powerful neighbour.'

On the last rainy day of the rainy February of 1927, John Pavernen's embassy had already required six trips through the dense barbed-wire that ringed the International Settlement. Behind him lay a community guarded by the greatest concentration of foreign troops and warships ever assembled in China. Before him in Chapei, north of Soochow Creek, lay the headquarters of the nearest of those potentates justly called warlords because their only claim to rule was armed might.

Despite his boasts, Quick Jack's embassy had been sanctioned only by the powerful but unofficial group of taipans who met at the Long Bar of the Shanghai Club. It had, moreover, been conceived in desperation.

Although the enemy was still hundreds of miles away, the foreign community already felt itself beleaguered. The atmosphere of siege was intensified by the continual arrival of ground forces and by the big warships steaming up the Yangtze to strengthen the permanent naval forces of nine nations. Some forty thousand foreigners were already protected by more than twenty thousand soldiers (including two thousand Volunteers) under the command of a British general and by forty-four warships (including an aircraft-carrier) under the command of an American admiral. Yet the more protectors the foreign concessions attracted, the more frightened their inhabitants became.

The great powers' apparent resolution was largely illusory. While reinforcements streamed up the Yangtze in mid-February, the British had yielded to the Nationalists permanent control of the British Concession at Hankow. With Hankow gone, Shanghai was logically next. Despite barbed wire, pill-boxes, aeroplanes, and cruisers, most foreigners were terrified by visions of Chinese Bolshevik hordes trampling down those defences to pillage, rape, and slaughter.

The spectre of betrayal haunted the more sophisticated. The pretensions of the Chinese had in the past been scotched by foreign military power, which reached throughout China. Yet the previous year British

176

gunboats had withdrawn from a prolonged confrontation with a local warlord up the Yangtze River, satisfied with a stand-off. Only clear cut victories could convince insolent natives that foreign power was unchallengeable – and foreign property therefore untouchable.

Private messages from European and American governments candidly underlined the moral: *The intrusive press, the hypocritical League of Nations, and moralizing do-gooders have made aggressive tactics outmoded – and impossible. Foreign Shanghai will, perhaps, be defended, depending upon circumstances. But there is* no possibility *of carrying the battle to the enemy.*

That unpleasant realism so dominated John Pavernen's mind that he was virtually unaware of the raw weather as his black Studebaker touring car crossed the Garden Bridge from the Bund to Hongkew. Despite the Manchurian fox coat that had been Tommy's birthday present, Julia shivered in the damp gusts that rattled the leather-and-isinglass side-curtains. Co-opted as her uncle's secretary and interpreter, she had brought her own aide. Respectably dressed by John Pavernen's generosity, Little Pow was balanced on the jump-seat. The larger an ambassador's suite, the greater his face.

The burly figure beside John Pavernen on the rear seat was as impressive as a half-dozen ordinary attachés. The forty-two-year-old soldier, invalided out of the British Army as a major, called himself Brigadier-General Sutton. That rank had been bestowed by his patron, the Old Marshal of Manchuria, who was for the moment also master of North China. Most foreigners, however, called him One-Arm Sutton because he had left his other arm at Gallipoli.

Sutton's greatest asset was his manner. His six foot two inches awed a short-statured nation, and his Old Etonian hauteur subdued even the arrogant Chinese. He was avidly promoting the trench-mortar he had perfected in a Manchurian arsenal. Only eighteen inches long, the miniature weapon flung a finned shell high into the air to fall almost vertically on enemy positions. One-Arm Sutton said he could supply one hundred and fifty patent mortars, each one with a full thousand mortar bombs. John Pavernen's quasi-diplomatic status had not affected his love for a quick deal.

The Studebaker swept past the North Railway Station, where an armoured train awaited with steam up. The Stars and Stripes fluttered on one mudguard and the Union Jack on the other, although neither Pavernen nor Sutton was entitled to display his flag. The local warlord, General Soo, was, however, unlikely to jibe at technicalities. Technically subordinate to One-Arm Sutton's patron, the Old Marshal who held Peking, General Soo was ferociously independent in pursuit of his own interests.

Some hypercautious soul had woven barbed-wire through the formidable spikes that topped the brick walls surrounding General Soo's commandeered mansion. Despite its flags, the Studebaker waited almost five minutes at the chained-and-padlocked wrought-iron gates, which were backed by sheets of corrugated-steel.

A pair of guards carrying Lee-Enfield rifles with fixed bayonets sauntered to and fro. Their lax discipline just prevented their retreating from the rain into the candy-striped sentry-boxes beside the gates. Their hair and their faces gleamed wet, though their uniforms were protected by peasants' straw capes.

'The real defence is inside,' One-Arm Sutton observed. 'Look there, Jack.'

Wooden towers reached above the brick wall at twenty-foot intervals, and guards in mustard-yellow tunics pointed their Tommy-guns at the Studebaker. Their broad peasant faces were self-consciously ferocious, but they were sheltered from the rain by exceedingly unmilitary oiled-paper umbrellas.

'Looks after himself, don't he?' Little Pow stage-whispered in Shanghai argot. 'Damned semi-feudal rotten egg!'

'Shush, Pow!' Julia cautioned. 'Your tongue'll get us all into trouble.'

Julia did not feel soiled by the dirty work of espionage. It was no more than her duty as a decent human being to report the foreigners' plans to the Communists, as she had done since the May 30th Incident. She had, therefore, accepted her uncle's invitation to interpret with alacrity, although she was by now weary of his schemes and his promises. She would report this day's intelligence not only to the Dean, who was the strategist, but directly to General Chou En-lai, who was deputy-chairman of the Shanghai General Labour Organization. The handsome political commissary had detached himself from the dissension-ridden National Revolutionary Army to become the effective commander-in-chief of the militant Shanghai underground. He was mobilizing the trade unions, the craft guilds, the People's Militia, and the left-leaning secret society lodges for the uprising that would seize Greater Shanghai.

The wrought-iron gates creaked and parted. A tall Cossack officer stepped through the crack, bandoliers crossed over his white tunic and a grey-caracul cap rakish on his blond head. He flicked his silver-handled riding-crop against his gleaming boots and leisurely examined the touring car with ice-blue eyes. Still unspeaking, he rapped the driver's door and pointed the riding-crop at the opening gates. The Studebaker rolled between the green-black pines that palisaded the driveway and half-hid a dozen Cossacks cradling Tommy-guns.

'The Old Marshal's got his Russian bodyguard, too.' One-Arm Sutton's Etonian vowels were languid. 'Big face, for him. The white man serving the yellow man. The Russkies, poor sods, will do anything for a few dollars.'

'They don't have much choice, do they, General?' Julia was irritated by the Englishman's condescension. 'I have heard that they're brave and loyal.'

'They've got to be brave, my dear. They can't desert and merge into the people of the countryside – not in China. But loyal? At least, the warlords think so. Because the Russkies can't talk to the enemy, they're meant to be unreachable – unbribable. Tommyrot! Silver and gold are the same colour in any language.'

The emerging sun lit the mansion at the end of the driveway, and the iridescent tiles on its cupolas and domes gleamed. The inspiration by the Taj Mahal was obvious in the long pool that reflected those arabesque splendours. Julia was almost as impressed because the warlord was waiting in the entry-hall to honour his visitors.

General Soo was not the burly bandit she had imagined, but stooped and frail. The pinpoint pupils of his slate-dull eyes explained his near emaciation, for the most brilliant chef could not tempt a man who loved the near oblivion of opium. Bushy for a Chinese, his snow-white moustaches accentuated his frailty and made him appear even more cadaverous. Had this elderly gentleman actually beheaded fifty-eight farmers for concealing the non-existent hoard of gold bars he believed buried in their fields?

Yet few field-marshals had ever been so gloriously uniformed. Massive epaulettes of diamanté-starred cloth-of-gold burdened his narrow shoulders, their metallic-gold fringes almost meeting the gold-braid twining on his green-barathea sleeves. Broad ribbons, enamel stars, shining medals, and cascading aiguillettes hung so heavy he leaned on the arm of his Cossack aide for support.

'My dear General!' John Pavernen gushed. 'We are profoundly ... inestimably ... honoured. That you should receive us yourself. . .'

Though that florid greeting almost choked her, Julia dutifully translated. She was equally revolted by the warlord's oleaginous reply.

'Not at all. I am unworthy. I fail to honour Your Excellency sufficiently. Yet how could I be ceremonious with my elder brother?'

Strewing 'unworthinesses', 'esteemeds', and 'honoureds' like Roman victors throwing coins to the crowd, they paraded down a long corridor with a chequered marble floor. The sitting room was so magnificently vulgar that Julia could not take in all its crass splendours. Through double doors she glimpsed a round table set with a gold Chinese-style service for eight. An inlay of semi-precious stones on the dining room's pink-marble walls depicted a pair of unicorns and a pair of phoenixes. Since the mythical beasts had been drawn by sensible Chinese, there was none of the hypocritical Occident's nonsense about their being asexual. The larger unicorn possessed unmistakable – indeed gigantic – male attributes, while the larger phoenix was, again unmistakably, gaudily male.

'Can take off and take with! Easy to load on train.'

Noting Julia's fascinated gaze, the General was addressing her in pidgin Shanghainese. He apparently wished to impress her not only with his great wealth, but his prudent provision for its preservation.

Did he believe he could pile all his loot into the armoured train waiting at the North Station? Impossible! The National Revolutionary Armies, now more than 300,000-strong, already held most of South and Central China. Moreover, their pincers were closing on the only gateway to North China, Nanking, where railway passengers crossed the Yangtze by ferry to board the Peking train.

The warlord soon wearied of inane small talk and turned to One-Arm Sutton's patent mortar. His words obliquely denied the readiness for flight he had earlier implied. He was evidently not on the point of packing up his hoard and running away when he talked about buying new weapons.

Nor was he feigning interest. Chinese etiquette frowned upon discussion of business until the overfed company was soothing its overburdened digestion with nicotine. Yet they were just picking at the smoked duck's tongues that began the gluttonous repast when the warlord asked: 'General Sutton, how many rounds a minute does your mortar fire?'

Julia talked her way around the military terms she did not know. Technical Chinese used new combinations of old ideograms for new objects. A trench-mortar was *po chi pao*, literally: intense attack cannon. Surprised by the warlord's technical knowledge, Julia was startled when he declared as the shark's fins and oyster soup arrived: 'All right, my friends, I'll take a hundred.'

'And, shall we say, a thousand bombs for each, my esteemed friend?' One-Arm Sutton purred over his first firm order in seven years of hawking his mortar around China. 'Ambassador Pavernen will discuss terms.'

'If they're to be any use,' General Soo stipulated, 'delivery no later than a week from today!'

Orderlies presented a platter under a silver dome on which a scaly dragon coiled. The Cantonese delicacy was called Dragon in Spring. Thumbnail slivers of white cobra meat on a bed of crisp lettuce were sprinkled with yellow chrysanthemum petals.

Gulping manfully, Quick Jack Pavernen forced down the snake-meat. The orderlies' silver-gilt ladles and gold-chased chopsticks immediately provided generous second helpings. Fearful of offending his host, Quick Jack lifted sautéed cobra to his mouth with his silver-and-ivory chopsticks – and smiled. His sallow cheeks were almost green, and greasy perspiration speckled his forehead.

Unable to force himself further, he laid his chopsticks down and asked: 'Can we talk about the big deal now? Ask him softly, Julie. Don't shout it out to the whole world.'

The warlord waved the orderlies out. After the latch clicked, he waited until the commander of his Cossack bodyguard returned and nodded confirmation that there were no eavesdroppers. The benevolent smile on the warlord's bluish lips then invited the unofficial ambassador to speak.

'I am happy to report that your conditions are acceptable,' John Pavernen declared. 'The mortars will be the gift of the Municipal Council, a contribution to the common welfare. And whatever crates of personal belongings Your Excellency cares to confide to us in trust will be stored in locked and guarded warehouses.'

After Julia's translation, General Soo's wrinkled features beamed goodwill, and he asked: 'What of the cheque? Remember, cheque, not gold!'

'It wasn't easy, my friend. You know how merchants hate to pay out. However, a certified cheque will be drawn on the Hong Kong and

Shanghai Banking Corporation. The sum is . . .' John Pavernen paused dramatically, '. . . exactly one million silver dollars.'

'Good! Good!' The General raised his porcelain wine-cup. 'Your fifty thousand will be paid in gold, Excellency.'

He tapped his cup with a chop-stick to summon the orderlies. Just before the door opened John Pavernen insisted: 'In return, General? Just for the record . . . for the Municipal Council.'

The warlord flicked a long nailed index-finger, and the door closed. His reedy tenor pledged: 'I shall defend Greater Shanghai and the foreign concessions to the death against the Red Communist bandits. Whatever the cost, myself and my hundred thousand brave soldiers will defend Shanghai.'

John Pavernen knew General Soo could muster no more than 65,000 men. He also knew that One-Arm Sutton could not possibly produce a hundred mortars in a week's time. None the less, both would be paid for full performance, and he would receive his broker's commission on both transactions from both sides. Those transparent deceptions demonstrated mutual goodwill. Moreover, the warlord's treasure stored in the Settlement would ensure his keeping his word, and the certified cheque would be his surety from the Council.

The door opened, and two orderlies carried in a golden-red suckling pig shoulder-high on a gold platter. Another pair brought silver wine-coolers from which peeped magnums of Veuve Cliquot. Though General Soo thought bubbly wine fit only for women, his Cossack officer had told him foreigners always drank champagne to celebrate.

While the orderlies were distributing crisp morsels of honey-roasted pork and filling crystal goblets with foaming wine, General Soo reached into the side-pocket of his bedizened tunic for a small packet. On his urging, Julia undid the silk cord – and gasped at the double strand of pearls glowing like miniature moons on a scarlet-silk wrapper.

Even if she had been less preoccupied, she would not have understood the orderly who whispered into the warlord's ear in rough Shantung dialect: 'Colonel Chang has decoded the telegram. The ship will be at Woosung for loading ten days from now.'

23

Elizaveta Alexandrovna Yavalenka glanced unhappily at the open touring car waiting for the traffic light beside the Haleevies' new canary-yellow Hupmobile limousine. Her carmined mouth curling in distaste, she played with the tassels of her cashmere shawl, which she had prudently thrown over her light shantung dress, although the evening was unseasonably warm for early March.

An enormously corpulent Chinese occupied the entire rear seat of the open automobile, his soft bulk oozing across the kidskin upholstery. His sparse grey hair looked like a cheap toupée, and rolls of fat encircled his neck like a ruff. His features were as bland as a face stamped on a child's balloon.

The faces of the two young women on the jump seats were covered with white powder so thick it would crack if their minute rose-bud mouths smiled. Almost obscured by eye-shadow and mascara, their eyes glinted like cats' in a dark cave. Sing-song girls, Elizaveta noted with professional disdain.

A footman sat beside the driver, and two guards perched on the running-boards. All were Russian. All were dressed in white riding-breeches with matching brass-buttoned tunics, and all were armed. The footmen, she saw with horror, were a count and a former brigadier-general, once colonel of her brother's regiment. The flower of the Russian aristocracy were now bodyguards for Chinese plutocrats and their tarts!

'Who's that fat fellow?' she asked. 'He looks as if he ought to be rendered down for lard.'

Emily glanced incuriously at the touring car as the light changed and replied: 'Never saw him before. He's certainly greasy with prosperity.'

182

To lighten her depression, Emily had worn a fire engine-red blouse and a striped blue skirt that swirled gaily around her knees. She did not quite know why she was glum. She was riding a wave of triumphs at the Women's Bank, and her physical relationship with Richard Hollings had been particularly satisfying lately. Quite remarkably, they had not quarrelled for several weeks.

'He ought to be, Em.' Joshua Haleevie observed from the jump-seat. 'That's old Zee Veeon. Cut-purse Zee, they call him. He's king of the pickpockets – among other things.'

'You know him, and Emily doesn't?' Richard asked. 'How's that?'

'He's a big investor in real estate.' Joshua fingered the blue paisley scarf knotted around his throat. 'We had the devil's own time turning him down. But he's into too many rackets.'

'Rackets?' Richard asked aggressively, his olive face flushed. 'Can a single rich man in Shanghai honestly say he's *not* a racketeer?'

'Steady, old boy.'

'Don't steady me, Haleevie!' Richard rasped. 'You know I'm right, don't you?'

'And don't try to patronize me, Hollings.' Joshua's voice was even. 'I'm afraid I just don't believe you know enough to judge whether. . .'

'Gentlemen, please!' Elizaveta said briskly. 'I didn't come out to referee a childish fight. You're worse than my cooks.'

Depressed by the degradation of her fellow Russians – a trifle, too, by her own condition – Elizaveta was inordinately irritated by their sharp words. She snatched at a diversion to relieve her depression, sensing that Emily's mood matched her own.

'I want to see a fortune-teller,' she demanded. 'Anyone know a really good one?'

'The one at the Great World, the amahs say,' Emily replied. 'He's called Gold Mountain.'

'We're only a few streets away.' Joshua's good temper appeared restored. 'What about it?'

In response to his instructions, the chauffeur steered the big yellow automobile towards Avenue Edward VII. Elizaveta threw Joshua a grateful glance. She already felt her spirits rising, for she had never failed to be amused – and slightly awed – by a fortune-teller.

The Hupmobile skirted the blockhouse that projected into the intersection. The four-square concrete structure that looked like a mausoleum behind sandbags was intended for a last-ditch stand against invaders – and to control street mobs. Even the optimists, who considered such precautions fanciful, admitted that the concessions faced the worst crisis of the twentieth century.

Elizaveta shuddered. Her world had been destroyed by Russian Bolsheviks, and Chinese Bolsheviks were now marching on Shanghai. She could not read the propaganda posters that had mysteriously appeared on buildings, but the stark drawings were like those she had seen in Siberia. A peasant fled a tiger with blood-dripping jaws that, Emily told her, was labelled 'Northern Warlords'. A cleancut Whampoa officer broke the chains that bound an emaciated coolie to a whipping post. Even poor Chinese, Elizaveta feared, would find the reality of Bolshevism utterly different.

The rasping of a dozen buzz-saws drowned out the normal din of the streets. A wood-and-canvas biplane swooped low, the Lewis gun behind the rear cockpit swinging menacingly. The scout-bomber was one of the six that made a brave display to intimidate the Nationalists, who possessed only a single aged Fokker.

However the enemy might feel, that show of force frightened Elizaveta. She could not endure another major dislocation of her life.

She glanced at Joshua, who was gawking at the warplane. She feared that he was growing tired of her obsession with the Ikra. Although he had not said a further word, she also knew from Julia that his parents were now pressing him very hard to take a suitable wife. Not just Rachel, but Sir Judah now sang the praises of Charlotte Gubbai, whose family was just as orthodox – and almost as wealthy – as the Haleevies.

When Elizaveta's eyes met Emily's, they exchanged conspiratorial female smiles. They were allied against the jagged, dangerous male world of warplanes, sandbags, barbed-wire and guns. Perhaps big boys had to have their toys, but why must they disastrously involve grown-up women in their gory games?

Emily's thoughts were running in much the same channel. Yet she supposed she should be grateful for the crisis. Without the revolution, Richard Hollings would have been testing his nerve in his new journalistic empire, which stretched from Japan to India.

He was increasingly irritated by her professional competition. She would have given up the *Philadelphia Public Ledger* without a tear – if he only asked. But Richard would *not* ask.

No more would he again ask her to marry him. Having been rejected so often, he was obviously waiting for her to speak. Yet a girl liked to be asked – even if she had to decide in the end that she could not marry a foreigner. Watching his rapt expression as he watched the warplane, Emily realized that she must take the initiative if she wished to marry him – or even keep him. Her vague depression began to dissipate. Although her situation was hardly cheering, she felt better for defining it. Normally undemonstrative in public, as her Confucian heritage dictated, she reached across to take Richard's hand. His olive cheeks, which were actually darker than her own, flushed and he squeezed her fingers hard.

Moved by that gesture, Elizaveta momentarily envied the young Chinese woman. If only she could reach across the gulf of social and religious prejudice to Joshua as easily as Emily had just reached across the gulf of racial prejudice! But did she really want to?

'By jove, that *is* a new wrinkle!' Untouched by the women's unspoken tension, Joshua mocked broadly. 'Just look at that, ladies and gents!'

A hexagonal four-storey building of brown brick occupied the entire city block at the broad intersection of Avenue Edward with Tibet Road. Beneath the six-tiered white tower that pierced the sky, illuminated red ideograms read: TA SHIH-CHIEH. Beneath that name, which meant Great World, lounged Annamese soldiers wearing dark-blue serge uniforms and steel helmets with metallic crests like scalp-locks.

Towering above the Annamese was the device that so amused Joshua. Apparently constructed of riveted armour plate in a naval dockyard, it looked something like a destroyer's turret pierced with rifle slits and capped by a rotating machine-gun. It was painted grey and was mounted on four solid-rubber tyres.

'My word, what a picture!' Richard Hollings exclaimed. 'I must get my photographer chap around. What in heaven does it do?'

'Per . . . per . . . perhaps,' Joshua stuttered with uncontrollable laughter. 'Perhaps they expect a U-boat attack.'

'With a surfaced U-boat, they could fight it out with machine-guns,' Hollings grinned. 'But a Chinese crowd would swarm all over it. Probably set it alight with petrol. Only the French. . .'

The Hupmobile swung across the boulevard and drew up under the white tower. The chauffeur looked respectfully dubious as he opened the door of the passenger compartment. He advised in emphatic pidgin: 'Great World b'long only Chinee men. Foreign peoples more bettah no go visit.'

Emily laughed, but Joshua wondered whether he should have yielded to Elizaveta's whim. He did not feel threatened, although foreigners shunned the amusement grounds. Nor did he feel unwelcome in the vast, circular interior, where dumpling hawkers competed with tea-shops while strolling jugglers vied with traditional operas. He was certainly not intimidated by the puppets performing old Chinese melodramas.

He was, however, half-stunned by the tumult and half-choked by the miasma of stale cooking oil, ancient sweat, and rancid pomade. When Richard shrugged in dumb-show exasperation, Joshua turned his palms up in mute sympathy. Transfixed by hostile stares because of her foreign clothing and her foreign companions, Emily instinctively turned towards the entrance. But Elizaveta clutched her arm.

'Come along, Emily!' she directed. 'Help me find the fortune-teller.'

Emily scanned the signboards and finally saw one declaring: GOLD MOUNTAIN READS FACES. She was jostled repeatedly as she led Elizaveta through the throng to the booth. Waiting for the dirty red curtains to open, she heard loud stage-whispers behind her: 'Foreigners' whore! . . . Rich bitch! . . . A disgrace to the race! . . . The Uprising'll fix her!'

Uncomfortable and slightly apprehensive, she followed Elizaveta into darkness that reeked of cheap incense and cheaper perfume. A woman's voice spoke behind the red veil she saw hanging over a small blackwood table when her eyes adjusted to the gloom: 'Please be seated and allow me to gaze upon you, esteemed ladies.'

'For my friend, not me,' Emily hastily interposed. 'Read her fortune, not mine!'

The red veil parted, and a bony hand with long, pale fingernails placed a tortoise shell on the table. The shell rocked restlessly on the black surface, halting only when Elizaveta laid down a second silver dollar. A

Chinese working girl would pay twenty coppers. She would know the predictions to be spurious, yet believe them implicitly.

'It's very difficult with foreigners,' the clear voice answered Emily's thoughts. 'Their features are so craggy and unrefined. Their faces display no proper pattern. So I must charge more.'

The voice trailed off into a low keening, which became a low mutter, and the seer resumed. 'I can now tell the foreign lady several things. She will live a long time, but never where she chooses! She will be admired by many men, but she will never possess the one she wants! She will have many children, but none will be her own! Her enemies will be her friends, and her friends will be her enemies. And she will be very happy.'

Emily duly translated. To Elizaveta's puzzled questions, the voice replied only: 'I am very tired. I can tell you no more!'

24

Like all fifteen-year-olds, who never get enough sleep, Little Pow awoke
slowly and unwillingly. He hated the chill dawn of Monday, March 21,
1927. Mondays were always worst, because long association with
foreigners had accustomed him to the Sunday holiday unknown to most
Chinese. The boy of all work resentfully knuckled his eyes and reached
out to pull the long ears of his bed-mate, Johann Adam Schall von Bell.

He was not alarmed when his hand touched the cold floor. Even an
earlier riser than himself, Adam sometimes strayed. Forcing his sleep-
gummed eyelids open, Little Pow jerked upright and almost toppled off
the bench on which he lay. He remembered then that he was far from the
loft-apartment on Kiukiang Road. He had spent the night in the offices
of the Shanghai General Labour Union in Chinese-ruled Chapei a half-
mile north of Soochow Creek. Before leaving the apartment the previous
evening, he had urgently advised Missy Joo-li and Missy Yuelin to stay
at home until he returned – and to keep Adam locked in the apartment.

Little Pow slipped his bare feet into the virtually new golf brogues
Julia had given him when she discovered they wore the same size. He felt
his way down the steep staircase to the communal sink in the rear courtyard. Still half-asleep, he barely heard the clatter of wooden soles or the
swishing of cloth soles around him. Dutifully plying a worn toothbrush
and scraping his tongue with the handle, he was virtually deaf to the
guttural gargling and the phlegmy hawking of his neighbours at the long
stone trough.

His eyes at last fully open, he whistled 'The Internationale' through
his front teeth. He knew he would get nothing for breakfast like the
delicacies Lao Zee gave him. Only a bowl of rice gruel with a sprinkling

187

of salted cabbage and with luck a sliver of gristly pork. He was, none the less, in high spirits. His big eyes sparkled in his triangular face when he slipped his brand-new armband out of his pocket. Admiring its splendour, he hardly heard the grumbling of the hungry men whose path to the kitchen he was blocking.

The red armband read *Chuan Shih*, Special Messenger, and in smaller ideograms underneath: *Workers' Inspection Corps*. Finally moving when a hard thumb dug into his ribs, Little Pow picked up a rice-bowl.

His task today was vital. Even before the General Strike and the Mass Uprising began at noon, he would carry the orders of Comrade Chou En-lai to the heavily armed militia known as the Workers' Inspection Corps. The dashing Chou En-lai was in command because Dr Tom's friend Chang Kuo-tao was involved in urgent negotiations with the left-wing Nationalists in Wuhan. Anyway, there would be glory enough for all today. Not only for the people's militia, now called the Workers' Inspection Corps, but for the half-million workers who were to march through the streets. Glory enough for the guerrillas from the countryside and for the black-shirted strongarm men of the secret societies.

Little Pow put his bowl down. Although he had not finished the rice-gruel, he was no longer hungry. His mouth was dry – but even thinking of food made his stomach turn over.

Today's offensive would be a total success. He smiled confidently while cold crab-claws nipped his throat. The fiasco of mid-February would not be repeated. Despite his confidence, Little Pow felt a griping need to relieve himself. He could still see the warlord soldiers from the north slipping their broadswords from the slings on their backs and scything a path through the workers just a month ago. Blood-spattered, he had only escaped because he was so small and so agile.

But today the National Revolutionary Army was almost at the gates. Besides, the Workers' Inspection Corps had been trained to a high pitch by Whampoa Academy officers in plain clothes. After a series of defeats in the interior, the warlords' defences were crumbling and their crack units were defecting. Although the warlord General Soo apparently stood firm in Shanghai, his position was eroded. Neither the police nor the garrison had impeded the Communist build-up in Greater Shanghai – perhaps because their information was inadequate, perhaps because they were afraid.

Taut discipline, modern arms, and meticulous training had made the National Revolutionary Army superior. But armed force only appeared decisive. The all-important factor was not guns, as Chou En-lai had repeatedly explained, but spirit. Guns were essential at this stage of the revolution, yet power did not ultimately grow from the barrel of the gun. Great political power, which controlled the guns, sprang from mastery over the hearts of men and women. General Chou summed up: 'Psychology is our chief weapon. We are fighting a psychological war.'

Parades and mass meetings, posters and leaflets, travelling singers and dramatic troupes – all were essential to win the hearts of the people.

Newspapers and magazines, radio broadcasts and town-criers, planted rumours and beautiful promises – all undermined the enemy's resolution. When the enemy fled, the revolutionary army swept forward. Because of its expert psychological warfare, the National Revolutionary Army was advancing confidently against retreating warlord forces that were still three times more numerous than itself.

His fear vanquished, Little Pow forced down the remaining rice-gruel and returned his bowl to the female comrades in the kitchen. In the big office on the first floor, the commander was briefing his sub-commanders.

'Victory is certain!' Chou En-lai was reiterating when Little Pow slipped into the crammed room. 'Then why go over the plan for the twentieth time? Victory is certain *because* we plan meticulously, drill hard,

and adhere strictly to our plans. ... Now the details again. At Chapei West Police Station, two detachments will advance in separate columns. They'll be wearing ordinary working clothes, and their weapons will be concealed in carrying-poles, valises, and parcels. At precisely 11:35 the converging columns will . . .'

Little Pow yawned profoundly and revealed dingy molars to the female propaganda cadre who was jotting down every word the commander uttered.

'No manners, these street urchins!' She shot him a scandalized look through thick-lensed spectacles. 'None at all!'

Little Pow grinned derisively and replied in broad Shanghainese: 'We are all comrades, Missy, all equal, is it not? Even spoiled and frustrated daughters of the blood-sucking bourgeoisie are now equal to street urchins!'

The female cadre blushed crimson and looked down at her note-pad as Chou En-lai declared: 'More than three million people live in Shanghai. Half in Greater Shanghai under the warlord rule, half in the imperialists' enclaves. Forty thousand foreigners in the foreign concessions – and the rest all our brothers by blood.

'Now we muster perhaps half a million workers – maybe five thousand armed. Not so many to take over a city of three million, eh? Against us the warlord troops and their police number, say, sixty thousand. The imperialists have about twenty thousand ground troops and twenty thousand more aboard their warships. Formidable odds, eh?'

Little Pow had heard lesser orators inflame men's courage by promising that victory would be easy because they moved with the tide of history, whatever that was! He had never before heard an orator inspire troops to battle by gloomily reciting the odds against them.

'None the less, our victory is inevitable, because our correct strategy is invincible!' Chou En-lai declared, and Little Pow released his pent breath.

'We shall break one stick at a time: first, Greater Shanghai, then the foreign-occupied territories. The imperialists will disgorge their concessions when the pressure hurts them – just as the British did at Hankow.

All but a handful of almost three million Chinese are on our side. And the National Revolutionary Army is hardly a day's march away. The odds are actually with us – overwhelmingly. Victory is inevitable!'

After that spirited re-dedication at dawn, the exhilaration slowly leaked out of the day. Little Pow was disappointed at not accompanying Chou En-lai on repeated sallies into the city that was to be the battlefield. He was, instead, instructed to stand by to carry messages to the fighting units. But there were no messages for him to carry. Shrill telephones executed that mission, since, by some proletarian miracle, the temperamental Shanghai telephone system was operating flawlessly.

Little Pow had volunteered his life to the revolution, and all the revolution asked was that he answer the telephone. Occasional rifle shots and bursts of machine-gun fire made him feel even more useless. The mass roar of political rallies and the choruses chanting the songs of the revolution reproached him.

When Missy Joo-li asked how he had served the glorious Shanghai Uprising, he would have to confess that he had only answered the telephone – as any fearful girl could. Simmering with indignation, Little Pow none the less logged all the messages precisely:

Monday, 21 March 1927
11:41: Friendly units converge on West Chapei Police Station.
11:59: Our forces drawing heavy fire, request reinforcements.
12:18: Additional units attack.
12:36: Police evacuate West Chapei Station. Most escape owing to our lack of sufficient men to surround them.
12:59: Fifty rifles and six sub-machine-guns found in West Chapei station.
1:16: Policemen seen throwing discarded uniforms into Soochow Creek and donning workers' clothing.
1:31: Resistance weakening. Our units taking control of all police stations.
1:58: Little resistance by warlord troops. General Soo Lang-hai has vanished from his headquarters. Most warlord troops flee, though some join the revolutionary forces.
2:15: Resistance stiffening around armoured train at North Station.
2:36: Units at North Station request reinforcement. They report: No Chinese warlord troops involved. Enemy are Russian soldiers commanded by tall, yellow-haired man with short whip. He ignores bullets and never unholsters his pistol.
3:06: Our forces at North Station urgently require assistance in repelling counter-attack of ...
(Line went dead)

That was Little Pow's last log-entry on the day of the Great Shanghai Uprising. All telephone communication had broken down, perhaps because shells had hit the exchange. A few minutes later, Comrade Chou En-lai dashed up the stairs to demand reports. Concluding that the general situation was overwhelmingly favourable, he concentrated upon the battle at the North Railway Station.

'I need a runner to the units at the North Station,' he declared. 'They are to draw back until reinforced. I would rather General Soo Lang-hai escaped with all his loot than lose a single life unnecessarily. . . .'

'Comrade, we've just had information regarding General Soo's whereabouts,' a staff officer interrupted. 'The Wharf Workers' Union reports he boarded a ship at Woosung at dawn. They had no orders to intercept and . . .'

'Then the Russians are fighting on their own?' Chou En-lai pondered before directing: 'We must give them a way out. Not sacrifice our own men to kill them. They are White bandits, but they are also politically insignificant. Now, Little Pow, you're the one I want.'

Quivering with pride, the special messenger straightened his red armband, pulled down his oversize blue-cotton tunic and stood at stiff attention, just as the foreign soldiers did before their officers. But Chou En-lai draped an arm around his shoulders and led him to the big wall-map. The commander's tapering index-finger traced patterns on the streets of Shanghai.

'Now, Pow, take this route,' he directed. 'You want the commander at the North Station. He is to pull out any men he has in blocking positions. When the Russians retreat towards the Settlement, he is not to interfere. The White Russians aren't worth a single drop of Chinese blood. Besides, the example of our lenient treatment will be a powerful weapon against the foreigners. Now move!'

The fortified boundary between Chinese-ruled Chapei and the International Settlement ran between the Municipal School and the Public Market on Elgin Road. Hectic Chapei itself was a maze of narrow alleys intersected by occasional wider streets. It was home for hundreds of thousands of poor Chinese, who lodged in jerry-built tenements and worked in clangorous factories.

As he trotted towards the North Station, Little Pow was astonished by the silence. All the workaday noises were hushed, and all activity had ceased. Spindles no longer sighed through the windows of cotton mills, and looms no longer clattered. The tinsmiths' hammers had stopped pounding, and the axles of man-drawn carts did not squeal. The purveyors to the dead had put up their shutters to hide their fragrant camphor-wood coffins. Even the food stores were closed, as were cafés, tea-houses and restaurants. The General Strike had hushed even clamorous Chapei.

Yet a bass throbbing like a thousand muted kettle-drums underlay the silence. At mass meetings and in parades the voice of a resurgent people shouted the slogans of the revolution. Red flags hung from every building, and demonstrators marched under triumphal arches flung across the streets on bamboo poles. The five-barred flag of the Peking warlord government was everywhere supplanted by the banner of the National Revolution: a white sun shooting out short, triangular rays on a blue field.

Little Pow's darting eyes searched for openings through the throngs. His splayed feet in their incongruously feminine brogues leaped across

191

pot holes and flew over ruts. He pounded through the exultant crowds, gesturing imperiously with his scarred hands and shouting: 'Special Messenger!'

Greater Shanghai was *en fête*. Dandling infants with pink ribbons in their jet-black hair, gulping yellow rice-wine from earthenware jugs, and chanting brave slogans, the largest proletarian city in Asia had transformed a *coup d'état* into a holiday. Jubilant spectators cheered the almost inaudible words of street-corner orators. Young female propagandists were hailed rather than jeered, though older women pointed disdainfully at their bobbed hair. Mass rallies boomed exhortations and cheers through tinny loudspeakers. Youth groups, women's associations, and trade unions marched in vast processions while funeral bands blared. Almost all the procession paused before the barricades protecting the International Settlement to taunt the foreign sentries.

On the edge of Chapei, the North Station offered a pocket handkerchief of open space. Today that small park was bereft of its usual pleasure seekers, its usual coolies, and its usual petty criminals.

Little Pow crouched behind the low brick parapet above the tracks. Peeping cautiously over the top, he felt a macabre thrill. Twenty or thirty men in blue workers' clothing lay still, as if flung haphazardly across the gleaming rails. Their red armbands glowed around General Soo's armoured train like drops of blood.

The funereal black armour-plates riveted to the train's steel beams were scarred by bullets' silver tracks, as was the big steam locomotive whose bulbous nose pointed towards Nanking. Four Cossacks lay still at the foot of the ladder leading to the locomotive cab, but rifles protruding from the loopholes in the armoured carriages spat smoke.

Just out of range, armed militiamen in railway uniforms with visored caps stood in a semi-circle grinning proudly. At their centre a self-consciously grim conductor squatted behind a heavy Browning machine-gun on a metal tripod. As Little Pow watched, a young fireman crumpled to the stony ground. His mouth open, the wounded man stared in amazement at the blood welling from his thigh.

The machine-gun's muzzle moved lazily, and puffs of grey smoke drifted prettily in the sunlight. Little Pow could hear the copper-jacketed bullets ricochet off the train's armour-plates. But some shots clearly struck home. A rifle slipped through a loophole and crashed onto the gravel roadbed. When the train's machine-gun turrets rotated in their direction, the idlers around the Browning scurried for the shelter of a large concrete tube. Bursts of fire pursued them. Two fell so near the abandoned Browning they were soaked by the jets of water from its punctured cooling-jacket.

Little Pow scuttled away behind the parapet. At the entrance to the terminal building, he wasted several minutes convincing two stupid guards that he carried an urgent message for their commander. Still crouching, although his guide strolled nonchalantly upright, Little Pow finally reached the improvised command post behind the ticket windows.

The young commander wore the uniform of the National Revolutionary Army. A sharp-faced southerner with the look of an alert squirrel, he was evidently a Whampoa Academy graduate. When Pow's Shanghainese was translated for him, he immediately directed: 'Comrade Chou En-lai gives the order! Withdraw all our units and let the Russkies go freely.'

Little Pow settled down to wait for the militia to disengage and the White Russians to seize the opportunity to withdraw. The suspicious Cossacks left the armoured cars two hours later. The dusk obscured the widely separated figures marching towards the Settlement's perimeter fence half a mile distant. Sporadic rifle fire harried them despite the commander's orders. Two Russians fell, but the gates in the barbed wire surrounding the Settlement opened when the Sikh sentries saw the Caucasian faces seeking asylum.

Among a rush of curious militiamen, Little Pow tumbled into the armoured train. To his astonishment, it was empty. The crates of booty he expected to find had either been removed or had never been loaded. His short legs fully extended, the youth climbed the metal ladder to the cab of the locomotive. He sat on the engineer's perforated iron seat and tugged tentatively at the control levers.

'Whee-whee! Chuff-chuff!' Little Pow imitated the howl of the whistle and the puffing of the engine. 'Chuff-chuff! Whee . . .'

No longer a soldier of the revolution but a happy child, he swung around to shout orders at an imaginary fireman: 'Faster, you addled egg! More coal, son of a turtle-bitch! Before night falls, we must reach . . .'

The clear light that flares in the instant between dusk and darkness flooded the cab and lit the figure seated against the heaped coal at the rear. A grey-caracul cap perched rakishly on the blond head, and bandoliers crossed the white tunic. The left hand rested casually on the silver head of the riding-crop tucked into the boot-top. The black muzzle of the revolver in the right hand, which pointed directly at Little Pow, wavered no more than did the ice-blue eyes.

For thirty seconds, the youth sat frozen in terror. The revolver did not move, and the blue eyes did not blink. Nor did the commander of the warlord's bodyguard speak. Not even the trail of blood moved, the red trail that reached from his temple to his jaw.

Little Pow hurled himself out of the cab in mortal haste, stumbling and skinning his hands. The corpse was even more terrifying than the apparition he had thought alive. The malevolent ghost of a foreign devil could haunt him all his days. Through streets vibrant with rejoicing workers he trotted back to the well-lit offices of the Shanghai General Labour Union.

John Pavernen and One-Arm Sutton later worked out exactly what had happened before the warlord General Soo sailed for Hong Kong at dawn on the day of the General Uprising. They concluded that he had never had any intention of defending Shanghai. He had stayed just long enough to preserve a scrap of face – and to collect the money the credulous foreigners were eager to pay him to defend Shanghai. He had then, as previously arranged, loaded his concubines and his choicest treasures on the coaster for Hong Kong along with a fifty-man bodybuard to protect them all.

Fortunately, General Soo did not receive the entire bribe promised him to do his duty. The taipans had cannily decided to pay the warlord in instalments. The certified cheque of the Hong Kong and Shanghai Banking Corporation had been drawn for $300,000. That was one-third of the full million less a preliminary payment of $15,000 to One-Arm Sutton for the mortars and $15,000 to John Pavernen as broker. The mortars had, of course, not been delivered. They did not exist.

John Pavernen was righteously indignant, having been cheated of the additional commission owed by General Soo. But eighty-five large wooden crates were being held for the warlord in the godown of the Hong Kong and Shanghai Bank. Those valuables would be delivered only to their rightful owner, for the Bank's commercial morality was impeccable. Yet even General Soo Lang-hai might well claim them in vain, for the Bank's commercial realism was renowned.

Somewhere in that impasse, John Pavernen concluded, lay a sterling opportunity for an honest broker like himself. As a preliminary to negotiating with the Bank he arranged with discreet bribes to have the crates opened. Looking at the contents he exploded with rage – and then with laughter. Most were packed with paving-stones well protected by thick wrappings. Some, however, contained expended artillery cartridges. The market for brass was, unfortunately, moribund.

25

Colonel Thomas Tan-ssu Howe, Surgeon-General of the Sixth Corps of the National Revolutionary Army, waited uneasily for Commander Hugh England, captain of HMS *Emerald*. Commander England's frigid aloofness was as disconcerting as his ship's presence in the Yangtze River near China's sometime capital of Nanking. *Emerald* was 9000 tons and 570 feet of brand new heavy cruiser. Capable of thirty-three knots, she could hurl explosives from seven six-inch surface guns, five four-inch anti-aircraft guns, and sixteen torpedo tubes. If any other warship anywhere were as powerful for her size, the omniscient Royal Navy was not aware of her existence.

Tommy Howe had been regaled with those details by *Emerald*'s gunnery lieutenant, who recalled being two forms behind him at public school. Old Radleyan camaraderie had breached the wall of taciturn courtesy behind which the captain wished to pen his unwelcome visitor. To the lieutenant it was inconceivable that an Old Radleyan could be anything but a gentleman, whatever flag he sailed under. Manifestly, a gentleman visiting *Emerald*'s wardroom must not find its hospitality grudging.

The unexpected welcome had somewhat alleviated Tommy's discomfiture over his grim mission. In the company of the young naval officers he had briefly reverted to the casual good fellowship of his school days. He had also concluded wryly that he had more in common with English gentlemen like those with whom he had grown up than he did with the half-savage soldiers of the revolution who had killed, raped, and pillaged in Nanking. The Chinese officers were hardly better. Most were incapable of disciplining their men, and some had joined the looting.

He now had to make amends. He was required to apologize for the unforgivable and to offer implausible assurances that the outrages against foreigners would not be repeated.

Tommy shivered in the wind that wailed across the ship's bridge and tightened the belt of his camel-hair greatcoat and wondered when the godlike Commander Hugh England would deign to take notice of his presence. He was anxious to discharge his business and rejoin his fellow officers, who distrusted his cosmopolitan knowledge as much as he deplored their provincial ignorance.

Upstream somewhat closer to Nanking, the setting sun silhouetted two warships. The identical destroyers had gigantic American flags painted on their hulls just beneath their four raked funnels. Like the guns of HMS *Emerald*, the guns of those destroyers were now silent. Even the three Nationalist gunboats that had earlier shelled the railway terminus at Putow on the warlord-held right bank were now gone.

Dusk on the Yangtze was still, except for the lowing of water buffaloes and the barking of dogs. Nanking, too, was still, but smoke drifted above its walls. The black plumes were thickest over the hillock outside the city walls that was crowned by the compound of the Standard Oil Company of New York.

By God, Tommy reflected, the newspapers'll make a bloody great meal of this day's work. It won't help the cause one little bit. Shanghai's foreigners'll be frightened out of their wits. Good job Julie doesn't know I'm here.

He could envisage headlines throughout the world: THOUSANDS EVACUATED FROM NANKING AS BOLSHEVIKS RAMPAGE/US AND BRITISH WARSHIPS SHELL CITY TO SAVE FOREIGNERS/SCORES KILLED AND RAPED/CITY BURNS AS WARLORD TROOPS FLEE/'NATIONALIST' REDS TRIUMPHANT.

It was just about over now, but in Nanking foreigners had been harassed for days – and a dozen or so had been killed. Tommy, who had seen the incident develop, was still not sure who was primarily responsible, but he was certain the 'Chinese Bolsheviks' of Generalissimo Chiang Kai-shek would be blamed abroad.

He had watched appalled as the retreating warlord troops began killing Chinese civilians. Peering through his binoculars from the southern district, which the Nationalists had already taken, he saw the soldiers in mustard-yellow uniforms loot buildings and set them to the torch. The Nationalists could not prevent tens of thousands of warlord soldiers escaping northwards across the Yangtze with their loot. A few hundred Russians were conspicuous in their distinctive blouses. Tommy had seen those hardbitten mercenaries weep when they were forced to abandon their two armoured trains. He had not seen the Russians killing civilians as had Chinese troops on both sides.

Nanking was a scandal – an atrocity, but also a great victory. The Northern Expedition had fought few pitched battles, since its reputation and its propagandists terrified the enemy. Temporarily unified by fear, the warlords had, however, made their stand behind the massive fourteenth-century walls of their last stronghold south of the unbridged Yangtze, which bisected China. They were fighting with their backs to the river to keep the Nationalist tide from sweeping unopposed to Peking bearing Generalissimo Chiang Kai-shek to power over all China.

The Nationalists' resolution, political warfare, and discipline had again proved irresistible. After weeks of skirmishing, the warlords were driven out of Nanking on March 23, 1927. The Generalissimo boarded a gunboat for Shanghai, and the Sixth Corps occupied the city.

All that night the seven hundred foreigners in Nanking, among whom more than four hundred Americans were the largest group, had feared marauding warlord troops. In the morning Nationalist soldiers bent on loot invaded the British Consulate and reportedly killed the Consul himself. Coming upon the heels of previous outrages against Americans, that attack frightened all the foreigners out of Nanking. Some seventy men, women, and children fled the American Consulate for the hilltop redoubt of the Standard Oil Company outside the city walls. Their steps were hastened by machine-gun fire inside the walls and the smoke from burning buildings, but all felt they were protected by the Stars and Stripes carried high on a bamboo pole. They had further been assured by Nationalist officers like Colonel Thomas Tan-ssu Howe that foreigners would not be molested.

Tommy had watched their slow progress through his binoculars and seen them come under sniper fire. He was angry and ashamed when he picked out the squad of Nationalist soldiers gleefully aiming at the hated imperialists. An American sailor in blue dungarees stumbled and clutched his back. After the American landing party from the destroyers fired three volleys, the renegade Nationalists fired only one more shot before retiring to look for revenge and loot elsewhere. They had evidently deserted their units and broken away from their officers.

Despite his passionate commitment to the revolution, Tommy Howe at that moment felt far greater kinship for the bedraggled foreigners than his brutal countrymen. He felt personally humiliated when he saw soldiers in Nationalist khaki pounding on the door of the big white house on top of Socony Hill. They were obviously demanding protection money from the beleaguered foreigners, who he had pledged would not be molested.

Returning to Sixth Corps Headquarters, Tommy protested strongly to his general, at the risk of confirming his reputation as a foreign-devil lover. Afterwards, he got the response he had expected – indifference.

The afternoon was extraordinarily quiet. For the first time in weeks the field-guns were still. Only sporadic small-arms fire and occasional shouts broke the silence of the conquered city.

At half past three, the afternoon erupted. For a quarter of an hour, an artillery barrage rocked Nanking. From the roof, Tommy saw the British and American warships shelling the approaches to the Standard Oil compound on the hill. He was not surprised when his general summoned him.

'Get yourself aboard that big ship, the English one,' the general commanded. 'And stop them! They'll tell you they fired only to cover their people's withdrawal to the ships – and no more than a hundred

197

rounds. But the foreign devils have tasted blood. Promise anything, but get them to stop.'

Thus Tommy found himself setting out for HMS *Emerald* to make more empty promises. He had commandeered a sampan and gone aboard the cruiser after a prolonged confrontation with the officer of the deck. Somewhat soothed by his fellow Radleyan's welcome, he now waited on the wing of the bridge for the captain to condescend to talk with him.

Bulky in a bridge-coat with gold-striped epaulettes, Commander Hugh England finally appeared and offered a perfunctory salute before speaking: 'Colonel Howe is it? If I talk slowly . . . very slowly . . . can you . . . understand?'

The Commander bared his stained teeth in a patronizing smile when Tommy nodded and continued: 'All right, then. I shall spell it out to you. We will not fire again unless we are fired upon. We will soon have brought all our people safely aboard. But there will be merry hell to pay. Your troops have killed more than fifteen foreigners. You Chinese will regret this day's work. Are you the Johnny who made all those promises to the Yanks?'

'I'm afraid so, Captain. The troops got out of hand.' Tommy remembered the officers he had seen looting. 'However, I can assure you there will be no repetition. I should also like to offer my personal apology for that misbehaviour.'

Startled by Tommy's public school accent, Commander England studied him in the glow of the bridge lights before replying: 'Your personal apology. Not an official apology, eh?'

'I regret that I cannot unless instructed . . .'

'Well that's that, then.' The captain was finished with him. 'Just as long as you understand: any more nonsense and we'll really let go – make the last barrage look like a damp squib. You'll be going ashore now.'

Tommy was further humiliated by that abrupt dismissal after the Englishman's contemptuous rejection of his apology. Infuriated, he squatted on the scale-speckled deck of the sampan amid the reek of fish. To be scorned in his own country by an arrogant foreigner like a nightsoil coolie! He had never been so treated in his entire life. For a moment, he felt joy at the foreigners' humiliation – and sympathy with the soldiers who had looted and killed.

The moon had not yet scattered the darkness, but the jagged silhouettes of the foreign warships dominated the Yangtze River. The cruiser and the destroyers were starkly outlined by the orange-and-blue oil fires leaping on Socony Hill. Their greasy black smoke billowed over newly liberated Nanking.

'Since the Nanking Incident your coverage has changed, Dick. You're becoming biased, almost anti-Chinese and white supremacist. You're becoming an old fashioned damn-the-natives British imperialist like the taipans at the Shanghai Club. I just don't know how . . .'

198

Emily stopped in mid-sentence. She could not drop the matter, though she knew she was on dangerous ground. Their bitter disagreements on journalistic ethics could well be projection – as defined in her psychology classes at Bryn Mawr. Perhaps they were arguing an abstract issue because the fundamental personal issue between them was so explosive. None the less, the question of fair reporting on the National Revolution was too important to gloss over – even though she might be courting disaster.

'For God's sake, Emily, don't talk such bosh.' Richard erupted into the silence. 'You're getting so emotional about local politics it's almost impossible to talk to you.'

'Local politics to you, but not to me!' she retorted. 'It's my own future – and the lives of my people. China needs . . . deserves sympathetic reporting – not biased sensationalism. You could start a war. Bring the foreigners into the civil war. And where would your precious Shanghai, your Model Settlement, be then?'

'My dear girl, it's *your* Shanghai. Even *your* Foreign Settlement. *My* family didn't get rich hiding behind foreigners' skirts and squeezing their countrymen. My family hasn't. . . Damn it, I'm sorry. I . . .'

Emily paled with fury, and her pallor made her appear even more fragile. Yet she half-agreed – as her brother Tommy would largely – with Richard's characterization of the Howes. But the same fundamental question arose again. Was his attack on her family not also projection, a substitute for a direct attack on herself?

'Look here, Em, I'm truly sorry!' he repeated. 'But I promise you, I'm just reporting the way it is. I wish China weren't a bear-pit – a dirty great arena for dirty fights. But I can't change that. I'm not God. Only a humble reporter.'

'You're as humble as Caligula, Richard Hollings. One minute you act as if you invented the Revolution, as if you are the demiurge. The next you're oily humble, another Uriah Heep.'

'Don't parade your learning, young lady. Blue-stockings aren't very attractive.'

Richard knew his Emily very well. Always amused by her stilted manner of speech when she was angry, he discounted her vehemence. She was invariably vehement in abstract discussions, particularly when her naïve patriotism was touched. He was, somehow, unaware that his condescending pleasantries infuriated her, particularly when he mocked her crusading feminism.

'Don't patronize me, Dick,' she snapped. 'I don't like it. And I don't like your airs of superiority to China and to me. We Howes were here long before you foreigners appeared. We'll be here when you're long gone.'

'I have no travel plans, my dear. Except to worm my way back into your good graces.'

Emily smiled despite herself. Yet she wondered again whether he could be jealous of her modest success in journalism. He unquestionably resented her substantial success in the Women's Bank. Richard called himself a Bohemian and asserted that he was not shackled by convention. Yet, like his Victorian father – and her Confucian father – he demanded that his woman be modest, retiring, and, above all, devoted to no occupation outside himself.

At least he was consistent in his prejudices. Taking her consent for granted, he was again chivvying her to set a date for their wedding. He really did want to look after her – to protect her. But he also wanted to confine her. He did not mind her little pieces for the Chinese-language press, since they did not affect him. Once married, however, he would assuredly curtail her freedom to file to the *Philadelphia Public Ledger*, which implicitly competed with his coverage for the *Boston Globe*. His outmoded idea of marriage could stifle her.

Yet she did love him, and she would be delighted to live with him. Even in the enlightened 1920s, however, her Shanghai was too hidebound. In London or New York, which meant Bloomsbury or Greenwich Village, cohabitation without benefit of clergy was not merely tolerated, but virtually conventional. Yet she could not fulfil her parents' worst expectations by becoming the 'little wife' of a foreigner. Marriage would, at least, allow them to live together openly, which would be a great relief. But one didn't take nuptial vows like asprin.

Emily was reluctant to face Richard, for she did not want him to see that she was thawing. She glanced down at the Bund from the office he had rented in the *North China Daily News* building. He said he wanted to be near the cable office and to read the *Daily News's* wire service reports. She knew he also needed the tension and the sense of being at the centre of events only a working newspaper office provided.

His own office was big, and he had invited her to set her new Royal Number Ten on a vacant desk. He had given her the typewriter – for Chinese New Year, he said – when the ancient Underwood once salvaged from the wreckage of JPEnterprises finally proved unrepairable. Emily's eyes misted. For a moment she saw a blur instead of the small pagoda that glowed in the afternoon sunlight amid the industrial slum called Pootung across the Hwangpoo River.

Although often scathing about her deficiencies as a correspondent, he had given her the Royal. He had also given her office space. Was it because he wanted to keep an eye on her during the evenings, when they wrote most of their despatches because of the thirteen-hour time difference to Boston and Philadelphia?

Perhaps he was trying to woo her away from her work. She laughed aloud, and Richard glanced at her quizzically. If he should give her an ivory abacus to facilitate her work at the Women's Bank, she should by that same reasoning be doubly suspicious. Anyway, she was a little tired of the Bank: the female lusting after money and the fluting female voices and the female preoccupation with trifles.

'I promised I'd crawl to get back into your good graces,' he said without rancour. 'Since then, you've gazed out the window, blotted your eyes, and laughed out loud.'

'I was thinking of something else.'

'What's so laughable?'

'I can't tell you. But, since you raised the subject again, what do you think now of your piece on Chiang Kai-shek's press conference?'

'A pretty good story.' He was defensive. 'Not anti-Chinese, though maybe a little pro-imperialist. But even you don't want the Foreign Concession overrun by that Red rabble, do you?'

'Not just now, Dick. It would be a terrible wrench. Of course, China *must* take the concessions back in time. But the Nationalists're no rabble. They're a disciplined army – as you well know. The Communists are, thank God, a minority!'

'So you do want us overrun by the fine Nationalist army?'

'It's inevitable in time. But just look out this window. You'll see why it's impossible now.'

He stood beside her. His arm proprietorially encircled her waist, which was supple under her pink *crêpe de chine* blouse, and he stroked her hip through her light heather-tweed skirt.

Moored to the men-of-war buoys off the Bund were two American cruisers, one flying the flag of a full admiral; two British cruisers, one flying the flag of a vice-admiral; a Portuguese sloop; two Japanese destroyers; and a Dutch cruiser. Most of the international fleet of forty-seven warships assembled for the emergency was lying off Woosung on the Yangtze River.

'Nobody's going to trifle with that lot,' Richard agreed. 'Certainly not Chiang Kai-shek and his one gunboat.'

He gazed speculatively at the flotilla, and Emily surreptitiously studied his profile. His usually mobile features were pensive, and the untamed lock of dark-brown hair fell unhampered over his high forehead. His sombre dark eyes moved her deeply. She lifted her hand to touch the vulnerable patch above his cheekbones where one or two bristles had escaped the razor-blade. When he turned to her, her hand dropped.

'None the less,' he demanded, 'just exactly what is wrong with my piece? You haven't shown me your blacks, so I can't compare them.'

'By all means,' she replied, 'read this if you wish.'

032727 CHIANGKAISHEK CCINCC VICTORYWARDING CHINATS ADUNISTATES PRESS GUARANTEED SAFETY FORNPERSONS . . .

Richard read the smudged carbon-copy and automatically translated into plain English the terse cablese used because press messages to the United States cost thirty-five cents a word: *Shanghai, March 27, 1927: Generalissimo Chiang Kai-shek, Commander-in-Chief of the Nationalist armies sweeping to victory in China, told American correspondents today that he personally guaranteed the safety of foreign nationals in Shanghai, as well as the security of their property.*

He requested that the foreign powers withdraw their troops and warships, promising the Nationalists would safeguard the International Settlement and the French Concession. He thus indicated that the Nationalists had no designs on the foreign concessions and would make no incursions into them.

'I suppose that's what he said – literally.' Richard grudgingly conceded. 'I don't see much difference to my lead. Of course, mine's livelier, but this is a dramatic story.'

201

'Yours certainly is lively. Practically jumps off the page. Let me see it again.'

Shanghai's more than sixty thousand foreign residents today, Sunday [she read aloud], *awaited invasion by Nationalist and Communist troops surrounding the international concessions. Despite a last-minute – and hardly unequivocal – promise of non-interference by General Chiang Kai-shek, who commands the revolutionary forces, leaders of the community were not reassured. Their ears still rang with the vehement demands for immediate military conquest of the Foreign Settlement and the French Concession shrieked at the gigantic Bolshevik rally held Sunday afternoon at the West Gate just outside the French Concession.*

She broke off and observed: 'It's all how you look at it, Dick, isn't it? Where you place the emphasis.'

'Of course it is, my darling ninny. Your copy's from a Chinese point of view, even though you're writing for an American audience. They can't identify with Chinese. They want to know about foreigners, particularly Americans.'

'So, I can't see the facts because I'm Chinese?' Emily flared. 'These wretched slant eyes of mine, they can't see straight.'

'Don't be so touchy, Em. You know exactly what I meant.'

'Well, if writing for a specific audience means twisting the facts, I'm glad I'm not so professional – not so quick with a lie.'

'Now look here, my lady.' Richard's olive skin was mottled by anger. 'I've never been a liar – to you or in print! Show me a single untruth in that piece. It's only the viewpoint. Yours and mine are different.'

'And not only on politics I'm learning. Why . . .'

'Em, let's not blow this up into something between us,' he interrupted. 'Just consider the facts: The foreign community *is* racked with anxiety. The Communists *are* getting stronger every minute. Who knows whether Chiang Kai-shek can control them? Has he really turned against the Communists, as your piece implies? I ask you again: point out a single lie in my story.'

'Not outright lies. But what you leave out is telling.'

'What did I leave out?'

'You don't report the Generalissimo's saying he wanted the barbed-wire barricades around the concessions removed because they're an insult to the Chinese people, makes them look like savages. He also promised no mob would sweep into the concessions as it did in Hankow. You didn't write a word about that!'

'My Lord, Em! I said he called in American correspondents to reassure the Americans. And there's nothing in *your* piece about the word from London. The weak policy followed at Hankow and recently prevailing in Shanghai is now reversed. If the Nationalists want a fight, we'll carry the battle to them. Everything's changed since the Nanking outrages!'

Emily turned abruptly to stare at the map of China hanging above the mahogany bookcase. She clasped her hands before her so that Richard could not see them tremble. She spaced her words deliberately, but her voice quavered when she finally replied: 'You know very well that your stories on Nanking in *The Times* fanned anger. Rapine, and pillage, indeed! Wanton slaughter! A massacre! But it was Chinese who died by the hundreds – died in their own country under foreign shells! As for rape . . .'

'Steady, Em. Don't go wild.'

'As for rape,' she continued as if he had not spoken, 'no single case has been proved. You should know by now that foreign women are abhorrent, disgusting, to ignorant Chinese soldiers. They're deathly afraid. They think white women are witches or evil female spirits which destroy men. Sometimes I wish *this* pagan Chinese woman felt the same way about white men – at least a certain white man.'

'Emily, there's no need for a tirade!' He ignored her final remark. 'I've already corrected any misapprehension. I've reported there were no provable cases of rape.'

She turned again to the wall-map to gaze as if entranced at the expanse of Manchuria. Realizing she would not answer, Richard spoke conciliatingly: 'About that certain white man, Em. I'm sometimes afraid you feel . . .'

'It's anti-Chinese prejudice! Bare-faced racism!' She slashed across his words. 'Anyway, who'll notice a half-retraction?'

'Emily, how could I possibly want to marry you if I was anti-Chinese?' Richard was no longer feigning indignation. 'How can you talk such tommyrot?'

'It is not tommyrot! That's how you feel deep down, even if you don't realize it. Don't you know *anything* about elementary psychology?'

'Forget that psychological claptrap. Just tell me! Why would I be begging you to marry me if I was really anti-Chinese?'

'Who knows? Perhaps to debase me.' Despite herself, Emily smiled at that absurd thesis. 'Maybe to humble all Chinese by making me your slave.'

'You'll never be anyone's slave, my dear. And don't try to sidle away from the issue with a joke. If I'm anti-Chinese, how is it I look forward to half-Chinese children? Not because they'll be half-Chinese, but because they'll be half-you. Answer me that, milady.'

'Oh, Dick, you know as well as I do that's a smokescreen. Men just don't feel the same way about children as women do. Men don't really think about children until they arrive – if then. But women . . .'

'So that's why you won't marry me.' He laughed. 'It's your anti-white prejudice. Your racialism! Now I know.'

She, too, laughed, but the embers of her anger flared once again before dying: '*If* you really want to marry me. Do you?'

'Of course I do. I've told you a hundred times.'

'All right then! If you really want marriage, I *will* marry you. Though, God knows, it's foolhardy.' She turned from the wall-map. 'Before the end of the year. Any day in December – *if* you truly want it then!'

26

April 10, 1927

Emily and Julia piled eagerly into the fire-engine-red Plymouth Convertible Coupé with the folding dickey. Emily had impulsively paid $754 US for the car, almost the entire first dividend just received from the Women's Commercial Bank. With canvas top down, the ride was exhilarating when they took the convertible out for its first run on Sunday, April 10th and raced at thirty miles an hour through streets that were preternaturally quiet for seven in the evening.

They could not try it in the country or even in Frenchtown. The nervous Municipal Council had barred all the gates in the barbed-wire entanglements that encircled the Settlement, cutting off not only Chinese-ruled Greater Shanghai, but its sister concession. The Chinese workers and pleasure seekers who normally swarmed into both concessions were effectively excluded.

The echoing streets were depressing. Even worse was the uncertainty as to how Generalissimo Chiang Kai-shek would move. His army was encamped outside the city, and Communist-run workers' councils exercised power over all Greater Shanghai. The uprising a week earlier had been a spectacular success. All the districts surrounding the foreign enclaves were now under Communist control, and the foreigners were appalled. Adding to the distress and uncertainty, the Nationalists themselves were split. The right wing which was loyal to the Generalissimo had its headquarters in Nanking. The left wing, which was still allied with the Communists, claimed to govern all China from the trio of industrial cities called Wuhan.

Cast down by the empty city, Julia persuaded Emily that the evening could better be devoted to what Richard Hollings called 'liturgical feminine tasks' since it would, after all, be no fun showing off the convertible when there was no one to see it. Those tasks were hardly onerous in Shanghai. Washing out stockings and underclothes; mending and brushing dresses; shampooing hair – such chores were inescapable in America, but not in China. Amahs looked after clothing, and the hairdressers who came to the apartment were so cheap it would be sinful not to employ them. There was really nothing left for Julia but shaving her legs and armpits. Emily remarked with mildly malicious satisfaction on the Chinese lack of body hair.

In their dressing gowns the two were companionably listening to music from XMHA on the Atterbury Kent console radio. Julia was correcting examinations while Emily made notes for a short story. Lying between them on the red-and-yellow carpet from Chinese Turkestan, Johann Adam Schall von Bell twitched his plumed tail. The telephone's jangle shattered that peace.

'I hope I haven't woken you, Em,' Joshua Haleevie apologized.

'Not at all,' she assured him. 'We were just sitting around doing a few odd jobs.'

'May I drop over? This barn is getting on my nerves. So I thought of my two favourite damsels.'

'I can't think of anyone I'd rather see, Joshua.'

'About twenty minutes then.'

Hanging up, Emily realized that she had told the literal truth. Aside from the long absent Tommy, both Julia and herself were happiest to see Joshua. Despite her latest passionate reconciliation with Richard, Emily needed a respite from the emotional storms she and her lover stirred in each other. After completing her notes, she made for the minuscule kitchen. Fortunately, Joshua's latest lavish present, a very large tin of fresh Beluga caviar, was barely touched.

Julia was left alone. The telephone tinkled, feeble as a sick lamb bleating for its mother, and then fell silent. When Julia picked up the handset, she heard only the static of a vacant line and Central's interrogative: 'Number please.'

The tinkle sounded again, and she realized that it was the bell. Releasing the bolts, locks, and chains, Julia flung the iron-grilled door open—though she had been repeatedly warned to find out who was calling first.

She belatedly recalled those warnings when she saw a tall man in nondescript uniform looming menacingly in the half-lit hallway. It could be a White Russian mercenary seeking refuge or money—and not too particular about how he found them. As likely, one of the reinforcements sent to defend the Settlement. Rogues in the uniforms of eight nations had made the foreign community wary. Tales of rape were not told only of Nanking.

'What is it?' she demanded. 'I warn you I'm not alone!'

'Not another man?' Tommy stepped forward, and his features were lit by the glow from the open door. 'That would never do.'

Julia flung herself into his arms. Her face pressed into the harsh khaki twill, she smelled harsh tobacco, soot and sweat. Only a whiff of anti-septics recalled the fastidious doctor.

'Tommy! Tommy!' she repeated. 'You scared me half to death. Oh, Tommy, I'm so happy!'

'Darling! Darling!' he murmured. 'Sorry I scared you.'

Recovering her poise, she stepped back to study his worn features and said: 'But you look exhausted. Come in. There's only Emmy here.'

'*Only* Emmy? A fine way to talk about your putative sister-in-law!'

Emily, too, embraced him fiercely, and together they shepherded him into the apartment. Amid a flurry of questions, he was finally seated on the cane sofa sipping a whisky and soda and gobbling caviar on toast.

'They thought I'd better come down.' He did not say who *they* were. 'The army's medical services are a mess here. So many different units. And, of course, everything is in flux politically.'

'How did you ever get through the gates in uniform?' Julia asked. 'They're barred, especially to Nationalist officers.'

'Money – not love – still conquers all in Shanghai. I simply flung a dollar or two about. Put my cap in my bag and my raincoat over my tunic. So I wasn't in Nationalist uniform.' He paused for several moments before asking: 'Have you seen the old parents? Anything new on that front?'

Emily shook her head, almost ashamed that her rift with her parents had not miraculously healed. Her guilt over that break was no longer acute, but it was always with her, as integral a part of her being as her arms and legs.

She was wistful when she saw her friend's unreserved joy in her brother's return. Perhaps too intellectual, perhaps emotionally cold, she could not give herself so trustingly to Richard – or, perhaps, to any man.

Even Julia's posture declared her delight in subordinating herself to Tommy. Careless of her nakedness under her scarlet kimono, Julia poured herself over Tommy's shoulder as if her bones were liquefied. Her small, competent hands with the long fingers fluttered around him like restless doves. She stroked his cheek and then lighted on his hand; she touched his thigh and grasped his arm.

Her unfashionably long mahogany hair tumbled across her forehead, and her eyes glowed gentle green. Her normally open features appeared to have softened, angles and lines melting into curves.

Tommy was grimy after the railway journey from Nanking, and his face was blanched by exhaustion. Despite the stained khaki tunic crossed by the scuffed Sam Browne belt, he appeared very young, Exhaustion blurred the outlines of his long scholar's face, but his eyes shone when he looked at Julia.

All three were intensely political beings: Emmy, the passionate Nationalist; Julia, who waged her secret war in the service of the Communists; and Tommy, his allegiance not as clear-cut, who had, none the less, enlisted under the banner of the National Revolution. But they did not speak a word about politics. Indeed, Julia and Tommy were virtually silent, their glances and gestures heavy with meaning and with longing.

Emily was rising, ready to plead weariness and retire, when the doorbell tinkled the jaunty refrain of 'Pop Goes the Weasel'. That tune always announced Joshua Haleevie's arrival. Emily and Julia looked down at their kimonos in dismay and scurried for their bedrooms.

'By God, Tommy, it's good to see you.' Joshua exploded with delight after his first incredulity. 'Just the man! Such luck!'

Joshua and Tommy had always rubbed along well, close, but not intimate. Tommy looked hard at his friend. At thirty-four, Joshua was lean and elegant, his authority enhanced by the touch of grey in his black sideburns and the faint crinkles around his light-blue eyes. In his cream-silk dinner jacket he looked like a dashing cavalry officer or a brilliant young diplomat. Normally restrained or breezily nonchalant after a few drinks, he was tonight agitated and talkative.

'What ho, Tommy!' he exclaimed. 'I'm absolutely delighted to see you. Missed the sinks of iniquity, did you? Revisiting the scenes of your sins?'

Tommy glanced apprehensively at the closed bedroom doors before replying softly: 'Just got in tonight. And do forget about the past. Lurid it may have been, but not that lurid. What's up?'

'I came by to drop a few words to the ladies, who have apparently decamped.'

'They're just slipping into something less comfortable.'

'Tommy, I reckoned Em and Julie could carry the word, but you're just the lad I need. I've a bit of a problem. . .'

'Help if I can.'

'Now, how to put it?' Joshua pulled his ear in thought. 'Tell me, what do you think of the Supreme Lord and the secret societies?'

'Vermin!' Tommy exploded. 'He's ruined more lives with opium than even the Japanese. As many in a decade as Jardine, Matheson in a century.'

Tommy's indignation was briefly diverted when Emily and Julia reappeared more suitably dressed to receive gentleman callers. They had changed into less revealing dressing-gowns and applied the lipstick, mascara, and rouge respectable young ladies now used without pretence.

'Our American Lord Mayor Sterling Fessenden's made a deal to save the concessions.' After bestowing compliments on them, Joshua returned to his purpose. 'I pleaded against it, but I'm only an adviser on Chinese affairs. Fessenden's mind is made up. The Supreme Lord is to be our saviour. In return for five thousand rifles and a free hand, his secret societies will move against the Communists on Tuesday morning. The night before, the Supreme Lord will assassinate the leaders.'

'Not Chou En-lai?' Julia had a soft spot for the dashing Communist leader. 'We must warn him – immediately!'

'I imagine,' Tommy said drily, 'that's the general idea.'

'Fessenden and the Supreme Lord,' Joshua continued, 'want to present Generalissimo Chiang with a *fait accompli*. They reckon the Nationalists will be grateful – and leave the concessions alone.'

'The Supreme Gangster would never make a vital move like that without the Generalissimo's knowledge,' Tommy observed. 'They *are* blood-brothers, you know. He's pulling the wool over Fessenden's eyes.'

'That's interesting, Tommy, but it's not quite enough. What else have you got for me?'

'Honestly, Josh, I can only offer you an informed view.' Tommy said. 'No top secret information.'

'Tommy, it simply hadn't occurred to me that the Supreme Lord was misleading Fessenden about the Generalissimo's not knowing of the plot. I need your insights. What else?'

'Very little, I'm afraid. I'm sure you know that the left-wing Nationalists are now firmly allied with the Communists. And their troops are marching against the Generalissimo. After coming back from France, the chief of the civilian government is taking over again. He's already relieved the Generalissimo of all his offices. The government at Wuhan is totally opposed to the Generalissimo. Naturally he's setting up his own government in Nanking.'

'The Generalissimo's setting up shop in Nanking? Not Shanghai?'

'Of course not. Shanghai's the ultimate source of power. Any government of China must depend on Shanghai for revenue. But the Generalissmo can't make Shanghai his capital unless he moves against the concessions. And the last thing he wants is war with the foreign powers!'

'You're saying there's no real threat to the concessions?' Julia asked. 'It doesn't look that way here.'

'Of course, there's a threat,' Tommy replied. 'From hotheads on both sides. But not from the Generalissimo.'

Emily nodded and observed: 'So May Soong insists. She says her Gimo knows he can't rule China without money. He needs dollars right now – and he can only find dollars in Shanghai. You've heard that T.V. Soong's coming here from Wuhan to raise the money?'

'This is *very* useful, chums,' Joshua purred. 'You'd be amazed at our ignorance.'

'Now enlighten me, old chum,' Tommy demanded. 'Not to put too fine a point on it: What's your game? Why are you spilling the beans?'

'Tommy, I'm a Shanghailander. Above all I want to avoid bloodshed. I don't want the battle for China fought in Greater Shanghai – and spilling over into the concessions. I want you to warn Chou En-lai.'

'Chances are the Communists won't believe me,' Tommy cautioned. 'They've got their heads in the sand. They're still trying to co-operate with the Generalissimo, even though he's purging radicals and leftists throughout South China – arresting them, if not killing 'em.'

'How tragic!' Julia exclaimed. 'And what are the Communists doing, Tommy?'

'Very little,' he replied. 'They're still talking about patching up their misunderstandings with the right-wing Nationalists. Misunderstandings? The Gimo's sharpening his knife for their throats. I'll tell them, but another warning's almost superfluous. I'll bet even Chou En-lai won't believe me.'

27

April 13, 1927

Late in the evening of Wednesday, April 13, Dr Thomas Tan-ssu Howe, Surgeon-General of the Sixth Corps of the National Revolutionary Army presently on detached service, recalled with melancholy satisfaction that he had, at least, alerted the Communists to their peril. Flushed with the vanity of his first major command, Chou En-lai, who was only twenty-eight, has naturally said he knew all about it. Naturally, for no politician would admit to such a vital deficiency in his knowledge. The commander of some five thousand well armed men of the Workers' Inspection Corps was, further, inordinately proud of his intelligence service. His agents were virtually invisible, he boasted, because they were so commonplace: coolies, servants, midwives, artisans, and street urchins like Little Pow, who had led Tommy to the headquarters of the Shanghai General Labour Union in Chapei early on the morning of Monday, April 11. Since the Commissar was so aggressively confident, Tommy had delivered his warning and departed without further discussion.

Tommy stretched to ease his back, which was cramped after bending for hours over an improvised operating table. Peeling off his blood-caked rubber gloves, he rubbed his smarting eyes. Flickering paraffin lamps had provided the only light after the electricity was cut off. He had never wished to practise the butcher's trade called surgery. Yet he had been awash in blood since joining the National Revolutionary Army. The two days just past had been the worst.

He had not had the heart to reject Little Pow's plea to man the emergency dressing station close to the offices of the General Labour Union. He had, therefore, been working with only amateur assistance for the past thirty-six hours. Yet he could not recall a single individual

209

among a hundred-odd gravely injured women and children, as well as men, he had treated.

Only, Tommy wearily corrected himself, Little Pow himself could he remember: both legs broken by a hand-grenade, and a fragment lodged near the tibia, which could pierce the artery. Without a doctor, the waif would have bled to death. Though his present condition would occasion no concern in a hospital, it would deteriorate without proper care. But there was no hope of getting him to a hospital immediately.

The dressing station had been the washroom of a building like the Union's headquarters. The concrete slab along the wall was scooped out for washbasins, and the charcoal braziers in the canteen had boiled water to sterilize instruments. Because the damp air was now so still, the stench of blood and excrement overwhelmed the odours of the sparse antiseptics and anaesthetics. The grimy brick walls and the gritty concrete floor littered with blood-stained dressings made Tommy feel he would never be clean again.

He tamped tobacco into his meerschaum pipe with a blood-rimed thumbnail and pushed aside the burlap curtain that cut off his makeshift operating theatre. He shuddered when the rough fabric prickled against his palm.

His remaining patients lay on straw mats on the concrete floor. Some were still, but others muttered and tossed. An old man with a bandage across his eyes keened a monotonous Buddhist prayer.

Little Pow lay under a paraffin lantern in the far corner. A crudely printed book of revolutionary cartoons was open on the tattered quilted-cotton coat covering him. One small hand with ragged nails guarded that treasure, though his eyes were closed.

When Tommy's soles grated on the concrete floor, the urchin's mulberry bruised eyelids lifted. The lantern above him swayed, and his features were haggard in its capricious light. His stubborn chin was slack in the inverted triangle of his face. But his fever-bright eyes welcomed Tommy, and his bloodless lips smiled.

Little Pow shook his head at the index finger Tommy raised to enjoin silence and spoke slowly: 'Tan Yee-sheng ... Dr Tom, I can't sleep any more. Please come and talk to me.'

'All right, Pow. Talking can't do you any harm.' As he squatted, the doctor realized that he, too, needed human warmth, for the world was not only wounds and incisions, pain and death. He added: 'Well, Pow, it's been quite a couple of days, hasn't it? After your performance, lad, we'll have to change your name. Not Little Pow any more, but Big Pow.'

By changing the intonation of the word *pow* Tommy changed its significance so that *pow* no longer meant a bubble, but a gun. Big Gun meant the same in Chinese as in English.

The youth's grin revealed his delight at that accolade from the man he loved almost as much as he did his saviour John Pavernen. Tommy's throat tightened. This battle-scarred veteran, who had survived three campaigns in just three months, was still a child.

'What's happening?' Little Pow demanded weakly. 'I can't remember much. . .'

'What do you remember, Big Shot? Tell me and I'll fill the rest in for you – what I know.'

It would be good for the urchin to talk, rather than brooding in silence on the catastrophe that had overwhelmed his small world. Besides, Tommy was eager to learn the details of the great events.

The terror had broken after weeks of manoeuvring – with the Communists and the left-wing Nationalists behaving foolishly and provocatively. Although the combined left had courted its own destruction, Tommy believed the burden of the guilt for the past forty-eight hours of bloodshed lay on the shoulders of the enigmatic Generalissimo Chiang Kai-shek. Little Pow had, however, seen the reality of the struggle while he was himself operating in the dressing station.

'You'll be safe here till morning, Pow,' he said. 'If you really can't sleep, why not tell me what you saw?'

'I've been trying to tell you for the past ten minutes but you keep interrupting,' Little Pow declared in exasperation. 'First, tell me, what do you know?'

'Let me see. You came for me about six yesterday morning, didn't you? We'd already heard from Hollings . . .' Tommy ignored Little Pow's grimace of distaste '. . . that it had started. Hundreds of secret society thugs had moved out of Frenchtown, wearing blue work-clothes, and armbands reading: *Worker!* All carried pistols or rifles. About the same time, the Generalissimo's regular Nationalist troops wearing the same disguise crossed the Settlement in big trucks. They were heading for Chapei, the workers' stronghold. At least a thousand, maybe more.'

'No need to guard the Settlement perimeter, our Communist leaders said,' Little Pow observed bitterly. 'They said the gates were all barred.'

'To stop your lot getting into the Settlement, *not* to keep the murderers in.'

'The first we knew at headquarters, Doctor Tom, was the shooting in the distance.' Little Pow picked up the tale. 'Soon we got reports that the enemy knew exactly where our posts were – and was attacking without warning. Everywhere from Chapei to Woosung, even way the hell and gone on the Yangtze. There were some Nationalist troops in uniform, the Generalissimo's troops, but most were phony workers, the Supreme Lord's musclemen. Headquarters was a terrible muddle. Even comrade Chou En-lai was dumbfounded for a few minutes. Then they hit us at headquarters. . . .'

Listening to Little Pow's slangy account, Tommy envisagd the embattled commander of the Workers' Inspection Corps. Chou En-lai's self-confidence turned to confusion and fear when the windows were smashed by the enemy's first shots. He dropped to the floor, immobilized by the volleys, and looked in vain for an escape route. He could not counter-attack because surprise was overwhelming and his strong-points were being crushed.

'Little Pow!' he shouted.

211

'Comrade Chou!'

'Throw away your armband and wriggle out the back way. Save yourself. But first get to as many posts as you can – and tell them to save themselves. Also, your friend Dr Howe. Take him to the emergency dressing station.'

Disobeying orders, Little Pow crept round to the rear of the attacking force after regretfully hiding the golf brogues Julia had given him. Crouched behind a dustbin in the brilliant dawn, he watched the men in workers' blue firing at the Union's headquarters. Volleys replied through the improvised loopholes where the defenders had pushed the ventilating grates out of the walls.

Little Pow's hopes flared for an instant. But the defenders could not hold out against an enemy now reinforced by Nationalist soldiers in uniform. Two squads were setting up tubes that looked like bigger versions of One-Arm Sutton's trench-mortar. On the point of firing, they were stopped by a colonel with a sunburst of medal ribbons and an anachronistic sabre. He pointed at the neighbouring buildings, obviously afraid that they would be damaged by mis-aimed mortar-bombs.

Little Pow then knew the enemy had won. He had learned at the Workers' Night School that the enemy cared far more for property than for human beings. The Nationalists must none the less be certain of victory when they did not use all their weapons because they were afraid of damaging buildings. He was convinced that he would never again see his comrades – particularly comrade Chou En-lai, who had joked grimly about his name's standing first on the enemy's death-list.

Slinging his faded cotton jacket around his neck, Little Pow rooted beneath the bamboo scaffolding that clothed a tenement under construction. The site was deserted, for all Chapei's workers had gone to ground when they heard the first volleys. He found a bamboo carrying-pole, an empty paraffin tin, and a sack of plaster. He slung the tin from one end of the pole after filling it with water and the sack from the other end.

Settling that burden on his shoulder, he trotted past the North Railway Station towards the gate on Elgin Road that gave passage through the barbed-wire, the sandbags and the pillboxes sealing off the International Settlement. Any reactionary thugs he encountered would dismiss him as a young coolie too stupid to stay under shelter.

But the ferociously bearded Sikh sentries guarding the Settlement refused to open their gates. Little Pow shrugged at the confirmation of his fears, and water slopped on the dusty road.

He turned and trotted eastwards towards the vacant lot between the Public Works Department depot, which lay inside the barbed wire, and the Municipal School, which lay outside. Seeing no sentries, he loped boldly towards the weed-grown chain-link fence.

His small figure vanished from view when it dropped into the nullah, the concrete storm-ditch that carried off flash floods. Crawling through the mud and debris that clogged the nullah, Little Pow found that he could just squeeze through where the ditch crossed the chain-link fence.

He squirmed under the wire, drew the carrying pole after him, and set out for Kiukiang Road.

'I couldn't stay away from our headquarters, Doctor Tom,' Little Pow whispered hoarsely. 'I went back after I brought you here to the emergency station. If I'd stayed away, I wouldn't be lying here all broken now.'

That laboured confession carried Tommy back to the reality of the half-lit dressing station in the building two streets from the conquered headquarters of the General Labour Union. Having finally stopped keening, the blinded old man slept – and the air bubbled harshly in his throat. Tommy poured tea from a thermos, and Little Pow spoke compulsively: 'After I left you here, Doctor Tom, I went back to headquarters to see what . . .'

Little Pow joined the crowd gawking at the pock-marked headquarters of the Shanghai General Labour Union after the shooting had stopped. He was still playing the ragged young coolie, the bamboo carrying-pole still cocked over his shoulder. That protective camouflage was hardly necessary, for a careless festive spirit ruled the victors. Phony workers and uniformed regulars were gleefully toasting each other in looted beer and rice wine.

Dishevelled and grimy, Chou En-lai still stood out among the captives straggling between files of soldiers commanded by a sergeant-major. His well-cut grey tunic was torn, and one sleeve was ripped away. But his undaunted authority still commanded his subordinates – and invited the blows of his captors.

Chou En-lai smoothed his hair and smiled easily. His expression did not alter when a Nationalist captain wearing the aiguillette of a general's aide informed the sergeant-major: 'I'll take charge of this prisoner. They want him at Garrison Headquarters immediately.'

'So you're my gaoler now?' Chou En-lai lightly asked. 'You were a good student, Shih, but who would have thought at Whampoa . . .'

'I'm afraid so!' The officer glared at the sergeant-major, who was patently unhappy at being deprived of his chief prisoner. 'Fate makes its own rules.'

Six soldiers with bayonet-tipped rifles formed a box around the Communist leader, and the detachment moved off sharply. By the time the bemedalled colonel commanding the Nationalists emerged from the captured building, guards and prisoner had vanished around a corner where stood a shuttered herbal medicine shop. After questioning his sergeant-major, the colonel shrugged elaborately at the vagaries of the high command.

Observing that gesture from the corner of his eye, Little Pow scurried down a lane that was a short cut to the road to Garrison Headquarters. A half-dozen gunmen wearing the armbands of counterfeit workers were lounging in cane chairs in front of a wine-shop whose shutters had been pried open. Otherwise the road was empty.

'Come 'ere, boy!' A gunman with a scarlet face waved an earthen-ware flask. 'Come 'n 'ave a drink.'

'Did you see a file of soldiers?' Little Pow asked. 'Not a minute ago?'

The gunmen shook their heads, and Pow darted towards the junction. That street, too, was deserted. Twenty seconds later, the detachment debouched from an alley. The tattered prisoner had disappeared.

The bewildered urchin counted six soldiers and two officers. Curiosity driving out fear, he slipped behind a wall plastered with cigarette advertisements. The detachment marched briskly past his hiding place, hob-nailed boots striking sparks from the cobblestones and arms smartly swinging in unison. Both officers were rigidly erect.

Little Pow muffled a gasp. The officers' peaked caps were low on their foreheads, shadowing their features. None the less, Chou En-lai's strong jaw was unmistakable between the choker collar and the black visor.

Little Pow did not follow the detachment. He did not want to know where his commander was hiding. If he were captured, he would not be able to tell anyone where Chou En-lai had taken refuge – no matter how he was tortured.

'Now, Big Shot,' Tommy commanded, 'it's time you had a sleep.'

'Only a little more to tell, Doctor Tom.' Little Pow shook his head stubbornly and resumed: 'On Tuesday night I didn't want to come anywhere near you. I was carrying danger on my shoulders. So I went to earth. You can always find a place to sleep behind a hoarding or on a construction site. The sidewalk's not so good. Some cops don't like it. They kick you awake all the time, so it's not very restful.

'Next morning the rumours were flying, mostly carried by the servants and the workers at Garrison Headquarters. General Chou En-lai had disappeared, and nobody knew who that captain was, the one who took him away. Also the rightists were already shooting prisoners in batches of five. Maybe a hundred – maybe a lot more. Maybe thousands lay dead on the streets.

'A lot of little union leaders were still alive and free, though. They didn't have the foggiest idea what to do. Finally somebody – God knows who – somebody decided to call a general strike. And somebody else got the bright idea of a protest march on Garrison Headquarters. Some great idea!'

A general strike, Tommy knew, was a last resort. That terrible weapon could hurt the working class even more than the exploiting class. Moreover, it could be impotent. After the May 30th Massacre of 1925, a general strike had briefly paralysed the Settlement and Frenchtown. But the foreign rulers were constrained by some morality. What good would it do against Chinese overlords who never dreamed they could some day stand before the bar of public opinion? The Nationalists would simply crush the strike with massacres – not caring at all what others felt and feeling no compunction themselves. How shame the unashamed rightists? How touch the consciences of secret society thugs who had no consciences?

The new general strike was already faltering when several thousand men and women assembled for the protest march at noon. But those militants were still confident.

Little Pow slipped on the armband with the red ideograms that read: *Special Messenger*. He straightened his threadbare jacket, clasped its choker collar around his skinny neck, and ran his fingers through his coarse hair. Although he was trying to act nonchalant, his large eyes opened even wider in astonishment. His neighbours on both sides carried old Mannlicher rifles with long barrels, which he had seen distributed surreptitiously by the Soviet Consulate.

'What are *those* things for?' he finally asked. 'Why rifles? The whole idea is a peaceful march, isn't it?'

'Little Comrade, we're not planning to shoot,' the man on his right replied. 'Not that we wouldn't if it came to it. But, for now, we're just showing that the people possess their own powerful armed force! Also demonstrating that the fearless soldiers of the revolution cannot be intimidated by clubs and guns. Got it?'

The dismayed urchin nodded. The pat slogans his neighbour parroted could inspire revolutionaries to defy danger and overwhelming odds. But mindless derring-do was precisely what the present situation did *not* require. The man on his left, who greeted him with a marked northern accent, was apparently a former warlord soldier. A number of deserters had been recruited into the people's militia by large bounties. He was marching between a fool and a mercenary into grave peril.

Yet the tread of thousands of feet in straw-sandals and cloth-shoes was the anthem of the revolution. Little Pow straightened his back and surveyed the moving ranks. Too many rifle barrels bristled above blue-clad shoulders. Still, all were slung; none was grasped ready for immediate action. The presence of women and children further demonstrated the peaceful intent of the march.

'Freedom or death!' Little Pow shouted. 'Victory to the Revolution!'

A parade marshal glared at that violation of collective discipline, and the urchin looked away. Along the top of an immense hoarding tattered posters proclaimed the virtues of Seven Star, Martyr, and Triple Longevity cigarettes. Other posters prudently recommended the healing magic of Special Number One Cough Syrup. Beneath that upper fringe, white paint had obliterated the Communist slogans printed only two weeks earlier.

Now a two-storey-tall hero in a Sun Yat-sen jacket flourished the white-sun flag of the Nationalists over figures representing the evils he had felled: militarism, capitalism, and landlordism. Unappeased, he was trampling a supine Communist Party with one foot and kicking a bloated imperialist with the other.

The enemy was even stealing the propaganda of the Communist revolution! Dejected, Little Pow looked down at his grimy feet in straw-sandals. He responded feebly when the parade marshal called out the next slogan: 'Free our innocent brothers!'

What possible impression could words make upon the stony hearts of oppressors? How could a peaceful demonstration win the release of the unjustly imprisoned?

None the less, Little Pow shouted loudly when the procession approached Nationalist Headquarters. His shouts helped dispel his fear of the atrocities perpetrated behind those yellow-brick walls topped with broken glass and wicked spirals of barbed wire. He undid his choker collar and shouted even louder: 'Free our innocent brethren!'

Little Pow could see only the back of the man in front of him. He was taken by surprise when a volley of rifle shots crashed in his ears. An instant later the man in front was hurled to the cobblestones, and Little Pow could see soldiers in Nationalist khaki working their rifle bolts and firing on their officer's command. He shrank in terror when the former warlord soldier on his left dropped silently. He turned to flee as the man on his right unlimbered his clumsy Mannlicher. That hapless hero was spun around and felled by a shot before he could level his rifle.

Little Pow dropped to the pitted cobblestones, where slimy straw and yellow hillocks of horse manure were all he could see. Lifting his head warily, he saw that volleys had scythed the revolutionary ranks like rice stalks. More than a third of the marchers lay on the cobblestones wounded, dying or dead.

To be captured would also be a sentence of death. He rose and bolted. A rattle of shots pursued him. He hurled himself down on the cobblestones, unintentionally performing a somersault.

The heavy military bullet took Little Pow in the left calf. Anaesthetized by shock, he ran on for several seconds unaware that he had been hit. Then an explosion flung him down. When the pain struck, he screamed. The next instant, darkness claimed him.

'So they brought you to me, Big Shot, and that's all there is to tell.' Tommy Howe wanted to put an end to the tale that was agitating his patient. 'Now you *must* rest!'

'All right. I'm sorry. I didn't see the comrades who brought me here.'

'That slug and the grenade fragments, they'll have to come out. But there's no rush.'

Actually, there was every reason for rushing. Infection threatened, and the metal splinters could shift and rupture an artery. An X-ray was essential. Yet tomorrow was only ten hours away. He could then shift the youth to Shanghai General Hospital, for the fighting would certainly have ended.

'Thanks, Doctor Tom,' Little Pow whispered. 'Many thanks. And I'm not even your servant. You care for me, though I have no claim.'

'You are a servant, a friend, of my sister and my . . . ah . . . Miss Joo-li. The Howe family will look after you, Big Shot.'

Embarrassed by his own emotion, Tommy laid the drowsy youth's hand on the quilted-cotton overcoat that was his coverlet. It was time to see to his other patients. When a groaning door announced a late arrival, he shook his head wearily. Another patient at this time of night was

216

almost too much to bear. He resignedly pushed aside the coarse burlap curtain.

The paraffin lamps were flickering low, but Tommy clearly saw khaki uniforms. The Nationalists were also bringing their wounded to him.

'Yes, sergeant!' he said peremptorily. 'What is it?'

'*Ha Yee-sahng* . . .' the sergeant asked in Cantonese. 'Doctor Howe, is it?'

'Yes. What is it?'

'You're to come with us, Doctor Howe. Under arrest. Garrison Commander's orders.'

'Do you know who I am?' Tommy demanded. 'You couldn't – not and come to arrest me.'

'Son of Howe Dan-erh. Colonel in Medical Corps. Surgeon-General of Sixth Corps now on detached service. That right?'

'Yes, of course. So you see, don't you . . .'

'That's the man I'm ordered to arrest. Come along, prisoner.'

'And my patients? Who'll look after them? Some are in critical condition.'

'And all are Communist pigs. Let them learn to pray. Maybe Buddha'll look after them.'

28

April 28, 1927

'They could always come to us, *mon cher*,' the rotund French colonel twinkled. 'No Frenchman has ever disappointed a lady in distress.'

Joshua Haleevie grinned down at him and replied: 'My dear chap, there's no room. You've already got all the bordellos in Frenchtown that'll fit. Besides, they'd soon go bust. Couldn't manage the squeeze.'

The forthcoming lottery, they had already agreed, was farcical. Where else on earth would the authorities yield grudgingly to pressure to padlock houses of prostitution – and then arrange that only one-fifth of some six hundred need close in the first two years? Only Shanghai would strike that fine balance between civic virtue and commercial enterprise. Only the International Settlement would select the first victims by drawing lots from a spinning globe made of brass wire.

'Squeeze?' the Colonel's round cheeks flushed pink like an angry baby's. 'Corruption is no worse than the Settlement's, *mon cher.*'

'Far worse, as you well know.' Joshua's grin veiled his distaste for a European enclave that was as corrupt as any warlord province. 'A little opium's fine. But an administration crammed with addicts! Natural, I suppose, since the Supreme Lord of the Floodgate – and the opium traffic – is your honoured resident.'

'Not a word against Monsieur the Supreme Lord!' The colonel's protest was superficially jocular. 'Without him where would we be? The Bolsheviki would have overrun us all.'

Had Tommy Howe, Joshua wondered again, actually relayed his warning to Chou En-lai? He did not know, for both the Commissar and the Doctor had vanished into the political maelstrom. The reasonably efficient intelligence service of the Special Branch of the Settlement Police

218

could only report ignorance regarding their fate, although it was two weeks since the rightists' counter-coup.

Shanghai was, however, nothing if not resilient – and callous. Shortly after the massacres, there came this ribald lottery. The director of the Revenue Service, who was supervising the drawing, had wanted to hold it at the Race Club. But the Committee had decreed that nothing involving houses of ill fame might sully premises hallowed by the presence of virtuous wives and daughters. The venue had therefore been shifted to the apricot-plush lobby of the new Empire Theatre overlooking Soochow Creek. The decor was a mélange of the 22nd Dynasty of Ancient Egypt, Art Nouveau, and Twentieth-Century Industrial, Joshua felt, while the spectacle itself was surrealistic.

Despite their official disapproval, several stewards of the Race Club were in attendance. At the chrome-and-crystal bar, a half-dozen ruddy taipans were drinking Veuve Cliquot with the two Emmenberg sisters. Those young matrons were reputed to entertain their intimate friends by bathing in champagne in silver hipbaths placed on their dining-room tables. A score of prowling madams were alert for fresh custom in the predominantly masculine throng. Sleek compradors in silk long-gowns, furtive secret society chieftains, and flashy modern businessmen dominated the Chinese contingent, within which remarkably intricate side-bets were already circulating.

Full, as always, of bravado, Elizaveta Alexandrovna Yavalenka had wanted to attend the drawing. 'I must be there to see my fate determined,' she had throatily declared, herself chuckling a little at that melodramatic statement. Joshua had persuaded her that she would make herself ridiculous if she appeared at the drawing quaking with fear that her house would be closed. Such a public appearance, he had stressed, would make it absolutely impossible for them to marry if she should ever change her mind. She had finally yielded – upon Joshua's promise to telephone the instant the drawing concluded.

Neither Emily Howe nor Julia Pavernen felt any inhibition at attending. To Emily the great bordello lottery was a choice tidbit for the readers of the *Philadelphia Public Ledger*, in the nicest way, of course, and a prime slice of life for her largely female Chinese readers. Julia was candidly fascinated by this latest aberration of her beloved Shanghai. The pair drifted through the throng, nodding to acquaintances and smiling at friends.

Emily's green-satin *cheongsam*, slit to the thigh, daringly accentuated her high bosom and her rounded hips. The miniature white-jade sceptre pinned at her shoulder was set with rubies as brilliant as her fixed smile.

She was deliberately – and uncharacteristically – flamboyant in the hope of quashing any rumours about her brother's fate. She believed that public notice of his disappearance would make his unknown captors more obdurate. Fortunately, not ten persons were aware that Tommy had returned to Shanghai at all. Richard Hollings had agreed after a brief struggle not to speculate about Tommy's whereabouts, neither in print nor conversation. Amid great historical events Richard was, for-

219

tunately, not concerning himself with trivia. He had even disdained to attend the lottery, leaving Emily free to make a show of her false gaiety.

Julia herself staunchly refused to admit that her lover might be dead. Because Little Pow had also disappeared, her idiosyncratic logic concluded that both must be held in secret by the same abductors, probably the Floodgate Fraternity. It was only a matter of time, she firmly believed, until Donald Howe received a demand for ransom.

Although she was neither wife nor fiancée, she could still help Emily prop up the carefree façade. The flame-red sheath that flared into pleats at her knees was a declaration of joy, as was the long string of pearls that filled the deep V décolletage and the peacock feather in her mahogany hair. Her heavy make-up camouflaged the ravages of two weeks of near terror broken by sodden slumber when Lao Zee pressed tiny black opium pills on her.

Emily drifted away to talk with a middle-aged lawyer called Mouthpiece Woo. He had good secret society connections and might know something about Tommy. Beside Joshua, Julia smiled and smiled and smiled like a demented chorus girl – and watched the spectacle with horrified fascination.

Under iridescent chandeliers of Czechoslovakian crystal, slabs of sandstone divided the apricot-silk walls into three murals. In one side-panel golden unicorns flirted with pink dragons amid silver birches. In the other the emerald eyes of rainbow phoenixes regarded a carpet of sea-anemones with astonishment. The central panel enshrined a figure that combined Michelangelo's God in the Sistine Chapel with the Jade Emperor of Heaven in cheap lithographs – and also managed to suggest a go-getting entrepreneur.

Tart-tongued Dick Hollings had taken a long look and declared that it embodied Shanghai's motto: 'For God, for China, and for Mammon!'

The brass-wire globe containing the ballots stood before a curved wall covered by orange satin flecked with gold. Hanging against that medieval background were dazzlingly chromed wheels, pistons, drive-shafts, and axles that celebrated the industrial Twentieth Century.

A gong sounded. Deserting the chrome-and-crystal bar with its caviar, smoked salmon, oysters and lobsters, the company moved towards the globe: taipans and their Chinese compradors; ponces, gunmen, and gang-lords; commanders and colonels. Tense with apprehension, twenty or so proprietresses of the more notable houses of pleasure were already standing before the shining wire globe. Each of the six hundred and eighty-three brass capsules within the globe contained a slip bearing the name of a different house.

A Portuguese croupier from the Golden Wheel Club rose to bow to half-mocking applause. Only him did all trust, albeit grudgingly, to draw the names. Taipans were excluded because every major firm had connections with the houses – as landlords, creditors, underwriters, insurers, or sponsors. Municipal employees were excluded because their notoriously low salaries made them eminently bribable. For various good reasons other categories were also excluded: compradors, military officers, lawyers, bankers, and even physicians.

The lamps dimmed, and spotlights lanced the smoke-laden air. Their beams splashed red, blue and yellow on the globe, which was now spinning so fast the brass wires seemed to melt together. Six hundred and eight-three brass capsules crashed in a prolong peal of thunder.

'Little Orphan Annie!' The corpulent croupier drew the first capsule. 'Little Orphan Annie's to fold!'

'Pipped at the post.' A disgusted British vice-consul tore up the slip recording his bet on the survival of Orphan Annie's, which boasted: *A friendly welcome, a reasonable price, and a warm embrace!*

'Eskimo Nell's! Eskimo Nell's is for the deep six!'

A Swedish procuress shepherding two seventeen-year-old platinum-blondes grinned with delight. She not only hated the buxom Berliner who owned Eskimo Nell's, but considered the name an infringement upon her monopoly of the frozen north.

'Venus!' the croupier called out. 'Venus of Lappland is going to shut up shop.'

The Swede started in shock. Recovering rapidly, she began calculating how soon she and her friend from Berlin could club together to set up a gentlemen's boarding house.

'Hop In Woe!' The croupier intoned the name of the Chinese-owned house, but only the blank-eyed gang-lords cared. Then he selected the next capsule, opened it and paused almost imperceptibly before calling out: 'Starlight! Starlight's wiped out!'

Accepting a goblet of champagne from Joshua, Julia was surprised to see his hand tremble. A froth of bubbles spilled down his sleeve. A moment later he was smiling unconcernedly – and she wondered if she had imagined his momentary discomfiture.

The sphere spun again, and the croupier extracted another capsule. Deftly unscrewing its cover, he smoothed the rice-paper slip with his thumb before reading: 'Little Redwing! Little Redwing's grounded!'

A Japanese major in dress uniform flourished his winning slip and demanded champagne for his party of seven. Though a petite geisha in a green-satin kimono put her finger to her lips, her countrymen's whoops of joy drowned out the name of the next unfortunate.

'Star . . .' The croupier appeared nonplussed, but recovered to read firmly: 'Sturgeon! Virgin Sturgeon's for the high jump!'

Joshua turned abruptly to Julia and remarked: 'No point in hanging about all night, is there? When you've seen one drawn, you've seen them all. I'm off.'

Julia waved to Emily, who was standing frozen-faced beside the lawyer called Mouthpiece Woo. She had learned nothing regarding Tommy.

'Whew, I'm glad that's over!' Joshua patted his forehead with his handkerchief. 'Never again!'

Emily lifted her eyebrows, and Julia asked: 'What's over, Josh? They're still in there.'

'And will be half the night,' he acknowledged. 'But I suppose I can tell you two. Mum's the word, though. When he called Starlight the first time, it was bad. But when it came up again! Whew! Lucky he's

221

such a quick-witted little chap.'

Emily was still preoccupied, but Julia exclaimed: 'You mean the first Starlight was really the Ikra?'

'Go to the head of the class. When the Ikra came up, he palmed the slip and substituted the one he had already written out – the Starlight Club. Then he almost called it again when Starlight really came up. Miladies, the strain has hurt me more than the pay-off. However, our croupier friend can now set up his own house if so inclined.'

'*You*, Josh?' Emily emerged from her reverie. 'You bribed the croupier not to call out the Ikra? How underhanded! How gallant!'

'Never again! I'd be better off if the Ikra was padlocked.'

'Joshua, do you really believe Liz would . . .'

Emboldened by the compulsive confidences of the normally reticent Joshua, Julia almost told him she was convinced that Elizaveta would never marry him. She was saved from that indiscretion by a glimpse of Donald Howe's emerald-green Rolls Royce parked before the theatre. Beside the uniformed chauffeur she saw the silver mane of Old Woo, the major-domo of Harmony Hall.

Emily dashed forward, her hands outstretched. Old Woo stepped out, majestic in his white long-gown with the green seal of the House of Howe on his breast. He took Emily into his arms for an instant. The next instant, he was again the impassive upper servant.

'*Yuelin Hsiu-yjeh, ho-jyeow* . . .' He spoke softly. 'Miss Emily, it's been so long. It seems even longer than when you were in America.'

'You've come to take me back?' The crusading feminist reverted to the dutiful daughter. 'They want to see me, the parents? At last, they want to see me!'

'Miss Emily, I have not come for you.' Old Woo dropped his voice so that the Small Mistress's barbarian friends would not overhear him. 'Whatever they wish, your esteemed parents cannot send for you. Not until you stop your foolishness. But they do miss you – terribly.'

'Then what have you come for?' She was almost brusque in her disappointment. 'Something about Tommy? Is there news of Tommy?'

'I'm sorry, Miss Emily.' Old Woo reluctantly crushed that new hope. 'I have been instructed to take your foreign friend to see the Master and the Mistress. She will come, won't she?'

'Oh, she'll come all right. But why, Old Woo? You must know. You know everything.'

'I really couldn't say . . . not even for you. I just don't know.'

Julia regretted her frivolous red dress when she entered the circular foyer of Harmony Hall. Although the *cheongsams* of emancipated Chinese ladies flaunted their beautiful legs, Emily's mother would undoubtedly be shocked by the expanse of thigh her short skirt showed no matter how carefully she sat. She was even more conscious of the valley between her breasts bared by the plunging V neckline. Not even the most daring Chinese women showed their bosoms.

222

Taboos, like fashion itself, were a matter of taste. She feared, though, that Eurydice and Donald Howe would believe her brief scarlet dress demonstrated that she was untouched by Tommy's disappearance. Yet why should she care what the Howes thought? They would in any event never sanction Tommy's marrying a woman who was foreign and, therefore, odious.

If she herself should eventually wish to marry him! Emily and Dick's stormy relationship was no testimonial for life with a Chinese partner. Tommy was, of course, totally different. Still, it was not just because Emily was high-strung. Chronic guilt at her relationship with a foreigner also made her irritable. Would Tommy also feel guilty? For that matter would he still want to marry her when he returned?

Donald Howe was rotund in a grey-cotton long-gown when he rose from the purple-flowered cretonne sofa to welcome Julia. His expression was bland, but he repeatedly wiped his black-rimmed spectacles. Eurydice's smile was tentative, easily outshone by the diamond-rimmed lavalière watch on her green-satin bosom, and she blotted her forehead with a scrap of lace. Her hesitant greeting conveyed the same message as her husband's excessively firm handshake: the Howes were just as ill at ease as Julia was.

But traditional etiquette calmed them. Eurydice poured straw-pale tea and offered pastries filled with crystallized dates. Donald punctiliously inquired after not only Julia's health and her Uncle John, but the health of her parents, whom he had never seen. After their urgent summons, the Howes appeared totally unhurried.

Eurydice shattered that illusion by asking: 'My miserable daughter? She is well?'

Touched by that breach of Confucian reticence, Julia told the anxious mother how Emily spent her days. Somehow, she managed to omit any reference to Richard Hollings, who took up a good part of Emily's days and a greater part of her nights.

'Emily loves you dearly,' Julia concluded. 'I know she misses you terribly!'

'Tell her . . .' Eurydice began, but Donald broke in: 'You need not tell our disobedient daughter that she has broken our hearts. But you *must* tell her something else.'

Although she resented his autocratic tone, Julia nodded docilely.

'We must have Yuelin's assistance,' he continued. 'She is our only remaining hope of finding Thomas. Otherwise . . .'

Moved by Eurydice's muffled sob, Julia silently choked back her own tears. Clawing in her clutch-bag for a handkerchief, her fingers encountered her ivory cigarette-holder. She jammed a Chesterfield into the mouthpiece and accepted the lighted match Donald offered with obvious disapproval. Though the smoke stung her eyes and throat, she listened with outward composure

'. . . just intimations, but it is our only information,' Donald said. 'It is possible that Generalissimo Chiang Kai-shek is holding Thomas. Our last report came from a wounded coolie who saw them take Thomas

223

away. The men were Nationalist soldiers.'

'Why can't you ask the Generalissimo?' Julia was still puzzled by Chinese indirection. 'Or T.V. Soong. He *is* Minister of Finance, after all!'

'T.V.?' Donald expelled a frustrated breath, and Eurydice interjected: 'He's only interested in one thing: extorting money from every Chinese capitalist to keep his precious Generalissimo going. You know . . .'

'Fifty million from Shanghai already – and no end in sight.' Donald was only momentarily diverted from his son's fate by the threat to his pocketbook. 'But that doesn't matter. Only Thomas is important. The *only* way is through Mayling Soong. Chiang Kai-shek cannot deny the pleas of the lady he's begging to become his wife. Now Yuelin must go to May and . . .'

'You really think May Soong will do it for Emmy? May's a pretty tough cookie.'

Donald continued as if she had not spoken: '. . . go to May and beg her to intercede. Also, she may tell May that a million dollars is available to . . . Perhaps more to . . .'

'Bribe May Soong?' Julia interjected. 'Is that a good idea?'

'A contribution, not a bribe. Generalissimo Chiang needs money to pay his armies and finance his new government in Nanking. A contribution is my patriotic duty. But I cannot embarrass the Generalissimo by approaching him directly. That *would* appear to be unseemly pressure, you see.'

Emily's heart hesitated, skipped, and then raced as she entered the office in the *Daily News* building with Adam the mastiff on her heels. He was worth it, she told herself, worth even the break with her parents, the lean figure with the smudge on his forehead where his ink-stained fingers had pushed back his rebellious forelock. His dark-brown eyes glinting, Richard looked like a cavalier on a disputed battlefield. He was not often comforting, and he was certainly not dependable, but he was always exciting.

'Bloody animal!' he intoned, and Adam rolled on his back in ecstasy, yipping in a falsetto ridiculous for his great size. 'Bloody, bloody animal!'

'Hullo darling!' Richard kissed her lightly. 'Back from the knocking-shop auction already? How'd it go?'

'Adequately, but I left early.' Somehow, his insouciant manner jarred upon her. 'What are you writing tonight?'

'The Generalissimo's moving fast, mopping up the Reds everywhere – except Wuhan, of course. A nice bloody purge: hundreds, maybe thousands already dead. And he's cobbling together his new government in Nanking.'

'Considering your gift for sensationalism, you really should have covered the lottery.' She laughed to show she was teasing.

'Of course, my love! Are you writing it?'

'I guess not. Too hard to explain to the sober citizens of Philadelphia – and too risqué. Definitely not!'

'Definitely yes! My dear girl, write it as farce or a moral homily, but write it. Titilate your staid Philadelphians. Sex and gambling, courtesans and champagne for the Benighted States of America, a country so hypocritical it outlaws both.' Richard grinned at his own eloquence. 'Anyway, the political story's getting too complicated. I'm afraid I'm losing thousands of readers.'

Emily was shocked. She could not imagine her country's epic struggle towards unity being anything less than compelling reading to Americans and Europeans. She none the less countered: 'Then why don't you write about the lottery? You love poking fun at the stupid heathen.'

'Em, the big story's running down here. I'll have to start travelling quite soon.'

'What's happening in Japan that's so fascinating?' she demanded. 'Or South-east Asia and the Indies? No big stories there!'

'They're fresh, Em – and different. Something new's essential if I'm to . . .'

'I know what it is, Richard.' Her anger flared. 'You're fed up with the rambunctious Chinese – *all* of us. The revolution's too untidy for your imperialist taste. The natives are getting too uppity.'

'Em, please don't whip yourself into a rage. It's only that my reporting badly needs some variety. Not just Communists and Nationalists, commissars and warlords, battles and massacres. China's not the centre of the world, you know.'

Although touched by his smile, which was at once defiant and wistful, she hardened her heart against his charm and continued: 'Centre of the world or not, you're afraid of the next stage in China. In the artificial paradise of Shanghai you've begun thinking like the taipans. You won't admit that Chinese brains and Chinese industry make the Settlement prosper. And you'd hate to see a strong central government leading China to prosperity. You're afraid of the power of a united China. . . .'

Richard Hollings was daunted by her outburst. He was also marginally amused. He knew his Emily, and he loved her – on his own terms. The sophisticated career woman could sometimes become a gawky American college girl or a shy Confucian lady. But the crusading patriot was the hardest to deal with.

'That's nonsense, Em!' He appealed to her sense of the ridiculous. 'Nor do I believe the earth's flat, and I've never smuggled an ounce of opium.'

'You would have, Dick, if you could.' She smiled despite herself. 'I grant you're not that bad. But the birth of a strong and democratic China is inevitable.'

'Inevitable, woman?' His humour was, as ever, tart. 'Not in my time. One day, but not this decade or the next. Not when your civil wars have got five or six sides all fighting each other. And China's so inefficient. . .'

'Inefficient? Why China was . . .'

'Was in the past, but is not today. You know your Yank friends call

225

total disorganization *a Chinese firedrill*! The Yew Ess Navy goes one better: *A firedrill in a Chinese whorehouse*. So please spare me...'

Richard Hollings broke off appalled. He felt as if he were falling through the air. He might as well have confidently stepped onto solid pavement and felt it disintegrate under his feet. He had previously used stronger language to Emily – and she to him. But he knew that his intrusion of such heavy-handed irony regarding her people was this time disastrous.

'I never realized you were a racist!' She spoke before he could shape a convincing apology. 'I should have seen it earlier. Just an old-fashioned bigot. How odd!'

'That was a bit strong, wasn't it?' He tried hard. 'But it was only a joke that got out of hand, no more. A joke in very bad taste. Em, you know...'

'Tell me, Richard, suppose I said *Yes* right this minute.' Her tone was still excessively reasonable. 'Would you marry me tomorrow?'

'I'd want to, but I couldn't, Em,' he rejoined. 'We need time to post the banns. That sort of thing, you know.'

'I'm not joking, Richard.' She turned to stare through the window at the Bund. 'Would you? I *am* asking now. After all your protestations, will you?'

'Tomorrow?' he smiled sheepishly. 'You know that's impossible.'

'There's my answer, isn't it?' She was soft spoken – and implacable. 'Are you tired of me, too? Not just China, but me, too?'

'Darling, I assure you I love you deeply. And I'm *not* tired of China, though what that has to do with. .... Anyway, I must take a trip very soon. But just as soon as I get back...'

'You needn't look for me when you get back.'

'Emily darling, nothing's changed. This quarrel's only a fantasy. It's all in your mind.'

'Take your damned trip!' she exploded. 'Leave tomorrow ... tonight ... for all I care.'

'I shall!' Richard felt surprising relief when he finally gave way to his just anger at her carping. 'I'll do that, and I'll start off right now!'

He snatched up his briefcase, yanked his jacket from the clothes-tree, and slammed the door so hard the glass panel trembled. Emily stared stolidly at the strings of lights that outlined the ships at the man-of-war buoys. Beside her, Adam Schall made a curiously uncanine noise in his throat, half-warble and half-purr. When she did not respond, he nudged her with his shoulder.

Emily laid her hand on his big head, and felt the hard bone beneath the silken coat. When she finally spoke, her voice was preternaturally calm: 'Thank you, Adam. I know you're here and you'll always...'

The telephone interrupted, and she lifted the handset to hear Julia sounding as disturbed as herself: 'Emily? Emily it is you? I'm so glad I've found you. When will you be back? I've got to talk to you.'

226

29

'Extraordinary!' Elizaveta's black-velvet Slav voice was velvety. 'Almost unbelievable!'

Joshua Haleevie looked up with a self-deprecating smile from the drink he was concocting at the white-lacquered cocktail cabinet. He was almost thirty-five and, Elizaveta felt, had never been more attractive. His royal-blue dressing gown and the slight frosting on his sideburns dramatized the light blue of his eyes. Before replying he judiciously added a measure of cointreau to the brandy and the lemon juice in the cocktail-shaker. The Sidecar was the latest rage in Shanghai.

'Thank you, my dear,' he finally said. 'I do like a heartfelt tribute. And may I observe that your own performance was brilliant?'

'Not *that*, my beloved.' Elizaveta grimaced delicately at his heavy-handed humour. 'Well, yes, I suppose *that*, too. My compliments to you as well. But I was actually talking about Emily and Richard. They're really interesting.'

He eyed her appreciatively before giving her the cue she obviously wanted. Her crow's wing hair fell loose over her shoulders in the intimacy of the mint-and-cream sitting-room atop the Ikra. Her eyes, so deep blue they appeared black, were still as soft as they had been in the seven-foot-wide bed. The pearly light of early evening in mid-June spilling through the split-bamboo blinds glowed on her scarlet dressing gown.

'What about Em and Dick?' Joshua asked lazily. 'They seem to be getting along famously. Quite a change that.'

'Precisely, my love. They used to be so tense I could see the sparks fly.'

'What's cured them?'

227

'Cured? Oh, they're not really cured. This calm can't last. But only a couple of weeks ago, they had a terrible fight. He walked out.'

'Together again, though, aren't they? How come?'

'I gather the fight cleared the air. They're easier together now. Both told me separately. He said he'd been childish. She said it was infantile of her to take out her worries on him. Both swore . . .'

'Then what's the trouble? Why are you so pessimistic about them?'

'The sparks have *all* died, Joshua. They're *too* comfortable together.'

'Come now, Bess. We're comfortable together.' He was deliberately obtuse. 'What's wrong with that?'

'We shall see. You know, there are times when I'm definitely uncomfortable with you. Thank God!'

Still playing the bluff cavalry officer, Joshua muttered: 'Funny thing to say, that.'

Elizaveta acknowledged his buffoonery by rolling her eyes. She sipped the amber cocktail and slipped a Murad into her lapis lazuli cigarette-holder. Blowing out a plume of scented smoke, she asked meditatively: 'Josh, do you ever wonder? What will it be like in twenty years? Possibly thirty?'

'Constantly, my love. And I'm terrified of growing old with Charlotte Gubbai. But I may have no choice. The Governor's pressing and, quite candidly, I don't fancy looking for another job.'

Elizaveta was not offended, for she had no right to be offended. Joshua now assumed that she would never marry him. He had pleaded too often and had been rejected too firmly. He now assumed that he would in time marry the eminently suitable Jewish heiress his parents had chosen. He knew he would always love the unsuitable Russian aristocrat who was his own unalterable choice.

'Poor dear!' Elizaveta finally remarked. 'Though it is the best of both worlds for you, isn't it? Charlotte and her shekels – with me on the side.'

'Give over, Bess. You know damned well I don't want it that way. But you don't give me much choice, do you?'

'Joshua, have you ever thought . . .' She paused tantalizingly '. . . thought what it would be like to grow old with me?'

'Often, my love. I firmly intend to grow old with you – no matter who I marry.'

'Then the prospect's not utterly revolting?'

'Revolting?' he snorted. 'How you can even ask such . . .'

'Joshua, sometimes I wonder.' She gazed at the dark smoke spiralling from her Egyptian cigarette and pursued her thought. 'Joshua, do you really want . . . That is, do you still want to marry me?'

'Only for the sake of poor Charlotte Gubbai.' He could not take her seriously. 'Only to relieve that foolish virgin of the affliction of a husband like me.'

'Joshua, forget about Charlotte. Do think seriously how it would be married to me.'

'Sheer heaven when we're at home, an idyll of bliss! But outside, constant jealousy! You arouse too much admiration.' He looked at her quizzically and asked: 'What's this all about, Bess? Are you just testing the water? Or are you seriously considering putting a toe in?'

'I'm not quite sure, darling. I really don't know. Perhaps I'm just wondering.'

Alone in the loft-apartment with the Tibetan mastiff, Julia Pavernen bleakly contemplated the glowing dusk in the high window above the rosewood desk. She had sent Lao Zee away, for she could no longer bear the amah's heavy silences and profound sighs. That melodramatic sympathy hurt too much when she yearned for news of Tommy. She ached to see him – and feared she never would.

To her surprise, she missed Little Pow almost as keenly. The urchin had been part of her life every day for five years, as Tommy had not. She had grown accustomed to Tommy's absence during the year and a half since he first left to go campaigning. Enthralled by the lingering twilight, she had just turned to point out its sad beauty to Little Pow, rather than to Tommy.

None the less, her thoughts dwelt only on Tommy while the luminous evening slowly drew on the black crêpe of night. Her ebullient temperament had kept her from despairing, although almost two months had passed since he disappeared into the maw of the evil city. Soon, very soon, it would become impossible to believe he was still alive. It would soon be plain that Donald Howe would otherwise certainly have had some scrap of news in return for his lavish bribes if his youngest son still lived.

Tommy could have been executed among scores of captives. In the frantic days succeeding the counter-coup, the rightists had 'processed' their prisoners as rapidly as a butcher stuffing suet-speckled Cantonese sausages. If he had died then, she would never know.

Julia was suddenly numb, and blessedly she felt nothing. She could sometimes forget for two or three minutes that Tommy had almost certainly been immolated in the cauldron of the revolution. The return of feeling was a snake coiling around her heart. Its scales were rough and very cold. She would, she swore again, do anything to be sure – and anything at all – to save Tommy if she could only find him.

Julia grimaced wryly when she remembered her appeal to Mayling Soong. Emily had insisted that they both call on the youngest daughter of the redoubtable House of Soong.

Mayling was in love with Generalissimo Chiang Kai-shek, whom she had finally permitted to address to her formidable mother, Mammie Soong, a formal suit for her hand in marriage. A young woman in love, Emily had believed, would warmly welcome another young woman who was deeply in love. May would naturally sympathize with Julia's anguish at not even knowing whether Tommy were still alive. May was still dewy-eyed, although a family council had rejected the Generalissimo's suit. May *knew* she would overcome that opposition, even though the formidable Mammie swore that no daughter of hers would ever marry a pagan like Chiang Kai-shek. Besides, May liked Americans.

The Soongs' relatively modest mansion on Seymour Road behind the Bund was familiar from previous visits. The sitting-room was like many others in well-to-do Chinese homes in Shanghai. A few English-language books complemented boxed editions of the Confucian Classics in the bookcase, and ox-blood vases of the Manchu Dynasty towered above blue-and-white porcelains of the Ming in glass-fronted display cases. Intricately crocheted anti-maccassars protected the easy chairs and the sofa of olive-green cut plush. A big-horned Victrola squatted on a side-table inlaid with mother-of-pearl. Also the clichés of middle-class American households: a stack of *National Geographic Magazines* displayed yellow-framed covers beside a bigger stack of *Saturday Evening Posts*. On top was a graphically detailed Norman Rockwell drawing of a freckle-faced boy dangling a fishing line with a bent pin for a hook and patting a shaggy dog. As Emily said, all the Soongs liked America.

May gave Emily and Julia coffee and brownies. She was, as always, totally self-possessed and minutely condescending. Her dress of navy-blue crêpe inappropriate for a spring afternoon, was loose, almost baggy. The model for the emancipated women of Shanghai was apparently shy of showing her figure, obviously still inhibited by the old male-dictated concepts of feminine modesty. Emerging from the enforced seclusion of the female quarters and casting off the enveloping garments that had made them sexless were major triumphs of Chinese women. They were now free to make themselves as attractive as they pleased. But May Soong was not inclined to celebrate that victory wholeheartedly.

Essentially serious like Emily, May was – again like Emily – a true daughter of the frivolous International Settlement. The two happily exchanged gossip while sipping black coffee from American mugs and toying with the chocolate brownies. Guiltily adding cream to her coffee, Julia looked at her closest friend as if seeing her for the first time. The glittering creature with the wide-set eyes, who concealed her laughter behind her cupped hand, was virtually a stranger – a very Chinese stranger. Emily was a wholly different person when she was with May, and Julia was momentarily jealous of their intimacy.

Since neither seemed concerned to get to the point, Julia reluctantly took the initiative in pleading for May's help in finding Tommy. Rather perversely May turned to Emily.

'What do you expect *me* to do?' She was almost petulant. 'Specially when you say you've tried every possible avenue.'

'May, dear, just ask the Gimo.' Emily was equally forthright. 'He's the only one we haven't approached.'

'What makes you think . . .' May demanded.

'Oh, we don't think he's involved!' Julia thrust in her reply. 'But he can find out – if anyone can. All we ask, May, is to learn the truth.'

'Well, I'll see what I can do,' Mayling conceded after a pause. 'Of course, Gimo's hard to get hold of. Always in and out of Shanghai. But I know how you feel, Julie. And I've always liked Tommy. I'll try.'

Since that afternoon four weeks earlier, May had not offered a word regarding Tommy. She had, of course, answered Emily's insistent phone

230

calls, but she offered no news. She only reported that Chiang Kai-shek had maddeningly said he would try to look into the matter when he had a moment free. Julia had taken what comfort she could from the Generalissimo's relayed observation: 'I like that young Doctor Howe.'

The mastiff placed his head on Julia's thigh, and she automatically stroked him. Remembering her fruitless quest, her thoughts began to chase themselves in circles. Unremitting speculation regarding Tommy's fate had worn a round groove in her brain. Like a cracked Victrola record the endless litany began: *We would have heard if he died. . . . No, they'd never tell us. . . . But he'd somehow get word to us if he were alive. . . . Yet how could he?* Julia deliberately turned her attention away from that agonizing – and pointless – round of conjecture to the common woes of China.

Ever since mid-April, the two antagonistic 'National Revolutionary Governments' had been fighting each other without mercy. Never mind that the warlords were again stirring in North China, the left-wing Nationalist government in Wuhan and the right-wing National-ist government in Nanking appeared determined to destroy each other.

In Wuhan, Comintern agent Michael Borodin raged: 'We must purge our revolutionary ranks before the revolution can succeed. Forget the Northern Expedition. We've got to march against Chiang Kai-shek right now.'

The Generalissimo was already wiping out all Communist organiza-tions in the vast areas south of the Yangtze River. Once again, political refugees flocked to the sanctuary of the foreign concessions. With many of its leaders defecting to the Generalissimo, the Wuhan régime of his diabetic chief rival was on the verge of collapse.

Julia partook of the agonies suffered by the radical friends she had made at Shanghai Labour Univeristy. Her mentor, the former Dean, had watched his plan for the Shanghai uprising succeed brilliantly – only to see the victorious Communists crushed by the Generalissimo's coup. Having spent two years in Moscow, the Dean was at odds with the China-first faction within the Communist Party – particularly with un-abashed nationalists like Tommy's friend Chang Kuo-tao and the zealous Mao Tse-tung. The Comintern's betrayal of the Chinese revolution festered like a thorn in the Dean's heart.

Julia's attention, however, swung to the reality of her solitary evening in the cavernous loft. Although recent political events had been cata-strophic, recalling them was still better than gloomy surmises regarding Tommy. But Julia's mind defied her will and her thoughts again whizzed around the same circular groove: *Tommy isn't dead because there is no word of his death. . . . But why not even a whisper of news? . . . Why no demand for ransom and no one offering to sell information? . . . Yet it's already more than two months, so he must be. . .*

The telephone's bell mercifully broke in. Julia lifted Adam's head from her lap, and rose from the cane sofa. She had sat so long with his head heavy on her thigh that her left leg was numb. She lifted her foot, and felt the excruciating stabs of returning circulation. Hobbling ludicrously, she lifted the instrument.

'Julie! Julie!' Emily's voice was shrill with excitement. 'Is that you?'

'Who else, Em?'

'It's wonderful news! Just wonderful! Tommy's alive! He's really alive! No question about it! . . . Julie? Julie, are you still there?'

Julia could not reply. Clutching the table with one hand and the telephone with the other, she slid slowly down to sit on the floor. A big paw touched her arm in concern, but she could only take in the single glorious reality: *Tommy was alive!*

'How is he? Is he hurt? Is he well?' The questions poured out. 'Where is he?'

'He's all right, I hear, but . . .'

'Emmy, I can't believe it! It's the most wonderful news I ever heard!' Julia broke in ecstatically. 'Who told you? Where is he? Why hadn't he . . .'

'Now, Julie, just a minute!' Emily laughed frenetically. 'I can't answer all those questions at once.'

'Then just tell me your own way. But, first, tell me again he's alive and well.'

'All right, Julie. Tommy is alive and well. That's all I really know. That's all May Soong could tell me.'

'May finally came through?'

'Like a lady – finally. He's been held . . . he's still held . . . by the Garrison Command, so the Gimo didn't . . .'

'When can he come home, Emmy? What do they want? Ransom or what? Why are they holding . . .'

'Whoa, Julie!' Emily's laughter was a shade less frenetic. 'Give me a chance. First of all, May has no idea when they'll let him go. Perhaps some time. She can't even say for sure they will let him go. She doesn't know why they want to hold him. She's promised she'll get after the Gimo to find out. But we must be patient.'

'Why in God's name? The Gimo's the boss, isn't he? This is crazy, Em. Why can't he set Tommy free? Why did he take so long to find out?'

'The Gimo's more like first among equals, Julie. Not the absolute boss. Not yet – if ever. So he's got to work around it. But May's ninety per cent sure it'll all work out all right.'

'Oh, God, I hope so! I pray so! I couldn't bear it – now that I know he's alive – not to . . .'

232

30

July 19, 1927

Outside on the circular terrace under the faint stars the dusk was stagnant. The heavy air reeked of mildew and sweaty clothing. Even for the French Club, that citadel of privilege, the slow fall of night promised little relief from the steam-bath atmosphere of mid-July. Everyone who could had already fled to the cool beaches of North China or the brisk hills of Central China, abandoning the dispirited stragglers to stew in their own boredom. Among missionaries, only the Jesuits still tended their flock and their observatory at Zicawei. Among businessmen, only raw juniors and a few unfortunate seniors remained, watchmen over a half-deserted city.

The heat blossomed like a rapacious tropical growth. The dense humidity hobbled even the rickshaw coolies, whose muscles were parched oak-hard by opium. They gasped for oxygen, and their rhythmic trot dwindled to an ungainly shamble.

Husbands who had yearned for freedom from wives and children sat lethargically at the metal tables on the Club's terrace and longed for summer's end. The hectic pleasures offered to summer bachelors had briefly delighted them. They had for a week or two revelled in the strange perfumes and the strange textures of strange bed-fellows. But the heat pressed down on libertines and virtuous alike, smothering all desire in its woolly, sodden embrace. Bored and contrite, some husbands planned chaste visits to the Olympia Cinema, which advertised a new device that might have been invented expressly for Shanghai: air-conditioning. But most looked with envy at the table where two men sat with three women who were manifestly not hired companions.

A number of the summer bachelors recognized Elizaveta Alexandrovna

233

Yavalenka. Uncounselled by their vigilant, censorious wives, none thought her presence untoward. She enjoyed that selective amnesia only at the French Club. Her aristocratic charm, feminine grace, and growing wealth would have made her acceptable there even without her powerful sponsor.

No one, of course, idly challenged Joshua Haleevie. His father's wealth gave him much power. Moreover, he was playing his own hand in municipal politics. And his astute activities in the booming property market and the construction trade were making him independently wealthy.

Joshua looked like a playboy or, more politely, an idler who had a taste for culture as well as pleasure. Few knew just how ruthless he could be when his vital interests or his protégés were threatened, for he was always nonchalant. Fewer knew that he was committed to certain endeavours that he would not call charities: educating the promising children of coolies and servants; providing sustenance for destitute White Russians; supporting maimed Chinese soldiers; and sponsoring a dozen medical students. Hardly anyone knew of his role in the Settlement's intelligence-gathering. To conceal his various commitments to the welfare of his fellow Shanghailanders, Joshua took pains to appear no more than a charming – and feckless – son of privilege.

Seated opposite him, Emily Howe twisted the yellow straw from her Tom Collins and wondered again why Liz and Josh got on so well that even their disagreements led to laughter rather than tears. Perhaps because both had been deeply wounded: he by the Great War and she by the Bolshevik Revolution. Of course, Joshua was hardly the fatuous playboy he strove to appear. Nor was Elizaveta the callous, grasping procuress, she deliberately acted in order to shield her vulnerability. Emily's thoughts became tangled. Liz *was* actually a procuress, and Joshua *was* a playboy in his leisure hours.

She smiled at Richard when the Filipino combo swung into 'Tea for Two'. He nodded towards the dance-floor, but she was still entangled in her snarled thoughts. The masks Elizaveta and Joshua wore concealed other masks – their complexity not merely Byzantine, but Japanese. Did their unvarying gentleness with each other, she wondered, camouflage the absence of the passion Richard and she felt? She and he were once again oscillating between ecstasy and anguish. Love on a trapeze was exhilarating, but also very hazardous.

Emily uncoiled the straw and leaned towards Richard to whisper: 'Dance with Julie first. She needs cheering up.'

Richard shrugged, and Emily read his meaning clearly: *No use asking. Julie'll only beg off. She's a frightful drear nowadays.* Since his own emotions were powerful but shallow, Richard was impatient with Julia's profound grief over Tommy.

'Tea for two and two for tea; it's me for you and you for me.' The Filipino singer possessed all the right props: a glossy black megaphone and glossier patent-leather hair, an orange-striped blazer and white-flannel slacks. 'A boy for you and a girl for me. Oh, can't you see how happy we will be?'

The familiar words evoked the familiar glow, and Emily rose to dance. Her fragility was set off by her white georgette dress with a deep V at the back. The top of her head was level with Richard's eyes and she was a column of ivory under the fairy lights strung above the dance-floor. Joshua Haleevie involuntarily recalled the execution of China's most celebrated – and corrupt – imperial concubine: 'She shone forth, lily-pale, between tall avenues of spears to die.' Yet Emily appeared as distant and as pure as a Vestal Virgin.

Caught in the toils of her own misery, Julia tried for a light touch. She was obsessed with Tommy's suffering at the hands of his Fascist gaolers, but she strove for gaiety. As a result she appeared frenetic, almost manic. She crouched defensively inside the dress she called her 'mad mauve confection' and Emily called 'a grotesque purple concoction'. Laughing too loud and too long, she crammed Chesterfield after Chesterfield into her ivory holder, stubbing each one out after two or three drags and immediately lighting another.

She saw without surprise the slight tremor of her hand. God knew she had tried to help him! And she would keep on trying!

Sometimes it seemed she was the only one who really cared about Tommy, except, of course, for the comrades of the Chinese Communist Party. But the Party had too many troubles of its own. Hard-pressed by foreign police and Chinese rightists, the Shanghai Apparatus could offer little but sympathy to the foreign girlfriend of a rich man's son. The Apparatus's intelligence service was in disarray, like the Communist Party itself. Themselves dispersed, the comrades could not even locate Tommy, much less arrange his escape.

Julia was, therefore, besieging the new right-wing government of Greater Shanghai, determined to win official admission that Tommy was a captive. The Howes, even Emily, appeared to have given up. Eurydice and Donald, after all, had three other sons – and Emily had three other brothers.

Joshua Haleevie was still seeking further information, but he had little leverage in an essentially Chinese matter. Julia did not believe Richard Hollings had really tried to use his influence as the correspondent of two powerful newspapers. Other expedients had yielded no results: her Uncle John, One-Arm Sutton, the American Consul-General, and the commander of the US Navy's Yangtze Patrol. Elizaveta had introduced her to municipal officers, magistrates, bankers, and gangsters. But she had gained no further information.

Julia felt herself soiled by her vain entreaties – and almost reproached herself for withholding the favours some gentlemen hinted could alter everything. In her black moods she feared that her strenuous efforts were making matters worse for Tommy – like a rescuer whose clumsy spade starts a landslip and buries trapped miners even deeper.

She looked up from the heap of butts in the ashtray and intercepted Elizaveta's glance. Seductive in a calf-length shift of cream lawn over a slim underdress of deeper cream pongee, the Russian had pulled her plaited black hair through a diamond clasp above her right ear. She wore no other jewellery. Amid that calculated splendour, her dark-blue eyes, sometimes as cold as the Siberian tundra, were now liquid with concern.

'We have in Russian a saying.' Elizaveta assumed a heavy accent. 'Moscow, she was not built in a day. This is meaning . . .'

'Robert Bruce and the spider,' Joshua interposed. 'If at first you don't succeed . . .'

'Put your nose to the grindstone.' Julia hectically capped the twisted maxims. 'But my poor nose is practically worn to a nubbin.'

'And a charming nubbin it is.' Joshua laughed. 'Now, Julie, I promise you it'll be all right. They can't really keep . . .'

'The Madam herself, as I live and breathe.' The speaker was unmistakably English and unmistakably drunk. 'Madam Yakavalnoka, is it? What in the world are *you* doing here, Madam?'

Elizaveta looked up with an artificial smile, and Joshua looked down at his hands. She had dealt with so many obstreperous clients that the four young officers in the khaki shorts and bush-jackets of a Sikh regiment of the British Indian Army should pose no particular difficulty. Joshua further feared that by intervening he would inflame the officers' tempers – and force a confrontation.

'Two of your girls, I presume.' The ringleader was a burly blond lieutenant. 'And *what* are they doing here, Madam?'

'Enjoying the night coolness, Lieutenant,' Elizaveta answered equably. 'Since we haven't met, perhaps you'd leave us now.'

'Don't know me, ah?' the lieutenant persisted. 'But I know *you*. Everybody knows you run the best little knocking shop in Shanghai. So come'n have a dance. You *and* the little ladies. They good crumpet, Madam?'

'Why don't you go and sit down like good chaps?' Elizaveta's tone was professionally placatory – and slightly desperate. 'I'll send you some champagne. But please don't . . .'

'Tart's holiday, eh? Not dancin'. Here you are. This ought to cover it.'

The lieutenant fumbled a handful of banknotes from his pocket. Contemptuously counting out crumpled ten-dollar bills, he flicked them onto the table.

'There we are, all present and correct,' he finally said. 'Two hundred and fifty Chink dollars – as near as dammit a month's pay. That'd better cover it.'

No longer an observer, Joshua was already pushing back his chair when the truculent lieutenant grasped Elizaveta's arm and Julia's shoulder.

'Let them go, lieutenant,' he directed. 'Deal with me instead.'

The lieutenant blinked owlishly and drawled: 'Oh, the Jewboy, is it? Well, you can't hide behind Daddy's moneybags. So . . .'

The roundhouse swing that only grazed Joshua's cheekbone, still set him back for an instant. He stepped forward again, his fists raised to protect his face. The next blow caught him in the stomach and drove the air from his lungs. Gasping, he side-stepped his opponent's rush and flicked a stinging blow at the lieutenant's eye.

'Hit me from behind!' the lieutenant bellowed. 'Dirty Jewboy. Get him, lads!'

All four subalterns surrounded Joshua, their code of fair play apparently abrogated by the false accusation. His arms were firmly held behind him, and the ringleader drew back a steel-capped boot to kick him in the groin.

'That'll do! You're a disgrace! Call yourselves officers?'

The cool voice of command arrested the assault. The subalterns turned to face Richard Hollings, who had from the dance-floor seen the confrontation develop with manic speed.

'Who's this, now?' The senior lieutenant recovered his poise. 'Why lads, we can cope with two of them just as well!'

Restraint having failed, Richard resigned himself to battle. He took a step backwards and raised his fists defensively. Seizing the diversion, Joshua turned and drove his fist into the mouth of the lieutenant who held his arms.

The ringleader roared in fury and hurled himself at Richard. Both feet left the ground as he leaped. He was snatched from mid-air and borne away by four white-coated waiters. Directed by their captain, Joshua's friend Fatty Woo, a dozen waiters simply lifted the belligerent officers and carried them off. Too surprised to protest, they were deposited on the melting tar of the parking lot.

Fatty Woo apologized profusely. Plump cheeks shaking, he snapped his fingers for a magnum of Joshua's favourite champagne: Krug 1912.

Emily was appalled by the sudden explosion of violence. She was compelled to recognise how helpless the three women had been, and she felt disdain for female weakness. Julia was obviously shaken, and Elizaveta trembled with humiliation.

'Is this what you want, Joshua?' Elizaveta composed herself and asked bitterly after Fatty Woo had poured the champagne. 'What you *truly* want?'

'Not every night, darling,' he replied lightly. 'A punch-up once a week is enough. Are you planning to arrange regular bouts?'

'Not quite, my dear.' Although she smiled at his levity, Elizaveta spoke earnestly. 'Do you really want to live this way? Do you really want a wife who provokes insults – and forces fights?'

'My darling Bess, I want *you*.' Joshua leaned across the table to cup her chin in his hand. 'If that's what comes with you, I don't have much choice, do I?'

'You're quite sure?' Her voice was tremulous. 'Absolutely sure? You've seen it again . . . seen how disgusting it can be.'

He nodded and said softly: 'I'm absolutely sure!'

'In that case . . .' She paused irresolutely, then took his hand in both her own. 'In that case . . . I will.'

Her voice was so low he had to lean across to hear her say: 'If you'll still have me, I will marry you. Joshua, my darling, I do love you!'

With exclamations and endearments almost unintelligible to male ears, Emily and Julia welcomed Elizaveta's projected return to the community

237

of respectable women. Joshua silently thanked God for the drunken subalterns and for the lottery, which had frightened Elizaveta and brought her to her senses. He thanked God, also, for his parents' pressing Charlotte Gubbai upon him and further alarming Elizaveta. Of course, he had never taken that prospect seriously. However, Elizaveta had been forced to make a choice: either to marry him herself or to see him married to Charlotte Gubbai. Gingerly rubbing his bruised ribs, the prospective bridegroom lifted his beaker of champagne.

'The bride!' His tone was almost reverent. 'I drink to the bride! Now and always!'

'That *was* odd. . . . Very odd, wasn't it?'

His dark brows knotted in concentration, Richard Hollings inserted the red convertible into the stream of traffic that clogged Kiukiang Road. Its canvas top folded to catch its own breeze, the runabout was almost comfortable despite the sluggish heat of the night. The cramped cockpit was almost spacious for just two, after the third passenger had left. They had dropped Julia off at the loft-apartment.

She had declined to join them for dinner because she had to prepare for her class at the Customs College. She was also very tired, and she had to be up at six to read the news on Station XMHA. Three excuses when one would do made it obvious that she simply did not wish to burden them with her misery. They had earlier left Joshua and Elizaveta alone to celebrate the unexpected betrothal, saying they had to check the latest wire-service reports.

Emily would have preferred a quiet meal nearer home, but Richard was determined to dine at Jeff Geoffreys's St Andrew's Café. He had recently developed a penchant for tumultuous nightclubs, where he was obviously stimulated by the constant nervous gaiety.

'Deuced peculiar, that lightning betrothal,' he reiterated, slotting the runabout between a crimson omnibus and a cart laden with cotton bales. 'Never thought an old Harrovian like Joshua would be so foolish, even if his ancestors did come from the ghettos of Baghdad.'

Emily's right foot in its silver evening-slipper pressed down on a non-existent brake. The convertible's nose was pointed directly at the uni-formed driver of a Chrysler limousine, but Richard's suede shoe was still heavy on the accelerator. The Chrysler's brakes squealed, and the driver was flung against the dashboard. Richard triumphantly wheeled the runabout around the stalled limousine and entered the traffic of Nanking Road.

'Their getting engaged isn't foolish at all,' Emily murmured when he glanced at her inquisitively. 'I think it's wonderful for them both.'

'Rash!' he exploded. 'Devilishly rash!'

'They've always been in love.' Emily filled the awkward pause. 'Since the moment they met. The only surprise, really, is that it took her so long. Otherwise, it's . . .'

Emily's voice trailed off. Her attempt to lighten the atmosphere was being met with sulky silence. She wondered if Richard had not had a good deal more to drink than she thought. Why else his volatile mood – his testiness and his recklessness? He probably shouldn't be driving. But she could not reclaim the wheel of her own car without enraging him.

Although he loved the red convertible, he could not be bothered to buy a motor-car of his own. He acknowledged that he could well afford one, but declared that it was 'just too much trouble'. That self-deprivation was akin to his failure to find more comfortable quarters. He preferred the large bedroom-cum-sitting-room he had rented in the Hongkew flat of a young *Daily News* sub-editor when he first came to Shanghai. His explanation was plausible: 'Between the office, your flat, and travelling, I'm hardly ever there except to sleep. And not always there to sleep.'

Smiling at that masculine bravado, Emily decided again she was wise in rarely allowing him to spend the entire night with her. One had to draw the line somewhere. Her love affair was often exhilarating, sometimes guilt-inspiring, and, upon occasion, depressing. But an affair was not cohabitation. It was certainly not yet – if ever – marriage.

She was, however, puzzled by her lover's self-denial. He was anything but mean. His gifts to her were lavish, and he allowed himself indulgences like fine clothing, good food, and superlative claret. His own car and his own quarters would make his life more comfortable. But he desired neither.

'Dickie boy doesn't want a car – or a millstone around his neck,' Julia had once remarked cryptically. Julia contended that Richard wanted neither car nor house because they would tie him down. And the last thing in the world he wanted, Julia said, was a wife, who would tie him down for good and all.

All bachelors flinched from marriage, but that normal wariness had almost become paranoia in Richard. Perhaps that was why he clung to her – why he grew ardent for marriage when she withdrew and became elusive when she was receptive. No matter how Westernized, she was undeniably Chinese. And only déclassé Englishmen married Chinese. She was not just a plaything; she was a shield for Richard. As long as he was with her, whom he could not marry whatever his protests, no other woman could manoeuvre him into marriage.

But Emily knew that Richard was neither as self-seeking nor as detached as he might appear. True, he had just shown himself without sympathy for either Julia and Elizaveta, insensitive to the one's suffering and the other's joy. Yes, he might appear self-centred, but he was acutely sensitive to her moods. Above all, he was far too complex to sum up simplistically.

'I can see your point about Josh and Liz.' Emily was briskly conciliatory, regretting the twenty or so seconds taken to spin her web of conjecture – regretting also her treacherous thoughts. 'It *was* a little abrupt, the way they finally decided to get married.'

'Abrupt! It was unchained lightning. She lured him into holy wedlock faster than old Borodin lured the Nationalists into Moscow's camp.'

'Both wanted to be seduced, though.'

239

'I suppose so.' He laughed. 'You've a tongue – and a wit – sharper than any Jesuit's tonight, Em. Pray God Josh and Liz don't end like Borodin and the Nationalists.'

'It's all over, I guess.' Emily gratefully fell back on their habitual professional talk of political events. 'That alliance is scattered to the winds. What about Borodin himself?'

'I hear he's only waiting for transport. When the motor-cars turn up, it'll be heigh-ho over the Gobi Desert to jolly old Moscow for *former* Chief Adviser Michael Borodin. Anyway, the Wuhan Government has just about gone out of business.'

'And high time, too.'

'High time, indeed,' he said. 'The Gimo's the only hope for China – such hope as exists. But why in the name of God has Rosamonde Soong booked passage to Moscow?'

'Dick, remember Rosamonde used to be Madame *President* Sun Yat-sen. She'd hate to have Mayling queen it over her as Madame *Generalissimo* Chiang Kai-shek.'

'That's not settled yet. Not by a long shot.'

'Don't tell May that. As far as she's concerned, it's signed, sealed – and about to be delivered. Mammie Soong'll have to run a lot farther than Japan to escape her would-be son-in-law's humble pleading for her daughter's hand. The way May's pushing him, maybe the South Pole.'

'Damn determined, you Chinese ladies, aren't you? If only *you* were determined to look with favour on my humble suit.'

Convinced by his quirky humour that he was far from drunk, she flirted lightly: 'All right, then. Why not give it a whirl? Let's get married tomorrow. What would you say to that?'

'Wonderful, Em! That's what I'd say – what I *do* say. I'd show you if I could let go of the wheel. You're serious?'

'I am, good sir. Tomorrow then?'

'Tomorrow . . . in principle.' He paused. 'But, practically, we'll have to wait till I get back. I'm booked on the *Koryu Maru* to Kobe day after tomorrow. I hated to tell you, so I kept putting it off. But I'll be back very soon – now that you've said yes. And then . . .'

'And then what, Richard?'

'And then we'll work it out. . . . We'll decide the best thing to do. . . . And when . . .'

As his words faded inconclusively into silence, Emily belatedly saw that he *was* drunk. He had obviously sought in the bottle the courage to tell her of his imminent departure. For one appalling moment, she also saw that he had no intention of marrying her – and never had. An instant later, she concluded protectively that he had little inclination towards marriage, but was unaware of his duplicity. He was negligent, but he was neither deceitful nor vicious.

Moreover, the revelations had clarified her own thinking. She now knew that she truly wanted to marry Richard. She could conquer her racial pride, for she loved him deeply. She knew she could in time remedy his few faults, even his rootlessness.

The convertible was passing Rafferty's funeral parlour, where the burnished coffin floated on a sea of light. Farther down Bubbling Well Road, lights glinted on the hammered brass letters: St Andrew's Café. Amid cars, trucks, and rickshaws Emily saw Jeff Geoffreys's big Daimler-Benz motorcycle and sidecar at the kerb.

'Of course, we will, Richard. We'll work it all out just as soon as you get back.' Her voice was firm, and she asked confidently: 'Could you drive a little slower, please? We're going a little too . . .'

'Dammit, Emily, stop humouring me,' he burst out. 'I know that tone too well. It's bloody condescending. Damned if I know what we'll work out. And you . . .'

He stopped talking as the black ghost of a rickshaw abruptly materialized out of the darkness. The red Plymouth swerved violently, but alcohol had blunted Richard's reactions. The rickshaw coolie rose vertically into the air after the fender struck him. He somersaulted with grotesque grace ten feet above the ground and began to fall. Richard's foot clamped down on the accelerator.

'Got to get out of here,' he muttered thickly. 'Too many enemies . . . they hate me for honest reporting. They'll crucify me if they catch me. Not just drunken driving, but murder. They'd try and pin murder on me.'

Afraid to speak, Emily never doubted that he would soon turn back. It was essential to get medical attention for the coolie – if he were still alive. If the unfortunate man were dead, common decency demanded an effort to help his family.

But the red convertible drew further away from St Andrew's Café. After two or three minutes, Richard sighed with relief and said: 'S'all right now. If anyone saw . . . couldn't get registration number. That's why I pulled away fast.'

He was actually congratulating himself on his cunning – on keeping his head. He showed no concern for the coolie and no inclination to turn back. Emily's body was rigid with distaste.

Most ironically, his fears were unfounded. No respectable foreigner who ran down a coolie would be punished by more than a *pro forma* reprimand, however drunk he was. He was not evading serious danger, but merely avoiding inconvenience.

'You're not turning back?' She could not suppress the appalled question. 'You don't care?'

'Why should I?'

'Why . . . why to see if you've killed the poor wretch. To help him . . . help his family. It's only the decent . . .'

Richard drew the convertible to the kerb, stopping by chance before the spear-tipped gates of Jade House, the Haleevies' mansion. He turned and looked at her in frank astonishment.

'Go back? And put my head in a noose?' he asked with unwonted vehemence. 'Never!'

'Richard, don't you care at all about the poor man?'

'Put my head in a noose for a miserable coolie who's probably better off dead?' He was aggressive, and his speech was thick. 'Why should I?'

241

'Because he's a fellow human being,' Emily pleaded. 'Because you're responsible.'

'Me responsible?' His words were heavily slurred. 'Responsible for a Chink coolie? Don't make me laugh.'

'You don't really give a damn about Julie or Liz either, do you? You don't care about anyone but yourself. Not even . . . even about me. Do you, Richard?'

Emily was enraged by his callousness and his racism, above all by his brutal selfishness. She opened the door and stepped into the heavy, dark night.

'Then you won't want this Chink girl anymore!' She turned in the yellow glow of a street-lamp. 'So there's nothing more to say.'

Moving with extraordinary agility for one so drunk, Richard sprang from the car. He seized her arm and spun her around. She stumbled, almost breaking the heel of her silver slipper, and fell hard against the car.

'You'd better get back to your poor abused countryman, hadn't you?' In his white rage, he spoke more clearly. 'All you Chinks stick together, don't you?'

'You'd better go, Richard.'

'To tell the honest truth, I'm happy to go. All this piety and patriotism's been getting up my nose. I'm glad to say goodbye.'

'I know, Richard!' she answered. 'I know.'

Emily got into the convertible and put her head down on the steering wheel. She gulped back her tears and lifted her head. Dry-eyed, she watched the solitary figure stride east on Bubbling Well Road under the street-lamps that lit the millionaires' mansions. When she no longer trembled quite so violently, she put the car into gear and very slowly drew away. In the rearview mirror she saw Richard waving a gleeful dismissal.

In that moment of parting she realized that he had for years deceived her. He was not only a racist, but a scoundrel. He had used her physically and emotionally; he had used her knowledge of China and her connections. He had ruthlessly exploited her – as Caucasians always exploited Chinese.

The car was approaching St Andrew's Café, where she would look for the injured coolie. She felt soiled and empty, used like a common prostitute. Yet her anguish was largely her own fault. She had flouted traditional Chinese decency. She had flung herself at the barbarian because she thought herself a modern emancipated woman.

She was finally free of Richard Hollings – free forever. And she was glad, very glad.

Still, she owed something to their years together. She would help the coolie and his family as much as she could, for her car had struck him. She would not implicate Richard if she could avoid it. But, her own woman again, Emily resolved that neither would she sacrifice herself to protect him.

31

The night of July 26, 1927 came diffidently to industrial Wuhan, the triplet cities lying on the Yangtze River amid a lacework of streams and lakes almost at the centre of China. The far bank of the river was a distant smudge beneath a glowing sunset.

Under that gaudy sky, the bulky young man at the rail of the river steamer was beset by black depression. Tommy Howe's friend and political mentor Chang Kuo-tao had embarked on this voyage most unwillingly. Boarding just before the gangplank went up, he had not noticed the white dollar signs on the spindly black funnels. He now looked with distaste at the ideograms on the bridge house reading *American Vessel* and at the Stars and Stripes flapping over the boxy stern. He needed no such reminders that the only security in anarchic China was provided by foreign flags backed by foreign men-of-war.

His melancholy deepened when the Dollar Line steamer swung into the channel and pointed her stubby prow towards Kiukiang, two hundred miles downstream. He looked glumly back at Wuhan, where the lights of the evening threw firefly trails across the river – and the best-intentioned government China had known for a century was dying. He smoothed the short hair on his domed head, and an ode of the Tang Dynasty came into his mind. The final couplet was the distillation of sorrow: *The yellow crane is flown forever, and the tower of the crane is derelict for all eternity.*

It suited his bleak mood. Chronically depressed by the suffering of his native land, he despaired of his immediate mission. The message he carried could determine the fate of China for decades to come. But he carried the wrong message.

Chang Kuo-tao was further depressed by the impending departure of

243

Michael Borodin, the Comintern's best agent in China. At the main station he had seen Borodin's special train, which was emblazoned with crossed Nationalist and Soviet flags framing a portrait of a beaming Dr Sun Yat-sen. The flatbed cars were loaded with the heavy-duty lorries and automobiles that would carry the party across the Gobi Desert to the Soviet Union. The Comintern's agent dared not venture across the warlord-ruled North China to the Trans-Siberian Railway. Defeated by China, Borodin was withdrawing to lick his wounds – and to advise urgently against all further intervention in that country.

Michael Borodin was an ardent revolutionary. He was also a realist who had opposed a *coup d'état* in Canton because the Communists could not hold the city. Released from Borodin's experienced guidance, the Chinese Communist Party had now decided upon a stroke that was at least equally audacious. Effectively in control of the Party was the man Julia had known as the Dean of the Shanghai Labour University, the man who had planned the Shanghai Uprising. Excessively confident because of the success of that urban insurrection, the Dean had advocated a military coup in Nanchang, the capital of Kiangsi Province. Success would give the Communists their own formidable army and control over most of South China. Almost all preparations having been made, the rising was scheduled to take place on July 31 – just five days away.

But Chang Kuo-tao had been despatched to countermand the plan. Moscow had vetoed the uprising, and the ever-obedient Dean had immediately agreed to kill his own creature. Even the independent Chang Kuo-tao was forced to concede that the Nanchang Rising could not attain its purposes if the Russians halted the flow of advisers, arms and gold to the Chinese Communist Party. He had, therefore, reluctantly agreed to carry the message countermanding the mutiny.

Chang Kuo-tao finally reached Nanchang on July 30th, after a bone-shaking journey from Kiukiang on the Yangtze River in a railway carriage with broken windows and splintered seats. His temper further frayed by long waits on sidings while troop trains rattled past, he was in no mood for nostalgia at returning to his native province. Besides, he had no time for sentiment. As soon as his train creaked to a halt, he was caught up in urgent discussions. Conversation did not cease on the ferry across the Kan River to Nanchang, for the Rising was scheduled for the next day.

The conspirators all came together in a weathered brick building beside the chief inn of the shabby provincial capital. Although the oiled-paper windows were open wide and the bamboo shutters were propped on sticks, no breeze relieved the hammering heat and the stifling humidity. The scent of the tropics hung over the city where jungle had once trailed arm-thick vines across tall palms while monkeys howled from the tree-tops at emerald and ruby parrots. Chang Kuo-tao recalled that the average temperature in July was 85 degrees. The thermometer might fall to 75 at night, but would rise over 100 in the daytime.

The long day in the airless room was exhausting and painful. Personal

244

rivalries influenced the mutineers almost as much as political necessity. The vinegar of jealousy seasoned the cold rice of strategy. Not only rebellious military officers argued with Chang Kuo-tao, but also Comrade Chou En-lai, who had been sent to Nanchang shortly after his miraculous escape in Shanghai.

Alternately mocking and affable, Chou En-lai dominated the interminable discussions. The former director of political training at the Whampoa Military Academy appeared untroubled by the mind-numbing heat. He was cool in crisp khaki drill, while his comrades were flushed in sweat-soaked homespun or crumpled labourers' blue. Wearing the clothing of the masses, they were like children dressed up for a masquerade. None was a son of the peasantry or the working class. The men who considered themselves the vanguard of the proletariat were almost all middle-class intellectuals.

Chou En-lai simply refused to consider cancelling the uprising. Still titular Political Commissar of the National Revolutionary Army, he was determined to incite it to mutiny. The sardonic smile on his mobile face presaged the failure of Chang Kuo-tao's mission.

As evening approached, the senior troop commander present suggested soberly: 'Perhaps we should postpone action for some time. Take more time to reconsider, as Chang Kuo-tao asks. After all . . .'

'This discussion's been going on forever,' Chou En-lai snapped. 'The Communist Party assigned me to do a job – and I'm going to do it regardless of second thoughts. If you won't go along with me, I'll be forced to quit – resign all my Party responsibilities.'

Chang Kuo-tao was distracted by noises outside. The cries of hawkers and the clamour of children were gradually supplanted by the sounds of the early evening. Where an itinerant knife-sharpener had clanged his shears, a noodle vendor trilled his bamboo flute. The squealing of pigs carried to market in wicker-work tubes had given way to the plaintive yodelling of a blind masseur. A hawker of sweetcakes cried his wares, and an itinerant storyteller pounded his miniature drum to summon his audience.

When he forced his attention back to the discussion, Chang Kuo-tao realized wearily that retreat was impossible. They could, perhaps, call off the Rising, but they could not call back the fact that it had been planned. So many people knew of the plan that the conspirators would be doomed if they drew back. He therefore yielded to the wishes of the comrades most directly concerned, asking only that the Rising be postponed one day to August 1. Declaring truthfully that he had never fundamentally opposed the Rising, he pledged his wholehearted support. Regardless of Moscow's misgivings, the Chinese Communists would dare to strike – and they would strike decisively.

As the night of July 31st fell, ladies of the evening clattered through the streets in wooden clogs that protected their finery from the mud puddles. A grove of green oiled-paper umbrellas bobbed between wood-and-brick buildings feebly lit by oil-lamps. In the inn next door, musicians rehearsed. An eight-tubed flute tirelessly repeated its scales while a nine-string lute was tuned interminably. A ten-year-old soprano vied for high C with a two-string violin, and a chorus of pi-dogs keened at the rising moon.

The scene, Chang Kuo-tao reflected, could have occurred a century ago – even five or ten centuries ago. The only modern note was the eerie moaning of a locomotive on the nothern shore of the unbridged Kan River. Medieval Nanchang on the south bank just beyond the railway's reach was the quintessential China, not industrial Shanghai.

Within the Communists' headquarters, apprehension crackled like heat. Worried staff officers and exhausted political commissars stared tensely at the wall-maps and the leather-cased field-telephones. The air was already rancid with the smoke of uncured tobacco, despite the occasional breeze that ruffled the moonlight.

The forced smile on the senior troop commander's face was transformed into a gargoyle's grimace by the blue-white glare of the acetylene lantern hanging above his head. The man who had argued that the Rising should be postponed could not completely conceal his doubts, although the fighting was already starting.

A field-telephone buzzed on the stained table where the city-map was spread amid dirty dishes, and the thirty-odd men in the room all stiffened in anticipation. The senior troop commander nonchalantly lifted the handset and listened with a strained smile. He fussily slotted the telephone back into its case before speaking.

'A dispatch carried by runners to the communications post on the north bank of the Kan River from the officer commanding our northernmost company. He reports that the Commander-in-Chief . . .'

Chou En-lai whispered into Chang Kuo-tao's ear: 'Old Ironsides himself. Our *nominal* Commander-in-Chief.'

'. . . turned up at a point seventy miles north of Nanchang headquarters yesterday afternoon. He questioned our troops' move south. May've suspected they were joining the Rising. He asked where they were bound – and on whose orders? Certainly not his, and he was their Commander-in-Chief. He then ordered them to halt.'

The troop commander lit a cigarette, and Chang Kuo-tao drew in his breath. Could a recrudescence of old-fashioned discipline have foiled the Uprising before it began? Beside him, Chou En-lai lounged insouciantly against a desk. But his long fingers drummed on the ebony top.

'The company commander fired a machine-gun burst just above the Commander-in-Chief's head,' the troop commander resumed. 'The Commander-in-Chief got the idea and left smartly.'

Guffaws and shouts of glee exploded across the room like a ragged artillery barrage. First blood to the insurrection! After exchanging excessively hearty congratulations, the comrades fell silent again.

What happened here in Nanchang this evening would be decisive, not a somewhat farcical contest of wills many miles to the north yesterday. Half the military units in the city and its environs were, at best, potentially hostile to the Communists. If those troops attacked before they were encircled or if they resisted strenuously, the fat would be in the fire. The Communists would no longer be worrying about the distant enemy, but about their own necks.

Headquarters was now powerless. During the new few hours the novice revolutionaries learned the hardest lesson of command: having cast their plans, deployed their troops, and issued their final orders, the staff officers could do nothing but wait for reports – and pretend that their mouths were not parched by tension.

Shortly after two in the morning, a telephone buzzed peremptorily. The troop commander extended a lean hand. He listened closely for half a minute, grunted non-committally, and replaced the handset. In silence he studied the city-map on the table for almost a minute before moving a red marker.

'That was Detachment Six,' he finally declared. 'Just reporting they've arrived at the jump-off position.'

A squeal of laughter from an adolescent runner transfixed the company. Deeper chuckles of relief followed, but were cut off by a volley of shots in the distance.

Louder shots scythed across the muted conversation, and a hush fell. Twenty seconds later, a rattle of rifle-fire sounded through the open windows. Volley followed volley. A machine-gun chattered for a few seconds. A second machine-gun answered, and the duet continued for a minute or two. It then abruptly broke off, and absolute silence descended.

Not a man spoke or moved. The silence lasted ten seconds, then twenty seconds, reached half a minute, and dragged its incorporeal length through the crammed room until almost a full minute had elapsed. The young runner lustily sucked a bleeding hangnail. Chairs creaked when their occupants shifted nervously. Chou En-lai yawned with tension, his jaws gaping wide. The troop commander's aide cracked his knuckles, and several officers jumped.

Hours later it seemed, though it was no more than four minutes, a telephone buzzed. The troop commander scrabbled for the instrument, his fingers, damp with sweat, slipping off the slick bakelite. Finally jamming the headset against his cheek, he barked into the mouthpiece. Listening to the protracted report he frowned, and his lean cheeks drew taut over his clenched teeth.

Before he could replace the instrument, its neighbour buzzed. The commander frowned savagely and shouted brusque questions into the mouthpiece. His right foot tapped impatiently as he strained to hear the response. His cheeks were mottled by anger when he slammed the handset into its case.

'It's those idiots!' He finally spoke. 'How many times have I dinned it into them – the proper form for a report? And the signal section isn't performing brilliantly. The lines are damned scratchy. . . .'

'For God's sake, man, what's happening?' Chang Kuo-tao exploded in frustration. 'Let us in on your military secret!'

247

'Sorry, Comrade.' The troop commander squinted through the rank tobacco smoke. 'Actually, it's going well. . . . But discipline and procedure, they're all important. These young officers! If they're ever going to amount to anything, they must learn. . . .'

'The report, Comrade? What was it?'

Chou En-lai's sharp interjection startled the rebel commander, and he said: 'Both reports concerned the garrison here in Nanchang. Some three thousand-odd men. We couldn't tell which way they'd jump. There was a dust-up – as you heard, a brisk exchange of fire. We suffered four killed and maybe ten wounded. Their casualties were higher. The garrison's all surrendered now, and we've got their weapons. The city is in our hands. Now for the outlying areas. Helluva lot more troops out there.'

The next half hour was enlivened by after-action reports from the Communist units within the city. Amid the clamour of relieved conversation the buzzing of a single telephone was almost inaudible. The commander's aide, however, lifted the headset and handed it to his superior. The crevices etched by strain around the commander's mouth deepened. The hushed room now clearly heard his brisk instructions: 'Disarm them first. Then we'll think whether we welcome them to the revolutionary ranks. Yes, it's great news!'

The troop commander flicked his battered lighter until the long cord kindled, and lit a cigarette from the smouldering end. He coughed with satisfaction before announcing with greater satisfaction: 'The 2nd Division reports no opposition. The fence-sitters all want to come over now!'

After the fourth similar call, the rebel commander leaned across the table and said: 'That's about it. The cadet regiment reporting. That old bandit their commander is in fine fettle. All the police have come over. And a clean sweep of all artillery batteries. Nothing can go wrong now.'

Although several superstitious comrades shuddered, that complacent observation was correct. When the early dawn cast a red glow into the smoke-clouded room, Nanchang and its environs were firmly in Communist hands.

The youthful leaders looked at each other with bloodshot eyes and rubbed stubbled cheeks with grimy palms. Their faces were ashen with fatigue, and their heads ached with tension and nicotine. But their hearts were filled with triumph. They could see the future clearly from the vantage point of their triumphant mutiny.

Chinese Communist military forces had just won their first clear-cut victory, and a glorious new stage of the Chinese revolution had begun. A mass uprising throughout the nation would inevitably follow the great victory at Nanchang – just as a prairie fire leaps from a single spark. The new Red Army, which had instantly sprung into existence on the morning of August 1, 1927, would conquer power everywhere in China within a year. Two years at most.

32

August 13–December 1, 1927

The Tibetan mastiff was still puppylike at the age of six despite his great size. The amah Lao Zee, who could not get her tongue around the foreign name Adam, called him Ah Dee, which fortuitously meant 'Younger Brother'. His playful 210 pounds constantly menaced the blue-and-white Ming porcelain his mistresses had been collecting since political disorder made it cheap. Rambunctious though he was, his jet-black coat with the white blaze on the chest gave him a priestlike appearance.

Adam was at his most dignified that mid-August evening. His domed head turned occasionally from the Gothic arch of the Atterbury Kent radio on the table under the window to check on Emily, who was stretched out on the orange-silk cushions of the cane sofa. All Shanghai was equally somnolent. The street noises, which could penetrate even the sixth-floor loft, were subsiding at 11 p.m., and the Strauss waltzes on Station XMHA engaged all Adam's attention. Emily was musing half-asleep, her bosom moving gently under her wipsy green kimono.

She should, perhaps, have accepted her parents' invitation to join them on the beaches of Peitaiho in North China. However, she disliked that resort because of the vulgar display of Hong Kong tycoons like the Sekloongs. She was also reluctant to strain the tentative rapprochement attained with her parents since her break with Richard Hollings. The wounds the elder Howes and she had inflicted on each other still needed time – and a little distance – to heal. Besides, she was irritated by her mother's constant sniping at all foreigners while meaning one foreigner in particular.

Her throat still ached when she thought of Richard. Yet she had sworn sincerely to her parents that she was through with foreign men forever.

She was, however, not quite ready for them to find her a good Chinese husband through a professional go-between in the good old-fashioned way. She did not like the idea of being hawked through the marriage-market like a prize mare. Besides, her vanity rejected the implication, however unintended, that she needed help in getting a man.

She also preferred the independence of the big flat in the loft to being stifled by Harmony Hall. Loath to leave Julia in the lurch, she was remaining to share expenses and hold her friend's hand while they worried about Tommy. Otherwise Julia would have been virtually alone to wonder when – if ever – he would be released. Elizaveta and Joshua were little help, totally preoccupied with their secret engagement. Julia's left-wing Chinese friends were less help. Still dodging vigorous anti-Communist sweeps throughout Shanghai, they were, none the less, obsessed with their joy in the stunning revival of Communist hopes since the Nanchang Rising two weeks earlier.

To Emily their jubilation appeared a delusion. Just four days after their triumph, the Communists had been forced to evacuate Nanchang by greatly superior Nationalist forces. The infant Red Army was presently withdrawing in some disarray towards Swatow on the coast, where the leaders planned to establish a base for the conquest of South China. Considering the common people's lack of enthusiasm for their self-appointed liberators, as well as constant harassment by hostile forces, Emily felt the Communists' enthusiasm was self-deceiving – not to say self-destructive.

An eager bark broke into her reverie. Adam pointed his muzzle at the imposing radio-set. The Strauss waltz had stopped abruptly, and a female announcer was saying: '. . . apologise for breaking into the concert. But the management of XMHA felt the news development warranted interruption.'

Adam was estatic – and puzzled – at hearing Julia's voice through the cloth-mesh speaker. Emily knew that Julia herself had decided to interrupt the concert, for only she and a lone Chinese engineer manned XMHA this late in the evening.

'Reuters News Agency reports that Generalissimo Chiang Kai-shek today resigned all his offices under the Nanking Government [Julia read, and Emily heard the rustle of the onion-skin paper of the wire-service file.] The dominant figure in the centre-right Nationalist Administration, the Generalissimo, is withdrawing from the political arena in order to break the deadlock that has set the three major factions within the Nationalist movement against each other. With the controversial Generalissimo removed, the rival groups are expected to reunite. Backed by the Christian General Feng Yü-hsiang, the Nationalist armies are expected to march against the northern warlords very soon. Other units are expected to crush the wave of rebellions in South and Central China which the Communists are raising under the slogan: *In Autumn, Harvest and Rebel!*'

The onion-skin sheets nervously rustled again, and Julia's voice quavered: 'The Generalissimo has already left Nanking for Shanghai,

250

where he will see personal friends before withdrawing to his home in Chekiang Province. It is understood he will spend the next five years studying moral and aesthetic philosophy. We now resume our interrupted concert. The next selection is "Tales from the Vienna Woods"!'

Of course Julia had developed a nervous quaver. Emily too, was dismayed by the Generalissimo's resignation. This time it sounded like the real thing, not just another threat made to get his own way. How would his withdrawal under pressure affect the Nationalist cause?

More immediately, the Generalissimo was the only hope for her brother's release – perhaps his survival. Cajoled by Mayling Soong, the Generalissimo had revealed that Tommy was a prisoner. Persuaded by Mayling, the Generalissimo had virtually guaranteed that Tommy would in time be released. Deprived of the Generalissimo's protection, Tommy was more likely to be shot than to be freed.

Emily lifted the telephone and gave the number of the Soongs' house on Seymour Road. Mayling might not be overjoyed at being called at ten minutes to midnight, but she couldn't help that.

'May, it's Emily.' They always spoke in English. 'Have you heard the news?'

'About my beau?' Mayling burbled. 'Of course, Emmy, and I'm delighted.'

'Why in the world? Not because he's out of power? Oh, I see. You mean it's another fake resignation?'

'Anything but! This time he really means it.'

'Then how can you be delighted?'

'Because it's the only way.' May's voice sparkled. 'The only way he can bring peace to the National People's Party. Then he'll come back to lead the unified Nationalist movement to victory!'

'So he *is* coming back soon. That's a relief.'

'I'm afraid not. Hardly soon,' Mayling responded. 'Not for some time. They've got to learn their lesson, those squabbling politicians. They've got to learn they can't do without him. Then . . .'

'So this is the decisive step?' Emily deliberately tested her friend's mood. 'You know, I still don't see why you're so bubbly.'

'There is something else. You know Mammie practically ran away. Well, Gimo's going to Japan to track her down and get her permission. He swears we'll be married before the end of the year.'

'Congratulations, darling. I'm so happy for you.'

'But what's up? Why're you calling at this time of night?'

'I just heard Julie on XMHA, reading the news of the Gimo's resignation. She sounded all broken up. May, what does this mean for Tommy? If the Gimo isn't around to help him . . .'

'Oh dear, Emmy. I didn't think of Tommy. I know Gimo promised to get him out. But he's been so busy lately. I just don't know. . . .'

'May, you've got to do something right now.' Emily sounded confident of their friendship, though she was never quite sure of the volatile May. 'Can you get to the Gimo tonight?'

'Hardly tonight, Emmy.' Was May's voice colder? 'But I'm seeing him tomorrow. As always, damn it, with an old aunt as a chaperone. At my age . . .'

'You *must* ask him about Tommy! May, darling, please! I'll never ask you for another thing. I'll be your slave for life. You *must* get the Gimo to intervene while he still can. If it's not already too late.'

'I'm sure it's well within his power – even now.' Hauteur frosted Mayling's voice. 'But he *is* very busy. Whether he can manage anything before he leaves for the country, I just don't know.'

'You will try, won't you May? I just know *you* can bring him round. Oh, May . . .'

'Of course I'll try, you ninny.' The presumptive fiancée of the most powerful man in China was cordial again, her own power having been acknowledged. 'I'll try hard. But I can't promise anything. . . . Em, I wouldn't get my hopes up if I were you.'

Quite unconcerned with the fate of Dr Thomas Tan-ssu Howe, Generalissimo Chiang Kai-shek disappeared at the end of August into the mountains of his native Chekiang Province just south of Shanghai. Like an Imperial mandarin out of office, he withdrew to the village of his birth to refurbish the tombs of his ancestors, above all his beloved mother's. Yet the couriers constantly trotting along the hillpaths between the tea bushes gave the lie to the pretence that he took little further interest in politics.

No pretence cloaked his failure to help Tommy. Her suitor had simply had no time whatsoever to look into the matter, Mayling Soong declared. She implied that he would have freed Tommy if he'd had a single free instant. Emily was duly grateful. Expressing her doubts would have mortally affronted Mayling – without helping Tommy at all.

The last faint hope had failed. If Tommy were lucky, a twist of fate might some day secure his release. If he remained unlucky, he would be locked in his cell indefinitely – or would be shot.

Even Julia, the ebullient optimist, stopped talking about Tommy. Then, despite herself, Emily resented her friend's apparent abandonment of her brother. At the other extreme, her father was being played for a fool. Although Donald Howe was paying large sums through the Floodgate Fraternity to buy Tommy decent food and small luxuries, he had no proof that his son was alive.

'It's costing me more than the royal suite at the Ritz,' he confided to his prodigal daughter. 'If only they'd let someone see him – even for a second.'

'Perhaps they can't, Father.' Emily did not spare him. 'Perhaps Tommy's not . . . not alive any more. They could be holding you up.'

'That's always possible, Yuelin. But what else can I do?'

Just before three on a humid afternoon in early September, Emily was drowsily reviewing the outstanding loans of the Women's Commercial Bank. Nothing more pressing required her attention in the dog days.

252

Leafing through the Ikra's file, she marvelled at Elizaveta's prompt payments. She also wondered idly what would become of Shanghai's glossiest bordello when its proprietress married.

Thinking of her parents in cool Peitaiho, she half-decided to join them – and to take Julia along. Her friend's days were empty. XMHA occupied her for only a few hours a week; the Customs College was still closed for the summer; and her left-wing friends were in hiding. Nowadays Julia rarely smiled and never laughed.

Emily's extension buzzed, and a sleepy operator reported Miss Mayling Soong calling. Since May's starling chatter about personalities, money, and politics was always diverting, Emily readily agreed to bring Julia to tea that afternoon. Since May never asked anyone else with them, neither bothered to change her simple day-dress. A dab of powder and a lick of lipstick were quite enough.

The Soongs' sitting room was, as always, undistinguished with its standard Ningpo-lacquer furniture and its heaps of *Saturday Evening Posts* and *National Geographics*. The electric fans blowing over big cakes of ice did, however, cool the room. Though the Soongs' enthusiasm for America sometimes seemed excessive, they had learned to make themselves comfortable in the American way. The chocolate chip cookies were delicious, and ice cubes floated in the refreshingly cold tea among slivers of lemon. Mayling proudly recalled that the Soongs had imported the first refrigerator Shanghai ever saw.

Their hostess was dressed for coolness. Her cream-linen smock with the scooped neckline was the antithesis of the assertively Chinese *cheongsam* she wore in public as if in dress-rehearsal for the role of the Republic of China's First Lady. Her slender ankles were set off by frivolous sandals that were no more than cobwebs of green and yellow leather strips.

Lulled by Mayling's gossip, Julia's thoughts drifted indolently. She casually noted the door-bell's tinkling and heard an amah's straw sandals flip-flopping down the long corridor to the front door. The amah asked high-pitched questions, which were unintelligible at a distance, and a deeper voice replied. An instant later, the amah shrieked – and a man laughed. Apparently deaf to that interchange, Mayling poured fresh tea from a frosted glass pitcher.

She looked up when leather soles trod the teak-floored corridor. A tall man appeared in the doorway. He was very thin and his white suit was baggy. Although the afternoon sunlight was filtered by split-bamboo blinds, he blinked repeatedly.

Dark spirals twisted before Julia's eyes, and she closed them firmly. She opened them again to see Emily's tan-pongee dress plastered against the stranger's white linen in a close embrace. Looking at his lean face, Julia knew she was hallucinating. Giddy and nauseated, she again closed her eyes to keep from fainting.

'Julie! Julie dearest! I've frightened you!' The crisp English accent was unmistakable. 'I didn't know either. They just brought me here. Julie dearest, I'm so happy to see you. I'm overjoyed!'

Julia opened her eyes to look directly into Tommy's. He was kneeling beside her chair. She clamped her arms around his neck and clung tight.

'Darling Tommy! My sweet! My baby!' she babbled. 'Oh, Tommy darling, you're back. You're really back?'

'Evidently so!' His tone deprecated his own emotion. 'Julie darling, it's wonderful. . . . And I've no idea how I got out.'

'You're so thin.' She studied him proprietorially. 'We'll have to feed you up. . . . And you're really all right? Only thinner, not sick or anything?'

'Fighting fit, though a little under my best fighting weight. Oh, Julie, I've got so much to say.'

But first Emily and Mayling had their turn to inspect the returned prisoner. Emily was bubbling with joy, and Mayling was unusually warm. When they finally settled down, Julia perched on the arm of the chair she had ceded to Tommy.

'Mayling Soong, you arranged this, didn't you?' Emily almost sounded accusing. 'It's all your doing.'

'Not entirely!' May came close to an unladylike grin. 'I didn't know he'd turn up when you were here – though I was hoping. A little bit of theatre . . . I could never resist . . .'

'They practically pushed me out of the door only an hour ago,' Tommy said, his voice hardening. 'I was the only one left. Forty-five men and six women in one lock-up. All executed. I saw them shot. All but me. Oh, I *am* sorry! I didn't mean to talk about that now.'

'Little Pow?' Julie demanded. 'Where is he? They didn't shoot him, did they, darling?'

'Not as far as I know. In the beginning, he kept me sane . . . looking after him. But they took him away a couple of months ago. God knows where. . . . But I'm talking too much. Why were they so eager to get rid of me? The two who brought me here were pretty sinister.'

'That's their trade!' May laughed. 'They're the favourite hatchetmen of the Supreme Lord of the Floodgate Fraternity. Gimo's blood-brother, you know.'

'I begin to see. . . .'

'If any one of you ever repeats a word, I'll be in big trouble.' Mayling laid down the law. 'You must promise me faithfully never to.'

She sipped her iced tea, and waved away the Chesterfields Julia offered. Tommy nodded emphatically. Indiscretion would increase the debt of gratitude his family already owed the imperious young woman.

'I decided not to keep after Gimo,' Mayling resumed. 'He was too busy and too far away. Besides, I didn't want him getting suspicious about my interest in Tommy. That wouldn't do at all. So I ran into the Supreme Lord. By accident, of course. He was happy to do a favour for his blood-brother. A couple of . . . ah . . . persuasive talkers called on the Shanghai Garrison Commander. They recalled the favours the Commander had received from the Floodgate. He would, they assumed, prefer the Supreme Lord's gratitude to his displeasure.'

'As easy as all that!' Emily marvelled, but Tommy interrupted: 'They turned me out, May. Dropped me like a white-hot coal. How come?'

254

'Well, Gimo had tried. He couldn't push too hard. Wouldn't do to irritate the Garrison Commander. Gimo could need his support later. But the Supreme Lord didn't give a damn. The Commander must have been terrified. Maybe afraid his opium would be cut off. So you see . . .'

Julia was only half-listening. Her eyes clung to Tommy. His mouth was vulnerable, and his narrow scholar's face was stamped with the pallor of imprisonment. Unshielded for once by plain-glass spectacles, his eyes were wounded. Her hand slipped out of his grasp and smoothed his thick hair.

Julia Pavernen, spinster of twenty-six years, knew then exactly what she wanted. Although the violent turmoil of China frightened her, she wanted Tommy Howe for the rest of her life – whether in Shanghai or in the wildest corner of his backward and turbulent country. Although she was exceedingly sensitive to her surroundings, she would go anywhere with him. The intensity and the simplicity of her emotion almost shocked her. She wanted only Tommy. She would happily accept everything that came with Tommy – violence or tranquillity, luxury or hardship.

The fugitive Communist leader Chang Kuo-tao had chosen the rendez-vous with his usual dash, as usual most reckless when he believed himself most cautious. The Majestic Café, halfway up Bubbling Well Road from the racecourse, advertised itself as 'the largest cabaret in Shanghai', and the enormous dance-floor was rimmed by dozens of white-covered tables. The Majestic also advertised: '100 charming dance hostesses'. But hardly a dozen couples were languidly foxtrotting when Julia and Tommy came through the double-doors.

No one looked up. Whether slumming or working as hostesses, young foreign women in party dresses were a common sight at the Majestic. So were well-to-do young Chinese men ritually sowing their wild oats. Most of those young men dutifully married the well-to-do Chinese brides their parents selected – and some even waited as long as six months before returning to the foreign women of the cabarets.

Perfectly camouflaged because they were exactly what they seemed to be in white sharkskin and chartreuse tulle, Tommy and Julia danced and sipped champagne. Neither noticed that it was already eleven, half an hour past the time Chang Kuo-tao had appointed.

They had just come from a formal Chinese dinner for five hundred guests, which Donald Howe had given to celebrate October 10th. It was the twenty-sixth anniversary of the Nationalist revolution that toppled the Manchu Dynasty. The delighted father could not declare that he was, above all, celebrating his youngest son's release from Nationalist captivity a month earlier. To acknowledge that Tommy had been held incomunicado for four months as a suspected Communist would have imperilled the Howes' good name. They were accordingly united behind the pretence that he had been engaged on secret service.

Tommy remarked that his father worried more about the two among his five children he had sent abroad to study than the remaining three.

255

His sister Emily's resumption of filial obedience had delighted their parents and proved the virtue of the old ways. She was admirably docile, except for continuing to work at the Women's Bank and remaining in the loft-flat.

Her mother had wisely prevailed upon her father not to ask that Emily give up her writing. When she was married, her scribbling would provide an amusing diversion – until responsibility for husband and children engaged all her energy and talents. And she would soon be married. Emily had at last suggested that her parents commission a professional go-between to find her a suitable husband. She was old, already twenty-six, but she was the only daughter of Donald Howe. His wealth and his power would ensure a good match.

'I hate to see her do it,' Julia said fiercely. 'But she won't listen. She hates herself for being duped by Dick Hollings.'

'She wants to punish herself,' Tommy agreed. 'If only she weren't in such a rush to marry. But no one can talk to her.'

While they chatted, they were weaving a strong fabric of mutual understanding to last them all their lives. Their protracted courtship had flared to its climax in that instant in Mayling Soong's dowdy sitting-room. They had looked at each other again and immediately known they would spend the rest of their lives together. Everything else was detail, lovingly filling in shadow and colour.

'No word of Little Pow?' After two months of negative answers, Julia was even more concerned. 'Nothing from Joshua?'

'Haven't I told you that he's been seen alive?' Tommy delighted in surprising her. 'I didn't hear from Josh, but from the Apparatus. They won't, maybe can't say exactly where. Got to protect their informants. But the Fascists are keeping him alive.'

'Darling, that's wonderful!' She squeezed his arm. 'The best news since you walked into May Soong's sitting room.'

Julia's new maturity no longer surprised Tommy. It still delighted him. She was eager for further news of Little Pow, but she did not press him. Otherwise, she had not changed. Her vitality struck him again with joy whenever he saw her – even if they had been apart for only an hour.

'By the way,' he said. 'Judge Allman says he'll marry us any time – with discretion. Just name the day.'

'Tommy, I'd rather wait. All this hole-in-the-corner business – to keep it from your parents. I don't like it. And I'd really like to have my parents at the wedding. Why not wait a while until we can be married in the open? It may be a pipe-dream, but . . .'

'You're telling me the truth, Julie? You're not worried about . . . ah . . . about something like Emmy's break-up with Hollings?'

'Naturally, I think about it.' She was relentlessly candid. 'But you're not Richard. And I'm not Emmy. So I'd just as soon wait till exactly the right moment. Till then, let's go on as we are.'

'We can't. Not entirely.'

'And why not, Doctor?' Julia's jocular tone did not conceal her sudden fear. 'What's to stop us?'

'Julie, I've got to tell you something.' He began gravely. 'There's something you should know about me.'

'Some secret crime?' She joked anxiously. 'Two wives hidden away – and a clutch of children?'

'Not that, darling. One is plenty!' He grinned and added with apparent irrelevance: 'You know Emily is totally committed to the Generalissimo.'

'What's that to do with us?' she demanded. 'Though I wouldn't be in her shoes.'

'Nor me,' he replied. 'That spell in the nick finished me with the Nationalists forever. Not that they were beastly to Donald Howe's son. They might have shot me, but they wouldn't mistreat me. For the other prisoners it was dreadful. Daily executions in the courtyard – men and women, even girls and boys. Mostly working people. The Nationalists don't give a tinker's dam for the common people – whatever they say. . . . But I got carried away. Where was I?'

'Finished with the Nationalists forever. And no wonder!'

'But I can't just lie doggo. Can't pretend politics are nothing to do with me and get on with healing the sick. So I've told the Apparatus I'd be more active – subject to your approval. They didn't like that, but . . .'

'My darling Tommy,' she interrupted, 'you're not being blindingly clear.'

'Not to put too fine a point on it, the Apparatus want me to do a lot more for them. I imagine that's why Chang Kuo-tao wants to see us. By God, it'll be good to see the big rascal again after . . .'

Tommy broke off when a bony hand thrust a tiny booklet at him. He grinned sheepishly at his alarm. The booklet was made up of flimsy white-and-red betting-slips on the National Lottery, which had recently been established on the irrefutable premise that the best way to extract funds from China's people to develop China's roads and airports was to offer them a flutter.

'Missy can catchee many many dollah,' the crone in rusty black exhorted by rote. 'Every time can catchee half million. Ticket no moren ten dollah. Missy no wantchee many many dollah?'

Tommy waved her away. But she stubbornly reiterated her litany and touched Julia's sympathy. Tommy dutifully laid a ten-dollar note on the table.

'*Kwuh-kwuh kan* . . .' the crone advised. 'Look at your ticket right now, sir. Make sure it's in order.'

Tommy incuriously turned over the slip. The hawker vanished into the gloom, as immaterial as the tobacco smoke curling around the beehive chandeliers. Scrawled on the reverse of the slip by a thick-nibbed fountain-pen were ideograms reading: THE CASINO AT 11:30.

Tommy grinned at the conspiratorial histrionics. If anything betrayed him, Julia reflected as they rose, it would be his irrepressible humour. Still, the struggle for social justice need not always be waged in funereal solemnity. Occasionally it could be fun.

Since the backroom casino was even dimmer than the dance-hall, they could for a minute see only grey shapes. It was almost deserted. Two Chinese men sat with four White Russian hostesses at the fan-tan table, languidly betting on the number of buttons that would finally remain at the end as the croupier removed four at a stroke from a random heap. A blackjack dealer had only three clients.

In a corner they saw the China Coast version of roulette: a larger ball and a smaller wheel with fewer divisions. Alone at that table sat a large young man whose sumptuous blue-silk long-gown marked him as the scion of a wealthy old-fashioned family. When Julia took the adjoining stool, he continued to stare at the motionless wheel. Finally he told the croupier to place his stack of chips on red. When the wheel whirled, he turned away as if disdainful of money and nodded casually to Tommy.

'Good to see you again,' Chang Kuo-tao said prosaically. 'The croupier's ours. Just keep betting as we talk. It's been a long time, hasn't it?'

'July of last year.' Tommy's pleasure was obvious. 'You're looking well. A bit thin, though.'

'So I should be.' The big man smiled wryly. 'All that healthy exercise in the fresh air. I've walked across half China since I saw you last. Only just got back. By Heaven, Tom, it was quite a walk. After the Nanchang victory, the South China débâcle! By mid-September . . .'

Julia had expected the dark glamour of the secret realm of espionage. The preliminaries had not disappointed her, but she listened with disappointment to the Communist leader's matter-of-fact tone. He might have been telling casual acquaintances about his summer holidays. Adjusting to the heavily accented Shanghainese which he spoke in deference to her meagre knowledge of Mandarin, she realized that he was relating high drama.

Chang Kuo-tao did not speak of his own gradual decline within the Communist Party from acting-chairman of the First Congress and director of the all-important Organization Bureau to second-class membership in the Political Bureau. A loyal Party member served gladly in whatever capacity the Party directed. Besides, where else did he have to go? The Party was his life. Without the Party he was nothing.

Chang Kuo-tao recalled that many of the ordinary soldiers of the fledgling Red Army had been captured and executed by the enemy. While a few had blended into the civilian populace, the greatest number had returned to brigandry or joined the enemy's ranks. Only one small fighting unit remained in existence. Some six hundred men under General Chu Teh, whose name meant Red Virtue, had gone into hiding in northern Kwangtung Province to reorganise. There were rumours of a band of peasant militia under the zealot Mao Tse-tung, but they could hardly be considered a fighting unit.

'It was nerve-racking getting back to Shanghai.' Without emotion Chang Kuo-tao watched his stake vanish. 'I had to go through Hong Kong, then take a coaster to Shanghai. Because I'm so thin, I've been masquerading as a sick schoolteacher. I only put on this get-up to meet you two.'

'Well then . . .' Tommy paused when the croupier's rake swept up the $500 he had perversely placed on black thirteen. 'That *was* quick. And, my friend, what do you want of us?'

'The Communist underground is in tatters,' the militant replied. 'We need help, and I was told to renew personal contact with you. You'll receive specific instructions through cut outs. We'll only use you for high-level work. And propaganda, of course! You've explained to Joo-li?'

Tommy asked deadpan: 'Who's going to make up my roulette losses, Kuo-tao?'

'Just mark them down to experience!' the big man chuckled. 'They'll go into our war-chest. The Party can use every cent it can get nowadays. What about Joo-li?'

'Naturally, I'm with you,' she interposed. 'You must know I used to run errands for the Dean. But I was never part of the regular Apparatus. What could *I* possibly do?'

'*That's* the next point on the agenda,' Chang Kuo-tao answered drily. 'A great deal. Your information's always been greatly appreciated. But there's a whole new field. Some day soon, public opinion abroad will be very important, perhaps crucial. Hacks like Anna Louise Strong and Agnes Smedley are useful. But they're too obviously Communists!'

Julia flared: 'What's propaganda to do with me? Tommy knows I can't write two coherent sentences.'

'That's the beauty of it, Joo-li. No one will ever suspect. You're both to appear a little to the right, even anti-Communist. Then you can work on the foreign reporters who're always drifting in and out of Shanghai. Chaps like young Vincent Sheehan. He already thinks he knows everything, so he's easy to flatter – and to steer. You do see?'

'Tommy, it's perfect!' she joked. 'A good excuse for my extravagance. To appear right-wing, we've got to have expensive right-wing tastes.'

'It won't always be beer and skittles. However, with two of us working together . . .'

'I suppose there's no hope of reconciliation with the Nationalists?' Julia feared the big Communist would consider her incurably naïve, but there had been extraordinary twists in political alliances during the past few years. 'There are some very good people like Mayling Soong.'

Chang Kuo-tao retorted: 'Just another rotten twig of the corrupt Soong clan.'

'That's not fair,' Julia protested. 'Look what she did for Tommy. Behind the Generalissimo's back, too. Just look at . . .'

Appalled at inadvertently betraying May's secret, Julia clapped her hand over her mouth. But Chang Kuo-tao showed no surprise.

'You really believe Mayling Soong got Tommy out of jail?' He laughed abruptly. 'Of course I know about the so-called secret deal with the Supreme Lord to free the doctor. Half Shanghai knows. And you actually believe Mayling . . .'

Julia looked imploringly at Tommy, disturbed at having thus betrayed May's confidence. He was, however, not concerned.

259

'You actually swallowed that fairy tale, Julie, didn't you?' Tommy's tone was fond, yet chiding. 'You really believed the Gimo couldn't find out where they were holding me – and couldn't spring me? You really believed May Soong went to the Supreme Lord behind the Gimo's back? Even if she were that foolish, he would never have played. He'd never take political action without consulting his blood-brother!'

'Then why ... why the play-acting?' Julia knew this question, too, displayed her naïveté. 'Why try to mislead us?'

'That's why you've got to look like rightists from now on,' Chang Kuo-tao asserted. 'The Nationalist secret police have their eye on Joo-li. And, of course, Chiang Kai-shek wanted Tommy held. He was purging all Communists – and he had a sneaking suspicion Tommy was a Communist. Funny how that suspicion and his imprisonment pushed him over the edge – made him one of us. Anyway, you've both got to reform. Got to be seen to reform. You must rise above suspicion if you're to be of any use. If you're to survive.'

'I'm still confused, Kuo-tao. Why did the Nationalists let Tommy go? And so suddenly?'

'Same reasons Chiang Kai-shek didn't shoot him in the first place – his father and his father's gold,' Chang Kuo-tao replied. 'Donald Howe is too rich and too prominent to cross lightly. But they'll be watching you two like a couple of microbes under a lens.'

Julia grimaced, but the ugly image drove his point home. For the first time, she understood in her bones. Waging the revolutionary struggle was not fun, but deadly serious. The penalty for negligence was not embarrassment, but imprisonment – or death.

The snub was a nettle hidden in a bouquet of roses, a stinging rebuff. Emily should have been one of the four bridesmaids who followed Mayling Soong down the red carpet between the massed flowers. Mayling had, however, explained at the last minute that the Gimo objected to Emily's inclusion in the wedding party. He would not insist, but Mayling could not displease him in the slightest on this day – regardless of her own wishes. She had, therefore, regretfully substituted her niece Pauline, the eldest daughter of her eldest sister and the Yale-educated banker-politician H. H. Kung.

The bride's attendants were now all to be blood relations. The Kung family was over-represented: Their younger children, Jeanette and Louis, were to be pages in back-velvet knickerbockers and white-satin waistcoats. Mayling would be able to boast that she had been attended on her wedding day by three lineal descendants of the Sage Kung Fu-tze, whom foreigners called Confucius.

The nettle stung again when May added: 'I'm afraid the Howes are under a tiny cloud. Not only Tommy's imprisonment but, quite frankly, Emmy dear, your own involvement with that man Hollings. A foreigner, after all. I know that's all past, and it was innocent, so to speak. But Gimo has to be very careful in his position.'

Emily could not in decency – or prudence – retort that the General-issimo was hardly one to make moral pronouncements. Aside from his secret society connections, he had cut a wide swathe among the Ikra's sister establishments. He was, moreover, not quite divorced from his second wife, who had accompanied him throughout the Northern Ex-pedition while he was writing devotedly to Mayling. Mammie Soong had had his own affirmation that no impediment existed to his new marriage. He had, of course, not based that affirmation on Chinese polygamy, which he actually practised. Instead, he argued that his second marriage had no legal validity because it had been contracted when his first mar-riage was still valid. One wrong apparently made a right for the foreigners – and blessed the private Christian ceremony at Mayling's home.

The public wedding in the traditional style was to take place here in the great ballroom of the Majestic Hotel. Emily glanced at Tommy on her left, who was fidgeting on the delicate gilt chair. Beside him, Julia smiled thinly. Her coolness towards May Soong, briefly warmed by gratitude for Tommy's rescue, had now frozen into dislike. Emily drifted into momentary resentment at her parents' tacit acceptance of Julia's relationship with Tommy. If they had been as tolerant of her own in-fatuation with Richard Hollings, she would never have broken with them – and she would have seen through him much sooner.

A quarter of the 1,300-odd guests waiting for the tardy wedding party were foreigners. They had turned out in force in homage to the powerful Soong family and to honour Chiang Kai-shek, their saviour from the Communist threat, which they had only lately believed he embodied. Under the benevolent eye of the American Consul-General, their doyen, the Japanese, Swedish, Italian, British, and French Consuls-General were sleek in morning coats. The admiral commanding the U.S. Asiatic Fleet sat beside the major-general commanding Britain's land forces in China. Both wore civilian clothing in deference to the bridegroom's nationalistic sensibilities, which had not prevented his marrying in the International Settlement, which was his bride's home. Foreign taipans, bankers, lawyers, and adventurous entrepreneurs with their ladies were in attend-ance in large numbers.

Having made their peace with the Nationalists, none of the foreigners was disturbed by the portrait of Dr Sun Yat-sen hanging between crossed white-sun flags. The Father of the Nation beamed over an altar table set in a bower of white flowers with green foliage. On either side, shields of white and red chrysanthemums displayed the double-joy ideogram to invoke nuptial bliss. Overhead, Emily saw in her boredom, hung en-ormous wedding bells made of tens of thousands of white blossoms.

A ripple of indrawn breath ran though the ballroom. The foreign band stubbornly completed its rendition of 'The Japanese Sandman' while Generalissimo Chiang Kai-shek and his best man strode down the snowy canyon formed by massed white flowers. The bridegroom's expression was at once ingratiating and defiant. His hairline moustache, his wing-collar, and the carnation in the lapel of his morning coat were all foreign. So were the kidskin gloves dangling limply in his left hand.

In the sudden silence Press Graflexes clicked, and newsreel cameras whirred to record the social occasion of the year, perhaps the decade. Scores of discarded flashbulbs popped underfoot when Mayling Soong came down the aisle on the arm of her brother T.V.

Behind her demure mask, as expressive as a porcelain doll, the bride's eyes blazed in fierce triumph. She had won what she wanted, and she was beautiful in her victory. Her gown of white-and-silver georgette, draped over the left hip, was accented by a train of silver-embroidered white satin. Her trailing veil of Honiton lace was secured by a chaplet of orange blossoms, and her enormous bouquet of blush-pink roses was tied with silver-and-white ribbons that matched her silver shoes and stockings.

'Trust the Soongs!' a male voice whispered behind Emily. 'They *never* let go of silver.'

Eminence always attracted envy, Emily reminded herself. The Generalissimo and his bride were beyond question the most eminent couple in the land. This marriage ceremony also crowned the personal triumph of Chiang Kai-shek. Even his chief rival had come to pledge the allegiance of South China and the progressive wing of the National People's Party to the new leader. In the north, the Generalissimo's ally, the Christian General, was on the point of driving the Old Marshal out of Peking. The Central Executive Committee of the reunited National People's Party was to meet in Shanghai in two days' time to restore Chiang Kai-shek as Commander-in-Chief.

The bride's entrance on her brother T.V.'s arm sealed these triumphs. Befitting the quasi-political occasion, bride and bridegroom posed for the cameramen even before the ceremony began. They then bowed to the portrait of Dr Sun Yat-sen within its floral bower. Oddly the bride's elder sister, who was the widow of the Father of the Nation, had ostentatiously absented herself.

Her features misty behind the cloud of lace, the bride listened gravely to the reading of the marriage certificate. Nodding his head benevolently, the bridegroom watched the witnesses impress their red seals on that certificate with jade stamps. Bride and bridegroom bowed first to each other, then to the witnesses, and finally to the audience. At no time did even their fingertips brush, for traditional etiquette forbade their touching each other.

The voice of an American baritone throbbing 'Oh, Promise Me!' confirmed the Chinese marriage. Mayling Soong Chiang's heart raced with pride as she and her husband stood under an enormous bell of red and white roses to pose again for the photographers. She smiled graciously. The swelling applause heralded the applause that would hail them all their lives.

While the photographers were pleading for one more shot, the bride slipped away to change into her travelling costume. Still puzzled by the strange music, the bridegroom followed. The Chiangs were to board a special train for Hangchow. That ancient resort was to be the gateway to the bright new China they were sworn to create – and to rule.

Transition
1928–1936

As the year 1928 began, the blackened stump of the sky-rocket that had been the Communist Party of China was dropping to earth in a sparsely populated mountain range in South China. At the same moment, Emily Howe and Julia Pavernen, inspired by Mayling Chiang's triumphant ceremony, were thinking chiefly of weddings. While delighted by the virtual eclipse of the leftists, Emily was deeply concerned about her own uncertain future. Julia had to pretend to share her friend's pleasure at the Nationalist high tide. While feigning satisfaction at the successive disasters that overwhelmed the Communists, she was also working hard to turn that tide. But it was to be a long time before the Communists were again serious contenders for power over China.

On August 5, 1927, four days after the Nanchang Rising, the new Red Army had withdrawn from that city. Two days later, a few members of the Political Bureau of the Communist Party had met in Wuhan to select a new secretary-general and to define a new strategy. The new man was Julia's old mentor, the Dean of Shanghai Labour University, who was responsive to Moscow's faintest whisper. The new plan was the old plan Moscow had previously opposed: to overthrow both the left-wing Nationalist Government at Wuhan and the right-wing Nationalist Government at Nanking and sweep into power a Soviet Government ruled by workers and peasants through mass insurrection backed by the new Red Army.

Deep in the morass of South China, Tommy's friend Chang Kuo-tao had learned of the renewed strategy and written in his diary: 'The Dean's plan for a general uprising is ridiculous – obviously dreamed up in a Shanghai attic. He thinks a single peasant only need set fire to a single landlord's house with a single match – and all China will rise in revolt.'

Chang Kuo-tao was, at that stage, still relatively optimistic. After he reappeared in Shanghai in late October, he confided to Tommy that he had no hope of a Communist victory for years to come.

From Swatow all down the South China Coast to Canton, a series of armed Communist revolts had seized large areas – and then lost them. Battering itself against popular indifference and Nationalist armies, the strategy of urban insurrection had failed catastrophically. Shortly after Chang Kuo-tao returned in disguise to Shanghai, Chou En-lai had escaped from the last abortive uprising, the Canton Commune, which had endured for just eleven days. Moreover the Red Army was shattered.

In the spring of 1928, no one knew that the nucleus of the army that was to conquer China already existed. Two splinter forces had coalesced in the mountain-range that straddled the border between Kiangsi Province and Kwangtung Province: the two hundred-strong Workers' and Peasants' Army commanded by Mao Tse-tung, and the five hundred-man remnant of the Red Army commanded by the former warlord called Chu Teh, which means Red Virtue.

In Shanghai, the Central Committee of the Communist Party was chiefly concerned to keep itself alive. Chang Kuo-tao confided to Tommy Howe: 'I could be picked up by the secret service at any time. But there's some hope. Because the special agents are paid by the foreigners and the Nationalists to root us out, they don't want to take too many prisoners. By dragging it out, they've got a perpetual fountain of gold. Also, the Party is using every last cent and all its energy for counter-intelligence – just to keep a step ahead of the secret agents. Nothing's left for revolutionary work among the masses.'

Tommy was invaluable to the hunted leaders of the Communist Party. His father was a major contributor to the Nationalist Party, and his sister was being drawn closer by Mayling Soong Chiang despite the snub at the wedding. He thus knew of most sweeps planned against the Communist underground. His sources were almost *too* good, too high-level. But he won entrée to the working level by the discreet medical assistance he provided at all hours. Through Joshua Haleevie, he also had some access to the Foreign Settlement's anti-Communist plans.

However, Julia did most of the spadework among the foreigners. She was well known as Quick Jack Pavernen's niece and as the announcer for Station XMHA. Police officers vied to impress the flighty young lady, even though she seemed stuck on that Chinese doctor. Hoping she would come to her senses and drop the Chinaman, the young bloods talked of their operations and their plans to dazzle her by their importance. No danger of the pretty flapper's passing on secrets. Whom would she tell?

The Communist Party was struggling to survive, and the Nationalist Armies, reunited under Generalissimo Chiang Kai-shek, were moving northwards. Mayling Chiang was attempting to make a home in raw Nanking and regularly summoning Emily Howe to the new capital. The impossible dream was becoming a reality. China was close to reunification under a forward-looking government. However, both Tommy and

Julia were appalled by the Generalissimo's march to victory over the corpses of hundreds of brave Communist comrades.

Another matter engaged Julia's emotions in the bright spring of 1928. She realized that she was more afraid of losing Tommy than of marrying him. Besides, a young woman of almost twenty-seven had to recognize that both marriage and children could evade her if she did not act now. And Tommy was pressing her hard.

'As Jack Pavernen,' he said, 'is given to remarking over the poker table: "You talk a good lay. But when it comes to the action, where are you baby?"'

'Tommy, I really resent that.' Laughing despite herself, Julia did not pretend not to understand. 'You of all people should know. About the action, I mean.'

Tommy actually blushed. Though the blood darkened his cheeks, he persisted: '*Touché*, my pet. Why not just say you'll marry me? We can't go on this way forever!'

'I suppose not,' she conceded for the first time. 'But, Tommy, I'm afraid.'

'What's there to be afraid of?' he demanded. 'The girl who bearded Chiang Kai-shek in his lair and sold him a load of old guns. The Mata Hari of the Foreign Settlement, what could she possibly fear?'

'Well . . .' she prevaricated. 'I've never been responsible for anyone except myself. And in a foreign country . . .'

'It means *less* responsibility for you, my beautiful idiot.' He was almost insufferably patronizing. 'And more for me.'

Julia disliked his assumption that husbands carried all the responsibility in marriage, But she could not arrest the swift passage of time. Nature was particularly unfair to women in so closely restricting their child-bearing years. She knew she wanted children badly. But did she want *Tommy's* children?

No, that was not quite the question. She did love Tommy, and she did want his children. But did she really want to bring into an unsettled world children who would suffer at the hands of both Caucasians and Chinese because they were both Caucasian and Chinese – and actually neither? The world would assuredly be more enlightened in ten or twenty years than it was even in the emancipated 1920s. But racial prejudice would hardly have vanished. Besides, marriage was gamble enough without loading the dice against yourself by taking a man of another race in an alien land.

'What can you possibly be afraid of?' Tommy impatiently repeated. 'Me, perhaps? Wicked Shanghai? Now, Julie . . .'

He was getting too close. Yet what was she actually afraid of? A revelation almost stunned her: she was already committed to Tommy, pledged beyond question by her deeds – public and private. Whatever might lie ahead, she could not repudiate that pledge.

Tommy and Julia were married in mid-April of 1928. Like Mayling

265

Soong, Julia was married twice to the same man on the same day. The civil ceremony performed by Judge Allman in his chambers was attended only by family, the Howes and John Pavernen. In the ballroom of the Palace Hotel an hour later a thousand guests watched the bride and groom lift their minute porcelain wine-cups before the red-satin draped altar: first to the witnesses, afterwards to his parents and her uncle, and then to each other. Finally, they exchanged cups and sipped, each from the other's, to seal the union. Julia felt only a little deprived because there was no Christian ceremony, although Judge Allman invoked a non-denominational deity after pronouncing them man and wife according to the laws of the District of Columbia.

Whatever Donald Howe said beforehand, he had accepted the marriage when it was clearly inevitable. He made only one condition in return for the father's blessing which would set Tommy's conscience at rest – and assure a struggling young doctor and his wife of luxury they would not otherwise have known for years. Donald had insisted upon the traditional Confucian ceremony and the formal reception. He wanted a public demonstration of unity, so that there would be no gossip about the Howes' falling out over his son's marriage to a foreign woman.

Public solidarity was essential after the public humiliation of Emily's protracted defiance. But she was striving to atone for her refusal to marry the man they had chosen. The crusader for women's rights was for a time eclipsed by the filial daughter who had returned to Harmony Hall from the loft-apartment on Kiukiang Road where Tommy and Julia were to start their married life.

Emily had advised Julia *never* to agree to move into the family mansion, 'not if they offer you a wing as big as Grand Central Station'. She could cope for a time with her parents' intrusiveness. But no daughter-in-law, above all no foreign daughter-in-law, could endure the implacable pressure they instinctively exerted.

Emily herself had no intention of remaining under the parental roof for long. She loved her parents, and she wished to please them. But she could not live with them for more than a few months. She was therefore determined to marry just as soon as they found her a suitable husband.

When she revealed that determination, the conversation broke down. Julia stared in perplexity at the three-carat diamond on the engagement ring beside her white-gold wedding ring, and Tommy threw up his arms in a display of emotion alien to both his Confucian heritage and his English public school training.

'Look here, Emmy, you'll destroy yourself if you let them arrange your marriage,' he admonished. 'God alone knows who they'll find. After all, you are "damaged goods". Only one thing's certain: whoever they dig up will be rich, elderly – and repulsive!'

Emily replied equably: 'I do appreciate your worrying about me. But the sooner I marry, the sooner I'll be *really* independent. I can't stand up to the parents any more. I used up all my resistance when I was defying them over . . . over Richard. And look where that got me! For me it's right to go back to the old ways.'

Supremely – and somewhat smugly – happy three months after she had married for love, Julia expostulated: 'Em, honey, why can't you hang on a little longer? Just stall them for a while. Somebody better is sure to come along. Tommy and I want you to be just as happy as we are. But there's not a chance if you rush into . . .'

'You still don't understand, Julie, do you?' Emily responded gently. 'Even now, you don't understand how Chinese women are trapped.'

'No, Emmy, I don't understand!' Julia exploded. 'I only understand that you're going to destroy yourself. With all the young men in Shanghai, the stream of diplomats and foreign correspondents you meet, I'd think . . .'

'I could *never* marry a foreigner!' Emily declared flatly. 'It would only prove I'd learned nothing from my ordeal with Richard. However, Chinese ladies are expected to marry – and I wouldn't be happy otherwise. That doesn't leave me much choice, does it?'

'Are you asking me or telling me? You've got all the choice in the world. Meanwhile, the Bank and your writing, they're enough to fill your life until . . .'

'Until I'm too old to have children, Julie? Or too old to be a good mother? I want children – now, not some vague time in the future. The last thing I need is so-called romance! The best thing is to marry the man my parents have chosen.'

She paused and reached for Julia's Chesterfields. When her cigarette was alight, she inexpertly puffed out a cloud of smoke and added mischievously: 'To tell the truth, they've already found a good man. He's called Ou-yang Hsiu, and he's a well-to-do banker with a good reputation. He also has a good disposition, a kind nature. I respect Mr Ou-yang Hsiu – and I know I'll never really care for him. So I'll be my own mistress.'

Julia retreated into the cave of her own thoughts. She disliked her sister-in-law's self-deceiving excuses for her foolish decision to evade life's normal uncertainties – and unexpected joys. Although Emily seemed undisturbed by the cool reception accorded her momentous news, she left shortly afterwards. Regarding her fiancé she would only add that he was 'an old-fashioned gentleman'.

After her departure, the normally imperturbable Tommy declared hotly: 'She couldn't tell us any more because she doesn't know any more. She's absolutely set on restoring the image of a perfectly united Howe family with perfectly filial children. Because she besmirched that image, she now wants to punish herself.'

'Why?' Julia asked when he wearily rubbed his eyes. 'And for the rest of her life?'

'There's nothing worse in Confucian morality than failing in filial piety,' Tommy explained. 'The old Sage's dead hand has still got a tight grip on us Chinese, even when we pretend to be modern and Westernised. Emily's going to atone for her treachery by making a living sacrifice of herself.'

'Let's drop the subject, Tommy. It's making you too unhappy.'

'Spoken like a good wife. But it isn't *talking* about Emmy's lunacy that makes me unhappy. It's her lunacy *itself*.'

267

The next day, Tommy was summoned to Harmony Hall, where Donald Howe and his four sons dined with the prospective bridegroom. Women were of course excluded. Tommy returned to his wife to report: 'Actually, the old boy they've lured into the net is a fairly decent type. He's even agreed to let her control her own money. She'll keep it in the Women's Bank. She's sacrificing herself, but she's keeping her money independent – and still working for female emancipation! Talk about contradictions! You women!'

Julia let that masculine arrogance pass with a raised eyebrow, and Tommy added: 'Of course, her dowry's not peanuts. A cool half million Pater's coughing up, a quarter of a million US.'

'Did he have to *buy* her a husband?' Julia asked angrily. 'Mr Ou-yang Hsiu doesn't sound like a very nice man at all. More like a greedy pig.'

'Julie, she *is* damaged goods!' Tommy explained again. 'Just being seen with a foreigner spoiled her reputation.'

'This marriage is the most hypocritical thing I've ever heard. But what's he really like? And exactly how old?'

'He's an old-style landowner, rather formal and very proper. Originally from around Soochow way. He's a kindly gentleman of fifty-three years. . . . What are you doing?'

'Counting on my fingers, naturally. Let me see now. He would have been twenty-four when Emmy was born.'

'A gulf, I grant you, but traditionally acceptable. And he *is* twelve years younger than Pater. Any rate, he always wears a long-gown, and he speaks nothing but Shanghainese and Soochow. He's very well off, though not in Pater's league. He badly wants the connection with the Howes. We're pretty big guns, you know. So he's happy to take on the slightly spoiled Miss Howe.'

'Has he been married before? What about children?'

'Five children, I'm told. He's had two wives. One died. The other he sent back to her family years ago. So he's free.'

'Not even a concubine?' Julia pressed. 'How unusual for a proper, old-fashioned Chinese gentleman.'

'Actually, my love . . .' Tommy looked away. 'Actually, there was a little country girl. Emily said she didn't care, but Mater insisted he sent his concubine away. And he agreed without a squeak.'

'So many sacrifices just to acquire spoiled goods?' Julie did not regret her derisive note. 'He must be a perfect angel!'

'He *is* eager. You see, he also wants more children.'

'More children? And he's got five already?'

'But they're *old-fashioned* children. Mr Ou-yang Hsiu wants *modern* children for the modern age. And who better to breed them from than a modern American-educated lady?'

'Tommy, it sounds crazy! Crazy and repulsive! It's quite mad! But, I suppose, it's also unavoidable.'

Emily Howe was a modern woman – a feminist and a supporter of the

National Revolution. The amiable man she married was a living fossil – and their wedding was an archaic pageant. As a concession to the times, her lavish trousseau was borne through the streets for display in open trucks bedizened with scarlet-and-gold ribbons, rather than on platforms carried by coolies, and Emily rode behind the drawn blinds of the emerald-green Rolls Royce Silver Ghost, not confined in a closed scarlet bridal palanquin.

For weeks, Harmony Hall was like a department store at Christmas. The circular ballroom with the glass dome was crammed with brocaded silks, embossed satins, crêpe de chine, and delicate gauzes, ranging from the palest pinks, greens, blues, and violets down to rich crimsons, deep greys, glowing chestnuts, and lustrous blacks. As the society editor of the *Evening Press* enumerated ecstatically '. . . and in dozens of glass cases: bracelets, rings, buckles, earrings, necklaces, and hair ornaments. Apple-green jade was the principal stone, but diamonds, rubies, pearls, sapphires, and emeralds shone resplendently. . . .' Ranks of furniture blocked the corridors. Huge wooden chests with gleaming brass locks stood beside bedroom suites of carved rosewood. One ornate brass bed was hung with silk curtains and silver ornaments. Furthermore, there were embossed gold and silver teapots, ivory and jade chopsticks, crystal bowls, silver-wire wine-cups, jewellery cases, hand-painted scrolls, and silk banners *ad infinitum*.

The dowry arrived early in ten trucks at the old fashioned house in Jessfield Park that was the home of the bridegroom – and his unmarried children. It was substantial but only a mansion, not a virtual palace like Harmony Hall. Within the brick-wall of the compound, the three-storey building enclosed a courtyard roofed with glass, where two bands were competing. Chinese in soiled long-gowns picked out arias from Shanghai operas on traditional instruments, and gaudily uniformed Filipinos rendered popular tunes. From the overhanging verandahs hung great octagonal lanterns, which trailed crimson-silk streamers with silver tassels. Scarlet banners covered the walls, and twenty-foot-long runners of fire-crackers hung from the eaves.

At half-past two, an hour past the bride's scheduled arrival, the Filipinos grinned and played 'Till the Sands of the Desert Grow Cold'. The guests really began arriving about three. Tommy and Julia Howe honoured the old ways by turning up at twenty minutes past three. Since Mayling Soong had been three hours late for her own wedding, Tommy predicted that Emily Howe would be three and a half hours late. But he began to glance irritably at his wristwatch shortly after four. The unseen bridegroom was enjoying the last hours of his second bachelorhood – his third or fourth, if one counted concubines – with his intimates in his private apartments. At twenty-five past four, when the intense heat of mid-July began to wane, Ou-yang Hsiu appeared to greet his guests. He was sleekly grey from shining silver-frosted hair to oyster-coloured cloth shoes. He would not look directly at Julia. He was obviously embarrassed at meeting a foreign woman, though she was soon to be his sister-in-law.

When the bridegroom left them with elaborate courtesy, Tommy glanced again at his wristwatch. He grimaced and exclaimed: 'It's twenty to five. Maybe she's changed her mind. Who knows . . .' He broke off in surprise and whistled tunelessly between his teeth: 'By God, I wouldn't have believed it. The real old way! Julie, my sweet, he's going off to kidnap the bride from her jealous family.'

Ou-yang Hsiu entered the emerald-green Silver Ghost that waited in the road. Four male friends piled in beside him, but the Rolls did not draw away immediately. Twenty-two Filipino bandsmen marched out, blaring John Phillip Sousa's 'Washington Post March' in jazz tempo. They crowded into one of the trucks that had brought the dowry and drove off behind the Rolls Royce.

Three-quarters of an hour later, the band marched back into the compound, still blaring the 'Washington Post March'. Saxophones, clarinets, and trumpets swung from side to side as they segued into Mendelssohn's 'Wedding March' to a polka beat, and the Silver Ghost drew up at the gateway.

Having been cast in the role of a traditional matron-of-honour, Julia stepped forward to open the door of the limousine. The bride smiled blandly in the late afternoon sunlight and clutched her bouquet of lilies-of-the-valley to the bosom of her long white-lace wedding gown. Her face was stark white beneath many layers of powder, and her lips glowed cherry red behind her veil.

When she entered the courtyard, thunder erupted and smoke billowed. Ou-yang Hsiu started when the second string of ten thousand firecrackers began to explode. Collecting himself, he stepped forward and waited beside his bride for the joyful din to end. Dogs howled, small children cowered behind their mothers, and bigger children jumped up and down in glee. For almost ten minutes, eighty-two strings of fire-crackers saluted the couple's combined ages by Chinese reckoning.

For some time afterwards, clouds of black smoke billowed through the courtyard. Peppered with red-paper fragments, bride and groom advanced to the altar table and bowed to the three men standing before its scarlet trappings. The three were the go-between and the official witnesses.

Tommy fiddled with his curved meerschaum pipe as the ceremony unfolded its apparently interminable length. After almost an hour, Julia saw with relief that Emily and her new husband were making their final bows to her parents. The ceremony was at last over.

Since Ou-yang Hsiu's mother was dead, Emily immediately assumed the full authority of the mistress of the house. She was, at twenty-seven, almost elderly, for traditional Chinese brides were normally nine, eleven, or even thirteen years younger. For both those reasons, she was spared the traditional bride-baiting. She would not be tormented by the female relatives and finally tumbled naked into the red-curtained marriage-bed.

Males and females drew apart in the pretence that ladies of good family still lived in seclusion. For half an hour the ladies had sipped tea and sweet wines while the gentlemen gambled and tossed down stronger spirits;

when the servants beat gongs to summon them, all made for the tables under the glass roof of the courtyard. Remarkably, the bride herself sat down with them in violation of traditional etiquette.

The groom's aged uncles nodded tolerantly. She was the daughter of a man insulated from even the possibility of error by his great wealth. The aged uncles' aged wives were not as tolerant. Shielding seamed and tinted lips behind liver-spotted hands, they whispered censoriously. She was no longer a Howe, but an Ou-yang after genuflecting to the sacred tablets bearing the names of the Ou-yangs' ancestors. She should, therefore, behave like an Ou-yang.

Emily won back the aunts' regard, which she was not so foolish as to undervalue, by punctiliously observing a new custom that they believed was hallowed by time. After every second course, she withdrew to her chambers, where her amahs waited. As the next course was served, she reappeared in a new costume. Ranging from the styles of the late 1800s, which were stiff, heavily embroidered, and set with seed pearls, to the latest *cheongsams*, some daringly slit to mid-thigh, each costume was wholly different.

Suckling pigs ushered in a dress of scarlet tribute-silk worn with glowing emeralds. Roast ducks, geese, and swans appeared with yellow satin that showed off cascades of baroque pearls. Conch, whelk, and terrapin accompanied a simple tunic of gold-shot black samite, the perfect backdrop for a necklace of blue-white diamonds. Those ancient delicacies, bear's paw, elephant's trunk, and humming-birds, almost outshone the bride's splendours.

Rising with relief a little past eleven in the evening after the red-date cakes that concluded the banquet, Julia and Tommy pushed through the crush to say goodbye to Emily. After looking at them without recognition for a moment, she bowed formally and smiled mechanically.

As they left the compound, Julia said abruptly. 'They put on a great show all right. But it was hollow. What can it all mean to Emmy? And what can they possibly have in common?'

'Blowed if I know!' Tommy's back was rigid, and he stared straight ahead. 'Not even bed, I'm afraid. Not really!'

All eyes and all hopes were focused on Generalissimo Chiang Kai-shek. He had regained supreme power after his marriage, and all his enemies had virtually disintegrated. Not only the Communists but the left-wing Nationalist Government at Wuhan. Allied again with that engaging opportunist the Christian General, the Generalissimo soon swept north to take Peking, the Northern Capital, and change its name to Peiping, meaning Northern Peace.

The Nationalist Government remained at Nanking, the Southern Capital. Although the diplomats loved old, refined Peking and detested raw Nanking, all the legations finally moved. Finally, all the foreign governments recognised the Nanking Government – and, for the first time in almost two decades, the world saw only one Republic of China.

271

The Generalissimo brought the warlords to heel, though he could not destroy them. Shortly after the independent Old Marshal scurried back to Manchuria rather than stand up to the modern Nationalist Army, the ambitious Japanese blew up his railway car. His son, the Young Marshal, acknowledged that Nanking was the capital of all China, including Manchuria. The Japanese threat, now becoming blatant, was subduing rivalry among Chinese factions – except for the maverick Communists.

It was not quite unity, and it was not quite peace. Yet the Generalissimo imposed greater stability than China had enjoyed for half a century. As a result the country was also moving forward economically. In the early 1930s, roads, railways, factories and schools were built despite major obstacles: feuding within the Nationalist ranks; the world-wide depression; the inherent weakness of the Central Government against the provinces; shortages of both capital and skills; and, of course, the menace posed by the Japanese and the Communists.

Emily was somewhat self-importantly preoccupied with her work for Mayling Chiang. She fervently believed that the Nationalist régime was leading China into a new golden age.

Tommy and Julia were not totally candid with her. They could agree that the Nationalists' accomplishments in road-building or rural electrification were a beginning to the Herculean task of remaking China. They could hardly confide that Tommy believed the Generalissimo was a viper in human form. Emily must never suspect that they were working to sweep away the weak Nationalist dictatorship and establish a united democratic China.

The Communist Party could, however, oppose a reasonably united enemy with only dispersed political activists and scattered military units. The Communist leaders disagreed bitterly among themselves – and were still tied to a policy that was not just ineffective, but catastrophic. Their troops conquered the vital communications centre of Changsha in 1931, but could, because of brutal losses, hold it for only a week. Yet urban insurrection was still not formally abandoned. The mutinies and sieges that took key cities were put down by determined Nationalist generals – upon occasion supported by foreign gunboats. Yet the Politburo clung to the same strategy. Like a string of firecrackers it sputtered dramatically – leaving bloodied corpses rather than shreds of red paper.

Politics aside, it was a very happy time. Tommy and Julia enjoyed themselves despite the distant thunders of the Great Depression. They were exhilarated by the danger of their assignment for the Apparatus, which had naturally forgotten the pledge to give them only high-level and low-risk missions. Withal, they blithely danced and partied and dined and gambled and made love and talked fond nonsense.

Tommy was highly intelligent, but no intellectual. He complained with a grin that he had consumed most of his intellectual capital in medical school – and was using up the rest in qualifying as an internist, a general physician. His leisure was devoted to the mindless amusements of the

Settlement's smart set. He played tennis and rode; he loved horse-racing, jai-alai, greyhound-racing, and rugby. With Joshua he competed in mounted paper-chases and murderous croquet matches.

Julia felt she was not as impulsive as Tommy. In serious matters like politics, her heart did not rule her head. Besides, she loved abstract argument, while he was intolerant of what he called 'hollow theorizing'.

Tommy could always surprise her, but he remained fundamentally the same – a rock of stability. Emily was, however, a true surprise. Immersed in her work with Mayling Chiang and her hopes for China, she was no longer the firebrand agitator. Instead she devoted her journalism and her fiction to explaining away the deficiencies of the Nationalist régime and to proclaiming its virtues. She even counselled her female readers to wait with patience for deliverance from male oppression – an attitude she had denounced as supine before her marriage.

Once, after too much champagne, Emily shrugged and declared: 'Hsiu is a good husband by the parents' standards. By mine, too, I suppose. Less of a household tyrant than most Chinese husbands. As you know, I didn't marry for love. So how can I be disappointed?'

When Julia responded with concern to that bleak statement, Emily warned her off. 'You don't understand, Julie, so don't waste your sympathy. I'm perfectly content.'

A detached wife, Emily was to become a deeply involved mother. In the beginning, Julia was puzzled by her sister-in-law's allowing the amahs to tend all her children's physical needs. But Julia understood when her own turn came. Infants required parental affection for emotional security, as that new breed, the child psychologists, counselled. That did not necessarily mean spooning food into messy faces or changing nappies. Julia, too, adopted Emily's motto: 'Leave the kids' mouths and backsides to the professionals.'

Emily, as usual, took the lead. Her son Jen-hsun, which meant 'perfect trust', otherwise called Jason, was born in August of 1929 thirteen months before Julia's elder daughter. Althea was a robust infant, who struggled for sixteen hours to emerge and finally required the assistance of forceps. Tommy called her Tien-tse, 'heaven's gift'. He swore that she was not only his first, but his last child because her birth punished her mother badly. On the other hand, Emily boasted that, despite her narrow pelvis, she delivered babies as easily as shucking peas.

She proved that boast by producing two more children by the end of 1934. She then informed her husband that three 'modern children' were all she intended to give him. After a splendid start with Jason, the next two had been disastrously female. Ou-yang Hsiu wanted more sons to carry on his name; to enrich the family by their talents; and to venerate him as their ancestor. Girls only required dowries.

Tommy Howe laughed when his sister reported her husband's candid reaction: 'Poor you. What a primitive attitude! I thought nobody except Pater thought that way anymore. Ancestor worship indeed!'

'Don't play the fool, Tommy!' Emily chided. 'You know very well *all* Chinese men feel exactly the same way. Hsiu just doesn't dare beat

273

me into agreeing to try for more sons.'

Tommy protested that he was beyond such egotistical and medieval nonsense. But he was delighted when Julia again announced herself pregnant in late 1932. He was not downcast when Persephone arrived in August of the following year, though later he candidly admitted he longed for a son.

Tommy and Julia had been blithely content with the loft-apartment's enormous sitting-room and two small bedrooms until Althea's arrival demanded more space. His parents again suggested that Harmony Hall could easily provide them with a wing of their own. Julia quailed, and Tommy told her his father would never help them buy a house of their own. Donald Howe believed firmly that a son's place was with his parents – no matter how old the son.

Joshua Haleevie solved their problem. He reminded them that he had perforce become their landlord when he bought the building years earlier. He offered them the four floors below the loft-apartment on very easy terms: Tommy was to serve as his personal physician, and they could settle their indebtedness any time after five years at the current property value.

Julia felt Joshua was creating an elaborate pretext of hard dealing to amuse himself. Tommy wondered if his spectacular generosity was entirely innocent. Both, however, happily agreed to solve their housing problem by staying where they were – and also adding a roof garden.

While Emily and Julia were caught up with the age-old preoccupations of young matrons, Mayling Chiang was preoccupied with great events. She was obsessed with the two forces that threatened the existence of the Republic of China: the resurgent Communists, whom her husband called a cancer eating away the country's vitals; and the aggressive Japanese, whom he called a skin-eruption – ugly and painful, but not a threat to life. The Missimo, as Tommy called her, became very demanding. Emily was repeatedly summoned to her presence, wherever she might be.

'What are amahs for?' May asked when Emily spoke of her children's needing her. '*I* need your help more. *China* needs your help!'

Tommy hated Chiang Kai-shek – not just for his own imprisonment, but for viciously suppressing the Communist-incited strikes that were flaring out of Shanghai into all East China.

'Along with skin rashes and stomach cancer, the Gimo's also suffering from another complaint: the recurrence of warlordism,' Tommy observed. 'Given a relapse this bad, there's virtually no hope for the Nationalists.'

The Christian General was the most conspicuous offender among the resurgent warlords. Aligning himself ideologically with the Soviets as he had once aligned himself theologically with the Christian powers, he periodically repudiated Nanking and proclaimed his own 'Revolutionary Government of China'. Each time, the Generalissimo patiently coaxed him and other restive warlords back into the fold. Chang Kai-shek thus managed to preserve the fragile structure of the Republic of China by bolstering egos, lubricating grudges, and bestowing lavish bribes.

274

He also tried to strengthen that structure with buttresses of modern administrators, technicians and soldiers. Those alterations annoyed the warlords, but did not impress either the Communists, who wanted to remake China in their own image, or the Japanese, who wanted to make China their colony.

Suavely capable in all else, Joshua Haleevie was hardly adroit in dealing with Elizaveta Yavalenka. She disarmed him with her mere presence. Occasionally she infuriated him so that he told himself the only reason he did not leave her was his deep interest in the Ikra as a rendezvous for Comintern agents and Japanese officers. He was a private citizen, but he took a quasi-professional interest in the activities of any group that could injure the foreign settlement. Shanghai was a paradise for spies, and he was becoming a remarkably adroit amateur at the thrust and counter-thrust of espionage. Since intrigue was second nature to her, Elizaveta enthusiastically assisted his surveillance of some of her guests. But she remained obsessed with the Ikra. Her obsession did not diminish after respectable sources of income allowed her to send away most of her ladies of pleasure. Shortly thereafter, the Great Depression forced the wealthy globe-trotters upon whose custom she depended to stay at home – and forced her to make the Ikra again a house of assignation.

Joshua unhappily noted that she enjoyed the reversion, for the raffish gleam flared again in her eyes. But he had hardly thought her conventional, just very difficult.

The sex lottery no longer threatened. After the first drawing purportedly closed down one of every five bordellos, the Municipal Council had tacitly postponed subsequent drawings indefinitely. After the world-wide economic collapse in 1930, neither the White House nor Number Ten Downing Street was much concerned about the morals of Shanghailanders.

For some time after the emotional storms of the lottery, Joshua and Elizaveta sailed through sunlit waters. She looked forward to becoming Mrs Joshua Haleevie, although her mother would have swooned at the thought of her marrying a *zhid*. Still, she would not set a date. She could not desert the Ikra amid the Depression and the general turmoil of the early 1930s. She also feared that Sir Judah would cut Joshua off for marrying her, rather than the eminently respectable Charlotte Gubbai, who was the Haleevies' choice. Yet she was now herself well-to-do, while Joshua's commercial acumen had made him independently wealthy.

'It's getting too much, Bess!' Joshua declared forcefully early in January of 1932. 'I'm happy to chance breaking with my parents, so you can't hide behind that danger any more.'

'My darling, I only want what's best for you and . . .'

'Later, after we're married,' he broke in, 'I'll do what's best for me. Whatever you say! But you haven't really got the right to tell me yet. So . . .'

'Joshua, darling!' She asked plaintively. 'How can you say that? How can you possibly . . .'

*

275

In Manchuria in the summer of 1931, Japanese paramilitary forces had killed several hundred Chinese farmers for defending their land from Japanese-sponsored Korean settlers. Not long afterwards, a Japanese army captain travelling in civilian clothing was mysteriously slain on a train. Since his mission was subversion in Chinese-ruled Inner Mongolia, the Japanese militarists were happy to assume that he had been murdered by Chinese agents. They were always alert for a pretext for aggressive action.

To make Manchuria safe for Japanese settlement, and Japanese agents, the Japanese Army took over China's three vast northeastern provinces. They drove the warlord ruler, the Young Marshal of Manchuria, into exile in North China, where he reaffirmed his loyalty to the General-issimo's Central Government.

Manchuria was to most Shanghailanders a faraway and cold place of no particular interest. Yet events in Manchuria drove Japanese troops to attack Chinese-ruled Greater Shanghai on the night of January 28, 1932. They obviously hoped to divert world attention from Manchuria by their action, reasoning that two wrongs might not make a right, but would undoubtedly make an ungodly muddle. The Japanese militarists were also concerned with their plans for future expansion into China proper. They were determined to give the defending Chinese armies a bloody nose, so that the Chinese would not again interfere with the doings of their betters in China.

It did not work out quite that way. The Chinese armies did not slink away, but resisted fiercely. Refugees again flooded the foreign con-cessions. The bark of artillery and the yapping of small arms made background music for smart dinner parties. It was all rather thrilling – and a bit too close. Diehard taipans, however, convivially cheered the Japanese on. Good idea to teach the Nationalists a lesson, they said. Give them a bloody nose. Keep the Chinks from getting uppity.

The Generalissimo was not uppity, but was satisfied with his local victory. He knew that China could not resist the Japanese invasion that would follow a major Japanese defeat at Shanghai. He also knew that no foreign power would help him. He therefore moved the government to a provisional capital further inland, began talking peace with Tokyo, and ordered the battered Shanghai defence force to pull back before it was wiped out.

Joshua did not cheer when the Japanese almost gave the Chinese a bloody nose. He was uneasy about Nationalist demands for a greater say in the running of the concessions and an end to extra-territoriality – the foreigners' privilege of governing themselves under their own laws in China. But he feared the efficient and single-minded Japanese far more than he did the bumbling Chinese. Despite her inborn Russian hatred of the Japanese, Elizaveta warmly welcomed the victors to the Ikra. She had to be at the centre of action – and they were making history gallop. Besides, it was always a good idea to be in with the victors.

However, she readily agreed to allow the Chinese secret service to mount surveillance over her Japanese patrons. She was not committed to the Japanese.

Nor did she demur when Colonel Ishikawa requested the Caligula Suite. Elizaveta did not know the Colonel's true name. She did know it was not Ishikawa. She further knew that he was not a colonel, but the major-general of intelligence who directed subversion by gold, narcotics, and intimidation.

Despite her professional aplomb, she shivered minutely when Colonel Ishikawa arrived. Although he had left off his uniform, he was, even in grey tweed, a commanding figure: tall, broad-chested, and aquiline of feature. Although she could see that women would find him handsome, she was repelled by the opaque stare of his flat-grey eyes and revolted by the tales told of him. He made a great show of his ruthlessness to terrify Japan's enemies, but visited the torture cells only when the subject was a woman.

'This will be a very glorious night,' he declared in his stilted English. 'I have escaped from my staff, and no one in the wide world knows where I am. I shall not be disturbed. It is glorious to escape all responsibility, even temporarily.'

Elizaveta closed the brass-bound door upon Colonel Ishikawa and his two blondes, one Russian and the other Norwegian. She had performed the formal introductions and taken his order for caviar and *saké*. She had also reminded him that he could obtain whatever he desired by lifting the telephone concealed behind the marble bust of the Emperor Nero sneering in the bed-chamber. Caligua himself leered in the bath-chamber.

Happy that she would hear no more from Colonel Ishikawa that night, she wondered at the revulsion he aroused in her. Well spoken and studiously polite, he paid extremely well for his pleasures – and his professional activities were not her concern. Nonetheless, he reminded her of the leeches used for blood-letting. Disgusting when shrivelled and hungry, they were equally loathsome when swollen sleek and black with engorged blood.

Elizaveta let down her hair for the evening. A little after ten, Joshua stepped from the private elevator behind the casino into her apartment. Although he was always interested in her political patrons, she did not mention Colonel Ishikawa. For once she wanted to forget her professional concerns entirely. For once her life seemed tawdry rather than glamorous.

She was enjoying the muzziness induced by a few goblets of champagne when the internal telephone buzzed. She lifted the handset reluctantly, but then sat bolt upright. After listening intently, she said in Russian: 'I'll be right there!'

'Trouble, Bess?' Joshua cocked an interrogative eyebrow. 'Need some help?'

He normally avoided involvement in the Ikra, but her tone had been urgent. She pondered an instant before responding: 'Not if you don't want to. You know, Josh, how you hate that side of things. But you could be a great help if you really . . .'

The Russian blonde had intelligently bolted the door after telephoning. She was trembling uncontrollably, and the paper mouthpiece of her cigarette was clenched between her lipstick-stained teeth. She dabbed ineffectually with a towel at her hair, which streamed like sodden flax around her shoulders. The Norwegian blonde was lolling in a scrolled gilt armchair. Her eyes glittered with cocaine. Her short platinum hair was plastered by water into a tight cap that made her head look small, vulnerable – and curiously sexless. Both blondes wore pink terry-cloth robes that somehow, recalled hot water-bottles and the nursery. Those robes somehow intensified the atmosphere of vice and depravity.

The Russian responded defensively to Elizaveta's sharp questions in Russian. Elizaveta finally shook her head in disgust, and her long black hair swished girlishly on her shoulders. She led Joshua into the marble bath-chamber, threw open the door and pointed dramatically to the sunken bath. When her gaze followed her index finger, she stared in horror. The woman of the world cowered into Joshua's arms.

'God!' she whispered hoarsely. 'Thank God you're here! She said it was . . . was bad . . . very bad. But . . . this!'

The naked body of the Japanese spy-master was floating face down in the scented water of the enormous bath, its wax-yellow back webbed with fine red lines. A whip of hair-thin wires lay among splotches of blood on the pale-honey marble floor.

Without speaking, the Russian blonde turned and lowered her robe. Blood oozed from the red web on her back. She faced them and delicately, almost modestly, lifted the skirts of her robe to her hips. Her pale thighs were blotched with bruises, and blood dripped from a wound the size of a silver dollar on her left hip.

'He bite hard, ver' hard!' She exploded in broken English. 'Filthy pig of Jap . . . he get us in bath, Marga and me. Then he try to hold us under. . . . We cannot . . . we struggle. And then. . . . And you see!'

The Russian harlot led them back to the sitting room, where she muttered crossly at the almost insensible Norwegian. Having told her story, she evidently felt absolved of all responsibility.

'It didn't, you know,' Joshua murmured. 'It didn't happen the way she tells it. It took two strong and determined women to drown him. No accident this.'

'What now, Joshua?' Elizaveta's eyes were almost black in their pale caverns. 'What can I do?'

They terrified the two blondes and sent them away. A single indiscreet word, they said, would mean delivery into the hands of the Municipal Police for trial – or the hands of the Japanese for beheading. Since the Japanese would demand vengeance for the death of the intelligence chief, they could not hush the affair up with official collusion – as they might a lesser crime. Besides, the scandal would delight Japanese propagandists and provide the militarists with an ideal pretext for action against the Settlement. The Japanese would scream to the world that

Colonel Ishikawa had not only been murdered, but his body taken to a brothel to discredit the Emperor's highly moral corps of officers. The Japanese might well move troops into the Settlement – creating a danger of war with the other powers. Certainly, the scandal would destroy Elizaveta, bringing bankruptcy and imprisonment – if the Japanese did not kill her first.

'He said something about being alone.' Elizaveta clutched at a straw. 'Let me think now. I forgot all about it in the shock. Yes, he said something about escaping his staff. They didn't know where he'd gone. A night of freedom, he said.'

'If that's true . . .' Beginning tentatively, Joshua concluded firmly: 'What have we got to lose if it's not?'

Elizaveta was heartened by the word *we*. She was not alone; they stood together. Rather, he stood with her, although he had no responsibility for the potential disaster.

'Yes, Joshua? What can we do?'

'If they *really* don't know,' he mused, 'we could do the obvious. Just get rid of him. Just as he is. The corpse collection service is picking up twice as many bodies now with the fighting. Another naked Oriental beaten up in a sailor's brawl – who'd care? They'd just dump him in a common grave.'

'It could really work? You'd really do it? Oh, Joshua!'

'My love, I must point out that it's not quite the done thing!' He regained his humour. 'Fair ladies shouldn't expect their admirers to dispose of murdered men. But, yes, I'll do it. If you'll just get Wang the bartender to come up.'

'Wang? Why Wang?'

'Bess, my love, even you know that Wang's been in the Red Apparatus for donkey's years. That is, when he's not picking up a few extra dollars from the Nationalists. But he's always a Chinese patriot, whoever he's working for. Wang's just the man for the job. Now go back and hold the fort.'

Joshua kept vigil over the drowned spy-master until the pulse of the Ikra slowed at three in the morning. With the delighted bartender, he eased the naked body into a canvas-sided laundry-hamper on coasters, which fitted neatly into the rear elevator. Wang pushed the hamper down the alley away from well-lit Kiangse Road.

When he turned into the side-street, Joshua dropped behind. A Chinese menial might well be collecting laundry at four in the morning in the city that never slept. A European in a velvet-collared chesterfield would have been wildly conspicuous walking alongside the laundry-hamper. The side-streets were relatively quiet, but eyes always watched through gauze curtains.

Wang stopped at the mouth of an alley two blocks from the Ikra and manoeuvred the hamper into the shadows. Together they lifted the rubbery corpse and laid it on the wet pavement. One waxen foot protruded into the light of a weak street-light, but Joshua was satisfied.

Colonel Ishikawa was known to frequent the Ikra. Suspicion would, therefore fall on Elizaveta if he were by some mischance identified. Rather paradoxically, her peril would be worse if his corpse were found far from his normal resorts. Joshua could not ensure that the corpse was not identified. He could enable Elizaveta to respond indignantly to any questioning: 'Do you really think I'm such a fool I'd dump him on my own doorstep?'

After a week, Joshua was satisfied that Colonel Ishikawa had been swept up among the unidentified corpses regularly collected from the streets. In a normal February, thirty to forty unknown vagrants might die of disease, starvation, and mischance each week. With the Settlement flooded with refugees from the demi-war, violence was endemic. Among forty to sixty unknown corpses, many bearing wounds, the Colonel's had obviously gone unremarked.

Joshua and Elizaveta were thereafter bound even closer by their common danger.

Joshua was protective, and Elizaveta happily sheltered in the citadel of his gallantry. He marvelled that a woman so fine-grained could tolerate the Ikra after that sordid incident, and Elizaveta half-agreed. There could be only one outcome.

Emboldened by Elizaveta's new dependence, Joshua yielded to impulse while they were toasting his fortieth birthday on March 2, 1932. Still young enough for new responsibilities, he was too old to delay an instant longer.

'You'll marry me now, Bess,' he told her. 'I know that. Let's set a day. Foolish to delay any longer.'

'I'm sorry, Joshua darling, but I can't.' She could no longer temporize. 'Please don't ask again. I'm very sorry. More sorry than I can say.'

'You're ... you're reneging?' He exploded in incomprehension. 'But you agreed we'd marry. What *are* you saying?'

'I can't marry you, Joshua. It grieves me ... deeply. If only ... but I can't.'

'Why in the name of ... I warn you, Bess, I'm not playing this game any longer. This is the *last* time.'

'I wondered when your patience would run out.' Her smile was melancholy. 'Why? All the reasons we've discussed. Your family and your circle, they'd never accept me. Besides, I *like* my present life.'

'Even after ... after Ishikawa? I can't believe it, Bess! How can you?'

'Anything else would be too tame. I won't string you along any more. I simply can't marry you, Joshua.'

'Well, then, my only love!' He spoke slowly, almost meditatively. 'I'll have to marry Charlotte Gubbai – if she'll still have me.'

'She'd be a fool if she didn't, as big a fool as me!' Elizaveta said. 'So you'll be leaving me? I expected that, but I hate it. Will I ever see you again?'

'No, Bess,' he replied slowly. 'I'm not leaving you. I wish ... I only wish I

280

could. I do mean to marry Charlotte, poor girl. But no, Bess, I don't mean to leave you.'

On the same day Joshua dolefully celebrated his fortieth birthday, the Imperial Japanese Army withdrew from Greater Shanghai. A Sino-Japanese Accord was announced on May 5, 1932, the day after two thousand guests at Jade House celebrated the orthodox wedding of Charlotte Gubbai and Joshua Haleevie.

Four months later, Sir Judah and Lady Haleevie gave a formal dinner for three hundred to welcome the couple back from a honeymoon spent half in Paris, Florence, and London to please the bride and half in Rhodesia, Kenya, and Nyasaland to indulge the groom's sudden passion for big-game hunting.

All the while China was changing rapidly, though appearing to remain the same. In the deep countryside the Communists were slowly building a following by equitable rule, by promises – and by fear. Fighting fire with fire, Red Terror opposed the White Terror of the Nationalists. In retaliation for the execution of captured guerrillas and peasant sympathizers, the Red Army buried landlords and well-to-do peasants up to their necks, leaving them to die of hunger, thirst, and exposure. They called it 'live burial', and the crows pecked at the living victims' eyes. The class struggle was a war without mercy against an equally merciless foe.

So Chang Kuo-tao had roundly affirmed on the night in mid-March, 1931, when he came to the house on Kiukiang Road to say goodbye to Tommy and Julia. He wore the clothes of a small merchant from the country, and he aped the manner of such a bumpkin. He was setting out on a long and hazardous journey to the northernmost Communist base, the Oyüwan Soviet Area. Sailing as a deck passenger to Wuhan, he continued by bus and finally walked scores of miles to reach the Communist pocket. Chang Kuo-tao was in constant danger from Nationalist agents and troops, even from the normally lackadaisical local police. All were alerted to prosecute the Generalissimo's latest campaign to exterminate the Communists, the fourth Extermination Campaign planned and directed by his German advisers.

'The net had a very fine mesh,' Chang Kuo-tao was later to recall. 'A fat fish like me was lucky to slip through. But everything went well for a while. Then my Fourth Front Red Army grew so strong the Nationalists concentrated on us. In October 1932 we had to decamp. Ours was the *first* Long March.'

Insensitive to the irony, he claimed the distinction of having been the first to flee. All eight Communist Areas scattered through East China were, however, to be rolled up by the Extermination Campaigns.

The largest Communist area held out longest in the mountains of Kiangsi Province under the political leadership of Mao Tse-tung and the military leadership of Chu Teh, the man called Red Virtue. Isolated from the Central Committee in Shanghai and sometimes defying that Moscow-dominated body, those two created a political machine and a disciplined army among the superstitious, illiterate, and suspicious peasants.

Warlordism was rising, and the Nationalists were rent by feuds. The people were alienated by extortionate 'special taxes' imaginatively levied on consumer articles of an amazing diversity from firewood to mules. The Communists should have been able to exploit widespread popular dissatisfaction more effectively with their promises of land to the landless and dignity to the hopeless. But they were not united – and they were under incessant attack. Mao Tse-tung was finally driven out by the Fifth Extermination Campaign in 1934. His protracted retreat became the revolutionary myth called the Long March. Before fetching up in late 1935 in a place called Yenan, with a few thousand men, he made himself master of the Communist movement. In the absence of his rivals, notably Chang Kuo-tao, he convened an emergency session of the Political Bureau. That splinter group duly elected him chairman of the Central Committee of the Communist Party of China.

The Extermination Campaigns did not cease when the Communists reached sanctuary in the arid northwest. Nor did Generalissimo Chiang Kai-shek linger over the self-justifying after-action reports of the field commanders the Red Army had evaded during the Fifth Extermination Campaign. In December of 1936, he flew to Sian, China's ancient capital, to assess the terrain and to co-ordinate the launching of the Sixth Extermination Campaign. The joint commanders were the Nationalists' Commissioner for the North-west and the Young Marshal with his formidable Manchurian Army in exile.

On December 12, 1936, the two generals took Chiang Kai-shek prisoner. They respectfully requested an immediate cessation of the Extermination Campaign, so that the Communists could join the Nationalists in all out war against the Japanese. The Generalissimo raged and refused. Their mutiny, he retorted, could destroy the Republic of China by destroying his face. If he were discredited, the nation would fall apart. No one else could lead China.

The Communists agreed, although little politicians and little generals in Nanking began manoeuvring to take over from the captive hero. On December 15th, Chou En-lai arrived from Yenan to greet his old chief and antagonist with the words: 'I have come to arrange a marriage between the National People's Party and the Communist Party.' After complex discussions, the two agreed to form a united front against Japan. On Christmas Day the Generalissimo returned to Nanking. The little politicians and the little generals cheered – and put away for another day their plans for *coups d'état*.

In Yenan, Mao Tse-tung happily feigned subordination to Nanking. The Soviet Area, so called from the Russian word for a ruling council of workers, was to be known as the Border Area. In theory, it had become a semi-autonomous subdivision of the Nanking Government. The Red Army was to fight as the Eighth Route Army under the nominal command of the Generalissimo but the actual command of Chu Teh. Chairman Mao smiled complacently and explained: 'We are finally on the high road to power. The United Anti-Japanese Front is the perfect camouflage for subversion in the White Areas – and for the rapid expansion of the Red Army. We are now certain to conquer all China!'

The piano in the bar of the Cathay Hotel was tinkling 'Beyond the Blue Horizon' when Tommy and Julia stopped by for a cocktail at Christmas 1936. The song expressed a generation's yearning to escape into exotic climes from the drabness of the Great Depression. Yet they were happy in a Shanghai milieu hardly touched by the cold winds of the Depression. Tommy's father was so rich he was virtually impregnable. His losses were all on paper. Julia's uncle, Quick Jack Pavernen, living always on the edge of disaster, was so nimble he could side-step even the Great Depression.

Although Tommy's practice was brisk, it could not have supported the self-indulgent, almost extravagant, manner of life the Apparatus had directed them to adopt to camouflage their underground activities. Tommy was not shy about accepting substantial gifts from his parents. He loved them, and he knew their generosity gave them much pleasure.

As 1936 ended, his practice promised to become very prosperous. After long preparation, Tommy was a fully-qualified specialist in internal medicine, a diagnostician who was called in when other doctors were puzzled. His public-school accent attracted the conservative British, and Julia was a lodestone for the Americans. The wealthy Chinese felt less apprehensive in submitting to the mysterious perils of Western medicine when it was practised by one of their own.

Although they had taken over the entire building on Kiukiang Road to make room for his consulting rooms, Julia was no more burdened by household cares than she had been as a giddy spinster. The number of servants seemed to increase twice as fast as their duties. The amahs would have spoiled six-year-old Althea and her three-year-old sister Persephone if Julia had allowed them to. She was proud that her daughters spoke Shanghainese well. She would have been ashamed if, like some British and American children, they were so rarely in the company of their parents that they barely spoke English. But, because she was afraid of smothering the girls with her attentions, she continued to present her record request programme every other day on XMHA.

Beyond those pleasant trappings, which were the fol-de-rol of daily life, she was exceedingly happy. Tommy could still surprise and delight her – and he swore she still had the same effect on him.

283

33

Julia would have received Richard Hollings amicably even if the Apparatus had not instructed her to offer hospitality – and guidance – to all foreign correspondents. He returned ten years after walking away from Emily's red convertible to begin a protracted tour of Asia that led in time to a plum assignment as roving European correspondent for the *Boston Globe*. Curiosity alone would have compelled her to see him when he returned as Chief Asiatic correspondent for the *Globe* and the National Broadcasting Company. Although she was not initially inclined to prolong their reunion, duty compelled her to spend time with him.

He was as casually engaging as ever – and even more attractive in his saturnine way. His baldfaced effrontery, which Joshua Haleevie called *chutzpah*, was even more outrageous than it had been.

Julia was not herself attracted, but she had never been. She was, however, glad that Emily was in Nanking with Mayling Chiang, the newly appointed Secretary-General of the Commission for Aeronautical Affairs. Emily's impetuousness might otherwise have flung her again into Richard's embrace, for she saw little of her husband nowadays. Fortunately, there would now be time to warn her to steel her heart against her former lover's insidious charm. She might even do so.

Julia selected the next record, silenced Richard with a glance, and spoke into the big black microphone: 'XMHA is pleased to respond to the umpteenth request this week for "Red Sails in the Sunset". It seems you listeners can't get enough of it. We'll have to send out for a new platter soon. But that's our worry, not yours. You only need tell us what tune you want to hear. Just call Julia Howe at 95040 or write me at Station XMHA, 445 Race Course Road. And now "Red Sails in the

284

Sunset" for Alma Wang and Danny Ho!'

Richard grinned at the words '. . . carry my loved one home safely to me', but did not comment. He had alluded to Emily only to remark that he had heard she was 'happily married and very fecund'.

Julia did not confide her own doubt that Emily was happily married. Yet her sister-in-law had displayed no interest in any other man – and little enough in her husband. Despite Emily's frequent absences, Ou-yang Hsiu uncomplainingly made it possible for her to enjoy the dignity of a married woman – and he unstintingly paid her considerable bills. Her own substantial funds were devoted to the service of Mayling Chiang and China.

Emily's heart appeared locked. Yet who was more likely to open it again than the man who had slammed the door and turned the key?

Richard Hollings might, however, not be interested. After obligatory inquiries about Julia's husband and children and the casual observation that Fiona, his wife of two years, would join him when he had settled into Shanghai, his conversation focused on politics and war. Since Julia was known as a first-class source of information, insight, and gossip, he said candidly, he was anxious to hear her views on Shanghai. It would not be a one-way traffic. He would be delighted to pass on his impressions after several weeks in North China.

'It's a whole new ball game, isn't it?' He smiled and added: 'I'm learning to talk like you Yanks for my new job. I could hardly expect NBC's devoted listeners to understand if I said: 'It's a totally new line of country.' But it is. Tientsin brought it home to me – exactly what the Japs are up to.'

Despite herself, Julia warmed to Richard. He now appeared so much more sympathetic to China and the Chinese.

'In Tientsin the police were offering $5,000 for information regarding one hundred and seven corpses. Yes, one hundred and seven males between twenty and forty, all found in the river. Not a mark on any of them. No sign of foul play, but all dead as mutton.'

Richard tantalizingly paused to take a cigarette from the round tin of fifty Senior Service clutched in his left hand. Julia silenced him with an index finger held before pursed lips. She pulled her yellow-shantung dress away from her bosom and fanned herself with a record-sleeve while waiting for 'Red Sails in the Sunset' to end. The recently installed air-conditioning could not deal with the mid-August heat. Even her lips felt as if they were perspiring under their coral lipstick.

'So we've seen those red sails for the ninety-ninth time this week,' she said brightly. 'They're pretty tattered by now, I guess. But we're off on another voyage. To "Blue Hawaii".'

Richard laughed and said: 'So you're the young lady who swore she couldn't write a word. No need to write – not with that slick patter. But to finish up. The police finally fished out a chap who wasn't quite dead. He was a contract labourer, and he'd been enticed to a so-called club in the Japanese Concession. Lashings of opium and heroin were on offer – dirt cheap. He smoked a few cigarettes – and woke up in hospital. Strychnine poisoning, the quacks said.

'The Japs are usually more patient. Just ordinary narcotics are subverting the Chinese everywhere the Japs have control, particularly Manchuria. It's drug warfare against civilians.'

He pulled hard on his cigarette, grimaced, and continued: 'Heroin's the leading item now in the Jap Concession in Tientsin. Their hostels have boxlike structures built in front. Just roll up your sleeve and pop in your money. A jab – and there's your fix. . . . Runners for the opium houses mob taxis on streets devoted solely to narcotics. And it's all run by the Japanese Imperial Army Special Services Section – for profit and to debauch the Chinese people. The Japs are as single-minded as a charging bull. They'll conquer China by any means – or bust!'

Julia nodded, wondering how best to put across her own message. China is finally fighting the Japanese, she wanted to tell him, only because Chairman Mao Tse-tung finally forced Generalissimo Chiang Kai-shek to stand and fight. But the Communists are fighting ten times as hard as the Nationalists.

The Marco Polo Bridge Incident of July 7th, Hollings observed, had fooled no one. The Japs obviously wanted to march, and they had obviously engineered a pretext.

Why else should a Japanese battalion have marched to the insignificant town called Wanping, whose dun-coloured walls overlooked the lion-head balustrades of the bridge named after the great Venetian explorer? Why else had they fired the instant the garrison denied knowledge of Japanese deserters? How else could the Japanese have immediately launched the co-ordinated attack that had subsequently conquered Peiping and Tientsin in a few weeks' time?

'You've got to hand it to them. I didn't believe Orientals were capable of such meticulous planning – or such dashing execution. I'll never look down my nose at the Japs again.' He ground out his cigarette in a flurry of yellow Virginia tobacco and directed: 'Now tell me how it looks like from Shanghai.'

Repetition had polished Julia's reply to that question. Wary respect for Richard's acuity, however, shaded her usual bold strokes. Playing on his dislike of the Generalissimo, she confided that the Nationalists were exerting ninety per cent of their military effort against the Communist areas, rather than against the Japanese. Moreover, semi-Fascist strong-arm men in blue shirts and thousands of special agents of the secret police were persecuting the Communists in Nationalist areas.

'So-called Communists,' she added. 'But really not even Socialists. Really agrarian democrats . . . social democrats.'

Themselves fighting the Japanese staunchly, the so-called Communists were even forcing the reluctant Chiang Kai-shek to fight the Japanese. They were mobilizing public opinion against the slothful Nationalists through student demonstrations, plays, movies and, above all, through indignant word of mouth.

'The Generalissimo's no fool, mind you,' Julia pronounced even-handedly. 'Nor is he a coward. He delayed the confrontation with the Japs because he wanted and still wants – to destroy the Communists first. Also, Mayling knew that war would interfere with peaceful pursuits. For the Soong family that means grabbing all the graft they can – tens of millions.'

She saw that 'Blue Hawaii' still had a half-minute to play and went on: 'The Gimo sincerely expected to strengthen China militarily while he stalled. But he hasn't done too well. For example, long before Mayling took over the Air Force, Nanking made a big deal with the Italians to provide warplanes and train pilots. In theory, China now has more than five hundred combat planes and a thousand-odd combat pilots. In reality, China has just ninety-one fighting planes and very few competent pilots, maybe a hundred. But Mayling has just brought in a retired US Army Air Corps officer called Claire Chennault who's supposed to be a hot shot.'

'Hold on, Julie, hold on!' Hollings held his palm up like a traffic policeman. 'You still go at things like a bull at a gate. Forget this Chennault fellow for a moment and tell me about Shanghai. There's a good girl.'

Julia lowered her head so that the curtain of her mahogany hair fell over her face. She did not want him to read her expression. She did not, she decided again, really like Richard Hollings, the ace newshawk. In the old days she had put up with his condescension for Emily's sake. Now, she supposed, she had to put up with him for the Apparatus's sake.

'Didn't that transport you to the spicy breezes of Waikiki?' She addressed the wire-mesh microphone. 'Next is my own choice, a brand new record just off the boat from San Francisco. Ray Eberle backed by Glenn Miller's band sings "The Nearness of You!"'

She spoke again to Richard, repaying his veiled insolence with her own: 'Naturally, you've looked around the streets as any good correspondent would! You've seen they're crammed with refugees. Sixty thousand foreigners plus a million and a half Chinese are normally resident in Frenchtown and the Settlement. Another three quarters of a million Chinese are now busting our seams. They always figure they're better off here.'

The syrupy melody of the 'The Nearness of You' made an incongruous background to her tough-minded exposition. 'And, dear Richard, the signs are pretty clear. An explosion's on its way. The Gimo let North China go. No dependable allies there, since he's finally learned he can't count in the Christian General. So he abandoned Peiping two weeks ago and Tientsin a couple of days later. But he's moved the crack 88th Division into Greater Shanghai. It's his pride and joy: Nazi-trained, every officer a Whampoa graduate, great at the goosestep, and sporting Nazi-style coal-scuttle helmets. Very glamorous and very sinister.'

Julia lifted the needle back to his first groove and told the microphone: 'I like this so much I'm going to play it again.' She slipped the microphone-switch off. 'The Gimo probably hoped the Japs would go easy because they're afraid of involving other foreign powers. But, when the Chinese dared prepare to defend themselves, the Japs responded. And that brings us to this scary Saturday afternoon. A typhoon hovering a few hundred miles out at sea, and the Japs piling troops and warships into Shanghai. Nothing like it since 1932 and, for sheer fright among foreigners, nothing like it since 1927, when everybody thought the big, bad Reds were going to eat us up.'

More than twenty Japanese warships, she told him, now lay menacingly at anchor in the Hwangpoo. They were modern and powerful, although their flagship HIJMS *Idzumo*, an old battleship the size of a modern cruiser, had been captured from the Imperial Russian Navy forty years earlier. Imperial Japanese Marines had reinforced the garrison in Hongkew, the old American Concession that was now Little Tokyo. Moreover, Japanese bombers from Taiwan were scheduled to 'make courtesy flights' over Shanghai.

That display of force should have induced the Generalissimo to back down – as he had in 1932. Instead, he had strengthened his units. The powder keg was full, and the Chinese had laid the fuse.

'And five days ago,' Julia said, 'somebody put a match to the fuse.'

The fuse had been burning fast since August 9th, when a Japanese Navy sub-lieutenant was driven westwards towards the Military and Civil Airport at Hungjao by a seaman first class. The black touring-car bearing the number 170 was not challenged by a single Chinese roadblock. Some twenty-five thousand foreign troops were prudently staying behind the barbed-wire-and-sandbag barricades that once again sealed off the Settlement and Frenchtown.

Neither the sub-lieutenant nor the seaman first class had reacted to the first shot. Both were intently studying the Chinese warplanes on the tarmac. They could not react to the volley that followed. The big car swerved as if slapped by a gigantic hand and hurtled into the ditch. When the rear door flew open, the sub-lieutenant's body was flung onto the road. His khaki tunic bore six small holes, and blood smeared his brass buttons.

Julia listened for the end of the melody and summed up: 'So the Japs had their martyrs. None the less, Tokyo magnanimously guaranteed the security of the foreign concessions – *if* the Chinese withdrew all their troops from Greater Shanghai. When the mayor refused, the good grey *North China Daily News* warned the Chinese against provoking Japan to worse excesses by resisting.'

'The *News* would!' Richard interjected hotly. 'The mouthpiece of the taipans and always preaching trade at any price.'

'. . . day before yesterday, Chinese employees of the Telephone Company cut off the Japanese Consulate. Also most Japanese firms,' Julia continued. 'The 88th Division occupied the North Station and blocked all roads. Yesterday the skirmishing started. Friday the thirteenth, by the way.'

'What about the bombing? The planes were so high this morning I could barely hear them, much less see them.'

'Maybe because it's so cloudy. The Chinese are gunning for the Jap warships, especially the *Idzumo*. There're no Jap pursuits around, but the pre-typhoon winds are not helping.'

The crooner was murmuring suggestively: '. . . not the pale moon that excites me, that thrills and delights me. Oh no! It's just the nearness of you!'

The skylight rattled, and the room trembled. The tall building seemed to sway, and the petulant buzzing of aircraft engines penetrated the studio's sound-proofing.

'They're flying lower.' Hollings's voice was heavy with apprehension – and anticipation. 'Can I get onto the roof? I must have a look.'

'Help yourself, Dick. One flight up to the tower – and you can see all Shanghai. I'll pick you up when I wrap up the programme. Another fifteen minutes or so.'

After his departure, she played four more songs. Glancing at the dog sitting rapt before the phonograph horn on the purple HMV label, she said flatly: 'And now an old song that's somehow always fresh: "There'll be a Hot Time in the Old Town Tonight". That melody appropriately closes our request programme for today, Saturday, August 14, 1937. It's just about 4.30 p.m., time for me to get back to my husband and my daughters. Goodbye till Monday. Also *tsai-chien*, *au revoir*, and *auf Wiedersehen*. I won't say *sayonara* again until I can say *sayonara* to all the Japanese soldiers who are paying us a strange kind of courtesy call. Here it is: "A Hot Time in the Old Town Tonight"!'

She smiled at the engineer in his glass cage, whom she left to close down the programme. It was faintly obscene to watch from an inviolate sanctuary as men and women were killed. But why else was she climbing the stairs to join Richard Hollings in the observation tower?

Binoculars clapped to his eyes, the correspondent was swivelling his head continuously. The big glass lenses capping the long black tubes made him look like a robot watcher against the overcast sky. But perspiration soaked his linen bush-jacket, for the atmosphere was heavily muggy even a hundred and fifty feet above the street.

'Can't see a damned thing!' he complained. 'I can hear them, but I can't see a single plane.'

Julia could not resist the gibe at his disappointment: 'You know, Dick, this war's not staged for your personal entertainment.'

'Sorry, Julie! But you're gawking, too.'

'Well, it *is* my town. And rubber-necking's free.'

The throbbing of engines grew louder and higher pitched as the aircraft drew near. In the overhanging clouds they remained invisible. Julia shivered at the unseen menace and looked down at Shanghai.

The Japanese had made the district northeast of Soochow Creek their fortress. Sullen beneath the leaden clouds, the close-packed tenements of Hongkew jostled each other. Amid the wisps of black smoke curling above the dingy rooftops Julia saw flames leap. Fires glowed bright among the brick buildings housing Japanese-owned cotton mills. The Chinese Air Force had not entirely wasted its bombs.

But the old battleship *Idzumo* floated unscathed in the centre of the Japanese flotilla off Hongkew, a toy man-of-war with three spindly funnels, square gun-turrets, and bright signal-flags. Through the box girders of the Garden Bridge, which spanned Soochow Creek, Julia saw a ripple like an enormous white-tufted caterpillar. Thousands of Chinese in white tops and dark trousers were scurrying into the sanctuary of the Settlement.

'It's coming back!' Hollings shouted. 'Look there. Over Frenchtown.'

A silver shape flashed through the overcast sky. Stubby-nosed and short-winged, it looked like a toy hurtling over the toy city. Engine yammering, the warplane swooped and levelled off. The jagged white-sun insignia of the Republic of China glinted on its wings when it banked. Two black-leather heads twisted within the perspex canopy, and a rear machine-gun menaced the empty sky.

'Northrops,' Richard declared. 'Light bombers. That first chap's damned low. He's not a dive-bomber, you know.'

Julia, who had not known, did not reply. She was mesmerized by these sleek modern warplanes, which were utterly different from the boxy biplanes the Settlement had sent aloft in 1927 to frighten away the Generalissimo and his Chinese Bolshevik hordes. Best of all, not foreigners, but Chinese were flying those American-built monoplanes.

The first bomber pointed its blunt nose at the Japanese flotilla. Just south of the Bund, it swooped low. Julia willed its bombs to hit the *Idzumo*.

'By God! No, it can't!' Richard pressed the binoculars into his eye-sockets. 'Oh my Lord! I can see it . . . see them.'

Two black cylinders were tumbling in the wake of the bomber. Free of the hand that had launched them against the *Idzumo*, the bombs drifted malignantly earthwards.

In the north the spent warplane passed unscathed through the loose-meshed curtain of grey-and-red explosions thrown aloft by the flotilla's anti-aircraft guns. The bombs vanished behind the dark-brick buildings of the French Concession, and a moment later an inverted cone of black smoke rose slowly above those buildings. An instant later, Julia heard a muffled explosion, and the tower swayed beneath her feet.

'Good Lord, look at that!' Richard shouted. 'Second one must be a dud. Otherwise, it would have gone off by . . .'

A plume of orange flame flared within the black cone, but there was no second explosion. At that moment a second bomber broke through the clouds in exactly the same place as the first.

The second Northrop followed the same course the first had flown, but no bombs fell. The bomber floated above the smoke of the explosion, its silver flanks glittering in the light from the west. Over the Bund, it appeared to leap forward to strike its prey.

Then Julia saw that two bombs had detached themselves. For several seconds they flew almost parallel to the bomber like skimming stones on the watery grey sky.

'Leading the target . . .' Hollings observed didactically. 'You see the velocity . . .'

The bombs fell abruptly, obviously moving too slowly to hit the Japanese flotilla. They plunged instead towards the Bund.

The black shapes disappeared behind the pyramid tower of the Cathay Hotel, and Julia let her breath out in relief. In an instant she would see geysers of coffee-brown water. Far better that the bombs should fall into the Hwangpoo, despite the danger to shipping, than among the refugees thronging the Bund.

Black smoke swirled above the Cathay Hotel. Julia heard the explosion, felt the shock-wave, and saw the plumes of flame. Five seconds later, the terrible sequence was repeated. Both bombs had exploded.

'Sir Victor Sassoon will be unhappy if they've damaged his nice new Cathay Hotel.' After almost half a minute, the Englishman had offered the obligatory jest. 'I believe I'll trot over to Frenchtown first to see just what damage's been done. Care to join me?'

Despite her loathing, duty drew Julia to the site of the explosion, which was a major international story. Many more correspondents would be drawn by the violation of the previously sacrosanct foreign concessions and one of the very first aerial bombings of a major city since the ineffectual raids mounted by Zeppelins on London in the Great War. Many of those newcomers would ask her exactly what it had been like.

Race Course Road was almost deserted. Pedestrians had scurried into buildings, and wooden shutters were going up on shopfronts. Preternatural silence cloaked the city inhabited by noise-loving Chinese.

A horn hooted cheerfully. Wang, Tommy's irrepressible driver, swung around in a dashing u-turn and flung open the back door of the Chrysler Airflow. She smiled involuntarily at Tommy's twin self-indulgences: the erratic Wang and the hyper-modern Airflow.

The driver's skill, Tommy insisted, justified both his regular disappearances and the 'loans' he cadged to pay his gambling debts when he reappeared. The Airflow's massive contours were broken for neither bonnet nor boot. The car was perfectly streamlined, a single arc from bumper to bumper. Julia thought it ugly, but Tommy the scientist insisted that it was beautiful.

Neither Julia nor Richard spoke as the Airflow rolled along virtually deserted Tibet Road towards the smoke columns rising from the plaza where it met the Boulevard de Montigny and Avenue Edward VII before the Great World Amusement Centre. Julia heard a sighing of breakers on a distant shore before clanging fire-engines broke the uncanny silence.

When the Airflow halted, she saw the source of that sighing. Hundreds of Chinese women squatting before hoardings advertising Crown Cigarettes and the National Lottery were keening, shrieking and sobbing.

Some wore dark-blue workaday tunics and others lighter holiday blouses. All those garments were blackened by soot, and most were speckled with blood. Stripped naked by the blast, a plump boy of seven or eight urinated with gusto into the gutter. The water flowing there was now tinged with pink.

Richard made for a French officer of the Fire Brigade. The pump-wagon stood beside the signal tower, which the blast had stripped of its metal covering. The traffic lights were switching from green to red quite normally.

Across the plaza, the brown-brick Great World rose comfortably solid. A protective wall some five feet high had apparently been erected around the hexagonal building against such a blast. Curiously mottled, the wall was evidently made of sandbags improvised from discarded garments.

Julia clutched her throat and gagged. The buffer wall was leaking red and yellow fluids. Standing straddle-legged, she vomited into the gutter.

The wall was made of shattered and charred human bodies. Despite her horror, she saw the undamaged soup kitchen that had been distributing rice to the several thousand refugees camped in the plaza. The explosion had piled hundreds of the refugees against the unscathed Great World – broken, bleeding, and dying.

Julia wiped her lips with a scrap of scented lace from her handbag and dropped the foul cloth into the gutter. The flowing water picked up the frivolous handkerchief and bore it away swirling gaily on the red-veined surface.

Julia was sickened by the savoury stench of roasting flesh. Beside three rickshaws three coolies lay unmarked, killed instantaneously by shock waves. The flimsy vehicles were shattered. Three grotesquely compacted bundles of blue cloth had evidently been their passengers.

'Either help or leave, Julie!' Tommy spoke brusquely behind her. 'You're doing no good just gawking.'

'Oh, Tommy!' She turned and opened her arms. 'Tommy darling!'

He embraced her and said: 'Sorry to be so rough, but you were going into shock. You *can* help, you know.'

Two ambulances stood beside the fire-engines and behind them three trucks that normally collected bodies from the streets. Doctors and nurses in incongruous whites were kneeling beside the figures strewn across the plaza. Occasionally, one shouted to summon litter-bearers wearing Red Cross armbands. But half the victims were obviously dead. Black-clad municipal corpse-handlers dealt with them. Those professional intimates of death hawked and spat noisily, but none mouthed the rough jests that enlivened their normal rounds.

Julia helped carry the injured, forcing herself to lift charred corpses in hope of finding the living beneath. All the rescue workers wore expressions so studiedly unemotional they were grotesque. They could function only by suppressing pity as well as revulsion.

Tommy touched her shoulder and directed: 'Time for you to go home. The amahs'll be worried sick, not to speak of the children. I'll call when I can.'

He did not telephone until the next morning, and he did not return to the house on Kiukiang Road until four that afternoon, when the tail of the typhoon was lashing Shanghai.

'At least the wind'll keep the blasted planes on the ground,' he said. '*All* the flaming warplanes – our gallant defenders of the Chinese Air Force as well as the Japs.'

He gulped his scotch and water and added tonelessly: 'They reckon twelve to thirteen hundred killed at the Great World. Maybe three hundred injured. Only a rough count of course.'

292

'Richard called, Richard Hollings. He called to thank me.' Julia was glad the high window of the sitting-room kept her from looking out on the anguished city. 'And to ask us to dinner. He's a little hard to take sometimes, though not quite as bad as you . . . we . . . thought, darling. He said they figured seven to eight hundred killed on the Bund near the Cathay Hotel. Maybe another thousand injured.'

'A good day's work for our noble Nationalist defenders!' Tommy Howe said savagely. 'God knows what they'll do when they really get into their stride.'

34

September 12–October 18, 1937

Richard Hollings revelled in possessing an advantage rarely granted a war correspondent. He could cover both sides as the battle for Shanghai spread. Enjoying easy access to the Chinese lines in Chapei, he was also a welcome guest aboard the Japanese commander's flagship *Idzumo*. The Englishman had diligently cultivated influential officers during his protracted visits to Tokyo, and he was known to them as a 'good friend of Japan'.

Richard preserved that impression just as diligently. Although he condemned Japanese aggression in conversation with Julia, his personal feelings did not colour his despatches. Almost inhumanly objective, he skilfully avoided giving offence to Tokyo. Yet Julia had warmed to him because of his expressions of sympathy for her beloved Chinese. But she could neither read his despatches in the *Globe* nor listen to his reports on NBC. His Japanese friends could, of course, not hear his private conversations.

To see them Richard had only to pass the barricades on the Garden Bridge over Soochow Creek. Unlike most foreigners, he was never delayed or harassed. Other men and even women who failed to bow to the Japanese sentries were detained for hours and, sometimes, forced to strip in public to show that they carried neither arms nor subversive material. The Emperor's soldiers were chipping away at the façade of Western superiority in the Orient. But a 'friend of Japan' was not harassed.

Covering the Chinese was actually harder. Although the mayor of Greater Shanghai was always good for a fiery quote, the Nationalist generals were prudently reticent. To see the men who determined Chinese policy in the critical autumn of 1937 he had to travel some 250 miles to

294

Nanking. By train or car, the journey was made hazardous by Japanese ground patrols and air attacks. But no one ever called Richard Hollings a coward, whatever their reservations regarding his character or his ethics.

At forty he considered himself only moderately successful. He had married Fiona Bradley, who was twelve years his junior, because she would make a highly presentable wife and an excellent mother. She had, above all, been recommended by her father's senior position in the organisation of Lord Beaverbrook, Britain's most enterprising newspaper proprietor. However, the highly paid and highly visible job of chief roving correspondent for the *Daily Express*, which Richard coveted, was not on offer. He had accordingly returned – alone for the time being – to China, determined to make his name an international byword for dramatic, daring and penetrating reporting.

That ambition brought him to the Chinese Air Force observation post on the roof of the Metropolitan Hotel in Nanking in the early afternoon of a hot September day. The Englishman understood his host's Louisiana drawl with difficulty. His host was the man responsible for the carnage of the terrible day of bombing in Shanghai now known as Black Saturday.

Claire Lee Chennault, who had recently passed his forty-seventh birthday, looked as if carved from seamed and pitted granite that defied time. His jet-black eyes were set so deep under his hooded eyelids that he almost looked Chinese. But no Chinese face was ever quite so aggressive.

Captain Chennault had flown pursuit planes – and preached the supremacy of the pursuit plane. Other military aviators insisted that bombers' machine guns would always brush aside the pursuits' harassment. Generalissimo Chiang Kai-shek happened to be shopping around for an air force at the time that Claire Chennault was involuntarily retired – in part because of those unpopular views. Lured by promises of a free hand and a large salary, Chennault became adviser on training to the Chinese Air Force, which came under the aegis of Secretary-General Mayling Soong Chiang of the Aeronautical Commission.

Waiting on the roof of the Metropolitan Hotel for Japanese bombers, Chennault chewed on a cigar and confided that he had ordered the attacks on the *Idzumo* that hit the foreign concessions.

'First combat action I ever initiated!' the flier said. 'And egg all over my face! My Chinese boys are long on potential, but they've been short-changed on training. You know the Italians were graduating every cadet. Only washouts were the dead.'

'You were telling me about the attack on the *Idzumo*, Colonel.' Hollings had unilaterally raised Chennault's rank. 'Could we come back to it?'

'Sure thing. The bomber crews were ordered to bomb from 7,500 feet, no lower – and only in level flight. They're not dive bombers. They were told *not* to make approaches over the Settlement. Nobody wanted an international incident!' Chennault surveyed the empty sky over Nanking and continued: 'When cloud cover made high-level bombing impossible, the boys were too damned eager. They violated orders three ways: flew over the Settlement, at 1,500 feet. Then they tried to dive-bomb.'

'A fascinating tale, Colonel.'

Chennault lit his cigar-butt with a wooden kitchen match and admonished: 'Sorry, but you can't write it. No more'n you can write about me. We put out a story saying the Nationalist Northrops were hurt bad by Jap fighters. Tried to jettison their bombs over the race-track, but missed. Tell the truth, the Japs never laid a glove on them.'

'Colonel, I didn't see a single Japanese plane.'

'You'll see plenty this afternoon. Our early warning net sounded the alarm. The Chinese use runners, drums, and even smoke signals along with telephones and radio. Maybe twenty-five bombers are on their way.'

From the rooftop observation post Nanking lay beneath them like a model city. The massive fourteenth-century walls enclosed eleven square miles still chiefly wasteland after the devastation of the Taiping Rebellion in the last century. Beyond the avenues of new government buildings, the populace lived in cramped houses huddled around the enormous city gates. Outside the moat on the east reared Purple Mountain, the tomb of Dr Sun Yat-sen gleaming white at its foot. To the west lay the grass airfield.

The field telephone buzzed, and the aviator thumbed the butterfly switch on the handpiece. Richard heard an excited male voice: 'Bandits! Bandits! At twelve o'clock and ten thousand feet. Estimate twenty to thirty. Bandits! Bandits!'

'All right Lee, don't shout. I hear you clear.' Chennault grinned mirthlessly. 'Canny little bastards, the Japs. They've gone and circled around! I didn't expect them to come from the north.'

He drew on the ragged stump of his cigar before thumbing the butterfly switch again: 'Lee? Hate to bother you. They're waiting above the clouds? . . . Well, just make sure. And remind them again. No one moves till the Japs turn back. . . . I know it's hard, but it's the only way. . . . Lee, just *do* it!'

Chennault looked at his cigar-butt in disgust and hurled it across the roof before remarking conversationally: 'I don't blame them. It's their city, their precious new capital that's going to get pasted. . . . Chinese pursuit pilots could be good as any. Better than most except for Americans.' After a ruminative pause: 'And maybe your Royal Air Force. But their training's piss-poor. So I've got to let the Japs come in and drop their loads. Then hit them from the clouds when their guard's down and they're worrying about their fuel reserves. It's hard on Nanking. But it's the only way to kill Japs!'

Preceded by the growl of air-cooled engines, three flights of bombers appeared on the northern horizon. The weak sunlight glinted on their long bodies as they descended and split up to confound anti-aircraft fire. They floated contemptuously low over the city, the blood-red suns on their wings enormous.

Twenty-six bombers roared down on the grass airfield. Enormous gouts of earth erupted, and, after a few seconds, fires leaped. Bright yellow flames spewed greasy petroleum smoke.

Engines yammered at full throttle in the clouds. Although not an aeroplane was visible, machine-guns chattered above the engines' clamour. After four or five minutes, the sky was again silent.

The aviator grinned, removed his cigar, and asked mildly: 'See what I mean, son?'

The field telephone buzzed again. Chennault's grin blossomed larger.

'You're certain, Lee? No doubt about it?' Then to Richard: 'There you are, son. They got eight. Eight big, bad Jap bombers are down. I see you're sceptical. Why don't we see for ourselves?'

They were driven by a jaunty chauffeur in Chinese Air Force uniform. Four miles into the countryside, which still wore its summer green, the first pyre of greasy smoke brushed the low-lying clouds. Chennault confirmed the obvious through his binoculars: the burning aircraft was a twin-engined Japanese bomber.

Like a macabre paper-chase, burning aluminium carcasses led them in the direction of the Japanese base on the island of Taiwan more than six hundred miles away. In the end they found four more burning bombers.

The country people stared, suspecting that the foreigners were Japanese crewmen who had parachuted to earth. When their driver explained that Japanese looked rather different, the farmers led them across the rough countryside. They saw two more bombers, blackened skeletons with their fires burned out. The farmers also led them to two aircraft Chennault grudgingly identified as Chinese pursuits. One cockpit was empty. The charred shape in the other was beyond help.

The eighth bomber claimed by the Air Force was never found – not that day or ever. Chennault searched for hours before finally conceding: 'Well, nobody counts just right – not in combat. Maybe they only got seven. But that'll do the trick. Look here, there ain't going to be but a couple more daylight raids on Nanking.'

'And then, Colonel?'

'And then, we'll see what happens next.'

Richard Hollings left the backwoods certainties of Nanking to return to the sophisticated scepticism of Shanghai. This second Sino-Japanese War, forty-two years after China's ignominious defeat in the first, was too complex to cover except from Shanghai, where the ground forces were clashing. The war was almost too complex to cover from Shanghai.

The action was three-dimensional, fought on the sea as well as the land and the air. The Imperial Japanese Navy proclaimed a blockade from the Gulf of Pohai in the north to the Gulf of Tonkin in the farthest south. Although the combined American, British and Japanese fleets would have had difficulty enforcing the blockade over the 3,000-mile-long China Coast, the Japanese hoped to frighten off timorous shipowners.

Except on the Shanghai front, Chinese armies were withdrawing. The Generalissimo had virtually conceded indefensible North China to the enemy, and the Communists were not ready to commit the bulk of their forces. Although both White and Red guerrillas harried the invaders, it was the Communists' 115th Division that inflicted the first bloody defeat on the invaders. Since Japanese generals could not believe the Chinese would stand and fight, column after enemy column blundered into the ambush laid in a narrow mountain pass in the North-west.

Julia Howe's rejoicing over that first Chinese victory was naturally even greater because it had been won by her own Communists. Her joy was not lessened when the Apparatus instructed her to whisper the tale that the Nationalist troops supposedly co-operating with the 115th Division had run away. For all she knew, the tale might even be true.

Richard Hollings was grateful for such inside information. He was also curious about Julia's sources, and he wondered about her apparent tilt to the left. But he did not quiz her, for she was too useful in Shanghai, which was the big story. The Nationalists stubbornly held – although outnumbered by a Japanese 'landing party' now 100,000 strong.

Hollings strongly believed that baldly reporting facts was, at most, half his job. He feared that his audience would be puzzled, bored and, finally, repelled by reports of indecisive battles in unpronounceable places between Oriental armies commanded by generals with unpronounceable names. He had an obligation to his editors – and to himself – to attract the largest possible audience by thrilling and inspiring, in short, entertaining that audience. Thus would the *Globe* and NBC prosper – not to speak of Richard Hollings.

The war in the air was irresistible, as inherently romantic as single combat between armoured knights. He therefore kept returning to Nanking and to Claire Chennault, who had promised to choke off the Japanese bomber attacks. After their first raid, the bombers returned three times in five days. They were harried by Chinese warplanes using Claire Chennault's new tactics. Three pursuits would attack a single bomber in close formation. Although they lacked rigorous training, the Chinese pilots proved Chennault's thesis. Bombers could *not* always brush aside the gadfly pursuits.

Claire Chennault asserted after the fifth day that the Japanese had lost three of their best bomber regiments, amounting to fifty-four twin-engined aircraft in all. Forty charred wrecks were actually found. The remainder, he declared, had crashed into the Taiwan Straits. On the sixth day Chennault remarked to Hollings: 'Now for the next stage – night raids.'

Working smoothly, the Chinese anti-aircraft command deployed its big searchlights in a grid the attacking planes could not escape. Impaled on shafts of light, the crews of the night bombers were blind to the pursuit planes 'rocketing up the beams like a monkey on a stick', as the American exulted.

The first night, however, there were no losses on either side. The next night one bomber was lost. On the third night, the Chinese shot down seven of thirteen bombers – and the bombers came no more by night.

The magician from Louisiana could not, however, overcome the three massive Japanese advantages: greater numbers, better aircraft, and seasoned pilots. After a respectful six weeks, the raiders returned on a wintry day. Out of thirty-six raiders, only a quarter were bombers.

Twenty-four modern single-wing fighters swept away eleven of China's remaining sixteen obsolescent biplanes. From the roof of the Metropolitan Hotel, they looked to Richard Hollings like clumsy bumblebees falling from the sky.

Claire Chennault, smiling grimly, acknowledged to Hollings: 'That's the ball game – for a while. They'll paste hell out of Nanking now. Remember, I never mentioned *escorted* daylight raids.'

'And Shanghai?' Richard pressed. 'Are you writing off Shanghai, too?'

'Well, if I can't defend Nanking, there's no way in hell I can defend Shanghai. At least we got the *Idzumo* before they put us out of business!'

'The *Idzumo*, Colonel? Why, she's back at her anchorage looking fine. If anything, better!'

'Ever think that was a mite funny? We hit her one night with three five-hundred pounders. All Shanghai sees the fires and the explosions. Next day the Japs tow her out to sea. And three days later the old battleship turns up absolutely undamaged! Did you know the Japs captured the *Idzumo* and her sister-ship from the Russians in 1904? I'm sure they repainted the name and sent the sister-ship upriver to the same anchorage. Too much face lost otherwise.'

'Be that as it may, what's next?' Hollings pressed. 'What can you do?'

'Now, don't write this up. *All* I can do is fight a guerrilla war in the air. Hit the Japs where they ain't expecting it. Give me time, though, and I'll sweep the Japs out of China. No need for ground forces.' Chennault's black eyes dulled, and he concluded: 'Take a while, but my boss is working on it.'

'Your boss, Colonel?' Richard asked.

'I'm the adviser to the Secretary-General of the Aeronautical Commission. My boss is Madame Chiang Kai-shek. Most correspondents, first thing they want is an interview with the glamorous Madame Chiang. She does more for China . . .'

'I suppose I should see her,' Richard mused aloud. 'I used to know her in the old days. Before she married.'

'Did you, by God?' Chennault's enthusiasm flared. 'You've got to see her.'

'I suppose I've been avoiding her.' Richard said softly. 'For personal reasons.'

The ebullient young man grinned, and the dark features he himself described as 'my monkey face' twisted in a comical grimace. He glanced out the tall window of the dining room of the Metropolitan Hotel and remarked: 'There goes Major Yee. An idiot, Dick, a dog's head generalissimo if I ever saw one.'

'A dog's head generalissimo?' Richard Hollings was always amused by his lunch guest, a government information officer called Jimmy Wei. 'You Chinese are awfully hard on dogs, aren't you? You're always swearing at running dogs, dog's legs, dog turds, and now . . .'

'A classical allusion, my dear boy.' Jimmy's mock-English accent was

299

ludicrous. 'A dog's head generalissimo is a bloody fool who thinks he's a flaming genius.'

'Tell me, why are you Chinese so hard on each other?'

'Major Yee is a disaster. So's the Army's public relations set-up. It's the worst of our . . . count 'em . . . five different PR outfits.'

'Which lot of professional liars do you recommend, Jimmy?'

'Only one, Dick.' He grinned. 'Madame Chiang herself picked Hollington Tong as Vice-Minister of Information. Myself, I'm not University of Missouri and Columbia Journalism School like Holly Tong. But our outfit's reliable.'

'And what've you got for me today?'

'Dickie, *absolutely* off the record. For your guidance only. Okay?'

The correspondent pondered for a moment before nodding. He disliked information he could not report, but it was better than no information.

'As Dan'l Boone says, the jig's up.' Jimmy's dark monkey face was solemn. 'That's it.'

'What?' Richard almost spluttered. 'Who?'

'Dan'l Boone is that old backwoodsman, Claire Chennault. You see, Daniel Boone was . . .'

'I do know, Jimmy.' Richard chuckled at a lesson in American history from a Chinese who had never seen that country. 'Also what you mean by the jig's up.'

'Not *all* Limeys are ignorant.' Jimmy Wei did not smile. 'Well we're pulling out of Shanghai. We couldn't stop the Japs, and we couldn't suck in the Western powers. It's going to be a long war. Without Shanghai, we can't hold the lower Yangtze Valley. We're pulling back – eventually to Chungking in Szechwan, about a thousand miles upriver. We'll kick and scream, fight tooth and nail, but it's inevitable.'

'Jimmy,' Richard demanded. 'Why are you telling me all this?'

'My friend, we trust you. Even if you do play footsie with the Japs, you're a straight shooter.'

'A miracle,' Richard retorted. 'You answered every question – except the one I asked: *Why confide in me?*'

'Sooner or later you'll come to Chungking. We want you to know you'll get the info straight from the shoulder. Not the bullshit the Nationalist Party and the army dish out. Also, we want you to know the ball game's not all over when we retreat. We'll be just starting to fight.'

'This isn't a bluff, Jimmy?' Richard suspected such damaging admissions so freely offered. 'You're not setting me up? I suspect you want me to report the Nationalists are pulling back to frighten the foreign powers into helping you?'

'Dick, it's the straight goods.'

'Tell me something else!' Richard tried a fresh scent. 'How can you ever win from . . . ah . . . Chungking? Where are the men and the guns to come from? Not to speak of the courage!'

'Courage is no problem, Dick. We've got millions of brave young men – tens of millions. We'll win if we can learn just one thing: A country can be corrupt or it can be inefficient, but it's doomed if it's both corrupt and inefficient. To survive, we'll have to . . .'

About twenty-five years old, Jimmy Wei was short, tough, bright and mildly libertine. He was also a connoisseur of food, art, and the Chinese classics. Those correspondents who knew enough about China to know how little they really knew called him the Number One Barbarian Handler. He could build bridges of at least partial understanding between the bull-headed foreigners and the arrogant Chinese.

Richard Hollings was, however, jaded after talking, writing, and, too often, dreaming about China for several hectic months. His attention was diverted by the sophisticated tinkle of the piano near the bar. The pianist was glissanding through 'The Nearness of You'. Fiona and he had danced to that sentimental ballad at the Café Royal on his last night in London.

It's just the nearness of you! The refrain made him see her wide-set grey eyes and her pale gold hair. On the P & O liner between Suez and Singapore he had to his considerable surprise discovered that he loved Fiona. He was mildly resentful at being reminded of that commitment by a pianist playing 'The Nearness of You' in a hotel dining room redolent of fresh paint, new carpets, and ancient mildew.

'Do you hear what I say?' Jimmy asked patiently.

Richard apologized: 'Sorry. I'm afraid I was in a brown study. Do go on, please.'

He hardly heard Jimmy ask what in hell a brown study was, for his attention was captured by a small Chinese boy of eight or nine in a khaki uniform who was skipping across the dining room. The elderly amah hobbling behind was berating him in Shanghainese.

The child was beautiful. His large eyes and high forehead dominated finely cut features that glowed with intelligence and mischief. His uniform bore the insignia of an Air Force major. Above his breast pocket, he wore miniature gold pilot's wings with the jagged white sun of the Republic of China in the centre.

As child and amah vanished into an alcove, tough Jimmy Wei dissolved into sentiment: 'That's what we're fighting for – China's future. You know, I thought she'd gone back to Shanghai. Now there is a lady you *must* meet – even if you can't see Madame Chiang right now. She's a good story herself.'

'Why?' the correspondent asked. 'What's she done?'

'For openers, she soloed last week. How many ladies in China who can fly a plane? She's got three kids, including that young fellow in the Air Force uniform, and she's Madame Chiang's right hand. She also does some publicity. In perfect English, not like my fractured lingo.'

'Who is this super-woman? Sounds like a new Hua Mu-lan – that Joan of Arc of yours.' Richard paraded his small knowledge of Chinese history to delay the answer he suspected he already knew. 'With all those accomplishments, she must be an Amazon. A big, brawny lady with thick ankles.'

'Boy, have you got it wrong! When you finish your coffee I'll take you over.'

301

The Englishman lingered over his bitter coffee, before finally following Jimmy Wei to the alcove. Only one woman in China could possibly fit Jimmy's impassioned description.

Richard was annoyed by his own hesitance. He had nothing to be ashamed of. He had not deserted her, but she had left him far out on Bubbling Well Road in the middle of the night. Besides, he was totally devoted to his young wife, Fiona, who would soon join him.

The crystal chandelier above the round table lit Emily Howe Ou-yang mercilessly. Her skin was still unflawed ivory, and her eyes still shone with wit, but her full lips were slightly parted in surprise. Her familiar fragility in a low-necked blouse touched him.

'Madame Ou-yang, may I present Mr Hollings?' Jimmy Wei's introduction was uncharacteristically formal. 'I'm sure you've heard of him. He's the famous foreign correspondent with great understanding of China. A true friend of China.'

Emily forced a smile, but did not offer her hand. Having also been dreading their inevitable meeting, she murmured a cool response to his proper 'How do you do?'

Hearty laughter brayed and a tantalizingly familiar American voice observed: 'Good God, kids, anyone would think you'd never met before. Sit down, Dick, and tell us what you've been up to since you pulled out of Shanghai.'

The man on the edge of Richard's vision rose and extended his hand. Irritated by the intrusion, yet grateful for the relief of tension, he turned up the interloper's name in his memory.

'Harrison Parker Smythe III, isn't it? Lord, Harry, I never expected to meet you here. I thought you were through with China for ever.'

'Hardest thing is getting my Mandarin back.' The man who had once been a vice-consul in Shanghai grinned. 'But Emily's a great help.'

Richard knew that his jealousy was wholly irrational, almost ludicrous. If he were to be jealous of anyone, it was not this brash American, but the husband to whom Emily had borne three children. Yet he had neither reason nor right to be jealous of Emily's affections.

'That's grand!' Richard told Harry Smythe. 'You must be a counsellor of embassy by now. I never thought the entrenched old China hands in the State Department would take back a deserter – not at that level.'

'I *was* first secretary in Rome, and a great life it was. You see, I'm not exactly in the Embassy here, Dick. Sort of . . . a kind of . . . it's a little hard to explain. To tell the truth, I'm on a special mission . . . on indefinite leave from the State Department.'

The correspondent looked sceptically at the diplomat. The tale *might* be true, although it sounded like a cover-story for a mission Washington did not wish to acknowledge officially. Yet it was hard to believe that Harry Smythe was not telling the absolute truth. His pale-blue eyes were candid, totally unaltered except for the minute crow's feet at their corners. He looked like an utterly sincere, albeit cheeky, altar boy.

The American was, at a guess, a few years past forty. None of them had grown younger, Richard told himself wryly. He was himself almost forty.

Even Emily, serene and unalterable, was – yes, just a year younger than the century, and therefore thirty-six.

'Dick, you know I never lied to you,' Harry persisted. 'And now you're such a big cheese in the newspaper game, I wouldn't dare. Between us, I'm here to do a little job for the President. Mr Roosevelt wants a first-hand assessment of Chinese capability – especially in the air.'

The correspondent reflected rather sourly that any official American abroad could claim presidential sponsorship. Every Foreign Service commission, like every military commission, was signed by the President as chief of state – in lieu of a real sovereign like King George VI. Somehow, though, he felt the hearty American was telling the truth.

'Dick, it's also turned out I can help more directly.' Smythe's enthusiasm mounted. 'I've kept up my flying hours, and the Army Air Corps made me a light-colonel in the reserve. Anyway, Madame Chiang thinks I should lend a hand, take some of the weight off Claire Chennault. That's why Emmy's being so nice to a beat-up old aviator.'

That mock-modest tone was more annoying than Smythe's normal brashness. Why, should the American feel it necessary to offer such an elaborate explanation of his *tête à tête* with Emily, who had not said a word after their stiff greetings?

Emily smiled levelly and regarded him with untroubled light-brown eyes. Her expression conveyed neither welcome nor antagonism. He was moved by the casual fall of her ebony hair, evidently cut short for convenience. Her long fingers lay quite still on the table, and the noncommittal inclination of her head expressed only the courteous attention she would give a casual acquaintance.

'We have very high regard for Harry Smythe,' she declared evenly. 'Madame expects great things of him. And I do not contradict her. We Chinese value our old friends very highly.'

Emily's smile momentarily cracked her mask of cool courtesy. He wondered at her equivocal observation about old friends. But she reverted to banalities: 'You saw my little hellion misbehaving, did you, Richard? Dear old Ven Jyeh is baby-amahing her second generation. She's so old she can hardly keep up with Jason.'

'A very attractive boy, Emily,' he replied as vapidly. 'Looks a lot like you.'

'We call him Jason because he's so daring, a terrible handful. Tommy thinks his Chinese name is very funny. It means true obedience. Obedience is the last thing on the little devil's mind. Though I do spoil him a little.'

'How could you help it, Emily? He's a fine little chap.'

Her lips compressed tightly, and her teeth clenched on the words she had almost shouted: *He should have been ours, you fool, mine and yours, not Ou-yang Hsiu's! If only you weren't ... weren't such a charming scoundrel, such a complete bastard, he* would *be ours!*

Appalled by her silent outburst, Emily went chalky-pale. That was not how she should feel – by no means how she had meant to feel – when confronted again by Richard Hollings. A cool smile and a flip reference to the old days should have done it. Perhaps a polite inquiry about his new wife to show that she no longer gave a damn about a discarded lover.

Why should she be disturbed at being accosted by this foreigner in the capital of her own country? Was she not a highly regarded journalist and writer? Had she not made herself a competent aviatrix? Was she not the cherished, though wholly independent, wife of a wealthy gentleman of ancient family and the mother of three beautiful children? Had she not made a resounding success as a woman and a patriot? She was no less than Mayling Chiang's right hand in the fight for the salvation of China and the liberation of China's women.

Emily despised her own confusion and resented her yearning towards Richard. She deeply resented her bleak realization that she had been living only half a life for a decade – despite all her busyness. Settled and content ten minutes earlier, she felt as if she had now been flung into an emotional maelstrom.

The next instant, Emily appeared almost unruffled even to shrewd Jimmy Wei who of course knew of her affair with Richard Hollings. He thought only that she was a little uneasy at the prospect of presenting her ex-lover to Madame Chiang Kai-shek.

'Okay then. I'll speak to Mayling this afternoon.' Emily completed a sentence she could not remember beginning. 'I'm sure May'll want a good, long talk, Richard. The North American Newspaper Alliance and the National Broadcasting Company, as well as the *Globe*?'

'And an occasional piece for *The Times*. The real one, *The Times* of London.'

'That's fine, Richard. But candidly we're interested above all in the States.' Emily knew she was babbling. 'Most Americans know little of China, but they all seem to have opinions on China. And Washington listens to their opinions. So we've got to reach them.'

She rose, offered him a crisp handshake, and declared: 'That's settled then. We'll call you. Now I must be going.'

Chilled by her brusqueness, Richard stared at the half-size Chinese Air Force pilot's wings pinned to the shoulder of her green-jersey blouse. The wings were gold; the white sun in the centre was seed pearls; and the blue-sky background was sapphire chips. Emily was evidently fighting a high-fashion war. It was rather like Joan of Arc ordering her armour from Coco Chanel. Moreover, her self-confidence now bordered upon self-assertiveness.

Yet Richard caught his breath as he watched her rounded hips and slender back recede. Behind her trailed the small boy in Air Force uniform and his aged amah. Head high, her dark hair bobbing on her neck, Emily strode across the lobby towards the main door, where a driver was standing beside an emerald-green Lincoln convertible.

She did not look back. But why should she?

35

October 27–December 12, 1937

Joshua Haleevie surveyed the late autumnal glories of his three-acre garden with gratification. The brilliant copper of the small Japanese maples made a vivid background for the crysanthemums of many colours. The long spearhead leaves of the rhododendrons were as shiny green as if polished weekly, and the plump leaves of the azaleas flamed autumnal red. The roses climbing the pergola were still in bloom.

Joshua guiltily returned the pruning shears to the pocket of his worn twill trousers. His head gardener was watching him with a stern eye. He had an inviolable agreement, Joshua occasionally said, with the gardener, whom the Chinese called King of the Flowers. The gardener might place small bets on horses, but he entrusted his savings to his employer to invest. In return, Joshua did not sabotage the gardener's life work by pruning so much as the privet hedge at the back of his own estate.

Another eye watched Joshua with complete approval and total trust. The mastiff Adam Schall was still lively at sixteen, a remarkable age even for the hardy Tibetan breed. His years were betrayed only by the grey hairs that powdered his black muzzle – and by his excessive sense of responsibility.

The mastiff had a week earlier accompanied Julia and Tommy Howe's two small daughters to the safety of Joshua's mansion off Avenue Road on the far edge of the Settlement. Julia somewhat sheepishly explained that she had sent him along as 'a kind of canine amah because he's so devoted to the girls'. Actually, Adam, too, had been sent away from exposed Kiukiang Road for his own safety. After her husband, her daughters, and her friend Emily, Julia cared more for Adam than for anyone else on earth. Sometimes, when she was fed up with

305

Tommy's protracted working hours, the girls' antics, and Emily's fervent pro-Nationalist sympathies, she felt she cared more for Adam than any of them.

Althea and Persephone Howe emerged onto the terrace, shielded from the evening chill by all-in-one pyjamas of thick grey cotton called Dr Denton's. Indignant at wearing such ungainly, babyish garments, they stomped down the stone steps to the velvety lawn. Adam moved protectively towards his charges and growled proprietorially when a young gardener offered them giant bronze chrysanthemums.

Twisting Adam's long ears, the girls trotted towards Joshua. Seven-year-old Althea's hair was pale blonde, and her eyes were light hazel. Four-year-old Persephone's hair was jet black, and her eyes were iodine brown. Otherwise, they were very much alike – with their father's pale-ivory skin and his wiry strength. When pensive, they looked like their Aunt Emily. When they laughed, they were transformed into miniature Julias.

Thunder rumbled in the northeast, and the fur around Adam's neck bristled in a thick ruff. The sky at dusk was clear except for the tufts of cloud to the south and the glow on the northern horizon, but thunder rumbled again over the jagged silhouettes of the tenements near the North Station. Adam opened his great jaws and bellowed defiance to that challenge from the heavens.

Like the Chinese, Joshua felt that dogs were useful as guards or even companions, but that foreigners were foolish to ascribe more than human devotion to their cherished pets. Today he envied the dog a little. He was a major in the Shanghai Volunteer Corps; a renowned big-game hunter; a prime mover in Shanghai's remarkable recent development; a millionaire twice over by inheritance; and a millionaire ten times over by his own efforts. Yet Joshua envied the dog whose only possession was a grandiloquent name. If only he could believe with Johann Adam Schall von Bell that the mounting din in the heavens was only thunder.

He wryly surveyed the hewn-granite mansion he had built for his bride, who had named it Zion. The splendour and spaciousness had seemed somewhat pointless since the specialists had told his wife Charlotte that she could never bear children. Yet no possible luxury was spared. The three red-tiled dormer roofs were crowned by twelve chimneys, but the fireplaces were supplementary to underfloor radiant heating regulated by electric-eye thermostats. The two-storey central hall with its minstrels' gallery, which could accommodate a chamber orchestra, was dominated by an African elephant's head with ten-foot tusks. In addition, Cape buffalo, lions, giraffes, and snow leopards had given their heads as trophies to adorn the hall. The great granite fireplace was framed by two towering bears, one grizzled, the other brown.

When he was still seeing Elizaveta, she had asked: 'What's become of my sensitive Jewish scholar, my reluctant warrior? I'm glad you're happy, darling. I'm just as glad you don't yet have a stuffed giant panda or mouse-deer!'

Joshua did not smile when he recalled that scathing comment. He knew how greatly he had altered since his marriage. The ostentatious mansion was a symptom of his alteration – as were the eight cars in the garages hidden from his three tennis courts by the twelve-foot yew hedge transplanted entire from the estate of a silk-merchant beggared by cheap Japanese rayon. He used only two automobiles regularly: the black Rolls Royce Phantom II with headlights as big as barrel-heads which could carry nine passengers, and the fire engine-red Packard Victoria.

His sapphire Delage runabout still sparkled because it was washed weekly and waxed monthy. But that jewel of the carriage-maker's art was immobilized on concrete blocks. Charlotte had jealously objected to his 'tootling around town like a young blade in that bug'. Since he was then still indulging her whims, he had given up that relic of his wicked, joyful bachelor days.

Besides, the twelve-cylinder Packard was more powerful, more comfortable, and more stable around the bends of the new road to Nanking. Few motor-cars, however, took that road nowadays. Carefree drives through open country had been one of the first casualties of the Sino-Japanese confrontation. The Settlement and Frenchtown were now even more claustrophobic under the virtual siege the invaders had imposed. The Japanese could not strangle China by isolating Shanghai. But they might well strangle Shanghai by cutting off its markets in the interior.

Yet an explosion of prosperity was the most visible effect of the gravest threat the foreign community has known since the Taiping Rebels turned back at the city gates in 1860. Julia's uncle, Quick Jack Pavernen, exemplified that curious phenomenon. The Sino-Japanese war and disorder in Europe were making him a rich man.

Thousands of Jewish refugees from Nazi Germany had come to the Settlement, where they could land freely and stay indefinitely. Most possessed funds, for they could not otherwise have bought their escape from their festering fatherland. Obviously they needed housing. John Pavernen and his partner in chicanery Gustav Vass were building, buying, converting and dividing properties. Some of those expensive dwellings were actually intended to last.

The real estate bonaza, which recalled the ill-fated Riverview Manor, was just a portion of the bounty bestowed by the goddess of fortune. Quick Jack was also engaged in selective – and profitable – philanthropy. Hundreds of Chinese industrialists who had moved their factories to the security of the concessions to escape the Japanese threat needed assistance in dealing with the foreign authorities. JPEnterprises had been revived to provide that assistance. John Pavernen had even cajoled his niece Julia into helping. Her Marxist hatred of capitalist bloodsuckers was tempered for the moment by her ready human sympathy for the human predicament of the Chinese entrepreneurs. Besides, their enterprises would provide jobs for the poor. Despite Julia's help, her uncle still bemoaned the disappearance of Little Pow, who would have been the perfect agent to deal with his own countrymen.

Quick Jack Pavernen missed Little Pow most when engaged in the complex negotiations that preceded the launching of another of his fleet of 'foreign flag companies'. A Chinese-owned company doing business in China was subject to the licensed depredation of Nanking's tax-collectors, to the covert demands of corrupt officials – and to the rapacity of the Japanese. But in October 1937, those harpies still could not touch enterprises doing business in China if they were owned by foreigners. The International Settlement's register of companies now listed John Pavernen as sole or partial owner of one hundred and twenty-three enterprises, ranging from bakeries and flour mills through ship's chandlers and slipways to a bus line and a Ford agency.

Having himself extended a helping hand to a half-dozen concerns, Joshua Haleevie chuckled at that bright patch on the grey fabric of recent months. But the reality of violence obtruded into the cheerless dusk. The conflagration near the North Station in Chapei glowed sombrely on the ashen sky. As if to propitiate fate, he stooped to pat Adam's silky head and to kiss Julia's daughters, whose cheeks were as soft as the dahlias beside the gravel path. They giggled when he explained that many plants were not blooming because they were having a sleep like good children. He sent them back to the house with Adam and sat down to smoke a Havana cigar on the bench under the white-flowered magnolia that draped the brick wall of his small estate.

Joshua's thoughts returned implacably to the all-dominating crisis, and images flickered in his head like a speeded-up motion picture. The Shanghai Volunteers had been on active duty for months. So many refugees had joined that they formed a full Jewish Company. They couldn't, after all, call it the German Company. The other Germans were still members of the international community, as, for that matter, were the Nazis' good friends, the Japanese.

The refugees had also strengthened the medical profession and invigorated the city's musical life, though the doctors were now busy attending the wounded and the musicians were carrying rifles instead of violins. The Empire Theatre no longer presented operettas. Sandbags protected the glass doors that faced on Chapei across Soochow Creek, and the marquee bore the bleak message: *Closed Owing To Hostilities*.

But Shanghai's commercial ingenuity had invented other diversions. The International Guides Bureau was advertising: *Shanghai's Most Enjoyable 'War' Feature – A Trip Around the Front on the Crystal Bus – including One Free Drink*. Never outdone, journalists were rushing out crisis supplements. *Oriental Affairs* had pre-empted the best title: 'Shanghai in Torment'. The *Shanghai Times* had to make do with: 'Pictorial Record of the Sino-Japanese Hostilities In and Around the City'.

Joshua Haleevie was forced to acknowledge the likelihood that the unique international community faced extinction. The Settlement's existence depended upon common agreement on common interests among all the foreigners. But that tacit agreement had been sundered by the Japanese attack on Greater Shanghai. Although Joshua feared the splendid game was just about up, the Western powers were acting as if they expected it to last forever. Troops shepherded by warships were pouring in to man the barricades. The berets of the Royal Ulster Rifles and the solar topees of the Durham Light Infantry paraded beside the pillbox képis of the French infantry. Rakish narrow-brimmed steel-helmets flaunted the anchor-transfixed globe of the US Marines alongside the jaunty scarlet pompoms of Italian sailors.

The commercial community was not reassured by the military build-up. Thousands of women and children had been evacuated to Hong Kong, and the flood of Chinese refugees was again damned by barbed-wire perimeter fences. The Bund and Nanking Road were parapeted with sandbags, as were the 'city's oldest victuallers and provisoners', Dombey and Son on Bubbling Well Road.

Although the show of resolution had prevented direct violation by Japanese ground forces, the projectiles of both sides dropped by accident on the foreign concessions. In mid-October, the bombs of an unidentified aircraft had blown up two adjoining department stores and killed well over a thousand mid-day shoppers. A rain of shell fragments regularly claimed victims, and disease flourished among hundreds of thousands of Chinese refugees. The concessions, none the less, remained highly privileged. Beside the carnage of Greater Shanghai their suffering was almost minor.

The glow of burning Chapei grew brighter as the dusk grew deeper, and the roar of artillery replied to the snarling machine-guns. The Chinese were still tenaciously holding their positions in the tenements, office buildings, and warehouses north of Soochow Creek. But how long could they last against three times their depleted numbers?

Despite two or three fragments of anti-aircraft shells that had fallen into the compound, Zion was a safe haven. Behind the rhododendron hedge Joshua heard high-pitched yapping. Turning the corner, he found the two small girls in grey pyjamas clasping each other in pretended fear. His head level with seven-year-old Althea's, Adam was crouching and barking in a ridiculous forced falsetto. He made a menacing dart, and the sisters squealed in delight.

'All right, ladies!' Joshua called. 'Time for bed.'

Despite their protests, he shepherded Julia's girls along the gravel path towards the three dormer roofs, which were stark in the first rays of moonlight. No longer playmate but guardian, Adam trotted behind, exhorting them with *basso profondo* barks to obey the master. The black mastiff was virtually invisible in the dusk, except for the white blaze on his chest.

The sparrows were debating shrilly in the darkness when Joshua heard the querulous metallic whine. Old instinct told him that it could only be an artillery shell. Scooping up the girls, he flung himself down. The displaced air boomed, and the red-hot projectile rushed by like a loco-motive with whistle blasting. When the whine receded into the west, Joshua realized that the shell had actually passed some distance away, never entering the air space of the Settlement.

He carried the girls towards the shelter of the house. Their arms were tight around his neck, and their warm breath tickled his cheeks. He remembered again that Charlotte could not bear children.

Why else had he married her? Why had he been such a pliable fool? Why had he not defied his parents and forced Elizaveta to marry him – and give him sons and daughters? Despite her skittishness, she really wanted a man with a strong will to command her.

Extraordinary! Such vain reflections when the din of the guns in Chapei battered at his thoughts. Despite that din, he heard the flight of trench-mortar bombs nearby. Yet Chapei was simply too far for any danger from mortars. He froze in astonishment when he heard a mortar-bomb explode at the far end of the garden two hundred yards away.

A second exploded closer, and Joshua flung himself down again, sheltering the girls with his body. Detached logic reminded him that hugging the grass would provide little protection if the train of shells drew closer. Even shrapnel shells threw fountains high in the air, but the vicious little mortar-bombs sprayed their fragments horizontally only a foot above the ground.

When a third exploded, Joshua decided to stay put rather than risk a dash for the house. He saw only the white flash of Adam's chest, but he smiled involuntarily at the mastiff's antics. Running around in circles, Adam was barking a falsetto accompaniment to the bombardment. And dogs were supposed to be afraid of the thunder of guns.

A fourth mortar-bomb exploded, blessedly still a hundred yards away. After almost a minute Joshua concluded that it was the last of the stick. Accentuated by the roar of the guns in the distance, stillness abruptly cloaked the garden. Even the falsetto barking had stopped.

Joshua carried the sisters up the stone steps, which were silver-grey under the tentative moon. His wife was standing just inside the French windows, and he spoke to her briefly: 'No, I'm fine! Not to worry, darling. Just get yourself and the girls away from the windows. I'll be back in a minute.'

Heavy with apprehension, Joshua retraced his steps across the lawn, which shone pale-green in the moonlight. Near the rhododendrons lay a black heap. Knowing what he must discover, Joshua trudged across the broad lawn with leaden steps. Adam was only a dog, he told himself, and the girls were untouched.

He lifted his foot to nudge the dark shape, but drew back abruptly. He forced himself to kneel and turn the animal over with his hands. Somehow, that gesture seemed more reverent. A ribbon of blood stretched diagonally across the white blaze like a scarlet sash across Adam's deep chest. The great brown eyes stared dully, and the silver bristles on the old dog's muzzle gleamed silver in the moonlight.

By the time he assured himself that Charlotte and the girls were unharmed, Joshua's mind had of its own accord explained the extraordinary salvo of mortar-bombs into his garden. He recalled a bizarre incident that had occurred in training in France in the Great War. An inexperienced corporal in charge of a trench-mortar had reversed his bearings and almost killed all his officers. His target lay at an angle of ten

310

degrees from his position, but he had aimed at one hundred and ninety degrees, the diametrical opposite. Only a similar error could account for the erratic volley that had killed the mastiff.

Joshua simply could not understand why he was so stricken by the death of a dog. Deeply troubled, he climbed the stairs to the attic in the gables. Through the mullioned window he saw a brilliant red glow illuminating the entire horizon to the north. The cliffs of black smoke over burning Chapei obscured the stars and the moon.

Joshua knew then why he grieved so deeply for Adam. The mastiff's violent death was a symbol – and a portent. Adam's passing marked the end of an era in which they had all been young and happy and optimistic.

He recalled Julia's house-warming in 1922. Already fizzing with champagne, Elizaveta and he had brought along five more crates and a primitive Victrola. Later that day, Tommy Howe's unlikely friend, the big Communist labour agitator Chang Kuo-tao, had delivered the black-and-white puppy. Joshua remembered Mayling and T.V. Soong expounding on the doings of the Jesuit missionary-scientist Johann Adam Schall von Bell in sixteenth-century China.

It seemed only yesterday, but it was fifteen years ago. And fifteen years was half a generation.

Joshua opened the small window – and recoiled from a blast of heat. The distant fires shone pink on his cheeks and his white sideburns. All Chapei was burning. The four-mile stretch from the North Station to the industrial western districts was a single sea of flame. The northern sky was the bright scarlet of arterial blood below enormous banks of black smoke.

Amid the towers of flame, a nine-tiered pagoda rose invincible, its tile carapace gleaming vermilion. Was that indestructible pagoda not another symbol? A portent that Japan could not defeat the indomitable will and the enormous expanse of China? In the next instant a gargantuan sigh rose above the roar of the fires, and the pagoda crumbled into the flames.

Richard Hollings was the odd man out on the American gunboat – and not because he was English. A joyful end-of-term mood ruled the crew, as well as the American Embassy officials and the correspondents who had embarked at Nanking. But he could not rejoice at leaving the doomed city, although even the indomitable Generalissimo and Madame Chiang Kai-shek had departed four days earlier for Wuhan, 600 miles upriver. The Nationalist rearguard was withdrawing, abandoning the capital and its people to the Japanese. The last foreigners to leave were safe on the USS *Panay*. The gunboat was protected primarily by the big American flags painted on her awnings and her hull, rather than her six thirty-calibre machine-guns and two three-inch guns.

The Englishman stared dejectedly at the placid expanse of the Yangtze near Ma-anshan twenty-five miles upstream from Nanking. On the afternoon of December 12, 1937, he was depressed because he was very

311

tired. He was, indeed, almost exhausted by the exertions and the emotions of the past week. He was, moreover, concerned about Emily Ou-yang, as he was still learning to think of her.

Since his first trip in September, Richard had visited Nanking frequently. His excellent relations with the Japanese had paradoxically oiled his contacts with the Chinese. Senior officials strove to win him over – and to obtain information on the enemy. He had seen both Generalissimo and Madame Chiang Kai-shek with no difficulty.

His self-appointed public relations adviser, Jimmy Wei, had confided: 'Your name jumped right to the head of the list because Mrs Ou-yang . . . Emily . . . insisted.'

He had, however, seen Emily herself only once after their meeting in the dining room of the Metropolitan Hotel. She had welcomed him politely – and distantly – to the Chiangs' suite, introduced him again to the Generalissimo, reminded Mayling of many earlier meetings, and departed. Mayling herself had interpreted – and interjected – in her soft American accent.

His repeated efforts to see Emily on her frequent visits to Shanghai had all been deftly turned aside. One day welcomed by Julia Howe as an important correspondent, he was the next day fended off as a threat. It was bad enough recalling how Emily had avoided him. It was far worse to be safe aboard the *Panay*, but not even know where she was.

A month earlier, the Japanese had occupied all of Greater Shanghai. Although a public personage like Madame Chiang Kai-shek could not cross the Japanese lines, her executive assistant Emily Ou-yang could slip through under false papers. One moment Richard hoped she was safe in Shanghai. The next moment he dreamed of finding her in Wuhan when the *Panay* finally reached that meeting of the waters.

If the *Panay* ever arrived! The Captain did not seem to know quite where he was bound. He had weighed anchor at 8:30 that morning, apparently on his own initiative, and steamed upriver in company with three Socony-Vacuum tankers flying the Stars and Stripes. Anchoring again where the Yangtze widened, he was behaving as if he had nothing to fear in all the wide world, as if both sides were not from time to time firing at neutral ships. While the long Sunday afternoon dragged towards dusk, he allowed a dozen crewmen to visit the tankers, where the US Navy's total prohibition of alcoholic drink did not apply.

The Captain was not disturbed when two military aircraft swooped over the gunboat. The Japanese were presumably searching for the ten troop-ships on which bazaar rumour had embarked a Chinese division fleeing Nanking. Armoured by his conviction of American inviolability, the Captain remained unconcerned.

'It's not real, is it, *caro*?' an American voice asked. 'A painted ship on a painted sea.'

Richard turned with a smile of welcome. The accent was American, except for that Italian *caro*, 'my dear chap'.

He was pleased to see the Roman profile of the correspondent called

312

Luigi Barzini, whose American idiom and anti-Fascist views both derived from his education at Columbia University. What a contrast to the other Italian correspondent aboard. The older man spoke in a hurdy-gurdy accent, but only to praise the dictator Benito Mussolini or to complain about the food. Barzini and Hollings had already formed a congenial little group with Harry Smythe, who was pursuing his mysterious mission, and Norman Alley, already famous as a daring newsreel cameraman.

'Just look at her!' Standing on the upper deck, Barzini gestured expansively at the length of the gunboat below them. 'A white-and-tan warship! Like something out of an opera – a comic opera. Madame Butterfly will turn up any minute. Have you ever seen anything less warlike?'

Hollings had been turning over the same thought for the story he would write when the US Navy condescended to take him to some place where he could file a cable. The Captain would not allow his under-employed radioman to send press messages to Shanghai. Despite that embargo, the Captain constantly volunteered information to the press – on one subject, the mighty gunboat he commanded. He also approved of laconic Norman Alley's practice of carrying a sixteen-millimetre hand-camera, even after completing his documentary on a Yangtze Patrol gunboat. After the Captain's lectures Richard could automatically recite the *Panay*'s facts and figures: 450 tons; 191 feet long; speed fifteen knots; built by Kiangwan Shipyard at Shanghai in 1928.

The buff-and-cream paint that so amused Luigi Barzini was intended to make gunboats so distinctive that no warlord could fail to identify them – or risk the wrath of the foreign devils by shooting at them. It was a theory which had, unfortunately, not quite proved watertight during the past decade, as Richard knew from the exasperated complaints of Royal Navy officers over pink gins.

He hoped the deterrent would work now. No ammunition filled the ready racks beside the three-inch guns mounted fore and aft. The after-gun was, moreover, so caged by the pipe stanchions supporting the indispensable awnings that it could not move to aim at ships or aircraft. After six months, the war between the Japanese and the Chinese was still something of a joke to the US Navy.

The anchorage the Captain had chosen revealed that state of mind clearly. His six obsolescent Lewis machine-guns were loaded for action against snipers, although the banks of the Yangtze were a brown smudge in the distance marked by the smoke of cooking fires. Only field-pieces could reach them, and illiterate Chinese gunners were notoriously poor shots. The *Panay* would have been perfectly secure – if the year were 1914, when the aeroplane was only an interesting toy.

Sixty miles to the north-east, two formations of the Imperial Japanese Navy's Air Arm were being hauled through the grey winter sky by their big aluminium propellers. The villagers below heard the clamour of their sixteen-cylinder engines twenty seconds after they glimpsed the V-echelons at ten thousand feet. The observers of the Chinese aircraft warning net could only spit venomously at the unoffending ground, for there was now no one in Nanking to report to. Shivering in the December breeze, several noted that the formations were very loose. The Japanese pilots had sacrificed their normal precision to the race for their objective.

In both bombers and pursuit escorts, pilots sucked in their breath in excitement. The naval aviators had narrowly missed colliding during their pell-mell take-off, elated at being loosed for the first time against their proper targets: ships. Reconnaissance flights had confirmed the rumour of ten troop-ships carrying a fugitive Chinese division. Intent upon being first to hit the target, the lieutenants leading the two flights leaned forward to urge their aircraft to greater speed.

Harry Smythe surveyed the sky with professional interest when the distant growl of aircraft engines heralded the Japanese flights.

'Some poor bastards are going to catch hell!' he said. 'The damned Japs own the sky. Not a Chinese pursuit plane for hundreds of miles.'

'It may be selfish, but I pray it's not us,' Luigi Barzini commented. 'I've had a bellyful of being bombed.'

'I'm in complete agreement . . .' Richard Hollings began, but broke off to exlaim: 'Why the devil are they coming so low?'

'Get down! For God's sake, hit the deck!' Harry Smythe shouted. 'It could be us.'

In the pilot-house near the bows, the Captain looked up. He had never seen so many Japanese warplanes flying into the interior. Even more curiously, they were losing altitude, diving like fools.

He did not see the bomb fall, but the explosion flung him across the pilot house. The flash blinded him, and the reverberation deafened him. Only half-conscious in shock, he saw that his left leg was bent at an extraordinary angle. As the delayed pain lanced his nerves, the Captain's professional eye assessed his ship. The radio-shack was stove in; the foremast was down; and the foreward three-inch gun had been blown off its pedestal. The Japanese were still diving, the red suns on their wings growing enormous as they bored closer.

Sprawled on the upper deck near the stern Richard Hollings actually saw the two bombs that smashed the prow drop from the twin-engined high-level bombers. When the ship shuddered under the double explosion, he was tossed half a foot into the air. He landed hard on the white-sanded deck, and for a moment brilliant cascades of light erupted before his eyes. Water raining down from the geyser thrown up by a near miss half-blinded him.

Blinking to clear his vision, Richard saw two dive-bombers hurtling towards the stern. Their big yellow bombs detached themselves at the low point of their dive. Both exploded in the water, but they shook the 200-foot *Panay* like a toy boat in a bathtub. The wooden hull groaned in mortal pain.

Richard smelled acrid cordite and heard the asthmatic wheezing of the old Lewis guns. A petty officer wearing a blue workshirt but no trousers was shouting orders at the gunners, while a nearly naked officer climbed the ladder to the pilot-house, his peaked cap perched jauntily on his head. A single sleeve on his right arm, a single shoe on his right foot, and the cap were all the bomb blast had left him.

Stronger even than the stench of gunpowder, the smells of China wafted across the water: frying garlic, stale cooking oil, and wood-smoke; the clay scent of the red laterite soil; and the nauseating reek of human excrement. In the brief intervals between the gunfire wild ducks cawed overhead, and the brisk wind whipping the muddy water carried the lowing of frightened buffaloes from the shore.

Afterwards, Richard remembered with some surprise that he had forgotten to be afraid. He also remembered Harry Smythe's knowledge-able commentary as the bombs fell around them and Luigi Barzini's ostentatious contempt for danger. Richard hardly remembered making the copious notes he could hardly read, but he clearly remembered Norman Alley standing erect and changing the film-magazines of his camera.

Later, Richard's memory yielded unconnected images: The radio shack behind the pilot-house hit again. A lieutenant hobbling across the deck with blood streaming from his leg, but still passing on his orders. Gouts of steam roaring from the funnel when the duty engineer tripped the safety valve to prevent the boiler's exploding. Luigi Barzini returning from a reckless sortie below decks to report that the older Italian cor-respondent had been badly wounded. And, constantly, the high-pitched clamour of the dive-bombers' engines; the blood-red sun flashing enor-mous on their wings; the defiant wheezing of the Lewis guns; and the contemptuous chatter of the warplanes' machine-guns in reply.

The order was passed when the warplanes turned their fire on the three tankers: 'Abandon ship! All hands abandon ship!'

Water lapped at their feet as they waited on the gunboat's deck to board the two sampans that were her only lifeboats. Luigi Barzini murmured a plea for gentleness to the sailors lifting his wounded Italian colleague into the motor sampan. Harry Smythe waited till last, from time to time shaking his head in disbelief – and admiration.

No one was in command. The Captain was unconscious. The Executive Officer, who had been hit in the throat and the hands, could no longer even scrawl brief orders with the marking pencil held in his bloody fingers. Yet the abandon ship routine proceeded smoothly. Efficient de-spite their shock, the crew took off not only wounded and passengers, but medical supplies and essential stores.

'Discipline!' Harry Smythe declared. 'Training and discipline!'

'Beginners' luck!' Richard Hollings added. 'And bloody lucky for us the Japs've gone away!'

At precisely five minutes past three, as Richard automatically noted, the last officer, the young lieutenant whose clothes had been blown off, stepped into the motor-sampan. He was still naked.

The survivors watching from the shore signalled frantically. The sampan drew away from the gunboat, her decks awash in the muddy water. Two barges crammed with Japanese soldiers were leaving the tankers they had been harassing to make for the *Panay*. As they approached, machine-guns in their bows repeatedly swept the stricken gunboat.

The Japanese boarded, but withdrew in haste. Shortly thereafter, the gunboat rolled wearily to starboard and exposed her flat bottom, which was green with long aquatic grasses and jagged with grey barnacles. Her white paint gleaming, the *Panay* dived, shattered prow first, into the Yangtze River. Slowly, almost deliberately, the gunboat subsided beneath the muddy water.

Richard Hollings automatically checked his wrist-watch. A single bar bisected its face. The time was exactly 3:45 p.m. The tough gunboat sailors could not weep – not even for the only home most had known for many years. But not one spoke for a minute. Finally someone said: 'Well, that's it! Let's get organized.'

Norman Alley wiped his soot-blackened face with the back of his soot-blackened hand and said softly: 'Terrific shots! Best I've ever made. Everyone will be able to see how close the Japs were, how they couldn't have mistaken those big Stars and Stripes on the awnings. Great shots, but never again I hope!'

36

Two hundred doves fluttered in the glass-roofed courtyard of the old mansion on Jessfield Road. Dyed red, green, and pink, they swirled like confetti beneath the leaden January sky. The bamboo whistles tied to their legs trilled joyously above the rattle of hanging clusters of fire-crackers.

The household was celebrating the betrothal of the eldest son of the wealthy gentleman Ou-yang Hsiu. But the mistress of the household, who was the youth's step-mother, was not present for the final eruption of fireworks. Ou-yang Hsiu rejoiced in the modern family of one son and two daughters his young wife had given him. However, the price of a modern wife with a foreign education was tolerating behaviour so independent it was sometimes unseemly.

Emily Ou-yang awaited her own guests in the big conservatory at the rear of the old house. If her duty to her country were a whit less pressing, she would not have left the family party. But Madame Chiang Kai-shek's instructions by courier from Wuhan had been urgent: *Because the American people believe our defeat is inevitable, the American government is hedging. If US opinion does not turn, even the meagre assistance we now receive will cease. You must work primarily on the Americans. You must convince them that we are fighting their fight – and that we can win. Drop everything else!*

Their own correspondents, Emily had concluded, must tell the American people that China was fighting for them because the Japanese were also their enemy. Then the Central Government would receive the arms and assistance needed to defeat the Japanese. She had, accordingly, drafted a plan of campaign with her sister-in-law, who seemed to have every foreign correspondent in China on a leash.

317

Julia had thrown herself wholeheartedly into the campaign – with the blessing of the Apparatus. Now, the National People's Party and the Communist Party were, after all, formally united in a front against the Japanese. Julia knew the Communists' reasoning, although she never mentioned it: Mao Tse-tung had manoeuvred to force that alliance because the Communists could have been destroyed if they had not diverted the Generalissimo's armies from their Sixth Extermination Campaign to the battle against Japan.

The reception for fifty guests that drizzle-sodden Sunday afternoon was the opening shot of the propaganda campaign Emily and Julia had planned. Consuls-general were to be fed titbits of inside information with the small chow and the drinks. Even more than newspapermen, diplomats loved a scoop. With the correspondents the conspirators would discuss high strategy, for newspapermen liked to think they were policy-makers.

Despite her dedication, Emily had bridled when Julia wrote Richard Hollings's name on an invitation to the reception. She had declared vehemently: 'I won't have him here. I can't bear his superior airs. And it wouldn't be fair to my husband. Not when the other guests will know that . . .'

'Emmy, I know just how you feel,' Julia had replied. 'I can hardly bear him myself. But I still see him a lot.'

'Julia, how can you? He's so grasping and hard.'

'I just think he'll come in handy,' Julia had repeated stubbornly. 'He's a big cheese now. Not only NBC and the *Boston Globe*. His despatches are syndicated by the North American Newspaper Alliance.'

'All right, ask him if you must,' Emily had finally agreed. 'But don't expect me to talk to him.'

Natty in a soft grey-flannel suit, Richard was among the first guests to brush past the scarlet poinsettias framing the doorway where Emily awaited her guests. She had chatted stiffly with him. Apparently unaware of her enmity, he had replied easily before giving way for other guests.

Greeting Julia like the close friend he believed her to be, Richard remarked genially: 'Emmy's really pushed the boat out. Not only a string quartet, but a strolling dumpling stand. And she seemed a little tense. Hostess's nerves . . .'

'You didn't . . . know, did you, Richard?' Julia interrupted. 'Em was caught in Nanking when the Japs marched in.'

'Poor girl! No wonder she's jumpy. How did she get away?'

'You'd better ask her. I think she's getting over it. It's only a month, but she's tough.'

Richard followed her glance. Emily was too thin, almost drawn. She was, none the less, striking in a royal-blue *cheongsam*. Her only ornament was the miniature gold Chinese Air Force wings of pearls and sapphires. Julia herself had defied wartime austerity because she wished to appear fragile, feminine, and a little frivolous. She wore a pink beaded dress with a round neckline. The long sleeves were secured by loops around her little fingers, and tiny gold buttons opened from knee to ankle.

318

'Dick, she's also dedicated.' Julia warned him off. 'She's working so hard for China she's got no room for anything else in her life.'

Emily was dressing down the American Consul-General, who could not take offence. The soft voice was Emily Ou-yang's, but he knew the message was Madame Chiang Kai-shek's.

'I'm sorry, Madame Ou-yang,' the Consul-General temporized. 'The United States is strictly neutral, favouring neither side. I don't understand how you can say we're helping the Japanese.'

'What about the *Panay*? The Jap aviators couldn't possibly miss the big American flags painted on the awnings. It's an open secret: Norman Alley's film – the sequence President Roosevelt personally suppressed – showed dive-bombers only a hundred feet above the *Panay*. They couldn't have mistaken an American gunboat for a Chinese troop-ship. But you did nothing!'

'I don't call stiff protests nothing, Madame Ou-yang.'

'Meanwhile, you're selling scrap-iron and aviation gas to the Japs,' she responded. 'And you're sniping at Claire Chennault and his men. Warning they'll lose their American citizenship by fighting for China.'

'The law,' he replied, 'prohibits Americans from serving in the armed forces of foreign countries. As I said, we're neutral.'

'Then, why can't you Americans act like *real* neutrals?'

'What precisely do you mean?'

'Military goods are flowing to Japan. Not guns or planes, which they don't need. They make their own. But gasoline and steel. And *we* can't get armaments. You Americans have even stopped obsolete rifles sold us by your own War Department. And you've forced us to unload Martin bombers in Manila – from a *Chinese* ship! You won't sell us explosives for construction purposes. America is really cracking down on us.'

'Madam Ou-yang, I shall risk being indiscreet. And you know that discretion is to a diplomat what chastity is to a lady.' The Consul-General lapsed into ponderous old world charm. 'A little unsolicited advice to you – and your . . . ah . . . associates. Just hang on and hope for the best. Policies do change, though slowly. It won't be easy and it won't be quick, but you can look for a change.'

'I'll try to hope,' she replied. 'But it's not easy.'

The Consul-General essayed an almost Continental bow. He had really told her very little, but he regretted those meagre confidences. He bowed again and excused himself.

'Never say die, Emmy.' She heard Tommy's light tone and crisp accent before she turned. 'It's not healthy, my favourite sister giving up hope. Definitely morbid. Bad for mental hygiene, as they call it in God's country. I prescribe two measures of gin, a half-measure of grenadine, and . . .'

'Tommy, darling!' she laughed. 'You only have *one* sister.'

'I suppose that's why you're my favourite,' he agreed amiably. 'No competition.'

'Jimmy Wei, you've been leading my brother astray.' Emily turned to Tommy's companion. 'How much have you two had to drink?'

319

'I assure you, my good lady,' Jimmy replied, 'only two or three little sips.'

Jimmy Wei was elaborately courtly when he was drinking, and the pink spots above Tommy's cheekbones had obviously been produced by more than 'two or three little sips'. Otherwise he would not have worn the ancient tweed jacket with the violent green-and-red check his wife hated.

Little Jimmy Wei's dark monkey-face was, however, unaltered. Accustomed to drinking as a reporter on the *Shanghai Evening Post*, he had become inured to liquor since joining the Press Office, where his chief Hollington Tong called him 'my utility outfielder'. He was today dressed in a pin-striped blue suit to play the suave diplomat.

Grasping their arms, he swept Emily and Tommy towards the bar. He demanded Black Jack Daniels and soda from the bemused bartender, plucked a turkey-leg from the buffet, and waved it like a baton to emphasize his points.

'So you want to know what it was like in Nanking after the Japanese dwarves marched in, Dr Howe?' he asked loudly.

Tommy nodded, although he had already heard the story of his sister's escape with Jimmy Wei. Besides, Jimmy and he had passed beyond titles to nicknames a half-year earlier. Drawn by Jimmy's raised voice, most of the guests moved towards the bar. Those who did not know him were attracted by the novelty. The correspondents, who knew Jimmy well, anticipated another virtuoso performance.

Jimmy flourished the drumstick and observed: 'You know, my friends, it's not fashionable to talk about right and wrong nowadays. We hardly ever talk about God. But Nanking made me believe in God. I saw evil – and I knew that good had to exist to oppose evil. And God let our hostess Madame Ou-yang and me get away.'

'Tell the story!' Tommy hissed impatiently. 'Or you'll lose your audience.'

'Emily and I were trapped in the basement of the Aeronautical Commission when the Jap dwarves marched in. We were lucky. The building had been pasted by bombs and looked like a ruin. So the Japs ignored it. And we had a grandstand seat.' He gulped his highball and continued: 'The Jap officers held a formation in the plaza right before our eyes. Then they turned their troops loose to pillage and kill. . . .'

'And rape!' Emily interjected. 'We had to watch. We had to know the enemy. . . . But, God, what we saw!'

'They turned maybe seventy thousand men loose to sack Nanking,' Jimmy resumed. 'Worse than the Mongols. *Bushido*, they call it, the way of the warrior. Some way! Some warriors! In the beginning, the killing was casual. The dwarves were stinking drunk. And they only killed those who got in the way of their looting. Not more than ten thousand.'

'Not more than ten thousand in the beginning, Mr Wei?' the American Consul-General asked. 'What is your estimate of total casualties?'

'Too many to count, but not less than a hundred thousand dead and injured. It started with swords and bayonets. Next they used pistols and rifles. And they finished with machine-guns and flame-throwers. I don't think I'll ever eat roast pork again.' Jimmy passed his hand over his eyes. 'The fires burned so high the whole city was lit like the stage of a theatre. We watched them line up the women. From young girls, maybe eight to ten, to grandmothers – old ladies with hair pulled back so tight they were a little bald in front. You all know the type.'

Jimmy shook his head as if in pain, the jester overcome by tragedy. He looked imploringly at Emily, who recounted in a monotone: 'Several hundred Japanese soldiers lined up. Rough men with cropped heads and brutal faces. Great barrel chests and long dangling arms – just like gorrillas. It might have been a general inspection. Many took off their trousers. Some folded them neatly. . . . But you can imagine the rest. Afterwards, they killed the women and girls. They hacked wildly with swords and rifle-butts – like threshing rice . . .'

'Emmy, that's enough for now!' Julia stepped forward protectively. 'No need to repeat every gory detail!'

'Just let me say . . . just add one thing.' Jimmy gulped the rest of his highball and said: 'You can't compromise with them, can't negotiate with them – no more than you can negotiate with a *tsunami*. Remember that for your own sake. And remember this: we Chinese are only the first. Like a *tsunami*, like a tidal wave, Japan cannot stop. Japan can only be broken by resistance. You're next, ladies and gentlemen. Southeast Asia, then India and . . . God only knows what after. You probably think I'm exaggerating. But I'm not. Suppose I'd told you twenty years ago that a country of sixty million like Japan would invade a country of four hundred million like China? Would you have believed me? It's going to be a very long war.'

When he stopped, the silence lasted for half a minute. The diplomats briefly withheld their ritual deprecation of his alarmism. The newspapermen stared down the dark corridor of the future, which was apparently to be lit with starbursts and explosions.

'If Jimmy's right, we'll be covering wars for the rest of our lives – if we live that long,' Richard Hollings finally observed, unsmiling. 'Peace and optimism aren't available in China right now.'

Tommy glanced at the guests who clustered around Jimmy and Emily, eagerly asking questions. He moved away, Julia and Richard with him, and murmured: 'They are, you know. If you know where to look. Ever hear of a place called Yenan?'

'We're all *heard*, but no one's seen what the Communists are up to,' Richard replied. 'It's impossible to get to Yenen. Anyway, they're not fighting for China. They're on the strings of Moscow and the Communist International.'

'I'm by no means sure about that, though I don't endorse their doctrines. Me least of all!' Tommy answered. 'I get the impression that doctrine – Marxism–Leninism or whatever you call it – isn't all that important to them since the Japanese invasion. Of course only the Generalissimo can save China from the Japs. But Chairman Mao Tse-tung and my old friend Chairman Chang Kuo-tao have really made the Red Army part of the Central Government's forces. The Eighth Route

Army, as you know, now takes its orders from the Ministry of National Defence.'

'What about the reports of the Nationalists still blockading the Communist areas?' Hollings demanded. 'Isn't the Gimo mounting a new Extermination Campaign on the quiet?'

'If that's true,' Tommy replied, 'I'm very sorry the Generalissimo still considers it necessary to contain the Communists. If he'd let up, both Nationalists and Communists could turn all their force against the Japanese. Mind you, I'm not criticizing the Generalissimo. But . . .'

'The hell you're not,' Richard laughed. 'But you hinted it was possible to get to Yenan.'

Julia looked at him blankly. Behind the smoke from his meerschaum pipe, Tommy lifted an eyebrow.

'Tommy, you're talking like a man who knows more than he says,' Richard persisted. 'Is all this theoretical? Or is there a way to Yenan?'

Tommy took his pipe from his mouth and nodded. The correspondent responded enthusiastically: 'What a story! The first eyewitness story of the mysterious Chinese Communists. Of course, I'd need to move round, and talk to everyone freely.'

'Dick, you're not there yet,' Julia laughed. 'If you make too many conditions, even my miracle-working husband won't be able to . . .'

'You mean you're not just flying a kite, Tommy? Julie, you really believe it can be arranged? A trip to Yenan?'

After a brief pause for effect, Julia nodded, and the correspondent demanded: 'Why are you involved? Why bother?'

Tommy had warned the Apparatus that open proselytizing could destroy their cover. The reply had been unequivocal: *It is priority one to lure an influential foreign correspondent to Yenan to refute Nationalist propaganda. Even at the cost of endangering your own future usefulness.*

'Why am I involved?' Julia mused ostentatiously. 'Only because we've been approached by an acquaintance who knows that some of our friends are foreign correspondents.'

'Julie, love, you haven't answered my question. Tell me, why are you bothering?'

'Because we believe in fair play,' Tommy broke in. 'We also believe in the power of the truth. If both sides are reported fairly and honestly, it's best for China in the long run.'

'When can I meet your acquaintance? The sooner the better.'

'It's not quite that simple, Dick,' Julia interposed. 'We can't just order him up like a hamburger. But we'll see what we can do! And meanwhile, keep mum.'

'Meanwhile what, Julie?'

'Don't tell Emmy! That would be fatal. You'll have to get through the Nationalist blockade, so don't tell her that . . .'

'I understand. Not, mind you, that I'm likely to get the opportunity to say anything to the Ice Queen beyond "Thank you and goodbye, Madame Ou-yang! What a nice party!"'

'My Lord!' Tommy Howe looked at the gold Rolex on his wrist. 'I'm due at ward rounds in fifteen minutes. Julie, say goodbye to Emmy for me. I'm off.'

'Not without me, Doctor,' she said. 'You haven't forgotten we promised the girls we'd be home to say goodnight. And we're due at Fessenden's at eight. I'll phone Emmy tomorrow.'

The Howes' victory in the skirmish of the propaganda war between the Nationalists and the Communists was marred by Tommy's misgivings. His sensibility, Julie sometimes felt, was too tender for their secret work. She herself could not completely still all pangs of conscience, but she would not let those irrelevant doubts affect her unduly.

'Bit ironic that, wasn't it, Julie?' Tommy asked as they bowled past the Race Course in the Chrysler Airflow.

'Ironic, Tommy?'

'Come now, Julie,' he said. 'You know bloody well what I mean. Not just ironic, but a little despicable. Seducing Dick Hollings at a Nationalist party.'

'Despicable or not, it's going to work,' she responded. 'Most correspondents would give their left arms for an exclusive on the North-west Soviet Area. And Dick is hungry for fame. Very hungry!'

Julia would have been less cocky if she had heard the conversation between Emily and Jimmy Wei as the guests were leaving. Jimmy, who took a benevolent interest in his friends' personal lives, was still playing Cupid. Disappointed in the results – or lack of results – after he brought Emily and Richard together in the dining room of the Metropolitan Hotel, he was still working for their reconciliation. He knew they needed each other. Ou-yang Hsiu was a stuffed shirt, he felt, while Richard's failure to send for his wife spoke for itself.

'You really ought to give Dick a break.' Jimmy drew Emily aside. 'After the *Panay*, he deserves it. Anyway, why did you invite him? Not to spit in his eye, I presume!'

'Julie wanted him,' she replied irritably. 'Not me.'

'And Julie's going to press our case with him, not you?'

'I guess so.'

'It won't do, my lady. You can't trust a foreigner to plead China's case – no matter how devoted she is. Anyway, I sometimes wonder about Julie's politics.'

'Don't be silly, Jimmy. I've known her since we were ten years old. Anyway, Tommy . . .'

'Sorry, Em. But Hollings is too damned important. Vital! The *Boston Globe*'s not all that important, though it thinks it is. NBC's where the power's shifting to. Radio's the wave of the future. And NANA with hundreds of papers in the States and abroad.'

'I know all that, Jimmy. I do write pieces for the newspapers from time to time. Remember?'

'Sorry again, Em. But aren't you fierce today!'

'All right, Jimmy. I don't want to, but I'll have a word with Mr Richard Hollings. What I do for China!'

'That's a good girl,' Jimmy responded gratefully. 'Of course, it's up to you whether you make the ultimate sacrifice!'

Emily glared at him, but then, reverting to childhood, she poked out her tongue at him. Jimmy only whispered: 'Now remember, my lady, don't spit in his eye!'

Emily was still smiling in the wake of that exchange when she found Richard among the half-dozen guests waiting to say goodbye to her.

'Can you stay a few minutes longer?' she asked. 'The farewells won't take very long. But do have another drink.'

Since Emily had consistently rejected his overtures for five months, Richard was surprised by her sudden amiability. They sat side-by-side on a wrought-iron bench embowered by ferns and orchids. His grey-flannel sleeve was two inches from her royal-blue silk, but they did not touch. Her fingers played with the Air Force wings pinned at her shoulder.

'We should have talked earlier, Dick – talked as friends.' Emily knew she had to get around his anger at her aloofness before she could influence him. 'It . . . whatever we had together . . . it was so long ago. It's ridiculous for old friends to keep away from each other like enemies.'

'None of my doing, Emily,' he replied. 'I'm delighted to talk with you – as an old friend.'

'And I want you to know that I bear no grudge.' She was heavy-handed, though the conversation required the lightest possible touch. 'None whatsoever!'

Because it would spoil the moment, Richard suppressed the riposte that sprang to his lips. It was he who might bear malice, since she had turned him out. Although he did not know quite what he wanted of Emily, her awkwardness gave him hope. She would not be so ill at ease unless the conversation was as important to her as it was to him.

'Anyway, for old times' sake, I thought you . . . That is, I wonder if . . .' She stumbled still. 'You see, I haven't told anyone everything I saw in Nanking.'

'You mean you haven't filed?' The correspondent was astonished – and suspicious. 'You haven't written it for your precious *Public Ledger*? No one could sit on an eyewitness story like that.'

'I haven't written a word, Dick. Honestly, I couldn't. I could hardly talk about it. Not till this afternoon.'

'That's a little hard to believe, Emily,' he mused. 'How could . . .'

'You always used to tell me I wasn't professional enough. Maybe you were right. But if you're not interested, I can find someone else to . . .' Recalling Jimmy Wei's warning not to spit in Richard's eye, she amended her words: 'But you're the one I want to write that story. Only you can do it full justice.'

Richard's suspicion melted in the warmth of her flattery. He leaned over and spontaneously put his hand on her arm. The familiar feel of the soft flesh and the delicate bone beneath the silk carried him back in time. A rush of tenderness swept over him, and his hand trembled. He withdrew it, forgetting whatever he had meant to say.

Emily looked up, her eyes wide in surprise. She moved towards him involuntarily, and he instinctively lifted his arms. She pulled back by an act of will, furious at that near-betrayal by her inconstant flesh. His arms fell, and he smiled nervously.

Emily shook herself and blinked as if awakening from sleep. She folded her hands in her lap and said cheerily: 'Now let's see. You do want to do the story, don't you? I can't tell you any more today. Must get back to my . . . to Hsiu's party. But tomorrow . . .'

'Could we meet for lunch?' he suggested. 'The French Club?'

'The French Club? It's so long since I've been there. But why not?'

There was as yet no need for further words – and there were no words to define the tentative understanding neither participant fully understood. They met several times during the next week, by tacit agreement avoiding the evening hours. They pretended to themselves and to each other that they were refining the story of Nanking, though either one could have written it in a few hours' time. Emily told herself it was her patriotic duty to ensure that his reporting was favourable to China, and Richard almost believed that his interest was primarily professional.

They had almost forgotten the exhilaration of being with each other, the preternatural heightening of all sensation. They were gradually weaving anew the complex strands of emotion that had formerly bound them. Despite the pressure of war, they felt no great urgency to reaffirm their still unexpressed commitment with their bodies. Yet, when they finally came together in Richard's suite in Broadway Mansions, it was the most profound pleasure either had ever known.

For almost two weeks, Emily virtually forgot the war for national survival. She had only one purpose – her reawakened love for Richard Hollings. She realized with wonder that the total impossibility of marriage had purged their relationship of all abrasiveness. She could now make no demand he could not fulfil, for she could neither expect constancy nor impose responsibility. Moreover, her conscience was clear. She had already given her husband everything he required of her, and she would avoid public scandal.

Richard could never wholly forget his work or his ambition, which were his essence. But he virtually forgot Fiona, whom he had married in England only two years earlier. He had always loved this jet-and-ivory Emily, he realized. It was not he but she who had initiated their earlier parting. He had never ceased to love her and to want her. The rebirth of love eclipsed all lesser emotions. From time to time he almost forgot his ambitions.

Emily imposed caution on her sometimes careless lover to forstall any scandal. As soon as they began to meet in private, they stopped meeting in public. After Richard wrote the account of Emily's experiences in

325

Nanking, it appeared to the curious – including a disappointed Jimmy Wei – that the former lovers remained estranged.

Only Julia and Tommy, who knew them best, sensed that something was stirring. Emily was radiant, and Richard was almost relaxed. Besides, they virtually ignored each other in public. And they vanished from view at the same time. Julia and Tommy also wondered about the strain they might impose on the reunited lovers by luring Richard to the Communist capital at Yenan. That fervent Nationalist supporter Emily considered Yenan the lair of the devil.

'Well, it's about time, isn't it?' Julia asked dully after dinner at home on the last day of January 1938. 'I hate to break it up. But I'm afraid I'll have to give Richard the green light tomorrow.'

'You could put it off a bit, couldn't you?' Tommy responded. 'It's your decision, after all. Not mine, thank God.'

'Tommy, what is that supposed to mean?' Her tone was ominously even. 'We're in this together, aren't we?'

'Of course, darling.' He agreed to avoid a quarrel. 'Though you're in charge of propaganda, aren't you? Or should I say liaison with the foreign press?'

'Say whatever you please, Tommy,' she snapped. 'Just remember, you got me into this!'

'You can always pull out,' he replied. 'They ... the Apparatus ... won't shoot you.'

'I'm not so sure of that. Anyway, I don't want to withdraw. We're doing great work ... essential work.'

'Then what's biting you, Julie? Why are you taking it out on me?'

'I'm not taking it out on anyone. We're doing the right thing.'

'Emmy hasn't been as happy in years, has she?' Tommy goaded her. 'And we're about to ruin it for her.'

'Not permanently. Just getting him away for a while won't ruin it. Not if they're truly in love.'

'I'm not so sure of that ...' he began, but she broke in: 'I'm fed up with your pinning the blame on me.'

'It was your idea to pick Dick,' he retorted. 'I've never really trusted him, and ...'

'You agreed though, didn't you? And you seem happy enough to go off to Yenan with him. I wonder why?'

'Now be reasonable, Julie.' He was alarmed by the course their quarrel was taking. 'Somebody has to interpret and ... ah ... guide him. Somebody he trusts. Remember, it's got to be plausible.'

'I could do it just as well. Maybe better.'

His Chinese conservatism shocked at the thought of a woman, his wife, travelling to the wild North-west with another man, Tommy regarded her with frank astonishment. She glared back defiantly, daring him to contradict her.

Tommy was suddenly cautious. For the first time since their marriage, they had for the past year been quarrelling regularly over their opposed approaches to political action. Julia attributed super-human wisdom to

326

the Political Bureau of the Chinese Communist Party. It was not her part to question the directives of the Party, she declared, but only to obey them. Tommy was more sceptical. He could not, he declared, justify lying, hypocrisy, theft, and murder just because the Party thought such outrages expedient.

Tommy now feared another bitter quarrel. But her glare dared him to contradict her – and, of course, he did.

'That's one of the most ridiculous statements I've ever heard,' he retorted. 'A foreigner? A foreign *woman* to escort a correspondent to Yenan? Preposterous! Besides, who's to look after the girls? Anyway, your Chinese isn't . . .'

She knew he meant her Mandarin, not her Shanghainese. But, deeply offended by his masculine rigidity and his racial arrogance, she snapped, 'Lao Zee is perfectly capable. As for my Chinese, it's not so bad you haven't trusted me to . . .'

'I didn't mean Shanghainese, Julie.' He was elaborately patient. 'But have you ever heard Chairman Mao Tse-tung speak Mandarin? You know he's damned near unintelligible. Not to speak of old Chang Kuo-tao's Kiangsi brogue. Why sometimes *I* can hardly . . .'

Julie's anger flared higher, fanned by her guilt at imperilling Emily's new-found happiness. She attacked him: 'You think I'm a poor weak woman, don't you, Thomas Howe? All right for producing kids. And better kept in the nursery with the kids. A stupid foreigner to boot! Better kept away from serious matters. Okay as a stalking horse for other stupid foreigners, a kind of decoy duck, but not . . .'

'Julie! Julie!' His laughter further fanned her anger. 'You just can't be a horse *and* a duck – not at the same time.'

'Don't laugh at me. I'm not a brainless toy. . . . You think a woman . . . all women . . . are fluffy-headed fools. You really despise all foreign devils, don't you? Even me! *Particularly* me!'

'Julie, darling,' he protested. 'This is becoming ridiculous. Can't we . . .'

'Don't try to sweet-talk me, Tommy Howe. I know what you're up to. And *you* can call Richard tomorrow. I'll be damned if I will. If I can't go, I damned well won't help. Go ahead, but don't be in a hurry to come back. I'm not sure I'll want you back.' She gathered herself for a final denunciation and said: 'Besides, I'll . . . I'll miss you *badly*.'

Julia was shocked by her own words. The mother of two coloured like a schoolgirl and grinned sheepishly. Against her will, she joined in Tommy's laughter.

'That's . . . that's quite the . . . the funniest thing I've heard in years,' he gasped. 'You don't want me back, but you'll miss me – *badly*.'

Julia chuckled in spite of herself, and her anger faded. But her heart still beat fast, and she was still a little indignant.

'Really, Tommy, I hate you going without me.'

'Can't be helped, darling. Somebody's got to look after the girls. Do you really trust Lao Zee alone for weeks?'

'Maybe not.' She was not yet defeated. 'But Charlotte Haleevie would be happy to . . .'

327

'You know, Julie, it's no cake-walk, the trip to Yenan. There is some danger. Is it really a good idea to put both parents at risk? What would become of . . .'

'All right, Tommy, I'm convinced. But it's so damned unfair. A woman's always tied down.'

'I'd hardly say that . . .' he temporized, but she interposed: 'Won't it blow your cover, Tommy? Our cover?'

'Certainly if you tagged along, darling. Too obvious by half if both of us went. Otherwise, I hope not. You know the Apparatus consider the mission so essential, they're happy to take the risk.'

'Thanks a lot – for nothing.' For the first time Julia spoke disparagingly of their controllers. 'They're bravely willing to risk *our* necks. Do they also give away ice in the wintertime?'

'It's not quite like that, you know. It's the old family doctor act again. My chum and former patient Chang Kuo-tao is complaining of general debility. Those years on the Tibetan Plateau during the Long March. Since we're all allied against Japan now, the Nationalists approve of giving him decent medical attention. And should I happen to run into Dick Hollings in Yenan . . . After all, we are old friends.'

'But, Tommy, they'll be even more suspicious of us.'

'Maybe it'll work the other way. The secret police are half-convinced I'm a reformed Communist. They're thick, but not impenetrably thick. They'll reckon I would never make the trip to Yenan – throw away my cover – if I was still a dangerous Red.'

'Why can't someone else go?'

'I *want* to go, darling.' Tommy's narrow face grew grave. 'Old Chang Kuo-tao's problems aren't really physical. He's clashing with Mao Tse-tung, seems to believe Mao's becoming a dictator. He's not happy with the Communist war effort either. Largely a sham, he believes. I *must* talk with Chang Kuo-tao – not only for his sake, but for ours, too.'

Although she still resented her exclusion from the pilgrimage to her particular Holy Land, Julia's anger cooled. She was no longer angry at Tommy, but at the general unfairness of life. She was, moreover, concerned about Tommy – and not just his physical danger. He seemed to be losing confidence in the wisdom of the Chinese Communist Party.

Life never worked out as one expected. Julia had for years fought to end the injustice and the exploitation that were integral to the Settlement and Frenchtown. She had laboured to mobilise public opinion abroad to demand the surrender of the extra-territorial privileges on which their existence rested. The Japanese were now clutching at the concessions, and she hated the thought of their being destroyed. Only fear that the other powers would defend the concessions with force kept the Japanese from closing their grip.

The dissension within the leadership of the Chinese Communist Party that Tommy had revealed was even more disturbing. But Julia knew with total certainty, that she would never surrender her trust in the leadership of the Communist Party.

37

February 13–March 2, 1938

Outside, the February wind whined dismally through the saw-toothed battlements of Yenan's city-wall and piled the snow drifts higher before the mouths of the caves cut into the yellow cliff crowned by the nine-tiered pagoda. Seated beside Chairman Mao Tse-tung, who had over-whelmed him with courtesies since his arrival forty-eight hours earlier, Richard Hollings peered disbelieving through the cigarette smoke that fugged the makeshift auditorium of the Yenan Academy for the Children of Senior Cadres. Elegant in a tweed hacking-jacket, jodphurs, and riding boots, Tommy Howe was sauntering through the cracked wooden side-door of the auditorium. The Englishman sprang from the rough bench to greet the friend he had thought nine hundred miles away in Shanghai.

'Dr Livingstone, I presume.' Richard extended his hand. 'Hardly an accident, I imagine, your turning up here.'

Tommy grinned and confided with disarming frankness: 'I've a patient to see, my old chum Chang-Kuo-tao. But frankly, Julie and I were worried about you. When I got the chance of a seat on an aircraft, I grabbed it.'

'You came by aeroplane? What luck for you! After a week in trains and lorries, I'm knackered. How on earth did you manage it?'

'You didn't know Emily was rejoining Mayling Chiang in Wuhan, did you? She was summoned to the presence just after you left. The Missimo also wanted advice from me on the Air Force's medical services. Not that you'll ever catch me in uniform again. Not if . . .'

'The aeroplane, Tommy?' Richard prompted. 'How did you actually get here?'

'Oh, yes! The Sian Garrison Commander was in Wuhan. When I heard

329

he was planning a visit to Yenan, I begged a lift. It appears he's carrying formal messages from the Generalissimo for the two chairmen – Mao Tse-tung of the Communist Party's Central Committee and Chang Kuotao of the North-west Soviet Area Government.'

'They now call it the Shensi-Kansu-Ninghsia Border Area.' The correspondent shared his newly acquired knowledge. 'Fits into the Central Government structure that way.'

'Interesting,' Tommy muttered. 'And lots of time to talk later.'

'You're staying, then? I'm delighted. It's all terribly fascinating, but they *will* go on in Chinese. And the interpreters! You have no idea what joy a familiar face can . . .'

Tommy prudently remained silent. He had come to the Communist capital because he had a very good idea indeed what joy a familiar face could bring to a foreigner alone in China's wild North-west. He had already digested the report of the university student whom Richard Hollings had providentially met on the second stage of his train journey.

The Englishman had virtually fallen on the neck of the young man who spoke intelligible English. He had been delighted to learn that the student, too, was going to Yenan. It was not Tommy's business to tell Hollings that his helpful guide, who had represented himself as a volunteer for the Communists' Eighth Route Army, was actually a valued employee of the Border Area's Public Information Department, which was, in turn, an arm of the Communist Party's Security Bureau, the directorate of the secret police.

So far, Richard Hollings had manifested all the right reactions. The correspondent had not for a moment been left unobserved – or unprotected – by relays of fellow travellers who concealed their knowledge of English. And the purported student had told him all the right things.

Richard's journey from Shanghai to Peiping had been uneventful. Although accustomed to the occasional absurdities of the Sino-Japanese War, the correspondent had jotted a note regarding the extraordinary *de facto* neutrality of the Chinese Post Office and the railways, which routinely crossed the fluid lines of demarcation between the belligerents. In Peiping, he was well inside Japanese-occupied territory, while the Peiping-Sian Railway took him back into the Nationalist-dominated areas. Finally, a truck had carried him through the undeclared Nationalist blockade of the Communist-ruled Border Area – with a load of smuggled newsprint and lead type for the Communists, who obviously considered leaflets as crucial as bullets.

Richard knew the seedbed of the Chinese nation was the wide fertile plains of the yellow soil called loess. The names on the land revealed the millennia-old yearning after elusive tranquillity: Yenan meant Extended Peace, and nearby Paoan meant Guaranteed Peace. Sian, the capital of Shensi Province, meant Western Peace. When it was the capital of all China under the magnificent Tang Dynasty a thousand years earlier, the city had been called Changan, Protracted Peace. A thousand years before the Tang, Chin Shih Huang-ti, the First Emperor, had chosen the same site for the first capital of a united China. But lasting peace was clearly unattainable. The First Emperor had built the Great Wall against nomadic invaders – and the Communists had only recently driven the Nationalists out of Yenan.

Richard Hollings was now to be convinced that Chinese civilization was being reborn in Shensi, its original birthplace, with the Communists as the midwives. To the Chinese, who were all history-struck, that return to the source was awe-inspiring. The correspondent, too, was deeply impressed, as the helpful student had learned from their discussions during the 200-mile ride from Sian to Yenan on roads carved twenty feet deep into the soft yellow soil by iron-bound chariot-wheels and cart-wheels over the centuries.

Tommy was gratified by that report. The hard journey to Yenan had suitably conditioned the correspondent. Tommy was also fascinated by the remote town propagandists were transforming into a legend. Having been a county seat, Yenan provided a few ramshackle public buildings for the rapidly expanding Communist bureaucracy. The auditorium of the School for the Children of Senior Cadres, the privileged offspring of the higher officials, showed its age by its crumbling plaster walls. Patches of fresh plaster merely emphasized the general decrepitude. The packed earth floor was, like every other receptive surface, filmed with the powdery yellow dust of the loess soil.

Acrid with the fumes of uncured tobacco, the long room was capriciously lit by the pale afternoon sunlight filtered through oiled-paper windows. Minute electric bulbs glowed ineffectually at the end of long wires with fraying insulation. The audience wore drab quilted-cotton jackets that made men and women look like chubby outsized school children. Slogans on the banners hanging on the walls praised the anti-Japanese United Front or extolled cleanliness, literacy, and discipline.

Close to the faded red curtain that veiled the makeshift stage, the senior leaders sat cracking melon seeds between their teeth and sipping tea from earthenware cups. Armchairs would normally have been provided for Chairman Mao Tse-tung and Commander-in-Chief Chu Teh of the Eighth Route Army, the man called Red Virtue. Today all sat on rough wooden benches without backs so that Richard Hollings would see only one big happy – and equal – family. The leaders' security guards had concealed their pistols under their jackets, and all the senior cadres had put away the numerous fountain-pens that normally bristled in their breast-pockets to declare their rank. The masquerade was well staged.

After paying his respects to Chairman Mao Tse-tung and his entourage, Tommy looked for Chiang Kuo-tao. But the friend he had not seen for almost eight years was not present. Tommy knew that Mao Tse-tung's presence at the public gathering was exceptional. The Chairman of the Central Committee of the Chinese Communist Party was already drawing around himself the cloak of aloofness China's emperors had worn. General Chu Teh might foxtrot with giggling female comrades at dance-parties while his pretty wife looked on undisturbed. Mao Tse-tung was more likely to seduce those awe-struck female comrades in private, although he had recently taken as his fourth wife a starlet of Shanghai motion pictures.

331

No longer the bumptious young careerist Tommy had first seen at the Students' Federation meeting some seventeen years earlier, Mao Tse-tung had discarded his homespun long-gown for the blue jacket and trousers of the peasants. Honed by danger and hardship, he was at forty-five no longer plump, but tall and gaunt.

Chairman Mao beckoned peremptorily to Tommy, complaining in his slurred Hunan accent: 'Interpreter's no damned good. Speaks English like a Cantonese talking Mandarin. Doctor, you interpret! I was telling this white-skinned barbarian about the League of Nations Resolution. It proves that our victory is inevitable.'

Tommy raised an eyebrow and omitted the racist slur. Another white-skinned barbarian was the mother of his daughters.

'Don't you know about the Resolution, old chap?' Richard addressed the conscripted interpreter directly. 'The Council of the League of Nations just voted to recommend that all members send aid to China. Chairman Mao's convinced that's a great victory. But what practical results can he expect? Could he be more specific? You know, I'm truly impressed by his grasp of foreign affairs. Do you think I should tell him so?'

'Honest approbation is always welcome.' Tommy tossed off that sententious observation in English – and then repeated in Mandarin Richard's question and compliment.

'The Resolution proves that all the world is behind our struggle against aggression and Fascism.' Mao Tse-tung's black eyes dulled as his attention turned inwards, and he continued in measured tones: 'I am aware that the League of Nations is derided as a do-nothing organization. Think of the difficulties the Soviet Union has met in attempting to forge a united front against Fascism through the League. But I am certain that this resolution will initiate major changes in the League itself. China's fight inspires all men who love freedom and justice.'

Richard began a new question, but the Chairman motioned for silence. His hand rose in benediction to the ten boys and the ten girls in freshly ironed blue tunics who had just appeared through the red curtain. The ideograms on their scarlet armbands read 'Young Pioneers'; they all wore scarlet neckerchiefs; and the girls' braids were tied with scarlet ribbons. A boy clapped his hands, and they began to sing: *'Chi-lai, chi-lai, pu yüan tso . . .'*

Mao Tse-tung beamed and beat time with his fist while Tommy put the Chinese Communists' anthem into English: 'Arise! Arise! All who hate to be bond-slaves. China's people face a great new day and great new dangers. Our flesh and blood will build a new Great Wall! . . . Forward! Forward! Forward!'

The chorus filed off after singing two folk songs that had been fitted with revolutionary lyrics and another two in their original form. Although the 'Internationale' normally concluded such performances, the anthem of the Comintern was not heard that day. The men who minutely planned the correspondent's reception had ruled out that avowal of solidarity with the Soviet Union. Those stage-managers could be in line for two-jump promotions in the Border Area's rigid bureaucracy. The operation was promising to be spectacularly successful.

The curtain parted for a young man of about twenty, who read in a shrill voice from a booklet he held in both hands.

'Comrades all, the staff and the pupils of the Yenan Academy for the Children of Senior Cadres welcome you.' Tommy translated softly. 'Today we are pleased to offer the salutary tale of the traitor Chang Mu-tao performed by the elementary classes. As you may know, the scene is set in . . .'

Tommy lost the thread when Richard Hollings pulled at his arm and demanded: 'Chang Kuo-tao? The traitor Chang Kuo-tao? What's up? You said this was a historical play.'

'For God's sake, Dick, shut up!' Tommy whispered. 'Chang *Mu*-tao, not Chang *Kuo*-tao. Chang Mu-tao is one of China's most famous and most despised traitors.'

In the easy tradition of the Chinese theatre, the audience joined in the drama. The 'oohs' and 'ahs' of fond parents competed with the comments of self-appointed connoisseurs as the centuries-old play unfolded. Sharp shafts of criticism alternated with the cries of admiration for the silk gowns of the beautiful court ladies, the fanciful armour of the generals, and the stately robes of the courtiers. The diminutive players all wore painted masks, and the audience speculated loudly on their true identities.

But all appeared to know the child-star who played the traitor Chang Mu-tao behind a villain's black mask. Tommy saw why he was such a favourite. His enunciation bell-clear and his gestures highly dramatic, the small boy dominated the stage.

Tommy hardly heard the side-door open. A ray of light intruded into the darkened auditorium, backlighting the newcomer, and Mao Tse-tung cackled: 'This is really art! How perfectly appropriate! What an inspiration it was to have Chang Kuo-tao's son play the *traitor* Chang Mu–tao!'

Tommy twisted on the bench and recognized the tall man whose entrance had evoked the Chairman's outburst. His old friend Chang Kuo-tao stalked towards the stage, sodden cloth-shoes squishing on the packed-earth floor. Stepping over the paraffin footlights, he ripped the mask from his son's face. He picked the frightened child up in his arms, and strode towards the door.

'You're barbarians!' Chang Kuo-tao shouted. 'It's wicked to trick an innocent child into baiting his own father! You're evil – worse than wild beasts!'

Tommy was shocked by that public clash between the two men who embodied the Communist cause. Established friendship and respect inclined him towards the upright Chang Kuo-tao, the Chairman of the Shensi Border Area Government. Yet Chairman Mao Tse-tung of the Communist Party's Central Executive Committee represented the collective will of the Party. A good Communist always gave his allegiance to the Party, not to any individual. But it would be profoundly un-Chinese – inhuman, in fact – for Tommy to turn his back on his old friend and political mentor Chang Kuo-tao.

After that clash Chairman Mao rather surprisingly attempted neither to justify himself to Richard Hollings nor to prevent the correspondent's talking with Chang Kuo-tao. Naturally eager to question the man he remembered meeting at Julia's house-warming in 1922, Richard grinned sardonically when Tommy suggested that the public confrontation might not be as significant as it appeared. He grinned broadly when Tommy reminded him that his own long experience should have taught him how hot-tempered the Chinese were.

Virtually Chinese in his delicacy, Richard did not embarrass Tommy by demurring. If the matter were trivial, he suggested, why should he not ask Chang Kuo-tao about it directly? Tommy agreed immediately. Since it was essential to give Richard the impression that free public debate was normal in the Border Area, he could not delay while he waited for permission from Chairman Mao and the security police of the Public Information Department.

The next afternoon Tommy and Richard strode briskly towards the north gate. The storm had passed, and the air was cleansed of impurity. The intensely blue Shensi sky appeared to extend to infinity. But the freezing wind knifed through the woollen scarves they had wound around their faces.

The snow-covered streets were deserted except for the waifs affectionately called Little Red Devils, who were busy on portentous errands. Two Red Devils stopped to tease a lean yellow dog. Then Tommy remembered the waif called Little Pow, who had vanished a decade earlier, and the mastiff called Adam, who had been killed only a few months ago. A sharp gust cut between his half-closed lids and brought tears to his eyes.

When Yenan was a Nationalist-held island in a Communist sea, the big wooden city-gates had been barred against guerrillas and brigands. Since its liberation, the city gates had stood open. The local brigands, the Party declared, were all now fervent converts to the Communist crusade. Was it really conviction or was it coercion and bribery? Tommy kept his doubts to himself.

The stunted sentry shivering under the city-wall looked like a brigand himself. Like Tommy and Richard he wore a captured Japanese Army greatcoat with a thick hood. His came down to his ankles, though Tommy's and Richard's did not reach their knees. Even the Japanese were not as undersized as the young Communist soldier, who had probably never eaten a decent meal in his life.

Beyond the gates, the dark-blue vault of the sky arched above the white bowl of the valley, and the February sun was a pale-gold disc above the yellow cliffs. The wind scoured the pallid earth, piling snow into enormous curved drifts like flying buttresses at the foot of the cliffs. Grey smoke drifted from the clusters of thatched hovels beside the frozen ruts of the dirt road. The valley of Yenan appeared hostile, poverty-stricken, and virtually depopulated.

The visitors were lanced by the cold despite their greatcoats. Their stick-figures cast faint shadows on the snowdrifts as they trudged towards the cave mouths. On the overhanging cliff the pagoda of Yenan sparkled against the deep-sapphire sky.

The placard on the terrace gouged from the cliff read: 'Office of the Chairman of the Border Area Government'. Tommy rattled the wooden door. Getting no reply, he pounded with his fist. An unintelligible voice called out within, and Tommy shouted: '*Wo-men chao Chang Chu-hsi* . . . we're looking for Chairman Chang.'

Bolts were drawn back with metallic snicks; the door grated open; and the Communist leader stood before them. He was scowling, but he smiled when he recognized his callers.

'Come in, my friends!' he boomed. 'Tom, I've been wondering when I'd see you. Nobody tried to stop you?'

'Not a soul, Kuo-tao. We might have been invisible spirits for all the notice anyone took.'

'Even they don't dare yet,' Chang Kuo-tao mused. 'There's still Moscow – and the world. Outside Yenan my name still counts for something. But I'm a bad host to keep you waiting.'

The passageway was dimly lit by the oil-lamp guttering in a recess carved from the soft soil. The main room was not much brighter. Desks and stools loomed formless in the half darkness, and from time to time voices sounded from the rear rooms. An oil-lamp flickered on a round table that also bore a chipped porcelain teapot, thimble-cups, a murky glass bottle, a red-and-yellow packet of cigarettes, and a battered tin ashtray.

'Our ancestors knew what they were doing. Living in caves in this vile climate.' Lit from beneath by the yellow lamplight Chang Kuo-tao's strong features glowed like a primitive mask. 'Caves are warm and dry and keep out the wind – most of the time. And there's only one way in. Nobody can take me by surprise.'

Tommy had forgotten how nearly impenetrable Chang Kuo-tao's Kiangsi brogue became under stress. Translating for Richard, he could reply to his friend's words only with occasional sympathetic grunts. But that did not matter. Chang Kuo-tao was a man with a grievance long deprived of a sympathetic audience. His indignation poured out.

'You saw what they did to the boy, a lad not even twelve years old. You saw it, didn't you?' he demanded. 'They're far worse than beasts. They're devils, demons in human form! . . . And Mao Tse-tung is the worst!'

His big head, sand-hued in the lamp-light, swung to and fro like an angry lion's. His fist smote the table, and the thimble-cups jumped. He forced a smile, which only made him look fiercer, and filled the thimble-cups with colourless spirits from the murky bottle.

'They still leave me some perks,' he observed without satisfaction. 'The business with the boy, you know, is only part of their harassment. It's vicious enough to trick a schoolboy into mocking his father. But they're even worse to my wife. You remember her, don't you, old Howe? Many's the time we've sat and talked the dawn in.'

335

He sipped his drink and continued: 'She's a very old Party member, a leading female cadre from the beginning. When I left Shanghai in 1931, she stayed behind working for the Central Committee. Then Nationalist special agents and the foreigners' police practically wiped out Party Headquarters. She escaped, but lost contact with the Party. So she went underground . . . changed her name and studied midwifery.'

He emptied his thimble-cup and glared as if daring them not to drink. After refilling their empty cups, he resumed, his deep-set eyes glinting above his broad cheekbones like the helmets of sentries on the battlements of a besieged city.

'When the United Anti-Japanese Front was formed, she immediately got in touch with our Liaison Office in Nanking, Chou En-lai's outfit. When she arrived in Yenan, we sent for our son. The three of us were together again after Heaven knows how many years! She started teaching midwifery, and doing regular political work. But Mao's blasted Central Committee refused to restore her Party membership . . . said they had to investigate her conduct after she lost contact in Shanghai. As if they didn't automatically restore the membership of dozens of others in the same boat! Naturally, she's damned upset! It's like losing her own identity! Like not knowing who she really is!'

He shook his head hard and looked regretfully down at his cup. He shook his head again after deciding against draining it and continued in a softer tone: 'You could say they're fleabites, this constant harassment. Though it's hardly a fleabite to be denied rightful Party membership. She's just lost! Even tricking the boy could seem trivial to somebody who didn't see it. A good joke!'

The correspondent's lean features twisted in sympathy, and Chang Kuo-tao for the first time addressed him directly: 'Mr Hollings, I don't deny the personal element. Candidly, personal rivalry and personal grievances stand between Mao Tse-tung and myself. We both have long memories. But his revenge is not at all trivial. He's determined to destroy me. He would've already if the Comintern hadn't stopped him. Last spring he mounted a formal anti-Chang Kuo-tao Campaign. The comrades were told to learn from my mistakes. Learn from *my* mistakes!'

Chang Kuo-tao fought to master his anger. Clamping a glowing cigarette between his thumb and forefinger, he puffed sporadically as he talked.

'When I formed my alternative Central Committee of the Communist Party several years ago in the wilds of eastern Tibet, it was the only way. We had to get the big decisions taken, and we were completely out of touch with whatever was left of Party Headquarters. I didn't even know if my wife and son were alive. How was I to know that snivelling careerist Mao Tse-tung had founded his own *permanent* Central Committee and bullied his way into the chairmanship?

'Issues of fundamental principle also divide Mao and me. Great issues! The stakes are life or death of the nation and the Party.'

He turned and called loudly: 'Lieh! Lieh! Let me have my diary, last year's.'

The twelve-year-old who had been carried out of the auditorium presented his father with a thick notebook, smiled dazzlingly, and vanished again into the gloom. Chang Kuo-tao flipped the volume open and read aloud: 'In November 1937, after three months of heroic fighting, the Central Government was forced to withdraw its troops from Shanghai. A few weeks later, the Central Government withdrew from Nanking to Wuhan. Even warlords like the Christian General pledged to fight to the death.

'And what of the hero Mao Tse-tung? He was elated after the fall of Nanking. He said: "All China will soon be occupied by the Imperial Japanese Army – and our guerrilla force will expand manyfold behind enemy lines. All China will fall to Japan from the hands of Chiang Kai-shek – and we Communists will later take China back from the hands of the Japanese."'

Chang Kuo-tao slammed the journal shut and rubbed his eyes before resuming: 'I was horror-struck when I heard Mao rant that way. Why should China become a Japanese colony, as he hopes? Why in Heaven's name isn't the Chinese Communist Party actively supporting Chiang Kai-shek's struggle against Japan? We're all Chinese together now, aren't we?'

The big man shook his head again. He was fierce yet bewildered, a wounded lion beset by jackals. Tommy's heart went out to his old friend. But what could he say? What could anyone say without defying the entire Communist movement? All he could do was interpret faithfully.

'How *could* China possibly rise again if the whole country became a Japanese colony?' Chang Kuo-tao demanded. 'Everything Mao Tse-tung advocates assists Japanese aggression. Everything mortally wounds the Communist Party and the Eighth Route Army – above all hurts the nation itself. I sometimes wonder if Mao isn't a traitor hiding under the cloak of Communism. You may feel that's absurd, but . . .'

The visitors had to leave before the early mid-winter dusk filled the valley with darkness. Fortunately, they had not brought a torch which would have lit the dirt road among the snowdrifts. Fortunately, because Tommy felt he had already spent too much time with his old friend.

At that time he had no intention of returning, above all not with Richard Hollings. He had felt almost physical pain listening to Chang Kuo-tao's grave doubts about the direction of the Communist Party. He could not completely refute those doubts in his own mind. He could, however, ensure that the correspondent took away from Yenan a picture of the Communist Party, its army, and its government that was not marred by Chang Kuo-tao's bitterness – whether that bitterness was justified or not.

Tommy and Richard returned the next afternoon to the cave of the Chairman of the Border Region. Because Richard insisted, they were to return twice during their two weeks in Yenan. Tommy had reluctantly concluded that denying the correspondent's wishes would only accentuate the conflict between the two giants of the Communist Party. Besides, part of him wanted to hear more. The Party, guided by Chairman Mao, was of course correct. But why not listen to the dissenting view?

Tommy also wanted to spend more time with Chang Kuo-tao, whatever his faults, and to comfort him in his distress. Failing to call again would only have intensified his old friend's paranoia by reinforcing his delusion that he was being abandoned. Besides, Tommy had to deliver the cashmere scarf and the fur-lined gloves Julia had sent to Kuo-tao.

He was appalled to find himself nodding reluctant agreement to some of his old friend's arguments. He tried to convey to Richard by his tone of voice that other statements were not to be taken at face value. As an interpreter, however, he could not intrude his own views.

'When the War of Resistance started last summer, I swore I would put all my bitterness behind me,' the old revolutionary recalled passionately. 'Otherwise, I would have had to leave the Party. Defecting would make me a man without friends or a home. Defecting would deny the purpose of my life. Yet I thought seriously about it. It was *that* bad! But it's worse now! Last Autumn another criticism campaign was launched by Chairman Mao.' The three syllables conveyed immense contempt. 'They were after me again, chivvying me to assume greater responsibility for the phony mistakes I'd earlier confessed – but only to bring harmony to the Party.

'One young fellow I'd never seen before got up in the meeting. Some newcomer, I gathered. He observed brilliantly that gold glittered, but not all that glittered was gold. Flies also glittered – like Chang Kuo-tao, who was a species of vermin within the Communist Party.'

Tommy was, above all, a patriot who believed the Communists were the best hope for China. He was dismayed by his friend's charge that Mao Tse-tung was working against the best interests of China.

Mao Tse-tung had ordered the Eighth Route Army *not* to fight the Japanese if there were the slighest risk of defeat, Chang Kuo-tao asserted. The Army was to husband its strength to strike against Chiang Kai-shek, not dissipate it fighting the Japanese. Mao had even reprimanded the general of the 115th Division who won the first great Chinese victory against the Japanese. That victory, Mao Tse-tung declared, was too costly.

Above all, Chang Kuo-tao charged that Mao Tse-tung was sacrificing all other considerations to making himself a dictator. Even minor dissenters were to be purged – regardless of their value to the movement. All Communists were to obey only Chairman Mao Tse-tung.

'His malice against dissenters is almost beyond belief,' Chang Kuo-tao exploded on the evening in late February when he bade his visitors farewell. 'He actually hates me more than he hates the Japanese – even more than he hates Chiang Kai-shek. His malice is turning Yenan into a sunless dungeon.'

Normally sharp-tongued, Richard had not commented on Yenan. He was maintaining his professional objectivity. Tommy was, therefore slightly taken aback when the correspondent grinned in the ruddy firelight and observed softly: 'One hell of a mansion, isn't it, for the ruler of thirty million people and the commander-in-chief of almost a million troops!'

Glancing around the cave-dwelling, Tommy agreed: 'Not like Number Ten or the White House. Can you imagine Neville Chamberlain or Franklin Roosevelt functioning in a place like this?'

Comrade Mao Tse-tung, Chairman of the Central Committee and the Military Affairs Committee of the Chinese Communist Party, was crouched before the big brick sleeping platform, the universal *kang* of North China. He was poking the coal fire underneath to ensure that the *kang* would be warm later. He was obviously enjoying the heat, and his bony features were dyed red by the fire's glow. Beside his low bamboo stool, his omnipresent cigarette smouldered in an earthenware ashtray. On the other side of the stool lay the quilted trousers he had just discarded.

'I can't believe it, Tommy. I just can't!' the Englishman declared in a strained whisper. 'I can't believe this chap's the monster our mutual friend talks about!'

Mao Tse-tung looked at the correspondent interrogatively and at the interpreter expectantly. He resumed his stool, reclaimed his trousers, and began to search their seams. He grunted in triumph, crushed a white louse between his fingertips, and flicked the tiny carcass into the coals. Turning away from the pyre, he looked at Tommy Howe again, silently demanding a translation of the correspondent's last remark.

'Chairman, he just observed that this was an extraordinary headquarters for a man burdened with your great responsibilities.' Tommy improvised. 'He marvels that you can discharge your responsibilities under such conditions.'

'Tell him, Doctor, it's not necessarily by choice.' Mao Tse-tung's open smile compelled respect and affection. 'Not that I'd want a palace, you understand. Men who live in palaces cannot hear the voices of the men tilling the fields. Sadly, the only tilling I myself have time for nowadays is my little tobacco plot.'

Since Tommy knew that Mao Tse-tung's early life had been a determined struggle to escape from his father's farm, he was not moved by the longing Mao expressed to return to the fields. He even felt a flicker of suspicion towards a man who invariably said the right thing. Yet, for all he knew, the man might truly yearn for the peace of the farm, but feel himself bound by duty to the tumult of politics.

'Chairman, I'd like to raise another matter.' Richard Hollings's introduction signalled that he was shaping an embarrassing question. 'There are rumours of rifts in the ranks of the Chinese Communist Party. Some say the Party is not fully committed to the war against the Japanese. Some say it is split by personal rivalry. What can you tell me?'

Alerted by the tone of voice, Mao Tse-tung cocked his head and studied Hollings's face while Tommy translated. He replied immediately: 'You've been talking to my old friend Chang Kuo-tao, haven't you. Naturally I know of your conversations with Kuo-tao. People tell me things even without my asking. But you will have noticed that no one

339

interfered – and no one was watching you. I can make a very good guess as to what he's been telling you. Above all that I'm some kind of monster. Isn't that it, Mr Hollings?'

Although he could not understand a word of Mao's slurred Mandarin, the Englishman nodded even before Tommy translated. Mao's expressive orator's voice had conveyed his essential meaning.

'My old friend's been telling you some strange tales, hasn't he?' Mao continued. 'It's very sad, Mr Hollings, but I'm afraid his time on the high plateau of Tibet was too much for Kuo-tao. He's suffering from delusions. He thinks he's being persecuted.'

He paused to allow Tommy to translate and then demanded, 'Do *you* think he's being persecuted? Is being appointed Chairman of the Border Region persecution? Although he himself recognizes he's incapable of fulfilling all the duties, we keep him on. His deputy does most of the work. But the last thing I ... the Central Committee ... want is to humiliate a veteran fighter, an old comrade who contributed so much in the past. We all hope his body will soon heal, so that he can again work side by side with all of us. I must speak with you *again* about Chang Kuo-tao's state of health, Doctor Howe. Do remind me please.'

Tommy was startled, Mao Tse-tung had never before that moment mentioned Chang Kuo-tao's physical health, which was obviously excellent. Richard, however, appeared impressed, insofar as any one could tell how he reacted when he was conducting an interview.

'I'm not denying that Kuo-tao and I have had our differences,' Mao Tse-tung added. 'Nobody claims there are never differences of opinion in the Communist Party. Frankly, Mr Hollings, there are many divergent views within the Party. One single policy must finally prevail, but it is shaped in open debate. That's why I eagerly await Kuo-tao's restoration to full health – so that he can again contribute constructively to that debate. Why, only last year we held a full-scale campaign to reconcile his views and ours. So you can see how much we esteem him.'

Could this be the same man who had cackled that it was an inspiration to have Chang Kuo-tao's son play the traitor? The correspondent would, of course, have noted that contradiction. But, Tommy recalled, he himself had been diverted by Chang Kuo-tao's dramatic entrance and had not translated that jibe. It was, however, too late now.

Tommy, too, was finding Mao Tse-tung's virtuoso performance not only impressive but convincing. Since flatly denying any conflict with Chang Kuo-tao would have been disbelieved, the Chairman had candidly acknowledged their differences – and thus enhanced his own credibility. The correspondent should, therefore, be taken in by Mao Tse-tung's necessary lies regarding his rival's health, the character of the Criticize Chang Kuo-tao Campaign, and the prospects for mutual reconciliation. It was, of course, no crime to lie for the cause. Actually, it was a major failing not to lie when lies were necessary.

Justly proud of Communist accomplishments, Chairman Mao presented them to best advantage in the talks with Richard Hollings that occupied his evenings for a full week. After the disasters that followed the Nanchang Uprising, the Chinese Communist Party had virtually recreated itself. Since their flight from Central China in 1934, the Communists had consolidated their independent realm in the North-west. They had also extended their underground organization throughout Nationalist-controlled and Japanese-occupied areas.

The Chairman's brilliant presentation transformed the Long March from a retreat into a triumph. Successfully disengaging from the Nationalists' Extermination Campaigns was undeniably a remarkable feat. Considering Nanking's bumbling pursuit, the subsequent flight was hardly the epic victory described by Mao Tse-tung and General Chu Teh, who lent his homespun charm to the wooing of Richard Hollings. Only six thousand of an original force exceeding 100,000 had actually reached their goal. Yet in the firelit cave in Yenan a legend was being created – the mighty myth of the Long March.

The Chairman further blended unabashed flattery with apparent candour: 'We chose you from all those who wanted to come, Mr Hollings. Quite frankly, because you can be most useful to us. We didn't pick you only because you are a brilliant writer, a keen observer – and possess sharp insight.'

The correspondent's saturnine face twisted in genial scepticism.

'Yes, Mr Hollings, I know your work. Most of your dispatches have been translated for me. Dr Howe has helped greatly.' Tommy omitted the last sentence, not primarily because it was false, but because it tied him too closely to the Communists. 'You didn't think I . . . we . . . would invite you not knowing what your work was like, did you? The risk would have been too great. We have nothing to fear from objective reporting, however penetrating. But we have everything to fear from inaccurate and biased reporting.'

Richard Hollings betrayed no gratification. Instead, he asked aggressively: 'Well then, just what do you expect of me? How am I supposed to serve your cause?'

'Please don't take offence, Mr Hollings,' Mao Tse-tung countered. 'We expect only that you will report fairly what you've seen and heard. No more! As I've said frankly, it was not just your personal qualities that recommended you, but your professional connections.'

Tommy glanced at Richard as he spoke those words. The correspondent's mask of indifference slipped for an instant, and he looked almost worshipfully at Chairman Mao. So much for journalistic detachment!

'I am a student of international affairs, as well as world history.' The Chairman waxed expansive. 'And I have come to one conclusion: America will control the future – until the final imperialist wars, when the imperialist powers destroy each other so that the Soviet Union and a Soviet China take the lead of all mankind. *Don't translate that last bit, Howe!* And you, Mr Hollings, represent the press of America. Quite frankly, we need friends in America – and we deserve friends in America. I believe you will help us win millions of friends in America!'

Mao Tse-tung stood beside the elementary-school map of the world hanging on the wall of the cave. Placing his palm on the pale-blue shape of the United States, he observed: 'We are fighting America's battle here and now. America will not have to fight tomorrow if she supports us today.'

The Chairman stared hard at the map. His fingers traced the outlines of the Japanese islands and moved west to encompass the great expanse of China. He turned and said: 'Goodbye, Mr Hollings. I'm sorry we can't talk more. You've listened patiently to the speeches of an ignorant countryman. But you undoubtedly have other pressing engagements. And I must attend to my duties. Goodbye, Mr Hollings.'

The correspondent would not take his dismissal without a final question: 'What about Communism, Mr Chairman?'

'Communism? I don't understand. What of Communism?'

'For China, Mr Chairman, what of Communism for China?'

'No one can say when, Mr Hollings. We naturally believe Communism will develop some day. Some among us doubt it. We are not now working for Communism. However, some day in the future . . .'

Richard Hollings already knew that the weeks in the Border Region were the most important weeks of his life. The untold story of the Chinese Communists could be his springboard to greatness – if he performed adroitly. Nor was he completely taken in by Mao Tse-tung's flattery. Even a politician less astute than the Chairman would have preferred the correspondent of the *New York Times* to himself. Richard assumed that he had been selected because the Communists believed the solidly conservative convictions of the *New York Times* would prevent its publishing a detached – much less a favourable – account of the Border Region.

Besides, the *Times* correspondent might have declined the invitation because he feared imperilling his relations with the Nationalists. Despite the united anti-Japanese front, the Generalissimo would hardly be happy about newspapermen consorting with the Communists behind his back. Richard made a mental note: he would have to mend his own fences with the Nationalists.

The correspondent moodily paced the perimeter of the airstrip, only peripherally aware of his surroundings. He had come to say goodbye to Tommy, who was leaving in the silver Boeing monoplane of the Nationalist area commander. He was by no means sorry to see Tommy go.

They had been together a little too much not to rub on each other's nerves. Besides, Tommy had displayed unpleasant curiosity regarding his own relationship with Emily. Brotherly concern had not quite overcome the reticence bred in an English public school. None the less, Tommy had been getting too close to the bone – close to asking about his intentions towards Emily. As if a happily married man could have any intentions beyond mutual affection and mutual pleasure towards a married woman who was the mother of three young children.

The Boeing lifted off, circled the valley, and pointed its shining nose south. He would himself have to endure the bone-cracking ride in a

342

supply truck to Sian the next morning. Tommy and he had already agreed to keep their association in Yenan a secret. Tommy's position as a fashionable physician would be imperilled if he were labelled a Communist sympathizer, however ludicrous the charge. For his part, Richard did not want potential competitors to know that the Howes could provide a passport to the Border Region. His own return by rail through Peiping would, moreover, handily confuse his back-trail. He wanted no one to know of his sojourn in Yenan until he was himself ready to reveal it.

The hammering of air-cooled engines in the west penetrated Richard's self-absorption. He saw in the distant sky a small transport aircraft. At the same time, a Cadillac ambulance appeared on the rough road from the town. Donated by the Chinese restaurant owners of New York City, it was used by Mao Tse-tung for personal transportation.

The big ambulance stopped beside him, and the Chairman poked his head from the wondow.

'Yes, Mr Chairman?' Richard asked in his rough Mandarin.

'You must make promise, Hollings,' Mao Tse-tung directed in pidgin Mandarin. 'You must not write up this aeroplane. I will tell you, it come from Soviet air base where Soviets train Nationalist pilots. Some old comrades return, some not seen for many years. We are very happy. But, Hollings, you will not mention this.'

'Can you say why, Chairman?'

'You English, you are so stubborn.' Mao Tse-tung's forced laughter was menacing. 'Stalin and Chiang Kai-shek sign treaty, you should know. Soviets only supposed to fly to Nationalist areas. Hollings, you not want get pilot into trouble. So no write about Soviet planes coming to Yenan. More better, you do not write anything about Soviets. They have no influence here. My Communist Party is only a Chinese party.'

38

June 7–8, 1938

Emily was not looking forward to the gala reception to mark the re-decoration of the private hotel Ikra. She was even less enthusiastic about the 'small gathering of old friends' to which she had been asked by the note written in mauve ink in a finishing school backhand. 'Countess Elizaveta Alexandrovna Yavalenka' had been slashed through on the embossed invitation and replaced with the single word 'Liz'. Emily was touched despite herself.

The pasteboard square crackled when she slipped it back into her beaded-satin evening purse. Lifting the silver-mounted mirror from the vanity case in the armrest of the limousine, Emily inspected herself. Unnecessarily retouching her lipstick, she was struck again by the contrast between her fragile appearance and her innate competence. But the tiny dimples still flickered beneath her cheekbones, and her expressive eyes were unclouded by time. She would do, Emily decided.

Returning the mirror to its plush nest, she glanced at Nanking Road, The traffic was heavy, although the anti-Japanese war was almost a year old in early June of 1938. War had actually created lucrative opportunities for greedy foreigners and unscrupulous Chinese. A mile from the gutted battlefield of Chapei, shop-windows displayed the greatest abundance of luxury goods Shanghai had ever seen. The Settlement and Frenchtown were booming while China bled.

She was almost ashamed of the Phantom VI, the latest of her father's Rolls-Royces, each bigger and more ostentatious. But she had borrowed it to overawe both the Japanese-protected thugs who plagued the Settlement and the arrogant Japanese sentries on its borders. The White Russian bodyguard who sat beside the old driver would not hesitate to use the automatic pistol in the black-leather holster belted over his quasi-military white tunic. Troubled times bred kidnappers and assassins, particularly in foreign-ruled Shanghai, which was a glittering treasure, actually grown richer amid the squalor of war and miraculously preserved, though perhaps not for long.

Emily shifted uneasily on the split-hide seat and pulled her *cheongsam* away from her thighs. Mid-calf in the latest fashion, the dress was a film of white lace over a silk slip. Yet the humidity made even those wispy garments oppressive. Regardless of the heat, silk stockings were also essential for the formal occasion. She yearned for the freedom of the wartime provisional capital of Wuhan. There she could wear sensible slacks which required neither the ladylike stockings with their cumbersome rigging nor a ladylike mincing walk.

She glanced out and quite unintentionally intercepted a beggar's malevolent gaze. His eyes were red-rimmed, and the crimson scar that pulled up his lip revealed broken teeth. Hunger had wasted his broad peasant face, and his skin was grey. With horror she recognized on his filthy tunic the badge of the crack 88th Division, which had so valiantly defended Chapei. His slashed trousers revealed cushions of inflamed purple flesh where his legs had been amputated above the knee. The board mounted on roller-skate wheels had presumably been the 88th's parting gift.

And she had been yearning for the freedom of the wartime capital! Emily was shamed by her own frivolity. The freedom of war! Some freedom!

She called to the old driver through the speaking tube. On her instructions one scrap of human jetsam would be saved by the rehabilitation clinic the Haleevie charities operated for wounded Chinese soldiers.

The traffic was already clotting on Kiangse Road, for Elizaveta had apparently asked half Shanghai to her gala reception. Emily would have come even if the firmly penned 'Liz' had not touched her. Emily was on duty. The reception at the Ikra was perhaps not precisely the kind of occasion Mayling Chiang had in mind, but it should prove fruitful.

May still refused to allow her to come to Wuhan to stay. Not because the Japanese were implacably closing on the provisional capital, since May expected her associates to display the same contempt for danger she herself did. But May still insisted that Emily was more valuable in Shanghai. Of course Jimmy Wei's office could easily handle normal liaison with the press, and the efficient secret service could provide routine intelligence reports. But only Emily could convey to China's First Lady the spirit of the cosmopolis. Only she could convince Shanghai's influential Chinese that their government would, despite its distance, overlook neither patriotic sacrifices nor unpatriotic crimes.

She was something between a tittle-tattle and the voice of conscience. Emily, however, enjoyed neither role.

When the emerald-green Rolls was halted by the crush of vehicles, she decided to walk the last few hundred yards. Even in fragile silver evening-slippers, that was no hardship for one who had hobbled out of burning

Nanking disguised as an old country woman with bound feet. Annoyed when the White Russian bodyguard insisted upon accompanying her, she was grateful when he cleared a way through the throng gawking at the rich at play. She felt vulnerable in her flimsy *cheongsam* amid the jostling crowd in serviceable workers' blue. Seventeen years after her return from the United States, she still did not feel at ease in a Chinese crowd. Like May Chiang, she could face danger with equanimity, even zest, but not discomfort.

Her bodyguard bowed at the entrance and promised to wait in the kitchens. Even denser than the throng outside, the throng inside induced almost the same claustrophobia, although it smelled better. The expensive fragrance of perfumes blended with the expensive aroma of Havana cigars, and the woolly scent of new carpets combined with the faint odour of fresh paint to testify to the Ikra's redecoration.

Although she was five foot seven in heels, Emily caught only glimpses of the new splendour. The corridors were too crowded. Giving her name to a red-coated footman, she found herself looking into the small elevator tucked under the stairs. The cut-glass windows and the heliotrope-satin curtains had been superseded by ulta-modern rhomboid mirrors and jet-black pendants.

A rotund footman ploughed a path for her through the packed corridor. The former saloon bar was now identified as the cocktail lounge in angular black letters on a mirrored background. The formerly red-plush restaurant had been transformed with swatches of tangerine, dove grey, and lime green. The semi-circular ballroom was, however, hardly altered. Only the woodwork shone whiter; the gilt Ionian columns glittered more golden; and the scarlet-velvet curtains glowed even deeper.

The Edwardian ballroom was obviously the heart of the reception. The choker-collared tunics of American naval officers gleamed snow-white beside the loose cut khaki-twill of their Japanese counterparts. The two groups were warily cool six months after the *Panay* incident. Some of the gentlemanly Italians wore the black shirts of Benito Mussolini's *Movimento Fascismo*, which were flaunted by the musclemen who beat up any Shanghai Italian who expressed any reservation concerning Fascism.

The Germans were better behaved, for the Nazi apparatus was still weak. Having withdrawn their advisers from the Nationalist army only a few weeks earlier, the Germans were not quite sure where they stood. Only one grey-blue *Wehrmacht* uniform was visible – and not a single swastika. However, the horizon-blue of the French and the scarlet of the British set off the rainbow evening-gowns of the ladies and the more presentable courtesans. Neither group of women was disturbed by the other's presence, as they certainly would have been only ten years earlier.

Most men wore dinner jackets, though a few diehards were in tails. A certain raffishness had crept over Shanghai in the tumultuous 1930s. Always avid for gain by any means, fair or foul, the foreign community had previously preserved a façade of starchy respectability. The exigencies of war now justified the collapse of standards – as if Shanghai had not known war in the past.

346

Only Soviet Russians were excluded from the reception – in deference to the handful of White Russians whose mothball-redolent cream-and-white uniforms made them appear the attendant ghosts of the dead Czar. Since Elizaveta hated the Soviets even more bitterly after learning how they had manipulated her in the 1920s, she was now flirting heavily with the Japanese. They were the enemy of the Bolsheviks, although also the hereditary enemy of Russia. She was also tolerant of the German Nazis and the Italian Fascists because they, too, were enemies of the Soviet Communists.

Joshua Haleevie had only raised an eyebrow at his former mistress's tangential involvement with the Nazi persecutors of Jews. He had no right to intervene, although he was actively assisting the Jewish refugees from Germany and Austria. Most could earn a living, for they were skilled, but all were nervous. Unlike the fatalistic White Russians, they did not look upon Shanghai as a permanent refuge.

Gritting its teeth at the newcomers' touchy arrogance, the established Jewish community was trying to help its co-religionists. Joshua had not objected when his father, Sir Judah, suggested three months earlier that his wife Charlotte should investigate the prospects for re-settling those refugees in Australia and America. But Joshua had evaded the suggestion that he should accompany her. His interests and his affairs in Shanghai, he declared, were in need of close attention. Sir Judah wisely refrained from asking precisely what kind of interests, affairs, and attentions his son meant.

Joshua's primary interest in Shanghai obviously merited the closest attention, Emily reflected with light malice, though she did not know whether Elizaveta and he had resumed their affair. Joshua was apparently not concerned because his presence at the reception would become known to Charlotte. His tentative approach to Elizaveta was, after all, only a little more dangerous than his recent foray against the tigers of Nepal. Besides, Charlotte was quite intelligent. She knew better than to make demands – or utter recriminations.

Dazzling in his white sharkskin dinner jacket, Joshua was trolling for information among the guests. Emily had almost overlooked his other role. He was not only a highly successful entrepreneur, but one of the best informed men in Shanghai. Nationalist secret service assessments had recently bolstered her belief that he was the brains of the International Settlement's intelligence service.

Joshua stopped to chat with a man almost as tall as himself, who wore conventional rimless spectacles and a humdrum little black moustache. A senior editor of Domei, the official Japanese news agency, Roland Yamaguchi was obviously valuable to his employers. He had acquired a Continental gloss from his European mother and colloquial American from the University of Missouri. He was highly intelligent and an excellent source for other correspondents, always ready to trade information. Emily found him a formidable antagonist in the struggle between China and Japan for the world's approbation.

Both Joshua and Yamaguchi were looking down, as if addressing a third person Emily could not see. When the crowd eddied, she glimpsed the shorter man. Gregory Hardin was the antithesis of the popular impression of a Texan. He was compact, trim, and shy, rather than tall, bulky, and loud. A tenacious and meticulous observer, he had recently joined the *New York Times*. Gregory Hardin's thoroughness was almost a match for Richard Hollings's flair.

After looking for Richard in vain, Emily drifted instinctively towards the trio of Hardin, Yamaguchi, and Haleevie. But she halted abruptly and turned away. She was very fond of Joshua, and she did like Gregory Hardin. Indeed, she almost liked Roland Yamaguchi. But she could entrust neither her temper nor her dignity to a public conversation with a Japanese.

A little flustered, Emily looked around the ballroom again. She did not like being alone. Madame Chiang Kai-shek's personal representative in Shanghai should for political effect be surrounded at all times by an aura of power, which meant supplicants and admirers. Regardless of that explanation, she felt just as she had at Bryn Mawr freshman dances. Somehow it was demeaning – and a little frightening – to be a woman alone at a party.

Roland Yamaguchi put his hand on Joshua's arm and drew him towards the bandstand, which was a gigantic pink scallop-shell. The move was obvious, indeed blatant, yet adroit. The astute Japanese had made it appear that the highly influential foreigner and he were exchanging confidences because of their mutual confidence. Meanwhile, the *New York Times* correspondent was left alone to wonder enviously what important news he was missing. But Gregory Hardin, apparently unperturbed, smiled in welcome when Emily joined him.

'What's new?' she asked automatically. 'What am I missing?'

'We were only chewing the rag,' he replied. 'Talking about Dick Hollings's copy from Yenan, Mrs Ou-yang.'

'Do call me Emily!' she chided reflexively. 'You make me feel like my own mother-in-law when you say Mrs Ou-yang.'

'Anyway, Mrs ... ah ... Emily, it wasn't important,' Hardin added. 'Just shoptalk – a little bitchy as always. Tell me, how was the Missimo ... ah ... Madame Chiang last time you saw her?'

'Now, Greg, you know I haven't seen her in months.' She wondered why he had so abruptly changed the subject. 'She's fine as far as I know.'

'You know there's talk of her going to the States for medical treatment?'

'There's also talk of a rift between her and the Generalissimo! Just nonsense. *All* China's enemies don't wear Japanese uniforms or carry guns. Rumour's a great weapon.' Feeling she had reacted too strongly, she returned to the original subject. 'What about Dick Hollings's copy?'

'Well, Mrs ... ah ... Emily ...'

Gregory Hardin paused in evident embarrassment, and Emily was pleased. Clearly reluctant to criticize Richard directly because he knew of their past affair, the sensitive *New York Times* correspondent had evidently heard no gossip about the affair's being renewed. Otherwise he would not have criticized Richard even indirectly. She would press him further if necessary. It was important – professionally as well as personally – that she know how his colleagues felt about Richard's six articles on the Border Region, which had initially puzzled her and ultimately, she supposed, not greatly displeased her.

The series had taken an inordinately long time to appear, in part because Richard was in no hurry to file. 'More important,' he'd insisted, 'to get it just right.' Swearing her to secrecy regarding his coup, he had not even cabled the exclusive stories. He had, instead, frugally confided them to the new Trans-Pacific airmail service provided by the four-engined flying boats Pan American World Airways called China Clippers. Since the series had not come clacking onto the teletype, his editors had been equally leisurely in publishing. Only during the past week had clippings trickled back to Shanghai.

'Don't you think, Emily, that his stuff was a little bland?' Gregory Hardin phrased his criticism delicately. 'A terrific opportunity he had. Anybody'd give his left arm to get to Yenan. But Dick made it sound like Boys' Town. His pieces were bland as rice-pudding. A raisin or a jujube here and there. But, otherwise, pretty tasteless – though very sweet.'

'If I may intrude on this culinary discussion . . .' Richard Hollings appeared at Hardin's elbow, lean and dark in a cream-silk dinner jacket. 'Madame Ou-yang I would hardly expect to approve – regardless of what I wrote. But you, Gregory . . .'

'That's not true, Richard.' She was glad of the public challenge, for he had in private consistently avoided discussing – or even showing her – his series. 'I don't disapprove. On the contrary, I think they're reasonably fair – as far as they go. Naturally I'd like more bite.'

'Bite, Emily?' he riposted airily. 'We seem trapped in culinary metaphors. What do you mean by bite?'

'The bite of truth, Richard. Truth has sharp teeth.'

'So we've moved from cookery to dentistry,' he sniped casually. 'Do tell me . . . us . . . what you mean.'

'Richard, we Chinese *know* the Communists far better than you can after a few weeks with them.' She had wanted to say certain things to Richard for some time – and a public quarrel was the best smoke-screen for their private life. 'You lived in Shanghai for years. Obviously you didn't learn as much as you should.'

'Is this a private fight?' Gregory Hardin inquired in his courtly manner. 'Do you want me to leave or to referee?'

Ignoring that conciliatory effort, Richard prompted sweetly: 'Do go on, my dear Emily.'

Her attack would undoubtedly draw him out. It would also confirm Hardin's belief that the former lovers now detested each other – as well as each other's politics.

'The Communists are all liars. They actually boast about it. Whatever they told you was mixed with lies. They're out for power by any means. Killing, torturing, raping – it's all the same to them.'

'I don't quite see where all this is going, Emily.' Richard was defensive – and patronising. 'What's the point?'

'You wrote about the Communists as if they were just another political party. A peaceful political party like the Democratic League. That's totally misleading.'

'Since the United Front against Japan, they *are* just another political party – all working with the Central Government to resist the invasion. Yes, they have their own territory – just like an American state. The Democrats hold power in Washington, but the Republicans hold certain states.'

'A political party with its own army?' Emily protested. 'Two armies in fact: the Eighth Route Army and the guerrillas of the New Fourth Army. Some political party!'

'I hear, Dick,' Hardin cut in, 'there's a lot more to be said on the Communists' side than you reported. How come you didn't?'

Emily realized this quiet question was more penetrating than her frontal attack. For once, Richard looked daunted.

'Why don't we drop this?' She was immediately protective. 'We're not getting anywhere.'

'No, Emily, I'll answer that one.' He passed his handkerchief over his forehead despite the air-conditioning. 'Just give me a second or so.'

While Richard pondered his answer, Emily glanced around the scarlet-and-ivory ballroom. Waiters in embroidered Russian blouses were weaving through the throng with silver salvers of champagne and vodka or large trays of smoked sturgeon and fresh caviar. The twelve-piece ensemble on the scallop-shell bandstand was playing the latest hit: 'Thanks for the Memory.' A Filipino baritone was crooning: 'You may have been a headache, but you never were a bore. So thank you so much.'

Appropriate, Emily mused when she glimpsed Julia's shady uncle, Quick Jack Pavernen, talking with Elizaveta beside the bandstand. He was sleek in a midnight-blue dinner-jacket. She was stunning in a ball gown that was obviously new, though it could have come from her mother's Edwardian hoard. Buttercup slipper-satin cascaded from a pinched waist into a swirling skirt; the bodice was a triangular wisp supported by silk-skein shoulder-straps.

What, Emily wondered, were they up to now? They were like a pair of drug addicts. John Pavernen loved to dabble in fishy enterprises, and Liz yearned for the thrill of danger.

But Richard was finally offering the *apologia* over which he had agonized: 'Emily has a point – a small point. Not, of course, her hysterical attacks on the Communists as murderers and rapists and God knows what else. I did note briefly that there were disagreements within the Communist ranks. But that wasn't a testimonial to democratic devotion to free debate . . .'

'Exactly!' Emily interposed. 'Devoted to free speech they're not!'

'I admit I fudged a little. Maybe I was a bit too kind – for a good reason. I'm not completely satisfied. I want to go back and get to the bottom of the Communist story. So . . .'

'Very laudable!' Emily jibed. 'Protect your access – even if you delude the reader.'

Ignoring her, Richard continued slowly: 'You see, the Nationalists won't bar me from their territory. They're too dependent on foreign goodwill to bar correspondents. But the Communists only have to hold back their invitation – not bar me. So it's just good sense to keep on their good side until I've got to the bottom of . . .'

'Porco Israelita!' The shout rang across the ballroom. Near the scallop-shell bandstand, Roland Yamaguchi and Joshua Haleevie were gazing in amazement at a stout blond man who wore the black-and-silver dress uniform of the Italian Fascists, complete to a ceremonial dagger. The company stared, and the Italian repeated his taunt in English: 'Swine! Jewish swine! Capitalist Jewish swine!'

Joshua glanced around the room, smiled apologetically at the by-standers, and shrugged contemptuously at the Fascist. Still smiling, he slapped the man's ruddy face with the back of his hand and on the return stroke with his open palm.

Joshua then turned away, still smiling apologetically as if to say: *I'm terribly sorry, but it had to be done.*

He had taken two or three steps when the Fascist bellowed in anger. Joshua disdainfully walked on. When Roland Yamaguchi uttered a sharp warning, he half-turned. The Fascist was charging like an infuriated rhinoceros, his dagger held before him. A woman screamed, and a man laughed in raucous embarrassment.

Awkwardly off-balance, Joshua raised his left arm to protect himself. Younger and more agile, Yamaguchi clutched the Fascist's arm, but could not halt the charge. The dagger pierced Joshua's upper arm, and the assailant pulled it back for another blow.

Yamaguchi's arm snaked around the Fascist's throat and jerked hard. The Fascist slumped against a gilt pillar. Materializing as if from the walls, a pair of White Russian guards in cream tunics grasped his arms and dragged him, boot-heels skidding on the dance-floor, to-wards the rear exit. Emily saw that the younger Russian was her own bodyguard.

Elizaveta rushed to Joshua, tears of rage starting in her eyes. Blood oozed through the rent in his sharkskin sleeve, which itself looked like the mouth of a wound. Her arms went around him, careless of her yellow-satin ballgown. Into the shocked silence, he ruefully remarked: 'Sorry, Bess! Afraid I've been misbehaving. And just look at the jacket. Damned well ruined.'

Elizaveta did not speak, but instinctively crooned consolations in her throat. She held him close, only looking up when Roland Yamaguchi bowed deeply before them.

'I am fearfully sorry!' the Japanese apologised. 'It is disgraceful that such a thing should happen!'

'It's not your fault!' White with delayed shock, Joshua spoke slowly. 'Nothing to do with you!'

'That sort of thing is very bad!' the Japanese murmured. 'With allies

351

like that, how can Japan . . .' As if himself at fault, Roland Yamaguchi bowed again and walked stiffly towards the door.

Tommy and Julia encountered him at the reception desk. They disliked Elizaveta's ostentatious redecoration, as well as such extravagant reception when China was struggling with the aggressor. Unable to bring themselves to snub her, they had arrived late, planning to go directly to her private apartment.

Julia wore a *cheongsam* of pale-green crêpe de Chine, which pointed up her mahogany hair and her green eyes. Tommy was not happy with her wearing the Chinese-style dress to proclaim her support of the Chinese cause. Unlike the less emphatic Chinese figure, her assertive breasts and hips were shamelessly voluptuous in a *cheongsam*. Himself resplendently colonial in a cream-linen suit, Tommy was handing his Gladstone medical bag to the receptionist when Yamaguchi broke stride to advise: 'Better hang on to your bag, Doctor. Your friend Haleevie's just picked up a nasty stab wound. He's in the ballroom.'

Tommy pushed through the crowded corridor. Behind him, Julia cursed the tight *cheongsam*, which hobbled her despite slits reaching three inches above the knee.

At the door of the ballroom, Jack Pavernen smiled in relief and said: 'You heard? She's taken him to her apartment. And already sent for Dr Rosenberg.'

'No need for amateurs!' grinned Tommy, who had not touched a needle or a suture since the accidental bombing of the Great World. 'The demon surgeon has arrived.'

In the small rear elevator, Julia observed testily: 'You're very jolly, my dear, considering we don't know how bad it is.'

'But I do, Julie lamb. No blood on the floor and no panic among the guests. Not so bad, you see, as it may have looked at first.'

It looked bad enough. When the elevator reached the sixth floor, they found a chalk-pale Joshua lying in his shirt-sleeves on the mint-green cushions of the cane settee. Elizaveta was kneeling beside him and holding a towel to his arm. Several red drops flecked her cheek, and blood oozed through the heavy green towel.

'Dr Rosenberg's not in. And they can't seem to find any other . . .' she said dully, before recognition lit her eyes. 'Tommy! . . . Oh, thank God! I was just . . .'

Tommy gently stripped the towel away. The deep wound was four or five inches long and was weeping blood. He replaced the towel and said to Elizaveta: 'He'll be fine. Nothing to worry about. But you're needed below. . . . You can't just abandon your guests.'

'But, Tommy,' she pleaded, 'I must . . . stay with him. To help.'

'You'd be more hindrance than help,' he replied with calculated brutality. 'Julie, get the smelling-salts and give her a whiff before she faints. Then help her get tarted up and send her down.'

Tommy cleaned the wound, disinfected it with alcohol, sprinkled iodoform, and sutured the edges. After a few months, the fair skin would show only a faint red line, which would fade to whiteness within a year.

Joshua had not uttered a sound since Tommy's arrival, but his face was pallid and clammy.

'A couple of codeines and a brandy'll fix you up nicely.' Tommy cocked his head and admired his work. 'What the devil have you been up to?'

'Playing the chump, Doctor!' Joshua answered as he sipped the cognac Julia had poured. 'I've been allowing myself illusions. Poisonous illusions, to tell the truth.'

'A canny old trooper like you?' Julia laughed. 'Impossible!'

'Old, yes. But canny? No.'

'How did you collect this little souvenir?' Tommy pressed. 'Who was trying to carve his initials on you?'

'Giancarlo Poletti, our local Mussolini.' Joshua smiled sheepishly. 'That was my poisonous illusion. I've been very annoyed at the new influx – all those arrogant, helpless German Jews. Of course, I helped them. I had to. But I wasn't Jewish, I told myself, not the way they are. I was British. So I am, but I've discovered I'm also Jewish. Then, I'm afraid, I lost my temper.'

'With that windbag?'

'Afraid so, my boy. Poletti's unusual for an Italian, but he was more vehement than Hitler about those cursed sub-humans, the Jews. I took exception. Very mild exception, you understand. Then he swore at me, and I had to slap him. You see the result.'

'It couldn't have happened in the old days!' Julia was mock-solemn. 'That's what my father-in-law always says.'

'And my father,' Joshua agreed. 'Ladies and . . . ahem . . . professional hostesses at the same reception. Comic-opera Italians with stage daggers. My word!'

Emily put her head around the edge of the door. Finding Joshua sipping brandy and joking with her brother, she opened it wide. Behind her, Gregory Hardin waited unobtrusively. He had asked Elizaveta why she had suddenly invited him to join the gathering of old friends, and she had replied: 'Not only old friends, Gregory my sweet. We're getting old and stuffy. We need new blood.' The correspondent was still wondering whether he was new blood or fresh blood.

Emily's white-lace *cheongsam* blended with the white carpets and walls, Julia's green crêpe de Chine with the green upholstery and curtains. When they kissed each other, they eerily vanished into that background for an instant. Seating herself on a green-cushioned chair, Emily reappeared and announced: 'Liz says she'll be along just as soon as she can. Meanwhile, we're to broach the champagne.'

The Krug 1932 popped discreetly, and the door opened. Richard Hollings entered with John Pavernen, whose patent-leather hair was obviously dyed, although his green eyes were still piercing. He was puffing luxuriously on an Upmann panatella, the rich blue smoke wreathing his head. In his late fifties, he was trim, except for the minute swell of a pot-belly beneath his white dinner jacket.

'Champagne, is it?' His baritone voice was remarkably resonant for a slight man. 'Well there's lots to celebrate.'

'Really?' Hollings cocked a patronizing eyebrow. 'I must confess, my dear Jack, that fact had escaped me. Aside from the Ikra's new furniture, I really don't see . . .'

John Pavernen strolled across to the white-lacquered drinks cabinet to kiss his niece roundly and take a goblet of champagne from her. He nodded cordially to Emily, whose nod in reply was restrained.

'Lots to celebrate, boys and girls.' He raised his goblet in salute. 'Not just the face-lift for the old Ikra. Though that's pretty snazzy when you consider that Liz was just another stinking poor White Russian taxi-dancer only a few years ago.' Quick Jack Pavernen's insensitivity was legendary. 'I also propose a toast to peace in China. Whatever Chiang Kai-shek says, he can't keep turning down every Jap peace offer. The Japs are reasonable, but he won't even be a Japanese puppet if he doesn't come to terms soon. He'll only be a grease-spot. He's got to make peace. Let's drink to peace!'

John Pavernen raised his glass amid frosty silence. Emily and Julia glared at him, while Tommy assumed an impassive Buddha-like expression. It was not for him to clash in public with his wife's uncle, who was the senior member of her family in Shanghai. Julia was opening her mouth indignantly when Gregory Hardin interposed a soft question: 'Are you speaking solely as a businessman, Mr Parvenen? Or as an American?'

'As an American businessman, Greg.' John Pavernen was happy to expound. 'Above all, China needs law and order – and the Japs are just the boys for that. Businessmen need peace and stability so they can make profits – and pull China up by the bootstraps. Only the Japs can give us that security.'

'You seem to have done pretty well,' Hardin interjected. 'Considering there's been no peace in China for three decades.'

'I'm not denying it. For a country boy, I've done pretty well. But why kid ourselves? The Chinese have been trying since 1911, but they can't set up a government that's worth a damn. None that lasts more than a couple of years. I won't deny I've done pretty well out of their feuding. But it's time for peace now. The business of Shanghai is business. And we're not going to do good business till the Japs clamp down.'

'Uncle Jack, I don't believe I'm hearing you right,' Julie burst out. 'Are you really serious? As an American?'

'Sure, Julie. What interest has the United States of America got out here except for business? The sooner the Japs bring the Gimo to heel, the sooner we can get on with business.'

Julia was too angry to reply, but Gregory Hardin's voice cracked like a lash: 'If you're speaking as a *legitimate* businessman, Mr Pavernen, you're an ostrich. As soon as the Japanese impose order, they'll impose their kind of order on all business dealings. When they're running the concessions, they won't put up with any competition. Unless you're useful to them, you'll find yourself out on your ear. Pull your head out of the sand, Mr Pavernen. At least, stop talking through the part that sticks up in the air when you bury your ostrich-head in the sand.'

John Pavernen filled his glass and laughed ingratiatingly: 'Now, Greg, this is just a slight misunderstanding.'

'If you really believe it's a slight misunderstanding, you'll believe anything. Speaking as an American, you're talking dangerous nonsense. Do you think the Japs'll be satisfied with China? Sure, they'll lie down for a while to digest China like a python with a pig in its stomach. But afterwards? South-east Asia is next – oil, rubber, and tin. Ever hear of the Greater East Asia Co-Prosperity Sphere, Mr Pavernen? Besides . . .'

Gregory Hardin looked in apparent surprise at the goblet of champagne in his hand and automatically sipped. Under the spell his anger cast no one else spoke, not even John Pavernen.

'And there's something more important than business or even national interest.' His Texas drawl was soft. 'Justice – morality, if you like. The Chinese are fighting for justice, not only to preserve their country. The Japanese militarists stand for the rule of naked force as in the dark ages. Mr Pavernen, I pray we don't get into this war. But the Chinese are fighting *our* fight.'

Gregory Hardin rubbed his upper lip with his forefinger, apparently abashed at his own eloquence. His youthful enthusiasm had, he felt, embarrassed the urbane company, for no one uttered a word. After ten or twenty seconds, however, Joshua Haleevie lifted his balloon glass and said: 'Hear! Hear! A most eloquent statement.'

Evidently unmoved, John Pavernen refilled his goblet, drained it, looked at his watch, and declared: 'Well, I can't wait all night for Elizaveta. Charming as she is, I've got business to attend to.'

He strode to the door, but was arrested by a murmur from Gregory Hardin: 'Mr Pavernen, I apologize for any personal references. But everything else I said stands.'

'I understand, Gregory. We all get het up sometimes. No offence taken.'

Beneath his show of joviality, John Pavernen was angry at being reprimanded like a schoolboy by a man thirty years his junior. He paused with his hand on the porcelain doorknob and asked: 'I'll be seeing you next week, Julie, the way we planned, won't I?'

After a perceptible pause, Julia replied faintly: 'Yes, Uncle Jack. Of course.'

Shocked by that grudging assent from his amiable niece, John Pavernen felt the full weight of the opprobrium he had called down upon himself. They were all fanatics! With the door half-open, he took his hand from the knob and turned to confront their silent condemnation.

'Maybe you couldn't figure out why the Countess invited me to your cosy little confab.' His tone was acid with resentment. 'Particularly since I'm not an old buddy like you folks. More of a business acquaintance. You see folks, we're still in business together, her and me. If Mitsubishi and the Kempeitai are good enough for the Countess, I guess they're good enough for me.' He looked accusingly at his niece and concluded: 'But I can see I'm not good enough for you fine folks. So I'll be going. Tell my partner in crime goodbye for me.'

*

355

'I must survive, Joshua! That is always my primary purpose. Survival!' Elizaveta was rarely less than dramatic. 'This I have told you many times. I've never made any bones abut it. Why are you shocked now?'

Joshua did not reply. Although some colour had returned to his face, his lips were pale and his eyes were distant. He reproached himself for eliciting such a passionate response to his question as to why she was collaborating with the Japanese. He almost disliked her when she talked such nonsense. Besides, he should have known from his own sources what she was up to. He would have known, if he had not allowed his profound concern for her to blind him, even during the years when they were not seeing each other.

Elizaveta felt that even a carping Joshua was far better than no Joshua after five years of separation. Her fear over his wound having been relieved, she was light-headed with joy over her new Ikra and her old Joshua.

A pity her intimate party had gone flat. Even Julia was reserved, though she normally bubbled with gaiety on festive occasions. John Pavernen, someone explained, had been called away on urgent business. Although she had ordered a lobster supper, her friends had all left after drinking the obligatory toast to the new Ikra. They had drifted away, and their farewells had been forced.

When she asked him why, Joshua had told her baldly of John Pavernen's revelations. He had then virtually demanded an explanation.

Although that explanation was obviously unsatisfactory, he spoke gently: 'Tommy warned me against getting upset. But I can't swallow that argument. You're much too well off to use survival as a pretext.'

'Oh my Lord, Joshua, I *am* sorry. So sorry.' She was totally remorseful. 'I almost forgot your wound. I'm evil, self-centred, grasping, rotten and selfish.'

'Let's not carry it to the other extreme, Bess,' Joshua grinned. 'But, I warn you, I'll come back to the subject in the morning.'

'In the morning? You mean you'll spend the night? How wonderful!'

'Not that wonderful, dear. You've got an injured forty-five-year-old on your hands. Obviously it's separate beds tonight.'

'Your bloody uncle takes the flaming cake,' Tommy exploded. 'The gold-plated copper-bottomed award for shit of the year – prime shit of the decade, in fact.'

'Sorry, darling,' Julia murmured. 'It's only an accident of birth.'

She switched her attention off. It would take about five minutes for him to finish swearing. Her gaze assessed the cavernous loft, to which they had retreated from the Ikra. The new rosewood settees and chairs were upholstered in glowing turquoise. Over Tommy's opposition, she had gradually disposed of the original furnishings: the rattan sofa and chairs, the barrel seats and the coffee-table that was really a packing case covered with an Indian shawl. The cheap prints had vanished, as had the five-foot copper-and-brass Tibetan horn that served as a standing lamp. Only the big old rosewood chair remained – and the folding leather Ming Dynasty chairs of which Tommy was implacably proud.

Tommy complained regularly. The new furniture was all so grand, he said, that he hated to defile it with his bottom, He was now lolling happily on the eight-foot settee, his feet on the new cushions.

'You know, pet,' Tommy finally said, 'it was really Josh's fault, that kerfuffle.'

'I thought the Italian, that Fascist Poletti, had . . .'

'Even so, Josh has only himself to blame. He needn't have hit Poletti. He's getting touchier all the time.'

'At least, he showed no sign of leaving the Ikra.' Julia sighed luxuriously. 'If this incident brings Josh and Liz together again, it'll have been well worth it.'

'Your uncle's blabbing is another thing,' Tommy pursued his own thought. 'If Hardin talks – or Hollings with his Japanese connections.'

'Gregory Hardin won't talk, I assure you. As for Dick, you can judge better than I.'

'I simply don't know, Julie. I still can't make him out.'

'Tommy, I've been wondering. How much damage would it cause if it did get back to the Japs? Uncle Jack's outburst, I mean.'

'For us, for the Apparatus? It would pretty well mess up our surveillance of Jap arms shipments to their puppets and their tame warlords. You know a good part are now shipped as American goods by JPEnterprises which is an American firm. If anyone asks, the wealthy and anti-Communist Countess Yavalenka provides supplementary financing. A sweet deal for Quick Jack, as he would say. And very convenient for the Apparatus.'

'Suppose the Japs do make some changes – *if* they learn Uncle Jack's spilled the beans?'

'Arms shipments to puppets – or potential puppets – is vital intelligence, Julie. We now know just where the guns are going. We know exactly which warlords the Japs are suborning – or attempting to suborn. And that indicates where the next Jap thrust is aimed. Armed with that information . . .'

'Yes, I know. The Eighth Route Army and the New Fourth Army can then take counter-measures. A pre-emptive attack, perhaps. Maybe a political counter-thrust. At worst, capture the arms.'

'Got it in one. So, you see, it would be damned awkward if the Japs caught on and changed their arrangements. You're certain Hardin won't gossip?'

'No, Tommy. He'll either write the story – or shut up. But I'll drop a word, steer him away.'

'On *those* terms already?'

'Not *those* terms at all, you smug beast. Someday, I will have an affair with one of my dashing foreign correspondents. Meanwhile, I simply find Gregory honest, hardworking, and idealistic. He finds me amusing, useful, reliable – honest in fact.'

'I hope he's never disillusioned.' Tommy's jests about their clandestine activities tended to be strained nowadays. 'Hollings I can manage. Maybe I'll hint that Yenan would bar all correspondents for all American outlets if Chairman Mao learned that American-flag companies were smuggling Jap guns. Dick's desperate for another trip to Yenan.'

'Do you think we should help him?' Julia probed delicately, wondering not only about her husband's assessment of the Englishman, but Tommy's own state of mind. 'Will the Party let him in again so soon?'

'Out of our hands, love. We're just cogs in the Apparatus. My guess is they'll leave him dangling for a while.'

'Well, he hasn't *offended* anyone by his pieces.'

'Nor pleased them too much either. Though he's certainly trying hard to please. You know, he asked old Mao Tse-tung about Communism. And Mao said certainly not now. Not tomorrow or the next day either. Not even in the foreseeable future. So the ace political correspondent writes that they're not Communists at all. Just social democrats with rural interests – agrarian democrats, in fact.'

'They'll laugh about that in Yenan, won't they? But it'll please the propaganda people. I'm using the line myself. What better way to win friends than to convince foreigners that the Communist Party of China isn't really Communist at all?'

'Julie, I told him! I explained to Hollings that Communism is an ideal for the future – the distant future. I told him nobody expects perfect justice in a perfect society for many decades. That's what old Mao meant, not that we weren't working for Communism. Perhaps I shouldn't have told Hollings. But I didn't want him to lose credibility. Who'll believe a word he writes if he makes such fundamental errors? He'll look a perfect chump.'

'Everybody'll believe every word, Tommy. Never underestimate the ignorance of the average reader. You're too theoretical, dear, far too idealistic. You expect too much from your fellow man. Perhaps you shouldn't have told him. But it obviously made no difference. Either he didn't understand or he didn't want to understand.'

'Perhaps it's beyond Hollings, but I explained at length, even over-simplified. Agrarian democrats! Some agrarian democrats!'

'Of course they're true Communists,' Julie agreed absently and added: 'Darling, I've been wondering. Wouldn't it be nice to have another dog? The girls would love a cuddly puppy. And it's almost a year since Adam . . .'

Tommy knew Julia was obliquely approaching some delicate issue, but he replied evenly: 'Not a dirty great mastiff. Something a lot smaller. A *shih-tzu*, perhaps. It's odd, though, to be thinking about dogs in the middle of a nasty war.'

'If the war is so nasty – so dangerous – maybe we shouldn't be here,' she said. 'Of course, you and I have work to do. But maybe the girls shouldn't be here. Lord knows, you were trying hard to make me leave a little while ago.'

'Julie, things have changed. The Settlement's quite safe for the moment. The war's moved on. Do you really want to go? Want the girls to go?'

'Anything but, my darling. I was just saying it was certainly safe enough for Adam's successor. And we won't call him Abel.'

Julia was relieved by her husband's equable response. She was ostensibly talking about the Tibetan mastiff, but Tommy knew she was referring indirectly to his old friend, Chang Kuo-tao. The Communist leader had enlisted them both in the Apparatus, and he also had brought the puppy Adam to Julia from Peking years earlier.

'I still can't believe it!' Tommy responded, speaking almost to himself. 'Kuo-tao leaving the Party. Quitting flat! I still can't believe it!'

Julie had been disturbed by Chang Kuo-tao's resigning from the Communist Party and leaving the Border Region. But her faith in the Party's leadership rested upon bedrock that was absolutely firm, though perhaps shallow. Appalled by his mentor's defection, Tommy, however, faced a fundamental crisis of belief in the Communist cause.

Chang Kuo-tao had chosen a dramatic occasion to escape from the 'airless dungeon' of Yenan. During the first week of April, the Central Government of the Republic of China offered symbolic sacrifices at the tomb of the First Emperor of China. As Chairman of the Border Region Government, Chang Kuo-tao naturally participated in the veneration of the common ancestor in nearby Nationalist-held Sian. He did not return to Yenan.

Tommy and Julia had just received full information on his spectacular defection. After Chou En-lai pleaded in vain for him to reconsider, Chang Kuo-tao was publicly censored by both the Chinese Communist Party and the Comintern. He had not resigned, they asserted, but had been expelled. On May 20, 1938, he replied with a devastating 'Open Letter to My Countrymen'.

'The only true goal of the Communist Party,' he wrote, 'is to conserve and expand its own strength. Support for the War of Resistance Against Japan and the United Front with the Nationalists are only propaganda devices to gain that goal. The Communist Party constantly works to destroy *all* anti-Japanese elements in order to clear its own road to power.'

'He *must* be wrong,' Tommy whispered in appeal to some unknown higher tribunal. 'He's only one man. The Party speaks with collective wisdom.'

'His whining about propaganda devices is pointless. Absurd!' Julia staunchly declared. 'Remember, Lenin himself said it was not just permissible but one's revolutionary duty to deceive the enemy – by all possible means.'

'Particularly when the enemy is begging to be deceived. Like your chum Hollings.'

'That reminds me, Tommy.' She diverted him from his dangerous brooding. 'The Soviets have been after the Apparatus. They know of our existence, though not our identity. And they want us to do some chores for them directly. Some specific inquiries. I guess we should, don't you?'

'Never, Julia!' Tommy exploded. 'Whatever I'm doing, I'm doing for China. Not for the Kremlin, the Soviet Union, or the Comintern. The Russians can get stuffed.'

Joshua had under-rated either himself or her, perhaps under-rated both of them, Elizaveta concluded smugly the morning after her reception. Although they had been slightly distracted by the care needed to avoid hurting his arm, coming together again had been blissful.

Elizaveta languorously surveyed the debris of their breakfast in her bedroom. Joshua was propped against heaped pillows in the seven-foot bed, happy but pensive. Was he repenting his betrayal of his childless – and loveless – marriage? Or was he brooding over John Pavernen's revelations and her own evasions?

'Bess, darling, you're more enchanting than ever.' He unwittingly answered her questions. 'And the other thing, my marriage? God knows, I tried. It's faded away, whatever it was originally. It was never much. No fault of Charlotte's, poor dear. All my fault. And yours! Bess, you're champagne to a man thirsting in the desert.'

She leaned over and kissed him, gratified as much by what he had not said as by what he had said. It's all over, she told herself. He's not going to remember that nonsense of Quick Jack Pavernen's. He's got far more pleasant things to think about.

'You're very eloquent, my darling,' she said happily. 'Now you're not to worry about anything. You're only to rest and pamper your arm.'

'You know, Bess, I've been thinking . . .'

'You're not to think today. Just to rest.'

'I can't make my mind a perfect blank,' he smiled. 'Oh, I almost forgot. Young Hardin said he'd ring you – wants to finish your talk. You used to be frantic to keep your name *out* of the newspapers. What's it all about?'

'My children!' Elizaveta declaimed. 'Only about my children.'

'Your children! Don't be absurd, darling.'

'They're not precisely *my* children. Not fruit of my womb, worse luck.'

'We could still change that, you know,' he interjected. 'It's not too late.'

'I'm a bit long in the tooth for that – almost thirty-eight.' She automatically deducted a year. 'Though it's very sweet of you. I was saying they're not precisely my children, but I am responsible for them. And four hundred are a pretty heavy responsibility.'

'Four hundred! Good God, woman, what are you running – a baby farm?'

'Not quite, darling. Only a crèche and a school for the lost children, the debris of war. Most never knew their parents. But it takes money – loads of money. I desperately need the goodwill of the Japanese.'

'So that's why you've been playing the Japanese game. This does put a different face on things. But still . . .'

'Also, Joshua, I'm on their side. Bad as the Japanese can be, they're a lot better than the Bolsheviks. And they're always getting into border clashes with the Soviet Red Army. So you see . . .'

'You're playing with fire,' he exclaimed. 'Have you forgotten 1932? Colonel Ishikawa, how he died?'

'No, darling, I haven't. Neither have the Japanese. They've a pretty good idea I was mixed up in his disappearance. That wretched Norwegian tart, the devil couldn't keep her from blabbing after two drinks. They don't know about you, though. The Norwegian thinks you were just another . . . ah . . . patron.'

'So the Japs are blackmailing you? How the devil I didn't know . . . didn't find out . . . I can't understand.'

'Only a slight case of blackmail. The occasional bit of information. Also, my appearing as the legal originator of certain arms shipments. They do pay well.'

'Yes, from their opium dives and their heroin traffic. Bess, it won't do. You're hurting a great many people to help a few hundred children.'

'Come see my orphans, Josh, and you'll understand why I must.'

'Look here, if it's the money, I'm sure the Haleevie charities could find . . .'

'Thanks, darling. But can you imagine the Japanese letting me carry on if I defied them?'

'We'll work out some way.'

'Also, don't forget the Japs *are* anti-Soviet. I'd make a pact with Satan himself to attack those devils who took my Russia. Yes, the Japs are sometimes beastly. Still . . .'

'Methinks the lady doth protest too much.' Despite the light quotation, Joshua's expression was grave. 'I can't believe you've told me everything.'

'There's an old Russian saying: *Only a foolish woman tells her man everything*!'

Elizaveta's voice took on the heavy Slavic timbre she assumed when she was clowning. She inclined her head in mock-submission and veiled her blue-black eyes with her long lashes.

Joshua chuckled, but persisted: 'And what else ties you to the Japs?'

'This may sound silly. But do you remember going to the Great World just before the Generalissimo took Shanghai?'

'Yes, early in 1927. Do get on with it, Bess.'

'Emmy took me to see a fortune-teller. Everything that's happened since proves the fortune-teller was right. So I know I have to wait for the proper time to get away from the Japs.'

'What did she say, if I may ask?'

'First, I'd have many children, but none of my own. As I do now. Also I'd be admired by many men, but never possess the one I want. I don't possess you, do I, darling?'

'Only my heart!'

'The other predictions I'm not so sure about. I'd be very happy. Who can tell about happiness till the end? I'd live a long time, which is very nice. But not always where I chose, which isn't so nice.'

'Any more predictions?'

'The last is already true. My enemies would be my friends, she said. So I've still got to go along with the Japs. They're the enemies of my friends, but they're also the enemies of my enemies.'

'Bess, you're a seething mass of superstition.' His amusement was tinged with exasperation. 'You can find a reason for anything.'

'Don't laugh again, Josh. I'm very serious. It's destiny.'

39

Richard Hollings propped himself on his elbow and took an emotional inventory of the slender body beside him under the scarlet canopy of the carved and gilded bed. Emily Howe Ou-yang was thirty-eight, and maturity had made her more beautiful. She was ripe in sensibility and intellect, as well as physically.

The small breasts were minutely fuller, and the pink nipples were a shade darker. Although her waist was nearly as slim as it had been when they became lovers fifteen years earlier, her hips were more rounded and the projecting bones were sheathed. Her shoulders no longer looked so frail that they would shatter under the weight of a swan's feather. The lean-muscled grace that underlay her apparent fragility was more evident.

Her eyes closed and her face devoid of cosmetics, Emily was as serene as a time-polished ivory statuette of Kwan Yin, the Goddess of Mercy. Her vivacity arose chiefly from her brillant eyes, now closed. Richard surveyed her tenderly from the high, smooth forehead framed by blue-black hair and dewed with perspiration, to the narrow feet with the incongruous crimson toenails. And he was happy.

He brushed an errant lock off his forehead. He was forty-one, but his skin was taut and his dark-brown hair was untouched by time. Still he was, rather remarkably, not concerned about himself that hot afternoon.

He was almost obsessed with the woman he had last seen half a year earlier in Shanghai a thousand miles away. They had just met again in Chungking, the new provisional capital, which lay far up the winding, gorge-choked Yangtze and was battlemented by mountain ranges. Beyond the reach of Japanese land forces, Chungking was secure. But Chungking was dominated by the urgency of war.

They had come together passionately, with few words, almost violently. On that humid Wednesday afternoon in mid-July, Richard knew – beyond self-doubt or even self-interest – that he loved Emily profoundly and irrevocably. He castigated himself for the searing quarrels and the wasted years. And he thanked his hearty Anglican God for the revelation of love, however belated. He also thanked God because she lay vulnerable and trusting beside him in the summer pavilion of the hillside compound overlooking the grey-and-dun city.

Abruptly, a vivid image floated unbidden before the rough-plastered wall. He saw the pale face and the blonde hair of his wife Fiona, who was seven thousand miles away in Berkshire. He fervently thanked his accommodating God that she was childless, for he knew that he would strive to keep Emily beside him all his life. Not that he did not love Fiona. Quite simply, he loved – and had always loved – Emily so much more.

A dog barked, and Emily's eyes flickered open. She smiled, momentarily surprised at seeing his face, and reached up languidly to touch his arm. Suddenly she sat up, unperturbed by her nakedness, and asked in apparent alarm: 'What was that?'

'Only a dog,' he answered. 'Startled you, did it?'

'My God, yes!' The dog barked again, shrill and insistent. 'But I guess it's all right.'

'All right?'

'You don't know, do you, Dick?' Suddenly aware of her nakedness, she pulled her blue-lace peignoir over herself. 'Barking dogs in Chungking mean an air raid.'

'Good Lord, why? Are they supposed to have extra-sensory perception, or do they hear the Japs' engines before we do?'

'No, my clever friend!' she laughed. 'You see, the fog is so thick from October through April that the sun never shines through. So dogs bark when they see the sun – as if it were an intruder, a burglar.'

'Perhaps I'm dense today. But I still don't see what dogs' barking has to do with the raids?'

'Simple, darling. The Jap bombers can't fly when there's fog. When the sun shines through and the dogs bark, the flying weather is good. And we get bombed.'

Her arms snaked around her neck and drew him down. His breath quickened and mingled with hers.

'God, Dick,' she whispered into his mouth, 'every time I see you, I just . . .'

Her mood abruptly altering, she pushed him away and sat up against the scarlet bolster. Luxuriously prolonging the moment, she took a cigarette out of his packet of Lucky Strike, shrugged into her peignoir, and primly buttoned it.

'Enough of this, my boy,' she commanded. 'For the moment, at least. You're to tell me all. First, when did you change brands?'

'That's easy. Can't get a decent English cigarette here – only the smuggled Yank brands. However, if I'm to tell you absolutely *all*, it'll take a week.'

'Well, all that's pertinent,' she compromised. 'You know it's almost six months since you left Shanghai? It was three months later when Mayling finally let me come to Chungking. I arrived in May, just in time for the first air raids. Here on the hill, well outside the city, the children are reasonably safe. But I'm talking too much. I always babble when I'm happy.' She paused and whispered: 'I *do* love you, Richard. God help me.'

'Emily, I . . . Em, I just . . .' Richard was hobbled by the inhibitions of his class and his nation. 'I just wanted . . .'

'Yes, darling!'

'I love you too. Deeply. More than I can say. I've just realized how much. I swear to you . . .'

'Don't swear anything, darling!' she cautioned. 'Who are we to swear everlasting love? In *our* circumstances? Tell me often, please, but don't swear to anything. That's tempting fate. Now, tell me everything that's happened since you left. You were on your way to London. . . .'

'I seem to have been in perpetual motion. Seven days by flying boat, Imperial Airways, from Hong Kong to London. Luxurious hotels every night. A few weeks in the Smoke seeing old friends and talking with chaps in the Foreign Office. Then to the States.'

Richard did not mention his wife, who had accompanied him to America and pleaded to return with him to Shanghai. He knew Emily would not ask about Fiona.

'The Yanks are frenetic . . . never stop talking business day or night. They've even got dictaphones by their beds in case a thought strikes in the wee hours. . . . I was rushing around, seeing all the grand high panjandrums. Most important to me, the editor of the *Boston Globe* and the people at NBC. But also President Roosevelt and the Secretary of State, a spry old fellow named Cordell Hull. He calls the Japs piss-ants, whatever piss-ants are. Washington is deeply concerned wth Asia – above all China.'

Emily took a long drag on her Lucky Strike, coughed amateurishly, and asked: 'What do they think about China? Where are their real sympathies?'

'There's no question about it. Everybody's cheering for the Chinese, from FDR to the lorry driver and the pullman porter. Except in the dead heart, the Middle West, where nobody's interested in anything but the next harvest. Everybody's wife is collecting money for China Relief and the Chinese Industrial Co-operatives. But you know all this better than me.'

'Hardly, darling. That's why I asked. It sounds very good. Just a matter of time!'

'Until what?'

'It's too much to hope the Japs'll be foolish enough to provoke American intervention. But it certainly sounds like only a matter of time till we get the help we need – and deserve. No more pettifogging about antiquated laws that keep us from getting the warplanes and arms we're happy to pay for. Maybe also large loans, substantial loans like the latest Soviet loan. It's only a matter of time, isn't it?'

'Sorry, Em, no! First, the Americans are determined to stay out of any war. Second, Japanese propaganda easily outdoes yours. Most important, the China trade is drying up because of the fighting. But the Japs'll buy anything: oil, scrap-iron, grain, even soya beans. The profits are fat and the Yanks swear they're just following George Washington's advice: *No foreign entanglements!*'

Emily was appalled by a portrait of the United States utterly different from her own memories. She drew on her cigarette and insisted: 'The presidential election is next year. Whoever runs must realize how important China is to America's future.'

'They're all talking about the two-term limit. Not in the Constitution, but hallowed by custom. If you ask me, though, Roosevelt's already running for a third term. He's strewing promises around, swearing to keep the United States out of all foreign entanglements.'

Her attention wandered from his unsatisfactory report, and she muttered in throaty self-parody: 'But we're not here only to talk.'

She leaned across to him, her manner deliberately provocative, indeed wanton. Richard unbuttoned the peignoir and took her in his arms, dismissing both past and future. Only the moment was real. Not only urgent, but overwhelming, he concluded muzzily when he sank again into sleep.

The keening of sirens awakened them.

Glancing at her minute gold wristwatch, Emily set her feet on the cool red-tile floor. She matter-of-factly opened the filigreed wooden shutter, looked out, and observed: 'An hour or so to twilight. Now do you believe me about the barking? Anyway, the Japs'll be here in about half an hour.'

'Shouldn't we . . .' He realized that he had no idea what one did in Chungking in an air raid.

'They never hit this hill.'

'There's always a chance of error. Remember the Great World.'

'The alternative is to jump out of the frying pan into the fire. The only air-raid shelters are down below in the old town, which they *always* hit.'

'Then let's sit tight. But can't we see them?'

'You get a grandstand view from here, looking right down at the bombing.'

She poured from the cylindrical teapot ensconced in its padded basket and offered a plate of crisp dried pork.

'Fatty Huang taught the Szechwanese to air-dry pork the way he likes it. You remember Colonel J. L. Huang, Mayling's all-purpose factotum – and leading gourmet in a nation of gourmets. And what food in Chungking! Not only Szechwan dishes, but Peking, Shanghai, Cantonese, Hunan, and God knows what else. It's fabulous.'

'For the rich!' he observed implacably. 'Only for the rich.'

'I'm afraid so, though sometimes I forget. But it's impossible to fight all the good fights at once. Till we drive the Japs out, I've got to forget about social justice – even about women's rights.' Sincerely contrite, she

366

then became impatient again. 'You haven't told me what kept you in the States so long.'

Richard made a prolonged business of lighting a cigarette before replying: 'Everyone wanted to talk about China. I did some lecturing. It was damned lucrative. And a lot of special broadcasts. Also. . . .'

'Also what? Don't be coy.'

'Also . . .' He grinned at her. 'It seems I've written a book. About China though I know it's presumptuous. Any rate, Random House want to publish it in the States. And Gollancz in the UK.'

'Richard, how wonderful!'

Emily flung her arms around his neck, kissed him hard, and released him to demand: 'When does it come out? What's it called?'

'And I thought you were only interested in my body,' he joked feebly. 'Towards the end of the year, I think. Maybe November. The tentative title is: *Yellow Earth, White Sun, and Red Star.*'

'Did you *have* to mention the Communists in the title?' Her pleasure was clouded. 'They're not really that important, you know. And you've only just got to Chungking. Will you be able to add a little? Without a section on Chungking, on the new war effort from the new capital, your book won't be complete.'

'I should think so, darling. I've still got months. I want to see everything, and I'll need your help.'

Richard Hollings did not himself know whether he was lying outright or simply modifying the truth. He did not intend to deceive Emily, but only to please her. Besides, he honestly did not know when the text of a book could no longer be altered. Since a newspaper could correct a story in ten minutes, he simply assumed that book publishers, too, could make major changes at almost the last minute.

'It's been chosen as a main selection by the Book of the Month Club,' he added. 'The publisher is terribly chuffed.'

'I *am* impressed.'

'I'm told it means a fair dollop of cash, so if we ever . . .' He let the hint hang in the air, though she would not pick it up. 'It also means new status for the author. Random House is begging for another book very soon. Apparently I'm now a respected author, not just a hack correspondent. Any rate, so they tell me.'

Richard's embarrassment was unfeigned. Although he was avid to advance himself, it was bad form to praise one's own accomplishments. Only bounders boasted.

'*Yellow Earth, White Sun, and Red Star.*' Emily tried the title on her own tongue, in part to turn the conversation from the hint that had made him sound like a suitor, which was unthinkable. 'Why not just *Yellow Earth and White Sun*? Much neater! It's shorter, punchier – and says all you need to say.'

'I'll give it a thought, probably drop them a line.'

The urgent sirens wailed again. Louder, shriller, more piercing, they sounded more like human sentinels shrieking warning of common peril than brazen-throated machines.

367

'*Ching-pao! Ching-pao!* Air-raid alarm!' Emily laughed edgily. 'Even the sailors off the foreign gunboats now know that much Chinese. It's only the second warning. Another fifteen minutes.'

'You know I'm developing a phobia. Bombers scare me stiff.'

'Darling, you'd better learn to live with them. We've averaged two to three raids every day since the beginning of May. But no point in dwelling on it. Tell me, did you see Tommy and Julie in Shanghai?'

'Of course, though on the hop. I was shifting frantically from the trans-Pacific liner to the coaster to Hong Kong to catch the Chungking flight. Shanghai's beginning to wither on the vine, you know.'

'And Tommy and Julie?' Emily pressed the question. 'How are they?'

'Seemed fine,' he answered airily. 'What else is there to say?'

'A good deal, I'd think. If you're trying to spare me, Dick, it's no use. Your tact has already alarmed me. What's wrong with them?'

'To be perfectly honest, Em, nothing I can put my finger on. Both are in good health, outwardly cheerful, and working hard. The girls are fine too. Though your niece Althea, the fair-haired one if I'm not mistaken, she's becoming a bit of a handful.'

'Richard, you're still being evasive. Tell me what you know or suspect. Otherwise, I'll imagine worse things.'

'If you insist. Mind you, I could be absolutely wrong, but I got the impression they weren't getting along.' He reflected before explaining: 'A little friction seems normal for you and me. But friction's most unusual for Julie and Tommy. He goes into brown studies. She doesn't laugh as much or as spontaneously.'

Her eyes remained insistent, and he added defensively: 'Devil take it, Em, it's probably my imagination. The war's moved on, but life in Shanghai's still a terrible strain. The Japs are all around. It's like a cage in the zoo with the Japs always peering in.'

'Why they won't come to Chungking I can't understand,' Emily mused. 'Or go to the States if that's the way the wind blows. Though Julie's anything but a coward. And Tommy? Well you know Tommy. Much too brave for his own good. He'd never leave China. But why stick in Shanghai?'

She leaned across him to stub out her cigarette in the ox-blood ashtray on his bedside table, and he stroked her hip suggestively. She smiled, shook her head, and leaned back against the bolster to muse further: 'Their letters are always cheerful. I think I'll write Julie and ask her point blank what's wrong. Worst she can do is tell me to mind my own business.'

Emily slipped off the high bed, leaving the ice-blue peignoir crumpled and flat like a sloughed-off snakeskin, and walked across the room to the chest where lay her hastily discarded clothing. Richard watched with delight the play of her taut buttocks, her tapering thighs, her rounded calves, and her slender ankles. Looking over her shoulder, she intercepted his gaze and – to his astonishment – solemnly winked. This was a new Emily, utterly self-possessed and occasionally ribald. As she shook out her flimsy undergarments, her cream-silk blouse with the jewelled Air

Force wings, and her beige-cotton slacks, he concluded that there was something to be said for war.

He pulled on his sweaty shirt and trousers, and she asked: 'Dick, when can I see your manuscript? I'd love to.'

'I'm sorry, Em.' He slipped the strap of his binoculars over his head. 'I should have brought a copy. But they make so much fuss about not weighing the aircraft down. The long and the short of it is I left my carbon in New York. I promise you, just as soon as I get a copy of the book . . .'

'I'll hold you to that.' She slipped her arm through his. 'Now shall we go see the war?'

Richard Hollings had paid little attention to his surroundings earlier that day when the sedan-chair coolies carried him on their shoulders up the narrow hill path to the stone-walled compound where the Ou-yang family was established in remarkable comfort for war refugees. The bamboo sedan-chair had repeatedly swung over the edge of the precipice – and fear had effectively distracted him from the view. Otherwise, his attention had been concentrated on his hope of finding Emily.

When she led him out of the compound at twilight, Richard was still intent on her. He looked down at her gleaming crow-black hair, not at the distant city. He hardly noticed the two green-uniformed guards on the gate salute with long Lee-Enfield rifles. Nor was he aware of his surroundings until they stopped on a rocky outcrop that looked over a river at the city and waved her hand at the horizon.

'There!' Emily pointed down. 'Extraordinary sight, isn't it?'

The centre of the provisional capital, whose odd name literally meant Twofold Felicitation, lay in the apex of the triangle formed by the meeting of the broad, dark Yangtze River and the narrower, sun-dappled Chialing River. The squat buildings with drab-tiled roofs within the crenellated city-walls were palisaded by bamboo and board fences. The triangle pointed east, and a sprawl of new construction tufted the hills rising to the west.

Chungking was protected against ground attack by its two rivers. Precipitous stone steps climbed hundreds of feet from the river's edge, where grimy wooden shacks perched on stilts like grey herons on skinny legs. Not only travellers, but every ounce of water and every grain of rice was carried up those time-worn steps on men's backs. Perched on the ridge above its moats, Chungking was a formidable – indeed almost impregnable – fortress-city.

Although the surrounding hills rose almost sheer from the rivers' banks to cup the medieval city in their palms, the provisional capital was naked to attack from the air. The batteries of anti-aircraft guns were hardly more effective against the swarms of bombers than the dark pines that stood sentinel on the hills in the encroaching twilight. The Chinese Air Force, Emily confessed, had been reduced to impotence – in fact, virtually destroyed. Claire Chennault was striving to rebuild the Air Force from the beginning in Kunming four hundred miles to the south-west, and the

Japanese bomber fleets were based at Yochow, four hundred miles due east. Through his binoculars, Richard saw confirmation of Chungking's vulnerability: the black scars that great fires had left branded on the city's coarse-grained face.

Without warning a million enraged wasps buzzed across the quiet landscape. He automatically turned east to look for the aircraft whose engines' roar shook the rocky outcrop upon which they stood. The sky was empty.

The opalescent dusk thickened into indigo evening, and the bombers came out of the south-west. They had clearly flown a great circle around the city to take the anti-aircraft gunners by surprise. Storming out of the sunset, the silver squadrons stretched from horizon to horizon. In precise Vs like wild geese, they swept overhead. The blood-red discs on their wings blotting out the sky, dozens of bombers swooped upon the virtually defenceless city.

Shocked by the immensity of the attack, Richard counted forty-six Mitsubishi twin-engined bombers. The half-dozen black specks circling above the sparse clouds were a token escort of pursuit planes. But Japanese dominance was contested only by the grey puffs of anti-aircraft shells that burst harmlessly in the air.

Darkness descended as abruptly as a roller-blind over a half-lit window, and fountains of scarlet tracers soared against the purple sky. The bombers disdainfully swung into a broad front wing-tip to wing-tip in order to saturate the target. The searchlights transformed them into precise rows of sequins glittering against the dark sky.

The bomb-bay doors of the first echelon dropped open simultaneously. The swarms of small incendiaries that swam downward through the searchlights' blue-white beams like fat minnows were followed by big heavy-explosive bombs like predatory pike.

Richard crooked his arm protectively around Emily's shoulders – and felt her tremble. Bereft of bravado, she buried her face in the crook of his neck.

The incendiaries' fires blossomed scarlet in the dark wedge of the city. Seconds later, the big bombs thundered.

The leaping flames glowed blood-red on the silver bombers. The second echelon's bomb-bay doors, too, opened simultaneously, but its bomb-aimers were not quite as accurate. Fountains of pink spray erupted around the foreign gunboats in the Yangtze.

Realizing that they were highlighted by the fires, Richard pulled Emily down to the ground. The great silver shapes passed directly overhead, their immense wings eclipsing the stars.

High-pitched reports rose over the engines' yammering, and scarlet torrents arched down at them. Richard glimpsed their assailant. Brightly illuminated within his transparent enclosure by the conflagration, the air-gunner thumbing the firing-levers of his twin machine-guns appeared to float alone in the dark sky. The enormous round goggles on the leather sphere of his head glared down like the eyes of a gigantic and malevolent fly.

370

When the armada had passed, Emily rose. Pushing her hair into place, she said: 'I mustn't forget my rule! Always be cheerful! Be cheerful or you'll cry!'

The north wind bore the fires' stench to their nostrils as they walked slowly back to the compound: burning paraffin, burning wood, and burning flesh. The billows of smoke shone dirty-red and black like blood smeared on charred wood.

'No matter how many times I see it, it's just as bad!' Emily murmured. 'Worse really!'

Before the green-tiled pillars she touched his arm and said: 'You might as well spend the night. Not with me, unfortunately, but in the guest-pavilion. Hsiu is tolerant as long as there's no scandal. It's easy not to try him – except when you're around, darling. And that hasn't been very often.'

'Not by choice,' he declared. 'If it were only up to me . . .'

'Maybe some day it will be.' She offered that first tentative hope casually. 'Perhaps when the war's won . . . But this is stupid talk. Your wife, after all . . .'

'No problem is insoluble, darling.' He said no more for fear of breaking the spell. 'I only wish I could tell you . . . tell you all I . . .'

'Hush, Dickie! You have already! You've told me! Don't say any more now. Later you can tell me over and over again. You know, I was never absolutely sure you'd come to Chungking. Not beyond all doubt!'

Harrison Parker Smythe III was lolling in an easy chair when Emily and Richard entered the drawing room of the mansion. He was rakishly dressed in suede chukka boots, chino trousers, a brass-buckled bush-jacket, and a campaign hat with a leopard-skin band. His cornflower-blue eyes beaming innocence, he grinned enigmatically in response to Emily's startled: 'I thought you were with Claire Chennault in Kun-ming!'

He had still not revealed his business an hour later when they sat down to dinner. British *sang froid* was, however, a match for American mysteriousness. Richard Hollings did not ask the American's purpose, but selected another morsel from the round bamboo steamer-basket and asked: 'What's this? If it's typical Chungking food, I may stay forever.'

'*Fen-cheng jou,*' Emily replied. 'Chunks of steamed beef, as you see. But first dusted with rice-flour and spices. The chef won't say exactly what spices.'

'Emmy's chef always makes it for me,' Harry said proprietorially.

He dipped a wing of the twice-cooked duck into the toasted mixture of Szechwan pepper and salt. Raising his highball in salute, he proposed: 'To the duck! To the miraculous duck and the chef! Dick, the real miracle is your scotch and my bourbon. Even the Embassy's run out. But Emily always . . .'

'My secret's simple,' she said. 'I tell my friends in high places I must have liquor to bamboozle the foreign press corps. Look at the enemy, I say. Just look at Chou En-lai's propaganda tea-parties! And imagine what *I* can do with liquor!'

'Seeing booze is sixty dollars a bottle on the black market, *if* you can find it . . .' Smythe wearily kneaded his chin. His carroty hair had lost its lustre, and his pale-blue eyes were clouded.

He added inconsequentially: 'Did you know the *Panay* was carrying a couple of crates of parts from shot-down Jap airplanes when they sank her under us, Dick? I was mother-henning them for Chennault – on their way back to the States for examination. It would've been an intelligence bonanza. Also a justification for the attack if the Japs only knew.'

'Why tell me now, Harry?' the correspondent demanded.

'My God, not to write about. Only to show we're not all asleep at the switch. Matter of fact, Chennault's just finished his own appraisal of Japanese pursuit types. Emmy's translating it from the Old Man's military jargon into English.'

'Can I ask about that, Harry?'

'Well, we *might* get Chennault to release it with a little pushing. You wouldn't be interested in the purely technical side, would you?'

'Not particularly. But I am interested in whatever story you're trying to plant on me.'

'Plant?' The American's truculent surprise might almost have been sincere. 'What do you think I'm trying to plant, my friend?'

'At a guess, something like this: *Don't be complacent, Mr and Mrs America. Your potential enemy is no slouch. The Japanese aren't short-sighted morons flying buckets of bolts, but hot shots in hot planes.* But why praise your enemy?'

Harry Smythe confessed: 'That's the story all right. Just the way we'd like to see it played.'

Emily laughed at his embarrasment and said: 'Claire Chennault tells about T.V. Soong watching a crack American pilot demonstrate a new pursuit plane. T.V. pointed at the plane and said, "What China needs is a hundred of these." Claire's reply was: "What China really needs is a hundred of those!" And he pointed at the American pilot.'

'Chennault needs American planes to fight the Japanese.' Harry Smythe was emphatic. 'He also needs Americans to train Chinese aviators. And he needs both right *now*. The American public must learn two things: It's already *their* war, and the Gimo is fighting it for them. Also Japanese planes and aviators are damned good – and only American warplanes and American-trained aviators can take them on!'

'What about American pilots to fight the Japs?' Richard asked.

'Certainly not now,' Emily cautioned. 'Maybe later, though.'

'Dick, the war in the air's going to be *the* big story until the Chinese counter-attack on the ground,' Harry interjected. 'And that could take years. Meanwhile, it'll be a gravy-train for a correspondent who's got the inside track.'

'That I presume,' Richard responded starchily, 'is meant to be a whacking great bribe.'

'I didn't mean that.' The former diplomat squirmed. 'You've got it wrong.'

'Harry, you should never, never try to bribe Richard Hollings,' Emily advised proudly. 'It just won't work!'

Emily's own embarrassment was relieved by a Shanghai manservant in a heavily starched white coat with sweaty half-circles under the arm pits. When he placed a covered porcelain serving-dish on the mahogany table, she said: 'I'll bet a hundred silver dollars you've never seen this before. Authentic Szechwan, it's called "Ants Climbing Trees".'

She lifted the cover to reveal a bed of fine, crisp, translucent noodles strewn with dark minced meat and garnished with chopped greens.

'Not much to look at,' Emily acknowledged. 'But just taste it.'

Anise, Szechwan peppercorns, rice wine, and wild onions were blended into a splendid new flavour. The crisp noodles crackled against the teeth, and the dark meat melted on the palate. Ambrosia, Richard mused, must be very much like this – at once delicious and tantalizing.

'Harry, why don't you fill Dick in?' Emily suggested. 'Whatever I say, he'll always suspect it's Nationalist propaganda. You tell him the good news.'

'All I can see is disaster.' The correspondent objected. 'A backwoods capital under terror bombing – too feeble to put up even a token defence. In New York they'd say, "Such good news I need like a hole in the head!"'

'You're wrong, kiddo.' Harry Smythe's brashness had not abated with the years. 'Remember Napoleon's drive to Moscow? The Russians kept falling back and sucking Napoleon in. Finally he had to retreat. The Gimo's strategy is the same. Only it'll take a mite longer to exhaust the Japs. Napoleon didn't have planes and tanks.'

'I've rarely heard such balderdash.' The Englishman was irritated by the American's condescension. 'Why don't you go peddle it to someone who's chump enough to believe it?'

'Now, Dick, I'm sure Harry isn't . . .'

'I'm surprised at you, too, Em.' Richard's jealous anger had been rising since they returned to find Harry Smythe in residence. 'How can you lend yourself to . . .'

'I only lie to diplomats, Hollings!' Smythe flushed. 'Never to newspapermen. And I'm not about to start with one who . . .'

'Whenever you two overgrown schoolboys are quite through! Or shall I send for the boxing gloves?'

Despite the pleasure she took in Richard's jealousy, Emily was angry. She was annoyed by his uninformed scepticism, and she resented playing the traditional feminine role of peacemaker.

'What about the enemy's figures?' she challenged. 'Will you believe them, Dick?'

Richard nodded. The gravest danger to their love, he realized, was neither her caprices nor his own selfishness. They were both too devoted: he to his craft of journalism, which compelled him to pursue the truth regardless of the damage; and she to the welfare of China, which could compel her to lie.

'I've typed them up.' Emily took a sheet of paper from the pocket of her slacks. 'Six hundred thousand square miles of Chinese soil and a hundred and seventy million Chinese under their control, the Japs claim. That leaves about three million square miles and two hundred and thirty million Chinese outside their grasp. Quite a nut to crack! Also confidential Japanese assessments admit they can't mount a new offensive.'

'Sorry about the dust-up, Dick,' Harry Smythe said. 'Of course you're not a wise-ass kid reporter who thinks he knows everything.'

'And you Harry, maintain that all this is the result of the Generalissimo's deliberate strategy?'

'What else, Dick? Otherwise why fight bitterly for every inch of ground you *know* you're going to give up eventually? Why sacrifice so many lives? Only to punish the enemy – deplete his forces and leave him only scorched earth and empty cities!'

'Harry, you've got the translation of the latest Imperial Japanese Staff Appraisal we captured, haven't you?' Emily asked. 'Show it to Dick later. If that doesn't open his eyes . . .'

When the dinner that had almost become a seminar ended with small Szechwan tangerines, Emily excused herself. Pleading exhaustion after a strenuous day, she told Richard: 'Harry'll show you where you sleep, maybe lend you a razor, too.'

She kissed him lightly on the lips and vanished, leaving him surprised by that casual display of affection before an outsider. Later, sitting up on his hard, wooden bed tucking in the mosquito net, he told himself that he would never fully understand female behaviour. Smiling at the banality of his conclusion, he turned up the wick of the oil-lamp on the bed-side table and skimmed the Japanese Staff Appraisal that Harry Smythe had handed him.

Despite inferior weapons, lack of training, and heavy losses, Chinese forces totalling some seven million harass our forces almost to exhaustion. . . . Their grand strategy is *retreating instead of advancing*. China's territory . . . is immense, and our forces are tormented by harassment and the length of our supply lines. . . . We cannot advance – and we dare not retreat.

After breakfast, Emily advised patience, although Richard was anxious to get back to work and Harry Smythe had business at the Ministry of Defence. No sedan-chair appeared, although two or three normally waited near the gate for fares. Surmising that all able-bodied men had been pressed into clearing the rubble left by the great raid, Emily offered her private sedan-chair.

When Richard said he would walk rather than dispossess her, she concealed her relief and directed her chair-bearers to the Aeronautical Commission. She preferred not to provoke Mayling Chiang by tardiness, although her old friend would have been happy with the excuse of lending the sedan-chair to a correspondent. Despite her increasing hauteur, Mayling never forgot the primary importance of American public opinion in the survival of China and her own position.

Her own pre-eminence derived largely from the American connection.

She was not only her husband's interpreter, but his collaborator in dealings with the United States – in good part because of her popularity with the American people. Since that popularity depended upon the American press, she would do almost anything for correspondents – even, sometimes, tell them the unvarnished truth.

While Emily's sedan-chair swayed down the precipitous path to the ferry across the Chialing River, her house-guests scrambled a few hundred yards behind. Burdened though they were, the chair-bearers steadily drew farther ahead of the two foreigners.

Harry Smythe stopped to examine Chungking's latest scars. The dense smoke rising from burning buildings was the funeral pyre of hundreds of men, women, and children. The brisk wind that chased the lamb's-fleece clouds across the sky shredded that smoke so that it did not lie in a funeral pall over the tortured city. But the clear skies were disastrous. Thick smoke cover would have hampered the Japanese aviators who were at that moment receiving orders for further attacks.

'You're not,' Harry asked, 'in a great hurry, are you?'

'Not frightfully,' Richard replied. 'Though I should see some people.'

The American hooked an arm around one of the dark pines beside the trail and said meditatively: 'Szechwan they call it, Four Rivers. China's most fertile province – and most heavily populated. Much of the romance of Chinese history started here.'

Richard realized that his jealousy of Harry Smythe's closeness to Emily was obviously misplaced. Harry did love her – not for herself, but as a daughter of China.

'Szechwan's also the end of the line.' Harry Smythe glared down at the bomb-scarred city. 'The Gimo's got his back to the wall, and he's cut off from the outside world. The Japs dominate the coastal provinces, so there's no outlet to the sea except the narrow-gauge railroad through Indo-China. An occasional plane from Soviet Central Asia or over the Himalayas from Calcutta. Mostly broken-down trucks dragging through the mountains on the Burma Road. More than half their load is their own gasoline. Not a great situation, is it?'

'And how do you square that with the glowing picture you drew last night?'

'Dick, an entire nation is at bay on this plateau. More than twenty million Chinese have swarmed into Szechwan – the ones with guts and imagination! And they're still coming – despite disease, starvation, accidents, and bandits!'

He stared at the peaks on the horizon and said softly: 'I saw it, Dick, the mass migration of a people. By ramshackle buses and by bicycle, ox-cart, and horseback. In jalopies and antiquated trucks held together with string and chewing gum. Thousands on junks through the Yangtze gorges –and a privileged few by plane. Most on their own legs. Toddlers and grandmothers with bound feet. Solid bourgeoisie from the treaty ports and dispossessed soldiers from Manchuria. Mule drovers from Shansi and tea-merchants from Amoy. Marine engineers from Canton and electricians from Tientsin.'

375

The American wrestled a cigarette from a limp pack of Camels. His chromium-plated Zippo lighter threw a flame three inches high. Blowing the smoke out, he looked down at his cigarette in apparent surprise and dropped it.

'Got to cut down,' he reminded himself absently. 'It's going to be a long war.'

'Harry, this is all terribly inspiring,' Richard interposed. 'But it's not winning the war.'

'Guess I got carried away,' the American confessed. 'Dick, it will win the war. Mechanics and engineers have brought their factories along – to make everything from matches and textiles to cement and guns. On men's backs or man-pulled carts. The heavy machinery on junks because the dirt mountain roads would have collapsed. Or by flatcar to the end of the tracks and then manhandled. You can't beat a people like that.'

Abashed by his own emotion, the American turned and loped down the trail to the riverbank. Waiting for the small sampan that sculled men and beasts across the placid Chialing River to Chungking, Richard pondered a story. The first sentence sprang into his mind: *The Chinese people are capable of anything – except surrender.*

He shrugged away that adulatory lead. It was ridiculous to make such a sweeping judgment so soon after arriving. He had hardly spoken to anyone except Emily and Smythe, both vehement champions of the Nationalists. He would have to wait and see and make his own assessment. Besides, it could be awkward waxing lyrical about *both* Chinese régimes.

The two foreigners jumped from the ferry's blunt prow onto the muddy foreshore – and into the reality of Chunking on the morning after a savage bombing raid.

Every second pedestrian held to his nose a crumpled cloth reeking of vinegar. Wads of cotton-wool protruded from the others' nostrils, as if half the population were afflicted with nosebleeds. The stench gripped Richard's throat like a giant hand, and bile rose bitter in his throat. The nauseating sweetness of gangrenous flesh overpowered the odours of the rotting excrement, the sour rice, and the fermenting chilies. Gagging, almost retching, he choked back the sour, coppery bile.

Harry Smythe extracted a flask of *eau de Cologne* from his bulging side-pocket and wet his own handkerchief before offering it to Richard. The cloying cologne intensified the sweetness of corruption. The stench was palpable – almost animate. It clogged his mouth with filth and almost stopped his nostrils. Although inured by many years to the stenches of Asia, Richard Hollings felt as if he were suffocating.

'I'm going the other way.' Harry Smythe clapped him on the arm. 'For the Press Hostel just follow that road. Don't let it get you down, buddy.'

Sampans were carrying heaped corpses to the far bank for mass burial, and small groups of men and women were searching among the dismembered bodies strewn on the muddy foreshore. Fragments of human beings spilled across the foul black mud like the leavings of a cannibal's feast. Eyes stared imploringly from bloodied faces, and bony hands clutched the air. A shapely leg neatly cut off just above the knee still wore an immaculate beige silk stocking and a high-heeled pump.

The searchers turned the bodies over like penitent monks and nuns. It was the least – and the most – they could do for their dead. Confucius had enjoined all Chinese to preserve unmutilated the bodies bestowed by their parents. Richard realized with sick horror that the searchers were hoping to reunite disjointed limbs and severed heads with original torsos so that the dead would go entire into the afterworld. Confucius had instructed all Chinese to preserve intact through this world the bodies bestowed upon them by their sanctified parents.

He turned away from the shambles and took the road to the Press Hostel. Despite the broken streets, the gutted buildings, and the burnt-out shrines, Chungking was vibrant with life. Workmen squatting among the rubble knocked mortar off bricks and stacked them for future use. Hawkers of food and drinking water loudly cried their wares through the pulsating alleys, and dogs barked defiantly behind bamboo palings.

In the busy lobby of the grey-tiled Press Hostel, the musty odour of mildew contended with pungent fresh paint. Opened a week and a half earlier, the Hostel was already showing hairline cracks in its plaster walls.

Jimmy Wei popped up to greet Richard with great warmth, his dark monkey-face alight with laughter and enthusiasm. Overwhelmed anew by Jimmy's ebullient personality, Richard finally broke away and found sanctuary in his room, which was somewhat larger than a monk's cell. He took the metal cover off his Hermes portable, rolled in a sheet of paper, typed the heading – and sat staring at the white surface for almost a quarter of an hour.

40

While Harry Smythe, Claire Chennault, and Emily Ou-yang, reluctantly assisted by Richard Hollings, plotted to win essential American aid for the Nationalist Government, the Soviet Union saw a great opportunity. Moscow promised arsenals of weapons and platoons of military advisers to Generalissimo Chiang Kai-shek, who had been transformed by a wink of the Soviet dictator's eye from 'a reactionary, feudal despot' to the 'democratic hero of the Chinese people'.

Joseph Stalin's reasoning was brutally simple. Japan, the Soviet Union's unruly neighbour in the Far East, was probing Soviet defences. Judging the Chinese Nationalists more likely than the Chinese Communists to kill a great many Japanese, Stalin made the Nationalists his protégés. He was, as always, impressed above all by power, which he felt the Chinese Nationalists possessed in greater measure than the Chinese Communists. Through the Nationalists he also planned to regain the influence the Kremlin had lost by the débâcle of 1927, when the Chinese Communist Party was crushed and the agents of the Communist International were driven from China. Naturally, he hedged his bet by continuing to support the Chinese Communists.

The paranoid First Secretary of the Communist Party of the Soviet Union graciously advised the Generalissimo: 'You must ensure that there is no treachery or disloyalty behind your back. The best way, in a country as large as China, is to shoot at least four and half million people. In the Soviet Union we pick up everyone who is suspect. Once they enter the gates of the Ministry of the Interior, there are only two exits: Siberia or the grave.'

By instinct a conciliator rather than a dictator, Chiang Kai-shek did not act on that advice. Besides, he felt that his secret police were already brutal enough. For his part, Joseph Stalin actually sent a trickle of war matériel to the Nationalists – along with a large military advisory mission. The Nationalists were, however, reluctant to take the advice of the Russians, whom they called the 'hairy barbarians' to distinguish them from the Japanese 'dwarf barbarians' and the Western 'oceanic barbarians'.

The pealing of the doorbell six flights below was relayed to the roof-garden Julia Howe had created above the cavernous loft sitting-room of the house on Kiukiang Road. Tommy and she liked to have advance notice of visitors in these troubled times. Yet they were weathering the storms of war better than most in late August 1939. Although the commercial beat of Shanghai was slowing perceptibly, that decline had hardly touched them. While Donald Howe's holdings depreciated, his son's practice had expanded.

It was curious, Julia reflected, but their life somehow seemed more *normal* than it had for some time – aside from more frequent and more abrasive disagreements with Tommy on political questions. Odd to consider invasion and partial occupation a kind of normality. Yet most of their lives had been spent amid tension and danger. Even the blessed years from 1931 to 1937 had been stalked by war and revolution, although those threats had seemed far from the charmed city.

She looked at Tommy with concern when the door bell pealed impatiently again. It pealed a third time, louder and longer. In residential Shanghai, unlike bawdy Shanghai, an unannounced caller at half past eleven in the evening was unusual. To the Howes it was mildly alarming. Their secret work for the Apparatus gave to their existence a deeper meaning – and the spice of danger. They feared not only the Japanese and the Settlement Police, but the special agents of the Nationalists, who worked closely with the indestructible secret societies.

'I'll go.' Tommy pulled his pongee dressing gown about his lean frame. 'Not likely to be a patient. They'd telephone, not come by. I wonder who . . .'

He revealed his nervousness by slipping on the plain-glass spectacles he rarely wore nowadays. Julia had almost succeeded in breaking him of using that prop to make himself appear older and more authoritative. But he reverted to the black-rimmed spectacles, not noticing that the lenses were greasy with finger-marks, and descended the spiral staircase to the loft. He opened the glass-and-mahogany door that now served where steel plating with folding grilles, locks, bolts and chains had once kept two young women safe. The hall, which had been dingy and gloomy, was now bright in lavender and yellow. Before his finger touched the call-button on the silver-painted grille, the lift began to rise, alternately whining and chuckling.

Tommy sternly directed himself to relax. His major-domo would not admit a stranger this late at night without inquiring on the house tele-

379

phone. It was a conscious effort to relax, and he marvelled at the irony. Why should a man such as he have to counsel himself to relax in his own house?

The inner grille opened automatically when the lift reached the fifth floor, and Tommy swung the door open. A vision confronted him: Countess Elizaveta Alexandrovna Yavalenka wearing a stole of white Siberian fox over the Cossack-inspired black-silk kaftan with gold embroidery that fitted her closely. She was burdened with a large wicker hamper. Where, Tommy wondered, was the uniformed White Russian footman who rode in the front seat of her twenty-two-foot Hispano-Suiza? She had recently acquired that limousine from an up-country warlord, presumably in return for services rendered by the Ikra, but more likely in exchange for machine-guns.

'Tommy, my own sweet darling!' Elizaveta regressed to the extravagant endearments of the 1920s. 'Do come and help, there's a perfect pet.'

'Are you joining the Communists?' He emerged from her embrace, which was scented with Mitsuoko perfume and Hine cognac. 'Do your own lifting and carrying now, do you?'

'I'll explain all when we're safely inside.' Her stage whisper was penetrating. 'I don't want anyone to know – especially not the servants. They're all spies, of course.'

Amused by her melodramatics, Tommy bundled the wicker hamper around the tight curves of the spiral staircase. When he reached the roof-garden, the two women ignored him. Julia was exclaiming over the white foxes Elizaveta had discarded in homage to the 86-degree heat after making her entrance. The jet-black and the tawny head close together, they were seated on the wrought-iron settee beside the gilded statue of Kwan Yin, the Goddess of Mercy, who was the patron of women.

Elizaveta opened the hamper to reveal two chill-dewed bottles of Taittinger *blanc de blancs* and an array of crystal goblets.

'Don't just stand there,' she directed. 'Pop one!'

'I never say no to a drop of bubbly,' Julia chattered happily as her husband attacked the cork. 'But it's nice to know why one's drinking it. What are we celebrating?'

'No one must know, my darlings. The Japanese have their spies everywhere.'

'The Japanese?' Julia asked in amazement. 'But you're working with the Japanese?'

'That's why!' Elizaveta declared cryptically; she accepted a brimming goblet with a regal air, raised it high, and proposed: 'A toast, Sir and Madam, to General Gregori Zhukov and his gallant soldiers! Defenders of the sacred soil of the Russian Motherland against the Japanese invaders! *Nosdroviya!*'

She quaffed the champagne and with the same motion tossed the crystal goblet over the parapet of the roof. Although Tommy raised a startled eyebrow, Julia and he also flipped their empty goblets over the parapet. Bubbling with excitement, Elizaveta burrowed in the hamper to find three more goblets, which she promptly filled.

'You are surprised!' she declared unnecessarily. 'Wondering, perhaps, what's got into me?'

'A bit startled, Liz,' Tommy conceded. 'Last week you were praying for the Japs to beat the Bolsheviks.'

'A lady can change her mind, can't she? After all, blood is thicker than vodka.' She grinned in delight. 'I suddenly realized that these men are Russians like myself – and they are defending the Motherland. To drive a Jap tank army from our sacred Siberian soil in a three-month battle is a heroic feat. Zhukov and his brave lads are true Russian patriots.'

'Look here, sweety, I'll drink to any Japanese defeat! But I don't like raising a glass to Bolshevik murderers.' Julia automatically reinforced her right-wing cover. 'You, of all people, Liz, know . . .'

'My dears, I am a realist. The Romanovs will never return to the throne. Hateful as the Bolsheviki are, they have united Great Russia – and they are standing against the Japanese aggressors.'

Tommy was thunderstruck by Elizaveta's calling herself a realist. She had never faced reality in all her life, not even during the fearful years in Siberia. Since that first exile, her faith in the ultimate restoration of the Czars had never wavered.

'Eternal life to Holy Mother Russia!' Elizaveta pronounced. 'The sacred soil of the Motherland forever inviolate!'

Tommy set his goblet down on the side-table and observed wryly: 'If you look hard, you'll find your sacred Siberian soil is really Chinese. Your Czars stole it from us at cannon-point. But I'll drink to the defeat of the Japanese.'

Pale arctic sunlight glinted in Elizaveta's eyes. She was, however, the guest of the man who dared question the boundaries divinely ordained for Great Russia. Moreover, his wife was her closest female friend. Marvelling at his Chinese chauvinism, she echoed Tommy's toast.

'My Lord, I must fly.' Elizaveta flipped open the jewelled lid of her Piaget wrist-watch. 'Must get back to the Ikra to keep the peace. The Japs'll be insufferable tonight, morose and quarrelsome.'

After dropping kisses on their cheeks, she floated down the spiral staircase to the big loft. Closing the door of the lift, Tommy shook his head in rueful admiration of her energy and her antics. Upon winding his way up the staircase, he was not surprised to find Julia chuckling with delight as she poured more champagne.

'You see, darling, it's true,' she said comfortably. 'Everyone sees the light in time – even a hardened reactionary like Liz.'

'What a performance! Logic be blowed!'

'Tommy, forget China's old imperialist boundaries. Liz is delighted because it's Russia that's won. I'm delighted because the vicious little Japs got their come-uppance – from the Soviet Union, which is also China's best friend.'

'I'm not so sure of that, Julie.' Tommy fished in his pocket for his old meerschaum. 'Almost all Soviet aid – what there is of it – is going to the Nationalists. The Kremlin obviously doesn't give a hoot for the Chinese Communist Party. You remember '27. Moscow bloody well abandoned the Chinese Communist Party. It could happen again.'

'Darling, please don't be morbid. This is an entirely new day – and not only because of the thriving Border Area. We must look at the objective historical conditions. We must also be practical. China has *no* other friend.'

'Julia, I've been thinking.' He lit the meerschaum, and a cloud of pale grey smoke hovered before his face like a smoke-screen. 'I'm worried about Shanghai. Anything could happen. I don't see why you won't take the girls to visit your parents. Just till we see which way the cat's going to jump. It's about time the girls met their . . .'

'Tommy, darling, how many times do I have to tell you I won't do it? I won't leave you here alone.'

'My dear girl, you know I can't leave China. Certainly not now. All the reasons that make it imperative for you to go mean I must stay. How could I desert?'

'You're not making sense, dear. You know very well I do my share for the Apparatus. A little more than my share because of your practice. If I go, you'll be hamstrung.'

'I never doubted that for an instant. But the time I now give to the family I could devote to the work. It would even out.'

'I think you want to get rid of me, Tommy Howe, and I resent the implication that I'm expendable. It's just as important for me to stay as for you to . . .'

The telephone on the marble side-table buzzed commandingly. Annoyed at the interruption, Julia snatched up the handset. She listened intently and twice asked: 'Are you sure?' She finally asked: 'And that's all it said?' and slowly replaced the handset. Her crimson lipstick was a garish scar on her chalk-white face when she turned to her husband.

'That was Billy Wang down at the station . . . XMHA.' Her voice was flat, but it quavered. 'He knows I'm interested in politics, he said, so he thought he'd ring me. Oh, my God! I can't believe it!'

Tommy was marginally relieved that the appalling news was political, rather than personal. None the less, he had rarely seen his wife so distressed.

'It can't be as terrible as it seems.' She tried to reassure herself. 'But it's a great shock. Tommy, Moscow and Berlin have signed a non-aggression pact. Stalin's concluded a treaty of friendship with the Nazis.'

'A pact with the devil!' Tommy was surprised, but he was not shocked. 'What about the Japanese? They're the Nazis' allies, after all.'

'Nothing said about the Japs. Billy Wang would've told me. Tommy, maybe I've got hold of the wrong end of the stick. Maybe it's a plan to split the Germans and the Japanese.'

'I doubt it very much,' he observed with asperity. 'Perhaps we should call your friends in the Soviet Consulate. Ask if they're going to make common cause with the Japs.'

'Tommy, you know that's impossible. The Soviets could never . . .'

'Just as impossible as a pact with the Nazis.'

'The Soviets *must* have a good reason.' Julia's faith was reviving. 'A very good reason. You do see that, don't you, Tommy?'

'I'm sure Comrade Stalin has a good reason – or thinks he has. That still leaves two questions: Is he right? And is it good for China?'

'If it's good for the Soviet Union, it's good for the working-class movement everywhere,' Julia affirmed. 'Without the secure base of the Soviet Union, the progressive movement is ineffective. Therefore, the highest priority is the welfare of the Soviet Union, which is the fatherland of workers everywhere. The Marxist-Leninist leadership of the Communist Party of the Soviet Union is the locomotive of history.'

'End quote - the Dean.' Tommy riposted savagely. 'Julia, please spare me the half-baked rationalizations of the Shanghai Labour University. Sometimes, I'm almost glad the Nationalists finally shot your precious Soviet toady, the Dean. How a decent Chinese . . .'

'You can be as sarcastic as you want, Tommy.' Her eyes were hard; her square chin thrust upward; and her small, competent hands were clenched in her lap. 'But I'm absolutely certain of one thing.'

'And what, my dear, might that be?'

She did not immediately answer. Most of their intense quarrels in recent months had arisen from her conviction that they should work directly for the Soviets. He had, however, never before employed that tone of cold, contemptuous sarcasm to her.

'And what's that, Julie?'

Although his tone was less hostile, she still did not reply. Instead, she twirled a Chesterfield into her ivory holder and studied him through the smoke. He was still a very good looking man. The two faint lines reaching from his cheekbones to his mouth made him appear even more scholarly, almost ascetic, but the faint wrinkles at the corners of his deep-set eyes relieved that severity.

'I was just waiting for you to simmer down,' she finally said. 'You know very well that the Communist Party of the Soviet Union *must* put its own interests first. And I think it was despicable – what you said about the Dean. But I'll let it pass.'

'Thank you, Julie. I'm grateful, I'm sure. And your revelation?'

'I'm certain of one thing: whatever forced Moscow to make this treaty, it's all the more reason for us to work with them . . . for them . . . directly. You've been stalling far too long. How much longer can you defy Party discipline? How do . . .'

'The Communist Party of the Soviet Union is not *my* party!' He spoke through clenched teeth. 'And never will be.'

'That's pettifogging, Tommy – and you know it. Moscow is our only hope, China's only hope, the world's only hope for peace and progress. So how can we refuse . . .'

'I do wish you'd take Althea and Persephone home till this blows over,' he said wearily. 'I really do, Julie. You're out of your depth here. The game's getting too dangerous!'

'Don't take that world weary tone with me, Tommy!' Her voice rose uncontrollably. 'Danger be damned! I'm not some little fool you've got to get out of the way as soon as serious matters come up. I've done as much as you for the cause – maybe more. And that gives me the right to speak. I tell you again we *must* work with the Soviets.'

383

'You're like the animal trainer who picked the wrong end of the forty-foot python.' His tone of light amusement was infuriating. 'He talked to the tail, stroked it affectionately until he was sure the python was devoted to him. But the front end threw its coils around him and crushed him.'

'What is that rigmarole supposed to mean?'

'The Soviet Consulate in Shanghai is the tail of the python. The head is in Moscow. No use making friends with the tail, which has little more idea than you what Moscow's going to do next. Go home, woman! For everyone's sake, go home!'

'You should have been a novelist, not a doctor,' she replied. 'What an imagination! But you're not getting rid of me. Shanghai *is* my home. I'm staying. And I'll make contact with the Soviets without you, if necessary.'

'Go home, woman!' he shouted. 'Go home before you get us all killed with your foolishness! How I ever ... why I ever thought you could ...'

Tommy's movements were tautly controlled despite his fury. He tapped his pipe out, rose deliberately and placed his foot on the first rung of the spiral staircase. Then he wheeled abruptly to face her again, scarlet splotches of rage glowing on his cheekbones. He snatched off his spectacles and hurled them at the marble side-table. The right lens shattered, and the tiny brass hinge of an ear-piece snapped.

'I'm going to the hospital!' He said softly. 'I don't know when I'll be back.'

Julia turned her head to avoid seeing him vanish inch-by-inch into the spiral staircase. She snatched up a book from the side-table and hurled it at the pale gold figure of the Goddess of Mercy standing amid the spearhead leaves of the miniature rhododendrons. The missile fell at the Goddess's feet, but Kwan Yin's expression remained benevolent – and withdrawn.

The Goddess's features suddenly blurred. Julia saw only an indistinct golden oval through her tears of rage. Refusing to blot those tears, she sat unmoving on the yellow-cushioned settee until the front door crashed shut.

It was their worst fight ever. Tommy's steely self-control had always been admirable. If his self-control had finally snapped, something was fundamentally wrong between them. She would have been glad to lay the blame on their political clash, but she knew that was by no means all.

Julia shivered. She was suddenly afraid, mortally afraid. Was it, she wondered, some failing of her own that had set off the explosion? Or was it some profound dissatisfaction within her husband? Was he resentful because she did not kowtow to him as Chinese wives – at least in public – kowtowed to Chinese husbands? Had she wounded his masculine pride by always assuming what seemed quite natural – her own equality?

Despite the muggy late-August atmosphere, Julia drew the scarlet housecoat around her and retied the fringed sash. Unthinking, she lit a cigarette and unhappily unrolled the scroll of her thoughts.

Tension was inherent in every relationship between female and male. Successful marriages kept that tension under control, and the most successful marriages utilized it. Her own marriage, however, incorporated another source of tension: her husband's innate conviction of racial and cultural superiority.

Any Chinese was bound to develop some degree of defensive racial prejudice in Shanghai, where Chinese were treated as inferiors, although they knew themselves to be immeasurably superior. When Tommy and she disagreed, did his racial prejudice focus on herself? Did he then regard her as a smelly uncultured female foreign devil? Did he hate her because she came of the race that had repeatedly humiliated his country?

Unwontedly introspective, she concluded that she herself had no racial bias. Anyway, it was not a Chinese she loved, but Tommy, who was a unique human being. Besides, unlike him, she had never in her youth had any need to develop racial prejudice. For his part, he had never showed any physical distaste towards herself. Quite the contrary!

'The hell with it!' Julia exhorted herself aloud. 'The hell with the whole business – male arrogance and Chinese superiority! Forget about subtleties, my girl. He was a bad-tempered spoiled child tonight. Stubborn as six mules and goddamned infuriating!'

It was a typical Tommy touch: the roses began arriving at noon. He had known that she would be numb with emotion and would take a nembutal capsule in order to sleep. She awoke shortly after the golden roses arrived. Her amah Lao Zee brought them with her breakfast tray to the bedroom that occupied half the fourth floor.

A subdued sniff expressed Lao Zee's half-incredulous displeasure at the note Julia had written in her clumsy ideograms: *Do not wake me before 12. Doctor had to go to hospital.* Lao Zee sniffed so expressively she might just as well have said aloud: 'It's been years since Doctor was so junior he had to spend the night at the hospital. I know you two have got up to some nonsense. Like spoiled babies!'

The golden roses came first, two dozen bound with a vermilion ribbon. Two hours later came another two dozen, blood-red bound with a golden ribbon. Tommy himself arrived at four with three dozen white roses still dripping dew. Having sent the girls off to the hospitable Charlotte Haleevie, Julia was embowered in the enormous sitting-room in green-tissue lounging pyjamas. The yellow roses and the red roses glowed in crystal vases among ferns from the roof-garden when Tommy pushed the door open.

'Lao Zee told me I'd find you here,' he said sheepishly. 'How are you feeling?'

'Fine! Just fine!' she answered. 'Tip-top! Couldn't be better!'

'All right, Julie.' He allowed himself a rueful grin. 'I take your point.'

'How do you expect me to feel? Like the Queen of May?'

'I'm sorry, very sorry. Inexcusable losing my temper that way. Whatever the merits of the ... ah ... argument, there was no reason for losing my temper.' He had obviously rehearsed his conciliatory speech. 'It was a filthy trick!'

'I suppose I shouldn't have goaded you,' she conceded. 'I'm sorry, too, darling. Sorry I egged you on. But you did frighten me.'

The stately gavotte of mutual apology and mutual forgiveness led in time to reconciliation. Yet, both knew that they had not agreed on the issues, but only on the futility of quarrelling over those issues. Tommy remained obdurately opposed to their working for the Soviets. He was also determined that she and the girls must get away from the dangers of Shanghai. Julia implacably refused to leave and was determined to collaborate with the Soviets. But bitterness was swept away by the passionate seal they put upon their reconciliation in the big bedroom on the fourth floor.

'Maybe we ought to fight more often,' Julia suggested dreamily. 'It's such fun making up. Who'd think an old married couple like us . . .'

'Not so much of that old stuff, pet.' He smiled. 'I maintain that was a most satisfactory demonstration of pretty vigorous . . .'

'Who would deny it, Doctor? Not me certainly.'

'Julie, maybe we could get away for a week or two. I think we both could do with a change of scenery.'

'What a lovely idea. Where shall we go?'

In the end, they went nowhere because there was nowhere to go for a week or two from beleaguered Shanghai. North China, their normal summer resort, was dominated by the Japanese. Japan itself was obviously out, as were Japanese-occupied Korea and Taiwan. Resorts in the interior like Kuling on Mount Lu were barred by the disorder, as was even the river-beach at Woosoong only fifteen miles away. Manila, Hanoi, Singapore, and Bali all were too far away – and no cooler than Shanghai.

'Only Hong Kong's left,' Julia observed disconsolately. 'But who in his right mind would go to Hong Kong in August?'

It was just as well that they didn't leave. If they had, they might have been out of touch with the news at the tumultuous end of August 1939. After the Russo-German Treaty of Non-Aggression, Europe was erupting. And the Howes were again arguing bitterly.

Tommy maintained that the cataclysmic events were the direct results of that malignant Treaty. Tommy said that Adolf Hitler had marched into Poland only because he was certain of the Soviet Union's benevolent neutrality. Tommy did not share Julia's pleasure when the Soviet Red Army began to take over eastern Poland. He was appalled by her open delight when Britain and France reluctantly declared war on Germany on September 3, 1939.

'I hate seeing more people killed,' Julia said. 'But you can't make an omelette without breaking eggs. And Stalin's strategy is brilliant. After the Nazis and the capitalists destroy each other, the Soviet Union will be the most powerful nation in the world. Then comes the triumph of the progressive cause! The non-aggression pact was a brilliant stroke.'

'Sometimes, pet, you sound rather like a propaganda play,' he replied

386

perversely. 'There's a Chinese folk tale about the man who sat on the hillside to watch the tigers fight. He got eaten! Anyway, you forgot the bloody Japs.'

'The Soviet Union will take care of the Japs. When the time is right, Uncle Joe Stalin will join China, and together we'll devour Japan.'

'Will your Uncle Joe join Chairman Mao or the Generalissimo? The way he's acting it looks like the Gimo. If I were Mao Tse-tung I'd be worried stiff.'

The next day, a secret message from Yenan reached the Howes after some delay. The Central Committee of the Chinese Communist Party had just issued urgent instructions to the regulars of the Eighth Route Army, to the guerrillas of the New Fourth Army – and to the subversive Apparatus. All Communists were ordered virtually to disregard the Japanese and to concentrate on driving the Nationalist forces from North China and the Yangtze Valley.

Little maggots of doubt gnawed at Tommy's faith, but Julia's faith grew even stronger. Their passionate reconciliation had not reconciled their increasingly divergent views. Friction was barely controlled.

That same week, Tommy picked up the American-edited *China Weekly Review* and saw its cover: *Japanese-American War Imminent!* Lieutenant-General Kiyokatśu Sato, the *Review* reported, had just published a book under that title. The dust jacket showed the United States Pacific Fleet being destroyed by the Imperial Japanese Navy and Air Force.

Tommy was greatly pleased at the prospect of the United States being compelled to become China's ally in battle. But Julia Howe was dismayed. Working – occasionally even praying – for a Japanese defeat, she had not believed her own country would become directly involved. Tension rose higher in the house on Kiukiang Road.

41

'That's the one lead you can't write, my friend,' Harrison Parker Smythe III declared magisterially. 'Not that!'

'Not to worry,' Richard Hollings riposted. 'I've got an even better idea: *President Roosevelt's personal envoy to China has already committed the US to hostilities with Japan by aiding and abetting the Chinese in every way – legal and illegal.* How does that strike you, my dear chap?'

'For Christ's sake, Dick, don't scare me that way. You've taken five years off my life.' The American's face was actually pale under its constellations of freckles. 'I didn't mean to sound like a tin-horn dictator. I really meant: Sir, we would be very grateful if you would not use that precise wording.'

'That's better, Harry.' The Englishman beamed in saturnine satisfaction. 'I could write: *The United States is already at war with Japan here in sub-tropical Kunming in China's extreme south-west. Predictions of the inevitable conflict, rife in Tokyo, have been overtaken by events.* Etcetera, etcetera. You get the idea?'

'I get the idea all right. Do you really want to give me a heart attack?'

Richard grinned and pressed: 'As you know, it's absolutely true. And I hate to give it up. But for you, chum . . .'

'I knew you were kidding, old buddy.'

Richard nodded, but pointed out: 'It's going to be dashed hard to do what you want me to without treading on your toes. You'd really like me to say it without saying it.'

Gazing across the grass airstrip of Kunming from Claire Chennault's thatch-shaded verandah, the correspondent added: 'But I think I can just about put across your message: *The United States will have to fight Japan*

388

openly because it is already fighting Japan covertly. The US should, there-fore, get in as many licks as it can before formal hostilities begin. Above all, it must give China all the aircraft and men China needs.'

Harry Smythe replied with a grimace of grudging approval. Between admiration and indignation, Richard reflected on the skill with which Harry and Emily had manipulated him. Yes, his own Emily, to whom he had two weeks earlier pledged eternal devotion – meaning every word.

The bullying was done by the American, while Emily was always sympathetic and encouraging. That obvious variation on the tough cop and the friendly cop routine amused Richard.

He had been proud when Claire Chennault turned the controls of his personal Beechcraft over to Emily for the flight from Chungking to Kunming. True, he had been terrified when the light aircraft rolled down the sandspit airstrip in the middle of the Yangtze River to take off be-tween the overhanging cliffs. But that was just for a moment.

Harry Smythe was rather engaging in his role of bear-leader, but Richard was still irritated by his casual intimacy with Emily. Yet Smythe was happily preoccupied with his 'French teacher'. That reed-slender young Vietnamienne had travelled six hundred miles to Kunming on the rickety railway from Hanoi to collect debts owed her wine-merchant father. Her gifts of champagne and burgundy averaged five times the amount Smythe paid for her tuition. Their night-time sessions were not only satisfactory, but gratis.

Emily and Richard had explored Kunming with mutual delight in the three days since their arrival. The city on the lake was a remarkable blend of nineteenth-century France and medieval China. The narrow-gauge railway with the miniature locomotives, which Emily called 'Toonerville trolleys', symbolised French influence. Unoccupied China's only rail link to the world wound from the Gulf of Tonkin alongside the Red River and through mountain passes to Kunming. The ornate houseboats on Kunming Lake were in early October already deserted by the French families who took refuge on the temperate plateau from the brutal summer of the Red River Delta. Those French had, however, left their legacy: the ample wine and tinned *pâté de foie gras* in the shops, as well as the bakers who produced crusty *baguettes*. The beige roofs, jalousied windows, and jaunty balconies of French villas peeped through the peeling trunks of eucalyptus trees.

The streets where the pepper trees dropped their fragrant green pellets were, however, thronged with the small dark men of the mountain tribes wearing faded blue turbans and their women wearing beaded black aprons over knee-length skirts. Pack mules that had struggled over the Himalayan Mountains to the noisy market place with basic manufactured goods were loaded again with tin, salt and opium. Pony carts rattled across the cobblestones, their unlubricated wooden axles shrieking. Rickshaws with tinkling bells wove among water buffalos and sway-backed swine. From time to time, the 'peanut whistles' of the miniature locomotives shrilled a lament for distant Europe.

'Helluva place for a flying school!' Claire Chennault said lightly while they were finishing their breakfast coffee on the verandah. 'Right out of the Middle Ages. Wouldn't surprise me if Marco Polo's ghost turned up for flying lessons. That old Italian came right through Kunming I hear. It's just as far as we can get away from Jap bombers. Sometimes not quite far enough.'

When Chennault grinned, his seamed cheeks curved like supple old leather. His face was the swarthy mask of a Pawnee medicine man after years of weathering in open-cockpit pursuit planes. Yet he bowed to Emily with the courtly grace of his Louisiana French ancestors and offered her his arm.

The incongruous pair then disappeared into Chennault's office. He was heavy-set in US Army summer uniform without insignia. She was slim in the beige-silk blouse and the leaf-brown tailored trousers that were her uniform. Both wore the Chinese Air Force's gold wings with the white sun and both worked for Mayling Chiang. The Missimo, as the Americans called her, had sent her Executive Associate to placate Chennault, who was once again explosively discontented with the facilities allowed him to create a new Chinese Air Force.

Mayling had delightedly agreed to Richard Hollings's accompanying Emily. Publicity for her training programme was a welcome bonanza. Mayling had smiled impishly, unbending with Emily as she could with no one else, and added in her soft American accent: 'Now, dear, you're not to exhaust the gallant correspondent. Leave him some strength for his work. And, for pity's sake, listen very seriously to Claire. Pretend you take his threats seriously. But only I can accept his resignation – and I *never* will.'

Emily now appreciated that admonition. The man seated at the rattan-and-plywood desk before the aeronautical chart of South China was no longer the gallant gentleman who had found her an ashtray and matches before taking his own chair. His lips curved downwards; his slit eyes were almost closed; and his head drooped on his powerful neck in profound sadness.

'I'm afraid there's no other way!' His normally robust voice was reedy. '*This* time it's really too much for me, Madam Ou-yang. You see . . .'

'Emily was good enough five minutes ago,' she interrupted.

'Emily, then. It's a sorry thing to lay my worries on the shoulders of a beautiful young lady.'

'I'll bear up, Claire. I'm not all that young, you know.'

'To me, you are – always.' His sorrowful expression contrasted so sharply with his gallantries that Emily could not suppress a smile. 'But if you don't take me seriously . . .'

'I take you very seriously. All Chinese do.' Her emotion was sincere. 'We're all in your debt.'

'That makes it even harder, Emily.' He paused histrionically. 'You see, I've got to resign. I'll go hunting in the bayous again, but I'll be sad when I think of my friends in China. But Madame Chiang can surely find another broken-down old pursuit pilot to run this place.'

'May . . . ah . . . Madame Chiang gave me full powers except for one thing,' Emily broke in. 'I can meet any reasonable request, even unreasonable. But I can't accept your resignation. Only Madame Chiang can. And she's going to be very busy for the next three months. So you may as well soldier on – unless you're ready to desert.'

A reluctant smile creased his thin lips; his iodine-black eyes glittered; and his thick-set body twisted in its chair. Finally, Claire Chennault threw back his head and chortled.

'All right, honey, you win,' he conceded. 'But you've really got to do something about tyres. Otherwise I will have to close up shop. Stones on the runways are cutting up tyres something terrible.'

'We've got two gross in the pipeline, Claire. We do read your memos.'

'Another thing, Em honey.' His face darkened. 'I've had to wash out seventy percent of the new class. Find me men with *no* flight training, instead of these hopeless dodos who think they're hot pilots. And for God's sake find me better liaison officers. Not grafters and useless lazybones.'

'We can always shoot a few of the worst cases, Claire. Make an example . . .'

'What good does shooting do? Just find me better men – or else.'

'You'll resign again, Claire?' She smiled her sweetest. 'Give up flying.'

When he failed to respond, she pressed her advantage: 'Mayling told me about the hour you spent telling the Gimo exactly what was wrong with the Chinese Air Force. Chapter and verse, pointing out every dishonest, incompetent, or disloyal subordinate. And he said . . .'

'He knew everything I told him,' Chennault interjected. 'He knew even worse things about those men.'

'So you asked why he didn't get rid of lazy, corrupt, inefficient officers. Even shoot them!'

The seamed cheeks creased in a slow grin, and Claire Chennault recalled: 'He said the Chinese are the only people he's got to work with. If he got rid of everybody who was at fault, who'd be left?'

'So there you are,' she declared smugly. 'We've got to do the best . . .'

'The hell we do!' His palm slapped the desk. 'Not for the Air Force. We've got to get other people – preferably Americans.'

'What's wrong with Chinese pilots?'

'I hate to tell a Chinese lady, but you asked for it, Emily.' Chennault apologized obliquely. 'Chinese could make great pilots – if we had all the time in the world. But it would take years before even the best were fit for flight training. Your educated young men look down on working with their hands. First, we've got to give them a feeling for machinery – the love and respect American kids develop for jalopies before they're fourteen. If the war lasts long enough, we'll produce great Chinese aviators. But we need real pursuit pilots right now to turn back the Japanese tide.'

'I don't like it, Claire,' Emily admitted. 'In the long run, we've got to have a Chinese-manned Air Force. Even if we have to train ten-year-olds from scratch. But in the short run I guess you're right. We need American pilots, not just American planes.'

*

391

When Claire Chennault set out to be charming, there was no one more charming. The authoritarian manner that cowed his toughest sergeant-majors fell away, and the backwoodsman gave way to the courtier. When Emily and he re-joined Richard and Harry on the verandah, it soon became clear that Chennault also possessed a great talent for publicity.

Richard Hollings listened attentively. He had already concluded that public opinion was as important in the new geo-political warfare now being fought as were weapons, strategy, and courage. Heroes had always fought villains. Today, for the first time in the annals of mankind, the struggle between good and evil was reported to the entire world within minutes of battles being joined. Public relations could be even more important to a military commander than strategy.

Chennault was demonstrating his instinctive mastery of public relations. With Chinese finesse, he had not yet mentioned his chief concern: the necessity to oppose modern Japanese aircraft with modern American aircraft. Instead, he was reminiscing about the early days of the flying school in Kunming not so long ago.

'First two Curtis Hawk squadrons that landed here, more than half cracked up. I had to go right up to the Gimo to get authority to give every so-called pilot a basic flight test – and wash out the hopeless ones. . . . Luckily, they can find the field. Old Baldy over there's some land-mark. Of course, it guides the Japs too.'

He pointed at the hill range beyond the amethyst waters of Lake Kunming, where the houseboats danced. Landslides had ripped both soil and vegetation from the highest peak, leaving a rocky cliff that shone rust-red in the late morning sun.

'Long way from Nanking in '37, when we knocked all those bombers down, isn't it, son? The Japs are so arrogant they landed pursuit ships on Chengtu airport, which is 165 miles *west* of Chungking. The pilots scampered across the field and set fire to the planes on the ground. Other Japs circled and kept the ground defences pinned down. Helluva note, isn't it?'

Richard nodded and jotted down a few words.

'Also deliberate cruelty to civilians. The Jap bombers open their bomb-bay doors and make three or four passes over a city before letting go. To show who owns the air – and make the Chinese people feel resistance is plain futile.'

'No Chinese resistance at all, Colonel?'

'Well, son, you couldn't really call it resistance. Most of the good pilots are dead. And the rest . . .'

Emily looked pained, and Harry Smythe rolled his eyes upward at the thatching of the verandah. Emily bit her lower lip, released it, and reluct-antly nodded her head. Her train of thought could not have been more explicit: She hated Chennault's deprecating Chinese pilots, even though his harsh judgement proved the need for greater American assistance, which was what she wanted Richard to report.

'Hell, things are looking up,' Claire Chennault observed amiably. 'My boys can now take off and land every time. They're not splattering themselves over the landscape the way they did at Wuhan. The Chinese Air Force isn't committing mass suicide any more.'

Emily clenched her teeth, but did not protest aloud.

'I've studied the best Jap pursuit, the Nate,' Channault added. 'Even got hold of one. The Nate is one hell of a fighter: fast, sturdy, easy to maintain – and so manoeuvrable it scares the hell out of me. They've got another one coming along. Something called the Zero.'

The aviator looked suspiciously towards the east. He cocked his head as if his eardrums, although thickened by the roar of engines in open cockpits, had picked up vibrations inaudible to the others. Seeing nothing moving in the pale-blue sky above the hills except fleecy clouds, he resumed: 'The new P-40 *might* just match up to the Nate. I don't know about the Zero. Anyway, tactics are going to be as important as planes. You see . . .'

He looked up at the sky again and frowned. He squinted at the clouds and glanced uneasily towards the thatch-roofed operations shack.

'Something's up,' he said. 'I can't . . .'

A lanky Chinese lieutenant in rumpled suntans loped out of the operations shack. When he came into earshot, he reported: '*Ching-pao*, sir. Estimate forty-two bandits closing from the north-east. Estimate arrival in twenty-four minutes.'

'Both squadrons to scramble in exactly fifteen minutes,' Chennault commanded. 'Mr Adair and Mr Alison to command. They know their orders. Only remind them: total radio silence.'

The lieutenant sketched a breezy salute and trotted away. Chennault grinned, and observed: 'If they were all like young Lee, we'd practically have the war won. Incidentally, Mr Hollings, Adair and Alison are Chinese names today. My American instructors aren't supposed to fly combat. Now we're going to be taking a hell of a pasting in a half-hour.'

'The ambush you were planning, Claire?' Harry Smythe asked.

'Hope so. You can see the dummy planes on the field. With a little luck, we could have us a turkey shoot.'

'I've never heard of a reporter seeing an air battle from above,' Smythe observed. 'How does that strike you, Dick?'

Richard smiled at the preposterous thought. But Harry Smythe, the old Jenny pilot, was obviously eager to take him up.

'Fine with me, Harry.' Chennault was off-hand. 'I want *all* aircraft in the air, including trainers. Only dummies on the field.'

Richard forced himself to say cheerfully: 'I suppose we'd better get on our horses, Harry.'

'I'm not your pilot, Dick. I never checked out on those Fleet trainers.'

'Well, in that case . . .' Richard was disappointed – and relieved.

'I've got so many hours in that trainer,' Emily volunteered, 'I can fly it blindfold.'

Richard knew he could not reject her implied offer. Because she was so touchy about masculine condenscension, he could not even hesitate.

'Where's the aircraft, pilot?' He grinned. 'I'm ready any time you are.'

393

'You'd think somebody'd ask me, wouldn't you?' Claire Chennault addressed the thatch ceiling. 'I'm only the fellow running the show. Take Baker Oboe-3, Emily. She's the only trainer with a radio. Go up to 10,000 feet and stay there. Don't descend – or you'll get mixed up in the dogfight. And observe total radio silence. Not a peep out of you. Just listen!'

'The first time I ever kissed the pilot before a flight.'

Richard Hollings laughed into the intercom microphone and craned his head around to smile at Emily. Her face was very small within the oval opening of her leather flying helmet, diminished by the round goggles and the big earphones. She pursed her lips in a kiss.

'Love you, my darling!' she whispered into her microphone, then added after a pause: 'We'd better not chat, though. Might miss something on the radio.'

As the biplane spiralled towards 12,000 feet, the postage-stamp aerodrome lay green beneath them. In the front seat of the tandem cockpit the correspondent's view was obstructed by the lower wing, but he could sweep the horizon simply by swivelling his head.

Neither Emily nor Richard could acknowledge to the other a sudden desire to be back on the ground. He was afraid of implying any lack of confidence in her competence. Emily was determined to show herself a dauntless aviatrix.

When the trainer passed through the first sprinkling of cloud at 6,000 feet, both consciously relaxed their cramped neck and shoulder muscles. Despite the proven efficiency of the radio-linked ground warning network, they had both feared attack by the Japanese armada while climbing and exposed. The white-sun rondels on their wings looked like bull's eyes for Japanese machine-guns, and they were alone in the sky. The two squadrons of Hawk pursuit planes that had taken off just before them were invisible in the layers of cloud above 10,000 feet.

When the trainer levelled off in the lower fringe of those clouds, the cold pierced their borrowed flying suits. Although it seemed hours, Emily found when she pushed back her leather cuff to consult her minuscule gold wrist-watch that the time was 11:32. Seven minutes had passed since their take off and just nineteen minutes since the young lieutenant had reported the air-raid warning. If the estimate was accurate, the Japanese would be over the field in five minutes.

The Fleet trainer flew great circles through the fringes of the clouds. With a minute to spare, Emily pulled the joystick back, and the trainer climbed four hundred feet.

The clouds enveloped them like damp cotton-wool and trailed clammy tendrils across their faces. Richard swore at the cloud cover. If he could not see the action, the risk was criminally stupid. Before he could ask Emily to go lower, the clouds parted. Craning his head, he could just see the aerodrome among the patchwork fields. The rifts in the clouds continually opened and closed beneath him.

The roar of the trainer's air-cooled engine was hardly muffled by the close-fitting earphones under his flying helmet. He heard no sound, but felt the trainer vibrate to the resonance of many other engines. A multitude of black specks on the horizon rapidly resolved into a host of silvery shapes.

The sun flashing on their wings, the Japanese drew closer, implacable and apparently invulnerable. Forty-two twin-engined Mitsubishi bombers, heavy-bodied as killer whales, and twelve Nate pursuit planes as their pilot fish. The armada circled the field contemptuously, ignoring the smoke-puffs of the Chinese anti-aircraft fire.

Open bomb bay doors hanging slablike beneath their bellies, the Mitsubishis made a pass across the field. But no bombs fell. The twelve Nates circled protectively over the bombers. But no Chinese warplane was visible.

On the airfield a Curtis Hawk darted out of a concealed revetment and streaked frantically down the grass runway. With no pause for final checks, the pursuit hurtled into the air. The jinking of the wings in erratic flight showed that panic gripped the pilot. High above the Japanese aviators, Richard envisaged the derisive smiles on their faces when the cowardly Chinese fled at tree-top level.

That wild break for safety was Claire Chennault's final dramatic touch. The scenery was already in place. Imperfectly camouflaged Hawks were scattered among three Northrop bombers and a brand new DC-3 transport. Although he had seen them on the ground, Richard was almost deceived by the bamboo-and-fabric dummies with oil-soaked rags and firecrackers stuffed into the cockpits behind their cellophane windscreens.

The bombers drew into line-of-battle formation six abreast. Precise as if guided by wires, seven elements in succession thundered across the field. Bombs saturated the runway and the hangars. Smoke rolled over the grassy expanse, and ground explosions flared red and black.

Richard tensed against his shoulder harness in impotent anger. The cloud banks above the armada were unbroken. When would Chennault call the Chinese pursuit planes down upon the raiders?

When the wind whipped the smoke, Richard saw that most of the dummy aeroplanes were still intact. Several anti-aircraft cannon still hurled feeble defiance, and streams of tracers from machine-guns flared feebly against the brilliant noon sun.

The bombers swooped lower, maintaining their precise formation. They were evidently more concerned with the danger of mid-air collision than with the ground fire. The air-gunners methodically sprayed the field with copper-jacketed bullets. A dummy pursuit plane erupted into flame. Fire-crackers sparked like machine guns, and viscous black smoke mushroomed from the oil-soaked rags. On the other side of the field, two more dummy aircraft exploded.

The safety harness cutting into his shoulders made Richard aware that he was straining forward tensely. He wondered at the patience of the Chinese pilots, who were still circling above the clouds. How long could Claire Chennault wait?

Seeing no opposition in the air, the sharp-nosed Nates broke off their protective patrol and swooped down to strafe the field. As the Nates made their last run, the bombers assembled again into six Vs for the flight home. The pursuit escort climbed above them in a formation as rigid as a ceremonial fly-past.

'Now!' The single word crackled in Richard's ear-phones. 'Now, Tigers. Go get them! Good hunting!'

The blunt-nosed Curtis-Wright Hawks dived out of the clouds before that final 'Good hunting!' The monoplanes flashing past the trainer looked like models – from the pilots' anonymous leather-encased heads under the perspex canopies to the Nationalist white-sun rondels on their wings and the flaring spats of their fixed under-carriages. The two leading Hawks displayed three white stripes on their tail-planes. Behind their American instructors, whose contracts forbade combat flying, twenty-four stubby-winged warplanes of the Chinese Air Force swooped on the enemy in the three-plane echelons Chennault had taught his pilots always to maintain.

The Japanese were majestically droning eastward, unaware of the Hawks. Streaking past the astonished Nates, the Hawks did not fire their machine-guns until they were less than a hundred yards from the twin-engined bombers.

To Richard Hollings above the battle, it seemed only seconds before the Mitsubishis began to blow up. The Chinese three-plane echelons twisted through the debris of burning bombers and, clawing for height, soared into the eye of the sun.

Their wings flashing, five bombers fell from the sky. Two spiralled as they desperately tried to regain control. Three plunged straight into the ground, white smoke streaming from their tails. All but one exploded on impact. The fifth pilot managed by a near-miracle of airmanship to make a belly landing, and Richard saw black ants scurry away from the wreckage.

The clouds closed beneath the trainer, and the correspondent for the first time heard in his earphones the cries of Chinese pilots interspersed with terse commands in English. When the clouds parted, the Nates had turned against their tormentors. They were surprised, outnumbered – and regretting the ammunition and fuel they had expended in attacking the ground targets. Three Nates abruptly broke eastwards and fled.

The remaining nine evidently had just enough fuel to meet the Chinese head on. Three Hawks fluttered towards the ground, their white-sun rondels stark as skulls in the noon light. Then the Japanese broke out of their loose formation in a challenge to individual combat – and the three-plane echelons chewed them up. Five Nates fell, spinning so rapidly the sun insignia on their wings were blood-red blurs.

Their exhausts flaring blue against the sunlight, the remaining four Nates followed the retreating bombers they had failed to protect. The Hawks still chewed at the bombers' formation. Abruptly the chase broke off. Chennault's recall echoing in their earphones, the exhilarated pilots hurled their aircraft into victory rolls over the smoking airfield.

The Fleet trainer still circled, and Richard tried to count the fallen. He made it roughly nineteen Mitsubishi bombers in addition to the five Nates and the three Hawks he had himself seen fall. Emily looked at her watch. The time was 11:46, just thirteen minutes since the Japanese armada had appeared on the north-eastern horizon.

Richard spoke into his microphone: 'Congratulations! It's a splendid victory!'

'They'll have more confidence now,' Emily replied shortly. 'Our boys.'

Her voice was flat – quite devoid of elation. He twisted in his seat to look at her. Behind the concealing goggles, Emily's face was contorted as if she were weeping.

42

November 26, 1939

The rickshaw-coolie's vein-knotted legs were bare in the dank chill of late November, when even beggars cocooned themselves in layers of filthy garments. The coolie's feet were blue-white from the cold in rubber-soled thong-sandals made from old tyres. His footfalls threw up puffs of white from the overnight snowfall. In the ten blocks from Kiukiang Road, Julia had with macabre fascination counted forty-six distorted corpses under that thin white blanket. Shanghai had not, she realized, lost its primeval power to surprise her – and occasionally revolt her.

She disliked rickshaws, but this one was necessary. Her reception by the students and the faculty of Kai Ming College would not be improved by her arriving in the Lincoln Continental Convertible that was her husband's latest toy.

Since the defection of his mentor Chang Kuo-tao, Tommy's ardour for the cause had diminished perceptibly. He still loyally served the Apparatus. But he had major reservations about the policies of the Communist Party.

The coolie's rubber-tread soles braked the rickshaw before a monstrously large brown-brick mansion. The four stories visible above the surrounding brick wall were plastered with yard-high ideograms declaring it severally: a university, a middle school, a kindergarten, a clinic, and an orphanage. Julia had heard that fifty universities, two hundred middle schools, and a thousand primary schools were now operating in the Settlement and Frenchtown. Refugees had nearly doubled the concessions' population. Joshua Haleevie estimated that more than three million human beings were now crammed into eleven square miles.

Marvelling at the number who must live in that one building, Julia absently counted out seven Mex, about two dollars American. The coolie instinctively lifted his hand to tug at her sleeve. Subduing that impulse, he stuffed the coins into his waistband and fled. The tail of the yellow rickshaw flicked around the corner as if pursued by ten thousand ghosts.

His train of thought was obvious. If the vast overpayment was a foolish mistake, she must be so wealthy she would never miss the money. If it was conscience-money, it would be no kindness to return it.

An arrow under the Y of the front stairs directed: 'President's Office'. Passing the iron-grilled half-windows of the basement, Julia idly counted twenty-four full windows in each of the five storeys of the left wing. The mansion must possess more than sixty bedrooms – and a dozen reception rooms. She was glad of her utilitarian wartime garb: a padded jacket, dark woollen slacks, comfortable low heels, and a bright-yellow oilskin rain-hat. The damp would have penetrated every cranny of the old-fashioned pile. Central heating – or more than two bathrooms for sixty-odd bedrooms – would be spendthrift luxury.

Central heating and bathrooms were not seen. Money spent on display, most Shanghai bourgeoisie believed fervently, was never wasted. Ostentation attracted business by showing how good business was. But unobtrusive comforts squandered money. Since they obviously revealed a reckless self-indulgence, such comforts drove customers away.

She had heard that theory from her husband some time ago. The witty, high-spirited Tommy she married had laughed loudest at the foibles of his countrymen and smiled at the foibles of foreigners. Nowadays, he sneered at foreigners and lamented the illogical ways of his countrymen. The war had made him so Chinese she could no longer anticipate his reactions. When she might have expected him to laugh, he was grave; when she might have expected concern, he laughed bitterly.

Their quarrel about her teaching at Kai Ming College showed how volatile he was. Once worried that she might be bored, he had volubly encouraged her to work – in addition, of course, to executing missions for the Apparatus. Yet he had exploded when she told him she was going back to teaching. He had insisted she was imperilling their cover because the college president, a former student of Julia's at Shanghai Labour University, was a camouflaged Communist activist on the educational battlefront.

Tommy had become too accustomed to finding her at home whenever his erratic professional schedule allowed him a moment of leisure. Unlike the frivolous Chinese wives he evidently admired nowadays, she could not devote her days to gossip, mah jong, beauty parlours, and entertaining. She had finally decided she must look after her own needs, since she could not understand his new needs.

Guided by the signs, Julia entered a small door and climbed a broad staircase with a dust-furred banister. She smiled when she came to the first floor. The high ceilings and the ornate plaster mouldings were all for display. So were the enormous bedrooms visible through open doors – with their three-colour marble fireplaces, their gilt mirrors, and their ornamental gas-jets.

On the first floor, she abruptly found herself in a jam-packed tenement. The corridor was littered with the paraphernalia of domesticity. Pots, pans, kettles, and tureens were strewn around terra cotta braziers. Bundles of kindling lay beside heaps of vegetables; tubs of washing nudged chamber-pots; and two sandalwood coffins leaned against the wall. Blue nappies were drying on lines that made a giant cat's cradle with lines from which salt fish and dried vegetables hung. Through half-open doors Julia heard the manic clatter of mah jong tiles and the ritual cries of men playing and betting.

Women froze over corrugated wooden washboards to stare at the foreign woman with the jaunty yellow rain-hat. Babies gaped – babies snug in baskets, babies slung on their mothers' backs, and babies fighting pet dogs for scraps. Young boys and girls looked up from the slates on which they were painstakingly inscribing ideograms. Two elderly men playing Chinese chess disdained to lift their eyes, but their liver-spotted hands were motionless. There were only two young men. Shifting sacks of coal, they stood for an instant as still as a statue symbolizing virtuous labour.

In the president's office, on the second floor, Julia stepped into a familiar world of ordered activity. Scrolls hung on the lime-green walls; plants blossomed in the south-facing windows; and filing cabinets were marshalled around the doors.

A neat woman in a padded rust *cheongsam* looked up from her desk at Julia's entrance. Her smile squeezed her eyes to slits behind her gold-rimmed glasses.

'Mrs Howe? I'm very sorry! The president was called away suddenly. He hopes you'll go ahead with your class.'

Julia accepted a cup of tea and glanced at her white-gold wrist-watch.

'It's not till one,' the secretary said. 'The president thought you might need time to think.'

Yellow light radiated from the big brass doorknob, which was turning slowly. The door opened to reveal a short man in a grey padded long-gown. His features were obscured by the brim of his black fedora, and he dragged his left leg. Julia had an impression of enormous eyes in a triangular face before he turned abruptly and slipped out of the office.

If he came from the Apparatus, his fear at seeing her foreign face was easily understandable. Although safer in the concessions than anywhere else outside their own rural bases, Communists were still persecuted by the foreign police. The secretary did not comment on the man's fleeting appearance, and Julia knew better than to question her.

However, she had a nagging feeling of familiarity. Had those large eyes flickered in fleeting recognition? The set of the shoulders was also hauntingly familiar. He was, she realized with a cold thrill, rather like Little Pow. But Little Pow had been dead for more than a decade. If he were alive, he would certainly have been in touch with Tommy and herself.

In the classroom, the smell of chalk-dust recalled her salad days at Shanghai Labour University, as did the paraffin whiff of the heater

Julia suspected was a concession to her foreign frailty. The big black-board on the wall stood ready for the maze-like diagrams illustrating the complexities of English grammar that the literal minded Chinese students loved to study.

Julia realized how much she had missed the interchanges with eager young minds. The Apparatus had instructed her to play the corrupt social butterfly, but she had never felt completely comfortable in that role. She was delighted that the Apparatus now permitted her to teach again.

But a new class was taxing. All that potential still unplumbed! She therefore decided to explore the class's ability through a dictation exercise followed by discussion. She had translated a passage from the Communist *New China Daily*, which was published in Nationalist Chungking by virtue of the United Front against Japan.

'Certain divisive tendencies have recently become apparent within the Nationalist-Communist United Front for the anti-Japanese War of Resistance,' she read aloud slowly. 'Wild Nationalist elements have repeatedly attacked elements of the New Fourth Army, the guerrilla forces in enemy-occupied areas. A particularly vicious attack was launched by infantry and special secret agents on November 11, 1939. More than 200 were wounded and their dependents brutally slaughtered. . . .'

Julia's mind strayed. Actually, the wave of fighting had begun a year earlier, when Communist units attacked a Nationalist regiment and disarmed and dispersed it. Although the Communist Party explained that the Nationalist regiment was secretly collaborating with the Japanese, the politically unsophisticated found it hard to understand why the Eighth Route Army had struck first. Since then, clashes had usually been initiated by the alert Communist guerrillas to forestall attacks. Occasionally, however, the treacherous Nationalists had struck first.

After a flurry of questions, the class earnestly corrected its transcriptions. Lulled by the warmth of the paraffin heater, Julia almost dozed off watching the jet-black heads bent over their work.

The sliding doors dividing the improvised classroom from its neighbour stood open an inch or two. An assured female voice was addressing the neighbouring class. Although Julia could not make out the words, she heard bursts of English interspersed with passages in a foreign language that was, at once, guttural and melodious.

Dismissing that minor mystery, Julia began the class discussion. Pretty Miss Lee, who spoke English best, obviously came from a well-to-do family. Her hair was permanent-waved, and her long nails glistened pearly pink. Her shaggy camel's-hair coat with a mink collar was spread on her chair to show off her saucy figure in an opulent orange-silk *cheong-sam*. Her flimsy pumps and sheer silk stockings displayed her neat ankles.

Julia's frivolous side warmed to the vain Miss Lee. Yet she was not amused when the young woman declared tartly that she had understood every word of the dictation, but not its logic.

'It doesn't make sense, Mrs Howe,' she insisted. 'If the Communists started the fighting, it must be their fault.'

A rather plain Miss Chang replied: 'You've got every right to protect yourself if you know I'm planning to steal from you. If you don't, you're helping me commit a crime. There's an English expression . . .'

'Compounding a felony,' the delighted Julia supplied.

'Thank you, Mrs Howe,' Miss Chang continued smoothly. 'You are compounding a felony. So, you see, it is your own duty to stand up to me. Even using force to stop me stealing . . .'

'What are the police for?' Miss Lee asked.

'But no police are higher than the political parties . . .' a young man vouchsafed. 'Who would stop this crime if Eighth Route Army is not doing so?'

Pleased with the homely analogy about stopping a thief, Julia beamed on Miss Chang, who was in every respect the opposite of the coiffed, curled, and cosseted Miss Lee. Her hair was plaited in two plump braids tied with red ribbons, and she wore a padded blue cotton long-gown on top of a second long-gown. She also wore a bulky cardigan, thick lisle stockings, and bedroom slippers with pink pom-poms. Against the chill of the old mansion she clutched a blue-rubber hot-water-bottle wrapped in a scarlet kerchief.

The reactionary Miss Lee was undeniably more attractive than the roly-poly rag-doll with the flat unpainted face who was the progressive Miss Chang. Julia reproached herself. Not only Tommy, but she herself was still tainted by bourgeois values.

Leaving the classroom, Julia saw another woman who was even less concerned with wartime austerity than the self obsessed Miss Lee. She was quite tall, her blue-black hair was caught in a chignon, and she wore a tailored suit of stiff canary-yellow tribute silk. The jacket flared over her hips, while the tight skirt was tapered to some three inches below her knees. The seams of her gossamer silk stockings and her canary-yellow silk pumps emphasized her sleek calves and moulded ankles. Flung negligently over her arm was a sable coat with a midnight lustre.

The fashion plate turned, and Julia smiled at her own obtuseness. Only Elizaveta Alexandrovna Yavalenka was endowed with the height, the wealth, and the daring to wear that extravagant costume. She had obviously been teaching Russian, the mysterious language on the other side of the sliding-doors.

'Julie, darling, I've been waiting for ages.' Elizaveta impulsively embraced her. 'Do you want a ride or is the dashing Tommy picking you up?'

The light snowfall that swirled on the streets in the morning had melted by late afternoon, and the dead bodies that defiled the streets in the morning had been carted to a common grave by the Corpse Collection Service. The shadows of the early dusk created caves of darkness at the foot of the walls along Jessfield Road, and Julia's quick imagination tenanted them with men and women suffering torture, disease, and starvation. She still loved Shanghai deeply. But she now loved it for the suffering it endured, rather than its spurious glamour.

Heads turned when the black Hispano-Suiza that Elizaveta candidly loved for its ostentation rolled slowly east after turning on to Bubbling Well Road. The twenty-two-foot limousine with the enormous headlights and the sweeping mudguards was conspicuous even in a city where the ageing Donald Howe still painted his Rolls Royce emerald green.

Having that morning endured the physical and psychological discomfort of a ricksaw to no purpose, Julia settled with a sigh into the most luxurious automobile in the Settlement. She ran her fingertips over the glove-leather upholstery. She was dedicated, she told herself wryly, but she was not a fanatic who hated comfort.

'You never expected to see *me* at Kai Ming College, did you?' Elizaveta demanded complacently. 'It's a long way from Kiangse Road!'

'Liz, dear, you'll never lose your ability to surprise me.' Julia was mildly sarcastic. 'Particularly by being virtuous.'

'It's all Joshua's idea. He decided in his own clever way that I was in danger of becoming boring – worse, boring myself. He also decided that only good deeds could save me, and the orphanage alone wouldn't do the trick. So I volunteered to teach a little Russian and a little English. My students are ragged, but not as mucky as the babies.'

Julia chuckled at the absurdity of her old friend's protestations and observed lightly: 'Liz, honey, you're getting just like Joshua. You two'll never convince me you do good deeds only for selfish reasons. By the way, how is he? It's been ages since I saw him.'

'He hasn't come back to me – not entirely. But he spends a lot more time with me now.'

'I asked about Josh, not you, darling.' Julia wondered why she was being so persistently – if lightly – malicious. 'Well, I suppose it comes to much the same thing. How does he manage with Charlotte, if it's all right to ask?'

'All right to ask? I'd be astonished if you didn't, my dear Julie.' Elizaveta repaid her with the same light malice. 'He apparently manages by telling the truth when his ... that woman ... is in town. That, fortunately, isn't very often. Russian peasants revolted against absentee landlords which my family never were. And Joshua has revolted against an absentee wife.'

'Whom he drove away in the first place, Liz. But let's not argue. Since you're in a confiding mood, tell me why you would never marry Joshua. For a time, we all hoped . . .'

'It wouldn't have worked, Julie. He's not ... I'm not ... the sort for formal obligations. This way, he'll cling to me. Joshua's like me. He gets bored very easily. The worst thing would've been children, though sometimes I've longed . . .'

Julia made an understanding noise.

'But any child of ours would have been a mess. Joshua's fits of depression – almost melancholia. And my black moods, my Slavic gloom. What a heritage for an innocent baby! He's worse now, you know.'

'Oh?'

'He loves the Settlement, the ideal of government by all nationalities. I think he loves it even more than he loves me. Without the Settlement, he's just another stateless Jew – though a wealthy, charming and able one. But the last few months he's just about despaired.'

'Why now in particular?'

'Alcibiades, Julie, the wretched man Dick Hollings nicknamed Alcibiades long ago. That miserable diabetic who's so handsome and so talented. Alcibiades, who's been the Gimo's chief rival from the beginning.'

'Sure as God made little green apples, Alcibiades'll be formally heading up a Jap puppet government in a couple of months,' Julie agreed. 'He's already got the job without the title. But everybody knows he's a has-been.'

'Darling Julie, everybody knows Alcibiades is a has-been – except those who matter: the Japanese and all those Chinese who want a quiet life at any price.'

'You're a chameleon, Liz. Not so long ago you were rooting for the Japs against the Bolsheviks. Then General Zhukov whips the Japs – and, suddenly, you're a Russian patriot. Now, you sound as if you hate the Japs. Bit of quick-change artist, aren't you?'

'I have had to be in my . . . ah . . . profession, darling.' Elizaveta's face was a white oval in the dim interior of the Hispano-Suiza. 'But we were talking about Joshua.'

'Sorry, Liz.'

'Just look at the international city he loves so. Not far from Kai Ming College, Alcibiades has his little Cheka headquarters. You've heard what goes on at number 76 Jessfield Road. Kidnapping, torture, extortion, murder. *Anything* you can imagine. Anything to break the will of Chinese patriots who want to hold out against the Japs. To force them to join Alcibiades – and the Japs. The Model Settlement's become a nest of stinging vipers – all under the cloak of extra-territoriality.'

'Also the Fascists, like that Italian with the dagger,' Julia mused. 'And the disgusting Nazis. The German-Jewish refugees thought they were safe here. But they're intimidated, slandered, and beaten up. Shanghai's now the centre for Nazi propaganda and espionage throughout the Orient. Shanghai's becoming a cesspool! I know just how Joshua feels.'

'I'm not sure you do, Julie.' Elizaveta was mortally earnest. 'None of us can know just what it's like for Joshua. His wonderful city dying – already rotting. . . . But what's all the fuss?'

Julia stared at the crowd that virtually blocked the intersection leading to the Laoza Police Station where the May 30th Incident had occurred in 1925. Despite the protests of her White Russian bodyguard, Elizaveta ordered the chauffeur to stop. Impelled by curiosity as well as her new commitment to civic responsibility, she was determined to learn why tens of pedestrians were staring at the cast-iron lamp-post that lit the intersection.

The two women plunged into the crowd behind the uniformed bodyguard, who flourished a long rubber-jacketed torch that was a formidable weapon. Julia saw a Chinese man lying on the kerb on the edge of the cone of light cast by the lamp-post. His chubby cheeks and brilliantined hair showed that he was no street vagabond.

The bodyguard shone his torch on the man – and a gasp of disbelief rose from the crowd. Julia's fingernails dug into Elizaveta's palm. The man's head, neatly cut off at the neck, was propped against the lamp-post. Blood was still trickling onto the kerbstone from the severed stump of the neck.

'Look!' a woman exclaimed in broad Shanghainese. 'Head just cut! Look! See drops of sweat on forehead.'

Julia forced her unwilling feet forward step by step. She could not just stand and gape. She noticed a number of foreign men and women in evening dress who had joined the crowd as if the atrocity were a diversion staged for their amusement. Her neck rigid with strain, she forced herself to look at the grisly sight. Suddenly she started in greater horror. She realized that she knew the young Chinese who had been killed on the spot only a few minutes earlier. He was a reporter and occasional columnist for the respected Shanghai *Shun Pao*, the oldest newspaper in China. Recoiling from his paralyzed grimace, her eyes moved to the crude ideograms on the yellow paper pasted to the lamp-post.

Warning to all editors [the message was headed]. *This just punishment, meted out by angry patriots, will befall all who sabotage the formation of the government that will make honourable terms with the Japanese Empire and restore peace and prosperity. This man was a traitor to China and a lackey of the war-mongering usurper government of Chiang Kai-shek. He dared write against the salvation of the country. Be warned by his fate!*

43

Richard Hollings had feared a cool reception by the volatile and imperious Chou En-lai, who was deputy minister of the all-powerful
National Military Council in Chungking. Richard feared that his close
association with the Nationalists through Emily would not please the
man who ranked highest among the many Communists who held offices
in the Central Government. But he was, on the contrary, greeted like a
long-absent disciple when he attended Chou En-lai's weekly tea party for
the foreign press in early December of 1939. Beaming good will, the
Communist chieftain trotted out his make-shift English to recall in fond
detail their brief meetings in Yenan.

'When,' he asked jocularly, 'will the Generalissimo allow you to return?
We are very pleased to greet you, always.'

'Any time you wish, Minister,' Richard replied. 'I'm longing to see my
good friends. That is ... I hope we're still good friends.'

'Dear Dickie, we are such great friends,' Chou En-lai affirmed. 'Very
good friends! Chairman Mao sends his chin-chins.'

Richard was bemused by a vision of the sometimes amiable – but
always autocratic – Chairman of the Central Executive Committee of
the Chinese Communist Party smiling coyly and wiggling his fingers in
greeting like a decadent Westernized dandy in Frenchtown. Anyone less
likely to send chin-chins than Mao Tse-tung it was hard to imagine,
unless, perhaps, Chiang Kai-shek. Richard was, of course, delighted to
learn that he again stood well with peremptory Chairman Mao. Their
last conversation had ended with a veiled warning not to reveal that Soviet
planes landed at Yenan – in violation of agreements between Chiang
Kai-shek and Joseph Stalin. Although he had naturally not done so, he

remembered Mao Tse-tung with some trepidation.

'Please present my respects to the Chairman.' The correspondent calculated his indiscretion to a millimetre: 'I'm delighted by your welcome, but a little surprised. Candidly, I was afraid you'd think I was in the Generalissimo's pocket.'

'Because of the charming Madame Ou-yang?' Chou En-lai reverted smoothly to the services of his Cambridge-educated interpreter. 'My dear chap, that's your affair, isn't it? We Communists don't apply outmoded bourgeois moral standards to the relationships between men and women. As Engels pointed out, marriage is no more than a bougeois contract to preserve private property. And property is theft!'

'You're refreshingly straightforward as always, Minister.'

'If that's my reputation,' Chou En-laid laughed, 'I might as well live up to it.'

Grasping the correspondent's elbow with affection, the Communist led him towards a window niche. They circled the huddle of newspapermen, most of whom were drinking scotch rather than tea.

'We like your candour and your accuracy,' Chou En-lai declared. 'If we had written your book, we could have avoided some errors. We would also have omitted some criticism. And that might have been a mistake. But, all in all, we're well pleased by *Red Star and Yellow Earth*.'

Delighted by that fulsome praise, Richard, none the less, asked: 'You've seen it? You know I haven't seen the book myself. . . . *Red Star and Yellow Earth*? That must be a mistake. The title is *White Sun, Red Star, and Yellow Earth*.'

'I haven't seen the book, Dickie,' Chou En-lai twinkled. 'But I have seen a fifty-page summary. Most detailed. I assure you it's called *Red Star and Yellow Earth*. Obviously a better title – and very prescient. Though it could get you into trouble with the Nationalists.'

'What can they do to a correspondent for American papers they haven't already done?' Richard shrugged off that concern. 'They can only be a little more obstructive!' He paused and added: 'Actually I like the title better. More punch! But they might have told me.'

'I *am* telling you, Dickie. I'm also telling you we won't hold your gravest error against you. Old Mao was quite annoyed, but I talked him round.'

'What's that?'

'We told you over and over again that we were Communists, true Marxist-Leninists. Yet . . .'

'I said almost as much in the book.'

'But not quite. You almost convinced *me* that we're not Marxist-Leninists at all.' From anyone less authoritative, Chou En-lai's laugh would have been a giggle. 'So it appears that we are agrarian reformers. At worst Socialists, good hearted Social Democrats. Mao was livid at the insult. He felt you'd accused him of bourgeois sentimentality . . . lack of revolutionary ruthlessness. But he finally agreed that, for the time being, that is just the image we require. I tell you this off the record.'

'I appreciate your candour, Minister. It does sound as if someone did a lot of editing behind my back.'

'Not to worry, old chap,' Chou En-lai declared. 'I can assure you that your editor in New York hardly touched a word. All your own work, I'm pleased to report.'

When Gregory Hardin approached, Richard Hollings thanked his host and left the party. He was puzzled by Chou En-lai's enthusiastic reception of the book. He was convinced that his reportage had been even-handed – by no means a hymn of praise to the Communist regime.

Waiting for a rickshaw, he was struck by an explanation of a puzzling incident. Two days earlier he had encountered Tommy Howe's old friend Chang Kuo-tao entering the compound of the Ministry of Information. The commanding figure with whom he spent so many hours in the cave beneath the nine-tiered pagoda of Yenan had ignored his outstretched hand and looked through him. The renegade must have had access to the report on *Red Star and Yellow Earth* – and must now hate its author for failing to trumpet his personal grievances and his malicious allegations against Chairman Mao Tse-tung.

That omission had proved wise. Former Chairman Chang Kuo-tao of the Border Region Government was no longer even a minor star in the constellation of power. The star of Chairman Mao Tse-tung, however, now shone almost as bright as the white sun of Chiang Kai-shek, which it might in time eclipse.

Richard wondered how Chang Kuo-tao could have seen the confidential summary Chou En-lai cited. But all things were possible in Chungking, even amicable private communication between former intimates who denounced each other poisonously in public.

Could Emily, too, have learned the gist of the report? Again, anything was possible, though, in this case, most unlikely. He could, of course, easily explain the awkward business of the altered title. She, too, knew at first hand the caprices of editors and publishers.

Chungking was a backwater a thousand miles up the meandering Yangtze River from Shanghai. It was, however, closer to the inactive battlefronts. As 1939 drew towards its close, retreating Chinese armies had worn down the Japanese to impose a near-stalemate. Both the Nationalists and the Communists were more interested in fighting each other. Chungking was none the less the capital of a nominally united Republic of China, where not only Chou En-lai, but the Christian General and other warlords worked in ostensible amity with the Generalissimo. Yet Chungking remained a backwater. Great events were occurring elsewhere, chiefly in Europe. By December of 1939 the Nazis had crushed Polish resistance, and the Soviets had reoccupied eastern Poland, which had once belonged to the Czars.

At the Ikra on Kiangse Road, Elizaveta Alexandrovna Yavalenka celebrated 'the restoration of the sacred soil of the Russian Motherland' despite her lover Joshua's derision. In the six-storey house on Kiukiang

Road, Julia Howe rejoiced at 'the strengthening of the workers' fatherland, the heartland of peace and democracy', despite her husband Tommy's scepticism.

At the Press Hostel in Chungking, Richard Hollings restively checked his pigeon-hole for messages. The world's attention was still focused on Europe, although that war had also settled down to a stalemate. Hardly twenty shots a day were fired on the entire Western Front. Bombers of both sides dropped leaflets appealing to the enemy to come to his senses and call off the war. As the first Christmas of World War II approached, a Paris seething with gaiety called it *une drôle de guerre*, a joke of a war. Neutral Americans read about the 'phoney war'. The little attention they could spare from their own affairs was directed primarily towards Europe.

Richard was, therefore, anxious to move on to the big story in Europe, where he could raise higher the edifice of his new fame. He was no longer a mere foreign correspondent, but an authority on world affairs – or would be just as soon as *Red Star and Yellow Earth* was published in mid-February of 1940. Since it would be just as well for him not to be in Chungking when *Red Star* came out, he decided to leave immediately after New Year.

Since Emily cherished her memories of their New Year's Eves together in Shanghai, he had promised they would celebrate the advent of 1940 with all the gaiety Chungking could offer. Although he had not yet told her he was leaving, she must know he could not linger in a backwater like Chungking while the world awaited his despatches from other fronts. He could wangle a seat to Calcutta on a China National Airways Corporation flight, though he would prefer Hong Kong. The night flight to the Crown Colony over territory tenuously occupied by the Japanese was not as hazardous as the white-fanged Himalayas, which pilots familiarly called the Hump.

Eager for his tryst with fame elsewhere, Richard realized that he was reluctant to leave Chungking. Having persuaded his joint-employers that he should go, he did not want to go. He hated to leave China, above all because he hated to leave Emily. Although she had once accused him of professional irresponsibility, the past was past. As soon as he could get back to England, he would set in motion his divorce from Fiona so that Emily and he could marry. The sooner he left, the sooner he could return a free man. But he could not in honour formally ask her to marry him until he was free.

With some surprise, Richard realized that he was also greatly attached to China. His material ties were as minimal in Chungking as they had been in Shanghai, and he had often derided the great affection old hands felt for China. But China was to himself no longer just a fascinating political and social laboratory – and a springboard to fame.

Sensitive to the English language despite almost two decades of journalism, Richard shuddered at that mixed metaphor. His immediate concern was, however, Emily's reaction to *Red Star*. She had obviously not yet learned of the new title or seen any summary of the contents. She was too straightforward – and too volatile – to remain silent if she had. Actually, she had not said another word about the book after extracting his promise to give her the first copy he received. He would cross that bridge when he came to it.

The pert youth who distributed the messages in the Press Hostel grinned at the correspondent's contemplative posture. One hand rested on the ledge of his pigeon-hole, and the other was tucked into the pocket of his well worn navy-blue blazer. It was, thank Heaven, a warm December, though raincoats were universal. But no dogs barked, and no bombers flew above the clouds that obscured the sky.

The messenger tugged at his sleeve and pressed the familiar blue-and-white envelope of the Chinese Government Radio Administration into his hand. Opening the cablegram, he read, first with dismay, then with elation: NATBROCAST CONCURS ADVISABLE YOU REMAIN CHINA TILL MARCH STOP TERRIFIC JOINT EUROPEAN ASSIGNMENT THEN AVAILABLE BEST REGARDS DAVIDSON GLOBE

He wanted to tell Emily of the reprieve immediately. But she did not like his ringing when she was with Mayling. In any event, the telephones were again out. But he had to tell someone. Jimmy Wei's assertively American accent rang from the dining room. Rearranging his features into his customary expression of mildly sardonic amusement, Richard sauntered into the small room.

A number of correspondents, attired as always like vagabonds, were gathered around the irrepressible Jimmy. Amid their derisive and occasionally obscene remarks, he stood unperturbed and natty in a pin-striped blue suit. He held aloft one of the under-sized, thin-shelled eggs produced by Chungking's long-legged, scabrous-yellow hens, which were starved of calcium.

'You'll never do it, Jimmy,' a Dutch photographer jeered.

'Impossible, my good chap,' contributed Reuter's correspondent, a Chinese who was fearfully Anglicized. 'No matter what you say.'

'My dear old chap,' Jimmy addressed Reuter's man in an impossibly plummy accent. 'The day before the winter solstice is the only time it's sure – and that's tomorrow. But we can give it a go today. Pity, old chap, that you don't know our ancient Chinese lore.'

Jimmy Wei was in full cry that afternoon, obviously inspired by the foul gin labelled 'Chungking D'. That meant 'Chungking Death', the correspondents insisted, although the distillers said it was for 'Chungking Double Strength'. Yet he managed to be assertive without being offensive. Even the snubbed Reuter's correspondent was grinning.

'Tomorrow for sure. The two days after probably. But let's give it a fling today. Any more bets say the egg won't stand on its small end? Step up, gents, and be relieved of your dough. Contributions to the James Wei emergency fund are always welcome!'

The offer was accepted by a visiting Dutch photographer and an Irishman noted for his constantly shifting journalistic affiliations and his constant thirst. The others knew Jimmy too well.

'All right then, men and boys, here we go!'

410

Jimmy closed his eyes, held the egg lightly between the extended fingers of both hands, and intoned a cabalistic formula he had confided was 'a Han Dynasty incantation unused for eighteen centuries'. Still murmuring that incantation, he balanced the egg on the fingertips of his right hand, flipped it over, and placed it on a table.

The pathetically small egg wobbled for a second or two. It teetered and almost fell over, but miraculously recovered. After ten or twelve seconds of tension, the egg righted itself decisively and stood firmly on its small end, trembling slightly.

The correspondents held their breath for a full quarter of a minute. Then someone applauded, and others joined him. The Irishman protested: 'Fraud!' But he was silenced by scornful stares. And the egg stood complacently on the table.

'Fifty dollars says you can't do it again with *my* egg,' the Dutchman proposed.

Banging on the table, he demanded two dozen fresh eggs, which the lean head waiter produced with surprising alacrity. With at least the care he would lavish on buying a diamond, the Dutchman selected the largest of the runt eggs. He presented it to Jimmy Wei with a complacent smile and purred: 'Now you'll see. I've nipped this fraud – in the egg, so as to say!'

Jimmy was nonplussed. His dark money-face frowned, and he shrugged elaborately. Finally he held the egg to his ear and listened intently. His expression brightened, and he said: 'I think this one's the real McCoy too.'

The Han Dynasty incantation was even more protracted, and the transfer from fingertips to fingertips was even more precarious. With a flourish, Jimmy placed the second egg on the bar, where it stood upright beside the first, hardly trembling at all.

'Any more takers?' Jimmy purred.

'Wait till I get my box,' the Dutch photographer demanded. 'Damned odd this business. Worth a picture, I think.'

The next hour passed in the most innocent entertainment the Press Hostel had ever seen. Jimmy Wei stood eggs on tables, on chairs, on stairs, counters, and shelves. Driven outside by the photographers' need for better light, he just as deftly stood eggs on the verandah, the paving stones around the banana plants, and, briefly, the hostel manager's bald spot.

Finally tiring, Jimmy declared a recess for a shot of Chungking Death and a cigarette. He drew the Reuter's correspondent aside, declaring grandiloquently: 'Only a Chinese can perform this wonderful feat. It's a clear demonstration of Chinese superiority.'

After smashing five eggs, the Reuter's correspondent attained harmony with the spirits of the land and stood ten on their ends. Finally, seventy-eight eggs were standing on their small ends in defiance of Newtonian physics. The hostel manager then instructed his waiters to recover tomorrow's breakfast.

'All in ca ... ca ... cahoots!' the Irishman protested. 'They'll not be letting us have a look at them eggs.'

411

Despite such scepticism, which Jimmy disdained to refute, the great egg stand became a major story abroad. Jaded correspondents and photographers were delighted after months of cables advising 'briefest coverage'. *Life* magazine's Christmas issue featured a full-page picture of a diabolically grinning Jimmy Wei surrounded by a gross of vertical eggs.

Even Richard Hollings, who felt he was not paid to cover such frivolous – and probably fraudulent – nonsense, was dragooned by peremptory cables from NBC. Throwing himself into the assignment with good humour, he produced an extremely funny seven-minute broadcast, which strayed in mock scholarship from the Han Dynasty incantation and Jimmy Wei's flamboyant personality to the alteration of the force of gravity in Szechwan at the winter solstice.

Although most correspondents wanted a neat end to the story, Jimmy refused to acknowledge – much less reveal – any trick. He would only repeat: 'Ancient Chinese wisdom, gentlemen. Not comprehensible by barbarians. Also the China story of the year!'

Jimmy was absolutely right about what the public wanted. Richard, who did not like covering trivial stories, was chastened. Jolly nonsense like the great standing egg miracle was intended for young and light-minded reporters. He was past forty and firmly established in his profession. In an advance review of *Red Star and Yellow Earth*, *Publisher's Weekly* had hailed him as 'a diamond in the crown of American journalism – one of our five most distinguished foreign correspondents.'

Random House, his American publishers, had airmailed him the cutting with an enthusiastic covering letter that did not allude to their arbitrary alteration of his original title. The letter was rhapsodic over the impetus given to *Red Star* by the Book of the Month Club, as well as widespread newspaper serialization. The letter concluded: 'Hollywood is also interested. But that doesn't mean a thing unless progressive elements on the Coast swing all their influence behind it, I'm afraid we haven't got a Chinaman's chance of a movie from a non-fiction book. (Sorry, I couldn't resist that.) But, remember Dick, we're going to sell one hell of a lot of books.'

Richard had replied: 'I am thunderstruck by the activity I seem to have generated. I am humbled by my apparent success in bringing to the world's attention the epochal changes in China – the new society rising from the ashes of mankind's oldest culture. I am awed by the thought of all those editors editing, printers printing, reviewers reviewing, and, above all, readers reading – not to speak of woodsmen felling acres of trees to make paper. To think that I did all this sitting alone with my little Hermes portable.'

The news from Britain was almost as good. Although the compact United Kingdom book trade could soon be cut off from the vital markets of the British Empire by the exigencies of war, the publishers Victor Gollancz had informed Richard of several triumphs in a letter carried by a sympathetic second secretary joining the British Embassy in Chungking. Gollancz's own Left Book Club had naturally snapped up *Red Star and Yellow Earth*. The Book Society had expressed interest, and there were prospects of serialization in the *Manchester Guardian*. *The Times* had, almost unprecedentedly, cabled to request regular columns and had, quite unprecedentedly, informed him that it was 'planning a good notice'. That was the same as an American editor's cabling: 'Rave review'.

That delightful flurry made Richard yearn again to be back amid the activity of the Western world, his *own* world. If the paeans of praise rang so sweetly in his ears ten thousand miles away, what must it be like in the middle of the chorus!

Fearful of Emily's reaction to the new title, he hesitated to share these long-distance triumphs with her. But he concluded during the last week of December that he could not much longer conceal the alteration from her. Accordingly, he offered her the letters from New York and London with the remark: 'I'm afraid they changed the title, Em. They're calling it *Red Star and Yellow Earth*.'

'I know what editors are like, darling,' she responded almost negligently. 'Don't worry about it – not as far as I'm concerned. But there's no point in kidding ourselves. It's going to be embarrassing explaining to some people what happened to the Nationalists' white sun. Of course it doesn't make any difference to me . . . to us. I won't let it!'

Richard wondered with relief why he had been so reticent about the new title. Emily was realistic, he decided, regarding the vagaries of the editorial pencil. Besides, she, too, was determined to preserve their love in a hostile world.

She did not tell him that Mayling Chiang had a week earlier remarked: 'Emily, I've seen some disturbing reports about your Mr Hollings's book from the Embassies in London and Washington. Sounds almost as if he's gone over to the Reds.'

No, Mayling had acknowledged when Emily pressed, none of the informants had actually seen the book. The diplomats were, as usual, relaying political gossip.

'Yes,' Mayling had agreed, 'we should withhold judgement. After all, your Mr Hollings is convincing the Americans that China desperately needs American warplanes and aviators.'

Emily knew she was fighting a rear-guard action when Hollington Tong confided that he, too, had received alarming reports regarding *Red Star and Yellow Earth* from the offices of his China Information Service abroad. From Singapore, George Yeh, who was an expert on Elizabethan poetry, reported leafing through an advance copy of *Red Star and Yellow Earth* sent to the *Straits Times* for review.

'I had to content myself with a quick once-over.' Emily translated Dr Yeh's elided cablese into normal language; the two American-educated Chinese officials communicated in English. 'What I did see made my hair stand on end. This pernicious book will do our cause immense harm. Mr Hollings has gone over lock, stock, and barrel to the Communists. He depicts Mao Tse-tung as an amalgam of George Washington, Oliver Cromwell, Abraham Lincoln, and Jesus Christ. Nationalist anti-Japanese resistance is minimized, while the Communists are battling valiantly. Mao and his henchmen are creating an earthly paradise.

413

'According to Richard Hollings, a new era has dawned for China. The novelist Ting Ling is lovingly depicted as the embodiment of the magnificent new Chinese woman. On military matters, Hollings is remarkably . . .'

Tears of rage blurred Emily's vision. Heaven alone knew what had gone on in Yenan, where all decency had been cast aside! She could not believe that more than smiles had passed between Richard and the woman called Ting Ling. Knowing both her man and the promiscuous left-wing writer, Emily amended her thought. *Anything could have happened.* She was furious. That Communist slut, that drab fanatic, to epitomize Chinese womanhood! What of Mayling Chiang? What, even if it came to it, of herself? The panegyric George Yeh described was an insult to every decent Chinese woman.

Then Emily saw a degrading parallel between her own role in Richard's life and Ting Ling's role. The Communist woman possessed a certain waiflike charm, the allure of the pathetic. She had probably made love to Richard to seduce him to her cause. But had she herself not done the same, she Emily Howe Ou-yang, who prided herself on her integrity?

No, that was not true! She loved Dick deeply – and had loved him for many years. Only when she was bleakly depressed by the hash her persistent and unconcealed adultery was making of her life did she console herself that love of China was her primary motivation. But patriotism was no excuse!

Only love was worth the bonfire she had made of her position in society and the respect of her peers. The war had delayed presentation of the final account, but it would soon have to be paid in full. The only justification was the love she would defend with all her might – whatever Richard had done.

Young girls dreamed of a grand passion, the overwhelming love that set the world at naught. Were the refined torments she was suffering a grand passion?

It was ridiculous at thirty-eight to be overcome like a giddy virgin of eighteen. But she had, it appeared, lost her freedom of will. Everything else was trivial: her work, her achievements, her family, and even her country. She would not let Richard go, whatever evil he had done.

Neither would she commit the mortal error of telling him how totally he dominated her life. He would devour her if she did. She could not make herself a part of him. She could not surrender her individuality to become an appendage, however cherished an appendage.

Emily and Richard both sensed that New Year's Eve was a great divide in their own lives, as well as a turning point in the affairs of nations. Although they did not confide their misgivings to each other, both anticipated the evening with vague apprehension as well as hopes of gaiety. On the last day of the fourth decade of the twentieth century, Chungking was joyless under its sodden cloak of grey fog.

The deprivation created by war was rendered more austere by the constraints on pleasure imposed by the puritanical New Life Movement. 'Not Strength Through Joy, like the Nazis,' Emily herself laughed. 'But Strength Through Abstinence.' Even dancing was forbidden, and the true Chinese New Year, the Lunar New Year, was still more than a month away.

The foreign community was particularly restive at the close of 1939. Many of the diplomats, soldiers, businessmen, and correspondents were as superstitious about *this* New Year's Eve as the Chinese were about *every* Lunar New Year's Festival, when all men and women were reborn and all debts – spiritual and material – were settled. Since their own countries were now at war, the foreigners knew that the coming decade would determine their own fate, as well as the fate of the Chinese. The foreign community badly needed an outlet for its tension.

A New Year's Ball was, therefore, to be held at the British Embassy. All but the French conceded that the British were unrivalled for parties and ceremonies, whatever muddle they might make of policy. Since the Embassy was legally British territory, it was under no compulsion to obey the Nationalists' repressive laws. Diplomats normally did so as a matter of courtesy – or pretended to do so. But New Year's Eve was different.

The Head of Chancery solemnly called at the Chinese Foreign Ministry to declare that the Embassy proposed to hold a gala dance, at which it further proposed to broach its hoarded stocks of champagnes, wines, cordials, and liquors. If the Chinese Government so desired, Chinese citizens would not be invited to thus breach wartime austerity. Such exclusion might, however, smack unpleasantly of antiquated social discrimination – even of the extra-territorial privileges at Shanghai and other treaty ports that the Chinese Government found so abhorrent.

The Director of Protocol had smiled and poured his visitor another cup of tea in tacit invitation to linger. The Chinese Government, he could state without further consultation, saw nothing amiss in the proposed entertainment. His Government was, in fact, pleased that its foreign guests could find ways to amuse themselves amid the rigours of wartime. He actually said 'tickled pink', being a proud alumnus of Georgia Wesleyan like Madame Sun Yat-sen, but hastily substituted a more diplomatic term.

On behalf of the Chinese Government he further agreed that the exclusion of Chinese citizens might recall old antipathies best forgotten. Speaking for himself, the Director was delighted – 'really tickled pink again' – to accept the personal invitation of the Head of Chancery. Finally, the Chinese Government would be greatly obliged if the Embassy would again convey to London the urgent necessity for the prompt renunciation of extra-territoriality.

As a leading British correspondent, Richard Hollings was naturally invited to the gala party. The British Ambassadress, who anticipated the New Year's Ball with the same queasy ecstasy as she had her first grown-up dinner party, considered Madame Ou-yang Hsiu's promised presence a major coup. Since Madame Chiang Kai-shek could not attend such a

415

frivolous gathering, her Executive Associate was the next best thing. The Ambassadress's sentimental heart was, moreover, wrung by Emily's tragic romance with Richard. Despite the ambassadors, the ministers, the generals, and the admirals who would attend the ball, the Ambassadress considered Emily and Richard her prize guests.

'Certainly your headliner,' the Head of Chancery had agreed, having spent too much time in Washington as a second secretary. 'The fellow's already famous – even before a single copy of *Red Star*'s got to Chungking.'

The Head of Chancery was misinformed. Six copies of *Red Star and Yellow Earth* had arrived in the provisional capital three days earlier on a China National Aviation Corporation flight over the Hump.

Richard Hollings had, however, wisely cancelled the cocktail party he had originally planned to display his two author's copies. Admiring the bright yellow dust-jacket with the five-pointed red star that cast its rays over his own name, he had further prudently decided to tell no one the books had arrived. He had smiled ruefully at his earlier naïve vision of himself laying the very first copy in Emily's lap.

None the less, he found very little he would alter or omit – and much to admire – when he reread his own words, which were, as Chou En-lai had said, virtually unedited. Perhaps, he had finally decided, he would have added a paragraph or two clarifying the defection of Tommy Howe's friend Chang Ku-tao, but nothing more.

Richard was, in turn, unaware that Hollington Tong had pressed on Emily one of the four advance copies his New York office had finally got hold of – and despatched to make the same CNAC flight. Fortunately, Mayling Chiang was preoccupied with her projected journey to Hong Kong to be treated for a persistent skin inflammation. She planned to spend time in the Colony with her two elder sisters and hoped to persuade them to return to Chungking with her. Otherwise she would have pounced on the book – and precipitated the crisis Emily feared.

Emily had only glanced into the preface to confirm that Richard had heeded her plea to delete the thanks originally accorded her. She had then closed the book and secreted it in a drawer. She could not evade the ordeal, but she would read *Red Star and Yellow Earth* in her own time. May was certain to demand a reckoning eventually, and Emily firmly promised herself that she would settle down to the book when the holiday season was over – after both the Western and the Chinese New Years had passed.

She thrust all thoughts of the future from her mind when Richard bowed her into the improvised ballroom in the British Embassy. The walls glowed with bright silks and Persian carpets beneath hanging lanterns with scarlet tassels. The company was just as colourful, for the Ambassadress had asked her guests to come in fancy dress. Emily was delighted that she could in conscience depart from the *cheongsams* Richard called her full-dress uniform. Her scarlet-chiffon evening dress with floating panels and plunging neckline was curiously set off by the grey cassock and the pectoral cross Richard had inveigled from the Papal

416

Nuncio's houseboy. His lean face ascetic beneath his black half-mask, he was playing Cardinal Mazarin, the Grey Eminence.

Emily was Ginger Rogers in *Flying Down to Rio*. Although she stopped at dyeing her hair red, she had lavishly combed in henna powder. Her natural vivacity was just right for the part, as were her slightly garish make-up and her swirling skirts. Her brief scarlet bodice was tight over her small, high breasts and her cinched waist.

The design was Elizaveta's and, like her own evening dresses unashamedly derived from the trunk of her mother's pre-1914 gowns that had been her chief asset when she arrived in Shanghai, Elizaveta had pressed the dress upon Emily when she left Shanghai, declaring: 'I had it made for you, pet. There'll be a time when you desperately yearn for – really *need* – something utterly frivolous up there in the backwoods.'

That New Year Emily did *need* the scarlet dress. She shimmered like a flame around the half-lit ballroom in Richard's arms. And she trod the hearty group-dances the British loved: the whooping Gay Gordons, the whirling Lancers, and the pick-new-partners Paul Jones. Richard's eyes never left her, wherever she was.

The champagne flowed in astonishing profusion from bottles that had to come by narrow-gauge train from Haiphong or by overburdened aeroplane from India. Most embassies had, however, been foresighted in laying in stocks by the last steamers and gunboats up the Yangtze. They were now generous, eager to make the night bubble with gaiety. The war encouraged hectic gaiety, since no one knew where he would be next New Year's Eve.

Not for years, Emily realized, had she been so unreservedly happy. Not, in fact, since her foolish marriage.

Only once was the enchantment marred. An earnest, pink-cheeked lieutenant off the *USS Tutuila*, who held her like a fragile Ming vase, observed without malice: 'Your friend Mr Hollings, we've been hearing a lot about him lately. Folks are saying he's written a wonderful book about China. Lord knows when we'll see it. I guess, though, you've read it already.'

'Sorry, sailor,' Emily replied shortly, 'I haven't read it either.'

She thanked God that Harry Smythe was still in Kunming, for he would not have been put off easily. None the less, the music, the perfumes, and the champagne restored her joyous mood. She was again bubbling when couples came together a few minutes before midnight.

She came into Richard's arms for that dance. Her eyes dwelt on his lean cheek, where the beard shaved hours earlier was again asserting itself. Behind the half-mask, his eyes were actually darker than her own. He looked down at her straight centre-parting, where her scalp shone pearl-white dusted with red henna.

'Darling!' he said softly. 'Always, my darling!'

She smiled, almost afraid to speak, and whispered: 'Forever!'

They did not hear the countdown to the New Year swell around them, and the midnight gong was a distant reverberation. Unmasking, they kissed lightly once – and once again.

'All will be well!' Richard assured her. 'All will be well beyond doubt – always!'

'Of course!' she echoed. 'Always!'

Around them the entire party was singing 'Old Lang Syne'. They kissed again more urgently. And both were suddenly afraid.

No matter how Emily tried, her eyes kept returning to the bottom drawer where the unopened copy of *Red Star and Yellow Earth* lay under her scarves. She was afraid that a time-bomb was concealed under the frothy silk – a time-bomb or a cobra's egg. She could put off the explosion, but not indefinitely, while only Heaven knew when the egg would hatch. The mixed metaphor amused her momentarily, but her thoughts reverted to the inevitable confrontation with her lover's book.

On a damp, chilly afternoon in late February she opened the drawer. Holly Tong had again been demanding her opinion of the book. She could no longer plead that she had not found time to read it when even Jimmy Wei rolled his eyes. After locking her bedroom door, her reluctant fingers fumbled with the pages.

Normally a fast reader, Emily took a full week to plod through the 416 pages. Her initial reactions oscillated wildly from approval to horror. Although she knew she was searching for mitigating evidence, she found some passages strikingly accurate – and she was moved by Richard's insight into China.

Some passages, the greater part in fact, she read with mounting incredulity. Since she knew Richard was not blind to reality, she was forced to conclude that he had deliberately distorted it. She knew from her talks with Tommy's friend Chang Kuo-tao the stark truths that underlay the bright, specious picture of the Communists Richard had painted. She also knew that Chang Kuo-tao had discussed those truths with Richard.

Emily's chief reaction to *Red Star and Yellow Earth* was incredulity. Since she could not believe Richard's account was as biased as it appeared, she put the book aside for a week and then forced herself to read it again. The distortions were even more glaring the second time, and the few redeeming passages seemed thin or shoddy. Richard, she concluded sorrowfully, had done irreparable harm to China in order to advance himself.

During the two weeks she was engaged with the book, she refused to see the author. Her excuses were almost deliberately transparent, but she dared not talk to him. Besides, she wanted him to suffer a little while she was suffering profoundly. Desolate because she was deprived of his presence and his love, she was furious at him for forcing her to make such a harsh and painful decision.

It was not primarily being compelled to choose between Richard and China, though that choice loomed large. It was not even being compelled to choose either Richard or her present work – as well as all her friends and associates – though that choice galled. It was, above all, his compelling her to choose between him and her self-respect.

418

Before reading his book, she had decided that she would, if necessary, sacrifice her work, her reputation, and, perhaps, even her children to be with him. But she had further decided that she could not sacrifice her existence as an independent human being. Since choosing Richard would clearly negate all the meaning of her life, Emily finally concluded that she had no choice. Having agonized and delayed for weeks, she *knew* she must break with Richard Hollings – this time permanently.

Too much of her being was, however, entwined around the man she still loved. She dreaded the confrontation with him as she had dreaded nothing since she sailed for America at the age of ten. If she were a shade more cowardly, she would inform him curtly in writing that it was all over. If she loved him a little less, she would end it with a brief note. But she could not spare herself that way.

She would see him soon, Emily told herself, although her long silence had already spoken for her. Richard must have concluded that she was avoiding him because she had read his book – and despised it. In the end, she did nothing, and the month of March was upon them.

Richard has not pressed her for a meeting. Was it tact or fear of rejection that had induced him to make a second visit to Claire Chennault in Kunming? Perhaps he did not feel strongly enough to demand that she allow him to plead his case. The ardent lover of New Year's Eve had given way to the craven who was afraid – or unwilling – to see her.

Emily was again furious. Not her withdrawal, but his cowardice was keeping them apart. It would serve him right if she let him go off without another word.

Yet she had, perhaps, already punished him sufficiently. Perhaps he had really been deceived by the Communists, who were brilliant pro-pagandists, which at rock bottom meant convincing liars. Herself a seasoned propagandist for the Nationalists, Emily respected the enemy's professional skill. Perhaps Richard had not fully realized how damaging his hymn of praise to the Communists would be to the Nationalist Government.

Emily was still searching for excuses for Richard when he returned in the first week of March. Anticipating her reaction, he had gone to Kunming to gather material. He hoped to allay her anger by balancing the scales with a glowing book about Claire Chennault, who was talking about forming several squadrons to be called the American Volunteer Group. An American foreign legion of the air fighting to keep China free would make brilliant copy.

Richard's literary agent had, however, cabled with reckless disregard of expense: I CANNOT REPEAT NOT PREVENT YOUR DOING BOOK ABOUT CHENNAULT. NO ONE CAN STOP YOU EXCEPT YOURSELF. BUT PLEASE BEAR THIS IN MIND: YOU ARE ABOUT TO BECOME INTERNATIONALLY FAMOUS AS THE WORLD'S LEADING AUTHORITY ON CHINA – AND MAJOR AUTHORITY ON INTERNATIONAL AFFAIRS IN GENERAL. RANDOM HOUSE WANT ANOTHER BIG REPEAT BIG BOOK, NOT REPEAT NOT LITTLE ADVENTURE STORY ABOUT A JOHNNY REB BIRDMAN FOR SCHOOLBOYS. RANDOM FEELS SUCH A MINOR SUBJECT WOULD IMPAIR YOUR STANDING WHILE A BIG THEME WOULD

SOLIDIFY YOUR REPUTATION. I AGREE. FOR EXAMPLE, THE SOVIET UNION'S ROLE IN THE WORLD AND THE WAR. SURELY YOUR FRIENDS IN YENAN CAN HELP YOU THERE. RANDOM PREPARED TO PAY THREE THOUSAND DOLLARS ADVANCE FOR CHENNAULT, OWING HIGH REGARD FOR YOU. THEIR INITIAL OFFER FOR SOVIET BOOK IS FIFTY THOUSAND, AND I CAN PROBABLY GET TEN THOUSAND MORE. NOT THAT I'M PRESSING. IT'S ENTIRELY UP TO YOU. CORDIALLY MOSS.

Richard winced at that aside about his friends in Yenan coming through the Nationalist cable office – and lamented the end of the Chennault project. His agent and his publisher were, of course, absolutely right. He could not allow himself the luxury of mending his fences with the Nationalists, but had to strike while the iron was hot. Wincing at the mangled metaphor, he took the inevitable decision: If they wanted the Soviet Union, they'd get the Soviet Union.

A pity he couldn't placate Emily with a book on Chennault. But she was professional enough to understand that he had no choice. Perhaps he could do the Chennault book later, when his reputation was so well established that publishers and agents had to take what he gave them.

A pity, also, that he could not linger in China. Knowing that he was working for their future together, Emily would understand that he had to move quickly. He had almost forgotten her long angry silence. But all that nonsense would blow away when he gave her the good news of the fat new commission from his American publishers.

Whistling cheerfully between his teeth, Richard drafted a telegram to his agent accepting the offer of fifty thousand dollars for a book – implicitly favourable – on the Soviet Union. Victor Gollancz in London would certainly snap it up.

His Hermes portable clattered out two more telegrams. Almost identical, they pointed out to the *Boston Globe* and the National Broadcasting Company that the China story was, for the time being, written out, while the Soviet Union was the key to victory – and, therefore, to the future of mankind.

Having briskly disposed of not only the future of mankind, but his own immediate future, Richard was in no mood to tolerate feminine caprices any longer. They had very little time before his departure, and they had to make the most of it. Having virtually expunged their tacit quarrel from his own mind, he simply assumed that Emily had got over whatever was bothering her.

Briskly he boarded a sampan-ferry across the Chialing River. Just as briskly he scrambled up the path towards the Ou-yang Compound, ignoring the reproachful obscenities of sedan-chair coolies done out of a fare.

Emily received him rather formally in the little used drawing room. He had, unknowing, found her in a regretful mood. She had almost convinced herself that she was unjust in her condemnation of *Red Star* – and its author. He saw that she had lost weight she could not afford to lose and that her wide-set eyes were suspiciously liquid.

'You took your own sweet time, didn't you?' She evaded his embrace. 'Anyone would think I had leprosy.'

'I thought you wanted . . .' His brisk self-assurance was taken aback by her lack of logic. 'I thought you wanted time to yourself. Any event, you could have sent a word or two.'

'I did need time. Maybe I still do.'

After this assertiveness, she surprised herself by asking plaintively: 'Richard, *how* could you do it to us?'

'Whatever I've done, Emily, I didn't deserve this.' He delivered the riposte just as he had planned it. 'I didn't deserve being banished from your presence. I've come to tell you I've got to leave soon, very soon. I'll be back of course. But God alone knows when we'll see each other again. Time is precious – and you're wasting the little time together we've got left.'

She did not reply, but busily rearranged the crocheted anti-macassars on the red-plush sofa, which was flanked by two red-plush easy chairs. Everything in the drawing-room was in the same style: lamps with glass-beaded shades; octagonal tables littered with bric-à-brac; still lifes of dead pheasants sprawled on over-ripe grapes; and dust-collecting plush chairs in shades of scarlet and mauve. On the mantelpiece, a magnificent ceramic Tang Dynasty mandarin looked down his almost Roman nose at the shoddy artefacts of the barbarous West.

'You sound as if it were only a whim on my part, Richard,' Emily finally observed. 'Just a female whim – refusing to see you.'

'No, my dear, not a whim. Far too drawn-out for a feminine caprice.' In his perturbation, he spoke ornately. 'I should count myself fortunate if it were no more than a whim. You do realize, don't you, that you've kept us apart for more than six weeks now?'

Despite her own tension, Emily smiled at the nervous pomposity that was so unlike his normal breeziness. She finally sighed: 'Oh, that mine enemy would write a book.'

'And what precisely is that cheapjack scripture quotation meant to convey?'

'If *you* don't know! Primarily, I suppose, that you did write a book and . . .'

'And a damned good book, too,' he exploded. 'But I'm not here for a seminar on literary criticism.'

'Perhaps you are. We'll talk about that later – the criticism.' Her voice rose ominously. 'And, I was going to say . . .'

'Please go ahead!' Richard prompted when her words trailed off. 'We've got to have it out, I see. The sooner the better.'

'I'm not so sure about . . . about . . . sooner being better,' she stammered, then burst out: 'Oh, Richard, how could you *possibly* do it? Did you for an instant think of us? Or only of yourself? You've betrayed me . . . betrayed just about everything! How *could* you do it to us?'

Striving to remain calm, he asked in genuine perplexity: 'Look here, Emily, I know you're unhappy about *Red Star*. Maybe you're right. Maybe some parts are a little over the mark. But it's not the end of the world. After all, it's only a book.'

'*Only* a book!' Emily exploded. 'My God, you might as well say *only* a life! *Only* the lives of millions of Chinese men, women, and children! My God in Heaven, *only* a book!'

'Steady now, Em!' He automatically fell back on banalities. 'Let's not go overboard.'

'Go overboard? What do you expect – an English gentleman's reserve? Well, Richard, I'm not English – and I'm not a gentleman. So to hell with reserve! *Why* didn't you think what it would mean to us? *Only* a book! My God, don't you *know* you've destroyed everything . . . ruined all we had?'

Richard plucked a cigarette from the pack of Camels on the marquetry coffee-table. After three wood-sliver matches had crumbled in his fingers, he succeeded in lighting the fourth. Drinking in the smoke, he looked at her in amazement.

'Whatever are you talking about?' he demanded. 'Destroyed everything? Ruined it all? I simply don't know what you mean, Emily.'

'If you didn't a minute ago, you certainly know now. You do know what I'm saying. Don't you?'

Shocked beyond speech, he nodded and, after several seconds, asked faintly: 'But why, Emily, why? You'd sacrifice us – everything – over a book?'

'I've got no choice, Richard. Everything else aside, anyone who could write a book like that! I don't know that person. I don't know you at all. How could I ever trust you again about anything? If you're ready to twist and distort and lie . . .'

'Steady on. That's just a little too much for me to take.' His voice rose. '*Red Star* is true, you know – just as true as I could make it. A few mistakes, of course. Even the best reporting's got a few mistakes. But, overall, it's a true picture and . . .'

'My God, Richard, I'm afraid . . . afraid you really believe what you're saying. If you do, you're a fool. And if you don't . . . if you're just lying again about not lying, I . . . I don't know what to say.'

'A knave or a fool?' His voice was now flat. 'Is that it, Emily?'

'What else can I say? When I look at the difference between what I know to be true and what you wrote. What else can I possibly think?'

'You might try thinking that *you* don't know everything!' he retorted. 'Because you're Chinese doesn't mean you know everything about China. Why don't you look at the inefficiency and corruption on your own side for a change? Aside from your precious Gimo, everybody's got his snout in the trough. Why don't you . . .'

'Richard, I do! Nobody says the Nationalists are perfect. But we can talk about it. Correspondents can write about it – and they do. That's one side. On the other side, you paint a picture of a rustic paradise. You *must* know that's nonsense. Why Chang Kuo-tao alone . . .'

'As you very well know, Chang Kuo-tao is a turncoat – a traitor. If you're going to listen seriously to the ravings of every defeated politician like Chang Kuo-tao . . . listen to opportunists and defectors . . .'

'Richard, this is becoming pointless. Why don't we drop it?'

'I'm all for that, Emily.' He was again conciliatory. 'That's why I

422

came today, why I didn't wait to be summoned. Not, I assure you, to debate politics. Let us indeed drop politics – agree to disagree. Then we can take up where we left off. We don't have much time, so let's just rub along now. If you must, we can discuss all this when I come back – discuss it calmly and coherently. But for now let's just rub along, and everything'll be fine.'

'You really mean that, don't you? You really believe it's possible! Love conquers all! Oh, Richard, you really do!'

He nodded stiffly, puzzled by her light, almost casual tone. Emily automatically took a Camel and clenched it between her lips. She nodded her thanks for his hastily proffered light as if they were mere acquaintances at a cocktail party.

'You always could surprise me, Richard.' She spoke softly, with little emphasis. 'And you still can. You really do believe we can just rub along. It's not only your self-absorption, is it? It's your *massive* insensitivity. You can't help it, I see that now. But you are undoubtedly the most callous human being I ever . . .'

'Emily, is that really fair?' he protested. 'How can you say . . .'

'You still don't understand what you've done to us, do you? To think I was in love with a creature I invented. You never cared enough for me . . . for us . . . to think for a single instant about the consequences.' She stared in bleak wonder at his uncomprehending expression. 'You don't really care now. You never cared in the past – however I deceived myself. And you never will care. Not if you live a thousand years.'

Richard was battered into silence by her brutal condemnation. Still staring steadily at him, Emily picked a shred of tobacco from the tip of her tongue and ground her cigarette out.

'Richard, there is no point . . . no point whatsoever.' She almost sounded detached. 'There was never any point, not really. I wonder why it took me so many years to find out. Richard, you've always been a gentleman in your own way. Be a gentleman now – and go quickly!'

44

March 29–April 30, 1940

The Red Ensign of the British Merchant Marine shielded the small coaster from the warships of the Imperial Japanese Navy blockading the China Coast. None the less, the twin four-inch guns in the forward turret of the destroyer *Tatsuta* followed the coaster as it turned into the Yangtze River from the South China Sea. Plodding up the Yangtze to the Hwangpoo for the turn to Shanghai would take several hours, and the guns of Japanese warships would follow the coaster all the way.

Warning Richard Hollings of this silent intimidation, the young ship's captain observed: 'They haven't fired yet. Does that make it more likely for us to get a red-hot shell in our guts? Because no one has so far, I mean. Or does it mean a better chance of getting by untouched? Bound to happen some day, though.'

The correspondent filed that remark in his memory. It summed up for him the mood of Shanghai even before he saw the queen city of the Far East again. Apprehension cloaked by bravado obviously dominated the great port that was slowly expiring in the Japanese grip – and also bleak resignation. The invaders did not interfere officially in the foreign concessions, except as members of the Municipal Council. None the less their heavy hand was stifling the trade by which the city lived.

Richard had come back to write a farewell series on the Shanghai no one would ever see again – regardless of the outcome of the conflict men now called the Second World War. His foreign audiences were, after all, more interested in the foreign-oriented cosmopolis than in remote cities with unpronounceable names inhabited entirely by Chinese or in battles fought entirely between Orientals. He planned to deal with Shanghai

424

expeditiously and then take up the roving commission in Europe his joint employers had offered their new star.

The white caps whipped by the stiff breeze made the dark-brown Yangtze look like a river of coffee topped with frothy cream. But Richard's heart no longer responded to the welcome of the junks on the water and the pagodas on the banks. He had seen too many rivers in China – and far too much of China. But he was almost done with China.

An era of his life was ending. He had come back to Shanghai to close the circle of his life in China where he had begun it. Moreover, the right introduction to the Soviet Union was worth travelling thousands of miles for – since it could means tens of thousands of dollars. He already had a title for his new book: *The Bear at Bay*. But he had to get his foot into the Kremlin's door.

He had, of course, spoken in Chungking to Chou En-lai, who promised to vouch for him with the Soviets after denying any special influence with them. He had also paid a courtesy call on the Soviet Ambassador. But formal introductions would take him only so far. He wanted to escape the net of protocol and bureaucracy.

The Soviet Consul-General in Shanghai was far more important than the Ambassador in Chungking, a hundred times more influential. Shanghai was the centre for Soviet espionage, diplomacy, trade, and subversion throughout Asia, and the Consul-General was the master-spider at the centre of that intricate network. Foreign correspondents' gossip, which was usually accurate in such matters, described him as a personal protégé of Joseph Stalin and a major-general in the OGPU, the security and intelligence service. His word could open the gates of the Kremlin for a sympathetic correspondent.

Richard had no illusions about the political position of Tommy and Julie Howe after Yenan. He had cabled Tommy his time of arrival in order to get off to a running start. He had a shrewd idea that Tommy was very important in the Apparatus in Shanghai. Tommy must, therefore, maintain close contact with the Soviet spymaster. If Tommy vouched for him, he would be within sight of his goal, which was the same privileged access in Moscow he had enjoyed in Yenan under Tommy's sponsorship.

Then he would be off. So many arrivals and departures! It seemed he had been travelling continuously since he left Shanghai in 1927 with Emily's angry denunciation of his selfishness still ringing in his mind. He sternly closed off all thought of Emily. His wife Fiona was always delighted to see him in England, grateful for his sparing her the time. And Fiona never railed at him. She never analyzed his shortcomings, never denounced his sins. Yet something was missing between them. Why else would he spend so much time away from her? He involuntarily thought about Emily again – and realized again that he was completely happy only when they were together.

Richard could not believe his second dismissal was any more final than his first had proved. He knew that Emily had spent the three weeks between their confrontation and his departure from Chungking oscillating between grief and fury. Harry Smythe had told him so, with savage satisfaction in making him suffer because she was suffering so profoundly. He had wandered around Chungking unable to work until he was unexpectedly offered a seat on a special CNAC flight to Hong Kong. Although he suspected that Emily had pulled strings to get him out of Chungking, he had accepted with alacrity.

He had not written her a farewell note. After much agonizing, he had instead sent her a copy of *Red Star and Yellow Earth* inscribed: *To Emily from the author with all his love forever. In the hope that she may some day want to read it again and, perhaps, change her mind.*

That dignified and civilized inscription had consoled Richard somewhat when he began the journey that was to take him to Shanghai by way of Hong Kong. A sampan had ferried him to the sand-spit in the middle of the Yangtze that served as Chungking's airport. Two worlds met. The shore was thronged with sedan-chair coolies, lantern-bearers, horse-grooms, messengers-coolies, and food-hawkers – all essentially medieval occupations. On the sand-spit, the airliner loomed huge, its silver flanks glowing red in the sunset. The newly-delivered Douglas DC-3 was the pride of China's national airline: it could carry thirty passengers 1400 miles at almost 200 miles an hour.

The cabin lights were off when the transport rolled down the sand-spit at dusk to twist into the open sky through the surrounding hills. When the DC-3 reached cruising altitude, even the navigation lights and the safety beacon were turned off. After five hours of darkness in Japanese-controlled airspace, the DC-3 sideslipped into Hong Kong's Kaitak Aerodrome.

When he disembarked, Richard saw why CNAC had risked the special flight. In the big black Daimler limousine on the tarmac the glow of the interior light silhouetted three women. Richard recognized Mayling Chiang when she leaned forward. Since the family resemblance was unmistakable, the others were surely her elder sisters: Eiling, called Nanny, who was Madame H. H. Kung; and Chingling, called Rosamonde, who was Madame Sun Yat-sen. Therefore the fuss and the secrecy. Mayling was returning secretly to Chungking after her medical treatment in Hong Kong. She had evidently persuaded both the fearful Nanny and the haughty Rosamonde to join her. Rosamonde had previously preferred to remain in the safety of British Hong Kong to snipe at her brother-in-law's Nationalist Central Government. Her visit to Chungking would please Chairman Mao Tse-tung. In combination with Chou En-lai she would undoubtedly enchant the foreign press and further gild the Communists' image.

Standing on the tarmac at Kaitak Aerodrome, Richard had congratulated himself on picking the winning side. He congratulated himself again when he stepped off Municipal Pontoon Six onto the Bund of the International Settlement after leaving the coaster that had brought him from Hong Kong. He saw Julia Howe waiting just at the end of the gangplank. They were practically partners now. Even before himself, she had picked the winning side.

Lit by the yellow cone of the street-lamp, Julia's costume made no obeisance to wartime austerity. Two long tassels hung from the apple-green pillbox cocked on the side of her head. The mulberry-linen bolero that matched her slim skirt flaunted the padded shoulders popularized by Joan Crawford, the Hollywood star of the year. Moreover, Julia looked glowingly happy.

She had reason to be happy. The prolonged war, which was a quagmire for the Japanese and the Nationalists, was providing splendid opportunities for the Communists. They were energetically expanding their territory, though their armies prudently recoiled when challenged. In Europe the Soviet Union was the only victor in the continuing phony war. After their victory in Poland, the Germans still faced the French and the British. But the Kremlin had painlessly extended its power. Julia must be delighted with the high tide of proletarian emancipation sweeping the heart of the Eurasian land-mass.

Contemptuous of appearances, Julia pressed against him and kissed his lips. This impulsive welcome was far warmer than he expected or had ever before received. She had never quite forgiven him for jilting Emily, as she believed, and flinging her sister-in-law into the ageing arms of Ou-yang Hsiu. Julia's first words revealed why he was back in favour.

'You're looking great, Dick.' She was remarkably enthusiastic. '*Red Star and Yellow Earth* is a terrific book. Tommy and I loved it. And how's Emmy? I'm so happy. I'm delighted that you two are back together again.'

'Emily's very well. But, I'm afraid, we're not quite back together at the moment. She's not at all pleased with me.'

'Of course, she couldn't forgive you for leaving,' Julia laughed. 'Even a superwoman like Emmy isn't always a hundred percent logical. Also, I guess, she's read your book. Dick, you could hardly expect her to *like* it, could you? But lovers' tiffs soon blow over.'

Requiring Julia's goodwill, Richard preferred to leave it at that. He had told her the truth, which she could interpret as she liked.

'And yourself, Julie?' he inquired. 'How are Tommy and the girls? All in the pink, I trust.'

'Absolutely thriving, Dick. We're all just fine. And very optimistic about the future. For China – and the world. It's all working out just right.'

The only undiluted truth in that sunny affirmation was Julia's optimism about political events – which her husband did not share. Nor were all the Howes thriving. Nine-year-old Althea was almost disabled by asthma, which her father ascribed largely to the foul Shanghai climate with its perpetual dampness. Althea's parents were passing through the unhappiest time they had ever known together. A decade of harmony had ill prepared them for the tension generated by their acute disagreements over personal as well as political questions. Tommy was goaded by Julia's optimism. She detested his dour pessimism regarding his nation, his city, and his family.

Like Joshua Haleevie, Tommy was depressed by the tawdry decline of their beloved Shanghai. The trucks of the Corpse Collection Service now picked up more than a hundred unidentified bodies every morning – and every day two hundred new refugees arrived. Women with wild eyes and matted hair led ragged, starving children in an endless hunt for scraps of food. Boarding houses, hotels, derelict mansions, and schools were crammed, and tens of thousands slept on the street. The overstrained charities simply could not provide for the horde of refugees.

The Settlement and Frenchtown were also tormented by criminals who were protected by the Japanese and their puppet, the Chinese traitor called Alcibiades. After the first beheading that had so shocked Julia and Elizaveta, political murder had become commonplace. The Supreme Lord of the Floodgate Fraternity could no longer control either narcotics or violence. His secret society battalions were outnumbered and outgunned by regiments of freelance thugs.

Julia had reserved Richard's old suite at Broadway Mansions. Since he was reluctant to talk about Emily, she expounded on the breakdown of law and order while sipping the first mint-sprigged Tom Collins mixed by the roomboy.

'As you've seen, downtown is practically a no man's land. Special constables patrol with their revolvers in their hands. You couldn't miss the armoured cars and tanks, could you? More guns are bristling out of more pillboxes than even in '27. Only this time, it's no false alarm.'

'No plans to leave, Julie? You're staying on, you and the girls? Of course Tommy's a Shanghailander born and bred. A doctor too. Perhaps he feels he has to stay. But isn't it a bit foolhardy for you to. . . .'

'He keeps harping on that, Dick. He wants me to take the girls back to America, and he's got a hundred reasons. My parents are getting old, and they've never seen their grand-daughters. Then the danger, and also Althea's asthma. I suspect he's exaggerating, but Tommy says she must live in a better climate for a while. And the uncertain international situation. We could be trapped here when war comes. So you see . . .'

'Slow down, Julie, slow down!' The Englishman raised his palm. 'You're going so fast I can hardly take it all in. Tell me, what does Tommy plan to do? Will he accompany you? To the States, I mean.'

'Sometimes he says Yes. Sometimes No. Anyway, he can't practise in the States. Even if he could cut through the red tape, he says, his place is here in China. But he wants me to go into exile.'

'A lot of couples are going to be parted if this war gets bigger, Julie. Hundreds of thousands already are. War isn't a family outing, you know.'

'So Tommy keeps telling me. He says the girls will get no proper schooling here as long as the crisis lasts – which could be many years. But I've got my work – and it's important. XMHA and teaching and . . . and other important work. But Tommy says cholera and typhoid are already bad – and they'll get worse. Also malaria's a certainty with the waterways blocked and stagnating. It's hard to argue with him, Dick.'

'Julie, I admire your spirit, though not necessarily your logic. Have you ever thought how much you can do in the States just now? For China . . . and for . . . ah . . . the progressive movement.'

Reading *Red Star and Yellow Earth* with delight, Julia had become convinced that Richard Hollings was, at the very least, a Communist sympathizer. She was further encouraged by Richard's using that code term, 'the progressive movement', to mean the Communists and their allies throughout the world. Still, she could hardly tell him that Tommy and she were quarrelling bitterly about working directly for the Soviets. She could hardly confess herself a spy to a journalist, no matter how sympathetic. Caution won out, and she only flourished her ivory cigarette-holder in a silent plea for a light.

'Can't we get old Tom to join us for dinner?' Richard lit her Chesterfield. 'I can't wait to see the old rascal.'

'Fat chance!' Her coarseness just missed the desired comic effect. 'Tommy's off healing the suffering rich. There's more illness among the wealthy than you can shake a stick at. Even two sticks! Particularly the glossy Shanghai ladies. *All* the Chinese ladies love my Tommy. Just as long as he's only *healing* them.'

Julia drew in a deep draught of smoke and accepted another Tom Collins.

'What about you, Julie? Are you free? Tom won't mind, will he?'

'Not as long as I leave a message with the houseboy like an obedient little wife. He's just as happy not to have to worry about me while he's healing the rich, you see.'

Richard realized that she had drunk a little more than she should and decided they would dine in the suite. Though he longed for the superb Russian food served at the Renaissance Café on Avenue Joffre, Broadway Mansions could produce the delicacies he had been longing for: fresh caviar, smoked salmon, oysters – and porterhouse steaks. After a few drinks, he recalled, the cosmopolitan Julia was apt to revert to a rather basic American taste in food.

Her bitter remarks about Tommy disturbed Richard. Their apparent rift was distressing to one who had until recently believed – and who still hoped – he would become their brother-in-law. Both Howes were provoking, Tommy apparently as much as Emily. They were virtual fanatics in their dedication to China. He still could not fathom why Emily objected so strenuously – and so personally – to *Red Star*. He wondered if politics were also a factor in the obvious friction between Julia and Tommy.

Richard did not mention Tommy during dinner. He preferred to answer Julia's questions about Chungking and to refresh himself from her inexhaustible well of gossip about Shanghai. But his thoughts reverted to the infuriating sister and brother when Julia led him onto the terrace to look upon the fairyland radiance of Shanghai at night.

Perhaps we'd both be better off if we'd never met the Howes, he reflected, neither Emily nor Tommy. They've got such high standards, other human beings can't possibly live up to them.

Julia looked at him strangely, and he feared he had spoken his thoughts aloud. He impulsively observed: 'They can be terribly provoking, the Chinese, can't they?'

'Can they not!' Julia affirmed roundly. 'Sometimes, Dick, I feel like saying the hell with them. To hell with *all* Chinese!'

She leaned back against the railing and stared at him. The lights of the Bund, glittering across Soochow Creek, cast a halo around her tawny hair. On her left, Nanking Road streamed westwards like the brilliant tail of a comet.

When she leaned back farther, he grasped her arm and cautioned: 'Careful now. It's a long fall.'

'Fall to where, Dick? Sometimes, I swear, I wouldn't mind falling.'

Julia's speech was excessively precise. The meal had not sobered her. Burgundy had followed the Tom Collinses, and they were now swirling liqueurs in balloon glasses: cointreau for her and brandy for him. After clearing the table, the roomboy had left the bottles on the sideboard.

'Exactly what did you say a minute ago?' she demanded after a prolonged pause. 'About Tommy and Emmy? I swear I heard you say something.'

'I only said the Chinese could be provoking. What else did you hear, Julie?' He teased her and realized that he was not dead sober himself. 'What did you think?'

'I thunk . . . I think . . . I was thinking about Tommy and Emily. You know, sometimes they're too good to be true. Certainly too good for ordinary mortals like you 'n me. Too hard to get 'long with. So pure . . . so patriotic . . . so logical . . . so . . . oh, hell, so superior and – and Chinese!'

'Don't be bitter, Julie. It'll be all right, I promise you.'

'It's not all right with you and Em, is't, Dickie? Not gonna be all right? Little Julie's no slouch. I can hear it in your voice.'

'No, my dear, it's not quite all right,' he confessed. 'She's miffed at me again. To tell the truth, she's furious about *Red Star* . . .'

'What'd you expect, Dick?' For a moment she spoke crisply, almost mockingly, 'A medal from the Gimo – the order of the White Sun and Blue Sky? Lord's sake, you knew exactly what you were doing, didn't you? And some people are proud . . . very proud . . . of you, Richard. Me for one.'

'I did try, Julie. I tried very hard to get the message across. I'm so glad you feel I've succeeded.'

'Succeeded? That's an understatement. From what I hear, you've changed the course of history. The reviews, I've rarely seen such raves. And the commentaries, even the editorials. Richard, my boy, you're a one-man agitprop team.'

'I'm so glad you liked it, Julie. You're not just flattering me? After all the flak I've been getting, I must say it's a nice change to . . .'

'Richard Hollings, just come a little closer so I don't have to shout.' Julia quaffed her cointreau recklessly. 'No need to let the whole world in on it. That's better. Now I'll just whisper . . .'

Setting the balloon glass down on the railing, Julia stood on tiptoes to whisper into his ear. She swayed slightly and leaned against him to support herself. He felt the soft weight of her breasts upon his arm and the warmth of her thighs against his leg.

Turning towards her, he told himself he was not really being unfaithful to Emily with her closest friend. He could not deprive Emily of that which she had already rejected. And Julia obviously knew exactly what she was doing after the eleven years of fidelity that had scandalized hedonistic Shanghai. Considering their relationships with the brother and sister, it was almost incestuous. But who else in the world could provide the other with revenge as exquisitely sweet?

Joshua Haleevie was amused by the cartoon from the London *Daily Express*. The broad pen-strokes of Herbert Low depicted Adolf Hitler and Joseph Stalin meeting to sign the Russo-German Non-Aggression Pact which had precipitated World War II. Both jackbooted and be-medalled dictators were smiling amiably and lifting their peaked caps. As he bowed to Stalin, Hitler remarked: 'The scum of the earth, I believe!' Also bowing, Stalin replied: 'The bloody assassin of the workers, I presume!'

Although the Russians and the Germans were getting along famously in Europe, they did not even meet in Shanghai. Although their consul-ates overlooked the Hwangpoo side-by-side in Hongkew, they avoided each other as they had when they were avowed enemies. Was that con-tinuing antipathy feigned, Joshua wondered, and why?

The anonymous director of the anonymous intelligence service of the International Settlement made a note in his pocket diary: *Ivan and Fritz?* He would have to look into the apparent antagonism between those allies. Shanghai was a remarkably fertile field for intelligence, upon occa-sion offering remarkable leads to major developments elsewhere in the world. The foreign powers controlled their espionage in the Far East from the concessions. All except two. The Americans had no intelligence operation, while Britain's secret intelligence service worked out of Sin-gapore. Joshua Haleevie, however, communicated directly with London.

He was presently involved with an intriguing lead regarding the Nazis. Elizaveta had casually remarked on the large funds apparently at the disposal of the Cultural Attaché of the German Consulate, one Johannes Witzer-Weidemann. He was hail-fellow-well-met not only with the Japa-nese and the Italians, but with diplomats and merchants of lesser countries. And he regularly gave parties at the Ikra that cost more than ten thousand Mex. Happy with the patronage, Elizaveta was, none the less, suspicious.

Like any well-brought up daughter of the Russian aristocracy, she spoke French, German, and Italian in addition to English and her native language. She did not parade her linguistic accomplishments. It was vulgar to boast – and it was often useful to understand without being known to understand. The proprietress of the Ikra had to listen discreetly so that she would know everything that went on under her roof.

Always voluble, the free-spending Herr Witzer-Weidemann became garrulous after a few drinks. She had seen him nudge the embarrassed German Consul-General and heard him remark: '*Die Maisache kommt hervorragend an.* . . . The May business is coming along splendidly.'

On another occasion, Witzer-Weidemann and a visiting brigadier general of the German General Staff had repeatedly toasted each other. Afraid to draw too close, Elizaveta had nonetheless heard two words repeated frequently: *Maibaum* and *Maibowle*. The Maypole and the May punch were apparently innocuous. But why the concentration on May?

Curious, Joshua had resorted to the hidden microphones he had planted in the Ikra with the internal telephone service. The bartender called Wang, who had helped him dispose of the remains of Colonel Ishikawa, replaced the spools on the new wire-recorder. Wang would, of course, report the electrical eavesdropping to either the Nationalists or the Communists, perhaps both. But Joshua did not care, since he was only trolling for information.

Though inconclusive, the recordings made Joshua suspect he had hooked a big fish. He ordered surveillance of Witzer-Weidemann and called in an informant who was the senior Chinese clerk of the German Consulate. The surveillance revealed that the Cultural Attaché had many unlikely friends in many unlikely places, people who 'probably think culture is a new kind of machine-gun' as one report observed sourly. The chief clerk believed Witzer-Weidemann was the kingpin of Nazi espionage in the Far East because the Cultural Attaché spent so much of his time in the radio room communicating with outlying posts – and with Berlin.

Routine instructions were given to the clerk, whose new sixteen-year-old concubine had expensive tastes. He was to obtain carbons or discarded copies of Witzer-Weidemann's incoming and outgoing messages. Although he would be liberally rewarded if he turned up paydirt, no one was optimistic.

Joshua now stared at the flimsy papers on his desk with incredulity. *It should not have happened; it could not have happened; but it had.* Messages had been sent to seventeen agents, all different and all in unbreakable code – except one. Extraordinary good luck, perhaps the Nazi's arrogant carelessness, had put into Joshua's hands not only the coded text but the rough draft in plain language of the seventeenth: *Confirm hereby decisive action first decade May. Remain alert for instructions regarding exploitation.*

The figure 37490, which must stand for May, appeared in every message. Further, a fragment of a coded message from Berlin repeatedly displayed that figure.

Marvelling that the Germans used the same code inward and outward, Joshua whistled through his teeth and took a Havana panatella from the crystal humidor on his desk. Herr Witzer-Weidemann clearly possessed information of far more than routine significance. Just as clearly, a major – perhaps apocalyptic – event was scheduled by the Nazis for early May. It was imperative to discover exactly what the Cultural Attaché knew.

Joshua drafted a cablegram informing London that he was pursuing a major lead and requesting authority to bring Witzer-Weidemann in. The risk was low, since the kidnapping would appear to be the work of Chinese gangsters. If he were skilfully questioned under drugs, the German would afterwards not even recall what questions he had been

432

asked. He could, if necessary, be 'rationalized', but it would probably not matter if he did know that the British had sucked him dry. The scheduled event was either so sweeping it could not be cancelled or Joshua was barking up the wrong tree.

Expecting no prompt reply, Joshua was not disappointed. He was still waiting three days after despatching his urgent inquiry. In mid-April it still appeared there was a reasonable margin of safety – still time to counter whatever great event was scheduled for the first ten days of May. He resolved to give London two more days before sending a scorching reminder – or acting on his own.

Joshua then relegated the Witzer-Weidemann affair to the back of his mind. When not occupied with normal business affairs or his balancing act between his wife and his mistress, he pondered the enigma recalled by the note: *Ivan and Fritz?*

Why, he wondered, did those totalitarians, the Soviets and the Nazis, so ostentatiously avoid each other, when their consulates were neighbours on the Hongkew waterfront? If their apparent antipathy camouflaged actual cooperation, they were very skilful. Not a hint of collusion had been turned up by the telephone taps or the loose surveillance the Special Branch of the Settlement Police maintained over those potential trouble-makers. Their communications were too subtle – and too obvious.

It was neither arduous nor dangerous for one of the junior clerks at the German Consulate to forget his copy of *Shun Pao* at his favourite tea-house – and to pick up the copy of *Shun Pao* forgotten by his counter-part in the Soviet Consulate-General. The same afternoon that Joshua resolved to wait only two days more before bringing Johannes Witzer-Weidemann in, the two young clerks adroitly exchanged newspapers. As Joshua, expected, Wang the bartender had reported the electric eaves-dropping to the Chinese Communists' Apparatus. After a week, the Apparatus decided that information was of little value – and had passed it to the Soviet Consulate. After brooding for another week, the Soviets had decided to pass it to the Nazis.

Johannes Witzer-Weidemann immediately asked the Soviets to find out who was so interested in him. Further delays occurred while the Soviets asked the Apparatus and the Apparatus pressed the bartender. The answer finally reached the German: Joshua Haleevie was responsible. The Nazi's request immediately bounced back to the Soviets: ESTEEM GREAT FAVOUR YOUR ARRANGING FINAL RATIONALIZATION OF THE INTER-FERING JEWISH SWINE. FOR OBVIOUS REASONS, WE PREFER NOT TO TAKE DIRECT ACTION OURSELVES.

Julia found the late afternoon traffic on Bubbling Well Road of no compelling interest. Shifting uncomfortably on the hot leather seat of the Lincoln Continental, she toyed with her ivory cigarette-holder. She was determined not to light another Chesterfield until her wrist-watch showed precisely five o'clock. She would just have to last another twelve minutes without nicotine.

If Joshua had not entered the victuallers Dombey and Son by that time, she had permission to end her vigil. Soviet Vice-Consul Pavel Egorov had, however, assured her that Joshua would make an appearance.

'He *always* goes to Dombeys on alternate Tuesdays to look over their new selection of cheeses,' the Russian had stressed. 'You understand, Mrs Howe, we only ask of you an introduction. No great thing.'

She had nodded impatiently, annoyed by the sun in her eyes and the slats of the bench cutting into her back. Their rendezvous, or tryst as Egorov melodramatically called it, had been in Garden Park on the Bund opposite the British Consulate. The only Chinese in that park were gardeners. No fear, therefore, of Special Branch detectives disguised as coolies or clerks. Their conversation had been strained because he held the *North China Daily News* before his face, while she pretended to be immersed in the twice-read copy of *Gone With the Wind* on her lap.

'To reiterate,' Egorov had said. 'You will accost Mr Haleevie as if by accident and detain him in conversation. When Mr Slavinsky comes by, you will introduce them and discreetly take your departure.'

He paused to turn the page of the newspaper before emphasizing: 'You *must* leave immediately. And you must *not* interfere – no matter what happens.'

'Why all the hocus-pocus?' she had demanded. 'And how am I to know this Mr Slavinsky?'

'You will know Mr Slavinsky by his white panama hat. Slavinsky has problems with the Settlement authorities, and he believes Mr Haleevie can help him. A social introduction is best. . . . And our interest? Slavinsky is a goddamned White Russian. By such help we are winning over the goddamned émigrés. But, Mrs Howe, the reason for the meeting is not your business.'

He had then folded his newspaper and stalked off, leaving Julia to brood on Soviet manners. It was not the first time Pavel Egorov had reproached her. When she brought Richard Hollings to the Soviet Consulate, he had said: 'Mrs Howe, you must never – never under any circumstances – come anywhere near this building again. Never!'

He had talked to her as if she were vastly his inferior, as to a chambermaid in a third-rate provincial hotel. When her anger cooled, she had seen that it was for her own protection. It would be disastrous if anyone learned she was so close to the Soviets, and the Consulate was under intermittent surveillance. It would be catastrophic if Tommy learned that she had six months earlier decided to anticipate his inevitable agreement – and place herself at the disposal of the Soviets.

She had so far only passed on information regarding Japanese troop movements and arms shipments acquired from her uncle, Quick Jack Pavernen, and tid-bits regarding American arms sales to the Nationalists. Leaving notes in dustbins at the Columbia Country Club was hardly conducive to intimacy. But she knew the Soviets were grateful. She had returned the $5,000 in old notes they left her, rather than signing the accompanying receipt. She was not serving the cause for gain.

The tryst in Garden Park was the first time she had seen Pavel Egorov since he had received Richard and herself at the Consulate. Why, she wondered, should the Press Attaché be involved with favours to White Russians? He was, of course, responsible for propaganda, and winning over his semi-Fascist countrymen would certainly make effective propaganda. Besides, someone had to undertake the unpleasant task of espionage if the Soviet Union, the fatherland of the workers of the world, was to be safeguarded against capitalist plots.

Egorov had also introduced Richard to the Consul-General, who promised to smooth the correspondent's entrée to Soviet leaders. Richard had left Shanghai elated.

Richard, indeed! Julia had not yet solved the problem of conscience Richard posed. Perhaps she never would. She smiled reminiscently and again assured herself that she did not regret her single indiscretion.

And Tommy? She prayed she would never know exactly how Tommy would react.

Without thinking Julia lit a cigarette, although it was only nine minutes to five. Tommy would be livid if he learned of her indiscretion with Richard. He would go berserk if he learned that she was working for the Soviets. One night was conceivably forgivable, but six months of deception were beyond the limits of his tolerance.

She tapped her fingernails on the steering wheel and searched the traffic again. No sign of the big red Packard Victoria by which all Shanghai knew Joshua Haleevie.

Julia leaned across to tap her ash into the ashtray and was struck by her own reflection in the rear-view mirror. Her own eyes regarded her with an appraising green stare. Or were they mocking?

She stubbed her cigarette out and fumbled in her big straw purse for the hand-mirror. She might as well salvage what she could from the interminable wait by repairing her makeup. If Joshua turned up, she would see him in her mirror.

What, she wondered again, had impelled her to make love to Richard? He had, above all, been so woebegone – deeply hurt by Emily's rejecting him although he tried to smile it off. Yet it was not really her responsibility to compensate for Emily's cruelty – or to take Emily's place in his bed.

She had, of course, been a little tight after gin and burgundy and cointreau. She had also been resentful of Tommy. No question about that. But that was hardly an explanation and was, certainly, no justification. In fact, it was rather frightening. She was naturally monogamous, innately faithful.

She followed Marxism-Leninism, but not its puerile theories on love and marriage. The act of love no more significant than a glass of water when thirsty? Horse-feathers! Marriage only a contract – an agreement to provide domestic and sexual services in return for bed and board and trinkets? What piffle!

Julia grinned and watched her lips curve in the mirror. Too much analysis, Joshua sometimes observed, was the death-knell of spontaneous feeling. How right he was! And where was he?

She turned to scan the rush-hour traffic on Bubbling Well Road, but coult not see the chalk-white canvas hood of the red Victoria. Her critical eyes returned to her own reflection. Though her forehead was still smooth, virtually unlined, she moistened her index finger and rubbed the minute indentation between her chestnut eyebrows.

Grinning in self-deprecation, she pushed her hair off her forehead, and looked up to see that the big red Packard convertible with the white-sidewall tyres had just been parked in front of her Lincoln Continent:.l. Joshua was strolling towards the recessed doors of Dombey and Son. They might, she saw as she got out of the Continental, have dressed for the occasion. His suit was the same cream-coloured linen as her dress. But he had clearly seen neither her nor her distinctive car.

'Joshua!' she called. 'Joshua, hold on!'

He turned and smiled warmly, when he recognized her. But his light-blue eyes looked beyond her, and concern ruffled his tanned features. Yet the expression vanished so quickly that Julia felt she had imagined it. Grasping her shoulders lightly, Joshua kissed her cheek.

'Dear old Julie!' he said. 'What are you up to here?'

'I've heard so much of Dombey's new shipment of cheese,' she improvised, 'I thought I'd see for myself.'

'We're on the same errand. May I take you in?'

She had obviously been mistaken when she thought he was troubled a moment earlier. He was in high spirits, gallant and playful.

Julia slipped her hand into the crook of his elbow. She heard her name called, and she turned. Dazzled by the declining sun, she saw as a dark silhouette the bulky man waving at her. But his white panama-hat was unmistakable.

'Oh, it's Mr Slavinsky!' Julia began the mummery. 'I haven't seen you in ages. How are you? Still studying English?'

'Ya, but you was my best of all teacher.' Neither the Russian's accent nor his syntax did credit to his teacher. 'I am so glad to meeting you again.'

Prattling a reply, Julia saw out of the corner of her eye that Joshua was grinning at her embarrassment. She would have to put up with a lot of teasing from him later. But it was in a very good cause.

'Mr Haleevie,' she said automatically, 'may I present Mr Slavinsky? A former student of mine, as you've gathered.'

'Mr Haleevie, I have so long admired . . .'

Julia wondered how soon she could leave. The White Russian would not discuss his purpose while she was present, but it was impossible to obey Pavel Egorov's curt instructions to leave immediately. She could not abandon an old friend with a stranger to whom she had just introduced him. That would look precisely the put-up job it was. Sometimes, the Soviets were very impractical.

The White Russian was tall, robust, and clearly an innocent. His blunt features were honest, and his hazel eyes were trusting. She had evidently done a good turn for a hard-pressed human being as well as for the furtive Pavel Egorov. Anyway Egorov wasn't important, only the cause he – and she – served.

Julia stood between the two men, who faced each other. The White Russian was curiously tongue-tied after finally gaining an audience with the man who could solve his problems. To fill the gap, Julia told of a funny incident in the classroom, casting the reticent Slavinsky in the leading role. She would remember an urgent engagement in another minute and leave them alone as Pavel Egorov had directed.

At that moment her eyes were were drawn by the movement of Slavinsky's left hand, which Joshua could not see because she was in the way. Clenched on a long leather handle, Slavinsky's fist was inching out of the side-pocket of his jacket. Paralysed by astonishment, Julia watched the shining blade of a knife slowly draw free of the pocket.

Shocked, Julia's thoughts moved just as fast. Pavel Egorov had obviously ordered the attack. Why else instruct her to leave immediately – and on no account to interfere? Whatever his motive, Egorov must be mistaken. Joshua Haleevie was not a foe of the Communists, but of the Japanese. Besides, Communists and non-Communists were united against Japan's aggression. She had to prevent a horrible mistake.

The knife was already thrusting underhand at Joshua's stomach. Julie threw her weight on the Russian's forearm and screamed: 'Look out! A knife!'

She felt flame arc across her thighs as the blade pulled back. Joshua was apparently untouched, though his jacket was ripped. Julia fell forward to the pavement, landing painfully on her hands and knees. Looking over her shoulder, she saw Slavinsky strike again. Joshua nimbly stepped aside, and the assassin overbalanced.

The next instant, his arms were pinioned behind him by two short burly Chinese in workmen's blue jackets. Simultaneously, Joshua scooped Julia up and carried her to his big red convertible. Without a word, he tumbled her through the door and slid into the driver's seat. After stamping heavily on the self-starter, he swung into the stream of traffic.

'You know,' he remarked conversationally a few second later, 'if it hadn't been for you, Julie, I believe that chap would've got me. Silly of me to be so careless.'

Fumbling in her purse for a cigarette, Julia could not answer immediately. She was buffeted by fear, remorse, and anger. How could Egorov have been so stupid – and so ruthless? Only luck had kept her from blowing her cover. She flicked her lighter and drew smoke deep into her lungs.

'Also, my dear Julie, if it hadn't been for me,' Joshua continued in the same light tone, 'one of that lot would have got you!'

'Got me?' she asked. 'I'm so sorry, Joshua. That man Slavinsky must be mad. I'm so sorry I introduced you. But he was after you, not me, wasn't he?'

'So *he* was,' Joshua agreed genially and turned into Avenue Road.

'But *all* the others were interested in you. Not only the Special Branch, who thank God reacted so quickly. Also, a couple of lads I know to be Nationalist special agents. And, if my eyes didn't deceive me, three thugs from the Apparatus as well. All in *your* honour, my dear.'

'My honour?' Julia was shocked. 'Why should they care about me?'

'Why, indeed? Julie, you've obviously offended a lot of people by your . . . ah . . . activities. It's lucky for me the Special Branch was keeping an eye on you. But it doesn't bode well for your future welfare, does it?'

Turning into the driveway of the mansion called Zion, Joshua murmured reassurances, but did not reply to her torrent of questions. Instead, he led her to a small room lined with books and instructed his number one boy: 'Give Mrs Howe a large brandy.'

Joshua returned after ten minutes, having changed his torn jacket. Julia had found the lavatory and washed her lacerated hands and knees. She had renewed her makeup, but could do no more about the slit in her skirt than pin it together. Across her right thigh stretched a hair-fine red line some four inches long.

'Well now, Julie,' Joshua asked, 'what *are* we going to do with you?'

Since the question was obviously rhetorical, she smiled shakily over her brandy snifter. Even medicinal brandy was served in crystal balloons in the Haleevie household, she reflected inconsequentially.

'Tommy's on his way,' Joshua told her. 'He said he was afraid of something like this. Julie, he agrees. You're leaving tonight for Hong Kong. The *Chusan* sails at ten, so there's just time to . . .'

'Leaving, Joshua?' she protested. 'That's madness. Why should *I* leave? You're the one who's in danger. They . . . he . . . was after you, not me. I don't see . . .'

'Julie, I can now look after myself very well, thanks to you. Your Soviet playmates won't catch me on the wrong foot again. I'm deeply indebted to you. You've also cast a glaring light on a couple of other matters that've been puzzling me. But as for you, my dear . . .'

'Joshua, please don't be silly.' She laughed unconvincingly. 'I'm glad you can make jokes so soon after. But I'm not feeling . . .'

'Julie, the time for fun and games is over,' he cut in. 'Among others, the Soviets will now be after you for spoiling their game. Also the angry Nationalists – the Apparatus, which will feel betrayed. That's a pretty collection of enemies, isn't it? Not to speak of Special Branch. You've got to leave, madam – right now.'

'I'm not saying you're right about my . . . ah . . . activities, Joshua. But, even if you are, what's the rush? Surely a few days longer, if I were well protected, wouldn't . . .'

'I *can't* protect you from the Special Branch, my dear. That's why I whisked you away so fast . . . to keep you out of their clutches. Be realistic. You're now a liability – a danger to Tommy and your little girls.'

She gestured in feeble protest, but he over-rode her: 'You used to be a shield. The Nationalists have good reason to be suspicious of Tommy, but they wouldn't touch him. Not with an American wife who was so well in with the foreign press. But now you attract danger. All bets are off as long as you're still in Shanghai. Afterwards, Donald Howe's son and Donald Howe's grand-daughters, will still enjoy National protection and tolerance. But not . . . not if their mother remains in town.'

'Joshua,' she asked faintly, 'aren't you being a bit melodramatic? You make me sound like Typhoid Mary bringing disaster wherever I go.'

'Except that you're not immune. You haven't already forgotten our little melodrama on Bubbling Well Road, have you, Julie? Would you like to attend the opening night after the botched dress-rehearsal?'

Wheels skidded on gravel, and a half minute later Tommy entered the room. He was carrying her small suitcase and her beige-cashmere spring coat. He appeared calm, aside from the slight whiteness at the corners of his mouth.

'Joshua's right, darling,' he said emphatically. 'You'll have to go, tonight! Now, Josh, if Julie and I can have a moment alone . . .'

When the door closed, Tommy said no more. He took her in his arms and pulled her close. He kissed her forehead and then her lips.

'My darling!' he said. 'Darling, daring, brave Julie! I do love you! And I'll miss you fearfully. But it's . . .'

She kissed him fiercely, drawing reassurance from his lips. He embraced her so tight her ribs hurt.

'I do love you, Julie! If you'd only told me about you and the Soviets. I could be very angry.' He broke off and resumed gently: 'Everything will be all right. You'll be away a while and then . . .'

She could not believe it would be so simple, but she nodded in emphatic agreement. He stepped back to arm's length to look hard at her face and noticed the rent in her skirt.

'I almost forgot,' he said professionally. 'Let's have a look at that cut.'

Transition
Mid-1941–Mid-1946

The cramped cabin of the coaster *Chusan*, all yellow varnish and threadbare puce carpet, depressed Julia during the three prolonged and solitary days before she reached safe haven in Hong Kong. Afterwards, the staterooms on the SS *President McKinley* crossing the Pacific were roomy and attractive, although she soon tired of repeating her tale of having gone to Hong Kong to say farewell to a dying friend and then returning to Shanghai on the *McKinley* so that her daughters could join her for the voyage to San Francisco.

Shepherded by an increasingly cantankerous Lao Zee, ten-year-old Althea and seven-year-old Persephone were as sunny as the Pacific Ocean itself after recovering with disheartening alacrity from the shock of leaving their father and their home. The twelve-day voyage was, however, marred by superfluity: too much food; too much time to think; and too much of the company of the ten American wives who had followed the Consulate's advice to remove themselves and their children from the war zone. Julia had to put up with far too much prying from those inquisitive women, who patently did not believe her story.

And she missed Tommy desperately. They had been able to snatch only a half-hour alone on the boat-deck of the *McKinley* while Lao Zee settled the girls in their cabin. Thank God there was no one besides Tommy, for he had sensibly concealed her second departure from her friends as well as her enemies. It had, though, been Tommy at his best. Not a word about the mess she had made, not even a glancing reference to her working for the Soviets in secret. He had simply pledged his love again and promised either to send for her 'just as soon as this nonsense blows over' or to join her for a while in the States. They would not, he had said confidently, be separated for more than six months. In the meantime the change of climate would help Althea's asthma, while both the girls and their maternal grandparents would be happier for finally meeting each other.

Things did not quite work out as they had planned while the *McKinley* tugged at her buoy and the gulls mewed around her portholes. The tedious voyage across the Pacific Ocean was to be the prelude to a protracted separation from the two beings Julia loved most: Tommy and Shanghai.

She initially believed her stay would be so brief that she leased an indifferently furnished apartment on Morningside Heights in Manhattan, rather than go to the trouble of buying new furniture. Her parents had agreed after a few months that she would be happier in New York City than in Puxatawney. She could meet congenial new friends in the neighbourhood around Columbia University, and the Horace Mann School offered the girls a first-class education. By September, 1940, they were settled in the spacious apartment overlooking the Hudson River, which even that fiercely loyal Shanghailander Lao Zee acknowledged was far more beautiful than the drab Hwangpoo.

In late October a letter from Julia crossed one from Tommy. She was already asking when she could return to Shanghai. He asked her to confirm by telephone the graduate fellowship in thoracic medicine offered by Columbia's School of Physicians and Surgeons. She was to cable him, for he was tired of waiting for the academic bureaucrats to send their formal invitation.

Tommy arrived on Christmas Eve of 1940, which was later than he would have liked because Julia had enjoined him not to entrust himself to aeroplanes. He was greeted not only by his exultant wife, but by two nearly delirious small daughters. Even dour Lao Zee bubbled. Julia's subsequent welcome was so uninhibited that Tommy complained with a straight face that he was exhausted by emotion – and exertion – when he began his work at Physicians and Surgeons in mid-January.

The fellowship seemed only a pretext for his coming to the United States, for he gave his family more time than he ever had in Shanghai. He further promised that he would not return until they could all go together. Discovering New York in Tommy's company was a joy for Julia, and the girls were just the right age to appreciate its tawdry splendours.

In late September of 1941 a cablegram shattered the idyll: Donald Howe had suffered a stroke, and the prognosis was not good. This time Tommy did entrust himself to aeroplanes. He vanished, it seemed, from one moment to the next, leaving a cupboard full of clothing, a spare razor, and a yawning hole in their lives.

Tommy cabled when Donald Howe died in mid-October. His father, he later wrote, had departed in peace from the world at the venerable age of seventy-eight. His mother Eurydice, who was five years younger, wished to retire to a Buddhist convent near their home village. He would himself remain in Shanghai until the estate was settled to keep an eye on

441

his three elder brothers. He trusted them implicitly, but it would do no harm to be on hand. He would also help carry out his father's final commitments to charities and clients. That task he could not in conscience leave to his brothers.

His subsequent letters promised faithfully to be back in New York by January of 1942. He had even managed to smooth over Julia's indiscretions, himself placating the Apparatus while Joshua squared the Settlement authorities. The entire family would return to Shanghai in the summer of 1942, when the girls had completed their school year and their father had concluded his interrupted fellowship.

Julia did not immediately think of the personal consequences when the bulletin interrupted the Philharmonic's concert to report the surprise Japanese attack on the American fleet at Pearl Harbor on December 7, 1941. Later, news of a minor naval action at Shanghai was buried amid spectacular reports of attacks on Singapore, Luzon and Hong Kong. That small item naturally focused Julia's thoughts on her own predicament. She now faced a protracted stay in the United States – a prolonged separation from Tommy. And only God knew what would become of him amid the expanded new war in Asia.

A cablegram from Elizaveta Alexandrovna Yavalenka received on New Year's Eve advised Julia that Tommy was well. GONE AWAY FOR HIS HEALTH, it concluded cryptically. After several agonizing months of silence, Julia received a letter from Tommy on a single sheet of coarse brown paper, forwarded by Harry Smythe in Kunming. It concluded: *Do not worry if you don't hear from me. It is likely that I shall not be able to write again for some time – and regular correspondence is obviously impossible. You will hear if something untoward occurs. You must therefore not worry about silence. I love you always.*

All the world was now at war, and the war was not going well. In the Pacific Theatre the Americans, the Dutch and the British were numbed by repeated blows. Attacking the concentrated military targets that had evaded them in China, the Imperial Japanese Army and Navy appeared invincible. If Julia had not already seen these same conquering Japanese sucked deep into the military quagmire created by China's vast size and enormous population, she might have despaired.

The defeats in the Pacific were shattering, but they were not as devastating as the German sweep in Europe. France had collapsed while Julia was steaming towards San Francisco on the *President McKinley* in the early summer of 1940. The shock was overwhelming, even to those primarily concerned with the Far Eastern front of the global struggle. France might not have fallen quite so ignominiously, Julia felt, if Britain's Secret Intelligence Service had given a whit of attention to its unpaid agent in Shanghai, Joshua Haleevie.

German Cultural Attaché Johannes Witzer-Weidemann had clearly been privy to the secret plan whose fulfilment was reported in screaming headlines on May 10, 1940. The 'business of May', which Witzer-Weidemann had toasted, was obviously the Nazi *Blitzkrieg*, the lightning attack against the Low Countries and France. If Joshua had been allowed to extract that secret, it might have been a different story. Forewarned, the French might, at the least, not have collapsed quite so fast.

Yet, Julia reflected, all the warnings in the world might not really have altered the outcome. France had actually been forewarned repeatedly during the years between the wars, but had not awakened to her peril. A society honey-combed with moral corruption could no more reform than its people could change the colour of their eyes. Innumerable warnings had also failed to avert the bleak fate of the International Settlement and the French Concession in Shanghai.

Julia later heard the story of the so-called 'last days of Shanghai' from Elizaveta, who was the perfect observer. Technically neutral because Russia was not in the war, Elizaveta was unobtrusive because of her obtrusive profession. In a cool upper-class English accent underlaid by a Scots burr she later spoke the elegy for the unique international community: 'It was a race between the Limeys and the Yanks to get out first. Right after the US Marines pulled out, the last of the American gunboats, bar one, disappeared downriver towards Manila. And the last of the British flotilla, bar one, churned off to Hong Kong. At the beginning of December 1941, but by the old Russian calendar . . .'

Implored to omit the vagaries of the Czarist calendar, Elizaveta smiled demurely and went on: 'Joshua spent the night of Sunday, December 7th at the Shanghai Club. He said he wanted to be near the action. Actually, he wanted to be near me. His . . . that woman . . . was of course away – either in Sydney or Washington. And Joshua was proceeding by easy stages towards a berth at the Ikra. He would have arrived after another night or two. About four o'clock that Monday morning, the night exploded. The Bund was rocked, and I was also awakened on Kiangse Road. I could see only the flare of explosions over the Hwangpoo against the sky. But Joshua had a grandstand seat. From his window, he saw Jap field pieces firing at ships and tracers flying over the river. To the north he saw the flash of big naval guns. The old Jap flagship *Idzumo* was exercising her ancient guns.'

Elizaveta inserted a dark Murad into her cigarette-holder and continued: 'Julie, all British and American warships were gone, except two. So the *Idzumo*'s targets were those wee gunboats, HMS *Petrel* and the USS *Wake*. Both were manned by skeleton crews, and *Petrel* was commanded by a sixty-three-year-old Naval Reserve lieutenant. So, my dear, one burned – and the Japs swarmed over the other. The war for Shanghai was over. Off the Bund, Joshua found the streets barred by Japanese sailors with fixed bayonets. Rather than argue with the inevitable – and cold steel – he went back to sleep after telephoning me. Yes, the phones and the utilities all kept working. The Japanese wanted to take over a going concern.'

Her midnight-blue eyes glacial, Elizaveta concluded: 'Next morning the Japs poured into the Concessions. Since resistance was impossible, the little men marched in unopposed. They posted proclamations telling us what we already knew: a state of war now existed between Japan and the allies: Britain, Holland, and the US. The posters urged everyone to carry on normal businesses. Well, *my* business was all right, despite competition from local amateurs and imported Japanese tarts who called themselves geishas.

'But who else could do business? Most could only mark time until the crackdown: confiscation of their property and internment of all enemy nationals. Did you know your uncle, Quick Jack Pavernen, refused an offer of liberty to work for the Japs? Later, civilians were exchanged – Japs from the US for Americans from Shanghai. But you know all about that end of it, don't you?'

'I saw the repatriated Americans in New York when they landed, Liz,' Julia answered. 'By that time, I was working for OWI, the Office of War Information. I came from San Francisco by second-class sleeping-car. Such were my sacrifices for the war effort! But you? What then?'

'Joshua had previously arranged to disappear – and he did. With his chum from the French Club, Fatty Woo, he drifted into the interior. Extraordinary, those two! They fought with the guerrillas and they rescued aviators shot down over Jap-occupied territory. I still had some unfinished business with the Japs. So I stayed put with my orphans for the time being.'

Ironically, China's destiny – and their own – was to be decided not by these dramatic Japanese attacks, but by apparently obscure events in the interior. Nationalist-Communist relations broke down, and the United Anti-Japanese Front ceased to exist, except in name, after the conflict called the New Fourth Army Incident. Julia recalled discussing with her students at Kai Ming College the beginning of major clashes between Nationalist units and the organized guerrillas of the Communists' New Fourth Army in 1939. Both Tommy and Joshua were to work with that Communist force as the war went on.

Operating behind the Japanese lines, the New Fourth Army was daily growing stronger – and more independent. Exasperated by constant insubordination, the Generalissimo finally ordered that Army to move north of the Yellow River. Rather than abandon large areas in the Yangtze Valley, the Communists mutinied. After a Nationalist attack early in 1941 captured the Army's commanding general, the Communists stubbornly appointed a new commander and consolidated their positions near Shanghai. Even the pretence of a United Front collapsed, and Chou En-lai left Chungking – not to return for several years.

While the Communists expanded their ground strength behind the fluid Japanese lines, the Nationalists took to the air. Harrison Parker Smythe III virtually licked his lips in satisfaction when he told Julia on a flying visit to the United States: 'Claire Chennault really got going in the spring of 1941, when he got orders from the Generalissimo to buy a hundred

444

American pursuit planes. Just as well our publicity campaign had prepared the people and the Administration. We'd finally convinced the American people the Chinese were fighting their fight. At last the legalistic obstructionism were swept away. And Claire Chennault was given *carte blanche* to recruit pursuit pilots from the US Army and Navy.'

By late 1941 the American Volunteer Group was flying Curtis-Wright P-40s. The small, swift, and highly manoeuvrable Japanese Zero was proving a better pursuit plane than anything the United States produced. But Chennault drilled his volunteers in his three-plane echelon. He also paid a bonus of US $500 for every Japanese plane shot down. The Americans painted grinning teeth on their engine-cowlings – and inevitably became known as the Flying Tigers.

Julia considered her own war effort almost laughable, quite minor and regrettably free of danger. The Office of War Information enthusiastically welcomed her in mid-1942 and posted her to San Francisco. Her radio experience and her association with foreign correspondents were considered ideal qualifications, although she warned she could hardly write a single original sentence. Her covert association with the Chinese Communist Party was evidently a further – and perhaps decisive – recommendation. Staffed by gifted amateurs, the OWI focused its output primarily on Asia – and secondarily on the American people's perception of Asia.

San Francisco was very pleasant. Althea and Persephone were avidly discovering America, and in Chinatown Lao Zee even found a family that spoke Shanghainese. San Francisco would have been delightful – except for Tommy's absence and Julia's constant anxiety about him. She heard from him at widely separated intervals.

In October 1942 her desk chief introduced a white-haired Chinese who taught sociology at Stanford University. Professor Han's courtly manner amused her, but the message he conveyed ruffled her. The Apparatus directed Comrade Julia Howe to place herself at the disposal of a Soviet controller. They were all on the same side now, Professor Han reminded her. The Chinese Communists, the Soviet Union, and the United States were all fighting a common enemy. Since Yenan lacked Moscow's chain of consulates and front organizations in the United States, she was to work directly for the Soviets.

Having been used as a Soviet cat's paw against Joshua Haleevie, Julia declared that serving as a Russian spy was no part of her commitment to the struggle to liberate China. Besides, the Russians were not fighting Japan, but only the Germans. Professor Han just said: 'You have received your instructions. It is not up to you to debate, but to obey.'

Julia did not obey. After a week of debating with herself, she simply ignored her appointment with her Soviet controller. To her surprise, she was subjected to no great pressure. Professor Han smiled coolly and declared: 'The Russians are, of course, the Russians – Communist or not. We understand. But, just remember: never defy *our* assignments!'

445

After several colleagues had made extended trips to Chungking, Julia felt it was her turn. She could certainly see Emily, whom she missed greatly. She could hope to find Tommy, perhaps even manage a visit to Yenan. The girls would be happy with their surrogate mother, Lao Zee, and their grandmother. Julia's mother, a vigorous sixty-three, had volunteered to come to San Francisco to look after them.

'It'll do the old fellow good to get away from cold upper New York State to balmy California,' she wrote. Julia smiled. Her father was exactly eleven months older than her mother, who knew that San Francisco was not balmy, but foggy.

Julia then awaited formal approval of her journey. Her desk chief was enthusiastic. What better tale to bring the human realities home to the American people than a wife seeking her Chinese husband, who was fighting in Japanese-occupied territory? What better way to touch the heart-strings of the Chinese people than the devotion of an American wife to her Chinese husband?

Bureaucratic delay was to be expected of any government operation, even one run by gifted amateurs. But Julia was indignant when her chief told her of further delay 'for reasons they won't tell even me'. A visit by the courtly Professor Han thereupon clarified the issue – to her fury.

'It has been decided,' he told her, 'that you can be of greater service here than flitting off to Chungking. What do you want with those reactionaries anyway?'

When her fury subsided, Julia glumly recognized that her personal desires could be thwarted at will by the revolutionary conspiracy to which she gave her total allegiance. She had made herself the pawn of men who had little regard for her wishes – or her welfare.

Still seething, she was delighted when Emily telephoned from Washington in late May 1943 to announce her impending visit to San Francisco with Mayling Chiang. Julia could not go to Chungking, but Chungking was coming to her in the person of her sister-in-law.

They met at the reception at the San Francisco Press Club where Vice-Minister of Information Hollington Tong waxed garrulous. By the club's tradition the statuette of a black cat standing before him guaranteed that his indiscretions would not be reported – neither his bitter comments on the Chinese Communists nor his slurs on the 'left-wing intellectuals who dominate the American press'.

Afterwards, it was like being back in the dormitory at Bryn Mawr following a long weekend apart. Her daughters were fast asleep after rediscovering their Aunt Emily, as was Lao Zee after a tear-stained reunion. Snug in quilted dressing-gowns, Julia and Emily looked down from Telegraph Hill at the swirl of fog where the lights of the Golden Gate Bridge shone in peacetime and talked the night out. They naturally dwelt on the one topic that had fascinated them at Bryn Mawr – men.

Emily had brought a long letter from Tommy, which began: 'My own darling Julie,' and closed: 'Forever, my love.' The letter would be her talisman in the uncertain future, but his news was already stale. Emily had taken nearly a month to reach New York, flying three quarters of the way around the world from Chungking to Calcutta through the Middle East to Africa and then across the Atlantic by way of Portugal. 'In Lisbon,' she said, 'I just managed to avoid Richard Hollings. No doubt he was up to something shady.'

No point in pursuing that topic. Emily only shook her head when asked: 'And . . . all this time . . . still no one else?' She was a woman of formidable constancy, completely – and pointlessly – faithful to her lost love.

Julia avoided praising Richard's new book *The Bear at Bay*, which had entrenched him in the front rank of serious journalists. She had her own reservations about the Soviets' operations abroad, but her sister-in-law had become a fanatical anti-Communist. Emily would undoubtedly have sneered at his wholesome picture of the Soviet Union united against the Nazi invaders. Nor did Julia confide that the OWI expected Richard to call into San Francisco in a few weeks' time en route to the Pacific Theatre.

'It'll be a new world when we go back to Shanghai after the war.' Emily inevitably turned to the world situation. 'Remember, it's only a couple of months since the British and the Americans renounced extra-territoriality. They hated to give up their privileges, but they knew they couldn't turn the clock back after the war. Even I shed a tear for the end of the Settlement and Frenchtown. Anyway, old Shanghai's finished forever. We can't go back!'

In July 1944 Sir Judah and Lady Haleevie came to San Francisco from New York, where they had lived since buying their way out of Shanghai. The old couple were a living link to the sunlit past whom Julia loved almost as much as her own parents. Joshua's estranged wife, Charlotte, the only member of their family to accompany them, was delighted to have Julia entertain them. Even dutiful Charlotte needed some time away from her demanding parents-in-law. Julia loved talking about the old days with the pair who had not just watched Shanghai grow, but had built a good part of the unique city on the mudflats of the Yangtze Delta. Their presence recalled earlier and simpler days.

In princely exile in an apartment occupying an entire floor of the Fairmont Hotel, Rachel Haleevie still treated Julia like a giddy twenty-year-old – and made her feel young and carefree. Julia was not greatly surprised, though she poignantly felt the futility of afterthoughts, when Rachel confessed with the candour of age: 'My dear, I'm very sorry I stood between Joshua and his Russian lady. It was another age, but even so. His marriage with Charlotte, it hasn't turned out so well, has it?'

On a chilly October afternoon, Julia found the six servants milling ineffectually in the enormous apartment. Immured in his bedroom, Sir Judah was a remote presence. Only seventy-one to her husband's eighty-three, Rachel Haleevie had died in her sleep an hour earlier. When he received Julia, Sir Judah was a grieving old Testament prophet with silver hair.

447

'It's better for Rachel.' His voice was steady, although his eyes were red-rimmed. 'She never wanted to be left alone. But, Lord, why did she leave me without saying goodbye?'

In accordance with Mosaic law, Rachel Haleevie was buried the next day. Her eldest son, Jeremiah, arrived the following day, having performed the miraculous feat for wartime of chartering a Lockheed Stratoliner. In the interim Julia had kept vigil with Sir Judah. All the curtains were drawn; all the mirrors were covered; and she was constantly on the verge of tears.

'We keep vigil for a week – to keep the survivors from brooding.' Sir Judah's outward composure was still unbroken. 'To keep them busy, particularly the women, looking after the guests. But for an old fellow like myself, virtually alone! It only gives the servants something to do. If we were in Shanghai, hundreds would be calling!'

Jeremiah Haleevie did not have to make another hurried journey. On the fifth morning after Rachel's death, the valet called him to his father's bedroom. Even more like an Old Testament prophet in his old-fashioned nightshirt, Sir Judah lay serenely back against his pillows. A secret smile lit his worn features, and his staring eyes revealed that he had joined his wife.

As 1944 slowly closed, Tommy contrived to write almost once a month. Julia could reply in care of Harry Smythe, who was, as he himself said, 'colonel, senior aide, chief cook, and bottle washer' to Major-General Claire Chennault, commander of the US Fourteenth Air Force in China.

The had to write very carefully because their letters could be intercepted. Harry Smythe would put out his eyes before he read their letters, but other Americans – and, of course, the Nationalists – were hardly as scrupulous.

Tommy wrote that he now truly appreciated the work Kit Marlowe did for Frank Walsingham in the field. Confirming her recollection of Elizabethan drama with a quick shuffle through an old textbook, Julia learned she was being informed – and warned. The playwright Christopher Marlowe had been an agent of the Tudor Queen Elizabeth's spymaster, Sir Francis Walsingham. Tommy's service to the Communist cause patently still involved espionage.

The suave Professor Han stood smiling narrowly in the doorway when Julia answered the bell of the apartment on Telegraph Hill the Sunday before Christmas of 1944. After taking the best arm-chair and happily accepting brandy that was grudgingly offered, he said: 'The Apparatus has not, my dear Mrs Howe, sent me with further unpalatable news. Only new instructions and a review of the situation so that you will be more effective. Also, Doctor Howe requested that you be fully informed.'

Julia felt a glow of pleasure at his being required to come to her on Tommy's orders. She nodded and settled down to nurse her scotch and soda.

'The Nationalists are doing the job for us by their vile deeds – convincing our friends and winning over our enemies,' Professor Han declared complacently. 'Very soon China will drop into our lap like a ripe peach. We must still struggle hard, but the outcome is certain.'

The first major Japanese offensive in years, that autumn, had been most beneficial, he explained. The large-scale offensive called *Ichigo*, Operation Number One, had driven the Nationalists out of most of South China, captured the forward bases of Chennault's Fourteenth Air Force, and threatened Chungking. After clearing a wide corridor from North China to Indo-China, the Japanese had stopped in exhaustion. Operation One had, however, savaged the Nationalists and precipitated the inevitable break between proud Generalissimo Chiang Kai-shek and his acid American Chief of Staff, General Joseph Stillwell.

'Stillwell behaved like a fool – much to our benefit,' Professor Han continued. 'How he thought he could force Chiang Kai-shek's hand! Another arrogant foreigner who thinks he knows China. I beg your pardon, Mrs Howe, but you will know what I mean. Stillwell demanded that Chiang Kai-shek withdraw the Nationalist units, more than 400 thousand men, blockading our Border Region. He wanted to use that force against Operation Number One. He threatened to cut off American Lend-Lease supplies if Chiang did not comply. That just hastened the inevitable. When the Generalissimo gave the President an ultimatum, Roosevelt had no choice. He had to relieve Stillwell.'

Julia restrained her impatience, although Professor Han's confidences had all appeared in the State Department despatches from Chungking she regularly read – and passed on to the Apparatus.

'Of course, that leaves Chennault the most influential American in China,' he resumed. 'Chennault is a great man in the air. On the ground he's not so hot. He's leading the Generalissimo down a blind alley. He's preaching that the Nationalists can defeat the Japanese – and the Communists – with air power alone. However, victory in China will come on the ground, not in the air. I pray every night for Chennault's continuing good health.'

Claire Chennault's supply-starved Fourteenth Air Force had signally failed to halt the Japanese assault on its own bases. Nor could millions of battle-tempered Communist infantrymen be stopped even by swarms of aeroplanes. Julia was elated. For the first time, she *knew* the Communists' triumph was inevitable.

Professor Han lifted his empty tumbler suggestively, and Julia readily refilled it. He sipped appreciatively and observed: 'The Nationalist split with the Americans is widening. The Americans in China are simply disgusted with corruption. Chiang Kai-shek's brother-in-law H. H. Kung is worth ten divisions to us. As Minister of Finance, he insists that the Americans pay one dollar US for twenty Chinese dollars. The black market rate, the *realistic* rate, is 800 Chinese to one US. And how much of the profits go into H.H. Kung's own pocket?

'I could almost feel sorry for Chiang Kai-shek. He still can't control his own Central Government. And he still can't bring the warlords to heel. He's like a juggler with too many bowls and glasses in the air. When exhaustion forces him to stop, the whole lot will smash to the ground.

'He simply isn't ruthless enough,' Professor Han summed up. 'Comrade Stalin told him he must exert iron control. Execute millions to ensure his complete control. But he didn't.'

'And my role?' Julia asked.

'As you know, we *never* deny that we are Communists, dedicated Marxist-Leninists,' he replied. 'Sometimes, though, it's better not to broadcast that fact. The Americans are determined to convince themselves that we are really agrarian nationalists or revolutionary reformers, whatever that means. A lot of earnest Americans have milled around Yenan – and seen very little. One colonel did question our military training and our effectiveness against the Japanese. Some State Department officers have warned that we would in time rule all China. But they've been ignored. . . . Mrs Howe, you might make a note or two – have you a pencil and paper?

'You will in the future concentrate on the Nationalists' failings: corruption, cruelty, ineffectiveness – and avoiding battles with the Japanese, even collaborating with them. Regarding our side, you will stress: patriotism, moderation, idealism, total dedication to the war against the Japanese, and constant readiness to talk with the Nationalists – on equal terms.'

Since Chou En-lai had just walked out of negotiations with the Nationalists for the third time, that last condition rang somewhat hollow even in Julia's sympathetic ears. Generalissimo Chiang Kai-shek declared that recognizing the Communists – and their Border Region – as equal to the Central Government would mean renouncing sovereignty over all China. Chairman Mao Tse-tung contended that the Communists were a political party like the National People's Party and that the Border Region was an autonomous government. The split was irreconcilable.

'Professor Han, I take it that the battlefield for public opinion is now primary.' Julia spoke with the formality the matter warranted. 'Do I also take it that we can win on that battlefield alone?'

'Never, Mrs Howe, never!' He was shocked. 'In some circumstances, public opinion can be the decisive factor. We must always attend to public opinion. But in China today propaganda can no more win alone than guerrillas can win alone. Both are the handmaidens of conventional military forces, the big battalions which alone can bring us to power. But the day of reckoning is very close!'

45

A little worn and a little scarred, Shanghai was manifestly still Shanghai. The fact that the Republic of China now ruled the International Settlement and the French Concession had altered neither the city's outlines nor its tough, wise-cracking natives. Something fundamental had, however, altered – something fundamental but not readily apparent.

Julia Howe puzzled over that elusive alteration while she and her family were borne down Nanking Road in Joshua Haleevie's Rolls Royce Phantom, which had been preserved through the Japanese occupation behind a false wall in his garage. Coming ashore in the launch from the new liner SS *President Wilson*, she had found the Bund wholly unaltered – ponderous, crude and assertive, as always. From Jardines and the Chartered Bank at the northern end to the Shanghai Club and the Bank of China at the southern, the temples of Mammon had suffered little. Naturally, the old Japanese flagship *Idzumo* was gone. Her three spindly funnels no longer dominated the Hwangpoo, but the American destroyer with the big white *DD 246* painted on her bow was a welcome replacement.

When the Rolls was halted by a traffic policeman, Julia's daughters leaned through the window. The elder's pale-blonde hair was a striking contrast to the younger's jet-black. Blasé at sixteen, Althea hardly allowed herself to display curiosity regarding the birthplace she had not seen for six years. To thirteen-year-old Persephone, Shanghai was an enchanted world. The sisters gaped at the crowds swirling on Nanking Road and at the profusion of silks, jades, furniture, and delicacies in shop windows and on open counters. Although shabby in mid-June of 1946, almost a year after the Japanese surrender, Shanghai was herself again: hectic, materialistic, and ostentatious.

Tommy, too, leaned forward for a better view. The city's pulse had quickened in the six months since he left for New York to resume his interrupted fellowship at the College of Physicians and Surgeons – and to reclaim the wife and daughters he had not seen for almost five years.

Julia was still nagged by the fundamental alteration she could not put her finger on. When the Rolls was released by the policeman's wave, she found the answer.

The police had always been natty in crisp khakis. They were now sloppy in crumpled cotton uniforms and ill-fitting peaked caps. The policeman at the busy intersection slouched, and a cigarette drooped from the corner of his mouth. Rather than the heavy traffic on Nanking Road, he might have been directing the sparse flow of a Chinese city. Julia smiled at her own lapse. He *was* directing the traffic of a Chinese city.

For the first time, the reality of the concessions' new status came home to her. After the renunciation of extra-territorial privileges by the U.S. and Britain during the war, the Settlement and Frenchtown were now integral parts of Chinese-ruled Greater Shanghai. Although she had worked hard for that change, Julia was saddened by the demise of that gorgeous anomaly, the multi-national metropolis. Being within the old boundaries of the Settlement, yet not being in the Settlement, was eerie, rather like being a ghost at one's own funeral.

Lao Zee, Tommy observed softly, would not have liked this new Shanghai that looked exactly like the old Shanghai. A fearful snob, the amah had been proud of the Settlement's foreign administration. She would have hated a Shanghai that was ruled just like other Chinese cities – inefficiently, corruptly, cruelly, and capriciously.

Julia took Tommy's hand. Lao Zee would be coming home a little later, after the *President Wilson* unloaded her coffin from the hold. When the only Shanghai family in San Francisco's Chinatown moved away, Lao Zee had pined. Although she described China as 'very dirty country with many bad men and many wicked mandarins', she had extracted the promise that her bones would be returned to that dirty country.

The Rolls drew up before the house on Kiukiang Road. Julia felt she was meeting an old friend who had suffered greatly, but survived triumphantly. The door and the windows were obviously new, and a crescent of pale bricks reached from the sixth to the third floor, a fresh scar against the weathered old bricks. Tommy had described the damage inflicted late in the war and the repairs that had almost been completed before his own departure. The work could not have been done with half the speed or half the skill in New York for twice the price. The old Shanghai spirit was still alive.

The red Packard Victoria with the white-canvas hood parked before the house belonged to Joshua, whose cars apparently bore charmed lives. A note sent with the chauffeur of his Rolls had sensitively suggested that the Howes would probably prefer to disembark undisturbed by a welcoming party. He would, he added, await them at Kiukiang Road. Behind the Packard exactly twenty-five feet of coal-black Hispano-Suiza

was gleaming as if just out of the showroom. Sometime Countess Elizaveta Alexandrovna Yavalenka was also waiting for them. The Cadillac
Fleetwood limousine a shade longer than the Hispano-Suiza was
unfamiliar, as was the metallic-silver Cord coupé with the boxy body
and the headlights sunk in the mudguards.

'Em's new runabout.' Tommy pointed the stem of his pipe at the
Fleetwood. 'She doesn't like driving herself any more. What with her
young – your nieces and nephew – as well as meeting dignitaries and
visiting firemen, she says, she really needs a decent-sized motor car.
Almost indecently large I'd say.'

Julia smiled with exaggerated sweetness and waited for him to
continue. When he looked guilelessly at her, she asked: 'And the Cord,
Tommy? You always wanted a Cord, didn't you?'

'Did I? I don't remember. Of course it's not much, not that one.
Practically an antique – more than ten years old.'

'I hope you and the Cord'll be very happy together.' Julia smiled
broadly. 'At least it's not as hideous as that old Chrysler Airflow, dear.'

'Hideous? Why she was beautiful. And, even now, very advanced technically – even after ten years. Do you know . . .'

Julia turned to her daughters, who were staring in disbelief at their
home.

'Gosh, it's only a brick house,' Althea marvelled. 'Mom, I always
thought of it more as a castle. Enormous and . . .'

Emily embraced them in the cavernous sitting-room that was a cave of
memories. She was not wearing her wartime uniform of blouse and
trousers, but the *cheongsam* she had earlier adopted, though with some
reluctance, as an affirmation of her patriotism. Julia was disturbed by
Emily's appearance. Her expression was strained, and she was so thin
her pelvic bones made little peaks beneath her tight, orange-chiffon
cheongsam. When she smiled, she appeared ethereal because of her translucent skin, but the line between her eyebrows did not vanish.

Tommy kissed his sister hard, frowned, and declared: 'I don't like the
way you're looking, Em. I've got a good man I want you to see. David
Chen'll give you a good going over and . . .'

'Don't fuss, Tommy, not now,' she protested. 'Julie hasn't seen the
children since . . . My, Althea, Perse, how you've grown. I know it's not
the thing to say, but . . .'

Dark-haired Persephone threw herself into the arms of her glamorous
Aunt Emily, the daring aviatrix she had always worshipped. Despite the
natural reserve of her sixteen years, Althea, too, yielded to her aunt's
formidable charm. Then she glanced with ostentatious lack of interest at
the youth and the two girls standing behind their mother.

'Jason, Patricia, and Eunice,' Emily directed, 'say hello to your Aunt
Julia and Uncle Tommy. By the way, Hsiu asked to be forgiven. He
wasn't feeling . . .'

They were not to hear how Emily's absent husband was feeling at seventy-two, for her voice trailed away. No one expected him to appear except at formal family functions. Julia and Tommy surveyed Emily's children, who were Ou-yang Hsiu's 'modern family'. Dutiful and embarrassed, their nieces kissed them. Their nephew offered a half-bow, a handshake, and flutes of champagne.

Studying Jason over the rim, Julia felt a rush of affection. Although his round head was like his father's, the seventeen-year-old was in manner, physique, and features uncannily like the young Tommy Howe. Tall and thin, he moved with engaging awkwardness. Although he did not wear spectacles as his uncle had, his stance, his shy assurance, and his gentle smile all recalled Tommy as Julia remembered meeting him twenty-five years ago.

Jason's worn cotton trousers and crumpled light-blue cotton tunic with a stand-up collar were like a clerk on holiday. He explained somewhat defensively that he was attending a student meeting that evening and did not want to look different. Tommy and Emily looked at each other. Julia knew they were, like herself, recalling student meetings in the 1920s. Jason, his mother said, was only demonstrating solidarity with his fellow students at American-oriented Yenching University in Peiping. Since the war had kept him from perfecting his English, he needed a thorough grounding before transferring to an American university.

Wondering idly why Emily had explained at such length, Julia turned again to her nieces. Patricia, who was fifteen, and Eunice, who was thirteen, were attractive in striped cotton dresses and saddle-shoes. Their heads were long like the Howes', but their features were small and neat like the Ou-yangs'.

'Let's go up to the roof.' Jason shooed his miniature harem up the circular staircase. 'Let's go up and let the grown-ups play.'

Humour as well as gentle charm, Julia noted. He would be devastating in a few years. Where, she wondered, had he acquired that understated self-assurance so like Tommy's or Joshua's? And where had Joshua himself got to?

She heard his voice and looked up to see Joshua behind Elizaveta. She was sweeping down the staircase, and she was wholly unchanged – as if time had no power over her. Even her dress was rather Edwardian, the style she had always favoured. In the early afternoon her blue-linen skirt swirled just above her ankles, and her waist was tiny. Of course, Liz would! The New Look just coming out of Paris featured long skirts, nipped waists, and full bosoms. That erotic, ultra-feminine style was a reaction against the skimpy, rather mannish clothing women had worn during the war. From what Tommy said Elizaveta, too, was reacting against her own war.

'My darlings!' She hugged Julia. 'My own darlings! My favourite American and my own guerrilla doctor. It's so good to see you together again.'

Responding to that Russian warmth, Julia felt her eyes prickle. She did love Liz – and it was uncanny how she had not altered. But close up her skin was suspiciously taut along the jawline and around the eyes. Liz had evidently had a face-lift.

And why not? Julia did not need such assistance yet, having led a less self-indulgent life. But she saw nothing wrong with it. Emily would probably never need it. Aside from that tension line between her eyebrows, Emily possessed the fragile, fine-pored, yet unlined skin that blessed so many Chinese women. As for herself, Julia would see.

Elizaveta swept across to coo over Tommy, but Joshua had not yet reached the foot of the spiral staircase. Stumping down step by step, he planted his left foot in its gleaming black oxford on the next tread and swung his right leg on the prop of a Malacca cane. When he reached the bottom, his forehead was damp with sweat. After a moment, he came towards them. His right foot dragged slightly on the golden Tientsin carpet.

'I see it did have to come off,' Tommy murmured. 'You might've let me know.'

'Shout the good news from the housetops, Doctor?' Joshua's smile was unchanged. 'I felt that news could wait. . . . My dear old Julie, how are you?'

Julia put her arms around Joshua and hugged him tight. Tommy had only told her that the compound, fracture of his leg, unheroically sustained when an ox-cart overturned, had not knit properly. They had also had a cheery letter from Joshua at the London Clinic. He had not mentioned amputation.

'It's wonderful to see you, Joshua,' Julia exclaimed. 'Just like old times . . . You poor dear, is it still painful?'

'Only hurts when I walk.' He grinned. 'Elizaveta also got some adjustments made, some mysterious female thing. The best quack for that was also at the London Clinic. Chap called Wolfe.'

Elizaveta threw her lover an irritated glance, and Tommy repressed his smile. Hereward Wolfe was a superb plastic surgeon. He had perfected his skill remaking the faces of Royal Air Force pilots who had been trapped in burning aircraft. Julia impulsively kissed Joshua again.

'Do restrain your passion, my dear,' Joshua urged. 'Not in front of your husband. Just as well that my wife's in Palestine with my sister Sarah doing good deeds.' Elizaveta nodded impatiently, and he proposed: 'A toast! To immortal Shanghai! And to us! Not quite immortal, but trying hard.'

The war years had engraved lines on Joshua's face and turned his hair quite grey. Although his hand trembled minutely, he was still a gallant figure in his white-linen bush-jacket.

Emily lifted her glass again and proposed: 'To Shanghai! To China!'

Evidently embarrassed by so much emotion, Tommy asked: 'Did I ever tell you about visiting Shanghai General Hospital the week the war ended? No? I thought not.'

He fumbled in the breast-pocket of his blue-seersucker jacket for the plain-glass spectacles Julia had finally persuaded him to give up three months earlier. His search frustrated, he began to fill his pipe and continued: 'There were several wards full of Japanese soldiers. When we entered, every man Jack sat up erect – at attention. Except three encased in plaster and two in coma.'

He lit his meershaum with a wooden kitchen-match and asked meditatively: 'Why? I don't really know. Respect for authority, perhaps. Definitely not toadying, not the people who blew themselves up in thousands rather than surrender. Imagine scores of wounded, sick, and dying, all sitting up at attention for the enemy.

Julia sat beside Elizaveta on the rosewood settee, whose cushions had been re-covered in the same turquoise Thai silk. Shanghai's material abundance amid poverty was even more striking than it had been before the war. All things were available to those who had the money, particularly the eager services of those who did not. The house actually looked fresher and more sparkling than it had when she left it six years earlier.

'The Japs are odd – damned odd.' Elizaveta lit the cigarette in her lapis lazuli holder with a lighter just like Jack Pavernen's gold-plated cartridge. 'They did the damnedest things.'

'Tell Julie how you got out of Shanghai,' Tommy urged. 'I told her a little, but I don't know the details.'

'After I closed the Ikra,' Elizaveta recalled, 'the Japs were aghast – no more gilded playground for brass-hats. But I was tired, and I'd lost most of my . . . ah . . . staff to internment, repatriation, and war marriages. And it was no longer fun, so I decided to. . . .'

'Getting out of Shaghai, Liz.' Tommy reminded her. 'You were telling Julie how. . . .'

'How could he reward me, the deputy garrison commander asked, considering my sterling services? Without thinking, I said I wanted to get the blazes out of Shanghai, but I couldn't go without my remaining orphans, a hundred or so. To my surprise, he immediately agreed to help. The orphans, he said were the future of China – and they would remember the kindness of the Japanese Army when they were older. The Kempeitai, the secret police, might be brutal but not the Imperial Army.'

Scented smoke spiralling from her Egyptian cigarette, she said: 'The general talked himself into it. Sending the orphans to the countryside would greatly advance Sino-Japanese amity. So I got in touch with Joshua and the guerrillas in the usual way.

'The convoy took the Soochow road, led by Japanese MPs under a white flag. Their motorcycles glittered, and the Hispano-Suiza gleamed like a diamond. My chauffeur and my footman were both in white uniforms. Then came five Imperial Army buses carrying the children. After we unloaded them at the rendezvous, the Japs duly left us. After an hour or two, the guerrillas turned up. The Japs never knew that every single one of the amahs and coolies looking after the orphans was a Chinese agent badly wanted by the Kempeitai.'

Emily's laughter at the hoodwinked enemy froze in her throat, and she said in wonder: 'The prophecy, Liz! Remember the soothsayer at the Great World. Her prophecy mostly has come true – so the rest is certain. You will live a long time, she said, but not always where you choose. Liz, you *will* live a long time – judging by the way you look. You hardly chose to live for almost two years in the hills. You have been admired by

456

many men – just as she predicted. I won't ask about possessing the one you really love. I don't really know what possession means. Not in that context.'

Julia glanced with concern at her sister-in-law, who was still in frenzied flight: 'Many children, but none your own. Right on the button. Of course, your enemies were your friends – the Japs. And you look very happy – just as the soothsayer said. I think it's wonderful.'

Julia decided she must very soon have a good old-fashioned gossip with her sister-in-law, who was closer than a real sister. The three years since they had last met seemed to have taken a heavy toll. Why was she so frenetic about a fortune-teller's lucky guesses?

Emily's extraordinary enthusiasm finally subsided. She was reasonably detached when the conversation turned to the Nationalist administration of Shanghai. Joshua and Elizaveta confirmed that the city was even more prosperous and even more pleasant for the rich and the privileged, but undeniably worse for the poor and the powerless.

'I think, Julie, you call them carpet-baggers in America,' Elizaveta said. 'There are hundreds of carpet-baggers from Chungking. They've expropriated everyone they could accuse of being a collaborator – and, naturally, all Japanese property. Me? One can get around anything with enormous bribes. The Ikra's reopening soon.'

'Just give us a chance, Liz!' Emily finally pleaded. 'It's a passing phase teething pains. Excesses have undoubtedly occurred, and there'll probably be more. But we're making progress. Things are getting better, so give us a little time. We've never run a cosmopolis like Shanghai before.'

When Tommy turned the light off, Julia turned towards him in the big rosewood bed. His lips brushed her hair as he leaned over to kiss her good night. She slipped her hand into his and within two minutes heard the regular breathing of sleep. Unable to tamp down the excitement of the day so quickly, Julia lay on her back watching light glimmer ghostlike on the white ceiling whenever an automobile passed four storeys below.

No one, she reflected, had said a word about the civil war between the Nationalists and the Communists, which had broken out with renewed virulence at the beginning of the year. The global war that killed tens of millions had only been an interval in the Chinese Civil War – no more than a distraction to Chairman Mao Tse-tung and Generalissimo Chiang Kai-shek. Despite the efforts at conciliation made by the American General of the Army George Catlett Marshall, the two were again at each other's throats. Battles ranged from the grassy plains of Manchuria to the paddy fields of the south, from the back alleys of Shanghai to the university campuses of Peiping.

Julia's thoughts leaped from the ocean voyage to the shape of Shanghai; from Emily's apparent strain to Jason's charm; from Elizaveta's unchanging beauty to Joshua's mutilation; from her daughters' diffident reunion with their birthplace to their future – and to the past. She

457

recalled that China's internal strife had been the backdrop for the first party she had attended in Shanghai, the reception for Eurydice and Donald Howe's thirtieth wedding anniversary. China had then already endured a decade of internal strife, which was to continue for another sixteen years before the Japanese threat briefly united the Nationalists and the Communists. As it had in the past, civil war today appeared the normal condition of China – though, she hoped, not for much longer.

The Apparatus flung Tommy and Julia into the skirmishing that was leading up to 'the final battle for China'. Now quite senior, they were to be involved in organizing new cells as well as espionage, subversion, and propaganda. Although instructed to stay away from Communist-sponsored demonstrations to avoid compromising their right-wing cover, both were determined to see the enormous protest staged against the civil war in late June.

Fortunately, Joshua asked them to the Shanghai Club overlooking the lower Bund, where the parade was to end. No one would look for leftists in that capitalist stronghold.

Before the war, Chinese had not really been welcome at the Shanghai Club. Before the war, too, demonstrators had faced the patient, British-officered Settlement Police, not the aggressive Nationalist police. It was a wholly new world.

Entering at the far end of the room, Joshua walked slowly to the window where they sat to greet them: 'Glad to see you got drinks. And when does the performance start? Are they holding the curtain for us?'

'Nothing much yet,' Tommy answered. 'Only a few dozen rather quiet demonstrators and a couple of squads of police. Nasty looking brutes, though.'

In addition to the revolvers at their belts, the powerfully built riot police were armed with three-foot ebony truncheons. Nervously rapping their truncheons against their palms, they tensed when a roar like breakers on a rocky shore resounded from a side road. An officer wearing mirrored sunglasses spoke sharply, and the ranks came to casual attention.

Heralded by the roar, a stream of demonstrators poured onto the Bund, having evidently marched unscathed from the Race Course. First in tens, then in hundreds, and finally in thousands, torrents of young men and women lapped against the façades of the temples of Mammon on the Bund.

The riot squads did not move. The students wearing crisply starched white shirts and many-coloured skirts or trousers were quite plainly not the children of the poor. The Nationalist police would not lightly attack those offspring of privilege, particularly under the eyes of foreigners. The riot squads were further restrained by Chinese reverence for the learning the students exemplified.

The breeze off the Hwangpoo, rather unexpected in late June, carried the salt tang of the sea and the stench of night soil. The muggy atmosphere stirred, and the gulls fighting for scraps from the ships soared on

458

lighter wings. The slogan-painted banners above the crowd flapped like titanic hands clapping.

END FRATRICIAL STRIFE, one exhorted in pompous English. RESIST THE NATIONALIST MURDERERS, another commanded in Chinese. AMERICANS, LEAVE CHINA ALONE, in English again, and beside it: DEMOCRATIC YANKEES MUST NOT SUPPORT NATIONALIST FASCISTS.

'Covering the waterfront, aren't they?' Joshua remarked. 'And naturally thickest around the *Daily News* building so the correspondents will have a good view.'

'The sooner we . . . ah . . . they crack down on this nonsense the better!' An anonymous American voice spoke among the group at the next window. An English voice added: 'But they're right. Sooner the fighting's ended, the better for business.'

Depressed by memories of three decades of such interchanges, Joshua grinned evilly at Tommy, who shrugged his shoulders. Julia threw them a fleeting smile, but her attention was commanded by the scene on the Bund.

They looked so young, those bright idealistic faces, so young and so vulnerable. At their age, she, too, had believed she could change the world totally. Though she now knew how hard it was to change the world, Julia was profoundly moved by their dedication. The new China was marching before her eyes.

The students were not only courageous, but ingenious. Two youths wearing US Army summer uniforms and flying helmets were throwing small bomb-shaped objects into the crowd of spectators. The banner lifted on long poles above them implored in English: YANKEES, STOP GIVING BOMBS FOR NATIONALISTS TO KILL CHINESE BABIES. Three young women in long skirts, staid blouses, and kerchiefs, who presumably represented colonial America, shouted unintelligible slogans under the cryptic exhortation: YANKS, REMEMBER YOUR OWN REVOLUTION!

'Good Lord!' Joshua pointed. 'Those two take the cake!'

The male figure was a veritable Uncle Sam: tall and thin in red-and-white striped trousers, claw-hammer coat, and white-starred waistcoat. An enormous papier-mâché nose protruded beneath the red, white, and blue top hat that hid his features.

The female figure beside him was even more extraordinary. She wore an intricately draped green dress that swept the ground, and she carried a flaming green torch. Green grease-paint coating her face, she was the image of the bronze Statue of Liberty. Somewhat incongruously, she wore a blonde wig beneath her green tiara.

The sign above the all-American couple cleverly declared: UNCLE SAM LOVES MISS LIBERTY – AT HOME! Behind them strutted General of the Army Douglas MacArthur wearing oversize sunglasses and a peaked cap festooned with gold braid. His hands were red with mock-blood. Two men with bloated stomachs wore waistcoats covered with dollar-signs. In his top hat one had a sign reading: WALL STREET BLOODSUCKER. The other's read: IMPERIALIST LEECH.

'Party's getting rough,' observed the American at the next window. 'No question who set up this show. Goddamn Commies!'

The demonstrators were chanting in unison: 'Americans, have a heart!
... Withdraw support from Nationalist killers! ... End the Civil War –
right now! Right now!'

The riot police still waited. But a ripple ran through their ranks, and
truncheons twitched in sweaty hands when the students taunted: 'Running
dogs of the imperialists! Chinese faces and barbarian hearts!'

A truncheon flicked at a student's head – and the squad surged forward
to savage its tormentors. A shouted order from the officer with the
sunglasses restrained them. None, however, took up the students' invitation to cast off the chains of servitude and join the patriotic masses.

Uncle Sam had clambered on top of a green Pontiac imprudently
parked on the Bund. Gallantly stretching out his hand, he helped the
Statue of Liberty to climb up beside him. Students formed a cordon
around the Pontiac and handed a microphone to Uncle Sam.

Julia nodded in approval. The manoeuvre had been well planned, as
had the emplacement of four loudspeakers, each protected by its own
cordon of students. Considerable preparation had clearly gone into this
demonstration.

'Fellow students, ladies and gentlemen, patriots and foreign friends.'
Uncle Sam's voice was distorted by the tinny loudspeakers. 'We have come
together today to demand a rapid end to the gory civil war which is bleeding
our beloved country white. We demand the Nationalist killers withdraw.
A true peace settlement can be attained easily if the murderer Chiang
Kai-shek withdraws his armies. The Communist Party offers reasonable terms. Only the stubborn Chiang Kai-shek clique impedes...'

A flying wedge of riot police struck the cordon around the green
Pontiac. Stubbornly battling their better armed but less numerous foes,
the students held them off while Uncle Sam denounced the Generalissimo.
The personal attack on Chiang Kai-shek, which had provoked the police
attack, grew more vitriolic. And the police attacked more fiercely.

Within seconds, the mêlée became general. All around the outnumbered
riot squads the crowd boiled into violence. Hands seized policemen from
behind, and flagstaffs smashed peaked caps. Truncheons flailed, and students retaliated all across the Bund. Demonstrators and policemen flung to
the cobbles were trampled indiscriminately by friends and foes.

Uncle Sam still shouted his appeals over the tumult, though truncheons
had smashed three of his loudspeakers. The tinny voice vehemently denounced not only Generalissimo Chiang Kai-shek, but US President
Harry Truman and General George Marshall. The Statue of Liberty
clutched Uncle Sam's arm in apparent fear, although the depleted cordon
around them was holding firm.

'Only a matter of time,' the American gloated at the window next to
the Howe's. 'They'll get that fresh kid. Serve him damned well right.'

The cordon protecting Uncle Sam suddenly broke, and the police
surged over the green Pontiac. Hard hands clutched his ankles and pulled
him from his perch. A club knocked off his top hat, and blood welled
from his cheek. Curiously, the police gallantly helped the Statue of
Liberty down from the car. Most curiously, the riot squad did not beat

the dishelvelled Uncle Sam and the weeping Miss Liberty, but closed ranks around them.

'Gonna make an example of 'em,' the American declared with raw satisfaction. 'Don't wanna muss them up too much. Look better in court unmarked.'

Tommy exclaimed unintelligibly, rose, and thrust through the group surrounding the window. Julia stared for another instant at the features half-revealed by the tear-smudged green grease-paint – and followed him into the violence of the Bund.

Tommy's white-linen sleeve ripped from cuff to elbow when a student grabbed at his arm. But Tommy's forearm clubbed those who stood in his way. Julia followed in his wake. She clutched her pearl necklace. The floral print of her dress was a bright spot in the drab throng.

'*Ho-ping! Ho-ping!*' The chant was ironic over the mêlée. 'Peace! Peace!'

His height enabling him to see over the crowd, Tommy made for the police cordon that guarded some two dozen prisoners. The stale smell of old sweat and the acrid smell of fresh fear rose to his nostrils. Swearing students struck at him with their fists. Cobblestones, bricks, and bottles flew at the police.

Tommy battled through the demonstrators to confront the enraged police. Ebony truncheons flailing, the police charged again. With pre-ternatural clarity, Tommy saw three policemen stretched on the cobbles with blood trickling from their heads. A truncheon glanced off his shoulder and flung him aside. As if he believed himself invulnerable because he was a doctor and was not a student, he confidently stepped forward again.

'Traitor!' A thick-set student shrieked and yanked him back. 'Never surrender!'

His blood up, Tommy turned and clubbed the assailant with his fist. Seeing Julia behind him, he grasped her hand and pulled her towards the gap between demonstrators and police.

'By God!' he shouted. 'We must get to them!'

Ignoring the eccentric foreign woman, two policemen closed on the respectable-looking Chinese man who had joined the rebels. A truncheon tapped Tommy's ribs – almost playfully, it appeared. But the blow knocked him off his feet. The second policeman wrenched his arm behind his back. Bent double, he was propelled through the cordon surrounding the prisoners.

Julia hurled herself at the policeman who held Tommy's arm. The startled policeman released Tommy and turned to face his new assailant. Tommy turned to see Julia being thrust down onto the cobblestones, her flowered dress incongruously gay. He raised his fist, only regretting, as he brought it down on the policeman's temple, that he had not carried a stick.

'Hold it! You mother-screwers, just hold it!' The bellow made Tommy turn and froze his startled opponent. 'Hold it right there!'

The stentorian voice continued: 'That's better. Now what have we got here? By God, I thought so. Dr Howe isn't it? Wasn't your father . . .'

461

Tommy nodded. His father's fame as an old Nationalist supporter had evidently bought him a respite. But the squat police officer with the mirrored sunglasses asked: 'You don't remember, do you, Doctor? You fixed up a wound for me years ago. Also, everyone knows of your father's contributions. You a Communist! What a ridiculous idea! You're not hurt, are you? And your lady, is she all right?'

Nonplussed by the abrupt alteration from violence to deference, Julia half-heard Tommy say: 'Thank you, Captain. We're both all right. But we do have a problem.'

Julia saw Tommy's hand extended with a green US$50 note protruding between his knuckles, and she heard him say: 'Two of your prisoners. Just high-spirited kids, after all. Badly misguided, but that's a matter for family discipline. You see, my nephew and my daughter . . .'

46

November 6–December 2, 1946

'We commit to the earth this husk, which was our brother. Ashes to ashes and dust to dust!' The American minister intoned the last words into the cold dusk and dropped the last clod on the mahogany coffin. The soil crumbled damply on the gold-plated plaque, which was inscribed: JOHN AUGUST PAVERNEN: JANUARY 6, 1877–NOVEMBER 3, 1946.

The tattered grave-diggers of the Shantung Road Cemetery were eager to escape the raw wind that knotted the fog into hanks of dirty wool. But the last mourners lingered around the open grave. They were eager to be gone, but loath to go.

Weeping unashamedly, Gustav Vass lifted his silver hip-flask and drank a solitary toast to his partner in construction and chicanery. Elizaveta Yavalenka lit her Murad with the gold-plated cartridge-lighter John Pavernen had given her on leaving Shanghai during the war and let it fall glittering into the grave. Expensively bundled against the dank cold in a cashmere greatcoat lined with mink, Harrison Parker Smythe III blew his nose loudly. His cornflower eyes were liquid.

Old and stout, the dead man's Korean mistress concealed behind a black veil the ravages her tears had inflicted on her gaudy make-up. She was rich, for he had left her all he possessed. But she was bereft.

Quick Jack Pavernen had returned to Shanghai in late 1945, delighted, as he said, 'to get back to civilization, business, and decent service'. He had died of influenza a year later at sixty-nine. His ingenuity had barely begun to exploit the great opportunities for shady business presented by corrupt Chinese rule, the massive American relief operation, and the spreading civil war.

As he had wished, he was buried in Shanghai after services at the

463

Union Church attended by a hundred foreigners and twice that many Chinese. The foreigners had cherished him because he was an engaging rogue. Even at his most sanctimonious, they felt, he was laughing at himself – as well as them. The Chinese had loved him because he was their silent benefactor amid their constant tribulations. The coolies who carried the enormous floral tributes left their own small wreaths on the grave. One stunted coolie, apparently half-blind, stumbled over a shovel as he turned away. All the mourners honoured John Pavernen's consistency: he had never slackened in his quest after the dishonest dollar, not even when he could have made many more honest dollars with much less effort.

Across the grave, the eyes of Julia Howe met the eyes of Emily Ouyang – and both hastily looked away. Julia coldly returned to her macabre thoughts. She had become accustomed to the abrupt cessation of human life in China. Yet nowadays there seemed to be more deaths. The generation just senior to her own was dropping away, leaving great rents in the lives of the survivors.

Julia raised her head and again met Emily's eyes. Ashamed of her previous coldness, she smiled tentatively. Emily returned her smile, and they turned in tacit agreement towards the lane where the cars waited. When they met at the foot of the grave, Emily leaned over and kissed Julia. Their gloved hands clasped, they walked on.

Ten paces behind his wife and his sister, Dr Thomas Howe also smiled. It was time to repair the breach with Emily that had opened after he snatched the children from the cold embrace of a Nationalist jail. Julia had given way to her anger at Jason for involving Althea when they took the unrepentant sinners to the house on Kiukiang Road. She was implacable because Althea's asthma, virtually cured by the years in America, had flared up again.

Althea had, however, been bruised chiefly in her pride. They had put her to bed and sent Jason home. The chauffeur carried a curt note to Jason's mother, for Julia had refused to telephone Emily.

'Let Emily find out from Jason that he's safe thanks to you,' she said. 'Let Jason explain what he was up to with *my* daughter. Let him do the talking – *if* he can find his mother. She's probably off in Nanking hobnobbing with that frightful Mayling Chiang. Ultimately, the Generalissimo is to blame for it all. But I blame Emily almost as much.'

'We should ring, but I won't press you,' he had replied. 'But, we should've known. We were forewarned.'

'Don't be silly, Tommy. How could we have known?'

'Remember last night? You told me you'd overheard a conversation between Althea and Perse.'

'More of an argument than a conversation. About Aunt Emily. Persephone loves her glamorous aunt devotedly. There may be trouble there some day, Tommy. Love auntie, love her politics.'

'We'll face that when we have to, Julie. Perse is only thirteen.'

'It's amazing what you don't know about girls of thirteen – or sixteen. *Aunt Emily says*. That's Perse's constant refrain. The girls almost came to blows when Althea said Emily was a right-wing harpy preying on the Chinese masses.'

'We should've guessed where that came from. I myself never. . . .'

'Nor I ever. I guess I've been afraid giving them political guidance would endanger our cover. Besides, in the States, there was no immediate need . . .'

'We'll have to see about that. We've played it so close to the chest our own children have no idea where we stand. But, of course, that line about right-wing harpies came from nephew Jason. His student meetings! Yet he seems to love his mother.'

'Darling Tommy, he can very easily love his mother and hate her politics. And he's convinced Althea that she is China's Joan of Arc. If it hadn't been for you . . .'

'I'd like to know what particular swine recruited my nephew,' he interrupted. 'I'd never have done so myself.'

Julia smiled mischievously, and Tommy grinned sheepishly. He had just denounced some unknown comrade for doing precisely what they were doing – recruiting young men and women for the Apparatus.

'It does seem ruthless, though,' Julia declared. 'Innocent children. Seducing them and flinging them into the political struggle. They're so young to be involved. And there's so much danger.'

Tommy's eyes glittered with self-deriding laughter, and he said with grave irony: 'It *does* look different, doesn't it? Quite different when it's your own child – even your own nephew.'

'Tommy, it's very confusing. I can't really tell . . . I'm not sure whether I'm angrier at Emily for her carelessness or her stubborn, stupid reactionary politics. But it's her carelessness that's worst. How could she *not* know what Jason was up to?'

'In the abstract, you approve of what he was up to. But not when your ox is gored – your daughter is at risk, I think.'

'I just don't want the kids dragged into it. But the Communists are the only answer for China.'

'Unquestionably, darling. We *must* carry on with the Apparatus, but . . . but . . .'

The repetition of that small *but* encapsulated Tommy's doubts. Nursing his scotch and water, he sat silent in the rosewood armchair – until Julia demanded: 'But what, Tommy? You were going to say . . .'

He took a long sip and placed his glass on the gilt-and-crimson rice-barrel beside his chair. She was on the point of prompting him again when he said slowly: 'What would you think, Julie, if I told you there was another way? Another approach, at least.'

'I'd listen, just as I'm listening right now. You know, darling, you mean more to me than any politics or . . .'

'And you to me. Which makes us bad Communists. More like bourgeois individualists. Please listen closely, Julie. During the war, it seemed only the decent thing . . . just natural . . . to work closely with Joshua. We were all allies, and I do have fond memories of England.'

'You sound as if you, too, were working for the British.'

'In a way. Actually a fairly active way. You know, darling, it *still* seems the decent thing. Our quarrel, yours and mine, isn't with the British and the Americans any more. Our enemy is Chiang Kai-shek. After victory, wouldn't it be a damned good thing for China to have very good relations with Britain and America? To counterbalance the Soviets, you see.'

'You *have* been thinking ahead. Yes, I can see that. Otherwise the Soviets . . .'

'I thought you'd agree.' He smiled at her detestation of the Soviets. 'Also I've been doing it for our own sake – yours, mine, and the girls! Did you ever think some day we may need Josh and his British connections?'

'As a kind of lifeline?'

'Perhaps. Anyway, it still seems the decent thing to keep on with Josh. For China's sake – and for our own.'

Julia had never been deeply frightened by the danger inherent in their work for the Apparatus – perhaps because she had assumed herself beyond the reach of Nationalist vengeance in the impregnable Foreign Settlement. She had been terrified upon occasion, above all when the Soviets manoeuvred her into introducing Joshua to their assassin. But she had never been dogged by day-in and day-out fear.

Her security was now shattered. Extra-territoriality no longer existed, and Tommy had just told her they could some day need a lifeline. Dire Nationalist vengeance would follow their unmasking. She might escape with prison or deportation, but he would not evade a bullet in the back of his neck. They were not playing a game they could quit whenever they wished. Only time would tell whether they had got away with it, but Tommy had taken what precautions he could for his wife and himself – and for his country. His mind returned to the cemetery, which was bleak in barren winter. His wife and his sister were walking arm-in-arm in front of him. Clearly the women were patching things up.

Julia had for some time been very unhappy about her quarrel with Emily. She had also been shaken by events. Her Uncle Jack's sudden death had shocked her. She had loved the rogue. Besides, her father, who was his elder brother, could also go soon. Her guilt at not having spent more time with her parents was exacerbated by their hearty declaration that they were happy as long as they knew she was happy – even if her happiness required her to live ten thousand miles away.

Emily and Julia waited arm-in-arm beside Emily's enormous Fleetwood. She had come alone, not even bothering to convey her husband's inevitable regrets. The Howes gladly accepted her offer of a lift and sent their car home.

But the women could not relax in the perfumed dimness of the Cadillac. They chatted lightly about fashions, friends, books, and children – carefully avoiding the Jason-Althea imbroglio. Tommy felt himself an intruder. If he had not been present, they would probably have had a jolly time dissecting husbands. His sister declined their invitation to come in for a drink, but bade them farewell warmly.

*

466

Located off the Bund on Foochow Road, the American Club always amused Tommy Howe because it was *so* American. Six four-square storeys of dark brick relieved only by white-stone lintels over the windows were a marked contrast to the very British Shanghai Club on the Bund – with its cupolas, pillars, and canopies.

Harry Smythe was waiting in the dining-room, which was also very American with its blond-maple furniture and its bright-print curtains. Harry himself was strikingly American in his single-breasted blue blazer, grey-flannel trousers, burnished cordovan loafers, and button-down blue oxford shirt. Tommy had warned him that they would not have too much time. His office hours began at 2:30, and he liked to mull over his patients' records beforehand.

'Seeing you're in a rush, Tommy, I won't beat about the bush.' Immediately after ordering, Harry plunged into business. 'We'd like you to join us.'

'You do get right down to brass tacks, don't you?' Tommy sipped his dry Martini. 'Do tell me, though, who are *we*? And why am I so honoured?'

When Harry grinned he was again the insouciant vice-consul. He extricated the toothpick from his Gibson on the rocks and nibbled the pearl onion.

'You said you were in a rush,' he reminded. 'There's a lot to talk about. *We* are Claire Chennault, a fellow called Whiting Willauer, and me – among others.'

'What can I possibly do for such a distinguished group?' Tommy signalled for a second dry Martini, which was his limit, grateful that Americans did not drink wine with lunch. 'You know I thought you were working for General Marshall, the great peacemaker.'

'The great peacemaker's getting nowhere. It's all off. So why should I tag along? I'll go with Claire Chennault. He gets things done.'

'What's he getting done?'

'Claire's starting an airline, no less. He's really going to do something for China.'

'So many people are doing so much for China,' Tommy murmured. 'We're inundated with foreign carpet-baggers. And most of them are doing very well by doing good. But Major-General Claire Chennault must be taken seriously, as must Harrison Parker Smythe III. Do tell me how I can help.'

'We want you to be chief flight surgeon. Not only to keep your eye on the aviators, but on health conditions wherever we fly.'

'Harry, where's your airline coming from?'

The middle-aged waiter placed a stemmed Martini glass before Tommy and a Gibson on the rocks in an Old Fashioned glass before Harry. He then served creamy clam chowder in red-banded cups.

'All right, I'll take it from the top.' Harry chewed his second pearl onion. 'You know Chennault came back to China at the beginning of the year. He was appalled – above all by the terrible suffering. He wrote some of us a round robin letter.'

Harry pulled a much-creased sheet of paper from his inside pocket and smoothed it in the tablecloth. After popping tortoiseshell half-glasses on his nose, he read: 'I have retraced my steps upriver from Shanghai through Nanking and Wuhan to Chungking – just as we did during the war. I was shaken by the devastation, disease, and starvation. Every city in the interior of the South except Changsha was completely destroyed – just black rubble. Only half of Changsha was in ruins.'

Harry sipped at his Gibson, lit a Camel and continued, his voice deliberately flat: 'It isn't just a passing famine caused by a single crop failure. It is *permanent* disaster – and no help in sight. The Japanese stripped the countryside bare of food – and killed all the pigs and chickens. The Chinese are eating bark and boiled weeds – as a delicacy, rice-straw bulked out with clay. The Japs swept up all oxen and buffaloes. So men and women now harness themselves to the ponderous wooden ploughs. But the Japs took even the seed-corn.'

'Not only the Japanese,' Tommy murmured. 'Also the local warlords and Central Government and Communist troops. No choice if the soldiers were to survive. I saw it in the countryside while you were revelling in the luxury of Chungking and Kunming.'

'Some luxury!' Harry smiled warily. 'And Claire wrote: The Yangtze Valley is almost a desert – and it used to produce half China's rice. Transportation is desperately needed. More than half the river shipping's been sunk, and there's no timber to build anew. Railroads are wrecked; roads are mostly potholes; very few trucks are still running. Air lift is virtually non-existent – forty medium-sized civilian air transports for all China. The hundred and twenty transports the US turned over to the Central Government at the end of the war are all hauling troops and supplies to the Nationalist armies in the field.'

Harry gulped the rest of his Gibson, stubbed out his cigarette, and said: 'Chennault concluded: Lack of modern transport is pushing China back to the stone age. Both trade and aid are paralysed. Millions are dying of starvation and disease – four million in Hunan Province alone – while trade goods and United Nations relief supplies pile up in coastal warehouses.'

The sandy-haired American carefully folded the sheet of paper and returned it to his inside pocket. He slid the half-glasses off his nose, closed them, and slipped them into his breast pocket. Placing his palms flat on the table, he looked at Tommy and said softly: 'Sure Claire wants an airline of his own. He likes his toys. His new Flying Tigers for peacetime – if you call this peace. He is also desperately concerned about China. I know it's becoming fashionable to make fun of Claire Chennault. But by God he does care about China.'

'No contest, Harry. Very few Chinese mock Claire Chennault – not even leftists. I'm with you so far.'

'Claire decided an airline was desperately needed. CNRRA, the United Nations' China National Relief and Rehabilitation Agency, has been pouring in food and supplies. But there's no way to move the stuff to the needy. So CNRRA's agreed to advance us US$2 million to buy planes.

And the Central Government's just given the go-ahead.'

'The transport aircraft, where do they come from?'

'The planes? Why Whitey Willauer bought them.'

'He simply popped down to the neighbourhood shops and bought them?'

'Whitey Willauer is ... was ... war surplus property administrator. He sold them to Claire.'

'And to himself, Harry? How enterprising!'

'It *was* a good deal. A few thousand dollars a plane – and we'll pay it off with the receipts from CNRRA shipments.'

'And what do you call this airline?'

'CNRRA Air Transport, CAT for short. Claire's chairman, Whitey's president, and I'm a vice-president. Can we count you in with us, Tommy?'

'As a consultant. I won't give up my practice entirely. But in principle I'm with you.'

Harry beckoned to the waiter, who replaced the soup-cups with the American Club's enormous T-bone steaks. Tommy waved away the French fries, and the waiter put a bottle of Châteauneuf-du-Pape on the table.

'It's not a bad burgundy.' Harry raised his glass. 'To a long and fruitful association.'

'To CAT,' Tommy duly responded. 'And now, tell me why you're disillusioned with General Marshall.'

'The General's going home right after the New Year, as you've heard.'

'Only because the President wants him to be Secretary of State. No one's said anything about the whole truce mission's packing up.'

'They wouldn't, would they? But Washington's definitely getting out of the peace-making business.'

'Why the rush for the exit?'

'It started with the Yalta Conference in 1944. But you don't really want to go into ancient history, do you?'

'Not really, since I've got to get back to my hypochondriacs.' Tommy glanced at his watch. 'Just tell me why General Marshall's going home in high dudgeon?'

'As you know he's gotten the Chinats and the Chicoms to the conference table a number of times. Every time, one or the other bridled – and blamed the U.S. Neither wants peace through compromise. Both are talking only to gain time – and the upper hand on the battlefield. So the denizens of the Temple of the Thousand Sleeping Colonels have concluded.'

Tommy chuckled at the nickname of the headquarters of the US Truce Mission in Peiping and prompted: 'But why now?'

'The General's tired of taking all the shit. No matter what he does, it's wrong. The Nationalist propaganda machine in the States screams that Marshall – and the President – are practically Communists. And Chairman Mao Tse-tung charges the US is *entirely* on the

Nationalists' side. Do you blame Marshall?'

'Harry, why doesn't the US understand its vital interests in China? Why do you Americans act like schoolboys taking their balls and bats home when the game doesn't go your way?'

Harry answered immediately: 'I call it the "Two Unwillings", Tommy. The US won't give up idealistic goals like creating perfect democracy and building a modern industrial economy in China. But the US is equally unwilling to pay the cost of attaining those goals.' He refilled his wine glass. 'Only a massive commitment of American weapons and a substantial commitment of American troops can halt the Communists. Chiang Kai-shek can't do it alone. But the US won't make the commitment.'

'So,' Tommy mused, 'the US tells itself the game isn't worth the candle.'

'That would be sensible, but American policy isn't sensible. We won't make the commitment, but we won't give up the goals. So we've left with the worst of all possible worlds.'

When he left the American Club, Tommy was bubbling with elation. Above all, American vacillation would ensure a Communist victory. He had valuable information for his controllers – for *both* the Apparatus and London. The Americans would maintain a substantial presence and bestow plentiful assistance – but not enough to affect the outcome of the Civil War decisively.

Emily had telephoned Julia five days after John Pavernen's funeral and announced that she wanted to drop by for a chat. Knowing her sister-in-law's fierce candour, Julia was not surprised when she declared without preliminaries: 'I've come to beg your pardon. Jason's behaviour was inexcusable – to involve a child like Althea in his political stupidities.'

'Althea could have told me.' Julia relented considerably. 'She was pretty irresponsible, too. And she's hardly a child. Not nowadays at sixteen. Em, you must be frantic about Jason's antics. So embarrassing!'

'God knows I've tried. But what can I do short of sending him to the States right now? And he'd undoubtedly get just as involved there. The Reds are very active among Chinese students in the States.'

'He is courageous,' Julia conceded. 'Though how he can truly believe the Communists' promises, I don't . . .'

'You've been away, Julie. *All* the kids are true believers now. They truly believe everything the Reds tell them – and nothing their own parents say. Anyway, Althea was pretty courageous, too.'

'I can't forgive her for not telling us. Besides, a well-brought up girl should never under any circumstances in public . . .'

'You know, dear, you've still got a female-slave mentality.' More confident of their reconciliation, Emily spoke with her normal frankness. 'Tommy may be the ideal husband, but that's no reason to become his docile handmaiden. Of course, you're so traditional – a

470

better Chinese wife than I've ever been.'

'Not so traditional, Em, not in politics.' Julia had given much thought to the alteration in her public political position necessary to preserve her credibility – and her cover. 'After seeing what's going on in Shanghai, I'm afraid the Generalissimo's not the answer.'

'*What* is going on in Shanghai?' Emily's voice was edged. 'Precisely what do you have in mind? And if not the Gimo, then who? Chairman Mao Tse-tung?'

'Heaven forbid, Em! Not the Communists. But somebody's got to do something when the Chinese dollar drops from 400 to 800 against one US dollar. How many people will starve when their money becomes worthless? I had the third force in mind. It's the only hope.'

'Are you on that kick too, Julie? The non-Communist opposition? Take it from me, dear, those well meaning liberals will never amount to anything . . .'

The conversation rapidly became surrealistic. Emily was a strong Nationalist supporter, but neither fanatical nor systematically self-deluding. Emily would have been suspicious of Julia's motives – or doubtful of her sanity – if she had continued to spout a hard right-wing line in the face of all the objective evidence. But it was a very complicated dance.

Julia was forced to deny some of her beliefs, while affirming others. Out of her own direct experience she wholeheartedly agreed with Emily about the danger of Chinese Communist involvement with the Soviets, but she had to say naïvely: 'Maybe Mao Tse-tung isn't so close to the Kremlin. You remember, Richard Hollings saw no sign of . . .'

'He *reported* no major Soviet influence!' Emily avoided the detested name. 'His reporting's always selective and self-serving. Please don't talk to me about *that* man.'

Julia could hardly confide to Emily that Tommy, who was an insider, was troubled by Soviet influence over the Chinese Communists. No more could she acknowledge that the Communists staged the 'spontaneous' demonstrations against the Nationalists and the US.

None the less, the discussion was obviously good for Emily. She could speak her mind – as she could not with her reactionary Nationalist associates. The flush on her cheeks and her vigorous voice were good signs. She was speaking freely, and she no longer appeared quite so strained.

'I should apologize, too.' Julia turned the conversation. 'I'm sorry I lost my head about Althea and Jason. It was cruel . . . stupid . . . to cut you off. I've been acting like a ninny.'

'Politics makes fools of us all, Julie. I think Jason will have to go to the States. But how can we keep him away from the radical Chinese students? There must be . . .'

The telephone's ringing rescued Julia from another surrealistic dilemma. Was she, of all people, to advise on keeping her nephew away from Communist influence? Amused by the irony, she lifted the handset.

'Julie? I *am* the lucky chap today . . . getting on to you first crack out of the box.'

471

She glanced apprehensively at Emily, who was happily stealing one of her Chesterfields. Although she knew full well, she asked: 'Who's that?'

'It's me, Dick Hollings, as you very well know, pet.' He was no less cocksure for the passage of the years. 'When can we get together? Are you lot free for dinner tonight?'

'I . . . I don't know. I'll have a look at my diary.'

His unqualified assumption that she wanted to 'get together' galled. Otherwise, she would not have resorted to the self-important pretence of consulting her engagement calendar. Her hand shielding the mouthpiece, she counted to fifty while Emily stared in amused speculation.

'I'm afraid not,' she finally said. 'We can't make it. And you'll have to escuse me now. I've got someone with me.'

Unabashed, the Englishman said conspiratorially: 'I fully understand, pet. A worthy and boring someone, no doubt. I'll ring back later.'

Emily blew out a cloud of smoke and asked idly: 'Who was that who wouldn't be put off?'

'You're not going to like this, Em. Naturally, I couldn't talk with him. Not with you sitting there. It was Richard, Richard Hollings, your old . . .'

'Julie, darling, I *do* remember Richard Hollings. The name hasn't completely escaped my memory. Even though that torch burned out years ago.'

'Quite sure, darling?' Julia responded to the heavy sarcasm. 'Are all the ashes dead? No glow at all?'

'Not an ember. Do you know why?'

'No, but I'm fascinated.'

'He never loved me. Never!'

'Never?'

'Julie, he didn't try very hard to make me change my mind. He hardly tried at all. He went off like a little lamb when I wangled him onto Mayling's special flight to Hong Kong. If he really cared, he would never have left me *just* because I told him to. He would've moved heaven and earth to make me take him back.'

Even with all Shanghai under Chinese rule, it was convenient to be a foreigner. Much safer, too, for the Nationalist police were far kinder to foreigners than to their own countrymen. Richard Hollings and Julia Howe were, however, the only non-Chinese among the thousands of street-hawkers demonstrating in front of the Municipal Police Station, and Julia, for once, felt conspicuous and exposed in her own city.

Richard's head swivelled within the turned-up collar of his trenchcoat like an amiable jack-in-the-box. He was approaching fifty, but looked youthful. His lean features were only a shade more saturnine, while his temper had improved. He was neither quite so cutting nor quite so obsessed with self-advancement. Success had improved him. He was however, just as persistent, unceasingly cajoling Julia to intercede with Emily on his behalf. His former mistress flatly refused to see him. Julia wondered why she had agreed to interpret for him today. Not

472

entirely because of his unforced charm. She, too, had wanted to see this latest of the mass protests that were eroding Nationalist power.

'Does this remind you of anything?' Richard shouted above the clamour of the mob.

'It's like watching the same movie again,' Julia agreed. 'We saw this back in 1925 – the May 30th Incident.'

His reply was drowned by the crowd's roar: 'Justice! Justice! . . . We protest! We protest! The Nationalists butcher innocent working people!'

The mass protests more than twenty years earlier had also been dominated by blue workmen's clothing and a show of banners. However, the inevitable slogans now denounced the brutality of the Nationalists, rather than the foreigners. Chinese Military Police had two days earlier, killed seven street hawkers among thousands rioting to protest against the new ordinances that barred them from many districts.

A modern municipality, the mayor's office declared, could not permit hawkers to cry their wares anywhere they pleased – and turn affluent residential districts into Oriental bazaars. The hawkers were naturally infuriated by the threat to their rice-bowls – and the Apparatus had naturally stepped in to organize the demonstrations. As if on schedule, the Military Police had lost their nerve, fired, and killed the seven. Martyrs were not essential for successful agitation, but martyrs were very useful.

PUNISH THE GUILTY, one banner read, and another: CHINESE MUST NOT KILL CHINESE. Although the demonstration had nothing to do with American intervention in the Civil War, a banner in English exhorted: END FOREIGN INVOLVEMENT IN CHINA.

The mob was now surging towards the Police Station, shrieking like primitive tribesmen screaming for their enemies' blood. The time for speeches was past.

Behind the barbed-wire, the Military Police waited. They wore American field-jackets and varnished American helmet-liners. Their American Mark I carbines were fully loaded.

Swearing that no one would do business if they could not, hawkers invaded the few open shops. Harsh smoke rose from the cars they overturned and set on fire. The crash of shattering glass and the groans of splintering shop shutters rose above the mob's shrieking. Waves of demonstrators lapped at the Police Station, thrust against the barbed-wire by the pressure of those behind them.

The Military Police nervously checked their ammunition. They faced a riot already more ferocious than the May 30th Protest that had provoked harsh police action. Why, Julia wondered, had this demonstration so quickly escaped the organizers' control? Perhaps it had not. Since martyrs were always useful, the more martyrs the better.

Shrill screams rose from the mêlée in front of the police station. A squad of MPs was making for the looters in the shops, hacking its way through the crowd with the butts of its carbines. At that moment, the mob crushed the barbed-wire barriers and rolled forward towards the station. Pressed against the brown-brick building, the MPs lifted their carbines.

473

The first volley cracked above the heads of the mob. The reports of the light weapons tore through their shouting like a jagged ripsaw through plywood. For several seconds, the demonstrators stood in silence. Then blood-anger exploded. The furious mob engulfed the MPs in its midst.

A second volley rattled from the police station, and Julia saw a youth crumple. The red bandana around his neck grew darker, and the grey-haired man shouting beside him stared in astonishment. But the youth was held upright by the pressure of the crowd. When his neighbours drew back in horror, he sagged slowly towards the pavement.

A third volley sounded, and the mob began to turn. The MPs advanced with flailing carbines. Individual shots punctuated the continuous screaming as the MPs trapped within the mob fought their way clear. The shiny green-and-white helmet-liners formed into a ragged rank, and their carbines rose.

Richard gestured towards the intersection behind them. Julia turned to follow him.

'Time to get out of harm's way.' His voice just carried over the din. 'We've seen this before. Same act under different management.'

'That's the only difference,' she replied. 'Chinese are now giving the orders to kill Chinese. You can see a little riot somewhere in Shanghai almost every day. The Nationalists are losing control even before the Communists arrive. It's all crumbling.'

While Tommy and Julia were dressing for a pre-Christmas ball at the Cathay Hotel a few days later, she said thoughtfully: 'The Nationalists are such fools. Twelve dead and more than a hundred and thirty hurt in the hawkers' riot. Well, it's all grist to our mill.'

'Aren't you a bit harsh, dear?' Tommy peered at the mirror and knotted his black bow-tie. 'They – the Chinats as Harry Smythe calls them – don't start the riots. And they don't *want* the deaths.'

'I'll *never* get used to the deaths, Tommy. I'd make a rotten organizer. I'd be shattered by every martyr I created. At least it's better in Peiping. The student demonstrations there. Nobody's been killed – so far.'

'There will be. If only because our comrades are afraid there won't be . . .'

'I'll scream,' she interjected, 'the next time anyone says: *You can't make an omelette without breaking eggs!*'

'Somebody's bound to get killed with the demonstrations and riots spreading like a forest fire. All the way from Chungking to Manchuria. And in Peiping no pretext was needed. That poor girl was undoubtedly raped by a half-dozen American soldiers.'

'You really believe that, Tommy?' Applying her lipstick, Julia glanced away from her mirror in surprise. 'Really?'

'What do you mean, Julie? You know bloody well that student at Peking University . . . what was her name? Yes, Shen Chung. Of course she was raped by drunken GIs. Just because you're American . . .'

'Darling, it has nothing to do with my being American. I know that the licentious soldiery can behave atrociously. But I'm sure Miss Shen made it up – or asked for it. Tommy, she's lying.'

'And just how,' he asked, 'do you reckon that?'

'No Chinese woman – lady or slut – would ever complain in public. Not about rape – especially by barbarian soldiers. She wouldn't cry rape unless she was getting something out of it. Justified or not, the public protest will destroy whatever reputation she possesses. Won't it, Tommy?'

'You're not completely wrong. So?'

'So Miss Shen Chung, who's probably no better than she need be, must have a good reason for screaming the house down. Remarkably, this terrible fate struck the one woman who *would* make a public fuss. So it makes little difference whether she was raped or not – though I doubt it. She – and the Apparatus – have a very good reason indeed for creating a public issue. Miss Shen Chung's shame is to be the nation's salvation.'

'It's working, isn't it, Julie? The anti-American movement is sweeping the country. Everyone's demanding that Washington stop supporting the Nationalists. Demanding that all Americans get out of China.'

'So American correspondents report the wave of anti-Americanism – and the American people want to get out. Good tactics. Old hat, but effective.'

'But I detect a note of unhappiness.'

Julie studied her face in her hand-mirror, smoothed an unruffled eyebrow, touched the glass stopper of the perfume bottle behind her ears, and confessed: 'I know I should be delighted. But, Tommy, deliberately creating martyrs. Isn't it a little like trading in human flesh?'

47

January 2 – December 14, 1947

The man on the bicycle was a living barometer of Shanghai's decline
during 1947. He pedalled eastwards on Kiukiang Road towards the Bund
about seven thirty on weekday mornings and returned westward about
six thirty in the evening. Julia never learned where he worked or slept,
not even his name or age. She only knew that he rode a venerable black
Raleigh and dressed with threadbare respectability, rather like a clerk in
an old-time foreign trading house.

She also knew that he was cautious. Stopping at a small tobacconist
on the corner of Honan Road, he immobilized both the handlebars and
the drive-chain with padlocks – and secured the Raleigh to a lamp-post
with two more chains. Despite the alarming rise of theft, it seemed excessive when he also detached the brake-pads and pocketed them.

Julia had first noticed the bicyclist when, muffled in an ancient tweed
coat, he was pedalling howewards through icy sleet on the first Friday in
January. From the Raleigh's handlebars hung a sausage-shaped string
bag about six inches long, which was stuffed with ten-dollar banknotes
bearing the portrait of Dr Sun Yat-sen. She surmised that he had exchanged the bonus that some foreign firms paid valued employees in US
dollars. A dozen illegal money-changers openly conducted their black
market transactions in front of the Bank of China on the Bund.

All through the spring, the string bag swelled. At the beginning of
March it was sixteen inches long. At the end of March two eighteen-inch
sausages of banknotes hung from the handlebars, although the clerk's
foreign-currency bonus undoubtedly remained the same. Inflation was
so virulent that the Chinese dollar was losing its value against the US
dollar at a hundred and fifty per cent a week.

476

By early summer, the string-bags on the handlebars had been exchanged for a small suitcase, which was strapped to the luggage rack over the back wheel. By mid-summer, it was a large suitcase. By late summer, the large suitcase was supplemented by two very large stringbags slung like saddle-bags over the rear mudguard – and the bicyclist was making his cash run twice a week. By early autumn, he was returning every day with a highly conspicuous load of banknotes.

Although cautious, the bicyclist obviously did not care who saw him carrying millions of dollars. Shanghai's swarms of thieves, who would steal a bicycle in an instant, were not interested in cumbersome bales of cash.

Confidence in the future fell as fast as the Chinese dollar. Shanghai was becoming pathetically shabby. Routine maintenance was virtually suspended by hotels, trading firms, banks, blocks of flats, and even the self-confident foreign clubs. Drab trams became ramshackle – their seats splintered, their paint peeling, and their motors clanking dismally. Untended roads were a punishing obstacle course for cars. Axles snapped in deep potholes, and passengers bounced like drops of water on a hot grill. While awaiting its fate, Shanghai was running down.

Not even Joshua Haleevie would put additional capital into the doomed city. The flow of capital was the other way – outwards. His beloved Shanghai was dying, and he was helpless.

Tommy Howe's older brothers were smuggling their funds to Hong Kong, New York, and London. Customs officials and bankers were easily bribed to ignore the Central Government's stern regulations against sending money abroad. Besides, cabinet ministers, senior civil servants, and generals were the worst offenders. They shipped gold bars and US dollars as official baggage. It all amounted to a resounding vote of no confidence in the Nationalists' Central Government.

Julia was afraid to look too close. The years had not completely inured her to Shanghai's hideous contrast between the pampered rich and the tormented poor. So many were suffering while a few still played.

Sing-song girls in sheer stockings and fur coats still haggled with bony rickshaw-pullers for half a cent – only the stockings were now nylon from the American army stores. The haggling had, however, taken on a new edge. Once good-natured, virtually a sport, it was now a fight for survival. The contenders were like sleek rats and emaciated rats slashing at each other on a rubbish tip.

The children were heart-rending. Thousands of families spilled into the streets when inflation made it impossible for them to pay elevated rents. Their sons and daughters offered their bodies for the equivalent of a bowl of rice. As young as six or seven, they were the lucky ones.

The crippled, the scarred, and even the ill-favoured were debarred from prostitution. They gathered in ragged packs at the doors of restaurants to beg from well-fed patrons. At the backdoors, they fought for the scraps waiters and dish-washers considered too mean to take home to their own hungry families. The ordeals endured by the waif Little Pow in the 1920s seemed benign when small boys and girls gleaned the streets where coolies carried rice-sacks – and rejoiced when they found a few spilled grains. Others shooed the sparrows away from the undigested oats in the steaming manure dropped by the few horses that still served the city. Despite municipal ordinances, hawkers everywhere cried wares ranging from fountain pens and tangerines to pornographic photographs and condoms. Few customers bought, for prices were soaring.

Julie Howe quite uncharacteristically became almost ferocious. When Tommy in mid-July reported confidential Communist Party plans for several more years of Civil War to wear down the Nationalists, she exploded: 'They *can't* wait! They *mustn't*! It's getting worse every day. God alone knows what Shanghai'll be like in a couple of years.'

'We're not ready yet,' he pointed out. 'We must be absolutely certain of victory before the final offensive.'

'Tommy, it's certain that tens of thousands of children will die in the meantime – in Shanghai alone. When I think of our own kids in the same . . . But there's one good thing. I'm certain nothing could be worse than this. I *know* we picked the right side years ago.'

Tommy looked down to see that his meerschaum was glowing nicely. She was, of course, right – regardless of his own doubts about the Communist Party. Nothing could be more appalling than the Nationalists' compounding of brutality and callousness with rapacity and ineffectiveness. He was ninety per cent convinced that Chairman Mao Tsetung would bring peace and prosperity to China. But that ten percent doubt nagged like a sore tooth.

'You know, it's a funny thing,' Julia resumed. 'I haven't seen my money man on the bicycle for a week now. That's a bad omen!'

Emily and Julia were as close as they had ever been. Both wished their children to spend more time together. Emily felt that no harm and – perhaps even some good – would come of exposing her children, particularly Jason, to the strong American influence exerted by Althea and Persephone. Julia knew that Althea liked masculine company at a very ripe seventeen, but Jason would be restrained by his regard for family honour. Besides, his idealism would be good for her bourgeois daughters. There was nothing wrong with Jason's politics – except that he was just too zealous.

The cousins were bored by long days at the wholesome Columbia Country Club and occasional evenings at the cinema. Since Jason had sworn to his mother that he would involve neither his sisters nor his cousins with the student movement, time passed slowly. The impasse was broken by an invitation from the aged Howe aunt who maintained a mansion she called a cottage on the Yangtze River at Woosoong, some fifteen miles from Shanghai.

Auntie Vi, who would not have a telephone, now wrote that she would be delighted to allow her nieces and her nephew to create as much tumult as they wished for as long as they wished. In addition to fishing, she offered swimming, sailing, tennis, and horses. 'Besides,' she wrote, 'it will do the

American girls a lot of good to see the *real* China.' Smiling at that description of his aunt's small estate Tommy agreed heartily. It would also do him a lot of good – by getting his daughters out of his greying hair.

The recluse Ou-yang Hsiu nodded benevolently when his daughters Patricia and Eunice returned under the protection of Aunti Vi's aged major-domo two weeks later. The girls were sun-tanned, chipper, and bursting with tales of their innocent adventures in the countryside. They did not immediately speak of their absent brother. But Persephone Howe had already told her parents: 'Althea and Jason were spoil-sports. Always saying they were bored. I'm glad they went back early.'

Tommy nodded automatically, and Julia said: 'That's nice, dear. You must tell us all about it after . . .'

'What did you say?' Tommy exploded. 'Jason and Althea went back early? When?'

'Why, nine or ten days ago, Daddy. They said you told them they could leave if they got bored. Where . . .'

The telephone's ringing breached their mutual confusion. Emily was on the line, frantic at her daughters' report.

'Tommy, *where* are Jason and Althea?' she demanded irrationally. 'You *must* know.'

'I don't, Em. But I'll find out – bloody quick,' he replied. 'And get your friends in the Nationalist police busy.'

He hung up briskly. He was ready for action, but had little idea what to do.

Ten days was a long time for two youngsters to be missing. He should already have had a demand for ransom if they had been kidnapped. Besides, they had set out together of their own free will after lying about having his permission. On their journey back to Shanghai they could, of course, have been abducted or injured. But he had to assume that Althea and Jason had deliberately run away.

He began his inquiries around Woosong – recruiting several dozen farmers and fishermen to search the district. And he asked for help from the Apparatus. Perhaps some comrade had seen the two youngsters where they should not have been.

Tommy assured the distraught Emily that he was making every possible inquiry. Her aged husband came to the telephone to demand that no effort be spared in the search for his youngest son. Curiously, the father, who had three other sons, sounded even more alarmed than the mother, who had no other.

Tommy grew gloomier by the day. No word filtered through the Apparatus, and the search of the Woosoong area was unproductive. Julia was irritable, and Emily was no help. She appeared and disappeared at odd hours, always dashing home in case her Nationalist sources turned up some information.

On the third day, a grubby tan envelope came in the post. The letter, posted from Soochow, read: 'Dear Elders, Please do not worry. We are safe with the patriotic guerrillas, and we are serving China. Jason is quite old enough to carry a rifle, and Althea can roll bandages or assemble hand-grenades – even learn to carry a rifle. It is glorious to make our contribution to the inevitable victory of the people's cause.'

Under her neat signature Althea had written: 'P.S. Mommy and Daddy, I'm sure you'll understand. We were afraid it would all be over before we could join.'

Tommy erupted: 'I only understand that bloody Jason's practically kidnapped her. Soft city youngsters like them will collapse . . . fall apart . . . under field conditions.'

Julia was so relieved she could even laugh at Tommy's indignation over his daughter and his nephew's doing just as he himself had already done twice: joining the army in a time of national peril. Now that she knew Althea was safe, she could even toy with the idea of letting her daughter suffer for her ideals for a while. But Althea's father was still swearing at his nephew for seducing her to the political cause he had himself served for decades. Besides, Tommy said, there was no reason for his daughter to endure primitive hardships and perform hard manual labour. There were plenty of peasant girls for that sort of thing.

Julia incautiously observed: 'I suppose we should really be proud to give our daughter to the revolution.'

'Pride be buggered!' he swore. 'And bugger the revolution, too! But *how* do we get her back? I can't ask the Apparatus. They'd laugh themselves sick.'

'Quite properly, too. You're quite sure you want her . . . them . . . back?'

'Don't be a fool, Julia. Of course, I'm sure. . . .' He noticed her mock-innocent expression and laughed grimly. 'God, I'm so glad they've turned up. Now what do we . . .'

'Let's go see Rosamonde Sun, Tommy. We owe her a visit anyway.'

Madame Sun Yat-sen held open house for the young liberals of Shanghai, foreign and Chinese. She also conveyed to foreign correspondents that information and those views the Chinese Communist Party wished to make known unofficially.

Tommy had never warmed to Rosamonde Sun. Julia, therefore, took the lead. She drew aside the woman she greatly admired and spoke softly for almost ten minutes. Rosamonde's doll-like features crinkled in agreement, and she impulsively kissed Julia's cheek. 'I'll do what I can,' she said, patting Tommy's hand. 'Your motives are estimable.'

After leaving the big house in the former French Concession, Tommy pointed the Cord's bonnet homewards and asked: 'What did you tell her about my motives? Blessed if I know what they are myself.'

'I told her we were, naturally, disturbed as parents. But, as patriots, we were very proud to have our daughter and our nephew serve with the guerrilla army. Certainly they were old enough, I said. So many others served when so much younger. We couldn't completely suppress our fears for their safety, but we'd strive to overcome that weakness.'

'Sod it, Julie, do you *want* them to stay with the peasants? Have you gone mad? They wouldn't last six months.'

'No, darling, I don't – and I haven't. Though I am a little ashamed of our selfishness. However, I didn't think Rosamonde would take kindly to a tearful plea to get our poor innocents out of danger. Not when so many are fighting and dying.'

'What *did* you say? What's all this guff about my estimable motives?'

'I told Rosamonde I'd been reluctantly persuaded by you – because you have a cooler head. Both of us were very proud, but you wondered if the kids wouldn't be wasted. Not everyone can carry a gun. But very few speak English – and even fewer have the chance to be educated abroad to serve the revolution even better. As Rosamonde herself has done.'

'Clever you. I never could have been that smooth. She'll pass the message on, then? Nothing now but to wait.'

Considering the guerrillas' poor communications, their wait was re-markably short. On the evening of the ninth day after their visit to Rosamonde Sun, the lift discharged two travel-worn and unrepentant sinners into the big sitting-room of the house on Kiukiang Road. Althea tearfully kissed her parents. Eighteen-year-old Jason was stiff-lipped. But he clasped his Uncle Tommy's hand hard, and he hugged his Aunt Julia.

'We swore to tell *only* you, Uncle and Aunt,' he confided solemnly. 'Comrade Chou En-lai *himself* directed us to return to Shanghai and resume our normal lives.'

'Chou En-lai himself?' Tommy echoed. 'How very strange!'

'Daddy, Comrade Chou knows everything that goes on,' Althea said. 'Even about two unimportant little soldiers like us.'

'And, Uncle, he wrote directly to us. He directed us to think of the future – not only of the present. Many brave young men and women can carry rifles or assemble hand-grenades. But very few had the opportunity to educate themselves abroad to better serve the nation.'

'How wise!' Julia exclaimed. 'Anything else?'

'Also, we are not to associate with leftists any more. Some people, Comrade Chou En-lai instructed, must learn to wait – and to serve in silence.'

Why, Althea's mother wondered, had Chou En-lai responded so handsomely to their plea? To repay Tommy for his assistance during the White Terror of 1927? Or to recompense them for their years of silent service? Perhaps Chou En-lai had simply done the sensible thing from his own point of view. Educated youth were truly too rare a resource to be squandered.

Jason's mother was relieved – and decisive. Emily directed: 'We've got to get the kids out of town immediately. If the Nationalist special agents learn the truth about this latest escapade, they'll both be in danger. I won't be able to hold the agents off for long. And I can't protect the kids – not with Mayling in her present mood. They've both got to be on the next boat to San Francisco.'

Two days later, Althea and Jason stood on the deck of the *SS President*

Wilson. The Blue Peter fluttering on the foremast signalled that the liner would depart within the hour. Patricia and Eunice Ou-yang, who were not sailing, clung to their heroic big brother, and their eyes were wide in worship. Persephone, who was sailing, tearfully blew her nose into a grubby handkerchief like a baby elephant trumpeting.

Emily and Julia touched their eyes with their handkerchiefs. Tommy was self-consciously poker-faced at being so soon again deprived of his daughters.

Ou-yang Hsiu was, as usual, not present. Emily explained that her husband's absence was not this time by his own wish. He had been deeply distressed by the youngsters' flight to the Communists and, at seventy-three, he was suffering the consequences of that distress. He had been bedridden for a week with acute indigestion and muscular pains. His condition was alleviated by neither his traditional herbal doctor nor by his friend, the equally elderly Doctor Chee, who had completed his medical training at Heidelberg in the 1890s.

'I don't like the sound of that.' Tommy retreated from paternal emotion to a professional problem. 'Did Old Chee take an ECG?'

'Doctor Chee wouldn't know an ECG from a boa constrictor,' Julia laughed and explained to the puzzled Jason: 'An electrocardiogram, dear. It measures the activity of the heart.'

'I'll see to it,' Emily declared. 'Shall I call that nice David Chen who found I was slightly anaemic last year?'

'Do that, Em,' Tommy urged. 'Just to clear the air, though Hsiu's a tough old bird.'

'Now, you've got it straight, haven't you?' Emily admonished the three voyagers. 'The Consul-General will meet you in San Francisco. But Aunt Julia's cousin Bob, who is your distant cousin, will look after you in New York.'

'Yes, Mother. Don't worry.' Jason was blasé; a Pacific crossing could not ruffle the patriot who had crossed enemy territory to join the guerrilla army. 'We'll be all right.'

'You won't forget!' Emily persisted. 'Bryn Mawr will certainly take Althea – even at the last minute. And the George School's already admitted Perse. She's just a term early. But Jason . . .'

'Yes, Mother, I remember. General Sun Li-jen is a distinguished graduate of the Virginia Military Institute. And General Sun has cabled them. So, it's virtually certain they'll admit me. But I'm not to talk of Communism or of joining the guerrillas. I'm to be on my best behaviour for the selection board. And I'm not to have anything to do with leftists, not that I'd want to. Is that okay, Mother?'

'Yes, dear, it's just fine.' Emily kissed him. 'And do try to write regularly.'

'It's okay, Mother.' Jason turned away to hide the tears that started in his eyes. 'I won't forget anything. Can we go down to the cabin now and drop our things off? This topcoat's killing me in this heat.'

Ou-yang Hsiu died in Mid-October shortly after even the cautious Dr

482

David Chen declared he had 'turned the corner'. He was apparently recovering from the minor heart seizures that had initially appeared to be indigestion when a massive attack carried him off. Mercifully, he died quickly. Fully conscious almost to the end, he complained: 'It feels like ten razors cutting up my chest.'

His wife, who was twenty-seven years younger, had faced his mortal illness with calmness, almost, it appeared to her brother and her sister-in-law, with detachment. Emily, who thought she knew her own heart, was herself surprised by her desolation after his death. She had expected to feel bereft, for she had come to love her husband in her own way. She had not expected to feel that the framework of her life had collapsed.

She had believed that light, almost casual affection bound Hsiu and herself. None the less, she felt lost without the paternal figure who had for nineteen years been the single fixed point in her life.

The deprivation coincided with a period of involuntary quietude in her public life. The great crusade had come to an end with victory over the Japanese. Like Mayling Chiang, Emily found that her knowledge of the United States of America was not as much in demand when all the guns were turned on the Communists. The Nationalists had never needed the United States more, but the old guard were sourly suspicious of all foreigners – particularly the brash Americans. When Herculean efforts should have been devoted to repelling the Communists' propaganda offensive in the United States, the Nationalists were almost paralysed.

In America, some former missionaries and some congressmen spoke up for Free China, as did a few journalists and businessmen. Many more men and women of greater influence espoused the Communist cause – primarily in revulsion from Nationalist corruption and brutality. When the Nationalists' champions were dubbed 'the China Lobby', the battle was almost over. That harsh name was its own condemnation. In any event, the men and women who shaped American public opinion preferred rosy Communist promises, which they barely understood, to the harsh face of the Nationalists, which they had come to know too well.

A great effort was needed, and the irrepressible Jimmy Wei jarred the apathetic Emily into returning to active service. At the beginning of a bleak and empty December he urged: 'Em, you've got to start living again. More than spending some time now and then with Julie and Tommy. That's okay, but . . .'

'I don't spend much time with them, Jimmy,' she interrupted. 'They're caught up with their own lives. Though what keeps Julie so busy, I don't really see.'

'Why don't you start doing again what you've always done best? You can make our case in the US better than anyone I know, except maybe Madame Chiang herself. You've got to get back into the mainstream.'

'How, Jimmy? You know I've cut myself off.'

'Let me do some spadework in Nanking. The best thing would be a tour of the States. Lectures, interviews, broadcasts – the whole shooting match. In the meantime, though, why not get to know the correspondents again? They're not *all* hypnotized by the Reds.'

'I'll see what I can do, Jimmy. God knows the job badly needs doing. Just talking about it makes me feel more alive. Yes, I'll . . .'

'You could start by dropping in on Madame Sun Yat-sen. One of her soirées for the press. You know, tea and Red propaganda.'

'I couldn't, Jimmy. I'd feel like a whore in church.'

'More like a saint in a brothel, Em. If only we could shut her up. But persecuting the sacred widow of the Father of the Country. Forget it!'

'Jimmy, I really don't see how . . .'

'You *are* an old family friend of the Soongs, aren't you? Why don't you act like one and see what develops?'

When the telephone rang, Tommy Howe was shuffling through the file of cuttings his secretary had winnowed out for him. He had to keep up with events, but he was hard-pressed. In addition to his practice, he was serving as CAT's chief flight surgeon – and, of course, carrying out the missions assigned by the Apparatus. Julia answered the telephone and mouthed the single word 'Emily'. While she talked to his sister, he reread two items that together said it all:

November 12, 1947: The general offensive of the People's Liberation Army captures Shiachiachuang on the Peiping–Hankoo Railway, the first major city in North China to fall to the Communists. [For him it all began, he recalled, with the strike by the workers of that same railway.]

December 8, 1947: Washington gives the Nationalists 140 warships including a heavy cruiser and several destroyers in exchange for American naval bases in China. [Perhaps too much, he concluded but unquestionably too late.]

When Julia hung up, she told him that his sister Emily had decided to venture into the camp of her enemies. But Emily was a little timorous. Would they, she asked, come with her to Rosamonde Sun's?

Like Julia, Tommy was delighted that his sister was shaking off her lethargy. He did not, however, share Julia's hope that Emily could be brought to see the light as they saw it – and he wondered at Emily's sudden interest in the left wing. But he would naturally help her. A week before Christmas 1947, Tommy rang the bell of the big house in the old French Concession. An enormous holly wreath tied with a red bow hung on the door.

'I'd almost forgotten Rosamonde was a good Christian.' Julia smoothed her mink. 'As the only believer among us three, I'll be right at home.'

Carols were pouring from someone's portable record player, and someone else had mixed a bowl of Christmas punch. Emily assumed that the guests had provided those bourgeois fripperies, since Rosamonde Sun was reputed to be above such frivolity. Since she had last seen her hostess very briefly in Chungking some seven years earlier, Emily could not properly assess the legend, perhaps myth, of the self-sacrificing, compassionate Madame Sun Yat-sen. That reputation appeared excessive – but saints always appeared excessive to their contemporaries.

On a record a choir was singing *Adeste Fideles*. A small fir tree was hung with miniature Chinese lanterns, whose red-silk tassels swayed when the old floorboards flexed and creaked. Smoke eddied in the subdued light, and the conversation was loud – just like every gathering of newspaper people anywhere. Emily was bemused by the familiar atmosphere.

'First a taste of punch, my friends,' Rosamonde directed. 'Then you must meet the interesting people. Gregory Hardin over there you surely know already. Everyone does. He's been with us so long.'

Emily waved to her favourite newspaperman. Favours or promises, even threats, could not influence him. It was a pity that a correspondent noted for his integrity was reporting more favourably on the Communists every day. Of course, he depended largely on second-hand reports, since he was virtually barred from the battle zones.

'The correspondents don't speak Chinese,' Hollington Tong, the perennial chief of propaganda, would explain. 'Unfortunately, I can't always spare a member of my staff to accompany them.'

A stupid policy, Emily felt. Even Jimmy Wei was starved of authentic information by the diehard Nationalist reactionaries, who despised all foreigners, particularly newspapermen. Such obstructionism left the field open to hardy campaigners like Rosamonde Sun. She could always provide the latest information, which was always favourable to the Communists.

Emily accepted a cup of punch and concluded that Jimmy Wei was right. A lot of work was needed. But could anyone even hope to reverse the tide? Yet any effort was better than none. She would have to strive to bring the truth about China to the outside world. Her sunny smile belying her bleak resolution, Emily turned towards Gregory Hardin – and felt Rosamonde Sun's hand cold on her arm.

'Emily,' Rosamonde said, 'I believe you know Richard Hollings?'

Emily just kept from replying that she knew Richard Hollings too well. Her smile no longer sunny, she murmured: 'Good evening, Dick.'

Richard, who had obviously arranged the encounter exclaimed: 'Emily! What luck running into you. I got back from India only yesterday. I *am* in luck.'

No need to tell him that since his return to Shanghai a year earlier, his every arrival and every departure had been reported by Julia, who at the same time denied that she was trying to promote a reconciliation. Despite Emily's resolve, the barbed words slipped out: 'The harpies of the press gathering for the feast, Dick? Or should I say carrion crows?'

'Correspondents may be queer birds, Emily, but we're not totally perverted,' he answered easily. 'If there were no wars and no revolutions, we'd happily dine on other meat – more agreeable meat. Anyway, I'm getting too old for these capers.'

He must be about fifty, she calculated rapidly and examined him under lowered eyelids. The grey wings that had spread from his sideburns to

485

his temples aged him only slightly and gave him an air of authority. The white wrinkle-line between his eyebrows and the crow's feet at the corners of his eyes made him look somewhat weathered – yet tempered, rather than worn. His eyes were, however, tired.

'I didn't mean you started the wars,' she replied. 'Just that you preyed on wars. Well, don't you?'

'A partial apology, which is *rather* uncharacteristic,' Richard ruminated. 'And a personal attack, which is *completely* uncharacteristic of the cool Miss Howe. . . . I *am* sorry. I mean Madame Ou-yang. What can be the reason?'

'Don't flatter yourself, Dick. It's not you. . . . But everyone else must be eager to talk with you if you're just back from India. Don't let me keep you.'

'Perhaps I'm not eager to talk with them, but only with you. . . . Incidentally, did Julie ever tell you about my wife? You remember my mentioning Fiona?'

'I believe I do recall. What of her?'

'Her divorce, the final decree came through a month ago. She's been fed up with me for ages. I was never there, and I was always thinking of somewhere else when I was there. So she finally decided to get rid of me.'

'How nice for you! No responsibilities at all. But why tell me all this?'

'Because it's important that you know.' Richard's dark eyes were grave. 'Because you're the only one . . . the only one I ever cared about. From the beginning, it's always been you. No one else ever! And I still hope . . .'

Emily's pulse raced in spite of herself. She could not continue to be casually unkind after that declaration, no matter how much she hated and despised him. She undoubtedly despised him, but did she really hate him? Why could he still stir her to great anger or, perhaps, to great joy?

'Don't say any more, Richard, not just now.' The implicit encouragement escaped of its own accord. 'I haven't really been up to scratch since Hsiu died. . . . Oh, you didn't know?'

'I'm so sorry, Em,' he said very slowly. 'No matter what others may think . . . what you may've thought . . . I know how important he was to you. I'm so sorry.'

Emily looked at him in astonishment. Did she really not know him, even after all these years? She would never have believed he possessed such sensitivity. Not merely to sense the depth of her feeling for her elderly husband, but never to have charged her with dereliction of affection when they were lovers. Richard was by nature jealous, but he had remained silent for her sake.

'Richard, I . . .' Emily knew she must be cautious because she was disarmed, but the words again slipped past her guard: 'You know, Dick, we can't just pick up where we left off.'

'I never hoped for that much.' He smiled ruefully. 'But Em, I'm dead serious. And we're both free now. Shall we give it a whirl?'

'And have more dreadful fights over politics? I wonder, Dick, I really do.'

486

'Politics isn't everything, Em. Damned nearly everything nowadays, but still not quite. Why can't we begin the experiment by having dinner tonight?'

'I came with Tommy and Julia,' she responded weakly. 'It wouldn't be right to . . .'

'All the better. They can chaperone us. Do say you will, Em. Don't stand in your own light.'

Touched by his familiar tart humour, Emily finally nodded.

48

Nothing in the world was quite like American coffee laced with thick cream. Coffee never tasted quite the same anywhere else in the world.

Julia poured herself another cup and lit her second after-breakfast Chesterfield. When she poured cream with a liberal hand, her daughter Althea frowned across the expanding table room-service had provided.

'It's all right, darling.' Julia anticipated the rebuke. 'I'm very careful about my figure when I'm at home. When travelling, a little leeway's . . .'

'It's not just the cream, Mom,' Althea said. 'But all those cigarettes. You know they make you cough. If you're speaking today, you don't want . . .'

'There, then.' Julia stubbed out the cigarette. 'Is that better?'

'Much better. But you really should cut down. I heard you coughing all night.'

'The way you talk, anyone would think the Commodore Hotel was going to throw me out for disturbing their other guests. Have I really become a public nuisance in my old age?'

'Now, Mother, don't try to make a joke of it. You really must . . .'

Althea had become so officious since entering Bryn Mawr that Julia felt as if their roles had been reversed. It was rather like having her own anxious mother around, rather than her daughter. Still, Althea meant well.

Besides, Althea had chosen to join her in New York for the conference on 'China in Crisis' sponsored by the Committee for a Democratic Far Eastern Policy. Her younger sister, Persephone, preferred to spend the entire Easter Holiday of 1948 at the grand house in the Virginia hunt

488

country loaned to her Aunt Emily by a wealthy Nationalist sympathizer. Persephone adored her glamorous aunt and shared her aunt's devotion to the Generalissimo. Althea was now very discreet – on the instructions of Comrade Chou En-lai himself. But she was dedicated to the Communist revolution – and to Chairman Mao Tse-tung.

Still, they would all be together in a few days at Emily's borrowed mansion. Since Jason would also be in Virginia, a pack of wolves could not have kept Althea away. She was fascinated by the conference – and absurdly proud of her mother's role.

Julia had, of course, not confided to Althea that both her parents were active Communists. Despite the child's own dedication, it would have been too dangerous. The Nationalists still ruled Shanghai – and the vengeance they exacted in the guise of justice was quick and gory.

But, like any normal nineteen-year-old, Althea was fascinated by New York as well as by the conference. A morning with a classmate in the big city was too exciting to miss, but she left in a flurry of promises to return that afternoon.

Julia's speech was to be called 'A Conservative Looks at China'. She had been told it was time for her to speak out against the Nationalists. The objectives of the conference were to halt American assistance to the Nationalists and to swing American support to the Communists.

Her own theme was, as directed, the recent opening of her eyes to the true situation after years of blind support for the Nationalists. She would point out: 'Even those Americans who want to keep the Nationalists in power are forced to admit that the so-called Communists are winning. There is no possible way to make American aid to the Nationalists effective, much less ensure a Nationalist victory.'

And she would conclude with a ringing appeal: 'Isn't it time we Americans stopped helping the wrong side? Isn't it time we stopped throwing tinder on the bonfire of civil war? Isn't it past time we stopped encouraging the bankrupt Nationalists to keep fighting – and to kill additional hundreds of thousands? Isn't it time to give the other side a chance to show what it can do? As you know, they're not really Communists, but national revolutionaries.'

She would not, however, give credit to the author of that masterly misdirection of truth: *national revolutionaries*. Richard Hollings, who had coined it, was known as a champion of the Chinese Communists. But the ostensibly academic conference on 'China in Crisis' was ostensibly independent. Deeply concerned scholars, journalists, labour leaders, and businessmen were discussing China's problems, ostensibly without prejudgment or political pressure. After much thought they would, of course, *independently* reach the inevitable conclusion that the Nationalists were finished – and the Communists were the hope of the future.

The telephone broke into Julia's thoughts. She lifted the instrument eagerly. A number of friends from the old days at the Office of War Information were coming to the conference. In addition to its vital purposes, it should be fun.

'Madame Howe? Madame Julia Howe?' She could not immediately identify the voice, though the suave pseudo-English vowels were familiar. 'Do you remember the friend who often brought news of your husband during the war. No need for names. A bellboy is bringing an envelope to your room. Please do not overlook it.'

What was Professor Han of Stanford University doing in New York? Julia smiled at her own naïveté. He would naturally be present, although he was evidently still under deep cover.

She gave the grey-haired bellboy a quarter, which was probably too much. She was nervous, a little apprehensive, for Professor Han always brought unpleasant tidings. She ripped the heavy manila envelope open, almost breaking a nail. The crisp bond paper bore neither salutation nor signature, but only the message in green ink:

The sponsoring Committee have been informed that you will not deliver a speech. You will, however, attend the sessions. You will express scepticism regarding the speeches – just enough to demonstrate that you remain a reactionary element.

It would be dangerous for you publicly to support the revolution. You will, therefore, not reveal yourself even as a well-meaning liberal.

After victory you will, however, publicly proclaim your discovery of your past errors – *after* seeing the reality of the New Democracy. Owing to your wide acquaintance in journalistic circles, your dramatic conversion will be highly effective. Destroy this immediately.

Julia's hand shook as she tore the paper into small pieces, which she flushed down the toilet. Although angry and frustrated, she smiled at the fantasies of thriller writers whose heroes burnt incriminating letters before consigning them to the sewers. A waste of time, she had been taught. Besides, the smoke and the residue of ashes could arouse suspicion.

Julia smiled, although she was deeply disappointed. She had hoped to throw off some of the tension of her secret work by partially revealing her true position – as she had originally been authorized to do by the Apparatus. She would now have to play her double role for some time to come. She would also have to feign laryngitis to Althea.

On cooler reflection, being forbidden to speak was a great honour. The Apparatus normally no more hesitated to discard an agent than she hesitated to discard a used Kleenex. But Tommy and she were evidently valuable enough not to be used up and discarded. The future role for which she was reserved was unquestionably far more important than adding another American voice to the tirades of American voices raised against the Nationalists at an American conference.

She could now acknowledge that she had not looked forward to speaking. An audience of several hundred was different from the impersonal microphone of XMHA. She was actually relieved – and pleased that she was not yet required to discard even a portion of her cover. She had feared a violent reaction when Emily learned of her denouncing the Nationalists. At least the danger of a breach with her sister-in-law was postponed.

Aside from her persistent political backwardness, Emily was in fine fettle. During the three months since their meeting at Rosamonde Sun's, she and Richard Hollings had attained a tentative reconciliation. Julia assumed they were again sleeping together, but that was not the heart of the matter. Although essential, sexual satisfaction would not alone determine whether they could stay together. They had to forge an emotional link strong enough to withstand the friction of two strong – sometimes abrasive – personalities.

Richard was determined to marry Emily. He argued that marriage would itself ensure a permanent relationship. Emily pointed to the failure of his previous marriage – and argued that only a prior permanent relationship could ensure a lasting marriage.

To that irrefutable wisdom, Richard gaily replied: 'But aren't you glad that my marriage didn't work? I am – profoundly. Otherwise I couldn't offer you my hand, soiled though it may be.'

Since they could not avoid politics entirely, they skirted political disagreement, sometimes dangerously. Yet Emily had become open-minded for a supporter of the Generalissimo. She could be reasonably objective, except for her iron-hooped prejudice against the Chinese Communists. Richard was, as ever, mercurial. But he would never force a confrontation on an abstract issue, whether political, moral, or intellectual. He was not the kind to sacrifice himself for a cause – or to inconvenience himself excessively.

The ties that bound Emily and Richard were already strong. Since she was determined to spend several months in the United States to see her son and to campaign for the Nationalist cause, he had for the first time in memory subordinated his career to his affections. He had arranged to join her during the final month, telling his tolerant employers that he must reacquaint himself with America attitudes.

What Richard had not told his employers that he also needed treatment in the US for a respiratory complaint that had defied even the miraculous new antibiotics. Tommy had referred him to the Presbyterian Medical Centre, which was affiliated with his beloved College of Physicians and Surgeons. Taking his ailment seriously, Richard had actually stopped smoking his Senior Service cigarettes. He had even stopped cadging cigarettes.

A few husky whispers convinced Althea that her mother had suddenly fallen victim to laryngitis. Although disappointed, Althea was fascinated by the conference. For the first time in her life, she confided a little tremulously, she was in the same room as 'men and women who make the world go round, really important people'. She was also delighted by the setting: the ornate red-and-gold ballroom of the Commodore Hotel. Perching on her gilt red-velvet chair, she craned her head like a child in fairyland. Enthralled by the oratory, she believed every word.

491

Julia automatically sieved the half-truths and the untruths from the rhetoric. Deceit was, of course, often necessary, just as she was deceiving her daughter about her laryngitis. But Althea was drinking in too many distortions, not to speak of outright lies. She would have a word with Althea that evening. A little frankness would actually strengthen her cover, just as the Apparatus had directed.

Some of the Chinese present Julia knew as fellow travellers. The unknown were probably secret comrades. The most important Chinese was, however, the most conspicuous person in the ballroom.

His grey-worsted suit stretched perilously over his heavy frame, Feng Yü-hsiang, who was called the Christian General, sat uneasily on a spindly ballroom chair with his enormous hands splayed on his powerful thighs. He had for decades been popping in and out of power like a jack-in-the-box. He had connived with warlords, monarchists, and Japanese, with missionaries, Nationalists, and Soviets. He was now seeking an arrangement with the Chinese Communists.

The Christian General was taking advantage of his involuntary exile to find new allies. Generalissimo Chiang Kai-shek had sent him on a world tour 'to study water conservancy measures' when his intriguing became intolerable. He now sat in the ballroom of the Commodore Hotel trying to ingratiate himself with the distant Chairman Mao Tse-tung by nodding his watermelon head in ponderous approval of speeches in English which he did not understand. That performance was, Julia supposed, no more bizarre than his earlier baptizing entire regiments with fire hoses to win over missionaries so that their home countries would provide him with armaments.

Yet Feng Yü-hsiang was a Chinese who had been involved in Chinese politics for a generation. Aside from the few Chinese students from universities, the handful of Chinese fellow travellers, and the sprinkling of unknown Chinese comrades, the participants were conspicuously non-Chinese. That was, of course, quite normal at an American conference, and nearly half the speakers were associated in some way with China. But the rest had no connection whatsoever with China.

'The usual bleeding hearts,' she had heard a round faced young man with heavy spectacles remark at the press table. 'They turn out for every worthy cause – worthy in Uncle Joe Stalin's eyes, that is.'

Julia resented the glib orators who were clearly innocent of any knowledge of China. She, too, was virtually certain the Soviets had recruited them. Soviet involvement was, however, her own particular bugbear. It would disturb few others.

The white-haired president of the Pullman Porters' Union had obviously not been selected because he was either a China specialist or a moving orator. He was, however, black. The Soviet racists were always anxious to parade as many coloured races as they could.

The Filipino who demanded removal of all American bases and businesses from his native islands was a more plausible speaker. Although he naïvely confessed that he knew nothing about China, he was at least an Asian. And he spoke with authority about American atrocities – a theme

492

the audience loved. Particularly eloquent regarding America's misdeeds was a large Indian lady in a purple-and-pink sari, who seemed unaware that America had never colonized India.

After such highly seasoned fare, Julia had feared boredom from the white 'labour leaders, progressive political figures, and democratic personages', as the Chairman introduced those who had nothing to do with Asia. But their oratory was fiery and moving.

Fervent applause and occasional tears promised enthusiastic approval of the prepared resolutions. The conference responded with shame and anger to American perfidy in supporting the 'Chiang Kai-shek remnant clique'. It responded with cheers to the promise of an imminent Communist victory in China.

'How you could possibly attend that . . . that shameless farce!' Emily exploded before Julia could touch her mint-julep. 'Even Richard stayed away. My old *Red* Hollings stayed away. But you went.'

Julia ignored the attack and sipped her mint julep. Shocked by her sister-in-law's vehemence, she knew they would quarrel savagely if she replied in the same tone. Yet Emily's second sentence pleased her greatly. If she could jibe at Richard's political leanings before a third person, they must have come a long way towards resolving their fundamental differences.

'Julie, sometimes I really do *not* understand your actions,' Emily persisted, almost as if she wanted a quarrel. 'And to take an innocent child – particularly one with Althea's record. I saw the list of speakers. They're a bunch of Communists and fellow travellers.'

'We were just trying to learn a little, Em.' Julia did not succeed in being wholly conciliatory. 'It might do you some good to come down from your ivory tower occasionally.'

'Ivory tower? Me? Chungking and Kunming weren't ivory towers, my dear. But some people spent the war in San Francisco . . .'

'Ladies, ladies, let us have peace,' Richard somewhat nervously intervened. 'No need to fight the Chinese Civil War here in Virginia.'

'Even though it's being lost next door in Washington?' Emily subsided sulkily. 'But really . . .'

'Peace, Emmy?' Julia smiled and slipped into her role of sceptic. 'You know, in a way you're not so far wrong. You'd think the Generalissimo had a forked tail and hooves the way they went on. But they painted Chairman Mao Tse-tung as an archangel – at the very least.'

'Actually, they did ask me,' Richard confessed. 'But some peculiar types were coming. That pullman porter leader is a nice chap. Quite a good mind, I've found. But what he knows about China is precisely nothing.'

'And they complain about the Nationalists' China Lobby,' Emily declared. 'Talk about us as if we were all devils, just as you said, Julie. But they ignore the tricks and the lies of the other side.'

'Em, the war's going to be won or lost on the battlefields of China,' Julie interposed. 'Not in the pages of American newspapers.'

'Maybe it can't be won in the newspapers, but it can be lost in the newspapers. If Congress cuts our aid any more . . .'

'If the Gimo used the aid better, he could win. And Washington wouldn't cut aid so much if he were winning. Americans love a winner, you know.'

'Julie, I nearly forgot,' Richard interposed. 'There's a letter for you. It came Special Delivery this morning. I'll fetch it, shall I?'

'You Americans don't know a winner from a loser.' Emily ignored the interruption. 'Why, you don't even know your own best interests.'

'Em, I'm the last person to want the Communists to win.' Though the flat lie was not new, Julia was a little ashamed of herself. 'But even you've got to admit the Gimo is primarily to blame.'

'He's not perfect. But who could have done better? If he'd executed all the Communists when he should have, the Americans would have made an outcry. Americans are destroying us. You're an exception, Julie. Most articulate Americans seem to want the Communists to win. But the people, the simple people who are the backbone of this country, they see it clearly. They're for us Nationalists because they fear Communism. They know we're fighting their fight.'

Julia's temper rose, and the words escaped: 'Em, if you Chinese would just stop blaming other people for your own failings, you'd be a lot better off. I'm getting sick of everybody always blaming everything on the Americans. What's happened to your admiration for this country?'

'Experience, Julie, experience taught me a lot. I've learned that Americans can't be trusted. Not even the best of them. Not even you, Julie. They seem open and frank, but they're not what they seem. They smile – and grab whatever they want! I trust *no* American now!'

Emily stopped abruptly, evidently disturbed by her own words. Her sister-in-law Julia was appalled. This quarrel could end decades of intimate friendship and split the family. Emily obviously knew more than she was saying.

Which of her own apparent betrayals had Emily discovered? Was it her secret life in the Apparatus – a discovery that could, quite literally, prove fatal? Had Richard Hollings sealed their reconciliation with a full confession? Her one rather unsatisfactory night with him had occurred years ago. But Julia knew Emily would find even that single lapse unforgivable.

'Here's your letter, Julie.' Richard had reappeared. 'Hope it's good news.'

Happy for the respite, she opened the flap and unfolded the brief note. She read it quickly and then reread it slowly.

'I'm afraid I'll have to leave, Em,' she said. 'Mother writes that my father's not very well. No cause for alarm, she says. That's why she wrote, rather than telephoning. But I'd better get up to Puxatawney. I can leave the girls here, can't I?'

As she and her bags were bundled into a car, Julia realized that she would not in the past have asked Emily's consent to her daughters staying on. She would have assumed consent – before that moment only minutes earlier when their friendship had radically altered.

494

49

September 5, 1948–January 8, 1949

A week after Julia's much-delayed return from America, Tommy was still inventing reasons to leave his consulting rooms on the ground floor in order to see her for a few minutes during office hours. Julia, too, discovered an excuse to intrude into his consulting rooms every time she left the house. They had been six months apart, their longest separation since the war, and they had celebrated their reunion in bed for almost twenty-four hours.

The servants were delighted, amused – and sceptical of Julia's claim that she had to rest after too rapid changes of time zones. They simply did not believe it had taken her only sixty-five hours to fly from San Francisco to Hong Kong in Pan American's China Clipper.

Their major-domo almost overstepped the line. They had always considered him ancient, although he was only five or six years older than Tommy. Then, shortly after Julia's return, he had slyly asked: 'Doctor, have you got more medicine to make old men act young? You haven't taken it all yourself?'

Flattered, Tommy had tossed him a bottle of multi-vitamin capsules. He remarked: 'At least vitamins won't do him any harm. Nor cost anywhere near as much as rhinoceros horn and ginseng. If he believes they will, the vitamins might even work for him.'

'Is that how you do it, darling?' she had asked. 'Vitamins?'

'No need,' he had replied. '*You* do it to me.'

He was, all in all, a most satisfactory husband, Julia complacently concluded again. When she was delayed in the States, he had telephoned repeatedly. Getting those trans-Pacific calls through, he later boasted, had been a greater challenge than harrying the Japanese with the guer-

495

rillas. Julia had given him little hope until mid-August, when her mother intervened.

'Darling, he is your husband – and he obviously needs you,' she had said. 'Your father will miss you, but there's little you can do for him. I need you, too, but I'm not going to be a selfish old woman. He could live another six weeks, Dr Creeke says, or another six years. He'll understand. Go home to your husband.'

Julia was torn. But when Tommy confirmed the uncertain prognosis, she decided to leave. His professional integrity would not allow him to misstate her father's prospects – no matter how much he might wish to. Tommy had told her bowel cancer could spread rapidly or, almost as likely, go into remission. Unless she planned to remain at her father's bedside for months, perhaps years, she really should return to Shanghai.

Julia had already spent so much time with her daughters that they were getting on each other's nerves. Four women alone were not much fun, particularly when they ranged in age from her mother's sixty-eight to Persephone's fifteen.

The girls had spent half their summer holiday with Emily and Richard, enjoying the company of Patricia, Eunice, and of course Jason. In response to her sister-in-law's precise and polite invitation by telephone, Julia had coolly declared that she could not leave her father. Besides, she had added truthfully, the children could look after themselves, but Emily would hardly want her around when she was worried about Richard.

The flexible author was resting. He was also writing his memoirs, an endeavour Julia thought rather pretentious for one only a year older than her husband. When she expressed some surprise, his laughter had snaked through the telephone lines. He had pointed out that he was accustomed to working hard, rather needed the money – and was for the moment physically debarred from doing anything else.

The radiologists at the Presbyterian Medical Center had initially found something they described vaguely as a 'spot on the lung'. The thoracic specialist subsequently told Richard with a faint air of embarrassment that he was suffering from tuberculosis, a disease prosperous white males simply did not contract in the enlightened 1940s. Furthermore, the new antibiotic, streptomycin, had virtually tamed what was once called galloping consumption. Social embarrassment aside, tuberculosis was rarely fatal nowadays. Still, a long rest was indicated – and an immediate return to China was impossible.

The specialist had sent Richard off with a clap on the back and the assurance that he probably need curtail his activities for no more than a year. Richard's question about China had restored the specialist to good humour. He had almost forgotten the protracted sojourns in that unhygienic country that explained how his patient had contracted a disease that was no longer fashionable – or even prevalent – in the West.

Julia now regretted not having stopped to see Emily and Richard on her way home. Next year seemed a long time off. She had, however, been distressed by her final parting from her father – and eager to see Tommy. Besides, not she, but Emily was primarily responsible for the coolness that had lasted longer than any previous disagreement between them. Julia hesitated to make overtures that were likely to be rejected.

'Julie, where are you?'

Tommy's voice startled her, for she had not heard the elevator's creaking. When he entered the enormous sitting-room, she saw that he looked tired. The air-conditioning was balking again, and the house was very hot. What else, however, did ninety-nine per cent of Shanghai's people endure in early September?

'Darling!' he called again. 'Oh, there you are. Bloody hot, isn't it?'

She nodded and lifted her mouth for his kiss. After mixing gimlets for both of them, he fussily lit his old meerschaum pipe. Although he had been at her to cut down her smoking, the meerschaum remained his constant companion.

'A funny business,' he said. 'The Christian General is dead, Julie. Do you think St Peter will roll out the red carpet? See that he's greeted by the regiments he baptized – and then sacrificed?'

'But I saw him only a few months ago in New York,' she answered unthinking. 'He certainly didn't look ill.'

Julie smiled penitently. Her husband had once pointed out that everyone said the same thing on hearing of the death of an acquaintance – as if having seen him last month, last week, or that morning should somehow have preserved him from death.

'He was only sixty-seven, and he wasn't ill,' Tommy answered. 'At least, illness didn't kill him. It was a fire on a steamer in the Black Sea. Did you know he was going to Russia?'

'It's not surprising. I told you the Soviets practically ran the conference on China in Crisis, probably picked up the tab. How did the fire start? Were many killed?'

'Now there's the mystery, my love. No one else was so much as singed. It seems the old boy was a photography buff, very keen. That's news to me, but no matter. All his inflammable film somehow caught fire, presumably by spontaneous combustion. Presto, no more Christian General. Nobody else even hurt.'

'That's fishy, Tommy. The poor old Christian General the only one killed in a fire at sea!'

'When you remember that film has been pretty fire resistant since the thirties, it's very fishy. But maybe not Soviet film.'

'They got rid of him, didn't they? I wonder why?'

'Presumably because they were afraid he'd queer their pitch in China. Or, maybe just tidying up the past. Maybe, Julie, on behalf of our own masters, the Chinese Communist Party. You know from your own experience how obliging the Soviets are in that way.'

Flowing out of the north like a great tide, the soldiers of the People's Liberation Army were flooding the Nationalist defences. On the map it looked like a vast blot of red ink spreading rapidly. First Manchuria and the North-west, then North China and, finally, most of Kiangsu

Province north of Shanghai – all fell to the big Communist divisions. The red tide halted on the northern bank of the Yangtze River, which bisects China. Just short of Nanking and Shanghai, it would quite obviously soon roll on.

'It's not quite panic yet,' Tommy observed in mid-August of 1948. 'But people are on the verge of it. They could go over the edge any time.'

The everyday actions of ordinary men and women amid the Nationalist collapse were tragic and macabre. Occasionally they were funny.

On January 31, 1948, three hundred taxi-dancers and sing-song girls had demonstrated in the streets against the decree that closed down all the nightclubs of Shanghai. They were supported by hundreds of nightclub managers, accountants, musicians, waiters, bartenders, and lavatory attendants. Two days later, the Ministry of Social Welfare reiterated the decree and announced a 'thorough ban' on all social dancing, private as well as public.

On the same day that purity was thus affirmed, the Military Police put down a strike of Shanghai cotton-mill workers, killing three and injuring more than sixty. During the succeeding months, students and teachers throughout China struck 'in support of the anti-hunger and anti-oppression movements', as their banners and circulars declared. Shanghai students actually discovered a new issue – and rioted against the American revival of Japanese militarism. As if to celebrate the American national holiday on July 4th, hundreds of students from Communist-occupied Manchuria had clashed in Peiping with Nationalist police. Eighteen were killed, and twenty-four were seriously injured.

'The litany,' Tommy said wearily, 'goes on and on and on.'

'I never thought it would happen this way,' Julia replied. 'I envisioned a mass uprising – and great armies marching.'

'The great armies *are* marching. But starvation, disease, and disorder are marching faster. So is inflation. While you were away, the cost of living sometimes doubled in twenty-four hours. Some shopkeepers changed their prices every other hour. Others closed down in despair.'

'The rich are on a buying spree.' Julia interjected. 'I've seen it everywhere. Food, clothing, even shelter, cost dozens of baskets full of Chinese banknotes. But a couple of US dollars will buy practically anything. Chennault's people use the CNRRA Commissariat. China's Nice Relief and Riches for Americans, they call it. A can of baked beans will buy a pair of beautifully made-to-measure shoes at Kow Hoo's. It's the same for the military and diplomats – anyone who can get into the Army PX. It's rotten, Tommy, just rotten!'

'Not for long, now, darling. Whom the gods would destroy, they first make mad.'

He fanned out a sheaf of back copies of the *China Weekly Review*, the American-edited journal that had been the bible of liberal foreigners since it began publication in 1917.

'Just look at the prices,' he directed. 'They really bring it home.'

The magazine dated March 1, 1941 bore the price of 80 cents Chinese National Currency, the equivalent of 15 cents US. On February 2, 1946, after wartime inflation, the *Review* had cost $150 CNC, and on July 10, 1948, it was $300,000 CNC, both just 15 cents US. The issue dated September 4, 1948 cost: 60 cents gold *yüan*, exactly 15 cents US.

'Remarkably consistent,' she commented drily, 'though I still don't understand exactly what a gold *yüan* is supposed to be.'

'It's the latest panacea that's meant to solve all economic problems: stabilize the currency, control prices and wages, restore confidence. You know, practically turn the disaster around.'

'Is it working at all, Tommy? Or is that a stupid question?'

The gold *yüan* had recently replaced the ludicrously inflated Chinese National Currency. All Chinese citizens were required to exchange all their gold, silver, and foreign currency for gold *yüan* – at four *yüan* to US$1. The economic supremo appointed to enforce those measures was General Chiang Ching-kuo, the Generalissimo's thirty-nine-year-old son, who had spent his formative years as a hostage in the Soviet Union. Taking office in Shanghai in mid-1948, Chiang Ching-kuo had enforced the regulations with great vigour.

'Ching-kuo's like Joe Stalin,' Tommy summed up. 'He believes the more people he kills, the more stable the country will become.'

Two days later, Julia strayed into the horrors of Chiang Ching-kuo's reforms. Driving in the Cord Coupé to Rosamonde Sun's house in the old French Concession, she was halted on Avenue Edward VII near the Great World by an officious policeman who said: 'All traffic must stop for fifteen minutes. Until after the punishment. You must wait.'

An American-made army lorry halted, and its tailgate dropped to reveal fourteen men in torn clothing under the American-made M-I carbines of Military Police wearing varnished American-made helmet-liners. Prodded by the carbines, the prisoners alighted painfully. Their hands were tightly bound, and their ankles were hobbled by chains.

The men were jabbed into kneeling on the gritty cobblestones. Their faces were bruised, and blood stained their grimy shirts. Tucked into filthy bands tied around their heads, hand-written placards proclaimed their individual crimes.

Julia could not look away. As Tommy had said, the Generalissimo's son was fighting inevitable economic collapse with mass executions. Despite Nationalist inefficiency, some of those men might be her comrades-in-arms in the secret war for freedom and justice. She shuddered, but gazed in terrible fascination.

Above the slack lips and the bloody cheeks of the nearest man, the placard read: 'Communist Bandit'. A thin man beside him displayed the pinpoint pupils of the opium addict and the verdict: 'Secret Money Exchanger'. A well-fed youth wearing the shreds of a Western-style silk shirt was labelled 'Gold Hoarder'.

An MP officer wearing wrap-around aviator's sun-glasses took out his pistol. The Colt 45 was standard American Army issue, and the initials US were embossed on the brown-leather holster.

499

Although she was half-nauseated, Julia still watched in her own silent tribute to those unjustly condemned. The officer halted behind the slack-lipped 'Communist Bandit'. Flame spouted from the Colt's muzzle two inches from the skull, and blood and bone gushed where the loose lips had drooped an instant earlier. The impact hurled the man to the cobblestones the 45-calibre bullets could stop a charging buffalo. His head had simply exploded, leaving nothing recognizable as human above the stump of the neck.

Julia closed her eyes and leaned her forehead on the hard steering-wheel. Although the Cord's cramped cockpit was hot, she shivered with a sudden chill. Shots sounded in staccato rhythm, and she smelled acrid cordite. When bile rose coppery and sour in her throat, she choked it back. Fearing she would faint, she opened her eyes again.

Ten of the fourteen men lay on the cobblestones. Some sprawled, and some were cramped into foetal postures. The MP officer was pushing a fresh clip into his pistol, and the remaining prisoners were staring straight ahead. Apparently dissatisfied, the officer removed the clip, pressed the bullets down on the spring, and snapped the clip back into the hand-grip.

The muzzle prodded the nape of a stout man whose placard declared: 'Economic Speculator'. Fear had not totally wiped the good humour from his bluff features. With new horror Julia recognized him. He was Joshua Haleevie's childhood friend, the sometime head waiter at the French Club called Fatty Woo, who had fought beside Joshua and Tommy with the guerrillas.

Julia closed her eyes again – and was terrified by a vision of Tommy in the same position. By Nationalist standards, her husband was a hundred times more culpable.

The fatal shot should already have sounded, for several seconds had passed since the MP raised his pistol to Fatty Woo's head. Julia glanced up fearfully. Fatty Woo was on his feet, solicitously supported by two MPs. They led him stumbling to an old Ford sedan, and he climbed awkwardly into the back seat.

A single shot sounded, then two more close together. Three more men lay in death on the cobblestones. The MP officer stood behind the last victim, reholstering his pistol. The sun glinted on his sunglasses, transforming him into a robot with photo-electric cells for eyes.

Julia started the Cord and began to put it into gear. She had been going to Rosamonde Sun's, she recalled. At that moment revulsion hurled her cowering against the leather seat. She trembled for several minutes before she could put in the clutch to flee to the refuge of her own house on Kiukiang Road.

When she told Tommy about it, he listened in silence, interrupting only to freshen her scotch and water. When she told him of the curious reprieve of Fatty Woo, Tommy smiled for the first time that evening, and said: 'I knew Josh was worried. Fatty's life cost him two thousand US. A fortune nowadays. But it worked.'

'Tommy, it could've been you.'

'Not a chance, darling. We've got the wherewithal. We could pay two *hundred* thousand US. If necessary, Joshua would lay out a million. And who could resist that? You can get away with murder if you've got the cash. Even get away with . . . ah . . . sedition. And if you don't have the cash? Well, you saw it.'

Tommy Howe sat at his desk and reflected that there was no need of a sooth-sayer to see the future clear. By November 1, 1948 the gold *yüan* had fallen from four to ten thousand to the US dollar, and the Generalissimo's son had resigned 'with deepest apologies for . . . intensifying the people's suffering'. On December 1st, the People's Liberation Army had taken strategic Hsüchow four hundred miles from Shanghai after the General-issimo squandered his veteran divisions by appointing generals who were political hacks. On the same day, with all Manchuria and most of North China in Communist hands, US$16 million worth of American arms arrived in Shanghai. It was the last delivery to the Chinese main-land. The Generalissimo had requested that all future shipments be diverted to the island of Taiwan.

By Christmas of 1948, the shape of the future was unmistakable. Setting the seal upon the imminent end of Nationalist rule, the staunchly anti-Communist Joshua Haleevie remarked on Christmas Eve when he stopped by for an eggnog: 'You know, Tommy, it's about time we told Whitehall what they'll need to do to get on good terms with a Communist régime. Besides recognition, what else will Chairman Mao want?'

Tommy duly passed the inquiry to the Apparatus, but he did not expect a quick reply. Even the far-sighted Chou En-lai would not be primarily concerned with foreign affairs when the Communists were rolling up the old map of China.

On that map the Nationalists still appeared to have some hope of surviving. South of the Yangtze River, China was largely free of the red ink-blot of the People's Liberation Army's advance. But the Nation-alists had lost the will to fight. Their leaders were either preparing to make their separate peace with the Communists or stealing more public money to ensure a comfortable exile. The white area south of the Yangtze was hardly more significant than the small white speck in the red north where the old warlord called the Model Governor stubbornly held Taiyüan, the capital of Shansi Province.

Tommy picked up the files of the patients he was to see that morning. Notwithstanding Christmas, Civil War, and the impending change of régime, personal illness still struck. All his patients were now genuinely ill. He had weeded out the hypochondriacs, in the process also weeding out his most lucrative patients. He was, as always, treating many who could not pay. But money mattered little nowadays. Very soon Shanghai would be liberated – and he would have no use for personal wealth. He would practise medicine as he had once dreamed, free of all pressures except the patient's needs.

The telephone buzzed, and his secretary advised: 'Mr Smythe on line two, Doctor.'

'Tommy, old pal, good to hear your voice.' The American was, as always, jovial. 'How do you feel about a little scenic flight this morning? We've got a problem in Taiyüan. A Dakota down and a pilot hurt. And no, I can't find anyone else. Otherwise I wouldn't ask you. It'll mean an overnight stay.'

Tommy agreed to meet Harry at Hungjao Airport within the half-hour. Leafing through his patients' files, he found nothing urgent. After instructing his secretary to refer any emergency to Dr David Chen, he took the lift to the fourth floor to change into warm clothing. Since Julia was out, he left her a brief note.

When the Curtis Commando lifted off the slush of the runway, the roar of the engines made the bare aluminium cylinder of the fuselage reverberate like a bell. Overcrowded, grimy, and licentious, Shanghai dwindled beneath the silver wings. The engines laboured as the aeroplane struggled for altitude. Uncomfortable on the canvas bench hung along the side of the fuselage, Tommy huddled into the sheepskin coat Harry had tossed him before take-off.

Despite heavy woollen socks, his feet were already losing sensation on the bare metal floor. The slush scraped off boot-soles had run into the grooves of the floorboards, where it was freezing again. Reaching under the bucket-seat, Harry produced a pair of sheepskin-lined boots. Tommy smiled his thanks, but even within the cocoon of the flight-boots his toes felt like frozen veal.

Harry mouthed a question, and Tommy shook his head. The hammering of the engines and the keening of the wind made it impossible to hear. When Harry lifted his cupped hand to his mouth as if drinking, Tommy nodded. Coffee or tea, anything hot would be very welcome.

The American clambered up the incline of the fuselage like a toddler climbing a slide, and Tommy craned through the small, round porthole. Beneath them the Yangtze River flowed lethargically through the severe winter landscape. He saw puffs of grey smoke on the northern bank, followed seconds later by flashes on the southern bank. Communist artillery was firing across the river that cut China in half. That was presumably why the pilot was climbing so high. Taiyüan lay more than eight hundred miles to the north-west, a minuscule islet lying amid an expanse of land held entirely by the People's Liberation Army.

Harry returned with paper cups clasped in his gloved hands after the Curtis Commando had levelled off, and shouted into Tommy's ear: 'Hope you like cream and sugar.'

Tommy did not even like coffee, much less that muddy beverage adulterated. But he nodded again. Clutching his cup, he stooped to tuck his worn Gladstone bag out of harm's way under the canvas seat. He then leaned back and contemplated the extraordinary spectacle of an overloaded CAT aeroplane in flight.

The rope-handled green boxes stacked in the forward area all bore the legend: *Ammunition, ball, .30-caliber, US Army.* At the rear where the fuselage tapered, heaped-up hay-bales fenced livestock to feed the defenders of Taiyüan. A rooster crowed, shrill above the din, and perturbed hens clucked in their wicker baskets. The hay barrier slipped, and a grey billy-goat pushed through it. Scimitar horns swaying, he picked his way on tiny black hooves around sacks of rice, baskets of vegetables, and two-foot-high earthenware jars of preserved eggs towards the green curtain that cut off the flight-deck. Poking his head through the curtain, the billy-goat contentedly surveyed the pilots.

The Curtis Commando carried just five other passengers, all young Chinese men. They were setting up a mah jong game on one of the twenty olive-drab US Army foot-lockers chained to the floorboards along the centre line of the fuselage. Wondering what the padlocked lockers contained, Tommy glanced at the long tarpaulin-protected object secured with wire-rope.

A CAT DC-3, an ever-reliable Dakota, had been raked by machine-gun fire during a rice-dropping mission over Taiyüan. The long object was a replacement for the Dakota's damaged engine, and the five young men were mechanics. The pilot had also been hit. Tommy was on the flight because Harry Smythe would not trust his fliers to the doubtful skill of Chinese military surgeons.

Although the twin engines' were revving more slowly at cruising altitude, the Commando's thin aluminium shell still clattered metallically against protruding aluminium ribs. Harry leaned over and asked in a half-shout: 'Everything all right, Tommy? It'll be a while. Four, maybe four and a half hours.'

'Fine, Harry,' he replied into the other's ear. 'Though I'm wondering what those foot-lockers are in aid of.'

The American grinned enigmatically and replied: 'Why don't you ask the captain? Meanwhile, what do you know about our Taiyüan operation?'

'Very little.'

'For five months now, CAT's been keeping Taiyüan alive, all alone in a red sea. The Gimo flew in the day after the siege started, and then gave Chennault his orders: *Drop everything else if you have to, but keep Taiyüan supplied.* We've brought in tens of thousands of tons of food and ammo. First time in history. Never seen a besieged city supplied from the air for so long.'

'And how much longer?'

'We can keep bringing the stuff in indefinitely.' In the freezing interior of the millimetre-thin fuselage at eight thousand feet, Harry's breath was instantly transformed into thick vapour. 'How much longer really depends on the troops – and the stubborn old Model Governor.'

He rose and gestured towards the flight deck. Tommy stepped gingerly over the lashing wires and nudged the billy-goat aside. An American with pale lashes framing light-grey eyes sat on the left in the captain's chair. A peaked cap was cocked rakishly over his left ear, its badge a grinning tomcat. In the co-pilot's seat, a grizzled Chinese was speaking into a hand-microphone.

'Welcome to my office,' the Captain said. 'Sorry the heating's on the blink back in the cabin.'

He spoke in normal tones, and he was in his shirtsleeves in the insulated and heated cockpit. Adjusting with difficulty to the lower noise level, Tommy offered the conventional response when Harry said: 'Captain Wessex Hakluyt Johnson. Everybody calls him Wex. Johnny Wang I think you know.'

'Anhwei Province is down there under the clouds,' the Captain said. 'At least, I hope it is. There's nothing much to see now. Why don't you come back up here when we land, Doctor? Could be interesting.'

'What number strip's this one, Wex?' Harry asked.

'Don't recall for sure, Harry,' the Captain replied. 'Johnny?'

The grizzled co-pilot hung up his microphone and counted on his fingers before replying: 'You know, Doctor Howe, every time the Communists get too close, the Governor builds a new airstrip closer to the city. I'd say this is about number six.'

'Then the siege ends when there's no more level ground for a new strip?' Tommy asked.

'I guess so, Doctor,' the Captain replied. 'Though we could support it with airdrops – for a while.'

The two passengers reluctantly left the warm cockpit to huddle again on the bucket-seats.

'They've got work to do,' Harry remarked. 'Tommy, old buddy, you didn't ask Wex about the footlockers.'

'I may be thick, Harry, but I'm not bloody thick. You were obviously trying to suck me in.'

'I really wanted to hear what Wex would say, Tommy. You know US dollars will buy anything, including money, in Shanghai. Well, US dollars will buy twice as much Chinese money in isolated Taiyüan, so the crews bring in fat rolls of greenbacks to exchange for Chinese banknotes. Back in Shanghai, presto, they sell the notes for twice as much in green. It's a sweet racket. Though I'm not supposed to know those footlockers'll go back packed with banknotes.'

'You don't mind?'

'Why should I? Worse things happen in Shanghai every day. And I've always got volunteers for the Taiyüan flight, which isn't exactly a piece of cake. It's sometimes very hairy. Only Taiyüan's left. A year ago there were ten to fifteen cities on the brink of falling to the Chicoms. Good pickings for my fly boys.'

'And for you, Harry?'

'It's not my act, Tommy. I can't see holding up people who're desperate to escape on a plane. Too much like robbing blind men's cups.'

At 3:18, the co-pilot leaned through the curtain and beckoned. Tommy took the folding seat behind the Captain and snapped the safety-belt. Through the numerous glass panes that made the cockpit a virtual greenhouse he saw a dark winter landscape sparkling with occasional fires.

'All settled, Doc?' the Captain asked. 'Here we go then.'

The bulbous nose dipped, and the Commando descended so rapidly

Tommy's ears popped repeatedly. The big aeroplane stood on one wing-tip in a sharp turn, then settled into an even steeper descent. The Captain turned the wheel and pulled it back. As the Commando climbed sharply to the right, a string of flaming spheres rose from the ground.

'Goddamn them boys,' the Captain swore. 'I heard they got themselves some flak guns. Goddamn!'

Two parallel rows of yellow lights flared in the darkness ahead, and the Captain pushed the wheel forward. The Commando hurtled downward, and a minute later the wheels threw up showers of gravel, which drummed against the aluminium skin like hail. The big aeroplane bounced high. As the wheels touched the ground again, the Captain was pumping the brakes.

Tyres squealed, and gravel spurted from the landing strip. The night was lit by flashes as the co-pilot flicked the landing lights on and off. When forward motion stopped, the Captain pointed towards the rear.

'Move fast now, Doc,' he said. 'Never know what surprises the Commies have got for us.'

Gripping his Gladstone bag, Tommy slid down the minute aluminium ladder hooked into the open doorway. He saw by hanging paraffin lanterns that the Commando had stopped in a revetment of sandbags roofed with corrugated iron. Outside mortar-bombs exploded.

'Welcome to Taiyüan!' Harry Smythe grinned evilly. 'Your patient will be in the dugout.'

The stricken pilot was a slight American knows as Walrus Reilly. Tommy set his broken arm, but left the machine-gun bullet in the flesh of the thigh to be extracted in hospital in Shanghai.

Stepping outside the revetment when the prolonged shelling that greeted their arrival had subsided, Tommy saw the medieval battlements of the walled city of Taiyüan against the moonlit sky. Within the revetment, the mechanics worked all night on the damaged engine. They were relieved to find no need for a complete replacement, only for parts from the spare engine. They were obviously as eager to leave Taiyüan as Captain Wex Johnson had been to reach the city.

The Commando was ready for take-off at dawn with Harry Smythe flying co-pilot. The repaired Dakota was to follow an hour or so later to avoid presenting the alerted Communists with a second target in quick succession. Tommy was to fly on the Dakota with grizzled Johnny Wang at the controls and with his patient on a stretcher. After watching the Commando loaded, Tommy would almost have preferred to remain in besieged Taiyüan rather than board that aircraft.

The cannibalized Dakota engine was the biggest single item aboard, but the double-padlocked foot-lockers were heavy with Chinese bank-notes. In the space left at the rear by the departed livestock stood a mound of chests, carpets, and trunks. The military cargo having been unloaded, cloth-wrapped bundles, canvas valises, and great wicker baskets filled every cranny, right up to the green curtain of the flight-deck.

'Where you're going to find room to sit,' Tommy remarked to Harry, 'I don't . . .'

'Just the beginning, pal,' Smythe replied. 'I've got to turn a blind eye. But you just watch.'

Standing before the aluminium ladder, Captain Wex Johnson and a squad of policemen were almost engulfed by a tidal wave of human beings. Truncheons flailed, and the throng recoiled. Reluctantly lining up, though still jostling each other and swearing, the passengers produced large red tickets. The Captain painstakingly examined each one.

'You're collecting fares?' Tommy asked. 'Who issues the tickets?'

'We've got a little office in town,' Harry Smythe replied. 'But old Wex Johnson is looking for a special chop. Every one of those people has ponied up. Not just our fare, but old Wex's special fare. He takes only greenbacks or gold bars. Same for the baggage. Every piece pays a tariff to Wex. He's going to be a very rich man when this is all over. I figure, after expenses and payoffs, he's clearing ten to fifteen thousand US on every turn-around.'

Beyond surprise by his native land or its friends, Tommy watched in disgusted fascination. Julia would have seethed, but he just counted. When eighty-five human beings had been crammed on top of the abundant luggage in an aeroplane designed to carry no more than fifty, Harry Smythe laid a restraining hand on Wex Johnson's arm. The double cargo-doors clattered shut, and the Captain climbed a tall ladder to the flight-deck.

Before following him, Harry rather formally shook hands with Tommy, who asked: 'You're not really going to fly in that overloaded whale? It'll never get off the ground.'

'Old Wex'll get off the ground all right.' Harry was nonchalant. 'He's got too big an investment not to. So long, pal. See you in Shanghai.'

As Harry clambered through the emergency door, the engines sputtered in the cold dawn. One finally coughed into life, then the other. Billows of dark-grey smoke filled the revetment.

Behind that opaque curtain, the engines' screams rose higher and higher until it seemed they must throw their pistons. When the slipstream cleared the smoke, Tommy saw the Commando straining against its wheel-chocks. The engines murmured low for a moment, and Wex Johnson leaned out the glass-enclosed cockpit to signal with a raised thumb.

When the engines screamed louder, Tommy plugged his ears with his fingers. Coolies jerked the chocks away, and the Commando shot out of the revetment like a pebble from a slingshot. The wheels hardly touched the gravel runway, it seemed, before the transport rose ten feet into the air. The next instant, it pancaked onto the ground inflicting an enormous strain on the under-carriage. Not until the very end of the runway did the Commando rise clumsily, hastened by the puffs of exploding mortar-bombs.

Tommy gulped cold air, aware that he had stopped breathing during that laborious takeoff.

The Commando rose slowly over the walled city, a gleaming intruder above the crenellated battlements and the high watchtowers of an earlier age. The climb was laboured, and the Commando wallowed. Lumbering through the air, the heavily laden transport slowly gained altitude.

Tommy turned to his patient, whose stretcher was propped on green ammunition boxes.

'Watch it, Doc! Watch it!' Walrus Reilly shouted. 'She's too heavy. Not answering the controls. Wex hasn't got her in his hands yet.'

The glass panes covering the nose caught the morning sun when the Commando dropped abruptly. The wounded pilot dug his nails into the canvas stretcher. The Commando recovered and climbed again towards the folded brown hills.

'He's too God damned close to the ridge.' Walrus Reilly agonized. 'But he should make it – just! . . . Oh, no! Oh, my God!'

Bright against the pale dawn, tracers licked at the labouring aircraft. The nose dipped lower, lifting again just before the ridge. Rising triumphantly, the Commando cleared the hill.

'Okay now, Doc,' Reilly said. 'By God, he scared me.'

Then one silver wing dipped inexplicably, barely clearing the second ridge. The Commando jerked in the air as if checked by brakes. The same wing dipped again, and the aeroplane appeared to halt.

The next instant, the big transport cartwheeled. It tumbled over and over again revolving ever faster. It was a silver cross flashing bright against the pallid sky. A wing-tip caught on a ridge, and the bulbous transport crumpled into the rocky hill.

'Oh my God!' the injured pilot repeated monotonously. 'Oh my God!'

Tommy saw flames flicker in the broken silver carcass. A minute later, a column of black smoke rose from the stricken Commando.

50

April 27–May 25, 1949

The baby grand piano had been lacquered black and set with hexagonal mirrors to go with the new ultra-modern decor of the dining room when the Ikra was completely redone a decade earlier. Although scratched and dented, the instrument still sparkled under the subdued lights that evening, and it responded nostalgically to the long-nailed fingers on the keyboard.

'The dear old thing's a night creature like me,' Elizaveta Alexandrovna Yavalenka observed. 'Not meant for daylight – or for Bach. But it'll do this last time.'

The piano player twirled his drooping bandit's moustache, settled his threadbare dinner jacket over his paunch with curious delicacy, and absently stroked the keys. No distinct melody emerged, but a euphonious tinkling like the gentle clashing of the crystal pendants on a chandelier.

Two bone-lean Chinese sing-song girls in long scarlet *cheongsams* were swaying before the upright microphone standing on the minuscule dance floor. Their mouths were shiny scarlet ovals; their hollow-cheeked faces were painted to make them modishly skull-like; and their stick-thin arms were garlanded with rhinestone bracelets, which glittered in the blue spotlight. Their cobra-like undulations were, however, growing slower. Their slitted eyes opening a crack wider in appeal, they looked hopefully over their shoulders at the piano player.

The tinkling resolved itself into a melody, and the piano player nodded their cue. The duo immediately began chanting in a minor key, and the plaintive rhythm made Julia recall children's retorting to taunts with the sing-song doggerel: 'Sticks and stones will break my bones, but names will never harm me.' The brave defiance did not quite conceal the fear beneath.

'*Maskee!*' The skull-women trilled the unique Shanghai expression. '*Maskee! Maskee!*'

'Can't be cured, must be endured!' Tommy insisted upon translating it. Julia felt that fatalistic resignation to an unjust – and implacable – fate was better conveyed by: 'What the hell, it doesn't matter!'

'*Maskee!*' starving rickshaw coolies declared with a grimace. '*Maskee!*' feckless amahs protested with grins at once servile and insolent when they could not hide a broken plate. '*Maskee!*' soldiers said, turning in helpless anger from a dying comrade.

The melody concealed within the piano player's stark – almost ascetic – rendition seeped into Julia's awareness. Her mother had crooned the lullaby when she was an infant. Yes, of course. It began, 'Hush little baby, don't you cry.' Then it offered consolations ranging from diamond rings to ponies. It closed with the promise that, despite all disappointments, 'You'll still be the cutest little baby in town.'

In their sibilant pidgin English the duo were actually shrilly singing:

> Me no worry,
> Me no care,
> Me going to marry a millionaire.
> And if he die,
> Me no cry,
> Me going to get another guy.

The poor sad little things, what would become of them? Millionaires were a diminishing, not to say vanishing, asset in Shanghai in late April 1949. Millionaires were going out of fashion – and would soon be as popular as skunks. The mindless jingle none the less caught the mood of the feckless city in its last springtime under capitalism.

The People's Liberation Army had swept across the Yangtze River on April 21st, meeting no organized resistance, only sporadic attacks from the demoralized Nationalist forces. The west wind that alone threatened the armada of sampans and junks had at the last and auspicious moment, shifted. As the Reds' New China News Agency reported, the boatmen said: 'Chairman Mao Tse-tung borrowed the east wind for the crossing.' On April 24th Nanking had fallen. The liberators were now regrouping to take Shanghai whenever they chose.

And Shanghai itself? Shanghai waited, and Shanghai still played despite the puritanical decrees of the expiring Nationalist régime. Shanghai also watched with sour envy those who could depart.

Generals and politicians naturally led the exodus, though some lingered to extract the last ounce of gold from the stricken city. Many Chinese capitalists followed their smuggled capital to Hong Kong, but many remained. Those who were loath to go placed their trust in the Communists' promises that they would be permitted, indeed encouraged, to carry on their businesses. Neither Communism nor even Socialism would be instituted after liberation, Chairman Mao Tse-tung had pledged, but the New Democracy. Private business would thrive when economic activity was no longer hamstrung by corruption, disorder, and brutality.

Some foreigners had left, but no great number. To most, Shanghai was their home, their native place as surely as it was to the settled Chinese community. Many foreigners also felt bound by their obligations to their Chinese staff. Others still felt themselves impregnable to the slings and arrows of Chinese strife.

The refugee communities were, however, very nervous. Most Chinese refugees had nowhere else to go, and the hapless White Russians were aghast at facing another Bolshevik conquest. As hypersensitive as they had been complacent in their native Germany, the European Jews were eager to bolt. The old, predominantly Sephardic Jewish community were, of course, not refugees. Some had, however, departed to watch developments in Shanghai from a distance before committing themselves. Joshua Haleevie's eldest brother, Jeremiah, who was the head of the family, had gone no farther than Hong Kong, where most of the Haleevies' liquid assets now reposed.

Joshua himself remained. Distinguished in his white dinner-jacket, he sat opposite Elizaveta and tapped out the beat of the artless ditty with a patent-leather pump. Joshua's wife Charlotte had drifted away more than a year ago to make her own life in New York and Jerusalem. But that no longer had much to do with him. He could not, he had told his mistress, leave the city that had given him life when it faced its greatest trial. Should the Communists behave well, he would look a fool if he scurried away. Should they behave badly, he would look a poltroon for running off.

Joshua had in 1927 been frightened away by neither Comrade Chou En-lai and his popular rising nor by Generalissimo Chiang Kai-shek and his army. He had stood firm before the Japanese in 1932 and again in 1937. He had left Shanghai after the Japanese attack on Pearl Harbor in 1941, but only to fight elsewhere. Why should he behave differently in the face of the present threat, which might be illusory?

Striving to be vivacious and gay, Elizaveta was pensive. When her lover laughed without apparent care, tears started in her midnight-blue eyes. Those eyes were no longer blinded by self-deception, for she had recently realized that Joshua did not love her enough. Believing that he would never leave her, she had often treated him cavalierly. She had been confident that he loved her just that much more than she loved him. She was now devastated by irrefutable evidence that her own love was marginally greater than his.

Ironically, he had formerly taxed her with loving the Ikra better than she loved him. Yet she had sorrowfully concluded during the past few days that Joshua loved Shanghai more than he loved her. Why else should he have casually declined to join her on the SS *Anson*, which was sailing for Hong Kong in the morning? He could always return, she had pointed out, just as she would certainly return if his optimism proved justified. He had finally given up urging her to stay and test the Communists' promises with himself. But he had obdurately refused to join her in the safe haven of the Crown Colony.

'It won't be the same thing if I have to come crawling back.' His explanation had rung hollow. 'The Communists are Chinese. They'll remember who stayed to welcome them. Besides, I've made some overtures – and I must be here to receive their response. . . . No need for dramatic farewells. You're not going forever, whatever you think. You'll be back, or I'll drop down to Hong Kong after a month or so. But what about the Ikra?'

'It's not so hard to give up the Ikra, darling,' she had replied. 'I should have done so years ago, instead of just talking about it. But I can't bear the thought of giving you up.'

'You never will have to, Bess. You've finally made your choice, it seems. Either the Ikra or me! And it's me. I'm overjoyed . . . even if you left it a little late.'

'Then will you come with me on the *Anson*?'

'Bess, I'm afraid that's out.' He was not brusque, but he was rather matter-of-fact. 'I must be here – whatever happens. I promise you I'll get away just as soon as I can. We'll take a wonderful cruise around the world. Whatever you want. We'll marry, if that's what you want. Though nowadays marriage doesn't make much difference, does it?'

'No difference, Josh?' She was startlingly vehement. '*All* the difference in the world. If we had only married years ago, everything would've been different. Of course I'll marry you.'

'Bess, you're making me very happy.' Forgetting Elizaveta's past inconstancy, Joshua's voice faltered with feeling for an instant. 'In Hong Kong, then, in a month. Sooner if things settle down here.'

With that modest commitment Elizaveta had to content herself. Still, her chest ached with cold despair. Not so much because she was leaving Shanghai, which had become her true home. Not at all because she doubted Joshua's promise. He always kept his promises unless it was physically impossible.

She despaired because she knew in the core of her being that he would not be able to come to her. The Chinese Bolsheviks would see to that. She feared that enemy so profoundly that her own great courage had failed. She knew she was losing Joshua, but she could not stay. And Joshua did not love her as she now knew she loved him. No other woman was her triumphant rival, but the hot-eyed and cold-hearted slut called Shanghai.

Elizaveta felt her fixed smile grow rigid on her lips. She lifted her goblet of the Krug 1936 that was the last of the vintage champagne. That gesture sealed the farewell that all the company, except herself and one other, were gaily pretending was only a brief parting.

Yet she could no more envisage the Howes' leaving Shanghai than she could the Bund's floating out to sea. Tommy looked almost as distinguished as Joshua in his cream-silk dinner jacket with the light-blue bow tie Julia had coaxed him into substituting for sombre black tonight. He had that piercing look again. That look made Elizaveta feel he knew her every shameful secret – yet was not shocked, but fondly amused.

Seated between Julia and herself, Jimmy Wei looked like a wise old

511

monkey in his old black dinner jacket. No one had actually invited Jimmy, but everyone had assumed that he would appear. He grimaced and tapped his fingers to the tinkling of the 'Anniversary Waltz' from the glittering piano. Across from him an empty chair stood before a full place-setting. His sprightly wife Mary should have been seated in that chair. But Mary had already left for the Nationalists' offshore refuge on Taiwan. Jimmy was himself to rejoin the Generalissimo on that island when he had, as he put it, 'finished saying goodbye to Shanghai'.

Three other chairs were empty. Had they been filled, their occupants would have completed the party that Elizaveta had joined at Jeff Geoffreys's St Andrew's Café in June 1921.

A champagne goblet was upended before one of those chairs. Harry Smythe would never again lend his cracker-barrel wit or his brash assurance to any gathering. His Curtis Commando had crashed out of reach behind Communist lines, but Joshua had established 'from private sources' that there were no survivors. No one had mentioned Harry Smythe that evening, and no one would. The down-turned goblet was monument enough.

The remaining chairs were reserved for Richard Hollings and Emily Ou-yang. Or was she Emily Hollings by this time? Perhaps it really didn't matter after so many years whether they had finally married. They were above all together in Washington, and they had finally accepted what everyone else knew from the beginning. They might fight bitterly and feel ill-used by each other, but they would be miserable without each other.

Although Richard's health still kept them from coming to China, he had repeatedly telephoned to gather material for the column on foreign affairs he was writing twice a week. He could not, he only half-joked, trust Emily's judgment because of her ridiculous prejudice against the so-called Communists. She was angry with the Nationalists amid her sorrow at their ignominious retreat. 'But she's just too doctrinaire an anti-Communist,' Richard had concluded mock-lugubriously, 'to offer any useful thoughts on the future.'

He would have written about China in any event, but in fact he had to write about China because the United States was fascinated by the country. Emily was, therefore, riding high professionally despite the collapse of her cause. Exemplified by the Generalissimo and Mayling Chiang, the Nationalists had been the darlings of the United States until the Communists usurped the sentimental affection so many Americans felt for China. Few Americans rejoiced unreservedly at the imminent Communist triumph. But their attention was focused on China by the spectacular collapse of a régime that had, only four years earlier, been considered one of the great powers.

That intense interest worked greatly to Emily's benefit. Her stories about Chinese women, although addressed primarily to Chinese women, had become the object of a virtual cult in the United States. Translated by the author into English even more evocative than her original Chinese, the episodes were strung on a single narrative thread. The novel provoca-

512

tively entitled *Tales from a Chinese Harem* was taken up by the Literary Guild after it became a bestseller by word of mouth. Emily had already contracted to write a second volume from the same material. Afterwards, she planned a raw novel on the Flying Tigers, though it might disappoint readers who expected only cosy women's books from her.

Initially resentful at being labelled a 'woman's writer', Emily now considered it a distinction. She was again fighting hard for female emancipation, although she was also determined to tread the greater literary stage where the author's sex was not all-important. Yet she had been born into an era when the struggle for women's rights made justifiable – and usually over-riding – demands upon whatever talent she possessed. Happily settled with a man for the first time in her life, she was again preoccupied with the problems of women.

To Emily's great relief, Richard had accepted her success gracefully – indeed with pride. He had confessed to her his initial surprise at his total lack of envy. Considering his own ambitious and competitive nature, Richard concluded, his delight must prove how deeply he loved her. Emily still wondered whether he would feel quite the same way if, rather than fiction, she were publishing reportage, which was his métier.

So much Julia knew from Emily's letters, which had virtually bridged the rift between them. She missed Emily keenly, but she was glad Emily was not in Shanghai to see the Nationalists' tawdry end. Of course, Julia was herself ebullient, bubbling with excitement and anticipation. She feared she might betray herself, but she was mindful of the assignment for which Chou En-lai had reserved her. Concealing her jubilation, she feigned resignation to the Communists' imminent victory.

Elizaveta, who was a past mistress of illusion, had conjured up an atmosphere of hectic end-of-term gaiety, not only the decadent piano player and his scarlet sing-song girls, but the balloons and streamers hanging from the mirrored chandeliers. She made them feel like a privileged few, rather than the last survivors in a deserted hostelry.

In rakishly formal Shanghai, the men of course wore dinner-jackets. Having commanded Julia to put on her most spectacular evening-dress, Elizaveta had appeared in a Schiaparelli creation – no lesser word would do – that combined her beloved Edwardian elegance with Victorian romanticism. A cloud of white organdie appliquéd with gold-and-silver flowers floated over the pleated bell of pink silk that was the skirt. The brief organdie bodice, which was almost an afterthought, admirably displayed Elizaveta's snowy shoulders.

Julia was not outshone. Her figure, which had hardly altered over the years, was outlined by a sheath of burgundy moiré. The stylized pagodas embossed on the fabric were like her six-tiered gold earrings. Relieving the severe cut, the skirt flared at the back into two stiff pleats.

Julia was still glowing with the memory of her tailor's tribute: 'Only perfect shape can wear such dress.' She might not be the most effective spy in Shanghai, but she certainly wasn't the least glamorous.

'You men all are so smug.' Elizaveta perversely addressed the one person who was patently not smug. 'All such optimists.'

513

'Doesn't strike me that way right this moment,' Jimmy Wei replied dolefully. 'What have you got in mind?'

'I've run away only once in my life,' Elizaveta declared. 'Twice actually, not counting the time the Japanese escorted me out of Shanghai. Both times when I was much younger. Both times from the Bolsheviks – first in Russia and then in Siberia. But here in Shanghai I've stood firm.'

Elizaveta was not inebriated, not even slightly. She was, however, exhilarated, a trifle manic.

'But I'm not waiting for the Bolsheviks to expropriate me,' she continued. 'Months ago, when Peiping was sold out, I knew it was all over. The Bolsheviks can have my poor old Ikra, but not me. I am no longer an aristocrat, but middle class. The Bolsheviks hate the middle classes worse than poison.'

'Liz, do you know where the gold *yüan* stands today?' Tommy was uncharacteristically sharp. 'Six million to one US. Remember when all Chinese were forced to turn in their dollars, their gold, and their silver for gold *yüan*? Remember when they were shooting the people who held out. And do you remember the rate? Yes, four *yüan* to one US.'

'We all know that,' Joshua interposed protectively. 'Why pick over old bones?'

'Liz says the Communists hate the middle class. What about the Nationalists? They stole the middle class blind. Stripped everyone who turned over foreign currency and precious metals for gold *yüan* – which are now worthless. Yet the Nationalists have always claimed to be pro-capitalist and anti-Communist. With such friends, why should the middle class fear its so-called enemies?'

'We Nationalists always appear even worse than we really are.' Jimmy Wei did not look up from his goblet. 'And the way it's ending – no dignity. The Gimo resigning. Worse, flitting off to Taiwan after eleven days of fantasy when he thought he could hold Shanghai, make it his last bastion. And the garrison's disgusting behaviour. Two hundred thousand soldiers acting like wild men – raping, pillaging, and killing. I'm too old to change my loyalty, maybe too stubborn. But it's disgusting. Why, the Shanghai Garrison . . .'

'The garrison commander had to have his reward, Jimmy. And he had to reward his troops or they could have mutinied,' Joshua interjected. 'After all, he did ship the Government's gold to Taiwan, as he was told to. Tens of millions – and only a few millions stuck to his fingers. So he let his troops play. What are a few thousand rapes and some wholesale looting when the world is ending?'

Jimmy did not respond, but Tommy bristled: 'Just don't say that it's the old Chinese way . . . always has been and always will be. Whatever else, the Communists don't act quite that way. Never mass misbehaviour. Not like these animals in uniform here.'

'Tommy, we only know what the Communists choose to let us know,' Joshua replied. 'Or what foreign correspondents write about them. You, of all people, know just how doubtful some of that reporting can be . . .'

514

'Gentlemen! Gentlemen and ladies!' Jimmy Wei lifted his head, and his manner was fierce. 'I sense a myth being born. Like most myths, it's got a basis in truth. I'll give you an example. The Gimo, everyone says, is personally honest, but has bad advisers and crooked subordinates. True enough on both counts. But the Gimo didn't have to tolerate *every* bloody-handed crook who pledged loyalty. As long as we Chinese live by myths, we'll never . . .'

'Jimmy, what myth is worrying you?' Tommy's voice was very gentle. 'We don't *know* it's a myth about the Communists' good behaviour.'

'My good doctor, that's not what I had in mind. I'm worried about the stab-in-the-back myth. Also the who-lost-China witch hunt. Both are already starting up in the States. Those myths'll poison the air for decades. . . . But I'm talking too much.'

'Jimmy, be a dear and say exactly what you've got in mind,' Julia coaxed. 'Among friends.'

'Among friends? Why not? If I can't trust you, who can I trust? I might as well be a lying Communist . . . never trusting anybody.'

Jimmy did not look at her, and Julia kept herself from wincing at his oblique condemnation. Instead, she prompted: 'Go on, please tell us just what you mean.'

'All right, I will. The United States hasn't lost China. The Americans never had China, so how could they lose it? Generalissimo Chiang, God help him, didn't lose China either. Even he never had China to lose. He was a kind of constitutional monarch. Or a chairman of the board who couldn't fire a single director. Not even a foreman. The Gimo never ruled China, so he never lost China. He did hold things together. No one could have done more. His so-called supporters ranged from Confucian monarchists and illiterate, feudal robber barons to wild-eyed Socialists and Trotskyites. How could anyone control China with a gang like that?'

'What about America, Jimmy?' Julia was intrigued. 'What about America's losing China?'

'I can see the stab-in-the-back myth growing. Yeah, I know *Comrade* Chou En-lai sometimes joked that Richard Hollings would conquer China for *Comrade* Mao Tse-tung.' He said *comrade* as if it were a curse. 'So old Red Dick Hollings and his buddies in the press want conquered China for the Communists. Uncle Holly Tong believes it, too. But it's just not true. Sure, their reporting helped turn off American support. But they didn't decide the fate of my country with their little typewriters. . . . Do you want to know who really lost China?'

'Please, Jimmy.' Tommy was respectful of his enemy's agony. 'Do go on.'

'*I* lost China, Tommy. *I* did because I didn't do enough to save China. Inefficiency and corruption lost China. Those who knew, those who cared, we didn't fight the graft and the muddling through – not hard enough to change them. We went along. So, no matter what anyone wrote in the papers, we would have lost anyway. The fate of China was decided in China – nowhere else.'

515

'Sure the Yanks kept sticking their noses into our business, which they didn't understand. Claire Chennault didn't help by preaching clean, easy victory through air power. Even last autumn, he was still telling the Gimo he could win with maybe fifty bombers. Not just a battle, but turn the tide of the Civil War.'

Jimmy Wei gulped his champagne and delivered his closing words to his empty goblet: 'Despite all that, American interference was never crucial – not really decisive. The issue was decided before the Yanks ever got into the act. You want to know who lost China? I'll tell you again. *I* lost China!'

At the beginning of May, Julia recognised that Tommy's elation by no means matched her own, although his country stood at the threshold of a wonderful new era. Yet the detached scientist in Tommy had often restrained the hot-headed patriot. That was not a bad thing. The revolution also needed men who could remain cool in the hottest crisis.

Tommy confessed that he still had misgivings. Not just generalized apprehension at sweeping change or even his old doubts about the Communist leaders. He was specifically troubled by several recent events.

From Peking, once more the Northern Capital, Chairman Mao Tsetung had issued a public statement regarding foreign policy on the eve of victory. Let there be no mistake, he had cautioned the world, New China would 'lean to the side of the Soviet Union'. Tommy and Julia had expected as much, though they both had grave doubts about unreserved co-operation with the Soviets. They were not alone. A significant group within the Chinese Communist Party was wary of drawing too close to the Soviets. Like Tommy and Julia, they remembered Soviet arrogance, Soviet slights, and Soviet opportunism – beginning with the First Congress of the Communist Party in Shanghai in 1921.

But the Chairman was assuming near-imperial grandeur in the rosy dawn of victory, and dissenters were powerless to prevent New China's cutting herself off from the West. The United States had by the late spring of 1949 became *the* chief enemy. The Apparatus had, moreover, failed to respond to Joshua's feelers regarding good British relations with the new régime. The Communist leadership was obviously preoccupied with the violent transition of power over the world's most populous nation.

Shanghai was waiting anxiously for the People's Liberation Army to end the dreadful suspense of the protracted transition of power. Unlike Julia and Tommy, most of the city's millions waited in apprehension – not expectation. For the Howes, the gradual Nationalist withdrawal heralded the beginning of the new era for which they had so long fought. For most Shanghailanders, it marked the end of an era that was familiar, however harsh.

Julia's joy was, however, broken by successive reminders that the globe still revolved while Shanghai waited. Since Western Union and Cable and Wireless were both functioning superbly on the edge of chaos, Shanghai was still in constant electronic touch with the outside world.

In early May a yellow Western Union envelope yielded a message from Washington. Frugally sent by cheaper night letter rate, it was extravagantly wordy: BLESS US COMMA BROTHER AND SISTER EXCLAIMER WE WERE MARRIED AT FOUR PEEYEM SATURDAY MAY SECOND AND IMMEDIATELY BEGAN LIVING HAPPILY EVER AFTER STOP LONG EXPERIENCE THUS CONFIRMS THAT COMMA ALTHOUGH RIDICULOUSLY BELATED COMMA OUR DECISION WAS AYE HUNDRED AND TEN PERCENT CORRECT STOP CAN HARDLY WAIT SEE YOU TWO STOP ALL YOUR CHILDREN AND OUR CHILDREN JOIN IN SENDING VAST QUANTITIES OF LOVE – EM AND DICK

That was very good news indeed – though long overdue. Julia telephoned Tommy, who expressed his delight and promised to open a bottle of champagne when he got rid of his last patient. Their glow of pleasure was obviously shared by their old major-domo.

'Look, Missy, have got one more piece telegram,' he carolled, lapsing into pidgin. 'Maybe b'long more good news.'

Julia took the blue-and-white Cable and Wireless envelope eagerly. With some surprise she saw that it was addressed to her alone, unlike Emily and Richard's message. It might be bad news after all. Although her father's cancer had apparently gone into remission, he was not a young man. Suddenly apprehensive, she tore open the perforated flap and slipped out the message. It came from Hong Kong and covered five telegram forms.

APOLOGISE DEEPLY FOR DISTURBING YOU [it began] BUT PRESUME YOU WOULD WISH TO BE OF ASSISTANCE STOP IF SUPPOSITION IS INCORRECT OR TASK IS TOO DAUNTING COMMA PLEASE ADVISE AND EYE SHALL TELEGRAPH DIRECT STOP NONETHELESS THE ENTIRE FAMILY WOULD BE MOST GRATEFUL IF YOU COULD UNDERTAKE THIS DISTRESSING TASK ON OUR BEHALF STOP

Puzzled and disturbed, Julia flipped to the last page to read the signature: JEREMIAH HALEEVIE. Recalling that Joshua's elder brother had taken charge of the family holdings in Hong Kong, she felt a chill of apprehension and read on.

SS ANSON DOCKED KOWLOON TWELVE HOURS AGO BADLY BATTERED BY ENCOUNTER WITH FREAK TROPICAL STORM BEATRICE IN STRAITS OF TAIWAN STOP SINCE ALL PASSENGERS HAD TAKEN TO THEIR CABINS ON THE CAPTAINS ORDERS COMMA NO APPREHENSION WAS FELT UNTIL DEBARKATION STOP SEARCH OF ENTIRE SHIP THEN YIELDED NO SATISFACTION STOP

CABIN OF COUNTESS YAVALENKA WAS UNDISTURBED COMMA INDICATING SHE HAD NOT RETURNED AS DIRECTED STOP COUNTESSES AMAH SUBSEQUENTLY CHECKED AND DECLARED ONE RAINCOAT AND ONE SET NORMAL GARMENTS ARE MISSING STOP MUST REGRETFULLY CONCLUDE THAT COUNTESS YAVALENKA WAS CARRIED AWAY BY WAVE BEFORE SHE COULD REACH CABIN STOP

EYE SHOULD BE TERRIBLY GRATEFUL IF YOU WOULD GIVE THIS APPALLING NEWS TO JOSHUA YOURSELF STOP IF ANY MESSENGER COULD ALLEVIATE HIS SHOCK AND SORROW COMMA IT WOULD BE YOU STOP FOR YOUR INFORMATION TO IMPART AS YOU JUDGE FIT COMMA CHARLOTTE HALEEVIE IS ALSO BEING INFORMED STOP GIVE HIM ALL OUR LOVE AND ALL OUR SYMPATHY

In shock, Julia neatly folded the message and tidily returned it to its envelope. Sorrowful, yet flattered by Jeremiah Haleevie's request, she lit a Chesterfield and drew in the smoke like life-giving air. A paroxysm of coughing struck her, and the meaning of the message struck home.

Elizaveta was dead, Elizaveta the survivor. The inconsequential thought intruded: the soothsayer at the Great World had been wrong in predicting that Elizaveta would have a very long life. In the next instant, Julia saw with stark insight that Elizaveta had courted her fate. She had not committed suicide, but she had with Slavic fatalism flirted with death.

Her bright courage had obviously faltered when Joshua demonstrated that he loved Shanghai more than he loved her. Elizaveta must then have felt herself deprived of the obsessive love that had sustained her all her life. Aboard the coaster to Hong Kong, the gallant aristocrat must have known hours, even days, of total desolation – the black, overwhelming Russian melancholy. A refugee once again, she had irretrievably lost her most precious possession – the Ikra. She must have believed in her despair that she had also lost Joshua.

No one would ever know precisely what aberration had driven her to the rail of a ship in a typhoon. Still, Julia knew beyond doubt that Elizaveta had not embraced death. But she had recklessly courted death.

Julia lifted the telephone again. The handset felt ponderous, and her finger-tip slipped on the dial. She irrationally hoped that she would fail to reach Joshua. Anything to put off the frightful task his brother had put upon her. But Joshua himself answered the second ring.

'Hello, sweetie,' she began, 'I wonder if you've got time for a drink this afternoon. . . . Yes, here. . . . No, nothing in particular. Just a whim.'

The three weeks that passed between those telegrams and the advent of the People's Liberation Army should have been lit by elation. But sorrow for Elizaveta and pity for Joshua clouded those weeks.

Joshua had aged before her eyes when Julia told him. He had said nothing at first, but simply shrunk into himself. His light-blue eyes filmed over; his smile became a grimace; and his skin turned ashen. His shoulders slumped, and he rubbed his stump where it fitted into his artificial leg.

'I should have gone with her, Julie,' he finally said. 'If I had, this would never have happened. If I had done other things earlier . . . who knows?'

Joshua said no more that afternoon beyond automatic courtesies. He sat silent for a long time. He said no more until he thanked her for telling him and wished her good-night.

The next morning, he briskly telephoned Tommy to discuss ways of protecting their employees from the depredations of the garrison troops. Later he came round to weigh the few snippets of information they had garnered for British intelligence. After a few words of commiseration, Tommy did not speak of Elizaveta – and Joshua did not mention her. He remained optimistic regarding relations with the coming rulers of

Shanghai, and he spoke confidently of new building projects. From time to time, however, he lost the thread of a sentence – and simply stared in mute appeal.

They had almost nothing to report that London could not have gleaned from the newspapers. The Apparatus told Tommy only that liberation was imminent. He was instructed to reassure all his associates as best he could without breaching his cover that the New Democracy was a threat to no one except the imperialists and their henchmen, the bureaucratic capitalists. He could, moreover, promise that the city would experience no immediate changes except, perhaps, emergency measures to alleviate public suffering. Therefore, no patriotic businessman need feel threatened.

'Finally it's certain,' Tommy declared on Saturday, May 21st. 'Liberation's only a matter of days, maybe hours.'

'How do you know?' Julia played up to him. 'Secret despatches from the front?'

'Better than that,' he answered. 'The last CAT flight is leaving Hungjao Aerodrome at this minute. CAT's always the last plane out – always overloaded with refugees and gold bars. Julie, your American pilots have got more courage than brains or scruples. . . . Still, it was very decent of them. CAT Operations called to say they were holding two seats for us.'

'What did you tell them?'

'Only that we were Shanghailanders – and would stay.'

That afternoon they heard shellfire from the south-west, where Hungjao Airport lay. Throughout Monday and Tuesday, sporadic small arms fire sputtered amid intermittent shelling. The tempo was leisurely; the volume was light; and the explosions were muted by distance.

'They're just seeing the Nationalists off.' Tommy spoke with the authority of a veteran of two wars. 'Hurrying up the lads we've seen scurrying towards the river with their loot. No serious fighting's going on, believe me.'

They locked up the house on Kiukiang Road at six on Tuesday evening. Tommy himself oversaw the shooting of bolts and the securing of chains to ensure that no member of the household would endanger himself by violating the curfew. Tommy and Julia went to bed early, almost exhausted by the tension of expectation and the slight apprehension that clouded their jubilation. Old Shanghai had been their life – and old Shanghai was perishing.

They fell asleep in the twilight of Nationalist rule and awoke to the dawn of Communist rule. The march of the People's Liberation Army into the city had begun during the night. By six on Wednesday morning, when Julia and Tommy climbed the circular staircase to the roof-garden, all the remaining Nationalist soldiers had exchanged their uniforms for faded blue workmen's clothing. By six fifteen, the scouts of the Liberation Army were entering Kiukiang Road.

Their rumpled and stained cotton uniforms darkly green against the ruddy brick buildings, the vanguard of the liberation advanced warily into the sunrise. Two by two for mutual protection, yet strung out against surprise attack, the soldiers darted from doorway to doorway. They held their rifles and their sub-machineguns in front of their chests, ready to reply instantly to hostile fire. But the morning was deathly still except for the chirping of the sparrows on the rooftops.

After half an hour, the liberators had grown in confidence. Loose columns of farm-boys in baggy green tunics moved eastwards towards the Bund and the Hwangpoo River. All were young, many no more than sixteen or seventeen. Most were bareheaded, though a few wore crumpled green-cotton caps bearing faded red stars.

The country boys gawked in amazement at the imposing buildings and the shiny cars. Identifiable only because their tunics had breast pockets, the officers did not reprove such unmilitary curiosity. The young officers, too, gaped at the opulent façade of the wicked metropolis.

The big wooden wheels of horse-drawn supply-carts creaked in the hushed dawn, and the small steel wheels of man-drawn heavy machineguns squealed as they jolted on the rough road. The first tentative columns swelled into a mass formation that filled Kiukiang Road.

Most soldiers of the People's Liberation Army wore canvas shoes with rubber soles, but some still wore straw sandals. They did not march in time, but each at his own pace. Thousands of soft soles scuffed on the hard city pavements like a great wind sweeping across an endless grassland. That immense and implacable shuffling was the loudest sound on that bright May morning when age-old rural China reclaimed Shanghai.

Epilogue

The grey-moustachioed porter glided into the velvet-curtained compartment of the train on cloth soles and poured green tea for the foreign woman. His tread was further cushioned by deference, for an ordinary man was wise to serve with downcast eyes the people's cadres of the new Common Wealth Republic – just as he had served the Emperor's mandarins of the Manchus' Great Pure Dynasty forty years earlier. Though excessively considerate, the foreign woman was clearly a personage of importance.

The Premier himself had escorted her to the platform. When she leaned out the window as the train began to move, he had taken her hand as if to keep her from leaving. Hallowed by the farewell tears of Madame Sun Yat-sen, she travelled under the protection of the young man and woman from the Premier's bodyguard in the adjoining compartment.

Protection, the old porter wondered, or surveillance? Really, it came to much the same thing today – as it had in the past.

As the train wriggled out of the hard shell of the city, tile-roofed, brick-built factories employing twenty-five to fifty workers gave way to shacks with corrugated iron roofs where three or four men beat out ploughs for peasants and sprocket wheels for bicycles from scrap metal. The countryside thrust its green tentacles into the industrial suburbs and gradually engulfed the city. Water buffaloes wallowed beside sampans in the creeks that drained the marshy Yangtze Delta, and trading junks lowered their masts to scull under hump-backed bridges. Aside from the cobwebs of telegraph and electricity wires against the horizon, the scene had been identical a thousand years earlier.

Julia leaned her head against the back of the worn velour-seat and tore open a red-and-gold packet of Gate of Heavenly Peace cigarettes.

American cigarettes had not been available in Shanghai for two years. Slipping the paper cylinder into her ivory holder, she lit the yellow Virginia tobacco with a sliver-thin wooden match. A moment later, she chuckled. Somewhere along this stretch of track stood an enormous hoarding, that had, before liberation, extolled Chesterfields. Anticipation of that advertisement had made her automatically light the cigarette, as responsive as Pavlov's dogs.

Still unaccustomed to the harsh tobacco, she coughed and ground the cigarette out in the cut-glass ashtray on the folding table under the window. Her eye was taken by the cornflowers growing beside the gravel roadbed, and she glimpsed a column of farm-boys marching under the orders of a green-uniformed recruiting sergeant of the Liberation Army – more conscripts for the Chinese People's Volunteers fighting the Americans in Korea.

The giant hoarding took her by surprise. She had been looking for a brightly coloured picture but she saw a white expanse with two blocks of vertical scarlet ideograms. On the left: OPPOSE THE US AND AID KOREA! BUY BONDS AND COLLECT SCRAP METAL TO RESIST AMERICAN IMPERIALISM! And on the right: ADVANCE THE CAMPAIGN TO CRUSH THE FIVE EVILS! EXPOSE THE CRIMES OF BUSINESSMEN WHO STEAL THE PEOPLE'S PROPERTY!

Presumably those exhortations were more wholesome than cigarette advertisements. But not necessarily. The war in Korea was killing hundreds every week. And the civil engineer Liu Zoongvee had only two hours earlier flung himself under the Premier's limousine to protest at the methodical extinction of the entrepreneurs China desperately needed.

Slowing arthritically from its leisurely twenty-five miles an hour, the train jerked to a halt. Ancient airbrakes huffing and puffing, it flung its passengers forwards and backwards. The first stop was Kasing, where the Communist Party of China had concluded its First National Congress forty-one years ago. The deserted platforms were funereal. Half the light bulbs were dead, and the rest flickered with the feeble current. The resort town on the South Lake had obviously been badly damaged by the Communists' brutal campaign to destroy all the bourgeoisie and seize all private enterprise.

China's new masters were determined to extract every last ounce of gold – and, if need be, every last drop of blood – from every industrialist, shop-keeper, and master craftsman. Those entrepreneurs were to be whipped into submission, and the workers were to be driven like mules. Even less than the Nationalists did the Communists spare the lash.

When the train pulled out of Kasing, the foreign lady gazed through the half-open window into the night. They had called her *wai-kuo tai-tai*, the foreign lady, so long she almost thought of herself in those words. She felt neither tired nor restive, neither happy nor sorrowful. She was for the moment totally detached.

She gazed into black-velvet darkness occasionally broken by the orange flare of a cooking fire. The immemorial odours of rural China drifted to her nostrils: wood smoke, fresh turned earth, pungent night-soil, fetid

522

pig-sties, and musty mildew. Aside from these haunting aromas, she might have been travelling alone through unpeopled blackness.

Julia rose mechanically and undressed for the night before removing her make-up. She slipped on her nightdress and creamed her face with automatic motions. After brushing her hair perfunctorily, she drew the light coverlet over herself and stared at the ceiling.

Without its lights, the compartment was indistinguishable from the enveloping blackness. Tommy had loved the dark mysterious night in the deep interior of China. He had always said: 'It's like another planet, except that the inhabitants speak my language – just about.'

She would not sleep if she thought about Tommy. She must not think too much about Tommy if she were to get through this final journey unscathed. She closed her eyes and listened to the high-pitched chatter of the wheels and the deep-bass creaking of the carriage.

'Leaving China!' The wheels condemned her. 'Leaving China! Leaving Shanghai!'

'Forever!' The carriage groaned. 'Leaving forever!'

The porter's timid knock startled Julia out of her reverie. She was glad of the fresh tea he brought, though irritated by his obsequious manner. A day after departure, the train was threading through the crumpled foothills of a mountain range. She asked the porter where they were.

'Quite a bit south of Nanchang,' he replied. 'Nothing worth seeing around here. Even Nanchang's just a wide space in the hills. . . . Will the Great Lady condescend to discuss the menu for luncheon?'

Because his exaggerated deference grated, Julia replied shortly that there was nothing to discuss. A bowl of noodles would do – no more than a bowl of noodles. The old porter was an original. Not only did he address her with titles suitable for a Manchu princess, but he was unaware of the significance of the city of Nanchang. How could any adult in New China be ignorant of the Nanchang Rising that had given birth to the Chinese Red Army?

She glanced out the window to see dense coal smoke. The train was labouring up a steep incline at ten miles an hour. Going downhill, they rocketed along at a dizzying forty – no more because the engineer did not trust the ancient airbrakes at a higher speed.

They were leaving the bare, dun mountains of Kiangsi Province for the great Central China Plain and Hunan, the native province of Chairman Mao Tse-tung. Julia felt her spirits lift. She had been depressed by the bleak hills that barely tolerated human habitation. The single track twisted through ravines hewn from the rock, almost scraping the jagged, fissured cliffs. These wounds on the living earth inspired Chinese folk-tales of gigantic dragons battling to the death. Gnarled Kiangsi Province was as deformed as the broken bones of those ancient dragons.

A far pleasanter aspect of the many-faced country she loved lay just ahead. The great rice-bowl of Central China glowed golden in her memory around the old city of Changsha. However, this railway ran twenty or thirty miles south of Changsha. It was, anyway, rather ridiculous to be going from the port of Shanghai to the port of Hong Kong by travelling some five hundred miles inland. China's railway system was still extremely backward – and three years of Communist rule had seen its further decline.

After a courtesy knock, the door opened for the old porter. He had a damask napkin draped over his arm. Startled by the intrusion upon her thoughts, Julia looked blankly at him. He stepped back and almost upset the tray carried head-high by the waiter behind him. His face chalky with anxiety, the porter lifted his eyes imploringly. Julia smiled in apology, and his face cleared.

'*Hsieh-hsieh!*' he whispered. 'Thank you!'

He was genuinely grateful for her relenting from her unprovoked rudeness. Subservience was ingrained, hardly to be altered by three brief years of egalitarian rule. Theoretically egalitarian rule. Premier Chou En-lai in a Zil limousine was no more like the common man than was an Imperial Grand Secretary in a golden palanquin. Less actually. Who had ever committed suicide by flinging himself under a palanquin?

The porter waved the waiter into the compartment with a flick of the damask napkin. On the silver tray, ivory chopsticks and sterling-silver spoons flanked a silver-gilt tureen.

Cupped in pale-green leaves, transparent vermicelli was intertwined with pearly sharks' fins and the translucent skeins of swallows' nests. For sharks' fins and swallows' nests Chinese aficionados gave great sums, and these were the finest. On that costly bed lay petals of whelk, rounds of conch, tiny oysters, rosy shrimps, and miniature lobster tails.

She had ordered a simple bowl of noodles – to be served this culinary extravaganza. It was like being presented with a diamond-studded Patek Philippe when one expected a Mickey Mouse watch.

She smiled her thanks and the porter confided proudly: 'It's called Dragons Mingling Amid Pearls in the Clouds. A dish created for the great Empress Dowager!'

Reluctant to mar the perfection with intrusive chopsticks, Julia meditatively, almost timidly, twined a strand of vermicelli around a minute oyster. The subtle flavours awakened her hunger, but she prolonged the pleasure by taking only a morsel at a time. She was enjoying the dish too much. Yet she was now leaving China – and such food – by her own choice.

Through the soot-smudged window, Julia saw flooded fields thrusting their silver fingers into the foothills and the rice shoots glowing green in the afternoon sunlight. Across the valley, wisps of smoke rose from a cluster of huts with straw roofs.

Worn brake-shoes squealed, air-lines coughed, and the ancient carriage lurched. Groaning piteously, the train halted and stood softly whimpering to itself.

The porter's knock on the mahogany door was measured, but he stuttered in consternation: 'Apologies, Great and Gracious Lady, profound apologies. How they dare! It is required that all passengers alight. I protested, but even the Noble Lady herself must . . .'

Julia was touched by his concern, but was herself unconcerned. Train journeys in China were invariably punctuated by unscheduled halts, whether for water-buffalo asleep on tracks, stolen sections of track, or barriers thrown up by men desperate to beg assistance. Desperate men also looted trains and held passengers for ransom. But such an outrage was less likely now, for the People's Liberation Army had imposed rough order on the countryside.

Inconspicuous in rumpled tunics of blue cotton, the Premier's young security man and security woman followed ten feet behind as Julia stepped down to the gravel ballast supported by the old porter's hand. Hampered by the tight skirt of her yellow spring suit, she was acutely conscious of the frivolity – and the fragility – of her red pumps and her sheer nylon stockings. She was warmed by the bright sun, and a trickle of perspiration crept down her spine. They were about fifty miles south of semi-tropical Changsha, on the same parallel as Miami.

Why, she wondered, the abrupt halt near the cluster of tumbledown farmhouses she had glimpsed from her compartment? Following the other passengers around the bulbous nose of the old sixteen-wheel locomotive, she saw several hundred men and women in patched work clothing squatting beside the tracks. On a rough platform of heaped boulders, three men occupied stools behind a battered table. They wore quasi-military peaked caps and relatively new blue-cotton jackets.

'They say they're very proud, and they want us to see.' A man spoke in rapid Shanghainese, showing off his understanding of the slurred Hunan dialect. 'You'd think they'd offer us a cup of hot water – no matter how poor they are. Such courtesy isn't capitalist. It's just Chinese!'

Julia craned her neck, but could not identify the speaker. Only an official secure in his authority would dare to criticize the 'great mass of farmers' who were, along with the 'industrial workers', hailed as the new masters of China. He was very sure of himself to imply that not all the old ways were bad. The old ways were everywhere under attack. In the cities, officials were being punished for succumbing to bourgeois temptations. In the countryside, land was being summarily redistributed.

Feeling perspiration soaking into her beige-silk blouse, Julia slipped off her jacket. Unfortunately, she could not make herself less conspicuous. Her tawny hair and her green eyes would set her apart even in the drab tunic now prescribed for women as well as men. Despite her Chinese name, she was irretrievably foreign in appearance – and, probably, in essential character. She was also blatantly bourgeois in the pretty yellow suit she had chosen that morning to lighten her depression.

For the first time, Julia felt uneasy. Her friendship with the grandees of the new régime would not protect her if the ignorant farmers – or the ignorant 'leading cadres' who controlled them – should conclude that she embodied their hated enemy: 'foreign imperialism'. Even a farm-boy from the next county was considered an intruder in the depths of rural China. Even the Chinese train-crew and passengers drew together for mutual protection.

The farmers hardly looked at their reluctant guests. They could not even offer cups of hot water, the last courtesy of the impoverished, and it would be discourteous to reveal their curiosity regarding the alien begins from Shanghai. But several farm wives did steal glances at the women among the outlanders.

The farm people's fear was even more powerful than their curiosity. Their eyes were fixed on the three cadres in blue tunics behind the table hung with slogan-inscribed posters. The senior cadre in the middle revealed herself as a woman when she adjusted her cap. Julia saw twin braids of black hair, once the emblem of virginity.

The farmers stank. The wind carried the stench of dried sweat, filth, and decay. Julia knew she was smelling rotting teeth and festering wounds. The wind swept over the silver paddy-fields – and the fermented human excrement that fertilized the rice smelled wholesome after the feral stench of the farm people.

Even the women who had dared glance at the visitors from another world swivelled their heads when two figures shambled forward between files of young men with red armbands and old Japanese rifles. The militiamen thrust the captives onto the platform. The man and the woman of middle years were plump. They bore themselves with confidence, although their cheeks were bruised and their mouths were bloody.

A roar rose from several hundred throats: *'Sha! Sha! Sha Low Ti-chu!'* For several minutes the farmers repeatedly screamed in their barbarous accents: 'Kill! Kill! Kill Landlord Low!'

The female cadre finally waved them to silence and spoke in Mandarin, her accent of the north. Julia had learned years earlier at Shanghai University how cadres were trained to rehearse the witnesses for public trials. Even if there had been no captive audience from the Shanghai train, that strenuous rehearsal would bring its own reward. Although manipulated by the agitators, the farmers would soon believe they were spontaneously erupting into fury at the landlord who had oppressed and exploited them all their lives.

'Comrades, we share your bitterness!' The female cadre spoke again in a high, sweet voice. 'But revolutionary justice gives even swine like these a hearing. You will all get your chance to testify. Only when the last one has spat out his bitterness will the masses pronounce their verdict on these bloodsuckers!'

Her twin plaits of maidenhood swinging saucily as her head turned, the leading cadre searched the crowd. The first witness should already be springing up. She frowned, but waited.

Without the peasants' militant participation, parcelling out the landlord's holdings was meaningless. The process was, above all, designed to force the farmers to make a political commitment. The cadres would thus break down the psychological props of the old social system – and clamp the Communist Party's absolute control upon the hamlet.

The peasants were, however, passive – almost sullen. Halting the train had not been such a brilliant stroke, for the shy countryfolk were obviously inhibited by the alien audience. They were overjoyed at owning the land for whose use they had formerly rendered the landlord the lion's share of the crop. But they were too timorous to speak against him.

'Hao-la! Ni-men yao fang . . .' Such simple language the peasants must understand. 'All right! You want to let them go – bloodsucker Low and his vicious wife? All right. The revolutionary masses are the boss. Landlord Low is to be given back his holdings. You farmers are very kind! To pardon the Lows for stealing . . . torturing . . . raping . . . exploiting . . . enslaving . . . murdering . . .'

The high voice, clear as a sing-song girl's, tolled the landlord's crimes – and the peasants squirmed. To be accused implicitly of cowardice and explicitly of magnanimity was an indignity. To be accused by a young lass was a humiliation. And, even worse than losing face, they were losing their newly acquired land.

A young man with a purple birthmark pushed towards the platform shouting hoarse imprecations. But a small woman with seamed cheeks pulled herself erect on the twisted willow branch that served her as a crutch and shrilled: 'I want to spit out my bitterness!'

The leading cadre beckoned to the gnome-like figure, although she had evidently not been rehearsed as the first witness. Women were a powerful force for destroying the rotten old social order that had kept them in subjugation.

The dwarfish farm wife was soon screaming. Her thick accent made her almost unintelligible to Julia, who heard a string of unconnected words: '. . . daughters . . . beat . . . sty . . . strangled . . . bean-curd . . . raped . . .'

The same male voice Julia had heard earlier explained in concise Shanghainese: 'The women's daughters were taken by Landlord Low as maidservants – and playthings. His wife beat them and made them sleep with the pigs. In a fit of rage, his wife strangled the younger daughter, who was ten. The elder, who was thirteen, was given nothing but watery rice-gruel, not even a sliver of salted cabbage or a morsel of bean-curd. When she complained, the landlord raped her. He then gave her to his strong-arm men to play with.'

Julia could only see the man's back, for he turned abruptly and, limping slightly, made for the guard's van at the tail of the train. Yet there was something vaguely familiar about the way he carried himself, the set of his shoulders at once proud and vulnerable.

Landlord Low and his wife obviously deserved what was coming to them. But she was repelled by the brutal destruction of their personalities as the cadres drew from tens of witnesses lurid details of usury, extortion, rape, torture, and murder. Landlord Low had certainly committed all – or most – of those outrages and atrocities. Local despots like him not only owned almost all arable land, but loaned money, monopolized trade, and collected taxes. He was also *de facto* judge, jury, gaoler, and executioner. Through war and revolution families like the Lows had exercised tyrannical power.

Almost all the witnesses wept. Many women were barely audible. They were deeply ashamed of speaking at all about sexual matters – and mortified at speaking in public. Some men shrieked in rage, their faces red and their fists raised against the cloud-flecked sky.

The young militiamen half-heartedly fended off the infuriated peasants who attacked the landlord and his wife. The Lows bled from jagged scratches, ripped mouths, and torn ears. They crouched defensively and had to be forced to stand erect when the female cadre asked the people's court for its verdict.

'Sha! Sha! Sha Low Ti-chu!' The roar repeated the words that had greeted the Lows' arrival: 'Kill! Kill! Kill Landlord Low!'

The militiamen relaxed their grasp, and the landlord's wife slumped to the ground. Two of the youthful militiamen with red armbands were struggling to hold the woman erect on her knees. Her parchment-grey face lolled on her shoulders, and her tongue protruded. She hung in their hands, shapeless as a half-empty rice-sack.

The female cadre's command was drowned by the women shrieking like vixens and the men roaring. When the throng surged towards the platform, the cadre gestured imperatively.

Two militiamen gingerly lifted old Mauser pistols from their wooden holsters. Blinking nervously, they ground the muzzles into the necks of the Lows.

Twin puffs of smoke rose an instant before the spectators heard the shots. Landlord Low and his wife crumpled on the rocky platform, and the farm people recoiled. The souls of those executed, just released, could wreak terrible vengeance.

Yet the crowd's fury did not abate. Inflamed by the cadres, the peasants would not easily relinquish their rage. They yammered for the bloody revenge the pistol-shots had stolen from them.

Militiamen and cadres scurried away when the mob turned upon the train. Someone fired a rifle, but he might as well have tossed a pebble. The old porter gasped: 'They think we're the enemy! These moronic dirt-farmers hate all outsiders!'

'Sha! Sha! Sha wai-ti!' The chant resumed: 'Kill! Kill! Kill foreign imperialists!'

Julia backed against the dust-streaked carriage as if the metal could divide and take her into its shelter.

'Sha wai-jen!' The shriek struck her like a gust. 'Kill the foreigners!'

No consolation that the Chinese passengers were also foreigners to the maddened peasants. She would not close her eyes. She would not go blind to whatever fate . . .

Shots crackled close by. A second volley seconds later obviously came from disciplined troops with rapid-fire rifles. The mob recoiled, voiceless except for women sobbing. When a third volley crashed into the sudden silence of the late afternoon, the mob turned and ran.

Julia looked for her saviours. A squad of a dozen Liberation Army soldiers was drawn up before the guard's van. Their trim tan uniforms and the semi-automatic American rifles they handled with accustomed authority marked them as élite troops.

'Cease firing!' The elusively familiar voice commanded in Shang-hainese. 'Cease firing and mount the carriage. All entrain immediately!'

Secure again in her luxurious compartment, the carriage-wheels rattling comfortingly, Julia shivered with delayed shock. So much for Tommy's old taunt that she scooted over the surface of China like a water-fly on a pond. She had descended into primeval China, and she was terrified. She was also conscience-stricken because she had so long served the political movement that now incited such brutal spectacles.

She abruptly pulled the window-shade to hide the abundant rice-fields beside the tracks and pushed the white call-button on the partition. When the grizzled porter appeared, she asked: 'That man . . . the Shanghai man with the limp who directed the soldiers. Do you know him? Who is he?'

' 'Nother passenger, Missy.' The walrus moustache trembled, and he retreated into pidgin. 'B'long only 'nother passenger. Me no savvy, Missy.'

Julia did not press the question. She would have the truth out of him in time – if he knew it. She smiled at the myth of Chinese impenetrability be-hind which so many old China hands concealed their inability to understand the people among whom they lived. And one Chinese had penetrated her.

Her mind strayed to some memorable occasions of Sino-American understanding, what Tommy exuberantly called 'passages of high venery and low lust'. Was that, too, all over for her forever? Was the fever of the blood never to rise again? If only Tommy had not . . . If she only knew . . . But those thoughts were unbearable.

She met the porter's uneasy gaze and flushed slightly. But he could hardly have followed her thoughts. She crossed her legs the other way, and pulled the yellow skirt down over her knees. She then spoke like a Chinese matriarch, whose imperious manner made foreigners' arrogance seem fawning.

'If you won't give me information, you can get me something to drink! Scotch whisky with ice and mineral water. However, I suppose that's impossible. Brandy then. You're sure to have brandy. Commissars or compradors – they all love brandy.'

'Nat'chly, Missy.' He clung stubbornly to pidgin. 'We got whisky. What kin' wanchee?'

'Not J & B.' She continued in Shanghainese. 'I'd like something with more body. What about Johnny Walker?'

'Can do, Missy! Chop-chop, Missy.'

When the porter withdrew, having reproached her hauteur with his ludicrously broad pidgin, Julia grinned sheepishly. He had made her feel an absolute bitch by accepting her bad humour so amiably. It was hardly his fault that she felt trapped on this apparently interminable journey.

After ten minutes, the door drifted open on oiled hinges. The old porter stood behind a small silver trolley.

'Quite like the old days, isn't it?' Speaking Shanghainese again, he beamed forgiveness. 'A delight to serve you, Madam.'

Ashamed of her bad temper, Julia smiled her thanks. On the trolley, cut-crystal goblets clustered around a crystal bowl heaped with crystalline ice-cubes. The white-damask table-cloth was so heavily starched it crackled as the train swayed. Before a blue-and-white vase flaunting a spray of scarlet azalea blossoms stood five unopened bottles: Cutty Sark, J & B, Johnny Walker Black Label, Chivas Regal, and Ballantine's Twenty-Four Year Old. Only the slight twitch of the porter's walrus moustache revealed his delight in over-awing the foreign lady. After serving her the Ballantine's, he wheeled the trolley out, smiling beatifically.

Julia laughed. He had deftly put her in her place. She sipped the smoky Scotch, and her expression darkened.

Why, she wondered, had Premier Chou En-lai commanded such grand treatment for her? Gratitude for her past services and old friendship could not entirely explain her being pampered like a princess of the blood royal. Could it be a mute apology for Tommy's disappearance? Or was he trying to ensure that she continued to praise the Communist régime when she could speak freely outside China?

Since she would never know, she sipped her drink – and waited with no great anticipation for her dinner. She was tired of inactivity and fed up with being crammed like a prize goose.

After dinner, she gave up trying to force herself to be cheerful. Resignedly, she slid open the door of the miniature washroom and removed her make-up with the coarse Chinese cotton wool. After sponging herself with a washcloth from the doll's house wash-basin she applied cologne liberally and drew her quilted scarlet-silk dressing gown over her thin nightdress. The night air could be cold on the Hunan plain. In slightly better spirits, she pushed the white-porcelain call-button. She would take a turn along the corridor while the porter made up her bed.

Julia set out briskly, her yellow mules swishing on the green carpet. The long corridor was lit only by glimmering lamps at either end. The doors of the eight compartments on one side of the passage were all closed, and the rows of windows on the other side were pitch black. The intense darkness hung like a curtain before her eyes, and she felt she could reach through the window and stroke its black-velvet softness. A single orange light flared momentarily in the distance, and the surrounding darkness appeared even denser.

The black night seeped through the windows into the carriage. Before her astonished eyes the corridor grew darker. Annoyed at the delusion, she stepped into the slightly wider vestibule at the end of the passage. The overhead lamp was very dim, so feeble it barely lit the translucent glass panel of the door leading to the next carriage. Not intrusive night, but the inevitable capriciousness of Chinese electricity was creating the gloom.

Tentatively, then with more authority, Julia ran through the warm-up positions of *Tai Chi Chüan*, the exercises foreigners called soft boxing.

Her right hand extended before her, she prolonged the stretching movement called Grasping the Bird's Tail. Pulling back slowly, she pushed both hands forward and swung into the threatening posture called the Single Whip. Her right hand was poised as if to swing a lash.

The overhead lamp flickered and died, but returned after a few seconds. Still, the vestibule was even darker. She resolutely ignored the illusion created by her apprehensive imagination. The outlines of the black shape on the other side of the door were distorted by the translucent glass panel. The amorphous figure contracted and expanded like a jelly-fish.

Hoping to banish the illusion, Julia swung into the posture called Playing the Fiddle. Her hands were extended like a violinist's, and her chin was cocked high. She stared through the panel and saw that the phantom-figure had not vanished. It appeared to be grasping the brass doorknob, which was slowly turning.

As the door opened a crack, she heard a noise behind her and glanced back to see the reassuringly burly porter. The door crashed shut. The black shape had no more been an illusion than had the slow dimming of the overhead light.

Angry at her own fear, she wrenched the door open. The sinister figure was just slipping through the door to the next carriage. He slammed the door behind him, and the bolt snicked shut.

'Must lock up ver'y good, Missy!' The porter reverted to pidgin at her compartment. 'Have got many bad men about these days!'

Gravel falling on a corrugated-iron roof awoke Julia. She slipped her watch from under the pillow and was startled to find it already ten. Easing up the window blind, she saw that heavy rain was pounding the carriage. When the downpour lifted for a moment, she saw that the train was inching through a narrow valley between rocky hills. The river foaming beside the tracks vanished when the rain descended again. She pulled down the blind and pushed the call-button.

Since they were running through mountains again, they must be in Kwangtung Province. Perhaps three hundred miles separated them from Canton, a journey of twelve to sixteen hours. The metropolis of the south was but a way-station for her. Hong Kong was again her destination, the first staging post of her second exile from China – as it had been for her first exile. She would, she supposed, then return to the United States for want of any other place to go.

At least she need not worry about money. The elder Howe brothers had removed most of Tommy's funds to Hong Kong and New York with their own.

At least, she would not be alone, for the girls would greet her. Althea at twenty-two would then do as she wished. Still coltish at nineteen, Persephone would be good company until she finished Bryn Mawr – and took up her beloved Aunt Emily's invitation to spend 'a few weeks, a year or more in Taiwan', the green island where the Nationalists had taken refuge.

Throughout the world, politicians and journalists were busily explaining – or explaining away – the Nationalists' defeat and the Communists' liberation of China. Some called it the Communist conquest, as if Mao Tse-tung and Chou En-lai were alien invaders, rather than native sons of the yellow earth. Many Americans were railing at the American culprits they blamed for America's 'losing' China.

They were, perhaps, moved by puritan guilt for other Americans having remorselessly exploited China; perhaps by a sense of obligation incurred because the Chinese had so lovingly responded to pioneer American missionaries. For many reasons, some real and some fantasies, Americans believed they had given more to China than had other peoples. They therefore expected more of China. They were now lamenting their loss of China – and looking for scapegoats to blame for America's losing what America had never possessed.

But the gentle knock must be the porter. Having double-locked and bolted the door, she had to dismantle her barriers against intruders in the night. She could almost see again the figure in the translucent glass panel change shape as it scuttled away. She hesitated before sliding the last bolt open, though she smiled at her own timidity.

The porter waiting outside in his crisp white jacket was the epitome of all the decent ordinary Chinese men she had known: from coolies and carpenters to bankers and merchants. Pleased to return to an everyday world of irreproachable solidity, Julia smiled her greeting. She asked for coffee, toast, 'and orange juice, if you have it'.

'Of course we have orange juice, Madame Howe!' The porter's smile virtually challenged her to ask for something truly exotic, perhaps soft-shell crab or fillets of moose.

After dressing, Julia fought her desire for a cigarette. She should no longer require the consolation of nicotine before breakfast. It was all over now. She was on her way out of China. The decisions – and the perils – all lay behind her. She was safe because she was unimportant, regardless of the phantoms her imagination had conjured up last night.

Brake-shoes squealed as the train slowed to a crawl around a tight bend. Looking down when she smelled fragrant smoke, Julia saw that she had lit a cigarette. She stabbed the long butt into the cut-glass ashtray and pressed the call-button. The porter had already kept her waiting almost half an hour. Hearing his deferential knock, she called: '*Lai!* . . . Come in!'

The light glanced from the gleaming brass doorknob, which was turning erratically, and she rose to help him. When the door swung open. Julia subsided onto the armchair beside the window-table.

Backing awkwardly into the compartment with the big silver tray, the porter appeared to have shrunk. His shoulders looked narrower within his white jacket, and he seemed much shorter. Besides, his hair was glossy black, no longer pepper and salt. The clumsiness of a new porter had apparently delayed her breakfast.

He turned, swinging the tray on the pivot of his slight body like an acrobat. His left foot scuffed the thick carpet, and a smile lit his big eyes so that his triangular face was a like a benevolent jack-o'-lantern.

'*Hsiu-jyeh!*' he said. '*Pa Hsieu-jyeh!*'

Not Madame, but Miss. Not Madame Howe, but Miss Pavernen. Julia stared uncomprehending. His spare, triangular face altered, becoming round and plump. Her normally acute vision was wavering, and the entire compartment was hazy. So much for cigarettes on an empty stomach.

Wiry fingers grasped her wrists and pulled her erect. She automatically sipped water from the glass that clinked against her teeth. She shivered, suddenly chilly in the warm compartment. The aroma of coffee partially revived her, and she gratefully grasped the hot cup put into her hands. She finally lifted her head to look at the apparition.

'Pow . . . can it be?' she asked in wonder. 'Little Pow? Is it really you, Pow? But you've been . . . It's so many years. We thought you were dead. How can . . .'

'Hsiu-jyeh . . .' The familiar light voice was only slightly heavier. 'Miss Pavernen, I'm very sorry I frightened you. But it was the only way. It's so good to see you, Miss.'

'Pow! Little Pow! It *is* you!'

Julia impetuously grasped his wrists and drew him to her. She felt him return her embrace, and, when she set him free, he stood beaming at her.

'Sit down, Little Pow, sit down!' she commanded. 'Coffee? A cigarette? Oh, Pow, why didn't you tell us? All these years and you never . . .'

'Joo-li Hsiu-jyeh . . .' He took a cigarette and spoke more familiarly. 'Miss Julie, I wanted to – many times. But it was judged not necessary for you to know. So I had no choice.'

Julia nodded. She understood precisely. The Apparatus had decided that its agents, Thomas and Julia Howe, need not know that its agent, Little Pow, still lived. Personal emotions and loyalties did not matter, only political necessities.

'And you, Little Pow?' She could not refrain from the question. 'You didn't mind?'

'Of course I minded. What other family did I have except you, the Doctor, and Mister John? But what could I do? You didn't see me at Mister John's funeral, did you?'

'Of course not. If I had . . .'

'I was the fourth coolie bringing flowers – my own flowers. And you didn't know me when I came into the president's office at Kai Ming College. I turned and left – even though my heart ached.'

'Oh, Pow, I'm overjoyed at seeing you. It's wonderful . . . like a new life . . . What do they call you? What have you been doing? What are you on this train? A porter? A waiter? Surely with your knowledge of English . . .'

'That is enough for questions.' He spoke one sentence in stilted English before reverting to Shanghainese. 'Miss Julie, I am not a waiter or a porter. And they do not call me Little Pow, though I hope you will still. But for others? Pow means a bubble. Am I a bubble bobbing on the tide? Pow was thought unsuitable. I am now called Lee Teh.'

Julia offered her lighter to the wiry man who was rolling a cigarette between his thumb and forefinger and grinning at her. There were few in the Communist movement who did *not* know of Lee Teh. The slender man in the waiter's jacket, who was no more than five foot two, was legendary. Pow was just forty, she calculated, but he had been a noted guerrilla leader for decades. He was also famous for his intelligence coups against both Japanese and Nationalists. It was said he could blend into any crowd or penetrate any stronghold disguised as a coolie or a scullery boy.

'It's hard to believe. So hard to believe, Little Pow. That *you* are Lee Teh. Such great deeds! I'm so proud of you, Pow!'

The veteran guerrilla blushed like a schoolboy. Pinching the cigarette between his thumb and forefinger, he took a deep drag.

'When you disappeared, when Tommy could not find you,' she continued, 'we thought you were dead.'

'Comrade Chou En-lai looked after me. I've been with him on and off over the years. You might say I was his man, the Premier's man.'

'Tell me, Pow, are you married?' she asked. 'Any children?'

'*Fu shi, Joo-li . . .*' More relaxed, he no longer called her Miss. 'No, Julie. I never had time. The revolution is a hard task-mistress. I've had close comrades-in-arms – and lovers. But no other family. Only the Doctor and you.'

His intensity illuminated Julia's insight. Her Uncle John had saved Little Pow from starving on the streets of Hongkew. Afterwards Tommy and she had been his father, his mother, and his teachers. In family-centred China he would naturally claim them as his family, and he would give them his loyalty – second only to his loyalty to the Communist Party.

'But why reveal yourself now after all these years?' she asked. 'It's not only because of longing and love . . .'

'Unfortunately not, Julie! Though I couldn't let you leave China without saying farewell. Also there are . . . ah . . . problems that must be dealt with. Some questions, you see, that . . .'

He looked down at the green carpet in embarrassment, and the toe of his black cloth-shoe traced a pattern in its thick pile. He was clearly torn by a conflict of fundamental loyalties. He should not even have made himself known to her, though he said fiercely that he could not let her leave China without saying goodbye.

'The Premier told me to look after you – as long as necessary.' Pow struggled with his conscience. 'He didn't forbid me to speak to you – or tell you who I was. So, I . . .'

'Protect me as long as necessary? Why do I need protection on a public train?'

'Julie, I must have your complete co-operation if we are both to . . . to come through with whole skins.' He ignored her question. 'I'll explain as much as I can. When I can.'

'Pow, I'm so thrilled . . . so excited at seeing you I can hardly think straight. But why the mystery? Why not explain now?'

'I'll get some more coffee.'

He slipped out the door. While she waited, Julia's uncomplicated joy gave way to more complex emotions. She was a little frightened by the riddles in which he spoke. She was also perversely relieved to learn that she had not necessarily conjured up the phantoms of the preceding night. He had hinted that she was threatened.

'I had to check on your bodyguards,' he explained when he returned after ten minutes carrying a silver coffee-pot. 'They're good watchdogs ... always obey the last order they receive. They're now obeying the Premier's orders – or seem to be. But they didn't move very fast when those wild peasants ... I wonder! Could Kang Sheng have ...'

'Pow, please tell me what this is all about.' Julia was chilled by his reference to the Communists' cold-blooded chief of security, who was known as the Executioner. 'Did I really imagine that business last night? The black figure and the nice porter coming to my rescue?'

'Not at all, Julie. Only that black figure was me. I was uneasy about the porter. After he saw me, he wouldn't have dreamed ...'

'You mean the porter was out to harm me?'

'To tell the truth, Julie, I don't know. But I had to scare him away. He'll be all right now. He's frightened half to death. But last night I hadn't yet decided when to speak to you. Perhaps just before the border, I thought.'

'Well you've done it, Pow. So please tell me what's going on.'

'All right, Missy.' His grin faded as he spoke. 'In a nutshell the problem is, first, what you know, and, second, what you're going to say when you're out of China. Kang Sheng ... the Executioner and his crowd say it's idiotic to take a chance. They wanted to liquidate you to eliminate any risk. The Premier blocked that. He said: *Don't be negative! Think of the good she can still do us—not the harm!* But he hasn't really made up his own mind. That's why I'm here. To make sure nothing happens to you before he's decided – and to help him decide.'

'As I understand it,' she replied, 'my old friend Chou En-lai hasn't quite decided whether to let me go free – or to dispose of me.'

'That's about right, Julie.' He studied the intricate pattern his toe was tracing on the green carpet. 'I'm ashamed to say. And Chou En-lai could decide to eliminate you. I don't know whether I can allow that to happen. You are to me my mother and ...'

'Pow, this is a nightmare,' she burst out. 'Why in the name of Heaven would they, the Premier himself, want to ... to ... kill me?'

'Because of what you might say, Julie. They're afraid you'll be very critical.'

'How absurd, Pow!' Her laugh sounded forced to herself. 'Anyway, what does it matter what *I* say? Not that I have any intention ...'

'No intention, not now. But later who can tell?' he said. 'As you know, Julie, we Communists are determined to restore the Motherland's good name. The People's Republic of China must be known as powerful – and just. We must regain all the face China's lost. So we're spending millions to entertain foreign delegations – and deceive them when necessary. Millions for fares, hotels, banquets, and transportation. More millions rehearsing every person the foreigners see. Also to build phony villages and factories. You know how it's done.'

'I still don't see what all this has to do with me.'

'Now, Julie. You've heard old Chou En-lai with a few drinks inside him. Remember what he says about your friend Richard Hollings and his book *Red Star and Yellow Earth?*'

'I've heard him, Pow. Richard Hollings, he says, conquered China for Chairman Mao by conquering world opinion. But it's only a joke, Pow. All the support of all the opinion in all the world couldn't have won China if it hadn't been for . . .'

'Yes, it's a joke. But not only a joke. We know it's not that simple. But world opinion is still crucial for us. Julie, you were very effective for years. You did wonders for the cause with the foreign correspondents in Shanghai. Later in the Americans' – what do you call it? – War Information Bureau.'

He took one of her cigarettes, lit it, and resumed: 'And after liberation, when you proclaimed that direct experience had convinced you despite your reactionary bias. Showed you the People's Republic was wonderful for China. You convinced hundreds of thousands, didn't you?'

'Perhaps,' she agreed reluctantly. 'But the analogy isn't . . .'

'Analogy be damned!' Little Pow exploded in his anxiety. 'Julie, just think. You're now famous as a great champion of the New China. If you let loose a blast against us, it would hurt us very badly. Chou En-lai's afraid you'd cite chapter and verse. You know too damned much about the inner workings, the seamy side. If you turned against us, you'd be damned convincing . . . do us irreparable harm. You can see why old Chou is having a hard time fending the Executioner off. And why I can't even guess how he'll decide himself. So, you see . . .'

'Pow, what happened to Tommy?' she suddenly demanded. 'I'm certain you know. You *must* tell me, Pow.'

'I did what I could for him, Julie.' Frowning in concentration, he stubbed his cigarette out. 'I can hardly say any more.'

'Where is he, Pow?' She was implacable. 'He is alive? You do know, don't you? Even if I can't see him. I don't care so much about myself. Only . . .'

'You *must* care about yourself, Julie,' Little Pow advised. 'For his sake . . . for the Doctor's sake, you must get away free!'

'Then he is alive. Thank you, Pow, thank you!' She could not pause to rejoice, but doggedly persisted: 'Now you must tell me where he is.'

'Julie, I swear I'd tell you if I could. But I can't. I can only tell you to be hopeful. Don't ever despair about the Doctor – or yourself!'

They sat no more than three feet apart, but Little Pow's words came to Julia thin and faint – as if spanning a great distance. She was isolated by her intense emotion. She felt wild elation and also relief. Her own life could begin again.

She had always refused to believe Tommy had been killed in his flight from Shanghai last summer. But she had not *known*. Now Little Pow had as good as said Tommy still lived – and had implicitly acknowledged helping him escape.

She still did not know whether Tommy was wounded or ill, whether he was safely holed up somewhere or was constantly pursued by the vengeful Kang Sheng, the implacable chief of public security, who was for good reasons called the Executioner. She did, however, know beyond question that, if Tommy were anywhere in China, he must be in grave danger.

After she left China she would not be able to help him. Yet she had been wholly unable to help him during the past year. She had not even been able to find him. She had been completely cut off, a virtual pariah until the day only a month ago when Premier Chou En-lai came to tell her he had decided to grant her an exit visa. No, she could not help Tommy by remaining in China. When she crossed the Hong Kong border, she would no longer be a hostage – and she should be able to help him more effectively.

Little Pow was a powerful ally. The revolutionary hero was evidently chafing under the inhuman discipline of the Communist Party, which had been his home since he was fifteen. His emotional loyalty had turned to Tommy and herself, who had virtually adopted him a quarter of a century earlier. But when would his ingrained loyalty to the Party reassert itself?

Little Pow's toe scuffed the carpet, and he awkwardly shook another cigarette from the red-and-gold packet. Forsaking Tommy, he reverted to his original topic: 'Julie, you do understand? Comrade Chou En-lai hates the idea of throwing you to the Executioner and his wolves. But even old Chou's hand can be forced. In twelve hours we should know his verdict.'

'Twelve hours?'

'When we reach Canton. On the military line I can then get to speak to the Premier in Peking. If I can't get through, my orders are to hold you.'

'I see!' Julia felt her new ally was somewhat less than ardent. 'And, of course, you'll obey your orders.'

'Many know my name, but few know my face.' He evaded her implied question. 'Your security watchdogs are here to watch you, as well as to watch over you. They mustn't know me unless it's essential. And, of course, the Executioner's gang. I don't know for sure they're on this train, but they mustn't know that I . . .'

Little Pow's voice trailed off, and he stared at the window, which was still obscured by sheets of rain. He scowled and rubbed his left thigh and said: 'It always hurts in weather like this. But without Tommy I'd have no leg. I probably would have died in 1927. So I'll do everything I can to . . .'

When his voice again trailed off, she glanced at him sharply, and he erupted: 'All right, Julie, if you must know! You've become a shuttlecock between rival factions in the Communist Party. Kang Sheng, the Executioner, is ostensibly concerned only with the danger you represent. But in reality he wants to get at Chou En-lai through you. You've been old Chou's protégée, and he decided to let you out. If Kang Sheng gets you, it's one in the eye for old Chou.'

'After all these years, still factional struggles? Even after liberation, just as vicious?'

'Julie, it's worse than ever.' He laughed sourly. 'And you're right in the middle of this fight.'

Little Pow rose and limped to the door, muttering about making sure the old porter was frightened into silence. Julia did not begin shivering until he had been gone for several minutes. Her forced composure endured until she looked down and saw her hands shaking in her lap. She lit a cigarette, took two quick puffs and ground it out. With tears of joy for Tommy on her cheeks, she smiled and laid her hand on her ribs. Her heart was beating wildly against her palm.

Above all else in heaven or on earth, Tommy was alive! Little Pow had enouraged her to hope that she would see him again, perhaps quite soon. She instinctively trusted the tough-minded little general who had been her protégé. She knew she would see Tommy – by God's grace, very soon.

And her own peril? She had acquired a staunch ally. If she were a shade more confident that he would defy the Party to save her, she would no longer worry. Little Pow was bone-loyal. But to whom? Yet he had already compromised himself by helping Tommy – and by revealing that help to her.

Dusk came more quickly to Shaogwan than to Shanghai, which was seven hundred miles farther from the Equator. At six in the evening, when the train shuddered to a halt, the semi-tropical twilight already obscured the station's damp-defaced wooden sheds. Julia decided to stretch her cramped legs on the cracked stones of the platform. Shaogwan was the last long halt before Canton.

The metropolis of the south lay five to seven hours away, depending on the condition of the track, on the priority troop trains bearing 'volunteers' for Korea, and on the engineer's courage in darkness lit only by a single feeble headlight. From Canton, Pow would telephone the nocturnal Chou En-lai to receive his final orders – either to detain her or to let her go free to Hong Kong.

Julia stepped warily into the steam-bath heat. An hour earlier, Little Pow had stealthily re-entered her compartment to sanction her leaving it briefly at Shaogwan. He had also warned her to be alert and to avoid her fellow passengers. There was only himself to protect her from any 'accident' staged by the Premier's enemies.

When Julia asked about the soldiers who turned back the enraged peasants, Pow had replied shortly: 'They're gone, Julie. They're a crack squad recruiting volunteers for the slaughterhouse – men to die under American bombs in Korea. We need a few real volunteers to leaven the surrendered Nationalist divisions and the regular divisions we've poured in. They got off at Hengyang to put on their show.'

Dusk over the hills was deceitful. The indigo dome of the sky, which was transfixed by the last pale shafts of sunlight, made the ill-lit platform seem a sanctuary, like a cathedral lit by the sun through stained-glass windows. Actually, the darkness would cloak any assailants – and she was not absolutely sure of Pow himself.

Watching the fiery rim of the sun subside behind the purple hills, Julia calculated coolly that the odds were slightly in her favour. Little Pow would almost certainly choose her welfare over Party discipline – if he were confronted with a split-second choice so that his instinct ruled. Given time to reflect, she feared he would take the easier way of following the orders of the authoritarian Communist Party.

The familiar bustle of a provincial railway station diverted Julia, who felt she was seeing it for the last time. Squat baskets stuffed with protesting chickens were being heaved onto a flatcar by coolies in sweaty tee-shirts. Intelligent pigs squealed in terror in the long wicker tubes that confined them, obviously aware that they were next. Big brown jars decorated with rampant yellow dragons were packed with preserved ducks' eggs. The bony farmers and coolies were sending those foodstuffs to Hong Kong. China's own people were hungry, but the British Crown Colony paid in hard cash. The People's Government badly needed foreign exchange – in large part to pay for Soviet supplies and arms for the war in Korea.

The coolies were arguing loudly under the flickering paraffin lanterns. When not toiling, coolies were always either arguing or gambling.

They ignored the figure that emerged from the station-shed. Jaunty despite the two large baskets of white cabbage suspended from his bamboo carrying-pole, the small, wiry coolie dragged his left leg minutely. The straps of his singlet revealed powerful shoulders. As he had promised, Little Pow was watching over her.

He shrugged off the thick carrying-pole and, unhooking his big baskets, stooped to set them down. His head was bent. A heavy-bodied coolie darted out of the shed, almost stumbling over Julia. The coolie's heavy carrying-pole swung in a graceful arc against the purple sky. Gleaming in the last rays of the sun, the long bamboo pole swept down.

'Pow, get down!' Julia screamed in Shanghainese. 'Pow, duck!'

He dropped to his knees, and the pole whistled viciously just above his head. Pivoting on one hand, Little Pow hooked his foot behind his assailant's ankle and jerked hard. The burly coolie almost fell on him, but he squirmed aside. His assailant lay still, apparently winded.

Pow could not see the second coolie launch himself into the fray. A knife shone dully in the flickering light of the lanterns.

'*Chiu-ming! Chiu-ming!*' Julia screamed. 'Help! Help!'

She snatched up a basket of chickens and hurled it at the second coolie. Startled rather than hurt, he drew back under the impact. The next instant, Julia raised a big egg-jar high. The yellow dragons writhed when she brought it down on his head. Appalled, she dropped the jar.

When the first assailant tried to rise, Little Pow flicked his own carrying-pole at his head. The impact thudded like a smashed melon.

Hands grasped Julia's elbows from behind. She instinctively brought her heel down, but missed the man's foot. She twisted in his grip and screamed again: '*Chiu-ming! Chiu-ming!* . . . Help! Help!'

'Madam, it's all right.' The anxious female voice speaking Shanghainese penetrated her alarm. 'Please don't shout, madam. You're safe now.'

Julia turned and saw that she had been pulled away from the struggle by the male bodyguard. His female partner was trying to calm her while the crowd on the platform gaped at the mad foreign woman.

'Why in Heaven's name interfere between coolies fighting?' the security man asked. 'You could have been hurt – badly hurt.'

'I thought . . .' she stammered. 'I thought he was trying to . . .'

'Now, madam, nobody'll hurt you,' the woman assured her. 'Not while we're here. Don't worry. You'll get home safe and sound.'

Julia allowed herself to be bustled back into the womb of the compartment. An hour after the train left Shaogwan, she heard a muffled knock, and a small voice called: 'Tea, Madame Howe. Hot water for your tea.'

She unbolted the door, and Little Pow slipped into the compartment. His mouth was cut, and his limp was more pronounced. He was clearly chastened, but not badly hurt.

'My thanks, Julie,' he said softly. 'My great thanks.'

'And my thanks to you, Pow. We make a great team. We could appear at country fairs.'

'They must be on to me. The real enemy, the Executioner's men. Not your tardy bodyguards. But have they connected the coolie with the porter?'

'We've got to assume they have. We're under siege, aren't we, Pow?'

'Looks like it. Anyway, I don't want to move around again. Let them come to me.' He fished in the pocket of his white jacket. 'I brought a pack of cards so we can play rummy. You never could beat me, Julie.'

The carriage rocked violently as the train clattered over the junction, and the fan of playing cards slid towards the edge of the table. Julia checked the cards' slide, studied her own hand, slapped down a ten of spades, and happily declared: 'Gin!'

They had been beleaguered in the compartment for almost seven hours, and this was her first win. Her opponent only nodded abstractedly and peered anxiously around the edge of the window-blind.

'It's not right, Little Pow,' she teased. 'When you win, you make a big fuss. When I win, you practically ignore it.'

'Sorry, Julie.' The small Communist general buttoned his sweat-stained workman's jacket over his grimy singlet and mustered a worried smile. 'That was the switch for Canton. Maybe a quarter of an hour now to Canton Main Station.'

'When the charade begins.'

'Where the charade begins,' he agreed. 'And we'd better make it good. No chance of rehearsing. It's the real thing.'

Perspiration ran down Julia's back beneath her blue cotton tunic, and the coarse trousers chafed her thighs. Her palms were clammy with tension. As Pow said, there would be no dress-rehearsal—only the single performance for which she was already in costume. His fate, as well as her own, could rest upon her credibility.

540

An hour ago, the female bodyguard had entered the compartment through the connecting door. Banishing the men, they had giggled like schoolgirls while they exchanged clothing. The young Chinese woman was obviously delighted to wear a frivolous foreign-style dress, sheer stockings, and high-heeled pumps again. Her performance would have to be even better than Julia's to make Little Pow's strategem work. At least the flame-red dress fitted her reasonably.

The hardest part was, naturally, their features. Only concealment could make the double impersonation convincing. The security woman had applied lipstick, rouge, and powder liberally. No point in mascara or eye-shadow. The black straw-hat's wide brim and fine-meshed veil should hide her Chinese eyes. Julia blessed her sentimental impulse to pack the hat she had last worn for her Uncle Jack's funeral.

Little Pow's solution to the problem posed by her foreign nose and green eyes was most ingenious – a two-foot straw cartwheel with a hole in the centre for the head. The strips of black cloth hanging from the brim to keep off the sun would effectively hide her foreign features. The Hakka woman's hat would mean carrying luggage, as those hard-working women did. But that was all to the good.

'We want the Executioner's men to suspect something's fishy,' Pow observed. 'So we'll divert them with an obvious fake. They'll believe you're hiding something else – not what you're really hiding. When they figure out that the security woman is disguised as a Hakka labourer, they won't wonder whether the foreign lady in red is the right lady in red.'

'And the security man?'

'He'll be got up as a coolie like me, recognizably disguised. You and he will shadow the lady in red. I'll carry her bags. I'm pretty sure they're on to me. They know me, and as a coolie. They *know* I won't leave you, Julie. So they'll be certain she is you.'

'Why should the two bodyguards want to disguise themselves?' she had asked. 'Wouldn't that look *too* fishy?'

'Anyone who has spent most of his life in the underground thinks it's only natural for agents to camouflage themselves. Especially Kang Sheng's mob. They're not called the Secret Executioners in fun. . . . First time you're *against* the Apparatus, isn't it?'

She nodded and lit a cigarette. The train was rattling across successive switches and bringing the ordeal closer. She ventured a glance around the blind, but saw only the dimly lit houses.

'Another few minutes, and I've got to leave you,' Pow said. 'The Executioners will break their backs to get me if they suspect anything.'

'You're really sticking your neck out for me, aren't you, Pow? More than I knew . . .'

'Julie, it was bound to happen some time. This isn't just a quarrel inside the Party. It's practically a civil war. The split is. . . .' The train slowly halted. 'No more time. The bodyguard will take you to a safe place, a quiet place. I'll see you soon – I hope.'

His back bent, he limped into the adjoining compartment. A minute later, the woman in red stepped down to the platform. Little Pow followed, Julia's leather suitcase dangling from one end of his carrying-pole and her crocodile train-case from the other. The security woman teetered on her high heels, and her waist was too thick for the dress. But, gaining confidence, she strode through the throng with the assurance of a foreigner who is always given precedence.

'Our turn now, Mrs Howe,' the security man said. 'You'll have to carry some luggage. Why you foreigners need so many bags I can't understand.'

Julia smiled at the familiar Chinese directness and followed him, stooped submissively. She carried a crocodile suitcase in her right hand, and a small Gladstone bag in her left.

Although it was past one in the morning, the noise struck her like a gale when she stepped onto the platform. The Cantonese were, as usual, transforming night into tumultuous noon. She lowered her head and followed the bodyguard up the ramp to the concourse. The flat heels of her cloth shoes made walking awkward, and the black pennants on her hat obscured her vision.

'Close, but not too close,' the bodyguard whispered while they waited to check the luggage. 'They must see us act as if we think our disguises are impenetrable.'

Julia inhaled slowly and deeply. She had been betraying her tension by breathing quickly and shallowly. Somehow, she felt less threatened.

'They're watching us,' the bodyguard muttered. 'Look at them if you want to. It'll make us seem clumsier, as the Comrade General wishes.'

Three men were chatting near the exit to the street. Their high-buttoned jackets of fawn tropical worsted, which were well cut and neatly pressed, identified them as privileged officials. They politely stepped aside when she and her bodyguard made for the trishaw rank outside. Two of the three-wheeled vehicles propelled by bicycle chains were receding down the street. The lady in red sat stiffly in the first. In the second, Little Pow balanced the luggage.

'Shameen Island!' The bodyguard directly loudly. 'Shameen Official Guest House.'

Twisting on the hard seat, Julia glanced nervously behind them. Having heard their destination, the men in fawn tunics were chatting nonchalantly. They were obviously not interested in a Shanghai security woman transparently got up as a Hakka working woman. Their quarry was the foreign woman in the flame-red dress – and they were now doubly sure that she had gone to earth on Shameen Island in the Official Guest House, which had once been the Victoria Hotel.

The Communists had evidently not yet succeeded in imposing on Canton the drab conformity that blanketed Shanghai. Lights still blazed in late-night restaurants, and the clatter of mah jong tiles was a cheerful obligato to high-pitched conversation.

'Heung jaw-been ...' the bodyguard directed in clumsy Cantonese. 'Turn left here. . . . Never mind Shameen, just turn left. . . . And right again. . . . Next left. . . .'

The trishaw threaded through a maze of houses with their upper storeys leaning companionably across the alleys.

'*Ho-la! Ho-la!*' the bodyguard finally grunted. 'That's fine! Just fine!'

When the trishaw had pedalled away, its red reflectors dwindling in the distance, the bodyguard led Julia into a lane. Turning and twisting, they walked for fifteen minutes before he pulled her into a shadowed doorway. After a brief wait, he tapped lightly on the door. A small woman carrying a candle opened it immediately.

'Goodbye, Mrs Howe,' her escort said. 'I'll see you tomorrow at the station.'

The small woman was very friendly – and completely unintelligible. Pressing tea and cakes on Julia, she chattered merrily in harsh Cantonese. When Julia replied in Shanghainese, her broad face crumpled into an incredulous smile seamed by a thousand wrinkles. When Julia tried Mandarin, she chortled with laughter at a ludicrous foreigner speaking the ludicrous northern language.

The woman cocked her head, apparently hearing a distant knock. She laid a small hand on her guest's sleeve, and beckoned. Julia followed her to a back door, where Little Pow waited with two cheap cardboard suit-cases and a small straw valise at his feet. He lifted the cases and sidled into the shadows cast by the overhanging upper storeys. Julia shuffled.

'No need,' he said, 'for the bodyguard to know where we are.'

'I haven't the foggiest idea, Pow.'

'All the better.' He grinned. 'Anyway, the security woman will stay in her . . . your . . . room at the Guest House, and the man will stand watch outside until tomorrow evening. By that time, we'll be safe – or dead.'

'Don't you trust them, Pow?' Julia lengthened her stride to keep up with his lope. 'After all they've done tonight?'

'They'll be fine until they liaise with the Foreign Affairs Bureau here in Canton. Then, if they learn Chou En-lai's changed his mind . . . But we'll get across the border somehow.'

'We? You're coming with me, Pow? Sacrificing everything. Pow, you mustn't. . . .'

'Suppose he says *No*, Julie. What then?'

She followed him in silence through the pools of darkness below the windowless ground floors. They saw no other pedestrians in the medieval alleys. But light streamed through cracks in doors, and the shouting the Cantonese consider conversation resounded from open windows.

Little Pow stepped abruptly into a courtyard, fumbled with a rusty key, and led her up a steep staircase hardly wider than his shoulders. Fried garlic, dark vinegar, and burnt sugar contended with musty mildew in the unaired room. He checked the window-shutters and lit a paraffin lamp to reveal foreign easy-chairs set around a low table inlaid with mother-of-pearl. He poured tea from a gallon thermos and lifted wicker-and-bamboo steamers from a larger thermos to reveal plump Cantonese dumplings.

'Eat first.' He picked up bamboo chopsticks. 'Then talk.'

'Eat and talk at the same time,' Julia riposted. 'Pow, where do we go from here?'

'To the station to catch the six o'clock train, the first train in the morning. There's a dress for you in the bedroom. Before we go, you must make yourself look as old as you can, slather on the make-up as if hiding a raddled face.'

'Little need to pretend,' she countered wryly. 'But why, Pow?'

'You're crossing as Miss Ethel McMurtry Phillips, an aged English missionary from a small town in the Kiangsi mountains, who's just been expelled. I'm crossing as a baggage-coolie – as usual.'

Julia smiled uncertainly and asked: 'Where on earth can you get a passport for Ethel McMurtry Phillips?'

'Tommy took care of that weeks ago.' He popped a dumpling into his mouth. 'Reckoned we might need one for you. So he sent it across. Even fudged a photo from an old picture of you.'

'I see,' Julia responded sensibly. 'So that explains . . . You said Tommy sent it? Then he is . . . is . . . all right?' Her voice rose. 'And he's in Hong Kong? Oh, Pow, is he really . . .'

'Calm down, Julie. Calm down or we'll have the police around our ears. I'm sorry. I shouldn't have surprised you that way.'

'Pow, darling, you can surprise me that way any time you want.' She leaned across and kissed his cheek. 'I knew it. I knew it when you told me to be hopeful. And he *is* all right? Pow, I'm so delighted I . . . But why didn't you tell me earlier? Why in the name of God keep me in suspense?'

'It's part of a very complicated arrangement, Julie. I really shouldn't have told you even now.'

'Why?'

'It's a long story.'

'We've got lots of time. And, I assure you, it won't bore me.'

'It's almost two o'clock, Julie. I've got to get through to Chou En-lai right away. I'll tell you all about Tommy afterwards. And, Julie, pray old Chou gives us the right answer.'

'Assure him that I won't talk when I get out. How could I?'

'And convince him? How am I to do that, Julie?'

He slipped out the door, and his cloth soles sighed up the staircase. A minute later, she heard his voice raised as if speaking to an operator. Annoyingly, she could hear bursts of talk, but could not make out a single word.

Alone for the first time after Little Pow had confirmed his hints about Tommy, Julia gave herself wholly to joy. Now she *knew* her husband was alive. Tommy was alive and active in Hong Kong. And she would see him tomorrow! Nothing else mattered. When she crossed the border, she would not be closing the best part of her life, as she had believed only yesterday. She would be resuming her life.

Julia found herself praying, as Little Pow had suggested. A word from her old friend Chou En-lai would mean that she was virtually safe in Hong Kong. She had no doubts regarding Little Pow's ability to get her across the border. But what if Chou En-lai directed him to detain her? Pow might already be torn by conflicting loyalties in the

544

room above her head, where he was still shouting on the telephone to Peking.

The shouting finally stopped. Her breathing suspended, she listened to him shuffling down the stairs. His expression was non-committal in the poor light, and he did not immediately speak.

'Well, Pow,' she demanded, 'what did he say?'

'I finally got through. But old Chou is out. I said I'd try again in an hour.'

If it were her decision, Julia concluded bleakly, she would *not* go free. Far safer to detain her or eliminate her, rather than risk so much on her promise to remain silent. Letting her leave China would be like turning one's back on a ticking time-bomb. Gratitude for her service to the revolution might impel the Premier to spare her. But gratitude was a highly perishable commodity.

'So we wait, Pow,' she said. 'Nothing else to do, is there?'

'We wait, Julie. And I try to make up my mind. What am I to do if I can't reach him?'

'Obey your last orders, Pow,' she urged. 'Get me out before Chou En-lai's enemies strike at him by ... by disposing of me. Pow, they could even grab me – and make me speak out against him. It's not so hard to make someone say what you want nowadays, is it?'

'Very easy, Julie,' he agreed. 'Especially nowadays.'

'Meanwhile, please tell me all you can about Tommy. Maybe it'll help make up your mind.'

'I'm sorry, but we had to keep you in the dark. And Tommy agreed. When the crunch came, you'd already started your performance. You were testifying loudly to the glories of the New China – and enjoying the limelight. So we couldn't tell you anything.'

'Tommy couldn't tell *me*?' She was shocked. 'But he knew I would never ...'

'Also, it wasn't his secret to reveal. A group in the Party is struggling to keep open our channels to the outside world. To keep China from becoming totally dependent on the Soviet Union – a Soviet colony, a danger to herself and the world. Little Teng Hsiao-ping, the new vice-premier, he's one of our leaders. Premier Chou En-lai can't throw all his weight on our side – not openly. The Executioner Kang Sheng and his faction are strongly pro-Soviet – with Chairman Mao's backing. It's a major fight about policy. It's also a struggle for power – and the Premiership is the prize.'

Little Pow refilled their minute teacups from the thermos and took up the thread again: 'The Executioner's mob was very suspicious of Tommy from the start. His association with Haleevie, for one thing. His release by the Generalissimo in 1927 and his sister's rabid pro-Nationalist activities. Also his American wife. But you get the idea. Yet Tommy was under Chou En-lai's wing. So they pecked away at him, that way also pecking away at old Chou. First they got rid of Haleevie. That was easy, you'll recall. All foreigners were being expelled except those who, like you, were working for us. They kept Haleevie on a string ... forced him to pay great sums for phony debts and imaginary back salaries. As well as atoning for his family's criminal exploitation of the Chinese masses.'

Little Pow waved his hand as if dismissing a banal subject and took another one of her cigarettes.

'You know all that. It was standard treatment for foreigners. Tommy was a lot harder nut to crack. Even if they could prove his connection with British intelligence, he could always claim he was acting on instructions. And the Premier would back him up. If old Chou repudiated Tommy, he'd be striking a blow at himself. So the Executioner took the long way round. Framed Tommy for trumped-up violations of Party discipline. Invented charges of corruption in his practice and in administering the remaining property of the Howe family.'

'And then Tommy disappeared,' Julia interjected. 'And I knew absolutely nothing after that. Not even how he disappeared.'

'It was simple, Julie. The old guerrilla network still functions well when it's needed. I got Tommy over the border to Hong Kong. I reckoned he could do more for China there. We need a man in Hong Kong the British trust. It was my decision – and I'd do it again. But we couldn't tell you. You do see, don't you?'

His defensiveness did not augur well for herself. If he had to justify rescuing his co-conspirator, he would assuredly balk at smuggling her across the border against express orders. She had no claim on his political loyalty. None the less, she *was* his surrogate mother, as he had said.

'I've made up my mind, Pow.' Her decision took shape as she spoke. 'I won't talk about the seamy side of New China when I get out. I'd only look a fool and a turncoat.' She had to convince him that he must help her. 'Instead, I'll work with Tommy – as always.'

'Julie, *why* did you decide to leave?' Little Pow probed gently. 'I don't mean now. You've got no choice, not with the Executioners after you. But why leave China in the first place? You didn't know about Tommy, then.'

'Frankly, I thought I was leaving him behind me. But there was no more I could do for him by staying on. I felt I could do more abroad.' She took a cigarette and gave him a grateful smile in return for his light. 'Somehow I knew I had to go when they changed the name of Avenue Edward VII to Yenan Road. Understandable, marking the end of an era. But also a gesture of exclusion . . . of isolation. I knew then I could do no more to help. It was up to the Chinese. Foreigners were only in the way.'

'What about those who've stayed on? There must be several dozen foreigners. And they must believe they can help.'

'Pow, I couldn't surrender my mind. I couldn't become a marionette, dancing when the Party pulled the strings – speaking only from the official script. Besides, I could no longer justify policies obviously bad for China, like the Campaign Against the Five Bourgeous Evils. Honest businessmen had been repeatedly promised they wouldn't be touched. Yet they were expropriated and driven to suicide – or to flight like Tommy. Intervention in Korea also stuck in my craw. I know Douglas

MacArthur was dangerous. But committing more than a million men was folly. And then to invade South Korea. China is Moscow's cat's paw – and cat's paws get burnt. This Korean business has set back economic progress – and strengthened Soviet influence. It's going to be hard to shake off the Soviet yoke. And very hard to convince Chairman Mao that leaning to the Soviet side is the biggest mistake he could make. But we must all work towards . . .'

Little Pow raised an admonitory palm and said: 'Enough, Julie! Enough! You've convinced me your motives and your intentions are pure. Now I've got to convince Comrade Chou. I'd better try again.'

Little Pow was gone for almost half an hour, but Julia could hear only a low murmur. Evidently the connection was better. She was initially cheered by his long absence. At least, he had not been peremptorily directed to detain her. Yet why was it necessary for him to spend so much time pleading with the Premier?

Little Pow's expression was glum when he returned, but he shook his head to allay her anxiety.

'Old Chou's not to be found anywhere. I should try again before we leave. But we can't waste much time.'

Julia did not ask what had taken him so long, but stubbed out her cigarette, smiled to put heart into him, and went off to transform herself into Miss Ethel McMurtry Phillips. The voluminous beige-cotton dress she found on the bed in the next room owed more to the tentmaker's art than the couturier's.

The Secret Executioners were waiting when Julia's trishaw drew up before Canton main station at five in the morning. Their fawn tunics were immaculate, and their cheeks were freshly shaven. But their eyes were red-rimmed. They openly looked her up and down.

She was hideously exposed, and she had never felt more lonely. Yet she had to begin this last stage of her journey alone. However disguised, Little Pow would have been a giveaway. The Executioners were looking for a foreign woman accompanied by an undersize Chinese man. By herself, she could blend with other foreigners belatedly being expelled. Three nuns in blue habits entered the station just after her, and a White Russian couple carrying coats of Manchurian squirrel were waiting at the passport control counter.

Julia stooped to tighten the rope tied around the battered cardboard suitcases that had replaced her expensive leather case. Her crocodile train-case had also been jettisoned, its cosmetics transferred to the cheap straw valise in her left hand. Her other bags would be left behind in the checkroom. Glancing up from the suitcase, she saw a fourth Executioner hovering near the left luggage counter.

How could she even think about luggage when his dull eyes scrutinized her? Yet he must have been informed that the foreign woman was still asleep in the Official Guest House.

The unworldly Ethel McMurtry Phillips would undoubtedly be very nervous, but Julia had no need to pretend. Sighing aloud, she awkwardly picked up her luggage and made for the passport control counter.

The Executioner followed her and extended his hand to take her passport from the immigration officer. He contemptuously flicked the gold lion-and-unicorn seal on the cover before studying the blurred photograph within. For almost a minute his eyes shifted repeatedly from her face to the photograph. As became a meek missionary spinster, Julia lowered her eyes. Then she stared straight into the Executioner's eyes – as became an arrogant foreigner.

Presumably the Executioners possessed a good photograph of her. All to the good! They would be looking for similarities. The only similarity between the smart Julia Pavernen Howe and the dowdy Ethel McMurtry Phillips was that they were both foreign and female. The sacklike dress draped her like a tarpaulin, almost concealing her ankles, which were thick in lisle stockings. Her old brogues, which Tommy called 'stout British walkers', completed the graceless costume, and a faded blue cotton scarf covered her hair.

Ethel McMurtry Phillips was, further, losing her dogged battle against the marks of age. From hairline to collar-bone her face was plastered with shiny pancake make-up so thick it was cracking. Behind her prim glasses, her eyelashes bristled with mascara. Small cupid's bow lips of greasy crimson were Julia's best inspiration. The discs of vermilion rouge on her cheekbones completed the portrait of a repressed spinster who still yearned after story-book romance.

The Executioner stared unblinkingly back at her. She saw in his eyes the respect for age no Chinese could quite shake off. She also saw hatred for a foreigner and disdain for a woman. When he returned her passport to the immigration officer, Julia was chilled by his contempt. But he had judged her beneath notice, which was exactly what she wanted.

Lifting her luggage with another weary sigh, she entered the next stage of the bureaucratic maze that led to the train for Hong Kong. She passed without incident through currency control, customs search, and the final Security Police checkpoint. Weighed down by her suitcase, she walked awkwardly down the ramp to the platform on legs wobbly with relief.

The grimy second-class carriage was a purgatory after the luxurious compartment on the Shanghai–Canton express. Each time the local stopped she was jolted violently on the wooden seat – and it made twenty-four stops on its ninety-mile route. Gnawing on the tangerines she had bought at Sekloong Station, she gratefully gave a few coppers to the slovenly attendant who poured fresh hot water onto the cloud of green tea leaves in her murky glass.

Yet she dreaded the arrival at Shumchon, the last stop, which was scheduled for 3:53 p.m. She would have to pass through controls at the border even more stringent than those at Canton. Finally, she would have to carry her bags some fifty yards across the covered bridge to British Lowu.

Since liberation, all passengers had to change trains at the border.

That was a political decision. The pigs and vegetables she had seen loaded yesterday would cross unhampered. That was a matter of business.

The last border guard in the baggy green uniform with red collar-flashes waved Julia on. Behind her lay the numbing formalities of departure from China, which had taken two hours. Every garment in her luggage had been pawed, fortunately by male customs officers, who could not see the vast difference in character between the dress she wore and the dresses she carried. She herself had been pawed by a female customs officer to ensure that she was concealing no contraband on her person.

She glanced back at the border guard. Standing beneath the scarlet flag of the People's Republic of China with its five yellow stars, he was idly fingering the sub-machine gun slung over his shoulder. At the other end of the covered bridge that crossed the shallow Shumchon River, she saw the Union Jack flapping over a square, whitewashed building. Before it, two Hong Kong constables were spick-and-span in khaki shorts and shirts with big black-leather revolver holsters on their belts.

Julia looked back again, anxious to imprint her last sight of China upon her memory. Through sudden tears, she saw the border guard languidly waving on a coolie in rusty black trousers, a stained singlet, and rubber sandals. His springy carrying-pole bobbed and creaked under the weight of the heavy earthenware jars of preserved eggs suspended from its its ends. Behind his grin, Julia recognized the triangular face and the big eyes of Little Pow – and slowed her pace.

She felt great joy, but no surprise. She had known he would not let her go without saying farewell when he bundled her off in the trishaw after failing for the third time to reach Premier Chou En-lai. She had known he would see her safe across the covered bridge to Hong Kong.

Loping to catch up with her, Little Pow grinned but did not speak. When they were almost halfway across, he glanced back at the bored Chinese guard and said softly: 'Drop the little case, Julie. Let it spill.'

She automatically obeyed. Bottles, tubes, jars, and brushes rolled on the splintered boards and tumbled into the trough between the railway tracks.

Little Pow knelt to help her sweep up her belongings and said: 'I had to say goodbye, Julie. Heaven knows when we'll meet again.'

'You're not coming over? Of course not. There's no need now. You weren't told to keep me. You never did speak to Chou En-lai, did you?'

'Julie, it's not that simple.' He let two curlers spurt through his fingers and roll away. 'I did speak to the Premier's chief of security. He told me to hold you. That's another reason I came – to make sure you got across. I was afraid those damn bodyguards would get the word at the Foreign Affairs Bureau. But you're safe now.'

'Pow, will you be all right?' she asked. 'Won't you be in trouble for disobeying? Shouldn't you come with me?'

'I take orders from Comrade Chou, nobody else. No jumped-up cop is going to tell me what to do.' He glanced at the complacent border guard.

'Julie, I've got to go back. Things are still getting worse in China, but some day they'll get better. I've got to go back and hurry that day up. In the long run, our revolution will prove the best thing for China in a thousand years. On that day, you and Tommy will return as honoured guests. Until then, I must say goodbye. But I'll be seeing you.'

He swept the last of her cosmetics into the straw-valise and handed it to her with a courtly little bow. She could not kiss him in public view, but their eyes met and clung for a prolonged moment.

Little Pow saw the commotion at the Chinese end of the bridge while Julia was still lost in an emotional reverie.

'Run, Julie, run!' he shouted. 'They're on to you.'

Sweeping up her bags, Julia saw the Premier's security man race past the border guard. Drab again in blue cotton, the woman followed. Behind her, two border-guards were unslinging their sub-machineguns.

Julia ran towards the haven of the British border post. Six Hong Kong constables emerged from the whitewashed building and trotted towards her. She heard Little Pow shouting apologies for hampering her pursuers with his carrying pole and its burdens.

Julia caught her toe in a crack between the boards and stumbled. The constables were drawing close, led by a tall man whose face was obscured by the black visor of his cap. Julia almost regained her footing, but the suitcase dragged her off balance. When she began to fall, the tall police-man stretched out his arm to catch her.

Julia fell heavily against him, shocked for an instant by the impact. When she raised her eyes, Tommy was looking down at her, his features rigid. He was clearly too moved to smile – or even speak.

'Tommy!' She at length murmured. 'Tommy darling! I knew you'd come!'

'It's all right, Julie, everything,' he finally replied. 'You're safe.' He paused. 'Can't kiss you here, not in this uniform. But I thought I'd better see you across myself.'

'I knew you would, darling. I always knew . . .' she began, but then demanded guiltily: 'And Little Pow? What about Little Pow?'

The Hong Kong constables had formed a khaki rank across the bridge. Two border guards in rumpled green were shouting at them, while a third gripped Little Pow's arm.

'Don't worry about Pow,' Tommy advised. 'He'll talk his way out of it. Undoubtedly persuade them he was trying to stop you. It helps to be a general.'

A constable swept up Julia's bags, and she walked beside Tommy towards the shelter of the Union Jack. A red-faced English police-officer waved them into the whitewashed guard post. The cool cube within was sparsely furnished with a yellow-shellacked desk and two rattan chairs. A small radio was playing softly.

Tommy put his arms around Julia and pulled her close. She clutched him fiercely and pressed herself against him. He kissed her very hard.

'Julie,' he murmured. 'Always you!'

Julia's guard was wholly down for the first time in a year. Tears came to her eyes, and she clung to Tommy. She tried to respond, but could not speak. To her utter surprise, she found herself trembling. The tremors became stronger, and the next moment she was shaking uncontrollably.

'Tom ... Tom ...' she finally stuttered. 'It's all over.... All we believed ... Our work ... and China. All ... all finished.'

Fearing the onset of hysteria, Tommy grasped her shoulders firmly. But her tremors became more violent.

'Stop it, Julie. Just *stop* it!' he commanded. 'It's *not* all over. Not by a long shot.'

He had caught her attention, but her involuntary spasms continued. Anything to divert her, since he could not force himself to slap her. He turned the radio to full volume, and the song reverberated in the whitewashed concrete cube: '. . . get you on a slow boat to China, all to myself alone.'

'Listen, Julie!' he commanded. 'Just listen to what they're playing. "A Slow Boat to China".'

She smiled blearily and said: 'Thank God, I've found you. . . . But it's finished, Tommy. We'll never go back.'

'We will, Julie. We certainly will. Slow boat, slow train, or fast plane – we will go back to China!'

135.$\frac{00}{net}$sp